THE
SENTINEL

About the Author

Mark Oldfield was born in Sheffield, and now lives in Kent. He holds a PhD in criminology.

THE
SENTINEL

MARK OLDFIELD

First published in the UK in 2012 by Head of Zeus, Ltd.

9 7 5 3 1 2 4 6 8

A CIP catalogue record for this book is available from
the British Library.

ISBN (HB): 9781908800183
ISBN (TPB): 9781908800190
ISBN (E): 9781781850435

Printed in Germany.

Head of Zeus, Ltd
Clerkenwell House
45-47 Clerkenwell Green
London EC1R 0HT

www.headofzeus.com

For Viv

Subdued by the remorseless violence of their captors, the first group of prisoners trudged across the dusty sand, halting in front of the wooden barrera. *The victors had torn open the shirts of many of the captured men and women to expose the right shoulder, seeking the telltale bruising left by the sustained firing of a rifle. Those who bore that mark were rapidly herded into the bullring. Some now stared defiantly at their captors while others wept, cigarettes held in shaking hands, their gaze fixed on a spot so distant it could not possibly be on this earth. They had suffered much, these beaten Republicans, but they had not yet suffered enough. The Moors guarding them slowly drew back, leaving the prisoners standing alone, casting long, stark shadows across the sand as they stared through the shimmering heat at their executioners.*

The sound of hooves echoed over the stone patio outside the gates and the victorious soldiers cheered their general as he clattered into the ring on his big white horse, its brasses gleaming, like some knight of the crusades. General Valverde reined in his mount alongside the two heavy machine guns, dark-oiled and glinting with dull menace, the sights adjusted for short-distance fire. A group of staff officers gathered around the general. A tall young teniente *took up position a couple of paces from the others, glaring at the ranks of condemned Republicans with sullen malice.*

The prisoners shuffled as they waited in the pitiless heat. Some of them exchanged final handshakes, others raised their fists in the Republican salute. Some merely stared, ashen-faced, at the machine guns pointing accusingly towards them. From somewhere behind the stands, there was a burst of screaming and from further away came the sound of muffled gunfire. The town was being sacked.

1

The men at the guns knelt, ready, the loaders cradling the belts of heavy bullets so they would pass cleanly into the guns without jamming. At the metallic sound of the guns being readied, many of the prisoners crossed themselves. But one woman stepped forward from the front rank, holding her torn blouse together across her chest. Twenty yards away, the troops could not see whether she bore the stigmata of a rifle: the sun was too bright. Little matter: where there was doubt about a prisoner's culpability, it was as well to assume guilt on the grounds of expediency.

The general's voice echoed around the stands as he gave the order to fire. Those standing immediately behind the guns saw the woman's mouth open, her fist rising in a final salute, but none heard her words as the machine guns exploded into their heavy staccato rhythm, scything down the prisoners, sending them tumbling backwards, smashed against the wooden barrera by the heavy bullets, some still trying to stay on their feet even as death tugged them down to the soaking sand. The firing lasted perhaps thirty seconds. Then the Moorish troops went in with their bayonets. It was surprising how many prisoners were still alive.

Once the wounded had been killed, the corpses were cleared away using wagons commandeered from the fallen town. Where the prisoners had stood, there remained only a patch of churned and stained sand. And then a new group shuffled into place along the barrera, its woodwork now riddled with the eccentric geometries of gunfire.

Outside the bullring, long lines of defeated Republicans waited to face the wrath of the victors. The battle was over. The killing had just begun.

CHAPTER ONE

The car turned another bend, climbing higher into a land of sun-scorched scrub, stunted trees and huge overhanging rocks. An arid landscape broken by sheer cliffs and sharp, boulder-strewn ridges. Stupefying heat. Galindez felt sweat soaking her shirt, trickling down her back. This had been the only vehicle left in the car pool, and now it had become an instrument of torture. Why no air conditioning? It was high summer, for God's sake. If she'd been a uniformed officer and not a lowly forensic scientist, they wouldn't have sent her out to the middle of nowhere in a vehicle without air conditioning. There was no point in complaining, she knew. No matter how reasonable the complaint, the same barrier always came up. The same look on their faces: *Women – always complaining. Don't they realise? This is what keeps the pay cheque coming.*

Galindez reached the crest of the hill and crossed a flat promontory leading to yet another steep winding road that curved around the flank of yet another ochre hillside. She slowed, seeing a small improvised shrine at the roadside a hundred metres ahead. Beyond the barrier, the sheer cliff fell into the valley far below. Tyre marks curved crazily from the centre line to the shattered gap in the wooden fence. Galindez drove slowly, taking in the profusion of cheap plastic toys, religious badges, a handmade cross and a portrait of Jesus, executed in luminous colours. Whoever ploughed through that barrier had friends with appalling taste.

A road sign: *Las Peñas.* Even the villages were named after rocks in this arid terrain. A two-hour drive in thirty degrees of heat. And waiting for her would be another heap of ancient bones. Another war grave. *Joder.* Why did they always send her? *No one else available in Forensics, Ana María. Good practice for you, Dr Galindez. Do me a favour with this one, Ana? It's not far, just outside Madrid.* She gripped the wheel, feeling a surge of resentment at what she was sure would be another wasted journey. In the mirror she saw beads of sweat on her face, the glint of her eyes behind the dark sunglasses. Her *guardia* ID swung gently on its chain from the sun visor, the small laminated photograph taken only a year ago: a picture of quiet confidence, her dark hair tied back, deep brown eyes bright with anticipation. Her name printed beneath the photo: *Galindez, Ana María, Forensic Investigator.* An image of her ideal self, calm and collected, just out of university with her doctorate, eager to start her career in the *guardia civil.* And this was how it had turned out. Collecting the remains of people killed in a war seventy-five years ago. *Good going, Ana María.*

It felt such a waste of time. All the years spent studying forensic science, developing skills of analysis and interpretation, peering at photographs of murders and suicides, learning the beguiling similarities between self-inflicted death and murder. Ways of avoiding the myriad opportunities to reach a wrong conclusion. All those skills focused on assembling a deeper truth. A truth no detective could ever piece together by observation alone. Time spent patiently gathering data. The hours of assiduous analysis devoted to identifying the logical sequence that would give up the secrets of a case. All the skills she'd acquired and yet so much of her time spent on these fruitless trips to recover the remains of people killed so long ago. Worse, Galindez knew she got these jobs because she was still the new girl. Last one in gets the shit jobs, they told her. Like that would make it better. *Life's unfair – and then you die. Papá*'s colleagues said he'd had that phrase painted on his locker. He thought it was funny. But then he died and it really was unfair. She took a deep breath, reminding herself it was all good experience, that it would look good on her CV one day. One day.

She glanced at the map lying on the passenger seat next to the pieces of her satnav. Almost there. A faded road sign confirmed she'd reached her destination. A bleached and faded sign: *Compañía Española de Minas, fundada 1898*. The remains of an old stone wall hinted at what once might have been an entrance. Behind the wall, an ancient wire fence wound through the scorched grass. Several sections of fencing had collapsed, the folded strands of wire intertwined with the dry scrub swarming over the rusted fence posts. Near the wall were several old buildings. Two of the buildings were in ruins, walls folded crazily inward over their fallen roofs. The remaining buildings were clearly entering the final stages of disintegration. The entire place was steadily decomposing, sinking sullenly into the harsh terrain.

Cautiously, Galindez eased the car up a rough track running through the parched scrub and seared rocks of the hillside. Five hundred metres of uncomfortable driving ended at a wire fence where several cars huddled in the steaming heat. One, a green and white Lexus with the insignia of the *guardia civil*, its windows closed. Galindez was willing to bet they'd got air con in that. The dry ground crunched under the wheels as she pulled to a halt in a cloud of arid dust. Slipping her ID around her neck, Galindez collected her case and the canvas equipment bag and stepped out into the leaden heat of the sun.

It was worse than she'd expected. Heat prickled her scalp and she felt it begin to scorch her neck and arms – short sleeves didn't help but then she'd dressed for the office today, not knowing she would be packed off to an abandoned mine. Everything about this place was unpleasant: the sharp desiccated soil working its way into her shoes; the clammy feel of the damp shirt plastered to her back; the dazzling white light bleaching the surroundings, painful even through sunglasses. An uncomfortable but familiar start to her working day.

The gate in the fence creaked loudly. Ahead was the disused quarry, a semicircular gash carved sharply into the hillside. A careless array of abandoned, rusty mechanical equipment littered the quarry floor. On the steep hillside overlooking the quarry she saw an arched area of brickwork that must be sealing the entrance to the mine. A group of people were standing by it. The hot air shimmered, making it hard to see them clearly. As Galindez approached, she saw a man wearing the olive green uniform of the *guardia civil*. Closer now, Galindez saw a ragged opening had been smashed in the bricks. An opening so small it obliged those entering or leaving the mine to bend almost double. The man in uniform came towards her. Typical officer of the *Benemérita*: middle-aged, belly straining over the top of a thick belt, eyes obscured by large round sunglasses.

'Dr Galindez? *Buenos dias. Teniente* Molina. We spoke on the phone.'

'*Holá*. What have we got in there, *Teniente*?' She held out her hand. Molina ignored it.

'As far as I can tell, fifteen corpses. Skeletons, I should say. Very little left of them.'

'A killing from *la Guerra Civil*?'

'You tell me, that's your job. I just need cause and approximate date of death to finish the paperwork and put this to bed. You've done this sort of thing before, *verdad*?'

'I've done lots of cases like these, *Teniente*. They get monotonous after a while.'

He shrugged. '*Claro*. That's police work, fifty-nine minutes of boredom and one of excitement an hour – if you're lucky.'

'Even so, I wonder why we bother. We catalogue them and then what? *Nada*. Usually there's no suspect and often no witnesses. *Dios mio*, it was seventy years ago. We aren't going to make arrests. God knows there's enough to keep us busy without digging up war graves three-quarters of a century old.'

'Maybe so, Dr Galindez. But in the *guardia*, orders are orders. Even for *forenses* like you. That's what keeps the pay cheque coming, no?'

'That's what they say,' she agreed. *All the fucking time. We should have it on the badge.*

Molina followed Galindez towards the mine entrance. A second *guardia* emerged, struggling from the hole in the brickwork. He saw Galindez and she felt the familiar sensation of being measured against that invisible benchmark her male colleagues carried around alongside their gun and their nightstick. Maybe it wouldn't be so annoying if they'd hide it a little. Especially since it was wasted on her anyway.

'This is *Sargento* Hernandez. Hernandez, Dr Galindez.'

The *sargento* gave her a cursory nod and stared at her chest. Clearly she met some of his criteria since he didn't even bother looking at her face. She folded her arms.

'You get back to the *comisaría*, *sargento*, I'll be along later,' Molina said. Hernandez took a last look at Galindez's breasts and walked back up to the cars parked by the fence.

Galindez looked at the ragged hole in the brickwork. 'Is it safe to go in?'

'*Absolutamente*. We've put up a couple of lights. You know, I think it shook the *sargento* when he saw what's in there.'

'I could tell he was the sensitive type.' Galindez took off her sunglasses, squinting against the white glare. She forced her way into the narrow gap, the broken bricks sharp against her back. Inside it was dark and the air smelled of earth. Molina followed, crawling awkwardly through the gap, panting from the exertion.

An electric lamp hung from a hook in the narrow passageway, throwing dull light along rough stone walls punctuated by the columns of bricks bearing the weight of the hillside above. Galindez's flashlight played over the dusty surfaces, a probing line of white light picking out rusty lanterns, heaps of broken tools and large coils of wire covered in lichen. Twenty metres in the passageway widened, ending in a brick wall with a heavy door fitted with a large rusty lock. There were storage spaces hacked from the rock on either side of the brickwork, most of the space occupied by piles of ancient equipment and tools, their form and function long erased by dust and cobwebs.

'That's the entrance to the mine,' Molina said, pointing to the door. 'But there's no key for the door and I don't fancy trying to force it open if we don't need to.'

Galindez nodded, her flashlight moving across upturned buckets, oil drums and wire netting. Dust flickered in the sharp beam. And there they were.

The killers must have piled the bodies on top of each other but time had changed the order of things. With the decomposition of the bodies, the skeletons had collapsed like a heap of firewood. Galindez knelt alongside them. She'd seen plenty of skulls in her short career yet she still felt there was a certain pathos looking into a face so denuded of its essential humanity. All that remained was this last unrecognisable vestige of its owner, the jaws open in the impossibly wide, astonished surprise of the long dead. Those where the jaw was still attached.

'From the look of it, none of these people died naturally, *Teniente*.'

Molina looked at the skull. 'That's a gunshot wound, isn't it?'

'Definitely. This is the entry point,' she pointed out a neatly drilled hole in the back of the head, 'and you can see the result here.' Turning the skull, she indicated the massive exit hole, a gaping expanse of the forehead missing. 'The bullet entered at the base of the skull, exiting through the forehead.'

'So what does that tell us?'

'*Hombre*,' Galindez smiled, 'someone shot him.'

Molina grunted humourlessly. He looked again at the dusty skeletons, so diminished in death, their essence long since drained away, the remains now crumbling slowly. 'There are no signs of identity.' He sounded disappointed. Galindez knew the feeling well.

She took latex gloves from her case and began to pull them on. 'I think it's best if I establish how many there are. Then we can get them bagged up.'

'There's no *we*.' Molina snorted. '*You* get them bagged up. That's what you do, *señorita*.' He got to his feet and headed back along the tunnel to the entrance.

Galindez felt the cold starting to seep into her damp clothes. It wasn't unpleasant now, but after a while it would be. And she was going to be here quite a while, she was certain of that. She pulled off the gloves. There were things in her car she needed and it was pretty clear she wasn't going to get any help.

Galindez climbed back through the ragged hole in the bricks into the simmering white heat. The light was painful after the half light of the tunnel. Two people were standing outside the entrance. An old man holding a sheaf of papers, and a woman: middle-aged, short dark hair. Quite attractive, Galindez noticed. She wondered if they were relatives of the victims. That would be good: she could try for a DNA match. The thought cheered her.

Molina introduced them. 'Dr Galindez, may I present *Profesora* Ordoñez, professor of contemporary history at the University Complutense in Madrid and *Señor* Teodoro Byass, former manager at the Spanish Mining Company. *Señor* Byass tells me a large part of the mine and the neighbouring quarries closed after the Civil War.'

Señor Byass was clearly pleased to have had his retirement interrupted to give the history of this godforsaken hole carved into the barren hillside. 'As you say, *Teniente*, although we carried on some operations in the area until about 1970 – the year the company shut down. But the mine was sealed off long before that.'

'Before the war?' the professor asked.

'No, *señora*. It closed in 1953. I've got the papers here. I kept the files when the company folded. Here you are, *señora*.'

'It's *señorita*,' Ordoñez said, glancing at Galindez. 'But if we're being formal, I prefer *profesora*.'

Byass mumbled an apology as he handed *Profesora* Ordoñez the yellowed papers with their faded official stamps.

She examined them carefully. 'Had the seam run out?'

The old man shook his head. 'Orders from above. As you'll see in that letter.'

Profesora Ordoñez turned towards Galindez to read the letter. Her finger moved down the faded typewritten sheet. 'Orders from the General Directorate of Security, January fifteenth, 1953. For reasons of public safety...' the *Profesora* skimmed the page, 'danger to passers-by, children and domestic animals... immediate closure of the mine entrance...'

'An order like that couldn't be ignored. Not back then,' Byass said. 'They sealed up the entrance within a few days.'

Profesora Ordoñez turned to put the papers in her bag and caught Galindez lightly with her elbow. 'I'm so sorry. Did I hurt you?' She squeezed Galindez's arm in gentle apology.

'*No ha pasado nada*, professor, my fault,' Galindez said, thinking it less of an accident and more an opening gambit.

Profesora Ordonez looked at the letter again. 'The letter is signed by the Military Governor of Madrid, General Antonio Valverde,' she read. 'As you say, *Señor* Byass, an order from the *Capitán-General* of Madrid wasn't something to be argued with.'

Molina sighed impatiently. 'None of that's important. As far as I'm concerned it's an open and shut case of a wartime killing. I'll leave you to do your job, Dr Galindez. I'm going to drive *Señor* Byass back to the village.'

'I may need some help,' Galindez protested. 'Those skeletons are going to fall apart once they're moved. If we could get a couple of officers in to assist, at least I could keep some of them intact. It would make the forensic investigation much easier.'

'A quick word,' Molina said, taking a couple of paces away from the *profesora* and *Señor* Byass.

Galindez followed him, knowing what was coming.

'Don't give me orders, Galindez,' Molina said in loud voice. 'You're just the cleaning woman here, as far as I'm concerned. You may have all day to spend on this but I don't. All I want is your report signed and dated and sent to the *comisaría* at Las Peñas by tomorrow morning. Get those bodies out of here and take them wherever the fuck it is you take them. And I want the hole in the bricks sealed up. I think I can trust you to arrange that, can't I?'

Galindez glowered at Molina, her cheeks burning with anger.

'That's settled then,' Molina said. 'I'll leave you to get on with it, Dr Galindez.'

'Just a minute,' Galindez said.

Molina stopped in his tracks and turned to glare at her.

'You registered the mine as a crime scene when you arrived, didn't you?' Galindez asked. 'And I presume you gave it a crime number?'

'Of course.' Molina was furious. Galindez could imagine what he was thinking: *who does she think she's talking to?*

'In that case,' Galindez continued, 'securing the scene is your responsibility. The regulations about crime-scene management are quite specific. You logged the crime – it's down to you to find a bricklayer.'

For a moment, Molina seemed on the verge of apoplexy. Realising the others were watching, he nodded curtly and walked sullenly towards his car where *Señor* Byass was waiting. They climbed into the green and white Lexus and drove off.

'What a charmer.' It was the *profesora*.

'He loves me really,' Galindez laughed, 'he's just playing hard to get.'

'Do you have to put up with that sort of thing often?'

'That?' Galindez shrugged. 'That was nothing, believe me.'

'You could complain, surely? Isn't there some sort of policy about these things?'

'Oh yes. We have anti-sexism policies, anti-bullying policies – all sorts of policies, *profesora*. But do you know what the most important policy of all is? I'll tell you: never – as in never even-in-your-fucking-dreams-ever – complain. Complain and you're a whinger. And that's not a good thing. You just take the shit and collect the pay cheque. That's what they expect and that's what you do.'

'What a depressing thought.'

'Believe me, the alternative's worse. You have to show you can take it. Otherwise they won't respect you. And then you can't do your job at all.'

'Don't you ever wonder if maybe you're in the wrong job?'

'I've only been in the *guardia* a year. I need to build up experience before I can get a transfer,' Galindez said, speculatively prodding a stone with her shoe. 'The trouble is, it's a family thing. My dad and my uncle were both *guardia*. My uncle still is. I need to show I can hack it. In time it'll get better.'

'I hope so. For your sake.' *Profesora* Ordonez knelt and opened the chill bag lying at her feet. She took out a plastic bottle of water and offered it to Galindez. The water was cold, the condensation on the plastic felt pleasant in her hand. She raised the bottle to her mouth, aware of the *profesora* watching as she drank.

'So it was you who located this place, *profesora*?' Galindez asked, wiping her mouth.

'Me and my research group.'

'How did you find out about it?' The intensity of the *profesora*'s look was almost embarrassing, Galindez thought. Almost.

'Well, there's a diary.'

'Whose diary?' Galindez asked, suddenly interested.

'Oh, someone who was a key player back then,' *Profesora* Ordoñez said. 'The diary of a man in charge of organising much of Franco's dirty work.'

'He documented it?' Galindez automatically began thinking fingerprints, DNA, handwriting analysis. Evidence. Even if it wasn't a smoking gun, she thought, at least it was some form of evidence for once.

'Some of the diary is autobiographical,' *Profesora* Ordoñez continued. 'There are also details of arrests and executions, although the locations aren't given in great detail. We've identified some of the places he refers to. This was one of them.'

'And he admits the killings?'

The *profesora* smiled. 'No. There's nothing to connect him to them directly. Besides, I don't think you'd be able to arrest him now, it's likely he's been dead for years. '

'So this is your speciality – tracking down Franco's hit men?'

Ordoñez laughed. 'Haven't you read my work? I would have thought someone working in this field would be familiar with it.'

'I don't specialise in war graves,' Galindez said. 'They're allocated to me. Frequently. There's a lot of political pressure to investigate them. But they don't put any real resources into it: I have a look, do a report and then it's on to the next one.'

'Make the most of them. They're fascinating,' the *profesora* said. 'Could I have a look at this one, do you think?' She nodded towards the hole in the bricks. 'Maybe a few photos for our records?'

'No problem.' Galindez picked up her latex gloves. 'I'll come in with you.'

'I hoped you would.'

Galindez took the lead, crouching to scramble through the hole. She felt the *profesora* watching as she struggled through the hole, wrestling her bag past the broken bricks.

The pile of bones intrigued *Profesora* Ordoñez and she listened carefully as Galindez outlined her view of how the bodies came to be in the mine: that it was likely they were killed somewhere else and then brought here and dumped in a heap before the entrance was sealed up permanently.

'How long would you say they've been here, Ana María?' The *profesora* asked.

'Right now, I'd date the killing sometime between 1952 and 1970, probably earlier rather than later.'

'And why do you say that?' The professor moved nearer, placing a hand on Galindez's shoulder to steady herself. Once she was comfortable, her hand remained in place.

'I'm not Sherlock Holmes,' Galindez said. 'The mine was sealed in fifty-three and the company closed down in the seventies. These people have been dead a long time and of course it's unlikely a pile of bodies was lying around while the miners came here to work the seams. So...'

'*Elementario, mi querido Watson?*' A hint of a smile in the professor's voice.

13

'It is when you know how.' Galindez tensed, sensing condescension.

'It's unlikely you'll find anything of much interest.'

'Over a dozen people shot dead and hidden in a mine? If it took place in the early fifties that was well after the war ended. We're talking about murder rather than a war crime surely?'

'This may not be a shooting carried out *during* the war. But that doesn't mean it wasn't connected to the war,' *Profesora* Ordoñez said.

'But why here? Why not just kill them in prison?'

'Things weren't so neat and tidy in those days.' The professor's flashlight wandered over the skeletons. 'Perhaps the killings needed to be covered up so they dumped them here. They knew one thing for certain: no one would come looking for these people. Not in Franco's lifetime anyway.'

'So the killers weren't worried about the law?'

Profesora Ordoñez smiled. 'It's quite possible they were the law.'

Five o'clock and the sun was remorseless. Galindez worked steadily and methodically, piling the skeletons on top of black plastic sacks outside the mine entrance. So many bones. Skulls, the strange curves of spines and ribcages, thigh bones, shins, the smaller pieces: toes, fingers – even a few teeth found in the dirt beneath the pile of bodies. Fifteen scrambled skeletons. Back at the lab Galindez could reassemble these bodies – given time. Whether the *guardia* would sanction the expense was unlikely, she knew. What good would it do anyway, she explained to the *profesora*. Apart from keeping the pay cheque coming, of course.

'You mean they won't investigate further?' *Profesora* Ordoñez asked, surprised.

'What difference would it make? That world has gone. Those people have been dead so long, who can possibly care now?'

'That's rather harsh, Dr Galindez,' Ordoñez said, 'Don't you have any interest in the past?'

'No, not really,' Galindez said, a little too quickly.

'None at all? Don't you care about how the past constantly

14

seeps into the present? How it nuances and shapes contemporary choices and options?'

Galindez laughed. 'You really do sound like a professor.'

'I'm in the right job then.'

'You mentioned something earlier about a diary, *profesora*?'

Ordoñez opened her bag and brought out a book bound in faded, scuffed leather. She opened it gently, almost tenderly. The writing was in a broad script written with a large-nibbed pen. The ink faint but still legible.

'We found this three years ago,' she said. 'Hidden under the floorboards in a house in the centre of Madrid.'

Galindez looked at the page. Strong, even pen strokes, the writing an exemplar of geometrical rigidity, yet with a bold, angry sweep to it. She saw dated entries, barely a hint of any correction.

'This diary is extremely important,' *Profesora* Ordoñez said, closing it. 'But I can tell you about him later. Look at you, you're filthy. You need to get out of those clothes and have a shower.' She smiled. 'And a cold drink or two. Tell you what, I'm buying when we get back to Madrid. In fact, we could go to my place. You can get showered while I fix us a drink.'

Galindez saw the look in the *profesora*'s eyes. The day might end better than it had begun. But she wouldn't be going anywhere until the truck arrived to take away the remains. And then there were photographs to be taken. 'That would be nice, *profesora*, but I've still a fair bit of work left to do.'

'I'll wait. And it's Luisa, by the way.'

'OK. Pro— Luisa. Listen, you've got me hooked, this man we've been talking about – the one who wrote this diary. Just who was he?'

Profesora Ordoñez smiled. 'So you're getting more interested in the past now? That can happen. He was very special, Ana María. This is him.' She opened the diary again.

Inside the cover was a pressed, yellowed newspaper clipping from the right-wing daily, *ABC*. The contrast between light and shade was so sharp the photograph seemed almost a sketch. In the

15

picture, a tall, heavy-set young man in combat gear was having a medal pinned on his chest by a short man in a uniform with big epaulettes, his spindly legs clad in gleaming riding boots. Behind them, neat ranks of troops were drawn up at attention. And beyond the lines of soldiers, the wooden *barrera* of a bullring.

Despite the blazing sun, Galindez felt a sudden chill, her skin prickled against her sweat-soaked clothes. She read the headline: *Hero of Badajoz decorated by* Generalísimo *Franco.* It was her first glimpse of *Comandante* Guzmán.

CHAPTER TWO

MADRID, 13 JANUARY 1953, PUERTA DEL SOL

During the afternoon the wind changed, and the scattered snowflakes that had spiralled down since early morning now turned to an insistent hail. Freezing rain clung to the shabby clothes of the crowds passing along the cobbled street between Plaza Santa Ana and Puerta del Sol. Guzmán watched the thin, hungry faces of the men and women who clattered past him, the sound of hobnails sharp on the frozen cobbles. Although his coat was thicker and of better quality than the majority of those around him, Guzmán was still freezing.

The lights of numerous cafés and bars illuminated the flurries of sleet and snow that dappled the vague light of the street lamps. Inside the cheaper places, Guzmán saw workmen in blue boiler suits, crowding round the bar, spearing tapas with toothpicks, others cradling cups of hot coffee in their frozen hands. In more expensive places he saw the middle classes, brilliantined and preening, taking coffee and cognac. In every establishment cigarette smoke rose in clouds around the lights, gently enveloping those within in an indistinct blue haze.

Guzmán stamped his feet to try to warm them. It was then he realised one of his shoes was leaking. Since the war, poverty encroached on the lives of all but the very fortunate. The idea he shared an experience with those grey, cadaverous workmen disgusted him. Their shoes might leak, but as far as Guzmán was concerned, it served them right. They were born to it. There was no reason why he should share in their poverty and deprivation if he could possibly avoid it. And he had so far.

Behind the market near the Plaza Mayor, Guzmán entered a plain small bar. The warmth washed over him as he stood against the bar watching the occupants with a practised eye. Behind the bar the barman was grilling large piles of mushrooms in oil and garlic on the hot plate. Guzmán nodded when the barman looked at him in silent inquiry before heaping a plate with sizzling mushrooms, dousing them with salt and topping them with slices of bread skewered by a couple of toothpicks. The plate was accompanied by a small stone pitcher of rough red wine. Guzmán poured the wine into the smeared glass. He tasted a mushroom and spat it to the floor as it burned his mouth. He damped down the pain with a gulp of the wine, glaring at the barman's back, wondering for a moment whether some retribution was necessary. A moment later the mushrooms had reached a more acceptable temperature and he wolfed them down, scooping them up with the bread and then mopping up the remaining oil and garlic. Guzmán finished his wine and then fastened his coat tightly before leaving. Outside the sleet was thickening again and passers-by hunched against the sharp gusts of clinging wind-borne snowflakes.

'Hey, that guy didn't pay,' the younger barman said as Guzmán left.

The old man pulled the young barman back. 'Police,' he said simply and the younger man suddenly deflated, shooting a worried glance after the dark bulk now striding into the snow-flecked late afternoon.

'You should have said before,' he complained.

In the street near the market, a dark Hispano-Suiza sedan was waiting, its engine running. Guzmán saw the wan face of the driver through the misted windscreen. He came alongside the car and opened the driver's door with one quick movement, reaching in and seizing the man's throat in his big hands. The driver's eyes jerked open as he struggled for breath.

'*Hijo de puta*, never go to sleep again when you're driving me, or I'll break you down to private and send you to the fucking Rif mountains where the Moors will cut you into pieces. *Entiendes*?'

18

The driver nodded. He was having difficulty swallowing.

Guzmán released him and climbed into the back seat behind the startled driver. 'Got the address?' The driver nodded again. 'Then let's go.'

The car moved away from the kerb. Guzmán felt the musty warmth seep through him as the car built up speed. The interior of the car smelled of leather, sweat and black tobacco and Guzmán relaxed as he inhaled the familiar odours. As they drove, he watched the architecture change as they left behind the impressive buildings surrounding the Plaza Mayor and passed through neighbourhoods of increasingly shabby, ill-kept buildings punctuated by the odd collapsed wall or bomb site. *Not as many as there used to be,* Guzmán thought. *Soon you won't know there had been a war at all. The city is starting to forget. If we let it.*

The streets were now decidedly working class, the dilapidated buildings dark and shadowed. Lines of washing hung across balconies like ships' flags, signalling the poverty of the inhabitants. There was less motor traffic now and they frequently encountered horse-drawn vehicles which slowed them, and from time to time carts and trolleys being pushed by sallow men in ragged clothes. The driver suddenly accelerated, forcing a pair of youths to abandon the cart they were pushing and leap out of the way.

Guzmán leaned forward. 'No rush, we're almost there.'

'*Si, mi comandante.*' The driver slowed as he took the next corner, keen to obey.

'There they are.' A hundred metres away, Guzmán saw a khaki truck filled with *guardia civiles*. The Hispano-Suiza glided to a halt by the rear of the truck and Guzmán looked out at the *guardia* crowded in the back of the vehicle, strange dark shapes in their tricorne hats and heavy capes, a mass of men bristling with long rifles. Guzmán climbed from the car into the freezing late afternoon air.

A uniformed *teniente* stepped forward. '*Comandante* Guzmán? *Teniente* Cabrera.' The man snapped off a salute. Guzmán ignored it.

19

'He's in a *piso* just up there.' Cabrera gestured towards a row of tall ramshackle buildings near the end of the street. Snow was falling heavily. Those few people braving the cold rapidly began to disperse, as they saw the *guardia civiles* climb from the lorry and move purposefully down the road. Bystanders melted away into the black recesses of the tattered buildings, recognising impending trouble. A tense silence accompanied the dark shapes of the *guardia* as they took up positions along the pavement, their breath steaming in the dwindling afternoon light. The noise of the city faded, muffled by the thick snow falling over the shadowed street.

'We need to get a move on. If it gets too dark he might be able to make a break for it,' Guzmán said. 'Five men at the top of the street there...' he indicated the far end of the road, 'another five in the alleyway at the back. The rest can go inside and break down his door. Any resistance and they shoot to kill.'

'Understood, *mi Comandante.*' Another snatched salute. Guzmán sighed.

Guzmán watched the first group of *guardia* move stealthily down the pavement to take up their positions. Several more troopers hurried along the alleyway leading to the back of the apartments. Escape from that end of the street would now be impossible, whether their quarry came out the front or rear of the building. When the man ran – and he would, Guzmán knew – his only escape route had now been decided for him. Guzmán waited until the remaining *guardia* started entering the building before he began walking towards the alley.

'Shall I accompany the *comandante*?' The *teniente* asked. Guzmán scowled and waved the man away dismissively. His work was best done alone.

Guzmán walked down the alley, barely noticing the rubbish strewn at his feet. At the end he came to the rear of the apartments. The space between the houses of the street and those at the back of them formed a high narrow lane. Fine for pedestrians, but there was no exit, particularly for a man fleeing from justice. That was how it should be, he thought. Looking down through the gloom,

Guzmán saw the *guardia* were now in position. He looked in the other direction, down another dark alley half filled with old packing cases and boxes. That was where the man would run when the *guardia civiles* broke down his door. He wouldn't risk going back out into the street once he had leaped down into the lane between the buildings – which he surely would because Guzmán had planned it that way. Guzmán ambled into the shadows of the alley. For a big man, he moved quietly and carefully. Taking up a position behind a large pile of boxes, he took out his pistol, an American Browning Hi-Power. Guzmán preferred the certainties of superior firepower to the vagaries of a smaller-calibre weapon. Some people carried a sidearm for effect. Guzmán's weapon was purely functional.

The silence was taut, charged with violent anticipation. Even the wind made little noise as it scattered snow in capricious gusts. For a moment, the faint sound of music on a radio. A car horn far off. The sound of the city in winter, a mute vague melancholy, held in place by the chill weight of the leaden cold.

A shot. Loud and sharp, echoing down the narrow alley. A volley of angry and confused shouts. More shots. A bullet whined down the alley above Guzmán's head. He scowled. Then he heard the sound of a man running, the shouts of the *guardia civiles* in pursuit. Guzmán listened to the fugitive's approaching footsteps. Just as he had expected.

The man came running at full tilt, briefly looking back at the civil guards clattering down the alley after him as he neared the jumble of packing cases. *Never look back.* It was too late to avoid Guzmán's outstretched leg and the fugitive stumbled and fell, his pistol clattering away on the cobbles. Before the man could get back on his feet, Guzmán brought the butt of the Browning down on his head. The man grunted and lay face down, stunned. Blood spilled into the dirty snow. The man groaned and struggled to raise himself.

'*Tranquilo, coño.*' Guzmán's foot pressed down on the side of the man's face, pinning him in place. The *guardia civiles* came running up, gasping, a bustling mass of tricornes, rifles and capes, their breath a pulsing cloud above their three-cornered hats. *Teniente* Cabrera pushed through them.

'Got him,' the *teniente* said, gasping for breath. 'Francisco Umbral, I arrest you in the name of Spain for crimes against the State and for treachery.'

The man on the ground tried to spit but Guzmán pressed his foot down harder on the man's face. '*Pendejo. Tranquilo.* Keep still or you'll really be sorry.'

'Shall we take him to the barracks?' The *teniente* was eager to be seen to be doing something.

Guzmán shook his head. 'Take your men to the truck, *Teniente*, I've a couple of questions I need to ask in private. I'll handcuff him and bring him along.'

The *teniente* gave him a look of furtive understanding. '*A sus ordenes, Comandante.*' He turned and led his men back to the street.

Guzmán released the pressure of his foot on the man's face. 'You took some finding, Umbral.'

'*Joder.* Take me away. I'll stand trial. Let the world hear what Franco's regime does to its people. Garrotte me. What will the world say, fourteen years after the war finished and you're still seeking revenge?'

Guzmán knelt and pressed the muzzle of his pistol into the back of Umbral's head. Guzmán knew the effect the proximity of a firearm had: he could hear Umbral struggling to keep his breathing under control. Guzmán reached into the fugitive's pocket and pulled out his wallet. 'Well look at this. Fake ID. Badly done. Want to tell me who did this for you? Maybe I could get your money back.'

'Beat it out of me in your cells, fascist. Cuts and bruises will look better at the trial.'

Guzmán stepped back. The daylight was almost gone now. 'Shame you weren't at the first trial,' Guzmán said, 'the sentence was passed in your absence.' He smiled. 'That was a long time ago. But the sentence stands. There'll be no more trials for you.'

Guzmán shot Umbral between the shoulder blades. The percussive bark of the Browning echoing down the alley, the smell of burning from the scorched clothing around the bullet wound in the man's back. A momentary twitching as Umbral's body accustomed itself to being dead. And then the blood. Guzmán retrieved the dead man's pistol and placed it next to the body. The *guardia civiles* came running, slipping and sliding on the icy ground.

'*Qué ha pasado, Comandante?*' The *teniente* struggled to keep his balance on the icy stones.

'Hidden pistol,' Guzmán said. 'I had no choice. Take him away, boys.'

Guzmán went back to the car and sank into its warm musty interior. He lit a cigarette.

'You got him, sir.' Less a question than a statement. At least it indicated the driver was capable of thought.

'I always do, Corporal,' Guzmán said. 'I always get them, because there's nowhere left for them to hide.'

The car's engine growled into life.

'Drop me at the Plaza Mayor,' Guzmán ordered. 'I'll get back to the *comisaría* under my own steam later.' He was hungry.

It was dark when the car stopped to let Guzmán out. He walked across the cobbled square of the Plaza Mayor, the lights of the bars along the sides of the square warm and inviting. Beneath a street light Guzmán pulled out the dead man's wallet. Fake identity papers, a repair bill for some clothes. And five thousand pesetas. *A man on the run with a lot of money*, Guzmán thought, putting the money into his wallet. *We'll have to find out who his benefactor was.* It wouldn't be too difficult.

He entered the Bar de Andalucía. The lights inside were poor and the selection of tapas on the bar despicable, but it was better than being outside. Guzmán treated himself to a brandy and then another, courtesy of the late *Señor* Umbral. The drink made him hungry and he ordered a plate of fried fish and then another brandy to keep out the cold.

At eight o'clock, Guzmán returned to the wintry darkness, strolling down into the small darkened square of Plaza Santa Ana, his footsteps muffled by the deepening snow. Pausing, he looked in through the window of the Cervecería Alemana, noting the warm glow from the lamps, the radiance of the stove behind the bar and the aroma of hot food that drifted out into the brittle cold each time the door opened. A couple more brandies wouldn't hurt. After all, he was on duty. Guzmán opened the door but was pulled up by a voice behind him.

'*Buenas tardes, Comandante. A sus ordenes.*' Two uniformed policemen jumped to attention. Guzmán had been so focused on the ambience of the bar he hadn't even seen them.

He scowled, his desire to ensconce himself in the warm fug of the bar and to order some hot food making him even more irascible than usual. 'Something wrong?' he snapped.

'No, sir, just that… it's me, Fuentes, from Calle Toledo. I worked for you last year on the Irate case. Doesn't the *comandante* remember me?'

Guzmán didn't remember him. 'Fuentes? That's your name, is it?'

'*Sí, mi Comandante. A sus ordenes.*'

Guzmán glared at Fuentes through the mist of sharp sleet. 'How the hell do you expect me to remember the name of every uniformed halfwit who opens the doors for me on an investigation? Carry on with your patrol, do your duty and don't fuck up my evening any further. Those are my orders. *Entiendes?*'

'Understood, *mi Comandante.*' The man saluted and Guzmán felt himself begin to rage when Fuentes stayed where he was, waiting until Guzmán returned his salute and dismissed him. 'Carry on, Fuentes, before a crime wave breaks out in your absence.'

'*Sí, señor.*' Fuentes turned away into the darkening square, glad to escape Guzmán's anger.

'Fuentes,' Guzmán called. 'Next time, speak when you're spoken to. That will make it easier to ignore you.'

'Understood, *mi Comandante.*'

Guzmán turned his back before the man could salute again. It was getting colder.

At the other side of the square, Fuentes rejoined his companion. The younger man cradled his carbine under his cape. He looked questioningly at Fuentes.

'That was Guzmán,' Fuentes said. '*Comandante* Guzmán.'

'The war hero?'

'That's him. The bastard. In the war they say he used to kill Reds and then cut off their ears – even from the women.' Fuentes looked back nervously. 'From what they say he would probably like to do that to most of us in uniform as well. My advice is to avoid him. It makes life easier.'

'Can't you get on his good side?' the younger man asked, watching uninterestedly as a legless beggar pulled himself past them, the stumps of his legs strapped to two wooden blocks, enabling him to half crawl and half slide over the cobbles. The beggar looked away, not wanting their attention. There was little chance of that, beggars were too numerous to interest them.

Fuentes laughed. 'Good side? *Madre de Dios*, he doesn't have a good side. He hates everyone: the *guardia civil*, the army, nuns, cripples, probably even the baby Jesus himself. Mind you, Franco himself pinned the medal on him so he must have seen something in *Comandante* Guzmán. God knows what.'

The policemen laughed conspiratorially and continued their patrol, boots crunching on the growing layer of snow that covered the cobbles of Plaza Santa Ana. The dull light of the street lamps struggled against the growing darkness. At the edge of the square, the two *guardia* passed into the shadows of the freezing night and were gone.

Guzmán watched the two policeman blend into the shadows bordering the square before opening the door to the Cervecería Alemana. The air was suddenly warm and moist with the smells of cooking meat and fish. Ignoring the '*buenas tardes*' from the barman who called out a greeting to each customer as they entered, Guzmán found a table and sat with his back to the wall.

25

The waiter came at once. '*Comandante. Buenas tardes.*'

'How's business, Salvador?'

The waiter blanched. If Guzmán made small talk it was a bad sign. Normally he would utter a stream of monosyllabic commands to which the only acceptable response was compliance.

'We manage, *Comandante*. As the *comandante* knows, times are hard. Produce is hard to obtain. But we do our best.'

'Well, do your best now. I'll have a plate of calamari, prawns with garlic and a glass of Rioja. And bring me a newspaper. *El Alcázar* will do.'

'At once, *Comandante* Guzmán,' the waiter nodded, happy to be dismissed so quickly.

Guzmán looked around, seeing down-at-heel students sharing a small plate of fried potatoes, businessmen immersed in newspapers or leafing through files, and a couple holding hands and gazing into each other's eyes, blind to the world. Guzmán looked at them contemptuously. *In this country, how is love possible? A constant preoccupation with someone else when what you really need to do to survive is look after number one.*

The waiter brought the food. He returned to the bar and brought the Rioja. He poured, taking care to fill the glass almost to the brim. Guzmán nodded approvingly.

'Tell me, Salvador, have you seen Dr Vargas in here lately?' Guzmán saw the waiter stiffen, taken off guard for a second. *Go on, lie to me, I'll kick you senseless.* The waiter swallowed.

'Well?' Guzmán was staring hard now. 'Before you answer, remember I still have your brother-in-law's name in my notebook. Once a Red, always a Red, they say. How sad if I have to reopen his case and go into his past a little more closely. I doubt your wife would forgive you if she found out you could have saved his neck but didn't.'

There was sweat on the waiter's brow. He had a look Guzmán knew well. He was scared, shit scared, his mind in turmoil between a desire not to inform on the doctor while also wanting to protect his brother-in-law from more detailed attention from Guzmán. It was one or the other. There was a certain calculation that had to be made and Guzmán waited for the waiter to make it.

'The doctor was in here two nights ago. He comes in every Monday and now and then on Fridays as well.'

'And what does the doctor talk about when he comes here?'

'Oh, the weather, rationing, students who won't try hard enough. Just day to day...'

Guzmán seized him by the wrist. The waiter froze, trying to mask the pain but not succeeding. 'Don't fuck with me, Salvador, or your wife's brother will be breaking rocks in Albacete until 1970. Unless of course the tribunal send him to the firing squad.' *This is where it becomes clear to him, where he can't tell me enough, where he doesn't hold anything back because he so wants to tell me what I want to hear and he doesn't want me to think he's leaving anything out. This is what fear does.*

'Dr Vargas meets with one man every week, usually Mondays. Bald, about forty with a short moustache. Well dressed, expensive clothes, sharp cut.'

'And what do they talk about?'

'*Comandante*, I would never listen in to our customers' conversations...' The waiter dried up under Guzmán's rigid gaze.

'Have you ever been in the offices of the *Brigada Especial*, Salvador?' Guzmán asked, taking a mouthful of wine. He waved a finger for the waiter to top it up.

'Me? No, sir. I served my country during the crusade, as the *comandante* knows. There has never been any reason for the—'

'What I mean,' Guzmán growled, 'is unless you drop the bullshit, you may find yourself down there, with me, my *sargento* and with your fucking teeth all over the room in the vaults where we take the faggots, the heretics, communists and pissy waiters who don't seem to want to do their patriotic duty.'

'From what I overheard, they talk about some sort of political stuff. I honestly don't understand it, *Comandante*. I swear. It's too complicated for me.'

Guzmán nodded. 'Give me a clue. You must have heard

something you recognised or can remember. Think. You're doing so well it would be a shame to send you home to your wife with your nose spread across your face and your balls like watermelons. Still, if you can't work, I expect your wife will be able to support you. Somehow.'

'Words, *Comandante*. Long words, *dialectical materialism, proletariat, hegemony.*'

'Even a moron like you knows what lies behind talk like that.'

The waiter nodded. 'The sort of things the Reds used to say, "Those without God—"'

Guzmán cut him short. 'Well done, Salvador. You've served your country yet again.' He gestured towards his glass and the waiter refilled it obediently. Guzmán lifted the glass, watching the light from the gas lamps illuminate the subtle colours of the wine.

The waiter stepped back, drained and eager to get away. Even though he had done nothing wrong himself, there was always the possibility the guilt of others could attach itself. Just knowing a suspect was enough to suggest complicity.

'Will there be anything else, *Comandante*?'

'Not for now. But next time the doctor comes in and meets this other man, call my office. We should talk with the doctor. Make his acquaintance more formally.'

With a stiff bow, the waiter turned and made his way to the bar. Through the haze of blue oil smoke from the large iron grill, Guzmán saw him say something to the cook. The cook glanced across the room, hurriedly averting his gaze when Guzmán stared back. Guzmán noticed Salvador put the empty bottle of Rioja on the counter and then pour himself a cognac, gulping it down before he disappeared into the steaming kitchen.

When he had eaten, Guzmán pulled on his hat and overcoat and left without looking at the staff behind the bar. Such niceties were not necessary here. Bracing himself, he opened the door and stepped out into the flat unrelenting cold. *There were winners and losers. And we won. To the victors the spoils. And to the enemy? Fuck them.* Those like Salvador were just as bad in their own way, always willing to defend or condone or excuse. The ones who would forgive and forget. Because they were weak. From there it was just another step to listening to the arguments of those who advocated Marxism, godlessness, Freemasonry or worse, democracy. Democracy, what a laugh. One vote for all? He stared at a beggar hunched in a doorway, a twisted hand holding a tin cup. Give a vote to that? What fool would let it happen? The war was fought to decide who would run the country. Franco won, and now things were done his way. And those who helped achieve victory reaped their rewards in turn. The *Caudillo* had called for an iron fist and it was people like Guzmán who wielded that fist. That was the way it was and that was the way it was staying. It suited Guzmán very well.

Walking back to the *comisaría* along Calle de Atocha, Guzmán saw the snow thicken in the lamplight, the bleak continuity of the flakes picked out briefly in their weightless descent through the greasy halo of the street lamps. Behind curtains, a weak glow occasionally fluttered from a candle or lamp. *It's as if the entire city is in hiding. Hiding in the dark, afraid and guilty. Guilty people, guilty for what they had done or guilty for what they had not done. Let them stay that way. Fear restrains them in a way no prison can. Some think they can hide their guilt in the darkness, but it's the darkness that will betray them.* And there were so many willing to betray them, he knew. And then he, Guzmán, would seek them out just as they had always feared, and he would destroy them. Just the knowledge this was possible was enough to keep most in their place, fearful and suspicious. They could never know who to trust. And when no one can be trusted, everyone is a suspect.

By the time he reached the main road, the snow had turned to slush, making the going less slippery. His feet were soaked. Guzmán cursed, cursing the entire brotherhood of cheating cobblers and bootblacks who conspired to create shoddy footwear and whose toxic polish destroyed the shoes it was applied to. The quality of shoes these days was third rate, the war had drained the country of just about every resource, particularly those which could provide even a minimal degree of comfort. *It's dog eat dog now*, Guzmán thought. Even so, he still had to make do with badly made shoes.

Outside the *comisaría*, Guzmán saw the two guards on duty. Sentry posts were always chilly affairs, but even more so tonight, he thought. The two men looked thoroughly unhappy, their capes drenched with sleet, rifles cradled with menacing affection.

Guzmán curtly acknowledged their salutes as he entered the building. Inside, a darkened hallway led to the ancient reception desk. A lamp glowed on the desk. The *sargento* looked up from his newspaper.

'*Buenas tardes, Comandante. A sus ordenes.*'

'*Muy buenas, Sargento.* Anything new?' The question suggested an interest but was entirely rhetorical: all Guzmán wanted was to light the stove in his office and dry his frozen feet. Then he noticed the *sargento*'s face. 'What ?'

'The general sir, General Valverde, he's here.'

Something must be wrong. Guzmán felt the adrenalin surge, his mind clearing, ready for action. *They always come for you at night.*

'Where is the general?'

'Your office, sir. I lit the stove and offered him coffee. He said he'd wait for you.'

'And how long has he been here?'

'Ten minutes, sir.'

'*Muy bien.* Listen, go to the kitchen and make some coffee. Use the real coffee in the officers' cupboard – but lock it away again when you've done, it's hard to get decent coffee even on the black market.' He pushed the key across the desk. 'I'll be with the general.' He turned to go through the double doors that led to his office. 'And I want the key to the cupboard back afterwards, *me entiendes*?'

The *sargento* grinned, an unpleasant act, since it gave an unwanted view of his broken and rotting teeth. '*Entendido, mi Comandante.*'

The bulb of the electric light in Guzmán's office spilled harsh white light over the sullen decay within. The ancient paper on the walls was peeling and an air of damp contested the other accumulated smells the old building jealously harboured. The general was sitting at Guzmán's desk, warming his hands by the small wood-burning stove. Guzmán looked round quickly, making sure he had left no papers lying about.

'*Mi General*, this is a pleasure. Had I known you were coming...'

The general's big ruddy face was not improved under the baleful light. His shaggy eyebrows contrasted with the neatly trimmed moustache. The immaculate uniform was ablaze with braid and medal ribbons.

'No need for small talk, Guzmán, thank you. I've no more time for it than you. What I have to say is best said in person, not on the telephone.'

'Of course, *mi General*. How may I be of service?'

'Sit down, *Comandante*.'

Guzmán pulled up a chair, aware of how the power balance between them was enacted, the general sitting at Guzmán's desk with Guzmán outside the warm radius of the stove, necessarily attentive. This was because the general thought his status was so much greater than Guzmán's. Guzmán did not agree. *Valverde knows his authority counts for very little here. We play this game; he thinks he is superior, I act as if it were true. But these are formalities. We both know who I answer to.*

'You're doing well, Guzmán,' Valverde said. 'I understand you've made a number of important arrests in the last few weeks.'

Guzmán nodded. 'The usual, *mi General*: traitors, agitators, Liberals. Enemies of the State who thought their conspiracies would go unnoticed. They may go unnoticed for a while but they don't get away. I don't let them.'

'Indeed. Your abilities in this field are particularly impressive, Guzmán. As I knew they would be when I first met you at Badajoz.'

'The general was very kind to me,' Guzmán said, without sincerity.

'Your physical and mental prowess were evident even then,' he said. 'That was why I recommended you to the *Caudillo*.'

'For which I'm grateful, *mi General*.'

'You've worked hard in this post, Guzmán. *Hombre*, you've been in the *Brigada Especial* since 1941.'

'As the general knows.'

'An excellent record in the army as well: and you attained the highest decoration your country could bestow on you.'

'Again, this is well known to the general. Even if it is, if I may say so, history.' *Nothing beats being modest*, Guzmán thought, knowing how much it would annoy a braggart like Valverde. *Why don't you just shit or get off the pot?*

'But a glorious history, Guzmán, Spain's history changed by the crusade against the Reds. By the actions of the *Caudillo* and, let me add, by men like you and me. That history will be told long after we are gone. Never forget it, *hombre*. And let no one else forget it, that's what I say.'

Guzmán nodded, despising the vanity of the man. *Cretin. After we are gone we are dust. Nada más. Does he think a few lines in the history books will give him immortality? Probably, since the man's ego is immense. General Valverde, hero of Badajoz, defender of the faith. Second in command to General Yagüe, architect of the first major victory of the Civil War. Valverde is still revelling in his role as hero after all these years. He remembers the times that brought him wealth and power. It's always as well to remember the other side of the coin. The real work. I wonder if he's already forgotten the dust of the bullring at Badajoz, as they herded in the beaten, the wounded, the women and children, shrunken, starved faces dirty and gaunt as they cowered before the bayonets of Franco's Moorish troops?* Guzmán remembered it very well. Standing next to Valverde and his officers, watching the machine gunners mow down the prisoners.

'You were appointed to this position by the *Caudillo* himself. That in itself indicates how highly he valued your conduct in the *Cruzada*,' Valverde said, interrupting Guzmán's memories.

The general was unusually talkative tonight, Guzmán thought. He was a man accustomed to giving orders, not inclined towards discussion and certainly not small talk. But he was boring and Guzmán's mind wandered, remembering again that afternoon at Badajoz. It had been very interesting to watch, Guzmán recalled, very colourful and well organised.

'The *Caudillo* was very kind,' Guzmán said. 'Because of my age I think he had a bit of a soft spot for me. And of course I'd been wounded.'

The general nodded, looking into the gloom at the edge of the circle of light from the bare bulb in the ceiling. He took out a packet of cigarettes and lit one, belatedly offering the packet to Guzmán. Both men exhaled smoke into the bitter light.

'He saw something in you, Guzmán, something that was needed in men who were to shape their country's destiny. He saw how you responded to adversity and he liked what he saw. The way you were willing to fight to the death for the Cause.'

Something's wrong. Suddenly Valverde's my best friend. He must want something.

'Guzmán, I too admire those qualities the *Caudillo* observed in you. Perhaps I haven't said so lately, but then in my position one can't have favourites nor can one single out a particular individual for praise no matter how worthy. I'm sure you understand that.'

As was so often the case when dealing with Valverde, there was nothing to do but nod in agreement. There was a knock at the door and an orderly brought in their coffee, pouring it into the ancient cups that were the *comisaría*'s best china. The orderly saluted and left.

'Perhaps you haven't had the recognition you deserve.' Valverde paused to wipe coffee from his moustache. 'That can change. I've got a business proposition for you, Guzmán. Something that will adequately reward you for your work on behalf of the *Patria*.'

Adequate reward? Does he think I'm stupid? He knows damn well I get by like everyone else: the bribes, the gifts, skimming off the deals of others. Not as much as a general can make, of course, but

33

then the secret of success is not to get greedy. Everyone, from high-ranking government officials dipping their snouts into the trough of public funds, right down to the local Falange members with their bribery and petty intimidation, all of them use the power available to them to get that bit more. It's how the country is run.

'If there is some matter in which I can be of service to the general,' Guzmán said, 'I would be only too pleased to help.'

Valverde leaned forward conspiratorially. 'Your talents are exceptional, Guzmán, no one can sniff out Reds and traitors like you. You would have done well in the Inquisition.' The general smiled stiffly. 'And make no mistake,' he continued, 'we still need an Inquisition in this country. After the *Cruzada* we dealt with many of our enemies. But there are those who still feel the *Caudillo* was too lenient, too...'

'Soft?' Guzmán tried not to sound incredulous.

'That's a soldier talking.' Valverde smiled, approvingly. 'Let's say, he was merciful. It's likely he was badly advised. Great leaders are always surrounded by a profusion of advisors and each of them has their own agenda. Decisions in such a context are always complicated.'

Treacherous bastard, Guzmán thought. *Is he trying to draw me into criticising Franco? What the hell is he up to? I'm having none of this. Franco – lenient? Fuck me. It would be easier to argue the Blessed Virgin had twins.*

'I'm surprised to hear the general considers that the decisions of the Head of State need to be revised, complex or not. If I may say so.'

Valverde flushed angrily. He finished his coffee, trying, with limited success, to calm himself. 'I put that badly,' he grunted. 'I wouldn't want you to take what I said as any form of criticism of the *Caudillo*. Naturally that wasn't my intention. But in a great country like ours, the business of government involves many people of lesser talent, with the result that decisions are often ill-informed. These are not faults of the *Caudillo*, of course.'

Guzmán revelled in Valverde's discomfort. *Pompous bastard.*

34

He's overplayed his hand. Now he's worried I'll inform on him. Valverde was right to worry. It was Franco who had elevated Guzmán to the command of this make-believe police station from where he and his men relentlessly hunted down the weary remnants of Republican opposition. It was Franco who trusted Guzmán to carry out work so secret and sensitive it could not be shared with the *Caudillo's* own generals. And Franco's trust in Guzmán caused great discomfort for many of those who were senior to Guzmán. In rank, that was: Guzmán was accountable only to the very top. This elevated status and the effectiveness of his constant pursuit and destruction of Franco's enemies made him a force to be feared. Guzmán well knew the effect he had on others – even those technically his superiors: *They fear me. They fear me because of what I do, the arrests, the beatings, the executions, and none of them are consulted on any of it. Not Valverde nor any other general, not the police or the guardia civil, no one.*

Valverde continued in a more conciliatory tone, 'The thing is, Guzmán, we're both men of action. We understand how these things work.' The general was smiling again.

Guzmán tried to appear as non-committal as his inherently suspicious face would allow.

'These have been hard times, Guzmán,' Valverde said. 'We've all worked hard to uphold what we forged on the field of battle, we who fought on the side of God and decency, now we reap a few small rewards for our labour. To the victor the spoils, Guzmán.'

Guzmán nodded. *Small reward indeed*, he thought. *Valverde controls the importation of foreign pharmaceuticals into this country. He was with Franco from the start of the War, and for a while it could have been Valverde who took command of the rebellion. But the other generals chose Franco, and, however unhappy he had been with that choice, Valverde had displayed a highly visible and vocal loyalty to the Caudillo ever since. After the war ended, the Caudillo made him Capitán-General of Madrid, to keep him happy. And quiet. Franco wanted to buy him and Valverde let himself be bought. And quite right too.*

'As you say, General. After the chaos of war we brought order. And we need to preserve order. A well-run country is one that will prosper. And if those in authority prosper, then so too will the lower classes in their turn.' Guzmán saw Valverde's nod of agreement and his contempt for the man increased. *No one in authority in this country cares a fuck about the lower classes, except in terms of making them work harder and for less.*

Valverde smiled. 'I have a proposition, *Comandante*. Nothing fancy or complicated and certainly nothing that would detract from your important work.'

'I'm at the general's service,' Guzmán said.

A sudden muffled scream of pain echoed from somewhere down the corridor. Guzmán was amused to see the general's discomfort as the screaming reached a loud frenetic climax and then stopped. There was some unintelligible shouting and the noise of boots in the corridor. 'My apologies, *mi General*,' Guzmán smiled. 'One of the prisoners. We think he was trained in Russia before the war. My lads are taking their time wringing the information out of him.'

Valverde nodded, getting back to the task in hand. Guzmán noticed the general had recovered his composure. *Just a little out of practice, General, I'm sure you could get used to it again if you had to.*

'Guzmán, I need help with a matter which needs to be handled with some delicacy,' Valverde said, frowning as the screaming started again. 'As you know, I have certain interests in the importation of pharmaceuticals into Spain.'

Certain interests? Guzmán thought.

'By using my administrative talents,' Valverde continued, 'the *Caudillo* has greatly improved the supply of medicine to the people. And naturally, being used to command and organisation, I deal with this importation in a highly efficient manner. Which is to say, in my own way. No man likes his work to be interfered with. Especially in business.' Valverde was scowling now, his cheeks reddening as he spoke. 'Which is why...' He paused, trying to quell his sudden rage. 'Which is why I need you to deal with these bastards, Guzmán.'

'Is someone interfering in your business dealings, *mi General*?' Guzmán raised an eyebrow. 'Those dealings are directly authorised by the *Caudillo*. Surely it's a matter which can be dealt with directly? Why involve my unit?' he asked. *Fuck, I didn't join the police to catch criminals.*

Valverde's puce face almost ignited, his eyes glittered, even his moustache bristled with fury. 'Because, Guzmán, I'm forbidden to take such action. That's why I want you to deal with this fucking mess and it's why I'm willing to pay you a great deal to handle these *hijos de puta.*'

This is probably not the time to ask how much, Guzmán decided. 'Who are these people?'

Valverde reached into his briefcase and brought out a cardboard file. Guzmán looked at the file cautiously. As far as he could tell, his name was not on it. That would have been a bad sign. The general took out a sheaf of papers and slid several black and white photographs across the desk. Guzmán saw various men, some posing, some clearly photographed without their knowledge. Dark moustaches, swarthy skin. One of them with a smile punctuated by a gold tooth. Yankee zoot suits: full baggy trousers, oversized jackets with padded shoulders.

'Dominicans,' Valverde said, biting his lower lip. 'These are who we have to deal with. You have to deal with, that is. These *hijos de puta* have been interfering with the sales of my products. On the streets – in broad daylight. They've even been dealing with my customers. Can you believe it?'

'I'm astounded,' Guzmán said, puzzled as to why the military governor of the Spanish capital would be bothered about a few foreign goons. 'They've been stealing from your pharmacies?'

'Grow up, Guzmán,' Valverde snapped. 'They've been interfering with some of the less official outlets.'

'I see.' Guzmán nodded. 'The pushers on the streets and in the bars?'

Valverde's puce face contorted. 'Never mind that, *Comandante*. You know how these things work. It's a service, in a way, for the degenerate and those in pain from their war wounds. The important thing is, these bastards have not only been selling their own products, they've attacked several of my most reliable,' he paused, 'sales people.'

'A bunch of half breeds dressed like pimps,' Guzmán sneered. 'Attacking your dealers. Shameful.' He arranged the photographs along the desk. 'Do we know anything about them?'

'A great deal.' Valverde nodded. 'This one,' he pushed a photograph towards Guzmán, 'is Enrique Garcia Melilla.'

Guzmán looked at the photograph. The man looked like a university professor down on his luck. Bald, with a scraggly beard and eyes hidden in deep sockets. 'He looks like a customer for the vice squad. Messing with little girls, playing with himself in public places – that's my guess.'

Valverde laughed. 'Wanted for murder in Cuba, Venezuela and Argentina. Served a sentence for murder in Bolivia, later commuted for unknown reasons. This one,' he pointed to the second photo, 'is Horacio Bienvenida. Apparently he's the leader. Was once a journalist, or so it seems. Served ten years in Panama for knifing his girlfriend.'

Guzmán snorted, 'I was right. Pimps and ponces. Why don't we ship them all back to their little island?' He thought for a moment. 'Or have them disappear?'

'This one,' Valverde continued, 'is Manuel Sanchez, the muscle of the outfit – for when knives and guns are not appropriate.'

The photograph was taken as Sanchez approached the doorway of a bar. Behind him was a stretch of glaring white beach and beyond a flat, gleaming sea. The man's face was largely in shade but Guzmán could still see the immense bulk under the tight-fitting cotton jacket. Sanchez had thick hair which extended down to his eyebrows. His jug ears stuck out from the improbable thatch, and below a simian brow the nose displayed all the signs of having been broken, probably more than once. 'Christ, what an ape,'

Guzmán said. 'When he was born I bet the nurse threw him a banana.'

'You'd underestimate *Señor* Sanchez at your peril, Guzmán. He trained as a heavyweight boxer, fighting bare-knuckle fights for pesos in Columbia, Peru and most of the Caribbean as well. According to reasonably reliable reports, he not only won forty-eight out of fifty fights, but left at least eight dead. He has convictions for manslaughter, gun running and an impressive record of almost ceaseless violence.'

Guzmán shrugged. 'If he was Spanish I'd offer him a job working here.' He picked up another photograph, a thin-faced young man with a large, floppy-brimmed panama that hid his face in shadow. The man's sunglasses prevented Guzmán seeing his eyes but he noted a thin pencil moustache beneath the aquiline nose. '*Maricón*, no?' Guzmán sneered.

'Diego Vasquez, aged nineteen,' Valverde said, looking at the sheets of typed information in front of him. And yes, as you say, a sodomite. A regular little debauchee. Convictions for violence, theft, pederasty and living off immoral earnings.'

Guzmán took the next photograph the general offered him, a mugshot of a pale-skinned black man with a wide jaw. 'His mother was too friendly with the hired help by the look of it.' Guzmán laughed.

'In the Dominican Republic, Guzmán, a large percentage of the population are of mixed blood,' Valverde said. 'It's even found in the upper classes, even the *presidente*'s grandmother was a slave. That gentleman is Salvador Bienvenida. Of whom we know very little so far other than he's Horacio's brother.'

Guzmán leaned back in his chair. 'So, we have five foreign criminals in Madrid, none of whom would be out of place doing hard labour, given their track record. Why not round them up? If it would help I'll take a squad of *guardia civiles* out and...' He shrugged, leaving the obvious conclusion unspoken.

Valverde sighed. 'If only. For some reason the word from above is that these Dominicans are to be tolerated. They came here with the American trade delegation. The *Caudillo* has been very specific: they must be allowed to conduct their business here, for the good of the economy.'

What the hell? Guzmán thought. *Valverde is planning to act against Franco's wishes and worse – for me – he wants me to do his dirty work.* 'The general is surely not going to go against an order from the *Caudillo* himself,' he said. It was a statement not a question.

Valverde looked uncomfortable. He sighed. Leaning down into his briefcase he produced a bottle of brandy. 'Glasses, *Comandante*?'

Guzmán went to a small cabinet by the window and took out two chipped glasses, putting them on the desk next to Valverde's bottle. 'Carlos Primero, General? A rare treat indeed.'

'Perhaps you'll develop a taste for it,' Valverde said, looking up from pouring two large shots. 'The finer things come to a man as he progresses through life.' He pushed a glass towards Guzmán. '*Salud y pesetas.*'

Guzmán took the drink, returning the general's toast. The expensive brandy was smooth and glowed on his tongue. He lifted the glass to the light and took another appreciative sip.

'An excellent brandy, Guzmán. I'll leave you the bottle.'

'The general is too kind,' Guzmán said, warily.

'I can rest easy then, *Comandante*?' Valverde said. 'You'll help me with this difficulty?'

Guzmán looked pained. 'General, I'll do anything in my power to be of assistance. But if these men are part of a trade delegation explicitly sanctioned by the *Caudillo*, then I must respectfully decline the general's request.'

He sat back and waited for the explosion. But Valverde shrugged, and took another mouthful of brandy. 'Of course, *Comandante*, of course. But you've seen from the dossiers on these men that they're exceptionally dangerous. As you say, they have every right to go about their *legitimate* business just as the *Caudillo* wishes. No doubt he's keen to preserve good relations with the Dominican Republic, given they're one of the few countries we're on good terms with at the moment.'

Guzmán noted the emphasis on 'legitimate'; it sounded as if the word were sticking in Valverde's throat.

'Just keep an eye on them, Guzmán, find out what they are doing. Do what you do best; a little information from here and there and then suddenly you have a dossier. And we know what dossiers can do.' Valverde smiled, far too smugly for Guzmán's liking.

'I certainly do,' Guzmán agreed. 'I'm happy to keep an eye on these men as long as it's clear I'm acting in response to your request. It's outside my normal remit, as you'll appreciate.'

'You're testing my patience,' Valverde growled. 'I want you to act without anyone else – and I mean anyone, Guzmán – knowing. In the meantime I want you to read the files and begin surveillance at once.'

Guzmán nodded. It was always difficult to turn down an offer of money. On the other hand, he had no wish to become involved in an operation that might be blamed on him if things went wrong. Something which would suit Valverde very well, given his loathing for Guzmán.

'One more thing, Guzmán.' Valverde stood up and rummaged again in his briefcase. 'Just so there are no misunderstandings.' He placed a brown paper parcel on the table. 'This should provide your motivation, *Comandante*. And I trust it will guarantee this remains between you and me. Discretion costs, I know, so I'm paying more than the going rate.'

He moved towards the door, Guzmán stepping ahead of him to open it. Valverde paused and looked at him for a moment. 'I have one further request, Guzmán, not nearly so difficult for you to agree to.'

'The general has only to ask,' Guzmán lied.

'My niece's husband Francisco has just finished his police training,' Valverde said. 'He needs experience but a copper's pay won't keep them, now the first baby's arrived. He's a bright lad, a good Christian and he'll obey orders. Everything you could want in an officer.'

41

'I have no budget for any more staff,' Guzmán protested.

'You have now.' Valverde smiled. 'Take him for six months, let him get some experience and then he'll probably be promoted and you won't see him again. Until he's chief of police.' He smiled again. *Which will probably be sooner than the poor bastard thinks,* Guzmán thought.

'If the general insists...'

'I do, Guzmán, I do. And I shall be very grateful. In fact, tomorrow night we're having a small soirée to welcome the American Trade Delegation. The *Caudillo* will be there, a few generals, politicians and some party members. Arrive between ten and eleven tomorrow evening.'

'In uniform?' Guzmán was horrified by the thought.

The general laughed at his discomfort. 'No, a suit will do, Guzmán, and not black tie, I assure you.'

'Very well.' Guzmán opened the door.

'You won't regret this, Guzmán,' Valverde said. He turned back for a moment. 'When shall I tell the lad to report to you?'

'Well, we have a raid at five tomorrow morning...' Guzmán began.

'Excellent. I'll phone him shortly. He'll be here an hour before. Name's Francisco Peralta. He won't let you down. He won't dare.' He smiled. 'I can see myself out.'

Fucking marvellous, Guzmán thought as the general closed the door behind him. *He dumps some rookie copper into a secret unit. The lad's in for a surprise, that's for sure.*

The clatter of Valverde's boots echoed down the worn flagstones of the corridor. Guzmán heard the swing doors open and close, heard the general's '*buenas noches*' and the barked reply from the *sargento* on the desk. There was the faint sound of running as the general's aides fought to open the car door for him. Guzmán looked around his office. This was how he liked it. Empty. A muted scream from below indicated the boys had started work again.

The anaemic light seemed more feeble than ever, the shadows pressing in around him as Guzmán locked the office door and sat at his desk. He took the bottle of Carlos Primero and pulled the cork, raising the bottle to his lips greedily. Yet even the expensive brandy couldn't overcome the sense of unease the general's visit had instilled in him.

The screams became louder and more frequent, now inflected with a desperate pleading tone. Guzmán looked at his watch. Eleven o'clock. He had ordered the *guardia civiles* to be ready at five in the morning. Raids were always best carried out while the subjects were in bed. It added to their sense of horrified anticipation as they were dragged away. He already had most of the addresses. The intelligence had been first class so far. The screaming represented the last pieces of information being obtained. Nothing must be overlooked. That was the way. His way. His men would have the information soon because Guzmán hand-picked his men. They could be relied on. Which, he reflected, was not the same as saying they could be trusted.

He picked up the brown paper parcel and tore it open, expecting to see a bundle of pesetas. But the bills were less ornate, though familiar enough: US dollars. He began to count. By the time he finished counting he had drunk two more glasses of brandy and sweat was running down his face. On the desk in front of him were ten thousand US dollars in hundred dollar bills. He was rich.

Scooping up the money, he went over to the metal filing cabinet and began to pull it away from the wall. It took a while and the cabinet was heavy but Guzmán was strong and had done this before. Behind the cabinet one of the flagstones was divided by a jagged gash in the stone. By inserting a knife blade into the crack, Guzmán lifted one half of the flagstone and placed it to one side, before removing the other half. Below him was a hollow a metre deep. Guzmán leaned down and pulled out a metal box. In it were photographs, assorted documents and some loose change. Souvenirs of his work which, in an emergency, might come in handy. He placed the dollars in the box and replaced the box in the dusty pit, nestling it amongst the other mementos he had stashed down there. He replaced the broken pieces of flagstone and then pushed the cabinet back into place. Didn't they say out of sight, out of mind? *Whoever said that never knew me*, Guzmán, thought. His shirt felt damp under the arms. He lit a cigarette, inhaling slowly. He knew the value of staying calm. But he also knew the value of the money now hidden beneath the filing cabinet. If Valverde was prepared to pay that sort of money for his services, there must be a lot at stake. Valverde was pushing his luck disobeying Franco. There were limits and he was paying Guzmán to push them. Guzmán took a drag on his cigarette and reached for the brandy. He needed to think.

A slight sound outside. Guzmán was instantly alert, veins pumping, the glow of the alcohol fading as his muscles tensed. Someone was sneaking along the corridor outside. He heard the slow drag of booted feet. He drew the big pistol from its holster and eased off the safety catch. *Always strike first.* He levelled the pistol at the door. The sound grew nearer. Guzmán moved silently to the door. His left hand reached for the handle, not grasping it until he had positioned himself, ready to leap forward into the corridor as he pulled the door open. He forced himself to breath slower. *Uno.* Outside, the slow, stealthy sound of boots on stone, and something else, indistinct, possibly more than one person then. *Dos.* Guzmán's hand closed around the door handle. *Tres.* He wrenched the door open, aiming the Browning into the corridor ahead of him.

In the pale light two men were dragging another by his arms down the corridor. The man was face down, his head hanging limply. Guzmán came towards them, pistol levelled. But only for a second.

'*Jesús Cristo, jefe*,' the taller man said. 'You scared the shit out of me.' The other man looked blankly at the muzzle of Guzmán's gun as it lowered and moved back to the shoulder holster under his left arm. The man hanging between them said nothing, a lengthening string of bloody saliva hung from his mouth, gradually stretching its way down to the floor.

'Sorry, boys,' Guzmán said. 'You sounded a bit suspicious from in there.'

They nodded, startled but not daring to complain.

Guzmán looked at the man hanging between them. 'Did he talk?'

The tall one nodded. 'We got it. Everything. He wasn't going to talk, *jefe*, told us to shove it. We kicked the fuck out of him, Juanito here told him we had his wife in the next room and he was going to let the night watch see to her unless he told us the address. Still nothing. We stuck his head in a bucket and then we broke his fingers. The bastard wouldn't say a word.'

'So what made him so cooperative?' Guzmán asked with professional interest.

'Juanito remembered the iron upstairs. We let him watch it warming up and then took some of the creases out of his chest for him. Want to see the burns? He couldn't wait to spill his guts to us,' the tall one said.

Guzmán looked at him incredulously. 'You used the iron from upstairs on him?'

The men's expressions confirmed they had.

'*Coño*,' Guzmán exploded. 'That iron's for emergencies like the last time we had the top brass visit the *comisaría*. Did you get flesh stuck to it?'

The dumb one, Juanito, nodded.

'*Hijos de puta*. So next time we want to press a uniform so we look like half decent servants of the State, we won't be able to because you ruined the office iron. *Cabróne*s.'

The men stood shamefaced. Guzmán shook his head. 'Tomorrow, when we pick up the Reds, I want you two to search each fucking house, once you've subdued the prisoners, of course, until you find a good iron. Bring it back, give it to the *sargento*, and I won't shoot you in the back next time you're about to go off duty. Is that clear?'

'*Si, mi Comandante*,' the men mumbled like schoolboys.

'Now get out of my sight. And *that*,' he pointed to the body, 'is he dead?'

'No, *jefe*.' The tall one shook his head. 'We thought you'd want him put in with those we're arresting in the morning.'

Guzmán shrugged. 'Up to you. But if you ask me, he looks suicidal.' He looked at the tall one again. 'No?'

'Very clearly, *jefe*.' The tall one nodded eagerly. 'These Reds, no concept of God, of decency, no values. Nothing to keep them in this world.'

'Thank you, Archbishop,' Guzmán sneered. 'I'll leave you to it. And see you at five tomorrow morning. On the dot.'

'Sir.' The men began to drag the man back the way they had come. Guzmán turned to enter his office.

'*Jefe?*'

'*Qué?*'

'The *comandante* wouldn't have any rope, by any chance?'

Guzmán whirled round. '*Cabrón*, don't test my patience any more. Let's have some of the sharp thinking the *Brigada Especial* are so well known for. Use the fucker's belt. That's what suicides do, no?'

'Of course. *Gracias, jefe*.'

Guzmán slammed the door on them, muttering florid curses about their mothers. He kicked the desk a couple of times until his anger subsided. Outside, he heard them dragging the prisoner back to his cell. *Amateurs*. He put on his coat and scarf, took a last swig of brandy and then put the bottle in his desk drawer, which he then locked. No point putting temptation in the sarge's way.

Guzmán's footsteps echoed on the stone flags of the corridor. The *sargento* snapped to attention as Guzmán entered the icy lobby.

'All in order, *Sargento?*'

'*Todo está en orden, mi Comandante*. The general seemed very happy when he left.'

Guzmán stared hard. 'Did he? I had no idea you were such good friends with General Valverde. I'll see you in the morning.'

'I'll be here, *Comandante*. Everything is arranged.'

Guzmán leaned across the reception desk. 'I would very much prefer you not just to be here but to be awake as well.'

'Of course, *Comandante*.'

'*Buenas noches, Sargento*.' Guzmán tugged open the door and went out into the street.

Snow was falling heavily and the street was white with thick snow, glistening in the baleful glow of the street lamps. He began to walk towards Puerta del Sol. Snow blew into his eyes, making him swear. The new snow crunched beneath his leaking shoes and he occasionally slipped, provoking a barrage of curses and threats into the freezing night.

Around the little warren of streets leading into Puerta del Sol he noticed the whores were still out. A pale thin woman in rags smiled at him, decaying teeth bared in a rictus of desperation.

'Some company for the *señor*?' she stammered through almost blue lips. 'Anything he wants for a duro. *Anything*,' she emphasised.

'No.' Guzmán moved on past the shaking woman, aware his rejection had only encouraged others to move towards him, hissing a chorused litany of desperation at him through the falling snow. One woman staggered forward, her breasts visible through the tattered clothing she was trying to pull across her scrawny frame. Another was so drunk she could no longer stand. Guzmán moved on, leaving the skeletal whores behind. They lacked the strength or will to pursue him further. And then, as he stepped into the pool of light under the next street lamp, a new group accosted him, promising everything, and yet, he thought, offering very little worth having, even if it were free.

Just before the Metro station he left behind the last group of whores and negotiated his way past a crowd of cripples sprawled against a wall, begging. Various combinations of amputation and disease were offered up for his inspection. But Guzmán remained firm. Charity was for the weak, those who gave out of compassion, that was, not the recipients. For Guzmán they were like the dead. Perhaps a little more animated.

Passing the entrance to the station, Guzmán ignored a couple of old crones who tried half-heartedly to solicit him. He crossed the road and made his way down into Calle Mesón de Paredes, the high walls of the buildings rising black and craggy above him. The snow was getting thicker now, clinging to the front of his coat.

And then he felt the adrenalin surge. Someone was following him. He was sure of it. He recognised the footsteps. He had heard them earlier after he left the *comisaría*, measured and muffled, keeping a steady pace, accommodating the rhythm of his steps. Pausing by a darkened shop window, Guzmán lit a cigarette, casually turning to look back towards the wide expanse of the Puerta del Sol. The wind drove stinging flakes of snow across his face and the street lamps were now shrouded by heavy falling snow. Guzmán could hardly see.

But he saw the man. A dark shape in a doorway. Not moving, just watching. Guzmán calculated he was about fifty metres away and began to walk towards him. Then he thought better of it. Turning, he continued down the road, his feet crunching on the thickening snow, ears straining to hear the footsteps behind him. And there they were again. Guzmán looked back and the man melted into the shadow of another doorway.

The blizzard was so strong Guzmán could see only whirling snow shadows, blurred lights and the dark outlines of the shops and houses in the street. When the wind dropped for a moment he was no longer sure the man was still in the doorway. Reaching the entrance to his building, Guzmán turned his key in the ancient lock of the entrance hall door and stepped inside, closing the door to the street immediately. He groped for the light switch. A dim bare bulb illuminated the hallway, the stone-tiled floors, the solid wood of the apartment doors, the sharp stone of the staircase. Guzmán made his way to the first floor, listening intently.

His door was large and crossed with iron bands at the top and bottom. It took time to unlock, given that he needed to deal with each of the three locks fitted at shoulder, waist and knee height. Anyone trying to batter down that door would have a long job. It finally opened on carefully oiled hinges. Again the fumble for the light switch and then the pitiful half-light from the tiny bulb.

It was a spartan room, dark, wood-panelled walls with a

threadbare carpet and dusty curtains. It had the air of a property whose owner had gone away suddenly, without making arrangements for its upkeep. Which, in a way, Guzmán recalled, was what had happened. A small kitchen to the left, a bedroom to the right and a small bathroom. A bathroom was still a luxury for many and Guzmán had been pleased to take over the occupancy of such a well-appointed flat. The owner had been on one of the lists sent to Guzmán by Central HQ in manila envelopes. Only the door had needed replacing – there was not much left after Guzmán's men smashed it down one cold morning an hour before sunrise. Two plain armchairs faced one another by the window. Against the wall was a sturdy table strewn with papers. On the wall next to the kitchen door a gaudy Madonna smiled beatifically from beneath a glowing halo.

Guzmán took a swig of red wine from an open bottle in the kitchen and then poured himself a large glass, drank it and poured another. He locked the door, securing the three bolts he had fitted, one above each of the locks. Kneeling by the table, he pulled back the carpet. The floorboards beneath were loose fitting and an icy draught rose as he removed them one after another, revealing a large space between the joists below. Two large boxes of papers. Several files, a shoebox full of French francs. A British Webley revolver. Two cartons of ammunition. He reached further under the floorboards, checking the sub-machine gun and the box of extra magazines. All just in case. Guzmán brought out one of the files and looked at the cover. The words were written with a broad-nibbed pen in a strong angry hand:

General Antonio Rodrigo Valverde

Guzmán put the file on the table. The electric light was too weak to read by. He brought out his matches and lit the lamp. A sudden gust of wind rattled the windows. He put down the glass and walked over to the light switch. The room plunged into shadow with only the spectral glow of the lamp on the table to guide him as he crossed to the window and pulled the curtain aside.

Snow was falling steadily, blown in irregular patterns by the freezing wind. Guzmán looked down the darkened street. Nothing. Just snow streaming down, blurring the detail of the buildings, hiding the city beyond. Then he saw it. The glow of a cigarette in a doorway, intensifying momentarily as its owner took a drag. Someone was down there in the shadows watching him. For a moment Guzmán continued staring at the doorway. Then he let the curtain fall back across the window. Someone was watching him. But then someone always was.

The battle had ended but the killing went on. For some of the defenders, it was a long time before they recognised the end had come. In the smoke from the flurries of explosions it was difficult to see which of the darting shapes was Republican and which was Nationalist. The savage ricochet of bullets from the baked ground and the jagged rocks obliged the men to crouch as they made their way back up the hill. Before the last barrage they had seen the Nationalists were gaining ground on their left and the men became increasingly nervous as explosions and clouds of dust to their right told them Franco's troops were advancing on that flank as well. The political commissar tried to keep the company together, exhorting them to stand fast and hold back the fascist tide, but his words lacked conviction. Some men threw away their rucksacks despite the threats from the political commissar to have them court-martialled. Bullets rattled around them and whined above their heads, increasing their determination to get to the safety of the trees above. Among the trees there would be shelter from the deadly fire of the enemy. Now and then a bullet found its mark and a man would fall, raising a cloud of dust as he slid down the steep slope, back towards the oncoming enemy troops. Paco the sargento *died like that: one minute he was next to the kid, helping him upwards, conscious of the lad's youth and intent on ensuring he kept up, the next there was the shrill whine of the bullet and Paco fell back down the slope, tumbling in a cloud of dust and pebbles until he came to rest against a large rock. The kid looked down at the* sargento, *the man who had protected him, ensured no one stole his rations and fought off the bullies. The* sargento *looked back, eyes wide as he realised flight was no longer possible. His rifle lay some six metres away and he stretched out a* bloodied arm towards it. He looked back to the kid. But the kid was already climbing again, his boots sending down small dusty flurries of dirt and stones. By the time the sargento died, his last view was of the remnants of the company passing from the scorching day into the welcoming shadows of the trees. Five minutes later, the first Nationalist troops reached him, barely pausing to bayonet the body before they continued their pursuit.

For a moment, amongst the trees it was quieter. The dull thudding of artillery and the crackle of small-arms fire faded as the men scrambled into the shadows of the little wood. The ground rose steeply and they quickly lost all sense of direction: all they could see were the stunted boughs, their clinging, low-hanging branches impediments to flight as the men struggled beneath the weight of their equipment. Soon, they began to throw off their extra ammunition, even their water bottles, and those who still had their packs dropped them to the ground. The political commissar tried to get them to stay together in a compact group, to fight a rearguard action to hold back the Nationalists until reinforcements arrived, unlikely though it was. He demanded three men remain in the trees to act as snipers, delaying Franco's men while the others continued the retreat. The men were on the verge of hysteria. They could hear the shouts of the Moors below on the hillside. The political commissar drew his pistol, threatening to shoot one of them as an example to the others. Realising the men were ignoring him, the political commissar fired a shot into the air, bringing down parts of the tree beneath which he was standing and showering those around him with leaves. The crack of the pistol echoed across the hillside. A sudden volley of shots told them the Moors had heard the pistol and were now pursuing them with greater precision as a result. It was then the political commissar was killed.

CHAPTER THREE

Daylight filtered warm and soft through the shutters. Outside, the bustle of the market and the chaotic tension of traffic were just beginning. It was early, though the heat was already enough to make Galindez kick away the sheet. The air felt cool on her skin as she slipped from the bed leaving the *profesora* to continue sleeping.

Galindez idly looked around the bedroom, hearing the street outside coming to life, watching the sun move slowly over the bookshelves. So many books on just one theme, several written by Luisa. The titles all suitably professorial – *Forgetting the Past: the grave secrets of the Civil War; Not So Hidden Secrets: war graves and complicity in everyday discourse 1940–1976; Where Do They Lie?: Geographies of Forgetting in Contemporary Spain.* She yawned and looked for another book. Luisa continued to sleep. Galindez stretched lazily, suddenly realising she was bored.

It wasn't that sex with Luisa wasn't good. Luisa's inventiveness was surprising. But something had come between them and, strangely, it was a man. The mysterious *Comandante* Guzmán. Luisa's research into the enigmatic police chief had begun to enthuse Galindez as very little else in her adult life had. Even so, something was starting to bother her about the *profesora*. The night before, Luisa set off alarm bells when describing the methods she used in her research into Guzmán and his activities. For Galindez, Luisa's most serious failing was her disdain for science: those templates of knowledge Galindez had assiduously incorporated into her life ever since she began to take science

53

lessons seriously in her teens. Although, she thought, peering down at the market through the soft gauze curtain, if she were honest, she owed her interest in science to *Señorita* Chavez, her science teacher.

Señorita Chavez enthused her, sharing with Galindez the thrill of seeking out and accumulating data, and then understanding it using complex models of analysis and interpretation. Science gave Galindez a framework of knowledge that eventually inspired her to train as a forensic scientist. And how she had loved that training. Learning how to tackle the challenge posed by intangible, incoherent strands of evidence and rework them, translating the chaos and confusion of the crime scene into a coherent, credible explanation. That challenge, she had realised, was missing in her work for the *guardia civil*. In fact, her only real challenge so far had been to accept that her junior status doomed her to the crappy jobs. Inevitably, that meant war graves, even though forensic archaeology wasn't her specialist field. But then, she thought, how much of a specialist did you have to be to wield a spade?

So far, all she'd done was catalogue sites and excavate remains, even though, very often, local people had known exactly who was in those graves since the day they had been shot. No one cared about the dead. The politicians wanted to be seen to be doing something about addressing the casual slaughter of the War. So the *guardia* sent her on these futile journeys because of pressure from the politicians. That way, something was seen to be done. Something visible but inexpensive. Her job summed up then: cost-effective but pointless.

She took one of Luisa's books from the bookshelf and sat by the window. A faint eddy of warm air moved the diaphanous curtain against her arm. Outside, the sounds of the street grew louder. She skimmed through the book. One heading caught her eye: 'How Should We Write the History of the Civil War?' She began to read:

Most histories of the Civil War are moral and political projections from a contemporary perspective to one from almost a century ago. Just as the abiding intent of the Franco regime, with its self-aggrandising and backward-looking hagiography was to align Spanish political and social life with quasi-mythical events and needs derived from a fictional golden past. This constant re-creation of a contrived and artificial history that justifies contemporary political ends clearly demonstrates the need for a history focused on the ways in which a society understands itself through its understanding of the relationship between 'now' and 'then'. Doing history with practical intent must involve writing a history which needs to be – as Foucault has shown – a history of the present. We need to identify the contribution of the past to the thoughts and deeds of the present.

A history of the present? Practical intent? The words appealed to Galindez. But the sentences which followed didn't as she skipped through the turgid, repetitive rhythms of academia in full flow. Where was the clarity? The argument? Why couldn't academics like Luisa write in plain Spanish? Reading further, Galindez noticed with annoyance that Luisa had little time for individuals in her grand theorising:

For too long we have accepted the notion that the slaughter of the war resulted from the murderous inclinations of individuals. Yet it is in the realm of ideas and ideologies that the seeds of destruction are sown: treating the war as a patchwork of disparate criminal acts lends nothing to our understanding and creates only a culture of blame intent on individualising culpability and stereotypically labelling its subjects.

Christ, Galindez thought, Luisa wouldn't make much of a detective. No role for the individual? Blame culture? She saw the implications clearly. No role for forensic investigation, or detailed inquiry, just a focus on ideas and grand theories. Luisa's approach rejected the principles of rigour and precision Galindez had worked so hard to apply to her own work. For Galindez, Luisa's work seemed more like storytelling, taking strands of dubious evidence and weaving them together with vague and insubstantial theories.

Galindez wondered if she could do it better. Rather than leave people like Guzmán as vague footnotes in the Civil War's catalogue of death, maybe she could use them as case studies, making their wartime activities public knowledge? She had the technical knowledge. Her background and scientific expertise would give her the necessary gravitas. She began to think about the opportunities: conference papers and journal articles bringing the darkest secrets of the Civil War to light. There would be benefits for others as well as a major benefit for her: a way out of the organisation *Papá* loved. The organisation that was grinding her down. She could leave behind the endless bagging up of remains, the hours of working alongside sweating men in fatigues who stood back to discuss her *culo* as she bent over the heaps of bones, debating whether she was a six or a seven.

Thinking of *Papá* kindled a familiar sadness. She recalled *Tia* Carmen telling her stories of how much he loved working for the *guardia*. Until the day he walked out of the door and climbed into his car without even a cursory look underneath. *Why would the Basques want to kill me*, he'd laugh whenever ETA was mentioned. *There are plenty of* guardia *nearer the Basque country for them to target*. He really thought he was safe. Until that morning when the explosion flung his car into the clear spring air, burning debris falling in an arc of fiery metal rain. The sound of the exploding petrol tank, the smoke, the lurid swell of the flames. Men running, *Mamá* screaming. Distant sirens. A little girl's frightened cry. *Papá*.

They got away with it, Galindez thought, her nails digging into her palms. No one was going to find his killers now, seventeen years later – least of all her. There were many in the *guardia civil* who'd tried – why had she ever imagined it could be her who would bring his killers to justice? That had been just an adolescent dream, though the thought that one day she might succeed sustained her through interminable nights of lonely study and revision. Hoping that by tracking down his killers she could become something more than that tragic little girl, Miguel's daughter. The one faces turned to when she entered a room. *That's her, pobrecita. So sad. First the father, then the mother as well. They say she drank, you know. But look at the child. Poor little thing.* Enough. It was time to acknowledge that *Papá*'s killers had faded into history. Impatiently, she wiped away a tear. *It seemed possible when I was fifteen. I'm twenty-five now. Time to get real, Ana María. Time to put that grief aside, although it's not as if I ever grieved for him really. Not the way people expected. There was an explosion and he died and so did everything I knew up to that moment. It wasn't my fault I couldn't cry at his funeral. Or Mamá's for that matter. God knows enough people tried to make me. Tia Teresa even pinched me to try and get the tears flowing. And afterwards, the shrinks treated me like I was a freak. As if a man in a white coat had the right to try and make an eight-year-old cry.*

But even if she'd never been able to express her grief, that didn't mean she had to abandon her longing for justice. Uncovering Guzmán's shadowy activities – and maybe others like him – might still be possible. She began to think about how it could be done. Develop a profile of the man, gather evidence of what he did, how he did it, who he did it to. A comprehensive catalogue of Guzmán's career. But that was where the problems began. Guzmán was in charge of a secret unit. They didn't have annual reports, didn't send out press releases on successful operations like today's *guardia*. Guzmán's secrecy was a challenge in itself, given its resonance with Galindez's own past: *He got away with it just as ETA did when they killed my father.* But, if she worked hard, maybe she really could drag Guzmán – alive or dead – into public view, deny him the comfort of hiding in the darkness of Spain's past, and, by doing that, enable society to recognise and acknowledge the pain he caused. And then move on. Closure. Surely, she thought, that's what people need. Closure for the lingering scars and the emotional damage of the War. Closure. It was what she wanted, she knew that much. Then she wouldn't have to struggle on in the *guardia*, taking the shit, bringing the pay cheque in, trying to show that Miguel's daughter could hack it. Maybe it might even put an end to the amnesia that blotted out all memory of her life before the explosion. Eight years of her life lost in a moment. Closure. Ironically, Guzmán might be the person to give it to her.

She looked distractedly at her scattered clothing on the floor as ideas began to spring to mind, light and airy and increasingly ambitious. The air from the window felt warm and sensuous. A car horn blared angrily in the street. Men shouting. Galindez realised she was being watched.

Luisa's eyes shone with wakening desire, making Galindez suddenly aware of being naked. She returned Luisa's smile, though she felt an urge to leave, to join the bustle in the street, to go somewhere, do something new. But Luisa had the key to that something new: *Comandante* Guzmán and all his works. Those works could also become hers if her plan worked out.

'Luisa, what would you say to me working with you on the Guzmán project? If I could get time off, a secondment maybe? I'd like to make a contribution to your research.'

'That would be great, Ana,' Luisa said. 'What sort of contribution?'

Where to start? 'I see from this book you don't believe in focusing on the individual in your studies?'

'Exactly, history is shaped by the larger realm of ideas. Understand those and you understand the actions of individuals.'

'But what about a perspective from someone from a different background? With a focus on the individual? As a counterweight to your approach?'

Luisa thought for a moment. 'Maybe it could work. A dissenting voice would give the investigation a dialectical tension. Forensic work – forgive me for saying so – is really about attributing blame and apportioning guilt. There'd be a theoretical conflict. Wouldn't you mind that?'

'*No para nada*. I want to collect evidence of his involvement in the activities of the *Brigada Especial*. And then assess the level of his culpability and the extent of his involvement in the crimes of his unit.'

'That doesn't sound a terribly sympathetic approach.' Luisa frowned. 'My own view is that Guzmán and others like him were functionaries, rubber-stamping the orders of those above them. Violent acts were informed by a much wider ideology. I'm more interested in discussing how those wider ideas came to be manifested at the practical level.'

'I don't intend to be sympathetic at all,' Galindez said. 'You said there's no hard evidence to incriminate him – but that doesn't mean there isn't. And after seeing those bodies in the mine at Las Peñas, I really think Guzmán merits further investigation.'

'And you won't mind if our respective interpretations clash?'

'Not at all. Because I don't intend to interpret him. I want to base my report on facts – just as if I was preparing a report for the prosecutor.'

Luisa reached over to her bedside table. 'You'd better start reading this.' She passed Galindez the musty leather-bound diary. 'Have a look while I make us some coffee.'

Galindez opened the diary. The entries consisted largely of lists. Lists of people, places, sums of money with comments about how they were spent – Guzmán was clearly punctilious in claiming his expenses – Galindez smiled: she could relate to that. So many names. Hopefully, she would be able to identify some of these people and the reason for them being in Guzmán's diary. With no time now to read the diary from start to finish, she turned to the last page, examining the final entry dated Thursday, 22 January 1953, a scrawled, cryptic sentence: *I am me and my circumstances*. She recognised the phrase from school: It was Ortega y Gasset. A literary quotation from a secret policeman? Perhaps there was more to him than she'd initially thought.

'Penny for them.' Luisa handed Galindez a mug of coffee. 'What are you smiling about, Ana María?'

Galindez looked up, her dark eyes shining. 'Luisa, did I ever tell you about my uncle?'

MADRID 2009, HEADQUARTERS OF THE GUARDIA CIVIL, JEFATURA DE INFORMACIÓN

The adjutant was waiting as Galindez stepped from the lift.

'Dr Galindez?' An unnecessary question. No one got to this floor without an appointment. The adjutant showed her into his office – dark wood furniture with brass fittings, a thick carpet – a world away from the functional austerity of Galindez's own small cubicle in the Forensic department several floors below. The adjutant gestured grudgingly at a leather chair. Galindez sank into the thick cushions, noting his measured look of disapproval.

'The general is on the telephone,' the adjutant said, indicating the door to the general's office. 'He's been very busy today.' The tone of his voice suggested not only a delay, it implied Galindez deserved the wait. She guessed he was wondering why the head of the Counter Intelligence Directorate would want to see a lowly forensic scientist. He was in for a surprise.

A few minutes passed before the inner door burst open and the general emerged. His uniform fitted him more tightly than the last time Galindez had seen him and the white hair was thinner but the bluff ruddy face was still the same.

The adjutant leapt up, giving the general a sharp salute. 'A sus ordenes, mi General, Dr Galindez from Forensics to see you.'

The general looked at Galindez, his eyes twinkling.

'A sus ordenes, mi General.' Galindez fumbled a haphazard salute as the general's big arms wrapped round her, hugging her to his barrel chest. The adjutant looked on, astonished. It was a fair bet most of the general's visitors weren't greeted this way.

The general laughed. 'It's all right, Capitán, young women always find me attractive.'

Now the adjutant was confused, sensing a joke but uncertain

what it was. The general hugged Galindez again, almost lifting her off her feet, and he ruffled her hair the same way he had when she was ten years old.

'*Por Dios, Capitán*,' General Ortiz said, 'you're slipping. If she'd been from al-Qaeda I'd be dead now.' Then, seeing the adjutant wasn't suddenly going to develop a sense of humour, he added, 'This is my little Ana. Always was, always will be. Right, *querida*?'

'*Absolutamente, mi General*,' Galindez said, stiffening to attention.

'Ana María, I can have you shot if you don't address me by my correct title.'

'Sorry, Uncle Ramiro.' Galindez extended a hand towards the adjutant. 'Ana María Galindez, *para servirle.*'

A flaccid handshake. '*Mucho gusto*, Dr Galindez.'

'She's Miguel Galindez's daughter,' Uncle Ramiro added, spoiling the moment for her. *Not so soon. Can't I just be the woman from Forensics for once?*

The adjutant stared at her. 'I admired your father a great deal, Dr Galindez. He's sadly missed, I can tell you.'

'Very true,' Ramiro said gravely. 'And wouldn't you agree she's the best-looking forensic scientist you've ever seen?'

'She certainly is, *mi General*. Of course, I could hardly say so before.'

'Women never object to a compliment,' Ramiro said, wrapping an arm around Galindez's shoulders. 'Now, hold all my calls while I'm with Ana María. Even if Prime Minister Zapatero calls. Ana's more important than he is.'

'*A sus ordenes*. Those are the exact words I'll relay to him.' The adjutant was more amenable now, Galindez noticed. *Papá's* name still carried a lot of weight.

Ramiro waved Galindez into his office. He closed the door and pointed to a seat. The cushions were even deeper and more opulent than those of the adjutant's office. Galindez inhaled the aroma of the freshly polished wood of Uncle Ramiro's huge desk.

'Drink, Ana?' Ramiro pointed to an impressively large drinks cabinet.

'*Agua mineral con gas*, please, Uncle.'

'Still teetotal then?' He rattled ice into a glass and poured sparkling water over it. Whisky for him. Some things didn't change. 'So, how's life in the *guardia civil, niña*?'

'I'm enjoying it.'

'Enjoying it? *Niña*, it's a calling. You don't enjoy it, you live and breathe your duty. Like I do, and my father before me. And yours, *niña.*'

'Don't call me that at work please, Uncle Ram. I'm not a kid any more.'

'*Venga*, Ana. Even though you're twenty years old, to me you're the same wide-eyed little girl I used to bounce on my knee.'

'Uncle Ramiro, I'm twenty-five and I spend most of my working day surrounded by dead bodies. I've grown up.'

'You certainly have, Ana. And it suits you – the *capitán* outside couldn't take his eyes off your *culo* when you walked in here. And to be frank, I'm not surprised, *querida*.'

Galindez laughed, shaking her head in disbelief. Ramiro was such a dinosaur. 'Look, Uncle, if you like, we can discuss the *guardia*'s anti-sexism policy – I'm sure you've only breached about half of it so far.'

Ramiro held up a hand in surrender. 'Have pity, Ana. I'm old school. Men like me see a pretty girl and it goes to our heads. Women take everything so seriously these days. Even those in uniform. They sue at the drop of a hat if a man so much as looks at them. Lesbians, most of them.'

Unfortunately that's not true, Galindez thought. She changed the subject. 'I'm sorry I haven't been in touch lately, Uncle Ram. I've been so busy, what with moving into the new flat and settling into this job. In fact, I haven't seen you or *Tía* Teresa since my doctoral ceremony last year.'

'I was proud to be there, Ana María. I know I'm not a real uncle, but I was your father's best friend and I still miss him.'

Ramiro rubbed his eyes. 'Sorry. It hurts to think about it even now.'

God, just for once, let me be Ana María. It's been nearly twenty years. Por Dios.

'We're both very proud of you, Ana,' Ramiro said. 'You put in so much work studying. You know, I don't think I ever saw you without a book in your hand in your teens.'

'I was a bit of a bookworm, I admit.'

'A bit? *Tia* Carmen told me you revised for one exam for two days without sleeping.'

'Oh, I don't think it was quite that long.' She laughed. *Three days more like.* 'By the way, thanks again for the car, Uncle. That was so generous.'

'My pleasure, Ana. Just let me know when you need another. If you park it anything like the women who drive our patrol cars, it'll be scrap inside a year.'

She thanked him, knowing she could never accept it. A graduation gift was one thing, regularly receiving largesse from the most senior operational officer in the organisation was another. If her colleagues found out, they'd think everything she did in the job was the result of Uncle Ramiro's favouritism. Credibility was hard enough to come by as it was.

'*De nada*. They pay me too much anyway. I'd work here for nothing.' Ramiro picked up a yellow folder on his desk. 'Right, let's have a look at this. See how you're doing.'

'What is that, Uncle Ramiro?'

'Your personnel folder, *querida*. Don't you want to know what *Capitán* Fuentes says about you?'

Shit. Galindez was suddenly uncomfortable. 'I thought those things were confidential?'

'Don't forget who's in charge, Ana María. Me. You can do anything you want when you've got the power. Let's have a look.' Ramiro skimmed through the papers in the folder, 'Independent... popular member of staff... persistent attention to detail... dedicated... team player... hard-working – *hostia*, willingness to

63

work late to meet deadlines. In fact, he says you have a tendency to overwork, *querida*. As if there's any such thing. Anyway, overall, it sounds like Fuentes finds you very acceptable, my dear.'

'That's very flattering, Uncle. Are you sure he was talking about me?'

'Oh yes, and coming from Fuentes, it's extravagant praise. You're doing well. Sure you wouldn't rather be in uniform and wearing a gun?'

'We've discussed that before, Uncle. You know my answer.'

'I do. Fuentes forgot to put stubborn in his list. So, how long have I got to enjoy the pleasure of your company today, *niña*?'

Galindez looked at her watch. 'An hour. Belén in Cryptography is going on maternity leave and we're taking her for a drink at four thirty.'

'Maternity leave?' Ramiro sighed. 'That means more overtime for someone. These pregnant women cost us a fortune.' He noticed Galindez's expression and changed the subject. 'Now, tell me, what's the favour you want? You didn't say in your email, so I assumed it meant you need to flutter your eyelashes at me before asking?'

Galindez gave her uncle a hard stare. 'As if. The thing is, I've been involved with a lot of war grave work over the last year and I wondered...'

'If I can get you out of it? Of course, *pequeñita*. Not fit work for a young woman. I'll speak to Fuentes, ask him to give you something office based.'

'No, that's not it. You see, I'm involved with a group at the university investigating war crimes and atrocities.'

'The Historical Memory people?' Uncle Ramiro snorted. 'They're just a bunch of lefties. raking over the coals of the past and whining about who shot grandpa.'

Galindez gave him a long look. 'Surprisingly, Uncle Ramiro, they don't refer to it like that. They need my skills to add a scientific dimension to their investigation of a *Comandante* Guzmán.'

Ramiro frowned. 'Never heard of him. What makes him so special?'

'He was a *comandante* in the *Brigada Especial*. His unit was involved in killing a lot of people in the years after the Civil War.'

Uncle Ramiro sipped his Scotch. He chuckled. '*Verdad*? That's what happens when you have wars, my dear. It's why we have them. Otherwise it would just be a sport.'

'Guzmán reported directly to Franco. He was in command of the Special Brigade yet there's no direct evidence of his involvement. I want to investigate—'

Uncle Ramiro held up his hand. '*Ya vale*, Ana. It's ancient history. As you know, my father, the late General Ortiz Senior, fought in the *Guerra Civil* and God alone knows how many people he killed or had killed. Iron Hand Ortiz, they called him. And with good reason. It was a war: end of story.'

'There were war crimes. Rapes and extrajudicial killings.'

'I know. I know. You've discovered the Civil War and you want to share its evils with the next generation. You won't be the first. Unfortunately.'

'I wondered if I could have a secondment to work on the university investigation?'

Uncle Ramiro laughed. 'I can just see Fuentes's face if I order him to second you to some lefty group. *Imposible*, Ana. He'd hit the roof. You've only worked here a year.'

Galindez pursed her lips. She hadn't expected outright rejection.

'Oh, don't give me that look, *cariña*. I can't bear it. If it's so important to you, then of course. I'll call Fuentes and tell him.' The general smiled. 'Order him, I should say.'

Galindez looked at him in surprise. 'I didn't give you any look, Uncle. But *muchisimas gracias*, I really appreciate it – and I promise I'll do a good job that reflects well on the *guardia*. And there is one other thing.' Save the biggest for last, she thought. 'I'd like access to some of the archives at Military Intelligence.'

'*Jesús Cristo y todo los Santos*, Ana. So would lots of people. Military secrets?'

'Only from the early fifties. To see if there's anything on Guzmán.'

Ramiro frowned. 'There is a possibility,' he said. 'They've computerised all the top secret records, though of course access to them is out of the question. Much of the material on the Civil War has been moved to the archives at Salamanca. But there's still a lot of old restricted stuff left. I can get you access to that – for what it's worth. You'd be working pretty much on your own. It's kept in an archive at the Institute of Military Culture.'

'Thank you, *Tio* Ramiro. This means a lot to me.'

'Well, make the most of it while I'm still in post, *chica*.'

'*Por Dios*, you're not retiring, surely?'

'*Que va*, Ana. I'm only fifty-nine. No, I'm going to be in charge of our NATO operation in Afghanistan from the start of next year. Unless some idiot stops the fighting before I arrive – which I sincerely hope won't happen. After all, it's rare for a general to get to shoot anyone nowadays.'

'I'm sure they'll keep it going until you get there, Uncle. Congratulations. Will you bring me back one of those rugs?'

'Dozens, *querida*. Listen, once I've sorted this thing out at the archives for you, you'll be on your own. They have very few facilities. You'll have to do all the work yourself.'

'I've had lots of practice, Uncle. I'll be fine.'

'Shame you never studied shorthand. That's always a useful skill for a young woman,' Uncle Ramiro muttered, signing the paper authorising the secondment.

Later, as Galindez prepared to leave, Ramiro pressed a wad of euros into her hand. 'A little spending money, *chiquitita*. Get yourself something nice.' He accompanied her to the door and waited as she thanked him once more and planted goodbye kisses on each of his ruddy cheeks. 'You should wear your hair down more often, Ana María,' Ramiro said. 'It suits you.'

Galindez smiled. She decided Uncle Ramiro wouldn't appreciate her explaining the importance of avoiding contaminating a crime scene.

It was a short walk to the lift and, as Galindez pressed the call button, she heard Uncle Ramiro's booming voice as he talked to the adjutant. 'Lovely little thing. They'll have to prise her husband off her with a crowbar after their wedding night. She'll make some man very happy. I'd say she was at least a seven or an eight, what about you?'

The lift doors opened and Galindez stepped in, wondering whether Afghanistan was quite ready for Uncle Ramiro. She pressed the button for the second floor and the lift descended slowly. She counted the money Ramiro had given her. Four hundred euros. Leaving the lift, she followed the corridor past Human Resources and down a short flight of stairs towards a small lobby with a dull khaki sign: *Capilla*. There was no one about outside the small chapel, just a sign giving the chaplain's hours of attendance. Galindez looked at the memorial on the wall by the chapel door. Rows of small photographs of the fallen, their names and dates of death. The later photos were in colour. Her *papá's* was in black and white. *Teniente Miguel Galindez, 5/4/1992.* Above the photographs, gilt letters bearing the words inscribed over the door of every *guardia comisaría* in the country: *Todo por la Patria*. Below the memorial was a collection box labelled *Las familias*. Galindez looked around to make sure she was alone before pressing the wad of notes into the metal slot of the collection box.

She returned to the lift and went up a floor to Forensics, stopping off in the women's changing room to tie back her hair. It was humid and she heard the dull rumble of thunder, far away, outside the hermetic world of Headquarters.

Opening her locker, Galindez took out her carefully wrapped present for Belén: a dozen romper suits wrapped in a riot of spangled wrapping paper patterned with storks carrying bundles in their beaks. The whole thing bound with a couple of vivid ribbons tied in frothy bows. Belén liked that kind of stuff. Galindez walked down the corridor to Forensics and opened the door.

The room was empty. Every computer logged out, blank. She frowned. Outside, she heard the scratching sound of rain against the windows as the summer storm picked up. Galindez walked through the unusual quiet of the empty office and noticed a light in the *Capitán*'s room. She knocked on the door.

Fuentes looked up. '*Holá*, Ana María. Not going to Belén's leaving do?'

Galindez lifted the gift with its sparkling oversized bows. 'I thought it was at four thirty?'

Fuentes shook his head. 'Two thirty. Belén sent everyone an email earlier in the week,' he said. 'Didn't you see it?'

'I must have missed it, boss.' Galindez shrugged. 'They'll have finished by now. I'll put her present in the post.' She turned to leave.

'Before you go, Ana María,' Fuentes said, 'that report you did on the grave near Getafe.' He held up a thick folder.

Galindez felt a sinking feeling. She'd cocked something up. For someone who prided herself on her fierce attention to detail, it was more than just disappointment: it was what *Tia* Carmen had told her was the bane of her father's life: *Sloppy work*.

'What was wrong with it, boss?' She waited for Fuentes to tear her off a strip.

'Wrong with it?' Fuentes said. 'There was nothing wrong with it. Nothing in all its hundred and fifteen pages – and I'm not even counting the pages of diagrams and photographs. Know how long your predecessor made his reports?'

So that was it. She had been too brief. That wasn't quite as bad as being sloppy but it was bad enough.

'Three hundred pages?'

Fuentes laughed. 'I was lucky if he did more than ten, Ana. I can present this report to the coroner's court without the slightest amendment. It's an excellent piece of work.'

'Thanks very much, boss.'

'To be honest, it's made even better by the fact that I know you don't like working on the war graves.' Fuentes smiled. 'But you've stuck at it and every one of your reports has been top notch. That's why I've put you down for a transfer to profiling as soon as a vacancy comes up. I believe that's what you were hoping for?'

Galindez wanted to punch the air. She contained that impulse. 'When do you think there might be a vacancy, *Capitán?*'

'There's one coming up in December. I hope you can wait that long?'

'Of course.'

'Did you speak to your uncle about the other matter?' Fuentes asked.

'I did. He agreed.'

'There you are then,' Fuentes said. 'You do your secondment on your Guzmán project until the post in profiling becomes vacant and then you move into a department dedicated to your specialism.'

'I don't know what to say, boss. You've been great about all this.'

Fuentes looked at her. 'You could have asked your uncle for that secondment and gone over my head. Many people would have. But you came to me first. I appreciated that, Ana. And besides, we like to keep our staff happy when we can – despite what you may think sometimes.'

Galindez nodded, lost for words. She waved the brightly wrapped present, unable to speak.

'Carry on, Dr Galindez.' Fuentes looked down at his papers, avoiding seeing Galindez quickly wipe her eyes as she left the *Capitán*'s office.

'Oh, one more thing, Ana,' Fuentes called.

'Boss?'

'The satnav. I'm sorry, but you're going to have to pay for it. That's the fourth in less than a year. I don't know how you do it: how can you run over a satnav?'

'It isn't easy, boss.'

'No. But you managed it anyway.' Fuentes laughed. 'They'll stop it from your wages at the end of the month.'

Galindez made her way back to her desk and slumped into her chair, putting Belén's gift in her in-tray. She sighed. *It's all good.* She'd stuck it out and now it was paying off. She punched the air. Then looked round self-consciously to make sure no one was watching.

She logged on to her computer and saw Belén's email reminder. How had she missed that? She stared at the email. It had been opened, so she must have read it. It wasn't like her to forget things. Little things. The doctors had told her to report any lapses of memory immediately in case they were signs of deterioration.

Anyone can forget things. Even amnesiacs. If it happens again, I'll tell the doc. No I won't, they might block the transfer. I'll wait and see. Christ it was only an email.

Galindez opened a file and set to work on her report on the latest war grave. At eight o'clock, Fuentes came out of his office and saw her still working.

'*Vamos*, Ana María, that's enough for one day.'

'OK, boss, you go, I'll turn the lights off.'

'No, Ana, if I go and leave you here, you'll still be here at midnight. Go home.'

'Coming.' Galindez waited until Fuentes began to turn off the lights in the main office. Quickly she put her report and the file into her briefcase. She could finish it at home.

CHAPTER FOUR

For most people, nightmares are a corruption, an interlude of unwelcome and uninvited mental images interrupting the gentle rhythm of their dreams. Guzmán, however, slipped from consciousness into the oblivion of an inferno in which the screams of the damned echoed his name in a demented choir. This was how he had slept since the war, lost amid the stench and corruption of death, crashing blindly through marshes where rotting eyeless faces stared up from charnel pools towards a sky traced with blood and darkened with the smoke of funeral pyres. He splashed through fetid mud spiked with clumps of decaying marsh grass, feeling skeletal hands clutch at him as he ran. But Guzmán was not fleeing. His pursuit across the fields of hell was always like this. Through the smoke and the stench, beneath the permanent midnight cast of the sky, he saw the vague shape of his fleeing prey. His mouth opened to scream, to scream for them to stop, to await their fate. And, as ever, as he felt the scream in his throat, he awoke, soaked with sweat.

By the time the alarm clock rang, Guzmán was already washing in icy water in the small kitchen. He shaved, cursing the cold yet lacking the patience to heat water. His toilet complete, Guzmán pulled on his clothes. The clock showed three thirty. Early. But then today they were hunting.

Despite the cold of his room he had almost forgotten the snow until he pulled back the curtain and saw the white expanse of the street below, the familiar angular shapes of steps, lamp posts and doorways now subtle and soft under ten centimetres of snow,

71

muted by the pale street lights. Guzmán saw no sign of the observer from the night before. No telltale footprints. Whoever the spy was, he had no patience.

Guzmán found a pair of boots that looked like they would keep out the cold and put on his thickest overcoat. The fifty-odd *guardia civiles* taking part in the operation could freeze in their khakis and capes but not him. Guzmán oiled his hair with the same oil he used – very occasionally – for cooking. The image in the speckled mirror looked respectable enough, although those he was after today would not remember him for his appearance, he was sure.

Outside, the cold was brutally sharp and Guzmán swore profusely, cursing again as he began to slide on the icy, hard-packed snow. His cigarette smoke hung in the frozen air as he slipped and staggered towards the end of the road, swearing in blind fury at the treachery of the snow, the inconvenience of the ice beneath it, at the whole world which seemed to conspire against him as he struggled to keep his feet. One thought comforted him. Someone was going to suffer. That much was certain. About thirty-six of them to be precise.

By the time he reached the Puerta del Sol, sweating with exertion and fury, a few workmen were clearing paths along the pavements. Guzmán glared at them with casual and unfocused hatred as he grabbed a lamp post to steady himself. After ten minutes he was still only halfway to the *comisaría*. When he saw the Café Ojalá, he felt justified in stopping off to regain his strength, ordering a coffee with milk and two stale cakes. At this hour the café's usual limited choice was even more limited. Guzmán asked for something hot but the owner threw up his hands and launched into a violent denunciation of the black market and the crooked party officials who facilitated it. Hot food was off the menu, Guzmán realised.

'Franco promised us once we'd beaten the Reds we would have bread and justice,' the man said, wiping a glass with a bar towel. 'Well, the Reds saw his justice, but where's the bread for those of us who fought for him?'

With whichever general handles the distribution of grain, probably, Guzmán thought. It was hard to argue with the man, and not only because it was four in the morning. More and more people were complaining about the lack of food. Guzmán heard it on the streets and in the bars and cafés where he met his informants or spied on his victims. It wasn't as if the hardship affected only those who had been on the Republican side: even members of the Falange were complaining their rations were inadequate, eroded by corrupt officials and administrators. *Franco should do something,* Guzmán thought. *There's a difference between taking a cut and bleeding the country dry.*

'Want to know what I think?' the man said, leaning across the bar, his rancid breath hanging in the frozen air.

'Not really.' Guzmán finished his coffee.

'Franco doesn't know the half of it,' the man continued, ignoring Guzmán's indifference. 'He has so much to do he has to depend on others, on the military and the Party members. They do what they want and take what they can. And what they do and what they tell him are different things. And *they* get away with it by using the *guardia civil* and the *policía* when things get bad.'

Guzmán nodded and paid the bill. Normally he would have baulked at paying but the man's complaint had been true enough. Guzmán thought he deserved a break for that – and for being open at this hour.

'Careful out there,' the man called as Guzmán stood up and made his way to the door, 'it's going to be a hell of a day.'

Guzmán paused in the doorway, noticing it was only marginally colder outside than in. 'I think you're right. For some people anyway.'

'Let's hope for once it's those who deserve it.' The man smiled, revealing a row of ragged teeth.

'I think today you can be sure of it.' Guzmán closed the door and stepped out into the silent blurred snowscape of the street.

*

73

The deep snow didn't improve Guzmán's temper as he trudged doggedly towards the *comisaría*. The hobnails in his boots gave him some purchase but he still slipped and stumbled at times, glad there was no one to witness his discomfort. The *comisaría* was ablaze with light when he finally arrived. Six trucks were parked outside, guarded by several *guardia civiles* wrapped in their capes, tricorne hats pulled well down. One asked Guzmán for his papers, stepping back and saluting when Guzmán thrust his identity card into the man's face.

'*A sus ordenes, mi Comandante.*'

Guzmán snatched back his papers and clattered into the entrance hall, stamping his feet to get rid of the cloying snow. It was a small, domestic gesture and it angered him greatly. At one end of the hall a table had been set out with a large coffee urn and a line of *guardia* waited in an unruly queue, even though, from the smell of it, the coffee had been made with wood shavings. Guzmán pushed through to the desk. The *sargento* saluted absently, eyes hollow from lack of sleep and, probably, lack of food. Or teeth, Guzmán thought. Still, the sarge obeyed him and that was enough.

'Who's in charge of this lot, *Sargento*?'

The sarge waved towards the doors leading to Guzmán's office. 'They went to the mess to warm up.'

'I'll have a word, make sure they know what they're doing. Anything to report?'

The *sargento* nodded. 'The Red prisoner. Died during the night. Suicide. Hanged himself with his own belt. Tragic no, *jefe*?'

'Got off lightly if you ask me.' Guzmán shrugged.

'He's arrived, by the way,' the *sargento* called as Guzmán walked to the double doors.

Guzmán turned, his hand on the door. 'Who?'

The *sargento*'s face oscillated between emaciated weariness and a strong desire to smirk. 'Acting *Teniente* Francisco Peralta.'

'Who the fuck is— of course. *Joder.*'

The *sargento* nodded. 'The *capitán-general*'s nephew, *jefe*. In the flesh.'

'And?'

'And what, *jefe*?'

'*Puta madre, coño.* What's he like?'

The *sargento*'s face twitched as he held back a smile. 'You need to see for yourself, *jefe*.'

Guzmán turned on his heel, pulling the door open with such violence it crashed against the wall. He stormed down the corridor and stamped into his office. *I'll kill that fucking* sargento. *I'll have him back in the ranks, give him double night shifts until he begs for mercy, toothless bastard.*

A man was sitting in one of the rickety visitors' chairs by the wall. He jumped up as Guzmán entered.

'*Comandante* Guzmán, Acting *Teniente* Francisco Peralta *para servirle*.'

Peralta was tall and exceedingly thin, his cadaverous face suggesting he ate nowhere near as well as his uncle, the *capitán-general*. Peralta looked older than his twenty-four years, his tallow hair already receding and thin. His dress sense left much to be desired, Guzmán noted. The overcoat was cheap and shabby, the cuffs of his jacket slightly frayed, his shoes soaked. Police wages. Totally impractical for ten centimetres of snow. He was really going to suffer, Guzmán thought happily.

He seized Peralta's hand in a quick handshake, quickly crushing any attempt to impress him with a firm grip. Peralta withdrew his hand with a pained expression.

'*Acting Teniente*, Peralta? That's a sudden promotion isn't it?' Guzmán slumped into his chair, pointedly not offering his new assistant a seat. On the desk was a sheaf of papers the *sargento* had left for him. Lists, maps, addresses. Interesting things.

Peralta remained standing. 'The temporary promotion came through yesterday. I was as surprised as you about it. May I say I very much look forward to working with you, *Comandante* Guzmán.'

'No you may not.' Guzmán gestured wearily towards a chair. 'Sit.' It was not a request.

Peralta indicated the green folder on the desk which Guzmán had been studiously ignoring. 'Perhaps the *comandante* would care to have a look at my file, if he has any questions about my experience...' His voice dried up under Guzmán's withering gaze.

'Look, son,' Guzmán said, 'if I want to read your file I'll read it, if I want to ask you something I'll ask it and if I want your fucking advice on something, then I'll ask you. Until then, speak when you are spoken to. *Entiende?*'

The younger man blushed, making Guzmán twitch with anger.

'I really must protest—' Peralta began.

Guzmán pointed a meaty finger at him. 'Understood? *Si o no?*'

'Understood, sir.'

'*Ahora bien*, let me outline the work of this department, *Acting Teniente*. Or better still, let's start with you telling me what you know about us.'

Peralta beamed. 'The work of the Special Brigade is vital to the preservation of the State, sir. Counter-insurgency and the prevention of sedition and rebellion. In short, maintaining the fight against the forces of godlessness, Freemasonry and liberalism.' He paused. 'And of course Communism.'

Christ, he could write speeches for Franco. 'You left out the bit about harassing Protestants but never mind, there isn't much of that. Didn't your uncle mention any of the specific tasks of this unit? What I do? Or, rather, what *we* do, since you're now part of it.'

Peralta shook his head. 'My uncle doesn't have much to do with me, I have to confess, *Comandante*. I think he decided to do me a favour by having me transferred here because of our new baby. We can certainly use the money. But in terms of discussing things with me... never.' His voice trailed away.

'You aren't the favourite nephew, then?' Guzmán asked, brightening considerably.

Peralta shook his head. 'Not at all, sir, he thinks I lack ambition and talent. He only informed me of the transfer last night by telephone. In about ten seconds flat.'

'*Muy bien*.' Guzmán pawed the papers on his desk. 'I'm about to brief the section leaders for the raid this morning. You'll come too. Before we do, let me tell you a little more about our work in the *Brigada Especial*.'

Peralta nodded eagerly. 'Should I take notes, sir?' He began to rummage for a pad in his coat pocket. Guzmán felt a murderous wave of rage but let it pass.

'No,' he snapped. 'The first thing you need to know is that this isn't an ordinary police station. It looks like it, but we're not part of the armed police. The *Brigada Especial* was set up at the end of the war to pursue the enemy beyond the battlefield. We were part of the *Segunda Bis* – Military Intelligence – that's where I started. Then we were made part of the General Directorate of Security but none of these were flexible enough for what we do. So now, we don't exist, which of course is why people call us the secret police. Other branches deal with the foreign threat. Our concern is the domestic front. The ex-leaders of the Republican movement, their generals, colonels, hell, every rank and everybody who fought or supported them during the Crusade. And, come to that, anyone on our own side who may threaten national security or pose a threat to the *Caudillo*.'

Peralta listened intently.

'I'm in charge here,' Guzmán continued. 'You may think it's a big task for a mere *comandante*. The *Caudillo* doesn't. We report to your uncle nominally on a number of matters but we take orders directly from the Headquarters of Generalísimo Franco himself and no one interferes in what we do without his authorisation. Any challenge to our activities, whether from the armed forces, the *guardia civil*, the armed police or any judicial power, is referred to the very highest level and then dismissed. When we decide to act, there are very few who can stop us.'

Guzmán looked at Peralta. The acting *teniente* didn't exactly seem thrilled to find himself in the heart of an elite secret police unit.

'These traitors, Reds, Anarchists – let's just say the enemy – we track them down,' Guzmán continued. 'Fourteen years on, many of them think they're safe enough to carry on their plotting and scheming. Some try to organise armed resistance and rebellion, others to provoke strikes. And some merely produce pamphlets and books aimed at spreading their ideas. There are a lot of them out there.'

'We'll get them,' Peralta said enthusiastically. 'Arrest them and bring them to justice. After a few years in prison, I've no doubt many can return to society to—'

Guzmán pointed a large finger at the *teniente*. 'Stop. You think we're going to arrest all of these men and reform them with a spell behind bars?'

Peralta's face suggested he did, though sensibly he kept silent with Guzmán's big fist raised a few centimetres from his face. Guzmán leaned forward conspiratorially.

'This only needs to be said once, Peralta. Your uncle presumably assigned you to me to enhance your future career prospects, so let me enlighten you.'

Peralta looked as if he was about to reach for his notepad, but settled instead for a look of absolute concentration, making Guzmán want to slap him all the more.

'Those people who supported the Reds,' Guzmán said, 'are the past of this country. A part of our history that's over. We made Spain what it is now and they have no part in what comes next. Those are the people this unit deals with. When we get our hands on them, they take their proper place in history. In the past. And of course the effect on those who have sympathy for their cause is...' Guzmán searched for the word he had heard the *Caudillo* use years ago, 'instructional. Never underestimate the use of terror, Peralta. It clarifies the choices people make, ensures conformity.' *Ten years on and I can still recall the Caudillo's phrases clearly.*

'I see,' Peralta nodded. 'We lock them away where they can never do any harm.'

Guzmán looked at him without blinking, his face expressionless. 'No,' he said, 'we don't. We bring them back here. Those who have information will give it to us, whether they want to or not. Then

78

for most of them, we end it.' He stared hard at Peralta. 'We kill them,' he added helpfully. 'At least, those the *Caudillo* indicates deserve to die. Which is most of them usually.'

Peralta frowned. Guzmán thought for a moment he might be sick. *And if you are I'll rub your face in it, you little fuck.*

'We kill them?' Peralta said with some difficulty, still digesting Guzmán's introduction to the squad.

'*Pues sí, Acting Teniente*, it's what we do. If you don't like it, join the Traffic Police.'

Teniente Peralta swallowed. His face was ashen.

'Churchgoer?' Guzmán asked. He'd already guessed.

A nod.

'Be careful how you phrase it at confession. Not all priests are as understanding as they might be in these matters,' he smiled, 'or better still, go to confession round the corner with Monsignor Vasquez, he's a real firebrand. I understand he personally killed several Republicans in the village where he was priest. He'll probably give you a few tips if you ask him.' Guzmán sneered. 'But he's very understanding in confession, I hear.'

'I'll do my best to do my duty, *Comandante*,' Peralta spluttered.

Guzmán nodded. 'You'd better, *Teniente*. Now, let's have a coffee and get this briefing out of the way.'

He went out into the corridor and Peralta followed, wiping a thin hand across his face as he hurried to keep up with him.

The small officers' mess was as shabby as the rest of the *comisaría*. Several dirty tables, an ill-assorted collection of chairs and very little heating. Guzmán and his new assistant poured coffee from a battered urn into chipped mugs. There were eight others in the room, six in the uniform of the *guardia civil*, another two wearing civilian clothes with the armband of the Falange.

'*Buenos dias, señores*,' Guzmán said. 'Let's get started – we want to catch these Reds in their beds where possible.' The others murmured agreement.

'May I introduce *Acting Teniente* Peralta, a recent addition to our unit.' Guzmán waved a hand at Peralta.

'You have our sympathy, *Teniente.*' One of the uniformed officers smiled.

'And I've had your mother,' Guzmán snapped. 'These gentlemen in uniform are the section leaders for today. And these,' he looked with belligerent disdain towards the two men with armbands, 'are from the Falange. They'll be accompanying us on the raid. Probably from the rear.'

'May I ask what role members of the party have in this?' Peralta asked.

The older of the two men, fat, ruddy-faced and bald, stood up. 'Gonzalo Guerrero, *Teniente, para servirle.* We're here to provide a support service to your work today. We'll document the area where today's arrests are made, take names, make inquiries and then pass on the information to the appropriate authorities for further investigation as is seen fit. Hopefully our involvement will free you gentlemen up for the more,' he paused for effect, and seeing no one was paying attention, continued, 'for the more, shall we say, *physical*, tasks involved in this exercise.'

Guzmán snorted. '*Señor* Guerrero will ensure once we have the fathers, their children are driven from school, their mothers are watched by the *guardia* to ensure they go to mass and those in work lose it.' Guzmán stared at Guerrero with contempt. Guerrero flushed, and Peralta noticed he seemed to be sweating.

'That's a little harsh if I may say so, *Comandante,*' Guerrero blustered. 'after all, we're only doing our duty.'

'Quite,' Guzmán said with disdain. 'Which is why, gentlemen, I must remind you this operation is under my personal command, and my authority will only be countermanded by the office of the Head of State himself. As for you gentlemen from the Party, I must ask you to wait until all objectives have been secured before you begin your important work.'

The two Falangists nodded, ignoring Guzmán's sneering tone.

'Because,' Guzmán continued, 'there may be shooting. These are dangerous men we are after and if they resist, they'll be shot.

80

And if any Party members are in the line of fire, my men will continue firing.'

The two Falangists exchanged nervous looks.

'*Muy bien*,' Guzmán said. 'You've all had information on this operation. We're going to hit three different targets in the Carabanchel area. You're all familiar with the location? That's good, because this isn't a guided tour. There are various wanted Republicans in the area – it has a reputation for harbouring Red sympathisers. Sections one and two will be dealing with the small fry, Reds of no real importance. Then there are several more important Reds, including a former Republican Officer, the anarchist Mendoza, known as *el Profesor* and various other luminaries from the Republican high command. Sections three, four and five will arrest these reprobates. Section six will block the road which leads back into the city. Papers to be shown by all, immediate arrest for anyone without identification. Anyone who flees is to be shot without warning. Anyone suspected of carrying a weapon will also be shot. These orders apply to men, women and children. Is that clear?'

Guzmán acknowledged their enthusiastic agreement.

'The *Caudillo* has emphasised these men should be taken alive.' Guzmán saw Peralta dart a glance at him. 'I want each prisoner searched at once for hidden weapons or poison. Once a man has been searched, bind him hand and foot and place him in one of the trucks. You have all been given a list of the addresses you are to target. Is everything clear?'

Again, a general nodding of heads. These men had done this before. All except Peralta. Guzmán grunted. '*Bueno, vamos*. It's a filthy morning for it but the sooner we get it over with the sooner we can be toasting our feet back in barracks. Let's go and get them. *Señores, por ellos*.'

'*Viva Franco! Viva España!*' One of the Falangists yelled, raising his fist in the air as he had seen Franco do on the newsreels. The Falangist raised his fist again and the *guardia civiles* joined in the old war chant of the Falange, shouting their response to the party member's call:

'*España! – Una! España! – Grande! España! – Libre!*'

The Falangist smiled, pleased by the rowdy response. As the *guardia civiles* began to tramp out into the stone corridor, the man patted them on the shoulder as they passed, wishing them well, encouraging them to do their duty. The Falangist didn't see Guzmán until he was about to give the *comandante* an encouraging slap on the arm. Guzmán stared at the man with undisguised malice. The notion of a Spain united, great and free was not one Guzmán found pleasing or desirable, nor was such a prospect likely. That was fine: Guzmán was quite happy with it as it was. The *guardia civiles'* boots echoed on the stone floor of the *comisaría*. Guzmán pulled on his overcoat and scarf and put on thick leather gloves. *Peralta is going to freeze, he's dressed for a day at the office.* Still, if Peralta froze to death, at least that would get him out of the way. He smiled at the thought.

The troops were already in the trucks by the time the officers left the building. The trucks' wheels had now been fitted with chains to enable a grip on the thick snow. It was still dark. Snow fell in desultory waves through the watery glimmer of the street lamps. Guzmán went to the first vehicle in the column and climbed up under the canvas cover. Peralta followed, squeezing himself in alongside Guzmán. Arranged along the seats on either side of the lorry were tightly packed *guardia civiles*. Some smoked, some had their eyes closed, trying to sleep. A trooper closed the running board and the truck cautiously edged down the road, the rear wheels skidding despite the chains.

'*Madre de Dios*, we'll take all day at this rate,' Guzmán sighed as he lit a cigarette. He noticed Peralta watching him. 'Do you smoke, *Teniente?*'

'Well, now and then, sir.' Peralta looked at Guzmán hopefully.

'Go ahead,' Guzmán said, turning away.

Snow fell in an unbroken white curtain as the line of trucks made its way through the wintry streets. Guzmán felt the cold creeping into him. At his side, Peralta was shivering violently and this kept Guzmán cheerful during the journey. The distance wasn't great but the snow made driving difficult and he fidgeted impatiently, glancing at his watch and cursing the lack of capable drivers. Peralta remained silent, miserably cold.

MADRID 1953, CARABANCHEL

There was a reluctant hint of light on the horizon as the trucks rolled through the dark streets. The few people who were about made themselves scarce as they saw the long procession of trucks filled with civil guards. A trooper jumped down to unfasten the running board and Peralta gratefully heaved himself down from the truck. The *guardia civiles* milled around him, threatening and bulky in their tricorne hats and large capes. The men formed quickly into their sections, eager to get started. Peralta saw barricades going up across the road behind them. No one was leaving this area – unless it was in handcuffs in the back of a khaki truck.

Guzmán checked his watch and looked towards the waiting *guardia civiles*. The men tensed, their weapons grasped tightly, ready for action. Guzmán raised his arm and gave the signal to begin. Peralta noticed how the different sections moved to their assigned apartment blocks, some entering hallways, others taking up firing positions. Guzmán stood next to Peralta, ignoring him completely. Apart from the muffled crunch of boots on snow, the road was silent.

And then shouting and noise. A woman screaming, the sound of glass shattering. A muffled gunshot. Guzmán looked up at the dark tenement, saw a sudden flash of light on the top floor. Another shot. Glass smashed and for a moment a man was framed in the broken window, struggling to get out onto the balcony. Unseen hands dragged him back inside and then a green-uniformed *guardia civil* peered down into the street and gave a thumbs up.

Events inside the buildings were having an effect. Groups of men and women were starting to run from the doorways. They were immediately confronted by knots of *guardia*. The Falangists scurried from their trucks, carrying ropes. There was some resistance, Peralta noted, seeing one man desperately kicking out against a *guardia*, struggling wildly to break away. Some of the occupants of the building were helping the man in his attempt to escape, swinging punches at the troopers. Other *guardia* pitched in, using their rifle butts to beat the attackers back. Peralta saw the man on the ground, still resisting, a struggling tangle of arms and legs until a guard raised his rifle and brought down the butt on the man's head.

Peralta ran over to where the man lay, his head resting in a pool of blood. He was still alive but barely conscious. One of the Falangists rolled him over onto his face, the second grabbed his legs and the man was quickly bound before being dragged away to the waiting vehicles. Looking towards the nearby building, Peralta was confronted by the contorted faces of the occupants, some still in night clothes, some half dressed, all shouting furiously at the *guardia civiles* and at him.

'*Hijos de puta.*' '*Sinvergüenzas.*' '*Policía asesinas.*'

Something hard struck Peralta on the head and he felt a trickle of blood run from his scalp. Dazed, he looked up, his bloody face drawing jeers from the people crowding the doorway. He felt faint.

'Don't fall down in front of these bastards,' Guzmán said, pushing through the mass of *guardia civiles* to get to Peralta. He bellowed for the men to fix bayonets and advance on the crowd. Then he grabbed hold of Peralta and manhandled him to the vehicles, shouting to the men standing by the trucks to come and help. Order was now slowly restored as the occupants of the building were beaten back inside with rifle butts. Many were in a worse state than Peralta by the time the area was quiet again.

Peralta leaned against a truck, trying to stem the blood with a cloth one of the Falangists had given him. His feet were soaking and frozen, his hands numb with cold and the wound on his head throbbed with a steady pulse of sharp pain. He looked into the truck. Some fifteen men lay face down on the floor of the vehicle, bound hand and foot. All were blindfolded with strips of white cloth. Peralta realised where his makeshift bandage had come from.

'Did we get them all?' he asked Guzmán.

'No, there's one left on the list. He lives in a street a couple of blocks away. He should be a lot less trouble than this lot.' Guzmán pointed towards the building and the churned snow at its entrance where bloody trails marked the flight of the residents. A thin dribble of gore in the trampled snow mapped Peralta's unsteady return to the truck. Guzmán watched as the first vehicles started to make their way back to the road block, many of the *guardia* walking alongside until more transport arrived, since the trucks were now filled with prisoners.

A corporal stepped forward with a list on a clipboard. 'I've checked them off, sir. We got them all, *Comandante*.'

'Any of our lads hurt, *cabo*?' Guzmán asked.

'Only the *teniente*.' The corporal turned to Peralta. 'That's a nasty cut, sir. I'll get one of our first-aid lads to come over and have a look.'

'Just one to pick up on the way back,' Guzmán said. 'Always save the best till last.'

More empty trucks had now pulled up at the roadblock and the *guardia civiles* began to climb aboard, ready to return to barracks. Guzmán pushed Peralta into the cab of their vehicle and climbed in after him, crushing Peralta between himself and the driver. Guzmán gestured to the driver and the truck eased forward over the frozen snow, hesitantly making its way into the road leading back to the city. Behind them, the other vehicles patiently began to form a convoy.

'Did the Falangists stay behind?' Guzmán asked the driver.

'No, they decided they'd come back another day.' The driver smirked. 'Last in, first out.'

'As ever.' Guzmán nodded.

The convoy made its way slowly towards the city centre. The canvas covers of the trucks were tied closed, shielding the prisoners from view. Passers-by paid little attention: military vehicles were a common sight. The long line of lorries slipped and skidded, making slow and painful progress through the snow. At a crossroads the convoy divided, the majority of trucks heading in the direction of the *comisaría*, while Guzmán's vehicle and another took a left, heading toward Lavapiés.

'Stop here,' Guzmán snapped. The truck drew to a halt, the engine still running. Guzmán got out. Peralta started to follow but Guzmán pushed him back. 'No, stay here. You'll only bleed on someone's carpet.'

MADRID 1953, CALLE DE LA TRIBULETE

Peralta watched Guzmán in the rear-view mirror as he walked to the back of the truck, shouting for the men to get down. Dark, caped figures began to clamber from the truck into the snow. Peralta continued watching as they moved towards one of the blocks of flats. The building was unlike those they had just raided; this one seemed well kept and middle class, not the sort of place a wanted Red would hide out. But then, Peralta thought, what did he know? Since he arrived at the *comisaría* that morning, he had been in a different world.

The entrance hall floor was an expanse of cheap tiles, lethally slippery under the *guardias'* hobnailed boots and Guzmán scowled as his men struggled to stay on their feet. In front of them a wooden staircase curved upwards into the gloom.

'Number ten,' Guzmán said. The civil guards began to climb the stairs. Guzmán ordered two men to stay behind, to block any attempted escape. Then he ran up the stairs impatiently, pushing his way through the plodding guards, muttering insults as he went.

They reached the first-floor landing. There were four doors; that meant their target was on the third floor. Guzmán detached two men from the squad to guard the landing and did the same on the second floor, taking the last six men with him to the third

86

floor. A cracked metal plaque announced '*Pisos* 9–12' in faded lettering. Guzmán pounded with the butt of his pistol on the door of number ten.

'Open up. In the name of the Spanish State. *Policía. Abra la puerta.*'

There was a faint commotion inside the apartment. Guzmán took a step back and then kicked the door against its lock. He staggered back, clutching his leg. The door remained unmoved. Guzmán glowered with incandescent rage as he rubbed his leg. 'Break the fucking door down. *Vamos, coño.*'

The door took some breaking down. It was thick and heavy and clearly bolted in several places. Several of the *guardia civiles* tried ineffectually to shoulder-charge it open while another kicked it with little success. There was a great deal of noise but the door remained unmoved.

A door on the left of the landing opened and a fair-haired woman in a dressing gown looked out at them disapprovingly. '*Qué pasa?*'

'Back inside, now,' Guzmán barked. '*Policía.*'

The woman retreated into her flat, her face showing her disgust. Behind her, Guzmán saw a thin child, stick legs in threadbare shorts, eyes wide with concerned interest.

'For fuck's sake.' Guzmán realised the men were getting nowhere with the door. 'Stand back.' He pointed the Browning at the door lock. 'Watch this. Just like Hollywood.'

The blast in the confined hallway was painfully loud and accompanied by a sudden cry of pain as the bullet ricocheted from the lock, taking off a piece of the nearest civil guard's ear as it went. The man swore and clutched his head, bleeding copiously. Guzmán scowled at the lock and cursed it. He kicked the door again, though more carefully than before, but it remained firmly closed.

'Fucking tough lock,' one of the men muttered.

'Five rounds through the door,' Guzmán barked, 'on my command. Aim...' the *guardia* eagerly aimed their weapons at the wooden door, the sound of the rifle bolts hard loud and metallic.

Inside the flat a woman screamed. Footsteps came towards the door. The voice of an elderly man: 'Don't shoot, we surrender.'

Guzmán gave the wounded *guardia* an 'I told you so' look, although it was lost on the man, who was now trying – without success – to bind a field bandage around his head.

'Stop bleeding, that's an order.' Guzmán's sense of humour blossomed at times like these. The civil guard didn't share it.

The bolts on the door slid back and a key turned in the lock. The door opened inwards. Guzmán thrust himself forward, still limping slightly, pistol in hand. He was confronted by a grey-haired man of about seventy, wearing glasses, and a dressing gown that had seen better days.

'Can I help you, *señores*?' He was clearly shaken but attempting to maintain his dignity. 'Santiago Mendoza *para servirles*.'

Guzmán smashed his pistol across the man's face, shattering his glasses and knocking him to the floor where he lay groaning as Guzmán and the *guardia civiles* crashed into the house, trampling the old man underfoot.

A woman's voice, 'Santiago? Santiago, *que pasa*?'

Guzmán stormed through the entrance hall and into a well-furnished, if shabby, living room. Every wall covered in books. Books reached up to the ceiling, shelf after shelf. Against the window two people sat on a divan, an elderly woman, and a somewhat younger man, wearing a polo-necked sweater under a sober tweed jacket.

'*Señora* Mendoza?' Guzmán asked. The woman nodded.

'And you will be Ernesto Garcia Mendoza, also known as *el Profesor*,' Guzmán said. 'We have a long-standing appointment, *señor*.'

The man stood up, releasing the woman's hand. 'That's me,' he said in a controlled voice. 'These people have nothing to do with any business you have with me, officer. I can assure you they have only helped me because I—'

'*Joder. Coño*. I know who you fucking are. You're a traitor and these people are traitors as well. You're all under arrest.'

The woman shrieked as a *guardia* dragged her husband into the room, blood running down the old man's face.

Christ almighty, why is everyone is bleeding today? Guzmán wondered. 'Take them to the *comisaría*,' he ordered. 'Arrange prison places for them.'

'We would like to remain together,' Mendoza said quietly.

'No you wouldn't,' Guzmán said, 'not where you're going.'

The couple were led away. *El Profesor* turned to Guzmán, 'I'd like to speak with your superior officer. 'I have information I'm prepared to exchange for their freedom.'

Guzmán's face reddened with fury and his big fists clenched as he pushed his face towards the professor, his words accompanied by a spray of angry spittle. 'I report to the fucking *Caudillo* directly, you little prick. *Generalísimo* Francisco Franco himself. I'm not some half-arsed copper come round to tell you you've parked in the wrong place.'

'The *Brigada Especial*? the professor said calmly. 'Clearly I underestimated my own importance.'

'You'll see how important you are,' Guzmán growled, turning to the remaining *guardia civiles*. 'Take him down to the truck. If he tries to get away, shoot him. It'll save time later.'

'I'm glad to hear Franco's justice remains so consistent in both its assumptions and its application,' *el Profesor* murmured defiantly.

Guzmán's reply was immediate. He smashed his fist into the professor's belly and the man crumpled, exhaling noisily. The two *guardia* kept the professor from falling to the floor. Even in pain, the man tried to make a last impotent protest, but failed. Taking his weight between them, the two *guardia civiles* frog-marched him down the stairs.

'Tie him before he goes in the truck,' Guzmán called after them. He waited on the landing until their footsteps died away and then knocked on the door of number eleven. No answer. He put his ear to the door. Nothing. Number twelve didn't answer either. Guzmán sighed. He pulled the shattered door to number ten closed as best he could. No doubt the place would be looted by tomorrow, and then the Falange would allocate the flat to someone else – friend, lover, relative, it didn't matter as long as you were connected to the elaborate mechanisms of power permeating every aspect of Spanish life. Still, that was how it worked and, for Guzmán, it worked very well. He knocked on the door of number nine. There was someone in there, at any rate.

The fair-haired woman opened the door. She looked at Guzmán with contempt. 'Yes?'

Guzmán ignored the tone of her voice. 'I want to talk to you about your neighbours, *señora*. We've just arrested them.'

'Ah. The old couple. That would explain why you needed so many men.'

'They were harbouring a dangerous criminal, *Señora*...?'

'Martinez.'

'*Señora* Martinez.' Guzmán pronounced her name slowly as if he were writing it in his notebook. 'Well, *Señora* Martinez, I want to know what you can tell me about those people.'

She looked at him impassively. 'There's little I can tell you. An elderly couple, very quiet. They have the odd visitor but other than that, they keep very much to themselves.'

Guzmán pushed the door. The woman resisted for a moment and then gave up as the door forced her back into her own apartment. The room was furnished plainly, the cheap furniture and the darns in her clothing evidence of her poverty.

'There's no need to force your way in, officer,' she protested. 'I'm giving you all the help I can.'

Guzmán sneered. He ran his eyes over her and watched how she backed away from him, how she squirmed uncomfortably under his blatant, hungry assessment of her body.

She was in her late thirties, he guessed. A long pretty face, high cheekbones, slightly lined and drawn from work and a lack of food. That was normal. His eyes ran over her breasts, her hips and then back to her face. She coloured slightly at his belligerent scrutiny.

From the back room a child's voice piped up. '*Quien es?*'

'No one, *mi vida*. Just a policeman. Stay there.'

Guzmán looked over to the door and saw the dark haunted face of a boy aged somewhere between six and ten. Like many kids, the boy was far too thin, his skin sallow and pale. He stood there like a little scarecrow, gangly and awkward.

'Are you a policeman?' he asked, unable to check his curiosity.

Guzmán looked at him. 'Yes. Are you a good boy?'

'*Si, señor. Me llamo Roberto.*'

'Then go back to your room and close the door, Roberto,' Guzmán said firmly. 'Like your *mamá* told you.'

The boy reluctantly went into his room and closed the door, his dark eyes still fixed on Guzmán as the door closed.

'Nice boy,' Guzmán observed. 'Just the one son, then?'

'He's not my son, my husband's dead. He's my nephew. I've had him since my sister died of cancer five years ago.'

Guzmán nodded. He could have offered condolences, but that was not his way. Besides, he didn't care.

'Look, I have things to do, is there anything else you need to know, officer?'

Guzmán looked around the flat. 'In my line of work you have to know everything. Sometimes it takes a while to get a feel for what it is you actually need to know.'

Señora Martinez looked confused. 'I have nothing to do with that couple next door, if that's what you are thinking. Only to say good morning now and again.'

'Really? Nothing else? Did you ever fetch their shopping, for example?'

He saw the answer from her expression. She struggled to answer and when she spoke, there was an element of sincerity, an attempt to convince, to justify. But for Guzmán there were just lies and the truth. And he could recognise both.

'A few times. As I said, they are elderly. The lady sometimes had problems with her knees: there are so many stairs in this building. I only collected a few groceries.'

Guzmán was again looking at the neckline of her dress, at her breasts. It was a predatory gesture, one of a cat to a mouse. She reddened, and he was pleased to see a thin line of sweat on her upper lip, despite the cold of the apartment.

'Groceries,' Guzmán repeated flatly.

It was very quiet in the flat. Quiet and cold. Guzmán towered over *Señora* Martinez. He reached into his jacket and pulled out his notebook. Without asking permission, he sat down at the cheap battered table with its faded lace tablecloth.

'Do you have a pencil?' Guzmán watched the woman's hips as she went to a cupboard and bent to a drawer. She handed him the pencil, avoiding eye contact, conscious of the fierce intensity of his gaze, aware of her own complicity in supplying him with the means of condemning her. He wrote in the book at length and without looking up, knowing her attention was now fully on him. There was something he enjoyed about committing people to writing, inscribing them into official memory, condemning their actions, their words, their entire being into the immutable history of a police file. He looked up, straight into her pale eyes which were, as he expected, riveted on the battered leather notebook and the chewed pencil in his hand.

'Full name?'

'Alicia Isabel Martinez.'

'Age?'

'Thirty-three.'

Guzmán looked up from writing as if needing to verify her age with his own eyes. He had thought she was nearer forty, but no matter. She was still attractive. At least attractive enough for him.

'Do you mind if I sit down?' *Señora* Martinez asked, annoyed by Guzmán's tone.

'Yes I do. Stand there. I want to get a good look at you.'

He stared at her. She tried to meet his eye, wringing her hands together in discomfort. Guzmán stared back. She looked away, flushed.

'Keep still,' Guzmán said. She froze. 'Well, *señora*,' he closed the notebook, 'let's just have a look at what we have here.' He sat back, never taking his hungry eyes from her. He saw her shiver. Not from the cold, he imagined.

'Firstly, you live next door to a couple with anti-Spanish sentiments. Traitors. Possibly agents of international Freemasonry or Communism. Possibly both of those.'

She started to protest, but shrank back under the threatening weight of his look.

'These traitors harboured a dangerous enemy of the State, a man who's been evading the law for years. A man condemned by the courts for his crimes during the Crusade.'

She raised her hands helplessly. 'The War ended fourteen years ago. Can't you stop fighting it now? Why can't you just let it all be forgotten? How can we ever have real peace if we stay locked in the past?'

Guzmán snorted. 'We don't forget, *señora*. There can be no forgetting because to do so would betray the great works achieved by the *Caudillo* and the people of Spain who rose up to destroy the Red menace. We don't forget, *al contrario*, we remember. We remember everything. Everything.' His voice was an angry growl as he got to his feet. He stepped towards her and slapped his notebook across her face. She gasped, shocked. 'It's all here. In files, books, ledgers, records, all manner of documents, all over Spain. The memory of what happened, who did it and when. And each time we catch another of these traitors, another obstacle to the greatness of Spain falls – like that Marxist bastard we arrested next door. We don't forget. We won and we have to maintain the victory. Even if we have to kill all of them. I'm surprised at you, *señora*, frankly, asking a question like that. Very surprised indeed.'

She was on the verge of tears now, afraid of Guzmán's huge presence, his malevolent intimidation, the barely controlled violence inflecting his voice. She stepped backwards as he advanced towards her. He came closer, forcing her against the wall. She was shaking violently. He could feel it.

'Be quiet,' Guzmán said. 'I have more questions.'

She nodded, her arms folded across her chest defensively.

'I notice you don't have a crucifix in the apartment. No sign of devotion, in fact. Not one.'

'I can't afford one. I can hardly make ends meet as it is.' Her voice trembled.

'And how often do you attend mass, *señora*?'

She stared at him, horrified, not knowing where this was going but knowing it was going very badly. 'Not very often. I work on Saturdays and so on Sundays I—'

'You don't attend mass. You have no trace of our Lord or His blessed mother in your house. I'd say you lack religion.'

'I know, I should go more often. I will go. I'll go this week. It's been hard.'

'It's hard for the ungodly, perhaps. But not for good Christians.'

'I'm not a bad person.' She was on the verge of tears. Guzmán was pleased.

'No?' His voice rose in the thick choked tone of the habitually violent. 'What the hell is that then?' He pointed to a small framed photograph on a shelf. A young man in uniform smiled at the camera, frozen in faded sepia on some day long gone. His hair shone with brilliantine beneath a summer sun. In the background there were blossom trees. But it was the uniform Guzmán noticed most. The Republican uniform. The enemy uniform.

'My husband.' She was starting to cry.

'Where is he?'

'Dead.' Tears fell down her face. 'He died in the war.'

'No one dies in wars,' Guzmán said sharply. 'They're killed. Who killed him?'

'He was a prisoner in Andalucía,' she wept. 'He was shot by the soldiers of Queipo Llano.' Her head dropped. Tears fell onto the threadbare rug.

'General Queipo de Llano,' Guzmán corrected her. When she didn't respond, he poked her with his index finger between her breasts. She recoiled, flinching back against the wall. Trapped.

'General Queipo de Llano,' she repeated obediently. He ran his

94

finger slowly across her breast in casual exploration. She pressed herself against the wall more tightly.

'General Queipo de Llano. May he rest in peace,' Guzmán persisted, his finger probing again. He felt the pounding of her heart through the coarse fabric. He rested his hand on her breast. He squeezed.

'General Queipo de Llano. *Que en paz descanse,*' she parroted, gasping with fear and pain. He felt the violent rhythm of her heartbeat and squeezed again, harder. She choked back a cry of pain and bit her lip.

'You were a fool to think I wouldn't notice that photograph. A man in Republican uniform.' Guzmán shook his head. 'A fool to even have it on show. God knows what else you're hiding.'

She whimpered, unable to speak through her tears.

'Stop crying.'

She tried unsuccessfully.

'Listen, *señora*, this looks bad for you. The neighbours, their traitorous nephew, your ungodliness. I've got enough here to send you to prison.' Guzmán's tone softened, the largesse of the victor to the vanquished. 'Look, even if I don't arrest you, and believe me, I don't want to because, frankly, I don't have the time, but there's still the issue of the Falange.'

She looked up, red-eyed. 'What about them? You're the law, surely...'

'The law, yes. But in civil terms, the Falange keep an eye on morality, they police public probity. Ensure children are well looked after in good, Christian households.'

He saw her eyes widen with sudden apprehension.

'Some of those people are cretins, *señora*, yet they hold positions of power. And when they consider a child isn't being brought up in the True Faith, or there's a history in the family of sedition, or radical politics...'

She looked at him with horror. He knew her worst fear now.

'They'd naturally intervene, take the child away – probably to a Jesuit orphanage, away from the moral contamination of the home. Where the child's habits can be undone and corrected. Where the rod won't be spared. Where the priests can remind him he comes from contaminated stock, that he bears the parents' guilt.'

'No, please...'

'That would be their duty, wouldn't it, *señora*? Their godly, Christian duty?'

'But...'

'Their godly Christian duty. Would it not?'

'Yes.'

'Yes what?' He touched her again, harder this time.

'It would be their godly Christian duty.' She broke into tears again.

'I have to go now, *señora*,' Guzmán said abruptly.

She looked horrified. 'Please, wait, please.'

'I really must be back at work. You'll hear in due course from the authorities.' He made towards the door but she grabbed him by the sleeve, pulling him back.

She lowered her voice. 'Please, I'll do anything. *Anything*. You shot my husband. Please leave me my sister's child. He's all I have. He's my life.'

'There is one thing.' Guzmán said.

'Anything.'

'Get on your knees.'

Señora Martinez shot a despairing look at the closed door of the back room, and then sank to her knees, her shoulders shaking. Guzmán leaned down and raised her chin with his hand.

'Listen, I've got a busy day today but I'll come back here tonight. It will be quite late. Make sure the brat is in bed. And that he stays there. We'll continue our discussion then, if you understand me. And, if you're a good girl, and do what you're told, then the Falange and the Church Child Care Authorities won't put your little boy in an orphanage. That's the price you pay for keeping him. Understood?'

'Yes.'

'Yes, *Comandante* Guzmán,' he instructed.

He lifted her face, his big hand cupping her reluctant chin, her red eyes spilling tears. 'Yes, *Comandante* Guzmán,' she whispered.

'Until later then. And don't think about trying to get away, we'd find you and then you'd both suffer even more.'

Guzmán let go of her chin. She slumped forwards, hands on the floor, gasping for air.

'*Tia* Alicia?' a reedy voice called. 'Auntie?'

She got up and ran to the back room.

'I'll see myself out,' Guzmán called, closing the door behind him.

He made his way down the stairs. Outside the truck was still waiting, its exhaust billowing dirty clouds of fumes into the freezing air. Peralta was chatting with the driver. When he saw Guzmán coming, he started to climb down from the cab.

'All well, *Comandante*?'

Guzmán pushed him back in the cab. He pulled out a cigarette and lit it. He looked round at the snow-covered tenements. Here and there, a curtain twitched. Another lesson imparted, he thought.

'Everything is very good, *Acting Teniente*.' Guzmán's sneering accentuation of Peralta's rank was now habitual. 'Everything is very good indeed.'

The sarge was standing in a nearby doorway talking to a man. Guzmán was already halfway into the truck when he noticed the *sargento* and impatiently shouted to him to hurry. They had arrested all those on their list and Guzmán saw no need for the numbers to be increased further.

MADRID 1953, COMISARÍA, CALLE DE ROBLES

Peralta noted the change in the stonework as he descended the stairs to the cells below the *comisaría*. The brickwork gave way to much older stone; some of the arches were inscribed with faded ancient carvings and the low ceiling reminded him of a sewer. The doors of the cells were made of thick metal, reinforced by iron bands, clearly more recent additions to the architecture of the *comisaría*.

The cells were guarded by a few *guardia civiles*. Down the corridor, Peralta noticed the Falangists, each with a large ledger. They seemed to be comparing notes. As Peralta reached the first cell, the *Guardia* snapped to attention.

'Where's Mendoza?' Peralta asked.

'Cell twelve, *Teniente*.'

Peralta nodded and walked past the other *guardia* and Falangists towards the end of the corridor. The atmosphere was quite cheerful. Amongst those outside the cells, at any rate. The corridor grew lower as he progressed along it. By the time he reached cell twelve, Peralta was obliged to bow his head. The cold sepulchral stonework of the walls seemed like that of some ancient church. At the end of the corridor was another door, much older than any of the others, its dark wooden bulk crossed by crude metal bands, the huge antique lock set in a swarm of ornate snakes. Outside the cell, the *guardia* saluted Peralta. On the door was a rough sign scrawled in an angry hand: COMANDANTE GUZMÁN ONLY.

'The *comandante* told me to begin Mendoza's interrogation,' Peralta said.

The guard pulled a set of keys from his belt. '*Pase, Teniente*.'

Peralta went in. It was a small windowless cell, with a low curved ceiling of ancient stone. The cell was cold and rivulets of water ran down the walls, patterning the stones with an elaborate network of green stains. In one corner, a battered bucket was the only sanitation. Against the far wall, Mendoza sprawled on a straw mattress. He looked tired. His hair was tousled and one of the lenses in his spectacles was cracked. He looked older than the faded photograph Peralta had seen a few minutes earlier in the mess room when Guzmán was splashing brandy into their mugs to celebrate the success of the raid.

'I would stand to welcome you,' Mendoza said calmly, 'but as you see I'm a little inconvenienced at the moment.'

Peralta's eyes were more accustomed to the darkness now and he saw the prisoner's hands were cuffed behind him.

'Stay where you are,' Peralta said. He looked round for a chair and then felt foolish for doing so. He tried to lean on the wall but abandoned that plan as he saw how wet the stonework was.

'Make yourself comfortable, *Teniente.*'

'I'm fine, thank you,' Peralta said stiffly. 'I won't be staying long.'

'Nor, I suspect, will I,' Mendoza said. 'This is how they do it in the American movies, isn't it?'

'What do you mean?' Peralta was becoming more annoyed. He was the one who should impose himself on the interview and ask the questions. He was used to interviewing prisoners, but they had always been small-time crooks or black marketeers, not enemies of the State.

'First the good policeman, then the bad one. You, then the *comandante.* It always works in those *Yanqui* films.'

'We're not in a film,' Peralta snapped. 'And I'm not sure *Comandante* Guzmán will be able to attend this interview.' He stopped, seeing *el Profesor* smile.

'He'll come,' Mendoza said. 'He won't be able to resist his need to gloat.'

Peralta frowned. 'Whether the *comandante* attends or not is irrelevant. I wish to ask you some questions, before...' He paused, recalling Guzmán's instructions not to inform the prisoner of his impending fate. The *teniente* ground his teeth in anger at the professor's smile.

'No trial for me then, *Teniente*? No report of my supposed crimes in *El Alcazar* or some other Falangist rag? Will it be the garrotte or the bullet?'

Peralta was sweating. 'The due process of law will be followed,' he snapped. 'Judgement will be based upon the evidence...'

Mendoza laughed. 'Evidence? Due process? You forget, *Teniente*, I've seen how it works. You don't want justice, you want to wipe out all those who opposed that whinnying little Galician.'

'You will not speak of the *Caudillo* like that,' Peralta shouted. 'You fought on the side of Communism and the anti-Christ, you burned churches, allowed the rape of nuns...'

'I made Molotov cocktails,' Mendoza said quietly. 'Wine bottle, petrol, rag in the top. That's why they called me *el Profesor*, because of my specialist knowledge. Before the war I was a schoolteacher. Then I joined up to support a democratically elected government against the treachery of Franco's military rebellion. Maybe it was a bad choice, but it was my choice and I was right to make it.'

'Not from where I'm standing.'

'No, I suppose not. And presumably until all of us who fought for the Republic are dead, this will continue. Endless punishment imposed upon those who opposed you – or even those who *might* oppose you.'

Outside the cell door there was the sound of a loud voice and boots clattering on the stone floor. The door flew open and Guzmán swaggered into the room, framed in the doorway by the pale lights of the corridor like some great ape.

He glared at Mendoza. 'Ernesto Garcia Mendoza, you are charged under the 1939 Law of Responsibilities which is applied retrospectively to all activities from 1934 onwards. You're charged with crimes against the Spanish State including supporting enemies of the State by subterfuge and force of arms. You were convicted in your absence by a military tribunal in Valladolid in May 1942 and sentenced to death. Do you have anything to say?'

'Yes,' Mendoza said quietly. 'Where are my aunt and uncle?'

Guzmán scowled, 'On their way to prison. Their apartment is confiscated and their pensions cancelled. And all because of ...' his face contorted angrily, 'you.'

'May I ask when you propose to execute me?' Mendoza said. 'Or are we going to have the torture first?'

'There will be no torture,' Peralta said, aware of how thin his voice sounded. 'Your dignity will be protected until sentence is carried out.'

Guzmán looked as if he was about to attack Peralta. 'There'll be no fucking torture because he's nothing of any importance to tell us. We learned all of that long ago.'

'I'm sure,' Mendoza nodded. 'But, I do have one confession to make.'

'Go ahead, just make it quick. We've a table booked for lunch,' Guzmán snarled.

Mendoza nodded. 'I hardly remember the war any more. Just vague detail. Names, faces, they don't come to me any more.' He paused. 'Now, I'm just me and my circumstances, *Comandante*.'

'That sounds like one for your headstone,' Guzmán said. 'Who said it first?'

'It was Ortega y Gasset,' Peralta said. 'He—'

'Shut the fuck up,' Guzmán shouted.

Mendoza sighed. 'It was all a long time ago. Now it's just history. And just as we grow old and die, so will the memory of your *Caudillo*.'

Peralta wished Mendoza would shut up and let Guzmán crow. And then wait quietly until it was time to go to the firing squad.

Guzmán snorted. 'That's where you're wrong and that's why you lost. You didn't want to win enough and we did. Let me tell you, professor, I remember every man I fought with and many of those I killed. Never a day goes by but I see the war, hear the noises, smell the carnage, the burning and the flesh. Hear the shots rattling around our trenches. I don't forget.'

'You're still in that war, *Comandante* Guzmán. Still fighting it. What will you do when all those who opposed you are dead. Retire on half pay and grow vegetables somewhere?' Mendoza said.

Guzmán turned to Peralta. 'We're done here.' Peralta moved towards the door.

Guzmán looked back at Mendoza. 'It will never be finished.' His voice was now more controlled and much more frightening. 'But for you, it ends tonight. One less stain on Spanish history.'

The door slammed. Mendoza stared at the wall, watching slow rivulets of water worming down their ancient mossy tracks to the damp floor. Outside, he heard the *comandante* shouting, heard his footsteps diminishing down the corridor and then a distant door closed with a dull thud. After that, there was only silence.

Peralta sat in Guzmán's office and waited while his boss raged. He raged about Mendoza, about Peralta and, after raging for a while about nothing in particular, he calmed down. It was lunchtime. The last thing Peralta wanted was to have lunch with Guzmán. In fact, the last thing he wanted was lunch. Mendoza's calm resignation had affected him more than he cared to tell Guzmán; indeed, more than he dared tell him.

Guzmán shuffled a pile of papers as he dialled the number of Military Headquarters.

'Thirty-six arrests. Let's see how many we can get rid of.' He winked at Peralta.

Peralta felt an uncomfortable sense of foreboding. No matter how he tried, there was no way he could think of to extricate himself from what was to follow.

Guzmán began speaking to someone, his tone respectful and measured. He gave a reference number to confirm who he was. Arranging the lists of names of those arrested on his desk, Guzmán began to place a mark against certain names. Finally it was finished.

'*Gracias, mi Coronel. Hasta luego.*' He replaced the phone in its cradle.

Peralta saw the list of names on Guzmán's desk. 'How many, *Comandante?*'

Guzmán looked up at Peralta, his heavy lidded eyes flashing with anger.

'Twelve. Can you believe it? Franco's spared most of them.' Guzmán sounded disappointed. 'It took weeks to get the information so we could get them all at once. We had dozens of plain-clothes lads following them around. We beat our informers senseless to make sure we could be certain. And then what?' He gestured at the paper on his desk. 'A few years in prison.'

'Perhaps the *Caudillo* decided that a few years in prison will be enough to straighten them out? You said yourself Mendoza had nothing worthwhile to tell us.'

Guzmán looked hard at Peralta. 'Mendoza dies.'

'How long do you think the others will get?'

Guzmán sighed. 'Nothing. Twenty-five, thirty years. For Christ's sake some of them could be out by 1976.' He sighed again. 'Fuck it. We do what we're told. It's not our fault if they get a slap on the wrist. Let's get some lunch.'

Peralta took his thin shabby overcoat from the coat stand. Guzmán rose ponderously and pulled on his own thick wool coat. The phone rang, metallic and shrill in the gloomy office. Guzmán picked up the receiver.

'*Buenos dias, mi Coronel.* Yes, I spoke to your colleague a few minutes ago,' Guzmán said, his face brightening. 'I have it here, *Coronel.* Go ahead, I'm ready.' Guzmán began to place marks against the names of some of the men on the list. 'I have all that, *Coronel.* Many thanks.' Guzmán hung up. He bounced up out of his chair. 'Well, that's better.' He began to wrap his scarf around his neck. 'Three more cases have been reviewed by Franco.'

'And?' Peralta asked.

'They die too,' Guzmán said happily. 'Probably the *Caudillo* received a plea for mercy from someone in the government or the church. It often happens. A cousin or some distant relative – Oh please, *Generalísimo*, spare my Juanito, he only killed a few priests. That kind of shit. So to show they have his ear, Franco spares them. Well, that's what he tells them. But then there's an administrative blunder at this end and the paperwork arrives too late to commute the original sentence. They die, but technically Franco has done their relatives a favour by ordering them to be spared.'

Peralta looked blankly at him. 'So they were never really going to be spared?'

Guzmán pulled his hat onto his head firmly. 'They were spared, Acting *Teniente.* Technically. Their deaths are just an administrative error.'

He stepped out into the stone flagged corridor and waited for

Peralta to follow him before locking the office door. At the reception desk the *sargento* was stamping his feet in an effort to keep warm.

'Off for lunch, Sarge,' Guzmán said. 'Need to keep our strength up for tonight.'

The *sargento* grinned. 'It's all on, then?'

'Naturally.' Guzmán nodded as he made for the door to the street. 'A bit of overtime for you and the boys.'

The *sargento* waited until they had gone through the two great doors into the frozen street before raising his right hand with the glowing cigarette cupped in it and taking a deep drag.

The freezing air was sharp and relentless as they walked the hundred metres to Guzmán's chosen café. As the door opened and Peralta followed him into the crowded room, the air was suddenly warm and thick with the smell of cooking. In spite of himself, Peralta felt his mouth water. The door closed behind him, momentarily framing in its painted glass the dark figure watching them from a doorway across the street.

They struggled through the trees with the panic of men trapped in quicksand: an overwhelming desire to escape shadowed by an increasing suspicion that escape might not ultimately be possible. The Moors pursued them, their voices foreign and hard as they came, firing through the trees in the hope of a random hit. Now and then they were successful.

The kid had ditched most of his equipment. Even his water bottle had been thrown down in order to lighten his burden. All he carried now was his rifle which he clung to with desperate attachment, as if his life depended on the fierce grip he maintained on the weapon. The muscles of his forearms spasmed with the exertion of carrying the rifle and his back ached from the crouching lope he was obliged to maintain in order to avoid the sibilant bullets whining through the trees around them. The wood began to thin out, giving way to steep stony ground that rose into a sheer stone cliff. Above that was a copse of fir trees offering new opportunities for cover. If they could make it that far.

The men ran across the scrubland. One man called out, a note of hope in his voice. Above them, curving up through the sheer rock face, was a path, rough stone steps carved into a steep narrow ravine rising through the vertical stone. The men looked back briefly. Shouts in Arabic and the crack of rifles from the trees sent them scurrying towards the path, boots rattling on the roughly hewn stone as they began their ascent. As the kid entered the shelter of the ravine and began to climb, the man behind him cried out. Turning, the kid saw the man sink to his knees, a rose of blood blossoming in the centre of his chest. There was no more looking back. Behind them was death and with every stumbling step, it was getting nearer.

CHAPTER FIVE

MADRID 2009, UNIVERSIDAD COMPLUTENSE, DEPARTAMENTO DE
HISTORIA CONTEMPORÁNEA

Galindez parked her car in the faculty parking lot and made her way across the campus to the Modern History building. The university grounds were tanned and dappled in the morning heat, the endless cascade of the fountain a stream of diamonds and ice fire in the thick warmth of the day. Students littered the campus, sprawling with practised informality amid the detritus of campus life: books, newspapers, fashion magazines, sandwich wrappers. A radio played rap, the bass reverberating around the campus buildings. Galindez followed signs that led her down a long corridor towards the department of Interpretative History. Galindez heard Luisa talking on the phone as she opened the office door. Luisa waved Galindez to a small couch by the window and finished her call.

'Hello, you.' Luisa sat next to her on the couch. 'Did you talk to your boss?'

'I did. He's keen for us to be involved in the project. Not only that, I can access the Military Intelligence Archive.'

'Fantastic,' Luisa said. 'You'll bring a new perspective to our work.'

'Good. I'm really looking forward to it. You're still sure you don't mind – now we're not seeing each other, I mean? I don't want there to be any friction between us.'

'I'm fine, Ana. We're both grown-ups. I must admit I was sorry when you said you wanted to break up, but that's life. And we can still be friends, can't we?'

'Of course we can,' Galindez said.

Luisa nodded. 'I'll introduce you to the team in a few minutes. It's not a big team, but that may change as the project develops. Let's go, shall we?'

Galindez followed Luisa to a door at the end of the corridor. A sign above the door told her this was Seminar Room B. A piece of paper was taped on the door: *Civil War Atrocities Project Team: Members only.* Luisa unlocked the door. 'This is our meeting room. We keep our photo library here as well. Have a look at our collection if you like while I get the others.' She strolled away down the corridor and Galindez entered Seminar Room B. And then the day changed as she stepped into a world over seventy years old.

The walls were covered with images of the Civil War. Sepia and black and white photographs everywhere, pinned to boards, mounted sequences of pictures with carefully annotated detail, others just propped against the wall. Photographs of men and women, worn faces turned to the camera, forever frozen in a variety of grins, salutes and scowls. Clenched fists raised by men in ragged uniforms crowded on a lorry, their bulging packs and long rifles held awkwardly as the truck wended its way along some unknown dirt track. Dark unshaven faces, flat caps, cigarettes dangling from their mouths.

Leaving her bag on a table, Galindez moved slowly along the array of photographs. The tone of the content began to darken. She saw huddled corpses, perhaps the aftermath of a battle. But she was wrong: here was the same scene but this time the corpses were still alive, standing cowed, their hands tied, unwillingly facing the camera, while a metre away a group of men aimed rifles at the prisoners. Did they really have to stand so close in order to shoot them, she wondered. And then she realised. The men were standing that close in order to get into the photograph. And, while they held their weapons aimed at the group of prisoners, each man in the firing squad was looking at the camera. Smiling.

The next photograph brought Galindez to a halt before its grainy, colourless image. The caption told her little: *Unidentified male and female, Granada, 1936.* A woman of indeterminate age – but then everyone looked older in those days, Galindez thought – perhaps thirty, fair hair. Clearly a prisoner. Standing next to her was a young man, thick, oiled hair and a thin moustache. The man had one arm draped around the woman's shoulder, a nonchalant gesture of affection but for the fact that he was pressing a small snub-nosed automatic pistol against her temple with his other hand. The woman's face was a complex landscape of pain and fear, the man's casual menace horrifying. Even so, Galindez wasn't prepared for the next photograph.

The same woman again, kneeling, leaning forwards, hands crossed across her breasts, looking up at the camera. Her dress had been torn and pulled down to her waist. Her face was bloodied from a large cut over her left eye. Galindez stared in macabre fascination at the transition from the fearful but intact persona in the first photo to this wounded, half-naked state in the next. Unwillingly, Galindez turned to the third picture. She froze, transfixed by the final image of horror.

The woman lay on her back, arms spread wide, as if crucified. She had been shot in the forehead and through the right temple, the left side of her face destroyed by the blast. The remnants of her dress and underwear had been pulled down to her knees in a last spiteful act of humiliation. Galindez had seen gunshot wounds to the face before. But they'd been corpses she'd observed during her training. They could never convey the sequential horror of this obscene transition from life to death captured in the faded monochrome sequence in front of her.

Turning away, Galindez tried to break the spell the triptych of death had put on her. To her side was an enlarged photograph, mounted on a stand. A heavy-set man with dark stubble, his lips set in a humourless line. Next to him, a rather skeletal younger man with thinning hair and a badly fitting suit, a thin, apologetic smile. Both seemed unaware of the camera, their stances suggested they were looking at something or somebody away to their left. Behind them was an arched, iron-banded, double doorway, and by the door, a man in uniform, looking intently at the other two. At the bottom of the photograph the caption: *Comandante Guzmán with Teniente Peralta and unknown sargento, c.1949–1954.*

Finally, Galindez thought, a clear image of her suspect. Perhaps it was the impact of the previous pictures or even a case of projection, but she sensed something far more threatening in Guzmán than in the grinning young assassin with his pistol to the woman's head. The room suddenly felt cold. Galindez had an urge to be outside, sprawled on the grass with the blaring radio and the translucent water music of the fountain, safe amid the vibrancy of the living, rather than here, surrounded by this exhibition of indifferent violence. Guzmán's dark hooded eyes glared at her, harsh and unforgiving. A sudden noise. Galindez turned, expecting Luisa, seeing instead a tall, heavily built skinhead, face bristling with piercings. The man didn't look like a student or a member of staff. Something felt wrong.

'Who are you?' she asked.

'I'm looking for the Guzmán book.' The skinhead gave her a long look. 'Know where it is?'

'Are you part of the team?'

He walked over to the table, scanning the assorted papers strewn across it. 'I thought it would be here. You have got it, haven't you?'

'You mean the diary?'

He scowled at her. 'No, the book. *Mierda.* Don't you know what I'm talking about?' He picked up her bag and casually started rifling through the contents.

'*Joder*, that's my fucking bag.' Galindez grabbed the handle of her bag, angry at his clumsy intimidation. The skinhead held on for a moment and she saw the tattoo on his arm: *SANCHO.*

He let go of the bag, grabbing for Galindez's wrist. She took a step back and then thrust the flat of her hand into his face, feeling the metal piercings as the heel of her hand connected with his nose. He staggered back in surprise, dribbling snot. He was lucky, she thought: if she'd hit him as she intended, his nose would be all over his face now. She saw his expression harden as he realised he wasn't dealing with some helpless admin worker.

'Fucking hell.' Sancho spat blood and snot onto the carpet. 'That's enough of that, *chica*, where's that book?'

She aimed a kick at his groin but he moved faster, turning and taking the blow on the outside of his thigh before spinning towards her. He threw rapid punches, trying to overwhelm her with speed and power. Galindez retreated, blocking the blows with her forearms, trying to keep distance between them in order to manoeuvre but the attack continued. Intent on blocking the blows to her face, Galindez opened herself up to a vicious punch to her right shoulder. A shaft of shimmering fire radiated down from her shoulder to her fingers, simultaneously numbing and agonisingly sharp. She moved back, staying out of Sancho's reach, her right arm hanging limply by her side. She tried to lift her fists to defend herself as Sancho approached, but her right hand no longer obeyed her and he laughed at her muted cry of pain.

'Stop now.' He spoke as if talking to a child. 'Just tell me where it is and I'll go.'

'*Hijo de puta.*' Galindez turned sideways, trying a kick to his knee while his weight was on it. Again, he anticipated the attack and twisted away before she could inflict any damage. 'I don't think you know, do you?' He said it casually, but she saw from his clenched fists and the way he was shifting his balance he was about to attack. He came closer. She smelled cigarettes and sweat.

'*Vamos niña*, I don't have time to play games,' Sancho grunted, feinting with his hands, trying to confuse her. 'Shame to mess up a pretty face like that.' His voice was almost pleasant. The dark malice in his eyes was not.

Sancho moved subtly, inching towards her, grinning as Galindez tried to keep herself at a distance. And then, as she'd expected, the attack began. He spun forward, his elbow coming straight at her face. Galindez ducked and the blow passed over her head. She tried to defend herself with her good arm but his attack continued and he batted away an attempted block, his other fist slamming into her belly. Galindez heard a strange percussive sound as the air was driven from her lungs. She tried to take a breath and could not. Clutching her stomach with her good arm she sank to her knees, gasping. She realised he was too good for her. *He could have finished me with that punch.*

'This is fucking ridiculous. Stay there,' Sancho ordered, moving to the door. He stopped in surprise, seeing Galindez struggle to her feet, her right arm dangling helplessly, her dark hair hanging across her face, and behind it, her eyes almost black with fury.

She glared at him. 'We aren't finished.' She raised her left fist: she was going to attack.

'For fuck's sake.' Sancho came at her, angry and fast. She braced, hoping to anticipate him. Contemptuously, he slapped aside her awkward punch, put his hand on the top of her head and pushed her backwards onto the table. The table gave way, its legs breaking noisily, photographs and papers scattering around her as she sprawled on the floor, shocked by the sudden impact. Sancho moved forward, placing his boot between her legs and then pressed down hard, pinning her in place. Galindez shouted in pain. She bit her lip, determined she would not cry out again.

'Stay still,' Sancho growled, maintaining the pressure, towering over her like some victorious gladiator. She lay helpless, clutching her abdomen with her good hand. Sancho's big combat boot pressed against her crotch, invasive and dominating. She wanted to kill him.

Sancho took his foot away and Galindez rolled onto her side with a stifled groan. 'Not so tough after all, then, *niña.*' He paused at the door, seeing Galindez trying unsuccessfully to get to her knees. 'That's probably the biggest thrill you'll get this year, *morena.*' He smiled, baring yellowing teeth. 'Unless you get in my way again.'

The door closed behind him. Galindez let out a low growl of pain and frustrated anger. She was still struggling to get to her feet when the door opened.

It was Luisa. 'Ana María? *Dios mio,* someone get a doctor. Ana? Speak to me, love. *Por dios, querida.*'

111

Galindez tried to find a position where things hurt a little less. She couldn't. 'Don't fuss, I'm all right.'

'What happened?'

'There was a man, a big skinhead,' Galindez said angrily. 'Didn't you see him? He attacked me.'

A young man with a goatee beard handed her a glass of water. He must be Toni, Luisa's postgraduate, she decided. In the background, she heard Luisa on the phone, talking to campus security.

Ten minutes later, the security men arrived. After a cursory discussion, they left in search of her attacker. Assuring Luisa she still wanted to attend the meeting, Galindez joined Toni and Luisa at the big conference table. Her right arm pulsed with raw pain. At least she was able to move it a little now. She knew it would pass: Sancho had known what he was doing: inflicting pain but no major damage. Apart from the humiliation of course.

Toni looked at his watch. 'Is Natalia coming?'

Luisa shrugged. 'I left a note on her desk. Let's start.'

The door opened and a woman entered. Galindez looked at her briefly. And then she looked again. The newcomer was perhaps two years older than Galindez, blonde hair in a loose ponytail, slim, her expensive T-shirt and skirt very smart compared with the dress of the other staff Galindez had seen so far.

'*Lo siento*, Luisa, I was held up at the library.'

'No problem, Tali. We haven't started yet,' Luisa said without looking up. 'This is Ana María Galindez, the forensic investigator from the *guardia civil* I told you about.'

Natalia took Galindez's hand in a surprisingly strong grip. 'Natalia Castillo. *Encantada.*' Pain ran up and down Galindez's injured arm. She tried not to wince.

Luisa gave Natalia a brief account of the incident with the skinhead. Natalia listened with concern, asking if Galindez felt up to staying in the meeting. The usual Galindez reaction would have been to dismiss such solicitude but she found Natalia's attention

112

rather pleasing. 'I'm fine now. Honestly,' she said. She picked up her pen. Her hand was shaking. She put the pen down again.

'Ana María shares our passion for *Comandante* Guzmán,' Luisa said.

Natalia nodded. 'We're a passionate bunch, Ana. You'll fit in well.'

Luisa began to fidget. Galindez suddenly realised: the avoidance of eye contact, the strained tension when either of them spoke. She wondered which one of them broke it off.

'Right.' Luisa shuffled her papers. 'It's probably best if we tell Ana what we've done so far in researching the activities of *Comandante* Guzmán. Toni, could you start?'

Toni peered at his notes. 'OK. I've been cataloguing operations carried out by Guzmán's men – trying to identify those activities that have traditionally been attributed to him and to see if there's any evidence to support such claims. Generally speaking, there isn't. Speaking of which, Ana María, did you come up with anything on those bodies found in the mine at Las Peñas?'

'Not yet, I'm afraid. The remains are at our lab but live cases take precedence. As soon as I can get a slot in the booking system I'll be able to examine the skeletons properly.' It sounded lame, Galindez thought, even though it was true.

'Fine,' Toni said. 'We'll leave that for another day.'

'How long was Guzmán's unit involved in these type of operations?' Galindez asked.

'At least fourteen years,' Luisa said. 'The Special Brigade's operations began at the end of the Civil War and continued well into the fifties. Guzmán was given carte blanche to suppress any resistance to the regime in Madrid. Franco did something similar in 1934 after he suppressed the miners' revolt in Asturias. He appointed a sadistic officer called Lisiado Doval to terrorise the local population. The difference is, there's evidence of Doval's direct involvement in that violence – unlike Guzmán. Guzmán reported straight to Franco. That's where the real blame should be attributed, Ana. The political level.'

'Trouble is,' Toni added, 'Guzmán was very secretive. So much so that he seems to have disappeared in 1953. We're lucky to know anything at all about him – although we have no idea what happened to him.' He flicked through his notes. 'We do know he operated out of the *comisaría* at Calle de Robles.'

'Calle de Robles?' Galindez asked. 'That's off Calle 30, isn't it, near the Vallecas bridge?'

'Yes, that's right, between the bridge and Puente de Vallecas Metro. Fascinating old street.' Toni slid a black and white photo across the table: an old building with an arched wooden door crossed with iron bands. 'This was Guzmán's HQ. He had a company of forty men, engaged in intelligence gathering and "hard hand" activities.'

'Franco said Spain needed to be governed with a hard hand,' Luisa said.

'Calle de Robles existed and didn't exist,' Toni continued. 'People knew it was a base for the *Brigada Especial*, but most didn't know just how secret or how powerful it was.'

'They probably didn't want to know,' Tali said.

Natalia had tawny eyes, Galindez noticed. 'The photo of him with the younger man. Where did that come from?' she asked.

'*Teniente* Peralta?' Luisa said. 'That was found in Guzmán's apartment. Hidden under the floorboards.'

'How did you know it was Guzmán's *piso*?'

'His name was on deeds dated 1947. There's no record of when he sold it since the documents are missing. The current owner bought it in 1971, and when she died, her daughter started renovating the place. The workmen found things under the floorboards and we got involved.'

'What did they find?' Galindez was suddenly impatient. For her, stories needed a proper order. This one was too fragmented. Although, she realised, that made it all the more intriguing.

Toni beamed. 'Guns. A sub-machine gun, some pistols, small amounts of money – dollars, Deutschmarks, a few francs. Various papers.'

'Hardly conclusive evidence,' Luisa said. 'He could have been selling those things on the black market.'

'So how did Guzmán come to be at the centre of all your inquiries?' Galindez asked.

'Narrative coherence,' Luisa said. 'I thought focusing on Guzmán would help us show how historians and politicians pass blame down the chain of command to their subordinates. Mainstream historians always assume Guzmán and others like him are responsible for various atrocities – but in many cases, there's never any substantive evidence to support those assumptions. I want to analyse his role using documents of the time – reports, policy papers and so forth – and develop a narrative, a better storyline if you like, locating Guzmán and others as nodes in a network of power.'

'Storyline? I thought you were doing history?'

'So we are, Ana María. We take real events and work them into a meaningful account using contemporary textual material.'

'Guzmán is a symbol of the Franco Era,' Toni said, with sudden intensity. 'A practical condensation of its theories and ideologies. But it's what is symbolised that we want to challenge. We,' he glanced at Luisa, 'that is, *Profesora* Ordoñez has advanced a counter-theory: that Guzmán and other middle-ranking functionaries are incorrectly blamed for the actions of their superiors and are unfairly pejoratively labelled as a result.'

'Which is to say, mud sticks,' Tali said with a faint smile. 'Often deservedly.'

'It's all very speculative.' Galindez frowned. 'Surely we need to link Guzmán to events by obtaining compelling evidence? Develop a psychological profile, collect forensic traces, gather witness accounts and so on.'

Luisa laughed as if Galindez had told a joke. 'The main thing is the narrative. A framework for reading events. We're dealing with myth and language as well as history.'

'There's little credibility in patching interpretations of events together without any sound evidence base.' Galindez was aware of the sharpness in her voice.

'You don't get it Ana,' Luisa said. 'We're talking about narratives of identity and dominance. We treat the war as a discursive episode in which we deconstruct motive and action as textual events. It gives a whole new way of representing what happened. People like Guzmán were caught up in the arguments and beliefs of those with far greater powers than them. These arguments, in effect, held them captive within a meta-discourse of domination. Against such structural and textual pressure, individual agency dissolves into conformity and compliance.'

Galindez felt a sinking feeling, realising just how alien Luisa's conception of research was to her own, both in philosophy and method. And, she realised, she was stuck here now for the duration of the project. Uncle Ramiro had pulled strings to get her this secondment. She couldn't back out. And she certainly wouldn't back down.

'Luisa, the argument that obedience to the State neutralises the moral responsibility of the individual was thrown out at the Nuremberg trials,' Galindez said. 'It isn't psychologically or morally sustainable.'

'I did tell you we'd disagree about these things.' Luisa shrugged. 'Just do your thing, Ana, and we'll do ours. Call it disciplinary diversity if you like.'

Galindez didn't like it. *Luisa said she wanted my expertise but it doesn't feel like it now.* There was a silence.

Natalia looked across the table at Galindez. 'Were those people at Las Peñas killed inside the mine, Ana María?'

Galindez tried to concentrate. 'They were killed somewhere else, in my opinion. There'd be the danger of ricochets in such a confined space. In any case, I found no traces of shooting inside the tunnel leading into the mine.'

Luisa coughed impatiently. 'I'm sure Ana María can provide us with any technical details in due course.'

Her tone was starting to infuriate Galindez. *Technical details?* Galindez looked at her notes. 'Luisa, you're certain there's no evidence of any atrocities being connected to Guzmán?'

'I said there's no evidence of his direct involvement. A number of execution sites are mentioned in his diary. One was excavated recently and contained half a dozen bodies. It's highly likely Guzmán's brigade carried out the executions. I'm sure he passed on orders from Franco's headquarters but that to my mind isn't the same as being physically involved.' Luisa consulted her papers. 'Let's move on to the next item on the agenda: Toni has some good news.'

'Indeed I have. I've been liaising with the *policía nacional*. They've given us access to Guzmán's old headquarters on Calle de Robles,' Toni said proudly.

Galindez felt a shiver of excitement. This was more like it: access to a potential source of real evidence. *Mierda*, his HQ. 'It's still standing?' She tried not to sound excited.

'It certainly is. Though it's not in use any more. In fact, it's rather run-down. Certainly not as it was when he was there,' Toni said.

'History isn't preserved in aspic,' Luisa muttered without looking up from her notes.

'Still,' Toni continued, 'it's worth a look. Up for it, Ana?'

'Of course. Will I be able to do some forensic tests?'

'The time available to us is limited at the moment. An observational visit is all for now, Ana María. The requirements of positivist science will have to wait,' Luisa said.

Puta madre. What is her problem? 'Naturally, I'm keen to visit it. Are we all going together?' Galindez struggled to contain the irritation in her voice.

'I've already been there.' Luisa's voice was smug. 'After Toni and I met with the *policía nacional* they took us over there. It's atmospheric – but very empty.'

Galindez bit her lip. Luisa could easily have phoned and invited her. She suspected she wanted to remind her who was in charge here. 'So when can I go?'

'We'll have the key by Thursday,' Toni said.

'Fine.' Galindez hid her impatience. 'Thursday it is.'

'And you, Tali?' Toni asked.

'By all means go, Tali,' Luisa said. 'We can't have Ana going alone. But you two shouldn't build your hopes up. It's quite empty.'

Galindez looked at Tali. Nothing wrong with building your hopes up, she thought.

'By the way,' Tali took a large document from her bag and slid it across the table, 'I made you a copy of Guzmán's diary, Ana María.'

'*Gracias*.' A sudden thought occurred: 'Luisa, when the skinhead attacked me, he asked where "the book" was – do you think he meant this diary?'

'I wouldn't think so. It's not a secret. We've discussed it with other academics, though we're not sharing all of its contents until we've completed the report. Perhaps we should keep the original under lock and key. Toni?'

'There's a safe in the admin office. I'll put it in there.'

Luisa checked her watch. 'You'll have to excuse me, I'm teaching in five minutes.'

Toni got up. 'Me too. How do you feel now, Ana María?'

Galindez flexed her right arm and winced. 'I'll live.'

'OK. *Hasta pronto*.'

Galindez heard Luisa and Toni chatting as they went down the corridor. She waited until their voices faded away. Tali was gathering her things together.

'Natalia, do you want to go for a coffee? We could talk a bit more about Guzmán.'

'Sure. But only if you call me Tali – everyone does. Where shall we go?'

'How about *guardia civil* headquarters? There's a new database that may throw up some information on Guzmán.'

Tali laughed. 'I've had more exotic offers, Ana, but OK, why not?'

CHAPTER SIX

MADRID 1953, RESTAURANTE GALLEGO, CALLE DE ROBLES

The restaurant was alive with the smell of food and Peralta salivated in Pavlovian harmony with the nuanced aromas. He and Guzmán took a table at the back of the room, near to the stove, basking in the radiant warmth, their shoes beginning to dry. The waiter came bustling over at once and Guzmán ordered a bottle of Rioja. Peralta noticed the bottle arrived remarkably quickly, given how busy the place was. Taking a mouthful of the wine, Peralta felt a surge of sudden warmth. Relentless cold and perpetual hunger were a constant background to all the other unhappiness and discomfort of daily life in Madrid. At least until the iron-hard heat of the summer came, bringing its own new planes of suffering. It was difficult to know which was worse, Peralta thought. Cold probably. It was inescapable whether at work or home. *But not here.* Peralta saw the generous portions of food, the smartness and affluence of the other diners. He looked at his own threadbare shirt cuffs protruding from his shabby jacket, feeling uncomfortable but not ashamed. You learned not to be ashamed of being down-at-heel, otherwise life would be intolerable.

A plate of fried fish arrived in an aromatic mist of garlic and lemon, the golden slices piled high.

Guzmán took several pieces and pushed the plate towards Peralta. 'For Christ's sake, man, eat. You look like you haven't had a bite all week.'

Peralta lifted a slice of fish onto his plate. 'To be honest, it's been hard recently. The *niña* was ill and María and I had to give her

119

some of our food to try to build her up a little. I'm hoping María gets pregnant again soon, though. I've always wanted a son.'

Guzmán looked at him inquisitively. 'Your wife's General Valverde's niece. Why doesn't she get him to help out?'

Peralta sipped his wine. 'She isn't in his best books. He was angry with her...' His voice trailed off.

'Don't leave me in suspense, *Teniente*. Why?' Guzmán said, chewing happily.

'Well...' Peralta looked sheepish. He took another drink. 'Her choice of husband. The general was so incensed when she married me that he has very little to do with us. He won't use any influence even for the sake of her or the baby.'

'*Mierda*. That's not true. He got you this job, didn't he? It pays more than pounding the beat or locking up tarts.'

'So it should,' Peralta said moodily. 'But when you put it like that, I suppose he did think I would benefit from joining you here, sir.'

'See, even for the general, blood's thicker than water.' Guzmán smiled. 'And you'll certainly see just how thick blood is, working with me.' He raised his glass, amused at Peralta's worried expression.

Peralta watched with intense interest as the waiter took away their empty plates and returned with a large bowl of steaming beef stew. Guzmán heaped stew onto his plate and then slid the bowl across to Peralta.

'They say loyalty is its own reward,' Guzmán said, spooning beef into his mouth, 'but there are plenty of other rewards in this job, I can tell you.'

'So all that's required is loyalty?' Peralta was distracted, his expression suggesting he could barely restrain himself from falling upon the stew. 'Remain loyal and there's jam tomorrow?' He raised his spoon and then added quickly, 'Not that I'm suggesting we should be anything but loyal – to the proper authorities, of course. But they always say good times are just around the corner and that's where they always stay.'

'Loyalty brings its rewards. Believe me. That and obedience.'

Peralta nodded uncertainly, his eyes averted while he began to wolf down his stew, undeterred by the fact that it was too hot to eat comfortably. Hunger did that to you, Guzmán thought, watching Peralta eagerly gobbling his food. Hunger concentrated your desire for something you once took for granted into a craving that narrowed your focus intensely. That was why starving prisoners was such a good idea. Starving people will do a great deal for a very small amount of food. It had been a long time since Guzmán had gone hungry, he had made sure of that, but he still remembered what it was like.

'Let me be straight with you,' he said. 'You were foisted on me by Valverde. It's possible he thought he was doing you a favour, though I'm sure this is hardly your preferred line of work.'

Peralta signalled his agreement through a large mouthful of well-cooked beef.

'However,' Guzmán continued, 'you can have the last laugh. It's very simple. All you have to do is buckle down, do what you're told and you'll get regular pay and plenty of perks. This is your job now. It's what pays the rent. You even get the thanks of the Head of State himself.'

'We can't eat thanks,' Peralta said glumly.

Guzmán shook his head. 'Jesus Christ and all His saints, *coño*, can't you see when you're on to a good thing?' He picked up the empty bottle and handed it to the waiter. A moment later the man brought another bottle. Guzmán filled their glasses. 'Many men would love to be in your position. Power, independence, freedom to do your job. More importantly, other men would know in a job like this you can fill your belly if you know how. In this line of work, people want to be your friend. They want to oblige you, to be on the right side.'

'You mean they want to bribe you?' Peralta asked, with a vague hint of reproach.

'No. That would cost too much and they can't be certain they can trust you anyway. But that's the beauty of it, Acting *Teniente*.

121

What they can afford is to offer something. The butcher gives you a cut of the best meat, the fishmonger the freshest of his fish, the baker always has a loaf warm from the oven and just for you. In cafés your money is no good. Not because they like you,' he paused, his face flushed with the drink, 'certainly not because they like you, but because they fucking fear you. And with good reason.' Guzmán watched as the *teniente* filled his plate again.

'See?' he said. 'You're getting used to it already. *Joder*, you're eating for two.'

'It seems wrong,' Peralta said. Guzmán noticed the *teniente* carried on spooning stew onto his plate anyway.

'It's the way it is.' Guzmán pushed his empty plate aside and pulled the bowl of stew in front of him, dispensing with niceties. 'From the top down. You know the stories about Franco's wife, *Doña* Carmen and her shopping habits?'

'Which ones?'

'About how she visits the jewellers' shops when she's in Madrid. Like some sort of queen. She descends on them, *buenos dias*, lovely piece of jewellery, how much is it? Oh really? How kind, thank you. And she's off with a new brooch or ring or whatever. Never has to get her purse out or ask her husband if they can afford it. Because they don't buy it. They take what they want. That's why they call her *Doña* Necklaces. Though not to her face obviously.'

'But...' Peralta struggled for the words, 'surely that just reflects the esteem we all hold for the *Caudillo*. People give her gifts to demonstrate their...' He stopped. Guzmán was moving his hand in a gesture suggesting masturbation.

'She does it,' Guzmán said simply, 'because she wants to and because she can.'

'Doesn't mean we can,' Peralta said.

Guzmán shrugged. 'Yes it does. Everything's relative, *chico*. The big fish take a big slice of the best. The little fish take a smaller slice of the not so good. That's how it works, just like the army: a hierarchy. We're not quite at the bottom either, *amigo*. You can be comfortable if you accept your place in things. Like a part in a machine. You work properly, you get oiled.'

'And if you don't?'

Guzmán snorted. 'You get replaced. Remember that, *Teniente*. Any time you feel this job is too distasteful or beneath you. Any time you think you know better or that your personal code of honour prevents you from doing something, I can walk out of the door of the *comisaría* and find someone who'd take your place in five minutes flat. And, let me tell you, if you fuck about and don't pull your weight, that's exactly what I will do.'

'Hardly good recruitment practice for the police,' Peralta said stuffily.

'*Teniente*, just remember we're not the police. We're not the *guardia civil* and we aren't the Little Sisters of Piety. We are what we are. People ask sometimes what I did in the war. Peralta, I never left the fucking army. For us, there's still a war on.'

He gestured to the waiter. The man came immediately, gliding through the crowded tables with practised ease.

'At your service, *señores*. I trust everything was to your satisfaction? *Algo más*? Coffee? A brandy?'

'Both,' Guzmán nodded, 'and make the brandy Carlos Primero.' The waiter took their plates and retreated to the kitchen, maintaining his vague professional smile.

'Nothing but the best for us today.' Peralta smiled sheepishly.

'You know who's paying for this?' Guzmán asked.

Peralta felt a moment of panic, wondering if perhaps this was a joke which would end with him as the butt of Guzmán's humour. 'Me?' he asked, uncertainly.

'Could you afford it?' Guzmán sneered. 'No, of course not, and I'm certainly not paying. It's on the house. Don't look so worried, they know it. I eat here a lot – as you can imagine, since it's free.'

'Just like that?'

Guzmán looked over to the bar. 'The owner's sister was inclined towards the Reds. She was arrested handing out leaflets about the need for democracy two years ago. Can you imagine? *Hostia*, it's like they're simple or something. *They lost.*' His voice thickened with anger. 'You'd think they'd try and blend into the background. But no. So she ended up at the *comisaría*. She was no real threat. But she'd mixed with those people, the ones who organised it, printed the leaflets. Those were the ones we wanted.'

'So she gave you the information in return for her freedom?'

Guzmán looked incredulously at the *teniente*. 'Hardly. We don't bargain with Reds and she'd committed an act of treachery. That carries a death sentence.'

'And how does that lead to you eating here for nothing?' Peralta asked.

Guzmán sighed. 'First of all we stripped her naked and then we put her head in a bucket of water. Well, the sarge did, he enjoys it so much it was a shame not to let him. Didn't take long. You just slowly increase the length of time they're under water. Then give them a few minutes to recover and do it again. Have a fag while they dry out and then back under they go. She didn't last long before we'd got every name she could remember.'

'And the owner paid for her freedom with free meals?'

'Not at all,' Guzmán said. 'One of the names she gave us was his. He was remarkably cooperative. Now he gives us information and we eat here for nothing. And, as long as he keeps his nose clean, he stays alive. The chef's excellent, as you'll have noticed.'

'But what about his sister?'

'She got ten years' hard labour. She's in one of the camps now, along with a load of other Reds, perverts, a few Jews and lots of gypsies, I imagine.'

'So him giving you free meals wasn't a bribe to try to save her?'

'Save her?' Guzmán laughed. 'He didn't try to save her. He saved himself.'

Peralta watched as the waiter poured coffee and then set down two large glasses of brandy. Raising his glass, he inhaled the rich aroma.

'Anything else, gentlemen?'

'Two Cuban cigars,' Guzmán said, gently whirling the brandy in his glass, 'the really good ones, Paquito.'

'At once, *Comandante* Guzmán.' The waiter's smile was definitely slipping now.

'I can't remember the last time I had brandy as good as this. Not even at my wedding.' Peralta said.

'Get used to it. But make sure you earn it. When a job needs doing, do it right.'

'You mean tonight?' Peralta asked.

'I mean all the time. But yes, tonight included. You'll need to pull your weight.'

'What time will it happen?' Peralta asked.

'We'll move them after it gets dark. The trucks will be brought up to the entrance and we'll load them up and then drive them out there.'

'Where?'

'The countryside. Mustn't offend sensibilities in the city. Especially with the *Yanquis* visiting. The war is over,' Guzmán gulped down his brandy, 'officially.' He caught the waiter's eye as the man approached with the cigars. 'Two more brandies, Paquito.'

The smile was gone. 'At once, *Comandante*.'

Peralta persisted, his cheeks flushed now. 'But what happens to the...' He was unsure of the word he wanted.

'Bodies?' Guzmán grinned. 'Normally, we'd dig a big pit and bury them. But the winter makes that difficult – ground's too hard to dig. So we've found a compromise. There's an old mine near Las Peñas. The entrance is just a long tunnel dug into the hillside. We'll put the bodies in, and brick up the entrance. Simple.'

'Who will form the firing squad?' Peralta asked, attempting professional interest.

'The usual people, they've done it before.' Guzmán smiled. Or possibly sneered, Peralta found it hard to tell the two expressions apart.

The brandies arrived. Peralta realised he actually felt warm now, and unusually full. He watched the waiter cut the ends off the cigars. The aroma was exquisite.

'Rolled on a virgin's thigh, Paquito. No?' Guzmán held the cigar to his nose.

'If you say so, *Comandante.*'

'I'd think virgins are even harder to find in Madrid than these cigars, *verdad*?'

'As the *comandante* says. Everything is in short supply at the moment.'

Guzmán sent the waiter away. Peralta saw him in deep conversation with an older man in a dinner jacket – the owner, he imagined, given the man's concerned look and the length of the piece of paper they were both studying.

'I wish María could be here,' Peralta said, inhaling the aromatic cigar smoke.

'Your wife?' Guzmán asked.

'Yes. It would be nice to share this with her. She's probably making do with a bowl of soup right now.'

'Well,' Guzmán said, 'there's a number of shops where they would be pleased to offer you a generous discount as a serving member of the *Brigada Especial*. I'll get the sarge to make a list for you.'

'When in Rome...' Peralta said, martyred resignation.

'Who said anything about Rome?' Guzmán snapped, exhaling a cloud of cigar smoke. 'Fucking Italians. They think they won the Civil War for us.'

Guzmán looked at his watch and stood up, pulling on his coat as he headed for the door. Peralta downed the last of the brandy and followed.

The head waiter opened the door for them. '*Hasta la proxima, señores.* I hope you enjoyed your meal.'

'Yes, thank you.' Peralta nodded. Guzmán ignored the man completely.

The cold closed in as they walked back. Peralta looked at his watch. It was almost half past two and, as they reached the door of the *comisaría*, the air shimmered as the great church bell sent waves of deep bass notes into the freezing day.

*

Guzmán was hunched in his office shouting into the telephone. Peralta sat in a room down the corridor, meticulously copying the names on Guzmán's list with a red mark against them into a leatherbound register. Against each name he filled in the charge: *Crimes against the Spanish State, Serious Apathy, Treason, Bearing arms against the Spanish State*, until the repetitive lexicon of capital crimes no longer held any surprise for him. His concentration was weakened by the large lunch, particularly the drink. His head ached and he took intermittent sips from a large mug of black coffee. It was foul.

Ernesto Garcia Mendoza, Bearing arms against the Spanish State, Assisting the enemies of Spain. Sentence: Death.

Peralta paused at the last column headed *Sentence carried out*. Later he would complete that. This evening. Something churned in his stomach. He cursed himself. Why could he not take Guzmán's advice and buckle down? He stared at the stained walls of the cold office with its chipped whitewash and drab militarycoloured furniture. Because he was not like that, he supposed. But he could not escape this place now: he worked here. General Valverde disliked him so much that, if he tried to get out of Guzmán's unit, the general would wash his hands of him. And then his career would be ruined. Unable to follow orders, too scared to watch them shoot a few Reds. And there was María to think of, María and little Luisa María. He began to balance the issues, stacking the justifications for the execution against his growing physical repulsion. These Reds would be shot anyway, whatever he did; no one cared, just as Guzmán said; there had been so much killing already – and these men were condemned to death by the courts; they had committed serious crimes – as defined by the law at least. As far as he could tell. So why was he squirming in a light sweat on a freezing day, concerning himself with the rights and wrongs of a legal process? Why was he worrying about criminals and not worrying about his wife and daughter? He sat back, staring at the pages of the ledger. *What will be will be,* he thought. *I must do my duty. My father fought against the Reds to save the country from Bolshevism. I've got to do the same.*

He looked down at the list Guzmán had received from Headquarters. There was Mendoza's name, with the letter 'M' indicating the sentence of death. There was another letter next to it, a red 'C'. He flicked back through the list. No other name had it. Peralta was inclined to ignore the mark, but his training at the academy came back to him: attention to detail was always key. He decided to check with the *comandante*. Overlooking anything at this stage would only attract Guzmán's wrath. He took the sheet down the corridor.

Guzmán looked up from his chair where he had been dozing by the wood-burning stove. '*Qué hora es?*'

'A little after five.'

'An hour to go,' Guzmán said. 'What do you want?'

Peralta pointed out the extra letter alongside Mendoza's name. Guzmán said nothing.

'I just thought...' Peralta tried to excuse himself, sensing another firestorm of anger.

'Excellent work,' Guzmán smiled. 'I'd missed this. *Joder.* That could have caused us some bother. Good work, Acting *Teniente,* if this had gone unnoticed we might have been digging latrines in Galicia in some pueblo with one goat and a dog. And the goat would outrank us. Well, you anyway.'

Peralta was taken aback by the unexpected praise. 'Just what does it mean?'

Guzmán's eyes darkened. 'Wait and see, *hombre.* All will be revealed tonight in God's own good time. In the meantime, I've a job for you.'

'*A sus ordenes,*' Peralta answered automatically.

'This is something you won't have any difficulty with,' Guzmán said. 'Go down the road to the church and inform Father Vasquez we've a job this evening for him. Give him this.' He placed a thick envelope on the desk. 'He's to attend at the usual time.'

Peralta took the envelope and placed it in his jacket pocket. 'Will Monsignor Vasquez be administering the last rites this evening?'

'He will. And when you go out, tell the sarge Mendoza will be a special tonight.'

Peralta nodded. 'I will. But may I ask—'

Guzmán placed his feet on his desk. 'As I said, all in good time, Acting *Teniente*. Now go and see the priest. We can't have all these godless bastards shot without a proper send-off. It wouldn't be decent.'

Peralta nodded; his stomach was churning again and he was sweating profusely. *Get a grip*, he thought.

At the door, he paused, turning back to Guzmán who was struggling in his chair to find a comfortable sleeping position.

'One question if I may, *Comandante*?'

Guzmán's look did not invite further discussion, but he nodded.

'Does this get easier with time?' Peralta asked. 'Will I get used to it, do you suppose?'

Guzmán looked at him blankly. 'No. Not for a second you won't, son. At least not unless you suddenly start breaking a few people's heads now and again just for the fun of it. And I can't see that happening somehow. It's the way it is. There are people like me – lots of them – and there are people like you. What you need to do is to make sure that while people like me do the dirty work, you make yourself as useful as possible without getting in the way. Keep your head down and keep quiet. Especially tonight when we shoot those traitors we've got downstairs. I know what I'm doing, *Teniente*, you're there to make up the numbers. Dismissed.'

Peralta stepped out into the corridor and closed the door, muffling Guzmán's laughter. He felt as if he was coming down with something. His head ached and he was sweating. He retrieved his overcoat from the meeting room and walked to the reception desk, the sense of dread still growing inside him. What had seemed distasteful work a few hours ago was now rapidly becoming a singular, terrifying reality.

'Evening, sir.' The *sargento's* voice was as contemptuous as ever.

'A message from *Comandante* Guzmán,' Peralta said stiffly. 'The prisoner Mendoza has been identified as a special case.'

The *sargento's* sullen face cracked into a harsh smile. 'Well, that doesn't surprise me, *Teniente*. Be a surprise to him, though, I bet.'

'What does it mean, *Sargento*, "special case"?'

The smirk grew bigger. 'The *comandante* didn't tell you, *Teniente*?'

'He said it'll be revealed to me in due course.'

The *sargento* smiled, revealing several missing front teeth and exposing disgusting shards of those that remained. 'I won't be the one to spoil your surprise, sir. Besides, the *comandante* would kill me.'

Peralta walked out into the icy darkness. A few flakes of snow drifted down through the anaemic glow of the street light. The windows of the shops and bars along Calle de Robles were pale and tired, much like the people in them. He walked slowly, breathing in the sharp icy air, making his way through bustling workers, preoccupied with the dull routines of daily life. The concerns of normal people, Peralta thought. Not for them the knowledge that in a few hours they would be involved in killing fifteen people and dumping their bodies in a mine.

Peralta had never killed anyone. That was what made the coming night's work so worrying. He had seen a robber shot once in his last year of training. He'd been on patrol near the Prado, accompanying a uniformed officer on his beat. A sudden shout came from ahead of them, the crowds parting near the window of a jeweller's shop. A man dressed in a dark suit ran towards them, pistol in hand, looking back at the shop where angry voices denounced his theft. Peralta didn't move. He felt the uniformed officer at his side raise his pistol and take aim, the blast a white starburst that drained the world of colour. Peralta saw nothing, heard nothing until time moved again as the man crumpled, legs flailing drunkenly, heard his pistol fall to the ground, strangely loud. And the voice of the policeman as he moved forward, still aiming at the man: '*No te mueves, coño. Manos arriba.*' The man lay twisted and broken, a dark bloody slick outlining his body. He didn't move, nor would he again.

That had been bad enough, Peralta thought. But to bind them, blindfold them and then stand them in front of a firing squad. Could he do it? Even though they deserved it. It wasn't that he cared, he realised. He just didn't want to be there. He rummaged through his pockets and eventually found a solitary, crumpled cigarette, black tobacco spilling from the loose wrapping in small flakes as he raised it to his mouth. He lit it gratefully.

MADRID 1953, CHURCH OF SANTA MARÍA DE TODOS NUESTROS DOLORES

The grim Gothic outline of the church towered over him. A slight glow within shone kaleidoscopic light through the stained glass window. Peralta looked round, finishing his cigarette. He saw a couple pressed close together in the shadows, an old beggar with his feet bound with rags sprawled against the wall. He turned back to look towards the *comisaría*. A man in a black overcoat with a wide-brimmed hat moved into a doorway. Peralta threw the cigarette away: it tasted foul.

Inside, the church was silent with an icy stillness in which the slightest move produced a whispered echo. Light glimmered from rows of candles, leaving the pews obscure in flickering semi-darkness around the penumbra of the altar. Peralta dipped his hand into the holy water of the font and crossed himself. He walked slowly down the aisle of the darkened nave, and crossed himself again, his footsteps loud in the cold silence. He stopped to listen. A faint noise. The sound of weeping. He turned towards the sound and saw the bulky shape of a woman, kneeling in prayer, her forehead pressed against the back of the pew in front. She was whispering hoarsely, her prayers interspersed by muffled sobs. The words clear and familiar in the darkness:

'I believe in God, the Father Almighty, Creator of Heaven and earth…'

Peralta felt embarrassed to be eavesdropping upon her grief. Each line was accompanied by more muted weeping and stifled sobs. He moved towards the vestry door which was lit by two small candles on a table piled with leaflets and tracts. Peralta decided to knock on the door but, as he moved forward a figure crashed into him from the side. Peralta stumbled and fell, struggling to get back to his feet. Above him a wild distorted face, florid and unshaven, the eyes improbably bloodshot. The man looked down at him, while from the darkness came the distant echo of the woman's voice as she continued her prayer.

'I believe in Jesus Christ, His only Son, our Lord, who was conceived by the Holy Spirit, born of the Virgin Mary, suffered under Pontius Pilate, was crucified, died and was buried.'

'You clumsy fuck,' the man spat, his florid face distorted with anger. 'What are you doing hiding there in the dark?'

'He descended into hell. On the third day, He rose again.'

Peralta dusted dirt from his coat and looked at the man. In the pale light of the candles he saw signs of physical decay, the damage wrought by a determined and sustained life of dissolution. The man had teeth missing, his hair was unkempt and his face unshaven and dirty with flecks of spittle at the corners of his purple lips. Peralta heard him gasping for breath and saw the way he staggered. He detested drunks and this one in particular.

'I'm looking for Father Vasquez,' he said coldly.

'He ascended to Heaven and is seated at the right hand of the Father. He will come again to judge the living and the dead.'

The man laughed with an asthmatic rattle and his attempt at a smile showed his few remaining teeth. 'Why, God bless you, my son. I'm Father Vasquez.'

Peralta saw the clerical collar and understood: this was Guzmán's priest. This wreck was to attend the execution and deliver final absolution. He felt sudden anger.

'*Comandante* Guzmán requires your presence, Father. You're needed in an official capacity this evening.'

The priest looked at him blankly and then his face folded into a smile.

'*I believe in the Holy Spirit, the Holy Catholic Church...*'

'Ah, the good *comandante*,' he beamed. 'How I love the work he does.'

Peralta looked at him with distaste. 'Really? Have you known the *comandante* long?'

The priest grinned. 'A long, long time, my boy. We've trodden the same road together, he and I, through blood, much blood. The blood of those without God. The blood of the Antichrist has washed around our ankles and always God has seen us through. He protects us in our work.' He crossed himself fervently though somewhat inaccurately.

'*... the communion of saints, the forgiveness of sins...*'

'Then you'll know what's required tonight.' Peralta's voice was tight with anger at this travesty of a priest. 'The *comandante* requests your presence in an hour. No later.'

Father Vasquez nodded. 'And the money?'

'Money?' Peralta echoed. 'What money?'

'*... the resurrection of the body, and life everlasting. Amen.*'

'The money from the pockets of the Reds, the rapists, the assassins, the child-killers, the nun-violators, the freemasons, the...' the priest's red eyes rolled as he searched for another category to add to his taxonomy of hate, 'those fuckers, the church burners...' He staggered against a pillar and clung to it gratefully.

'You're drunk.' It was a statement, not a question.

'And you're an arsehole. So what about my money?'

'*Comandante* Guzmán sent you this.' Peralta took the envelope from his pocket and handed it to Father Vasquez who took it with a reverential air. The priest clutched at Peralta's sleeve. 'I hate them, like you,' he slobbered. 'The spawn of evil and international Jewry and—'

Peralta shrugged the man's clawing hand from his coat sleeve.

'Get off me, you piss-head. Save your slobbering for *Comandante* Guzmán. Perhaps he puts up with it, but I won't. My advice is to sober up, you filthy bastard. There are men going to die and we're expecting you to give them the comfort of the sacraments.'

He turned and walked through the darkness towards the church entrance.

The priest's voice echoed in the shadows. 'Comfort? Comfort is for those who follow the way of God. These *cabrónes* will get no comfort, *señor*, I'm not there to tell them it will be all right: just a little bullet and then off to heaven. Oh no, I'm there to tell them they deserve to burn in hell for eternity and that I will pray every day for their continued suffering. The priests they killed, the nuns they raped. Those who lived without God shall die without him. Their suffering is a small atonement for what was done by their side. The fuckers, the—'

'Be at the *comisaría* within the hour,' Peralta called from the doorway. He stepped out into the cleansing cold of the night. Flakes of snow whirled through weak light. Like lost souls, Peralta thought in a moment of poetic invention. How nice it would be to read poetry again, to lose himself in the rhythm of words, their angular abstractions and emotional ambiguities. He apologised, shaken from his reverie as he bumped into a man in a dark overcoat. The man seemed vaguely familiar, but when Peralta looked back to see if he could recognise him, the man had gone.

Guzmán looked up as Peralta entered his office.

'Don't you ever knock, Acting *Teniente*?'

'I did knock,' Peralta snapped. And then he could keep it in no longer. 'Why, in a country awash with priests, use someone like him for this work? The man's a drunk.'

Guzmán grinned. 'And the rest. Thief, paedophile, you name it. But he's all we can afford.'

'For God's sake,' Peralta said, 'you're shooting fifteen men and you send them to their deaths with that bastard giving them the last rites?'

Guzmán looked at him. 'Firstly, *Teniente*, those men downstairs don't believe in God. They fought on the side that killed priests and burned their churches. These men supported communism and foreign corruption. Secondly, these are the fifties. The younger priests were only kids when the war began. They don't want to be involved in the work we do. And even some of the older priests no longer want to be involved with these things either. So we have to take what we can get. And we can only get what we can afford and what we can afford is Father Vasquez.'

Peralta exhaled angrily. 'I don't think it's right. There should be some dignity in these things.' He turned on his heel and went out into the corridor.

Guzmán looked at the closed door and smiled. 'Dignity?' His voice was edged with contempt. 'You'll see fucking dignity once the shooting starts. Lots of it. Spilled all over the fucking ground. A drunken priest is nothing compared to that.'

But Peralta had gone. Guzmán lit a cigarette and returned to staring at the wall. His breathing slowed as he drifted into a self-induced trance with only the slow monotony of the old clock on the wall to disturb him. Guzmán was getting ready.

Peralta heard the crash of boots on the stone of the corridor as he sat in the mess with a cup of lukewarm coffee. Several *guardia civiles* entered, followed by the dissolute figure of the *sargento*. One of the men was carrying a large bucket.

'Evening, *Teniente*,' the *sargento* grinned toothlessly.

Peralta watched with slight curiosity as the *guardia civiles* produced several large bottles of brandy and began to pour them into the bucket.

'Making punch, *Sargento*?' Peralta asked, exasperated at having to ask what was going on.

'Not one you'd care to try, sir,' the *sargento* said. 'At least not in a minute or two.' He placed several small cardboard boxes on the table. 'Sleeping pills, sir. For the prisoners. We dose the brandy, they have a last drink. Bingo. They go off happily. More or less.'

135

'Almost humane, *Sargento*. That will make them easier to manage, I imagine?'

'They'll be good as gold, sir' – another glimpse of rotten teeth – 'be all over before they know it.' He continued to fill the bucket with brandy. The smell was overpowering. 'Care for a glass, sir – before I dope it?'

Peralta shook his head. 'I don't think brandy would agree with me just now.'

The *sargento* laughed. 'It'll agree with those bastards a lot less. But I think I'll have a quick nip. How about you boys?'

The *guardia civiles* quickly agreed and waited while the *sargento* dipped a chipped cup into the brandy. Peralta wondered for a moment about the regulations concerning drinking on duty but decided this was not the time to raise the subject.

'Fuck, that's rough,' the sarge said, gulping down a large mug of the neat spirit. 'Down to business then.'

He opened a box, removed the bottle from inside and tipped its contents into the bucket. He repeated the measure several times. Peralta looked into the bucket. The dark brandy was covered with a white powdery scum from the dissolving tablets. The *sargento* stirred the mixture with a long wooden spoon retrieved from a drawer next to the stained, cracked sink.

'They won't drink that,' Peralta said. 'They'll see there's something in it.'

'Ah, but it's dark down in those cells,' the *sargento* grinned. 'Besides, they're desperate.' He hoisted the bucket by its handle and walked to the door. 'Pass me a cup, Rodriguez, I'm going to serve our guests.'

The *sargento* and the *guardia civiles* clattered down the corridor towards the stairs to the cells. They were laughing.

Peralta straightened up as Guzmán strolled into the mess room.

'*Comandante, a sus—*'

'My office. Now,' Guzmán ordered.

Once in his office, he motioned for Peralta to take a seat and opened a carton of cigarettes, lighting one. He put the carton back down on the desk before he saw Peralta looking at it wistfully.

'Christ, you can always buy some, you know.' He pushed the carton across the desk, and waited until Peralta had lit up. 'I don't expect too much from you tonight, Acting *Teniente*.' Guzmán exhaled thick smoke. He waved away Peralta's protests that he would strive to do his duty. 'None of that counts. It isn't pretty and only some people ever get used to it. The sarge, he's used to it. But then he's fucking crazy anyway. You'd better bear that in mind when you're talking to him, by the way. My advice is never upset him, and if you do, don't turn your back for a second.'

'The man's a non-commissioned officer,' Peralta said. 'He should obey his superiors, surely?'

Guzmán laughed. 'He's loyal and he does what he's told. By me, anyway. And in return, I excuse his little eccentricities. Usually.'

'And when you can't excuse them?'

'Then I beat him unconscious,' Guzmán said cheerfully.

'*Comandante*, is there anything I can do to help tonight?' Peralta offered. 'Help the men draw lots for the firing squad, for instance?'

Guzmán looked curiously at Peralta. 'Those arrangements are taken care of. Most of the lads tonight know what to do. I want you to observe and learn. Keep the priest in order. Make sure he does the absolution without attacking anyone.'

Peralta frowned. 'That man is a disgrace. He has no business in a house of God.'

Guzmán grinned. 'No, I suppose not. Although it was in the house of God where the Reds castrated him. Cut off his balls and left him to bleed to death. Except he didn't.'

'Unfortunately,' Peralta spat.

'He crawled several kilometres, at night, with his balls in his hand,' Guzmán continued. 'He thought the doctor at the *guardia civil* garrison would sew them back. When he'd recovered – physically anyway – he accompanied the *guardia* in the search for the Reds. They captured several. They say the priest killed four of them by hand. Slowly.'

Peralta shook his head in disbelief.

Guzmán nodded. 'It's hard to believe, I know. But then Father Vasquez claims he killed seven. He and the *sargento*. Mad. The war affected a lot of people, Acting *Teniente*.'

'I had heard,' Peralta said sarcastically. Guzmán's glare silenced him.

'Have some respect, *Teniente*. Someone has to do this job and our men are the best at what they do. Most of them have killed with their bare hands. I certainly have. Know what makes you able to kill someone like that? Someone you've never met before, never spoken to, no idea what they've done. Sometimes they might chat to you over a beer, show you pictures of their families. But at the back of your mind are the orders. So you get another beer, laugh at their jokes, eat tapas. And then you go to take a piss and they come into the toilet still laughing, still your friend. And they die with their dick in their hand. Or choking on vomit with your hands around their throat. And then you go back into the bar and finish your drink, pay the tab and stroll out. It's easy enough. If you know how to do it, people die very quickly. As long as you have the right attitude, you'll come out all right. But there's one thing you have to really want.'

'What?' Like a rabbit caught in headlights, Peralta's eyes fixed on Guzmán with anticipatory horror. Guzmán smiled and pulled hard on his cigarette. He exhaled slowly. Peralta waited, rigid and tense, not wanting to be part of this discourse on death and yet, simultaneously, enthralled by it.

'You have to want them dead,' Guzmán said at last. 'You really have to want them to die by your hand. By any means necessary. And after, you have to be pleased they're dead. They may be good fathers, wives, mothers. No matter. Orders are orders, and you carry them out properly, because otherwise you fuck up. And then they might kill you instead. That's all there is to it. You do a good job or not at all.'

Peralta no longer felt the anxiety and foreboding he had experienced earlier. Now it was much, much worse: the feeling of awakening from a nightmare to find it wasn't a bad dream at all but was real, very real. It was bad now and it was going to get worse.

'Look on the bright side, Acting *Teniente*.' Guzmán smiled. 'We've got a reception to go to at the *capitán-general's* later. Perhaps your uncle would like to hear all about what kind of a day you've had at work? He probably would, because he was never one to look away when the killing started. In the bullring at Badajoz, the blood was so thick by midday our feet were squelching in it. There was this one bloke, when the machine gun fire hit him, it cut him in—'

Peralta didn't ask for permission as he fled the room. He could still hear Guzmán's booming laugh as he reached the toilet. Holding his head over the evil-smelling hole set between two concrete footprints in the floor, Peralta noisily brought up the excesses of lunchtime. It took a while. Afterwards, he tugged the chain. Nothing happened. He waited for a moment, trying to compose himself but the smell of vomit combined with the ever present odour of shit started him retching again. When it was finally over, he slunk back to his temporary office and continued his paperwork, ensuring the night's executions were at least in order administratively.

The darkening shadows of evening merged into night and gusts of wind blew snow against the windows. For some time now, Peralta had been aware of increasing activity outside his office. He heard the low rumbling of heavy vehicles in the street, *guardia civiles* stamping noisily along the corridor, the *sargento* barking orders, reeking of brandy and swearing even more freely than usual. Boots clattered on the stone steps leading to the cells. He pulled on his overcoat and walked down towards Guzmán's office. Before Peralta reached the door, Guzmán appeared. He was wearing a trench coat and heavy boots, his neck swaddled in a scarf. When Peralta asked for orders, Guzmán seemed strangely distant.

'Just go with the sarge,' he said. 'He'll show you the ropes.'

Two *guardia civiles* came towards them from the cells, a drugged man slumped between them. Similar trios followed. Peralta saw the prisoner's faces: uncomprehending, eyes unfocused, their thoughts somewhere beyond the echoing stone walls of the *comisaría*. He saw the *sargento* approaching, wrestling a prisoner along the wall of the corridor.

'You come with me, *Teniente*,' the sarge said, struggling to keep the prisoner on his feet. 'The *comandante* said to look after you. You can give me a hand with this one.'

Peralta grabbed the prisoner by his arm. The man was a dead weight. Soon he would just be dead. The prisoner didn't struggle. His head hung loose, his eyes opening and closing, vacillating between a desire for sleep and a vague wish to know what was happening. The worst of both worlds, Peralta thought. Neither conscious enough to reflect coherently as his life moved towards a brutal close nor sufficiently drugged to be entirely unaware of what was happening. Instead, the man staggered drunkenly towards his death, bereft of even the dignity of being able to walk out in front of the firing squad without assistance.

'I surrender,' the man spluttered, drool hanging from his lips.

Clouds of greasy exhaust fumes met them as they bundled the prisoner through the front doors. Three drab green military trucks waited, backed up close to the doorway. At each end of the street a cordon of *guardia civiles* blocked access until the condemned men had been loaded into the vehicles.

'Here we go,' the *sargento* said, nodding towards one of the vehicles. A civil guard reached down to help get the prisoner into the truck. The man was a dead weight and it took some effort before he was rolled into the truck alongside the other bound and stupefied prisoners. Peralta was panting with exertion and a bead of sweat trickled down his face. He was shaking. He had been shaking for most of the afternoon.

It took a while to load the prisoners. Peralta watched and occasionally helped, as the drugged men were manhandled into the vehicles. There was no resistance. With all the prisoners loaded, the curses and shouts of the civil guards were replaced by a tense stillness. Only the low grumbling of the trucks' engines disturbed the freezing night, exhaling thick, stinking clouds of exhaust fumes into the dark air. Desultory flakes of snow fluttered in the headlights. Peralta saw the red pinpoints of cigarettes in the dark as the *guardia civiles* waited for orders. At the rear of each truck, troopers with sub-machine guns kept a watch over the comatose prisoners. A short walk away was the city, Peralta thought, lighting another cigarette. People living their lives. Getting by. Life went on. Here, all this activity centred not around life but death.

Guzmán emerged from the front entrance of the *comisaría*. The atmosphere changed, suddenly charged with renewed purpose. With Guzmán, hands bound and wearing only a light jacket, was *el Profesor*. He was clearly not tranquillised like the others. Guzmán pushed him towards one of the trucks with a meaty grip on the man's arm. Behind them staggered the priest, a black scarecrow in his flapping cassock, carrying his small bag, a squashed biretta jammed onto his lank tangle of hair. He had difficulty getting into one of the trucks and was finally manhandled into the vehicle by a burly *guardia civil*. The *guardia* retrieved the priest's hat from the ground and brushed the snow from it before handing it up to him.

'God bless you, my son.' The priest made the sign of the cross haphazardly over the trooper. 'God bless us all.'

'*Vamos, Sargento*, we've got a party to go to, once this is over,' Guzmán said.

'In we get, *Teniente*.' The *sargento* opened the door of the truck and Peralta slid across the seat towards the driver. The *sargento* clambered in next to him and slammed the door.

Peralta sat, trapped between the driver and the *sargento*, his leg jammed painfully against the gear stick as the truck manoeuvred slowly past the other parked vehicles and bumped over the snow-covered cobbles at the end of the street. The other vehicles followed, lights flickering balefully in the rear-view mirror. Ice was a problem and the driver swore repeatedly as he struggled to prevent the vehicle skidding. The convoy proceeded slowly through the back streets, scarcely noticed by the few passers-by braving the snow. The surfaces were slippery and the drivers cautious. After a while the street lights finally petered out as they nosed their way out into the countryside and began to climb uncertainly into the hills.

The road rose steeply and they saw only the dark shadows of trees, picked out in the limpid beams of the headlights. Inside the cab the air was thick with tobacco smoke. The three men sat in a shared silence that transcended the belching noises of the engine as the truck fought its way up the frozen country roads to higher ground. Peralta looked at his watch. Almost an hour had passed. It seemed much longer.

'This is terrible weather to come out here,' he said, peering with concern down the jagged side of a ravine.

'We'll make it, sir,' the sarge said. 'We had the road checked this morning. A couple of the lads drove there and back with no problems.' He exhaled cigarette smoke. 'Anyway if it had been too bad, the *comandante* had Plan B.'

'Which was?'

The *sargento* turned awkwardly in the cramped cab to face Peralta. 'Kill them in the cells. But then it gets messy. And someone has to bring the bodies up all those stairs and with all that blood we'd have to clean everywhere up and—'

'*Gracias, Sargento*, I get the picture.' Peralta once more felt the panic building.

'Mind if I ask you something, sir?'

Peralta did mind, but nodded anyway.

'You been involved in anything like this before?'

Peralta shook his head. The *sargento* continued, 'Well, a word or two of advice, if you don't mind then, sir. Just so you know what's coming. So you behave yourself properly, if you know what I mean?'

Peralta nodded. He had no idea what the *sargento* meant and no intention of asking.

'Firstly, let us do the job – you don't have to. All the lads know what they have to do, when to do it and what happens next. It's like a machine, almost. What I'm saying, *Teniente*, is that it would be easy to get in the way and disrupt things. Like if you was sick or something.'

'Does that happen often at these things?'

'All the time, sir. Especially when people are new to the game. Sometimes they've seen active service, which always helps, but often they haven't. Like those Falangists who came along on the raid. They can get a bit disturbed by it all, seeing it close up. And killing one person, let alone a bunch together, well, it can make you, you know, funny.'

'I don't see anything funny in it at all, *Sargento*,' Peralta snapped.

'Oh you'd be surprised,' the driver chimed in.

'*Callate coño.* Speak when you're spoken to. *Me Entiendes?*' The *sargento* leaned across Peralta and glared at the driver. The man stared ahead at the road.

'Anyway,' the *sargento* continued, 'all I'm saying is stand well back. Watch if you want but if you feel sick, fuck off out of the headlights where you can't be seen. The *comandante* wouldn't like it if you did that in front of the lads. Let the side down, so to speak.'

'Thank you, *Sargento*,' Peralta said, swallowing. 'I'll bear that in mind.'

'Haven't finished yet, sir.' The truck was slowing as they reached the top of the hill. The headlights flickered over a wall of roughly hewn stone. A flat patch of ground, with a large weather-beaten wooden sign nailed to a post, announcing in painted letters: *Compañía Española de Minas, fundada 1898.*

Peralta saw a few small warehouses and outbuildings. To the right of these, a rough stone wall ran along the side of a field and nearer still, running parallel to the wall, was a small drainage ditch. The truck stopped.

'The *comandante* said you mentioned something about a firing squad.'

'Yes, I asked if he wanted help organising it, that was all, *Sargento.*'

In the wing mirror, Peralta saw the other vehicles pulling to a halt, headlights picking out the crumbling stone walls, shuttered windows and half collapsed outbuildings of the *Compañía Española de Minas*, established 1898.

The *sargento* turned to Peralta. 'This may not be quite what you were expecting, sir.'

LAS PEÑAS, 1953, COMPAÑÍA ESPAÑOLA DE MINAS

Guzmán was already barking orders as the *sargento* got down from the truck. Peralta climbed out more slowly, stretching his numb legs and rubbing his left thigh, battered by the gear stick. The driver began to reverse, stopping at Guzmán's shouted command. The headlights picked out a stretch of the ditch and the stone wall beyond it, etching them in the freezing air, framed by the night.

Peralta waited by the truck. The driver clambered out and disappeared round the back. More shouting. Orders. Acknowledgements. Shouts aimed at the prisoners. Peralta took out his cigarettes and lit one, glad that the darkness hid his shaking hands. Guzmán was standing near him and, for a moment, Peralta was going to speak, to make some small comment, share some sense of mutual involvement in this. Then he saw Guzmán's face and the urge to speak to him was gone.

The *guardia civiles* manhandled the prisoners from the trucks, herding them forwards to stand by the ditch. Some were recovering from the *sargento*'s narcotic cocktail, others were whimpering, stumbling, dazed and dazzled by the battery of headlights illuminating their last walk.

'I want to confess,' a timid voice called. Peralta looked around for the priest. There he was, his bony hands clutching a cross and a Bible. *At least he will be some use now*, Peralta thought, *a man about to die surely won't care who administers to him.* The priest stood in the white beam of the truck's headlights, casting angular shadows onto the prisoners as they waited, heads bowed, breath smoking in the harsh light.

'Confess then, you murderer, filthy assassin, Soviet lackey.'

The screeching voice contrasted with the silence of the prisoners, now lined up a metre apart along the edge of the shallow ditch. They faced the low wall, their shadows huge and distorted in the pale septic light.

'You killed nuns, raped them, ate their flesh. Sodomites, catamites, traitors to God. Now you repent but it's too late. You fear the pains of hell but they wait for you, your names are damned and you with them...'

The priest moved forward, attempting to strike the nearest prisoner. Peralta looked at Guzmán for some sort of direction, but the *comandante* was standing outside the glare of the headlights, looking down. For a moment Peralta thought he was praying, but then, in the half light, he saw the big Browning pistol in Guzmán's hand. Guzmán had taken off his gloves and Peralta saw him slide off the safety and check the action of the pistol, the sound sharp and thin in the shuffling quiet.

'Just do what we asked, *padre*.' The sarge gently restrained the drunken priest who took a last lurching swing at the prisoner and then staggered back, cursing.

'Very well. Let them kneel.'

The *guardia civiles* moved quickly, forcing the prisoners to their knees with blows from their rifles. The line of men knelt along the edge of the ditch, facing the stone wall, their shadows stark against the pale stones. Peralta saw the professor at the far end of the line, kneeling as if in church, back straight, ready to receive communion.

The priest began to speak but the sarge tugged his sleeve, urging him to stand further back. The man tottered back a few paces, with the sarge's hand on his arm, steadying him. The priest finally spoke in a high cracked voice, trembling with emotion.

'*I confess to Almighty God, to blessed Mary ever Virgin, to blessed*

145

Michael the Archangel, to blessed John the Baptist, to the holy Apostles Peter and Paul, to all the Saints, and to you Father, that I have sinned exceedingly, in thought, word and deed: through my fault...'

The prisoners begin to recite the familiar prayer and Peralta joined in, clinging to the comfort of the familiar words, words that bound him to a different world, a place away from this freezing vision of hell.

'... through my fault...'

The *guardia civiles* withdrew, slowly retreating pace by pace until they were standing several metres behind the prisoners. As if avoiding something.

'... through my most grievous fault.'

Peralta looked at the stone wall. As if avoiding something.

'Therefore I beseech blessed Mary ever Virgin, blessed Michael the Archangel...'

The stone wall. Bullets. They were avoiding ricochets. Something sharp and unpleasant started to rise in Peralta's throat.

'... blessed John the Baptist, the holy Apostles Peter and Paul, all the Saints, and you Father, to pray to the Lord our God for me.'

'Amen.' Peralta tried to swallow. His mouth was dry. His breathing getting faster. A trickle of sweat slid down his face. He looked at Guzmán. Guzmán moved slowly, his right arm by his side as he approached the line of prisoners. He had removed his hat. Peralta saw the headlights glint on Guzmán's oiled hair.

The priest raised his hand.

'May Almighty God have mercy on you, and forgiving your sins, bring you to life everlasting. Amen.'

Guzmán was about a metre from the first prisoner. Peralta saw the steam of the prisoner's breath, his shoulders heaving.

'May the Almighty and merciful Lord grant us pardon, absolution, and remission of all our sins. Amen.'

'Amen,' Peralta mouthed, his voice a hoarse whisper.

'Hail Mary, full of grace. The Lord is with thee.'

Guzmán was behind the prisoner now, looking down at him. Peralta couldn't see the *comandante's* face, but he didn't need to.

When he had seen him a few minutes earlier it had been enough. His expression had been empty: beyond fear, or pity, beyond any human emotion, entirely focused on the work. On *his* work.

'Blessed art thou among women, and blessed is the fruit of thy womb, Jesus.'

The prisoners struggled to repeat the words as the priest's delivery grew faster, charging the words with a hysterical urgency. Peralta was sweating heavily, his gaze alternating between the kneeling figures and the dark bulk of Guzmán standing motionless behind the first prisoner, right arm raised as if pointing to the man's guilt.

'Holy Mary, Mother of God, pray for us sinners, now and at the hour of our death.'

Peralta crossed himself, his hand shaking. 'Amen.'

The blast of the pistol shot slammed the man forward into the ditch, the concussive echo bouncing back painfully from the stone wall. Peralta was breathing in short dry gasps now. Where there had been a human being, there was now a crumpled shape and the inverted outline of the soles of the man's shoes. The second blast was worse. Guzmán moved slowly down the line to the next man. Peralta fought a sudden urge to vomit. This time, the prisoner screamed before the explosion. His words were garbled, incomprehensible, suddenly sheared off by the blast from Guzmán's Browning.

There was a line established now. Just a metre or so separating life and death. Those kneeling on this side of the ditch were with the living. But, as Guzmán approached, each step brought nearer the short journey into the shallow ditch. Peralta saw them shaking, saw their involuntary spasms of fear at the next blast of Guzmán's pistol. And then the tinny sound of the ejected cartridge on the frozen ground as he moved on to the next victim. The shots no longer made Peralta flinch so readily, though his ears rang from the percussion. He placed a hand on the side of the truck. He listened to the crunch of Guzmán's feet on the icy ground, the loud terrified breathing, the sobs, the whimpers, the pleas, the violent blast that took away part of their head. And then the same sequence repeated. Many of the prisoners wept as their turn approached and the tension was reducing Peralta to a similar state. *Don't forget you'll be going home afterwards,* Guzmán had said. The bile in Peralta's throat was sharp and bitter as he struggled to keep it down. Guzmán paused. Peralta looked up, retching, as he peered through the white glare of the headlights towards the two prisoners still alive. Guzmán had stopped and Peralta heard the metallic noise of the pistol as he removed the magazine. In an unwanted moment of insight, Peralta realised what the problem was.

It was the Browning. The magazine held only thirteen rounds. There were fifteen prisoners. Guzmán was reloading.

Guzmán slapped the magazine back into place with his palm and Peralta heard the sound of the hammer as he cocked the pistol.

'Sons of Satan, Freemasons, communists. *Asesinos.*'

It was the priest, clutching a bottle pulled from his bag, lurching towards the ditch where fourteen bodies now lay in a neatly spaced line, face down in the drainage ditch, their feet still touching the road, the wall beyond spattered with blood and fragments of brain tissue, the stains black in the white arc of the headlights. 'Vengeance is mine, sayeth the Lord...' The priest was addressing one of the corpses, poking it with his foot.

The shot seemed even louder after the short pause in the killing. Scalding bile exploded from Peralta's nose and mouth. One of the civil guards turned and looked at him with disdain.

Only *el Profesor* remained. Kneeling, his back straight. Staring ahead. Facing the short journey across the line.

'This way, Father.' The *sargento* was pulling Father Vasquez away. 'That's a good chap.' The priest was trying to spit on the bodies but was mostly spitting on himself.

Peralta remembered the afternoon. *The prisoner Mendoza has been identified as a special case.*

By the ditch, Guzmán was holstering his pistol.

Peralta had found that mark in the ledger, had alerted Guzmán to it. Guzmán had thanked him. *The prisoner is a special case.* The sarge knew what it meant. He'd laughed.

'I'm waiting, *Comandante* Guzmán,' the professor called, his voice steady. 'Run out of bullets? That's Franco's economy for you.'

The *sargento* was struggling to prevent the priest from attacking Guzmán now.

'Kill the fucker, burn him, burn him like they burned the nuns, kill him.' And then, as a civil guard rushed forward to help pull him away, the priest screeched up into the frozen night sky: 'They cut off my balls.'

Guzmán was standing behind the professor, pulling on his gloves.

Peralta saw Guzmán take something from his coat pocket, draw his hands apart and jerk them, testing the shining wire now wrapped around each gloved hand. The *sargento* watched, enthralled, even as the priest struggled to kick him. The sarge knew what Guzmán had in his hands for the professor. *The professor is a special case.*

'*Comandante*, shoot and have done with it,' *el Profesor* shouted. 'You'll catch your death of cold out here.'

Guzmán gave an angry grunt as he launched himself forward, looping the wire over *el Profesor*'s head, pulling it taut around his throat as he thrust his knee into the small of the man's back. The professor pitched forward under Guzmán's considerable weight into the shallow ditch. The bleached headlights of the trucks threw their distorted shadows onto the stone wall. Guzmán knelt on the man, his right knee pinning him down, keeping his bound hands trapped in place while he strangled him.

Peralta stood transfixed. The sight of Guzmán throttling the man was bad but the noise as he threshed beneath Guzmán's great bulk, struggling to breathe as the wire bit deep into his throat was almost enough to send Peralta screaming back to Madrid on foot. Almost. Instead, he sank to his knees and began to puke, his harsh gurgling mimicking the dying man's last rattling attempts to breathe. The noisy struggle for air ended abruptly, leaving a silence broken only by Peralta's retching.

Guzmán stood up, sweating from the exertion. He walked back toward Peralta. The priest broke free of the *sargento* and ran towards Guzmán, gibbering in a voice cracked by drunken malice. '*Ya faltan menos.* Death to the Reds. Viva Franco. So die all—'

Guzmán's punch hit the priest on the temple, knocking him to the ground. Without breaking stride, Guzmán stepped over the unconscious priest and continued towards Peralta. Peralta looked up into Guzmán's expressionless face, saw the blank eyes. Holding his stomach, Peralta rose to his feet. 'You... you punched a priest,' he said weakly.

Guzmán nodded. 'Sometimes I have no sense of humour when I'm working.' He looked round. 'Where's the brandy, Sarge?'

The *sargento* held out a bottle. 'Here you go, sir, get a drop of that down you.'

'Not me, you idiot, him.' Guzmán nodded at Peralta. The *sargento* passed the bottle grudgingly. Peralta looked at the brandy. On the point of refusing, he suddenly grabbed the bottle and downed a mouthful, coughing as the fiery spirit burned his throat. It was almost like being sick again, only more painful. And then he vomited, sinking back to his knees to avoid spewing onto his shoes.

'Perhaps not.' Guzmán took the bottle from Peralta, wiping the neck with his gloved hand before taking a drink. 'Must have been something you ate, Acting *Teniente*.'

Peralta stood up again, mopping his face with a handkerchief. Guzmán offered him a cigarette and he shook his head. Guzmán raised an eyebrow in theatrical surprise.

'What now, *Comandante*?' Peralta asked, his throat sore from vomiting and brandy.

'We drive back into the city,' Guzmán said breezily. 'These lads can tidy up. Sarge, you know where that lot are going?'

'*Si, mi Comandante.* We've got the bricklayer with us. I'll sort it all out.'

'*Bueno.* Make sure he seals it up properly before you leave.'

Guzmán walked to the nearest truck and shouted to Peralta to join him.

He waited as Peralta climbed into the cab and then got in, crushing the *teniente* between his bulk and the gear stick.

'Early night for you, son,' Guzmán said to the driver. 'And no dirty work.'

'*Sí, mi Comandante*,' the driver grinned happily. 'Early night for you too, *jefe*?'

'Not at all. The *teniente* and I are off to a reception with the top brass.'

'*Vaya vida*,' the driver said, impressed. 'That's how to live, sir.'

Guzmán nodded in agreement. 'So they say. Then after that, I've got a date.'

'*Hombre*, what a night.' The man shook his head admiringly.

'With a decent woman, mind,' Guzmán said. 'I'm not paying.'

'It just gets better, *mi Comandante.*'

Peralta hunched miserably in the oily claustrophobia of the cab, hoping he had emptied his stomach entirely by now. He had not. The ride back was as twisting and tortuous as before and Peralta had to ask the driver to stop twice. Guzmán and the driver watched Peralta kneeling by the roadside, interrupting their conversation about the price of whores to listen to his retching with amused contempt. Time passed slowly. It was after ten when the truck rattled into the road behind the *comisaría*. Guzmán jumped from the cab as Peralta headed for the stark comfort of the building.

'Don't spend too long with your head in the toilet, *Teniente*, we've a party to go to.'

Peralta's pace quickened as he started to retch again. Guzmán let him run ahead, and strolled cheerfully after him, whistling. The driver turned off the ignition and locked the cab door, pausing to light a cigarette. His lighter spluttered and refused to light. He cursed. A man was standing in a doorway and the driver approached him for a light. The man lit the driver's cigarette, wishing him a good evening. The driver exhaled smoke into the thin night air, idly watching the man walk up the street and turn into Calle Gallegos. The man's footsteps died away and the empty street fell back into silence and shadow. Finishing his cigarette, the driver threw the butt away and entered the *comisaría*. The door closed behind him leaving Calle de Robles in funereal quiet. After a few minutes, the man in the black coat slowly returned to his vigil, this time walking a little further down the street before stepping into the shadow of a doorway.

Around them were pine trees, their sharp, pungent needles a soft carpet beneath the men's boots as they scrambled away from the rocky incline. Twelve still alive. One man wanted to surrender but no one else saw the sense in that. It wasn't that the Moorish troops might kill them – they almost certainly would – it was the manner in which it would be done that prevented them giving up there and then. Montesino the corporal took charge. The Moors had to come up the same steep stony conduit they had just scrambled up, he pointed out. Only one man at a time could emerge from the narrow ravine onto the plateau. They would make a stand here: it was a good defensive position.

The men fanned out in a widely spaced line in the soft grass, feeling the fragrant pine needles give gently beneath them as they took up their firing positions. The sun was behind them and, as the Moors emerged from the jagged rocks, they would be dazzled for a few vital moments while the men lying in the dappled shade beneath the trees would be almost invisible. It was a reassuring plan and the men waited with a renewed sense of purpose, peering intently through the sights of their rifles at the entrance to the plateau.

'Allahu Akbar.' God is great. Excited shouts, the voices of hunters nearing the kill. The corporal lay a few metres from the kid. He looked over, smiling and making a thumbs up sign. But the kid looked at him blankly and turned back to peer down his rifle sight. The sound of boots on stone grew louder as the first Moors began to scramble up the last few metres to the grassy plateau.

CHAPTER SEVEN

MADRID 2009, CUARTEL DE LA GUARDIA CIVIL

Tali took her visitor's badge from the officer on the desk and fastened it to her shirt pocket. Seeing Galindez's ID, the man waved them towards the metal detector. 'Nice to see another pretty face around here,' he grinned. For a moment Galindez's stomach tightened. Maybe Tali wouldn't tolerate the constant sexism that permeated day-to-day life in the *guardia* the way she had to. The way she knew she had to: otherwise, it would be a case of *Miguel's daughter: what a whinger.*

Tali ignored the man. Galindez was worrying for nothing.

The lift purred upwards.

'This is exciting,' Tali said. 'Inside the HQ of the all powerful *guardia civil.*'

'It's just one big bureaucracy, believe me.'

The lift stopped at the fifth floor. It was a short walk along the corridor to the forensic department. Tali followed Galindez into her tiny office.

'You know how to show a girl a good time, Ana,' she laughed. 'What is it you're going to demonstrate? You made it sound very secret in the car.'

'Our new database. It has all sorts of records from the years of the dictatorship. Material collected by the people working on historical memory, government departments, police and the *guardia civil* as well. It's a big project.'

Galindez logged in. The screen changed and a database search form opened up.

'Who goes into the database? Suspects? Criminals? Victims?' Tali asked.

'Everyone. All those old files will be entered into it one day. That's the plan anyway. Details of who they were, why they were recorded and any known outcomes.'

'What kind of outcomes?'

'Arrested, tried, accused, sentenced – things like that. If it was recorded it goes on the database.' Galindez reached for the keyboard. 'What shall we start with?'

'Guzmán, of course.' Tali leaned forward, watching as Galindez entered his name.

'OK. Leopoldo... G... u...' The name appeared, the name that haunted many of the documents she'd been reading lately. The name that was starting to haunt her.

She pressed *Enter* and the database began its search. A small box appeared at the top of the screen: *Espera Por Favor*. The computer suddenly displayed a list of names.

'All Guzmáns?' Tali peered at the screen.

'He's here,' Galindez moved the mouse, selecting a name five lines down. 'Leopoldo Guzmán, *Capitán*. That's his date of birth, 4 April 1920.'

'*Capitán* in what?' Tali strained to see the screen. 'Army? *Guardia*?'

'Army – this is from a payroll document dated 1943. *Hostia*, Tali, *Capitán* at twenty-three? He did something right.'

'We already have some of those documents at the university,' Tali said. 'They only tell us he was paid, nothing more.'

'True. None of these other matches relate to him either.'

'Try just his surname,' Tali suggested. 'Maybe he had aliases?'

'Just "Guzmán"? OK.' Galindez typed the letters again. Nothing happened. 'I could try including a date,' she said. 'Maybe the information links to events rather than people.'

'Go ahead, Ana.'

Galindez thought back to her visit to Las Peñas. 'They said the mine where we found those bodies closed in the early fifties: let's try "Guzmán1950". Nothing happened. 'OK, I'll try the next few years.' The first two years didn't produce a result either. Her fingers rattled across the keyboard again. 'Guzmán1953'.

The screen exploded into a vivid red with a flashing message at the centre:

**UNAUTHORISED ATTEMPT TO ACCESS
RESTRICTED MATERIAL**
ACCESS DENIED

'What the...' Galindez hit the escape key. Nothing happened. The screen continued to flash.

'Why is it doing that?' Tali asked.

Before Galindez could answer, the phone buzzed. It was Mendez from Technical Services.

Tali listened to Galindez's conversation with Mendez, watching her expression change as they talked. 'What's up, Ana?' she asked as Galindez hung up.

'Apparently "Guzmán1953" is a password for some highly classified material. It needs a higher level security clearance than mine. Attempting unauthorised access looks bad, and the system records who did it. I don't know what happens then. Probably a bollocking.'

'Can't you just tell them what you were doing? You don't want your bosses thinking you were up to no good.'

'I certainly don't. That's why it's good Mendez was monitoring the system today.'

'Who is this Mendez?'

'An admirer.' Galindez smiled. 'And because of that, I can get help from technical services that would be difficult to arrange otherwise.'

Tali raised her eyebrows in mock outrage. 'You little tease, Ana. Stringing the poor guy along like that. Is that what you're like? All talk and no action?'

'Do you want to find out?' Galindez said in a low voice.

Tali shook her head. 'Not here.' She turned back to the computer screen. 'Do you think this Mendez can do anything to keep you out of trouble?'

'Yes. Mendez is a real technical wizard.'

'He's worth knowing then – just don't go breaking his heart, will you?'

'I promise,' Galindez said. 'Shall we get some lunch?'

'All right. And then there's somewhere I'd like to take you. It's related to Guzmán.'

'Really? I'm game. Where are we going?'

'The Almudena cemetery.'

MADRID 2009, CEMENTARIO DE ALMUDENA

Tali edged the car out of the car park, slowing to pass groups of wilting students, all with the same torpid air of uninterest, clinging to the shadows of trees and buildings as they languidly negotiated their various routes beneath the scorching sun.

'I think you'll find this interesting,' Tali said. 'It will give you an idea of the things Guzmán was involved in.'

'I'm intrigued,' Galindez said.

'During the meeting, I sensed you'd got the Guzmán bug,' Tali said. 'You have, haven't you? Everywhere we look, Guzmán crops up – yet we know so little about him.'

'It's funny,' Galindez said, 'I never had any interest in the Civil War before. Trying to track down Guzmán has made things I only knew from history lessons start to feel a lot closer.'

Tali slowed at a crossroads, waiting for a lull in the traffic. 'So much of what Guzmán and his unit did has been kept secret for too long. It's time for everything to come out in the open.'

Traffic was heavy and the entire world seemed in an evil mood. Cars bounced to a halt, braking suddenly, arms waving from windows, a constant blaring of horns, flurries of obscenities.

Galindez sneaked a glance at Tali. Expensive clothes, arms tight with toned muscles: time well spent in the gym, her legs tanned and sleek.

'So you're in a relationship with Luisa?' Tali asked, breaking the spell.

'I was,' Galindez said, reluctantly. 'It didn't work out. I'm not good at relationships.'

Tali turned to look her, her hair a sudden cascade of gold in the bright sunlight. '*Mujer*, I doubt it was your fault. She's not the easiest of people to get on with.'

'No,' Galindez said angrily, 'she's not discreet either. I broke up with her because I didn't want it to look as if I was only involved in the investigation because I was her girlfriend.'

'*Tranquila*, I was only saying.' Tali held up a hand in supplication. 'Sorry, it's just...'

'*No te preocupes*. I know what Luisa's like from past experience. Didn't you notice how she behaved with me at the meeting?'

'I could hardly miss it.'

The car turned a corner and passed through the gates of the Almudena Cemetery. Slowing, Tali pulled into a vacant parking space. 'Just be careful with Luisa, she doesn't do rejection. I'd keep it quiet if you start seeing anyone else while you're working with her, that is.'

'I'll bear that in mind.'

Galindez's damp shirt clung to the hot plastic seat as she climbed from the car. The whole city was baking, the air shimmered above the huge cemetery, distorting the distant skyline of the city.

'Look at the back of your shirt, you're soaking.' Tali laughed. An easy laugh, bright in the thick warm air.

Galindez looked at her in subtle appraisal. 'So why are we here, Tali?'

'I'll show you. Come on.'

Galindez followed her along a pathway lined with rose bushes and ornamental trees.

'Ever heard of *Las Trece Rosas Rojas*?' Tali asked.

'Yes, it's a charity, isn't it?' Galindez said. 'Something to do with social exclusion?'

'It's named after the *Trece Rosas*,' Tali said. 'They were thirteen young women, members of an illegal radical workers' organisation. At the end of the Civil War they were held in the women's prison at Ventas. It seemed likely they'd be pardoned or have their sentences commuted, but then a *guardia capitán* called Isaac Gabaldón was killed. The women were shot in reprisal. Guzmán was present, although we don't know what his role was.'

As they continued along the path, the air grew heavy with the scent of blossom. The path opened out and facing them was a wall. A plain stone wall. And roses. The wall was covered in red roses. Roses in bunches, pairs of roses, here and there single flowers, attached with string or wire, pushed into cracks in the mortar. At the centre of the wall, amongst the roses, a plaque. Tali stood motionless. At first, Galindez thought she was praying. Then she realised she was crying, soft tears slowly falling onto her T-shirt, her body shaking gently with inarticulate sorrow. Galindez's arm moved around Tali's waist as she read the plaque:

The young women known as

THE THIRTEEN ROSES

gave their lives for freedom
and democracy here on 5 August 1939
The people of Madrid remember their sacrifice

5 August 1988

'My great-aunt,' Tali stammered. 'She was seventeen when they...' She leaned against Galindez, her shoulders rising and falling with the rhythm of sorrow. Galindez tried to say something of comfort, her arm tightening around Tali's waist, her cheek pressed against her hair, trying and failing to find the right words. And then it hit her: an unexpected wave of agony, the condensation of her tragic childhood experience. Taken by surprise, Galindez surrendered to the pain she had kept at bay for so long. And the wall, with its tributes of roses, the jars of flowers at its base, the simple plaque set into the dusty red brickwork, melted under a mist of shared tears.

They sat in silence on the stone bench. Galindez felt adrift, bewildered by her reaction to this inundating grief for a woman killed seventy years ago. And, she wondered, if Tali felt such pain for someone she never knew, how should others who lost someone feel? Those whose suffering was more recent, to whom the death was so much closer and more visible? *What about me?* For a moment, the sun-washed pathways of the cemetery were replaced by images of that spring morning: the pale lines of newly built houses across the road, horrified neighbours standing rigid and helpless, thick black smoke from the burning petrol enveloping the shattered car, oily flames spiking upwards from the wreckage. *Mamá's* screams, the articulation of a pain beyond words as she tried to get inside the car, thinking *Papá* could still be alive. But *Mamá* couldn't even find the car door. Only later did she realise the car was resting on its roof.

Galindez leaned against Tali, and her tears began again, tears she never shed for her father, not even at his funeral, the coffin wrapped in the vibrant colours of the flag, carried by six solemn *guardia* in tricorne hats, wearing sunglasses to mask their pain. Nor had she wept after her mother's suicide, when *Mamá* was too contaminated by her toxic grief to continue with the half-life she'd been trying to lead. Maybe the destruction of Galindez's young world had been so fast and unexpected it never hurt in any conventionally recognisable way. Suddenly assigned to being that tragic little girl, defined by absent others. *Always Miguel's daughter, never Ana María.*

So this was the pain of loss, she thought. How strange to feel it now, its visceral surges reducing the world to a small space delineated by undulating grief. Tali held her until the spasms passed. Galindez wanted to tell her, to share with her. But she couldn't. Not right now. Not until she was certain she could trust her. Things were no longer under her control, Galindez realised. And that could take some getting used to, after having been in control for so long.

A moment came when her tears diminished. Galindez held Tali tightly, her body tense with rising need. A few hours ago, she'd idly fantasised about this across the seminar room table. Now, she wanted more. But Tali gently pulled away, looking at her watch. '*Para*, Ana. It's getting late.'

'What do you want to do now?' Galindez asked, hopefully.

'I'll have to drive you back to the university to get your car. I'm seeing my younger sister tonight. It's her last night in Madrid before she goes back to college in Barcelona. Sorry, *querida*.'

'But another time. Soon?'

'*Claro que sí*. Anyway, you've some reading to do, no? Guzmán's diary.'

'That will have to do for now.'

The drive across Madrid was slow and hot. The university was quiet, with only a few torpid students still sprawling on the grass. Tali parked alongside Galindez's car. 'I wanted you to see,' Tali said, 'how what Guzmán and his men did still affects so many people. Including me.'

'I'm glad you shared it with me,' Galindez said, wondering if she would be able to share her own extensive history of pain some day.

She leaned forward and their foreheads collided. They pulled back in surprise, amused at their mutual awkwardness. Shared laughter. And then Galindez felt the warmth of Tali pressed against her, lost in a moment with no space or time outside their confined passion. Finally, Galindez climbed from the car, smoothing her tousled hair, waving as Tali drove away into the warm dusk. Galindez slid into her own car, flicking on the light to check her appearance. She struggled unsuccessfully to calm her wayward fringe. She abandoned her hair and started the engine. What the hell, it was night. No one would see it.

She was wrong. Luisa turned away from the small grassy slope overlooking the parking lot from where she had been watching them and slowly made her way back to the Contemporary History building.

MADRID 2009, CALLE DE LOS CUCHILLEROS

Gentle patterns of sunlight danced across the room. Galindez struggled to sit up. Her right arm still ached from Sancho's punch and the memory of the fight sparked an adrenalin rush that put an end to her soporific reverie. Awake now, she replayed the fight against Sancho in her head. He was really good, she realised grudgingly. Better than her. She needed more time in the dojo to prepare for the next time they met. *There is no problem that can't be solved through application.* She'd let her application slip of late.

She was too preoccupied to sleep. Guzmán, of course. It was such a fascinating case. The more so since Luisa seemed hell-bent on arguing that he wasn't responsible for what had happened. Galindez found that strange, though she relished the challenge of proving Luisa wrong. Preparing her coffee, she smiled. Things were going well. The Guzmán investigation was what she'd trained for: amassing evidence, interrogating complexities of background and context before drawing the threads together – a stark contrast to Luisa's literary inventions and projections. Passing the mirror, she paused, seeing the smiling woman looking back at her. It had been a long time since she had been this happy.

MADRID 2009, PLAZA MAYOR

A golden day with soft clouds shielding the sun. Crowds bustled along the sides of the square, browsing menus outside restaurants, filtering in and out of bars and cafés, taking a beer here, tapas or a fino there and then more tapas. Galindez sat with Natalia in the square, a glass of cold white wine glistening in front of her. Tali nursed a brandy with a shot of anise.

'You really like that? I don't see you as a *sol y sombra* type,' Galindez said.

'After all that emotion in the cemetery last week I felt like something strong.'

The square bustled with teams of Japanese tourists taking turns to photograph one another in front of the statue of Felipe Tres. Voices echoed along the shaded walkway lined with bars and restaurants around the edge of the square No need to talk. Just sitting back, listening, watching people go by, hearing the murmur of traffic in the distance. The liquid sound of a saxophone spilled from an open window, a sudden rush of silvery notes shimmering in the bright air before falling in an intoxicated cadence into silence.

The air grew rich with the drifting scent of cooking: smoke rising from heating oil, iron-hard notes of garlic, the seductive aromas of fried meat and grilled fish punctuated by herbs, blurred by the blue smoke of cigarettes. Cool almond milk splashing into glasses, waiters carrying cold pitchers of golden beer frosted with condensation. Restaurant windows bright with sleek rainbows of salad, crisp greens, bright peppers mixed with pungent chunks of onion, glossy with oil.

Tali leaned forward. 'Ana, when we were in the cemetery, you said something. Can I ask you about it?'

'Of course. What did I say?'

Tali finished off her *sol y sombra* and beckoned to the waiter. 'Well, when you started crying, you said...' She paused as the waiter arrived. Galindez asked for water, another *sol y sombra* for Tali. She turned back to Galindez. 'You said *"papá"*. I just wondered what it was that upset you so much. I didn't like to ask at the time.'

Galindez stiffened. She pursed her lips. There was no one apart from *Tia* Carmen she'd ever talked to about what happened. Not even the shrinks. Especially not the shrinks. 'It's a long story. I wouldn't want to bore you.'

'You won't.' Tali smiled. Galindez was vaguely aware of the waiter swooping through the bustling tables, leaving the drinks without a word.

'I've never talked about it to anyone I've been seeing,' Galindez said.

Tali nodded. 'Well, I'm glad that it's with me. If you want to?'

Galindez wanted to. It took her a while to get through her story. *Papá*, the car bomb, *Mamá's* suicide. Half a lifetime to cover. How she went to live with *Tia* Carmen, how Uncle Ramiro paid her way through university, how she'd joined the *benemérita* as a forensic investigator. And then the sad slow coda of *Tia* Carmen's decline with cancer. And how when Carmen died the previous year, Galindez bought the flat in Calle de los Cuchilleros. All that tragic detail. Galindez found herself relaxing, enjoying the warm intimacy between them. The strangeness of sharing.

'God, you didn't have an easy time of things, did you?' Tali said. 'And you really can't remember anything that happened before the explosion? Can't the doctors do something?'

'Seems not,' Galindez said. 'Retrograde amnesia, it's called. I had some therapy after *Mamá* killed herself, but the first eight years of my life are just a blank. I remember little things sometimes, playing with a ball with *Papá* in the garden, stuff like that. But it's always very hazy. My early memories went up in smoke along with *Papá's* car.'

'No wonder, Ana, it must have been terrible.'

'I know what you're thinking: tragic child, sad character – how can anyone have a normal life after that? It's what people at work think. Particularly since *Papá* was the perfect *guardia civil*. Did everything right by the book, loved by his men – you get the picture? Most of my colleagues think I went into forensics as a cop-out, rather than trying to live up to *Papá's* reputation working on the front line.'

'I don't see you copping out of anything, Ana María,' Tali said. 'You got through university despite everything that had happened and you've got a good job. Your dad would be proud.'

'Maybe.' Galindez shrugged. 'I wouldn't know. It's hard for me to imagine, because he's hard for me to imagine.'

'I'm sure you're like him in lots of ways,' Tali said. 'You're quite tough, aren't you? You know when Sancho flattened you? Luisa said all you were concerned about was that you hadn't hit him hard enough.'

Galindez sighed. 'With my history I learned to stand up for myself. Kids at school used to call me little orphan Ana and pick on me. For a while, anyway. *Tia* Carmen paid for me to have karate lessons. They stopped picking on me.'

Tali laughed. 'Good for you. You went through a terrible time, losing your parents the way you did, but you've got past it. Mind you, with your luck I wouldn't ask you to buy a lottery ticket.' She smiled. 'I wanted to know all about you, because you interest me. And now you interest me even more.'

A shadow across the table. A sharp voice shattering the moment of delicate intimacy. 'Filthy perverts. Get indoors, you dirty bitches.'

Shocked, Galindez looked up, to be confronted by a bizarre couple. An elderly man and woman, both with mercilessly dyed black hair, the woman's face an orange mask of crudely applied cosmetics and garish crimson lipstick. Their clothes dated back to the fifties, maybe earlier, lapels plastered with badges – Galindez saw the yolk and arrows of the Falangist badge, a gold swastika and the more recent fascist emblem of *Fuerza Nueva*. In the stunned moment before Galindez could react, the elderly woman snatched up Galindez's wine and tossed the contents over Tali. She shouted in surprise as icy wine soaked her shirt.

'It would take more than that to wash the dirt off you, you filthy bitch.' The old woman's voice was high-pitched and loud. Heads turned, people looking, staring, looking away again. The old woman began to reach for Tali's glass, but the waiter stepped in.

'Fuck off out of it, you lunatics.' He grabbed the old man's arm, pushing him after the woman. '*Joder*, piss off to Franco's mausoleum if you want to relive the old days. *Cabrónes.*'

'Leave them alone, *maricón*.' A sharp, nasal voice.

'Shit,' Tali muttered.

Half a dozen skinheads pressed through the café tables towards them, their clothes covered with predictable slogans: *Make My Day: Kill a Gay*; *Spain's not Black – Send them Back*; *Franco lives! Arriba España!* The skinheads halted, confronting the solitary waiter standing between them and Galindez and Tali.

'What's the problem?' a young skinhead demanded, tattooed face sullen with dull menace.

'Lesbians,' the old women howled. 'Practically fucking in public. Filthy animals. If they're going to do it, they should do it behind bars where they belong.'

'They're my customers,' the waiter said, coolly. 'They're staying. You lot can piss off.'

The skinheads began to mock his bravado with growing belligerence until they saw the ring of waiters quietly forming around them, several with baseball bats. The gang made a sudden collective decision and backed off, shouting insults as they went. A couple of officers of the *policía nacional* appeared, one talking rapidly into his radio, the other drawing his baton. The skinheads quickly began to melt away into the crowds around the edge of the square.

'Come on,' Galindez said. 'Let's go back to my flat.'

Shaken, Tali got to her feet, failing to see the old woman lurching towards her again, snatching at her with a wizened hand, seizing the neckband of her T-shirt and ripping it away from her body. There was the sound of tearing, a sudden moment of exposure and then Tali's anguished cry as she hurriedly pulled the sides of her ripped shirt together. Galindez moved quickly to push the old woman away – a little too hard: a metal table clattered noisily to the ground as the woman fell across it, glasses shattering. The ageing fascist pulled herself to her knees, her corpse-coloured face twisting into a mask of hate as she unleashed a barrage of obscenities. Focusing on the woman, Galindez failed to see the old man grab a glass from a nearby table and toss the contents over

Tali. She staggered back, shocked, cold liquid dripping from her face. Galindez grabbed the old man firmly by his lapels, giving him her opinion of his ancestry before shoving him away.

The afternoon had become a nightmare. The world seemed out of time, suddenly malevolent and unpredictable. Galindez steered Tali across the square, a protective arm around her shoulders. Tali leaned against her, holding her torn shirt together, letting Galindez guide her, ignoring the stares. And the catcalls: not everyone in the square was sympathetic.

Finally, they reached Calle de los Cuchilleros. The narrow cobbled street was deserted. Tali stopped for a moment, raising a hand to her face to wipe her eyes. Her ripped T-shirt flapped open. It made her seem even more vulnerable, Galindez thought.

'I'd give good money to see those,' a familiar voice said. 'But I can wait my turn, Galindez.'

Galindez turned quickly. Emerging from behind a builder's skip outside the old bodega across the street was Sancho, piercings twinkling, his eyes dark and flat like a snake. Galindez realised he wasn't staring at her, but instead was more intent on ogling Tali. Aware of his attention, Tali pulled the sides of her shirt together more tightly.

'Never mind her, Sancho, I'm the one you need to deal with.' Galindez's mouth was suddenly dry. She breathed deeply, trying to calm her anger.

Sancho laughed. 'I'll do what I want, Galindez. Who's going to stop me – you? I don't think so, you little dyke. I know who you are, where you live – everything. And I'll tell you what's going to happen, when it's going to happen and when it will stop. *Me entiendes, puta?*'

He was trying to wind her up, Galindez knew: threatening Tali, calling her a whore, all of it a distraction so she'd come into the fight with her head messed up – already a loser. She knew better than to let Sancho's insults put her off. They were things she had trained for in the dojo: *clarity of thought, detachment from emotion.* But those were ideals. Right now she wanted to beat Sancho to a bloody pulp.

Tali backed away from Sancho as he came towards her with his slow, reptilian gait. 'Ana, I'm scared,' she called.

'Not half as scared as your *novia*, blondie,' Sancho sneered.

A sudden playground memory. A ring of kids surrounding little Ana María, her dark eyes bright with fierce defiance, fists clenched, her cheeks glowing with anger as they pushed her down again and again. And every time, she struggled back to her feet, lashing out at them. Voices harsh with childish malice: 'Little orphan Ana. Where's your mum and dad, Ana? *Huérfanita Ana.*'

Sancho stopped, surprised by how quickly Galindez closed on him. His attention was on her now – just as she intended. Tali backed away, moving behind the skip.

Sancho grinned. 'Tell you what, Galindez. If your girlfriend doesn't want to show me her tits, show me yours. They're not as big but they'll do.'

'Fuck you.' Galindez knew she shouldn't let him get her riled but he wasn't easy to ignore. *He's saying it to mess with you. Focus.*

Sancho smirked. 'Think of it as the price you pay for pressing the wrong buttons, Galindez. Let's have a look, *niña*. The alternative is I make you cry in front of your sweetheart.'

Well if he wants it that much. 'If I do, you'll leave us alone?' Galindez asked quietly.

Sancho licked his thick lips and nodded. His eyes greedily followed Galindez's hand as it moved to the top button of her shirt. She fumbled with the button for a moment and then her foot lashed out, catching him in the groin.

Sancho's eyes bulged and he swore as he staggered backwards. He didn't go down, instead bending forward and taking a deep breath before straightening up, rubbing his crotch. 'Nice one, Galindez,' he spat. 'But your timing's all wrong: you should have taken me out with that kick. No attention to detail, *niña*.' He turned to Tali. 'Watch this, blondie. I'm going to take your girlfriend apart.'

Galindez was incensed. *No one says I lack attention to detail.* She launched herself at Sancho, aiming for his face. Sancho deflected the blow and punched her, connecting with her right shoulder, almost in the same spot he'd hit her in their previous fight. The pain was dazzling. A sudden thought occurred: *He is better than me.* And then another: *Shit.*

Swinging round, Galindez tried a kick to his head. Sancho ducked and caught hold of her foot, holding it just long enough to send her flying backwards across the cobbled street. It was a bad fall: her shoulder flashed with sparkling pain and she felt a sickening crack as her head hit the cobbles. Sancho came towards her as she scrambled to her feet. Her foot slipped on the smooth cobbles and she went sprawling to the ground again, shaking her head in angry frustration.

'Come on, I haven't finished yet.' Sancho turned to Tali. 'I hope she's not this lazy in bed, *amiga.*' He faced Galindez again. 'Get up, you idle little fuck.'

Galindez shook her head again, taking deep breaths. This was bad. He'd turned his skills up a notch. She was in trouble. The best she could do now was to keep him busy while Tali got away.

'Tali run.' Galindez's voice was tight with pain. She struggled to her feet just as Sancho came steaming in on her.

Sancho feinted, throwing tentative punches, keeping Galindez on the defensive. Suddenly, he caught her with his forearm, a blow that smashed against her chest, sending her reeling back, struggling to stay on her feet. Lights danced across her vision as Sancho leaped forward and slapped her, her head snapping to one side and then the other as he hit her with alternate back- and forehand slaps. Sancho laughed crazily as his blows rocked Galindez's head, her hair whirling with the impact of his blows. He kept coming, swapping slaps to her head for painful jabs intended to humiliate her, easily wading through flurries of her counterpunches. Galindez kept moving, desperate to keep a distance between them until her head cleared. If it cleared. She moved back a few steps and he followed. That was good. While he focused on her, Tali could get away.

Sancho grinned, his mouth open, strings of saliva hanging

between his lips. 'I've got you breathing heavy, Galindez, and you've still got your clothes on.' He dropped his hands to his sides and swayed his shoulders, mocking her. With a sudden angry shout, she leaped at him, trying to kick him in the throat. He moved, avoiding her easily. Galindez fell heavily, rolling quickly across the cobbles to stay out of his reach. 'Come on, love, let's cut the foreplay and give you that big bang you really want.' Sancho was laughing like a lunatic, sensing victory.

His hand shot out, grabbing for her hair. She ducked, desperately driving forward, striking upwards with a blow to his face that sent him staggering. Galindez saw motion behind him. Sancho stared at Galindez, her hair dishevelled, blood trickling from her nose, her body shaking as she gasped for air. With a laugh, he raised his hands, ready to attack again. The attack didn't come. Instead, he straightened, his head snapping back, legs folding under him as he fell to the ground. Tali stood behind him, holding the pool cue she'd pulled from the skip. Galindez saw the blood on the back of Sancho's head and wondered if Tali had killed him. But Sancho suddenly moved, dragging himself to his knees on the cobbles, shaking his head.

'Fuck.' He sounded surprised.

'Give me that cue.' Galindez's voice shook with anger as she snatched the pool cue from Tali. 'I'm going to fucking kill him.' Raising the cue, she started for him, her voice trailing away as Sancho pulled a pistol from inside his jacket and aimed it at her.

'Get the fuck out of here, Galindez. Both of you get lost.' Sancho struggled to his feet. His cotton jacket had come open. Galindez saw a shoulder holster hanging under his left arm.

'Go on. Your girlfriend saved you this time.' He backed off a few metres before holstering the pistol. Then he turned and began walking unsteadily up the hill towards the main square.

'*Corre coño. Cobarde.*' Galindez's shout echoed around the tall buildings. She staggered after him, still furious but then the pool cue clattered on the cobbles as her legs gave way. Tali rushed forward, taking Galindez's weight against her and lowering her to the ground. Galindez looked around drunkenly, struggling to get up. She saw Sancho had stopped. He stared down the hill at her.

'Don't meddle with things that aren't your concern, Galindez,' he shouted. 'You've been warned. You fucking mess with me again and I'll mess you up permanently.' He turned, and walked out of sight round the corner of the market.

Tali looked at Galindez with concern. 'Ana, can you make it back to your flat?'

'Of course,' Galindez said. 'He hardly touched me.' She tried to stand. The world rotated and she slid to the ground again. 'I'll be fine in a minute,' she muttered, the cobblestones cold against her cheek.

When she opened her eyes again, she was in her *piso*. In her bed. 'How did I get here?' she mumbled, struggling half-heartedly as Tali pulled a shirt over her head..

'With a great deal of help, *querida*,' Tali said, easing Galindez's arm into the sleeve of the shirt. 'Now shut up and keep still. Try and rest.'

'I always sleep in my—' Galindez began.

'*Ya lo se*. You always sleep in your Barcelona shirt. You told me several times. Don't worry. You're wearing it.'

'This is the home shirt,' Galindez mumbled. 'I sleep in the away—'

'Shut up.'

Tali applied antiseptic cream to the skinned knuckles of Galindez's right hand. It was strange, just lying there, having someone look after her, Galindez thought. An unusual experience for her. She started to analyse the feeling, remembering she needed to tell Tali something, wondering if she'd double-locked the door to the street. And there was a lettuce in the kitchen that needed to go in the fridge. And something else, probably, she couldn't quite remember. That was funny, she thought, an amnesiac who couldn't remember. She smiled to herself. Then she slept.

CHAPTER EIGHT

t was almost eleven o'clock. Guzmán was shaving over the sink in the dingy cold of the mess room. He was in his shirt, his sleeves rolled up, exposing his massive forearms. His braces hung down over his hips. The razor gleamed bright and new as it moved over the anaemic foam Guzmán had managed to raise from the worn bar of soap.

Peralta sat at a table, his hair dishevelled, his cheeks dark with stubble. His coffee was cold in front of him and he stared hollow-eyed at Guzmán as the big man cheerfully shaved. Peralta had been in this trance for some time. Guzmán ignored him. Finally, he stopped shaving.

'For Christ's sake buck up, Peralta. We're going to a reception for the Head of State. Have you ever met Franco before? No, of course not, because you're a fucking nobody. And you'll stay one if you don't mix in the right circles.' He stared at Peralta angrily, eyes glinting in the weak sepia light. 'You're sulking because I chinned that priest, aren't you? You were the one who said he was a disgrace.'

'I was thinking about what you did,' Peralta said in a subdued voice. 'You killed them all.'

'What did you think we'd do with them? Chat about the football?'

Peralta shook his head, trying to dislodge the recurring image of the prisoners kneeling, facing the stone wall, picked out by the beams of headlights. Guzmán standing behind them with his Browning automatic. The explosion of the shots. The stone wall splattered with blood and brains.

'The shooting was bad enough,' he said. 'It was what you did to *el Profesor*. That's what really gets me.' He took a drink of coffee. 'How could you do it?'

'It was personal.' Guzmán returned to his shaving.

'How could it be personal? You'd never met him before.'

Guzmán looked at him sternly. 'It was personal but not between him and me. Higher up it was personal. His escapes made him unpopular at the top.'

'Franco?'

'*Generalísimo* Franco,' Guzmán corrected him.

'*Generalísimo* Franco,' Peralta repeated.

'I can't say.' Guzmán smirked.

'So it was him who ordered it?'

Guzmán looked irritated. 'He doesn't say it. Why should he? He gives the nod and then someone tells me. In any case, suppose he'd been taken to trial and sentenced to death. How would he have ended up? Garrotted. Sat in a chair against a post with the iron collar round his neck while they tightened it until his neck snapped. At least tonight it came as a surprise. Shot, strangled, garrotted. They ended up dead just the same. You with your firing squad bollocks. Waste of time. What if the troopers can't shoot straight? You end up with someone with a bullet in the belly, lots of screaming. And then someone has to put a round in his head to shut him up. So we cut straight to that part. One bullet, one man. Said and done.'

'You can explain it all away, can't you?'

'Yes I can. Because I'm in charge. And because I'm in charge, I do these things myself. They say if you want something doing well do it yourself, no? Anyway, you'd better get ready because we're going to meet important people and you are my *teniente*. You need a shave. Come here.'

'What?' Peralta asked, horrified.

'Come here, I'll shave you.' Guzmán rinsed the blade under the tap. 'Your hands are shaking; you'll cut your own throat if you try it. Come on.'

Peralta stood up and walked to the sink. Guzmán pulled a chair from under the table and pushed him into it. Draping a dirty towel around Peralta's shoulders, Guzmán picked up the soap and his shaving brush and began to work up the semblance of a lather.

'Shitty soap, this, but it will do the trick. Would sir like a haircut as well? Something for the weekend? No, I suppose not.'

Peralta was suddenly afraid. Afraid of this huge man who earlier had shot fourteen prisoners and then strangled the last one with his own hands. This man who was now standing behind him with an open razor. Peralta felt an urge to run out into the frozen night, to flee this world of shadows and violence. Instead he inclined his head to the left as Guzmán moved the razor across his cheek expertly.

'I used to do this in the army,' Guzmán said genially, the blade gliding smoothly over Peralta's face. 'One of the Moors taught me. He used a big knife he carried. One time, he gave several of us a shave after a battle and his knife was dripping blood from where he'd used it on the enemy. Mind, many of them would have been dead already.'

'Dead?' Peralta asked, anxious to keep Guzmán in a relaxed state while he had the razor to his throat. 'Why did he stab the dead?'

'He didn't.' Guzmán stepped back and drew the razor in a sawing action across his crotch. 'He collected their balls.'

The blade returned to Peralta's throat. A dribble of sweat ran down the *teniente*'s forehead. Rigid with apprehension, he sat motionless despite the sour blast of garlic and wine being breathed in his face. Suddenly Guzmán's face contorted.

'Ah...'

'What?' Peralta almost screamed. Guzmán seemed to be having a seizure of some kind. The razor pressed against Peralta's throat and he felt it cut him as Guzmán contorted and then sneezed explosively over Peralta. Peralta mopped his face with the towel, anxious to mop off the sweat now flowing freely.

'*Joder.*' Guzmán sniffed. 'Sorry, *Teniente*, nearly cut your throat.'

Peralta looked at him. Guzmán's heavy face was breaking up in laughter. He put down the razor and leaned on the table, shaking with a convulsive cackle. Peralta wondered if he was going mad. At least the shaving had stopped, he thought gratefully.

'Sorry, it's just...' And then Guzmán cracked up again, just as he began to advance once more on Peralta with the razor. His laugh was infectious and Peralta found himself joining in, feeling the tension and horror of the night dissipating until suddenly he too was convulsed and breathless with the intensity of this unwarranted mirth. Finally he drew a calm breath and looked up. Guzmán glared back at him.

'I don't know what you think is so funny.'

'Sorry, *Comandante*.'

'Well, pull yourself together, man, let's get you finished off. You'll look a bit more human. Or you will do once you've washed that blood off your face. Funny, I can't remember ever having made anyone bleed by accident before.'

The driver knocked at Guzmán's door at half past eleven. By then the *sargento* had returned with a few of the men and they were now sitting drinking in the grimy mess room. Peralta wondered about the propriety of uniformed men drinking while on duty, particularly such copious amounts, but the men ignored his presence and so he said nothing.

Guzmán and Peralta, shaved, ties knotted neatly and hair combed into brilliantined compliance, walked to the elegant if somewhat battered Hispano-Suiza. The driver made to open the door but Guzmán swore at him and the man quickly scuttled back into the driving seat. Sitting in the back, the two men watched as they passed through a cold, skeletal Madrid.

'Avenida de la Asunción.' Guzmán leaned forward to remind the driver.

'I've got it, *jefe*.' The man nodded.

Peralta began to question Guzmán, feeling in need of advice on etiquette.

'Easy,' Guzmán smirked, 'just don't make a prick of yourself, be

175

polite and try not to commit an act of treachery – it carries the death penalty.'

Peralta sighed and focused instead on the hole in his shoe. Guzmán took his silence for anticipation and began to hold forth.

'Firstly, you address the *Caudillo* as *"Excelencia"*. Everyone does, even his son-in-law.' He looked at Peralta who was now exploring the hole in his shoe with some interest. 'Pay attention,' he said, driving his elbow into Peralta's side. Peralta paid attention.

'This is supposedly an informal get-together,' Guzmán continued, 'so it won't be. There will be important people dotted all over. Just don't think you're at some Christmas party and go over and introduce yourself. If the *Caudillo* wants to speak to you – which is extremely unlikely – he'll get some flunkey to fetch you.'

'Speak to me?' Peralta spluttered. 'Will he want to speak to me?'

'It's possible. Valverde only invited us along because he thinks I'm spying on him for the *Caudillo*.'

'And are you?'

'Of course,' Guzmán said. 'And maybe I'll come up with something one day. If I could get enough shit to drop him into once and for all – something that would have him up in front of the firing squad – I could retire and have the concession for checking the quality of service given by the country's brothels. *Capitán-general* of bordellos, that would suit me. I could do it part-time and spend the other six days of the week testing wine to make sure it was fit for consumption.'

'I'm sure you'd be very good at it,' Peralta said, bracing himself for another elbow.

'I would. I really would,' Guzmán agreed.

'So you honestly think you might do something else one day? When you retire?'

'If I live that long,' Guzmán said. 'And the way this *cabrón* is driving it may not be much longer.'

MADRID 1953, HEADQUARTERS OF THE CAPITÁN-GENERAL

The headquarters of the *Capitán-General* of Madrid had the appearance of a rundown Gothic museum. Outside the entrance, Peralta saw unformed armed guards and men in overcoats he presumed were secret police.

'Just remember, mind your manners and you'll be fine,' Guzmán said as they walked up the grand stone stairs to the entrance. Their way was barred instantly by two heavy-set men in plain clothes. Even as the two stopped their advance, Peralta noticed two uniformed guards at each side of the entrance move to block the doorway completely.

'Papers please, gentlemen.' The older of the two carried a clipboard and checked their names against the list, inspected their identity cards and then looked them over with what Peralta considered to be unwarranted disdain.

'Are either of you gentlemen armed?'

'Of course we are,' Guzmán snorted, 'aren't you?'

The man looked at Guzmán carefully. 'No one can bear arms in the presence of the *Caudillo, señor*. A matter of security. You of all people should see that, *Teniente*, if you don't mind me saying so.'

Peralta felt Guzmán stiffen.

'To whom do I have the honour of speaking?' Guzmán managed to make politeness sound like physical threat.

'I am *Capitán* Castells, *Teniente*. At your service.'

Guzmán towered above the *Capitán*. 'And I am *Comandante* fucking Guzmán, *Capitán*. Have a little respect for your superiors – otherwise you'll find yourself back in uniform in some village in the Basque country sharing the local goat with a group of senile inbreds, and before your Basque posting, I'll put you in hospital for six months. *Entendido?*'

The man snapped to attention. 'I understand perfectly, *Comandante* Guzmán. Apologies for my error. But you must appreciate I've been given orders by *Almirante* Carrero Blanco himself as to tonight's security measures. So I must respectfully

177

ask you both to leave your side arms with us. They will of course be returned when you leave.'

'When you ask like that it's impossible to refuse,' Guzmán sneered and reached inside his coat for the Browning. He handed the pistol over butt first. Peralta was amused to see the man's surprise at the weight of the weapon as he took the pistol from Guzmán.

'This has been fired recently.' The man sniffed at the pistol.

'Tonight. And every shot a hit, *Capitán*.' Guzmán smiled.

The *Capitán*'s face never changed. 'I have no doubt, *Comandante*.' The man stepped back, extending an arm towards the entrance. Peralta stepped forward but the man lightly touched him on the arm.

'Your weapon, *Teniente*.'

Embarrassed, Peralta took out his service revolver and handed it over.

Behind a trestle table in the lobby, a heavily made-up old woman took their coats. Guzmán adjusted his tie awkwardly while Peralta slicked down his hair with his palm, both like schoolboys about to go before the headmaster. Passing along an elegant but musty corridor, they heard the gentle sound of a chamber quartet. At the door to the reception room two more secret policemen checked their papers. Beyond was the wide open space of the ballroom. Peralta had expected a large crowd but there were perhaps only fifty people in small groups around the room. On one side of the room was a table filled with plates of food, and next to the food, a well-stocked bar with waiters in evening dress.

'This looks rather fancy,' Peralta said, following Guzmán to the bar.

'Not really. Otherwise we'd have had to come in black tie – or worse, uniform. Your uncle said this was going to be informal and actually it is – by his standards.' Guzmán turned and grinned. 'First time he's told me the truth since I met him.'

The barman inclined his head in a slight bow. 'What can I get for you, *señores*?'

'Whisky,' Guzmán said. He watched the barman pour it. '*Hombre*, not a small one.'

The barman nodded and half filled the glass, passing it to Guzmán who looked at it blankly. 'Fill it up, *cabrón*.'

The waiter obeyed and turned to Peralta.

'Do you have some Rioja?' Peralta asked.

'Indeed, sir, would sir have the ninety-eight or the twenty-two?'

Guzmán leaned towards Peralta. 'That would be 1922, in case you were wondering.'

Suitably offended, Peralta asked for the ninety-eight. 'I've never drunk anything this good,' he said, admiring the Rioja glistening in the thick cut-crystal glass.

'Good.' Guzmán nodded. 'I'll have that next.'

They stood at one end of the bar, observing the guests. Peralta noticed a number of generals and a few colonels in uniform. The rest of the guests wore civilian clothes, the expensive cut a good indication of their social standing.

'Isn't that Carrero Blanco?' Peralta asked, nodding at a dark-haired man who seemed to be holding a conversation with several people at the same time.

'It is indeed, the arse-licker. Don't get stuck in a corner with him, *Teniente*, he'll bore the pants off you. Christ he's dull. Someone should put a bomb under him. *Mierda*, he's seen me.'

The admiral came towards them, his face set in an unconvincing expression of pleasure. Guzmán downed his whisky in one swallow.

'*Comandante* Guzmán. It's been a while. How are you?'

'I'm—' Guzmán began.

'Excellent. Well, the *Caudillo* will be here directly. He was only asking after you just a little while ago.'

Peralta looked at Guzmán, impressed.

Carrero leaned forward conspiratorially. 'I understand you took care of that matter we contacted you about?'

Guzmán smiled and looked meaningfully into his empty glass. 'Said and done, *mi Almirante*. Just as your office requested.'

'And *el Profesor*? I believe he was to have special treatment?'

'And he did,' Guzmán agreed.

'Indeed. Indeed.' Carrero nodded. 'A job well done, no doubt.'

'Probably the Reds didn't think so, sir.'

'No? Well, they had it coming. Justice catches up in the end, eh? I'll bet it was a surprise for *el Profesor*?'

'Oh yes,' Guzmán said, taking a drink from the tray of a passing waiter, 'he was choked.'

Peralta looked around the room. Repeated images of the killing came back to him. His palms were slick with sweat and the nausea had returned.

'I'll see you shortly,' Carrero said to Guzmán. 'The *Caudillo* will be in very soon.'

Carrero sauntered across the room, drawing upon a whole repertoire of insincerity as he moved amongst the guests, greeting everyone but avoiding conversation.

Guzmán finished his drink and reached for another as the waiter passed. He emptied the glass, all the while keeping his eyes on Carrero Blanco. 'Cunt.'

'Maybe you should ease up on the drink until you've seen the *Caudillo*, sir,' Peralta said, instantly regretting it as he saw the change in Guzmán's expression. Guzmán leaned forwards, his face in Peralta's, his breath nuanced by the wide variety of drinks he had downed in the short time since they arrived.

'Once we're married, *Teniente*, you can talk to me like that. Until then, I advise you to go and fu—'

'*Comandante* Guzmán,' a shrill voice interrupted. Guzmán turned. Franco was wearing one of his many dress uniforms: tonight he was a full general, his spindly legs accentuated by riding boots.

'*Excelencia*.' Guzmán stood at attention.

Franco held out his hands. *Like the Pope*, Peralta thought as the dictator took both of Guzmán's big paws and then dropped them after a cursory shake. Two sycophants stood at the *Caudillo*'s heels, fawning and smiling in unison with him.

'It has been what, five years?' Franco asked. 'A long time. We're all getting older.'

'Yet you look so very fit, *Excelencia*,' one of the sycophants echoed dutifully.

'Remarkably so,' the other added in a rapid extemporisation.

'If you feel older, *Excelencia*, one imagines it's because you're carrying the cares of the country on those shoulders,' Guzmán said solemnly. Peralta looked at him, surprised by his sudden air of gravitas. The sycophants shook their heads in disagreement.

'You are as ever, *Comandante*, utterly to the point. And correct, of course.' Franco beamed. 'The weight of such responsibility wears a man down.'

'Yet one cannot escape destiny,' Guzmán said solemnly. 'And belated congratulations on your first grandchild, *Excelencia*. I trust she and her mother are doing well?'

Franco allowed himself a smile and patted Guzmán on the arm. 'Carmencita. A lovely child. And my little Nenuca, so proud and happy. Children are our gift to the future, Guzmán. You should have some.'

Guzmán smiled back. 'If work gave me time for such pleasures, *Excelencia*, no doubt I would. But...' He made an expansive gesture of helplessness.

Franco nodded sagely. 'I know, Guzmán, I know. For some of us life is mapped out in our duties. My entire life is one of work and meditation.'

Those around nodded in solemn accord. Guzmán's heavy face became heavier and more intense. *Your entire life has been spent furthering your career*, he thought. *No stone unturned in the pursuit of power, no trough you haven't dipped your snout in. An example to us all.*

Peralta noticed Carrero Blanco hovering behind Franco. The dictator turned, enabling Carrero to mutter something into his ear without the others hearing. Franco shook his head. Carrero nodded and stepped back in an exaggeratedly formal gesture of subservience and made his way across the room to a group of men in uniform.

'Now, Guzmán,' Franco said, 'a word in private if I may? Excuse us, gentlemen.'

Guzmán followed the *generalísimo* as he moved away from Peralta and the sycophants. Guzmán was aware of the envious gazes, the muttered, perplexed comments. It was hard enough for decent Christian businessmen to gain an audience with the *Caudillo* these days – unless he wanted a favour – yet this large policeman with his oiled untidy hair and his cheap suit had cornered Franco's attention.

Standing near the buffet, Peralta observed the thinly veiled hostility of many of those around him to Guzmán's audience with Franco. Then Peralta saw General Valverde. No thinly veiled hostility there: the general's florid face was set in a mask of pure hatred, his hard eyes following Guzmán and the *Caudillo* with malevolent intensity as they crossed the room.

Franco stopped in a remote corner, far enough away from the crowds to ensure no one would hear their conversation. Guzmán handed his glass to one of the passing waiters, noticing how discreetly Franco's bodyguards took up strategic positions around them without infringing upon the dictator's conversation. Civilians would not have even noticed their positioning, Guzmán noted, seeing two of the men had a direct line of fire at him without the risk of Franco coming between Guzmán and their bullets. Very professional, Guzmán thought, approvingly.

'You've noticed my faithful protectors.' Franco smiled.

Guzmán nodded. 'They do a very good job, Your Excellency.'

'Sadly necessary, *Comandante*. As you in particular know, there are those who would still challenge the Head of State's right to govern. A right bestowed by God himself and they still seek to usurp that.'

'Quite so,' Guzmán agreed.

'You took care of that reprobate they called *el Profesor*?' Franco asked.

'Personally. As always.'

Franco's face was deadpan as he spoke. 'And he was specially dealt with?'

'He was indeed, *Excelencia*.'

'May I ask how?' Again, no flicker of an expression that would indicate interest or, in fact, any emotion.

Guzmán shrugged. 'I gave him a necktie.' *But then you ordered it, Excellency.*

'With your own hands?'

'These very hands, *Excelencia*.'

Franco raised his eyebrows. 'Did he suffer?'

'No more than he deserved.'

Again the cold stare. 'Well, he's now being judged and dealt with for all eternity. The country is all the better for his removal. You did well, Guzmán.'

'You're too kind, *Excelencia*. I did my job.'

'As you always have. And we are grateful. Many these days have lost the notion of duty. Of fidelity to the cause. The cause, Guzmán. We must never let ourselves be distracted. Which is why you are so useful to us.'

I wonder when he first started using the royal 'we,' Guzmán thought.

'When people forget their values,' Franco continued, 'when they forget their place in society, their obligations, their commitments, when they forget the natural order of things, that's when the forces of godlessness thrive. Only the memory of what we were, what we are and what we shall be can hold the dark forces of Freemasonry, Protestantism, Libertarianism and the social cancer of democracy at bay. And you, Guzmán, play a vital part in the preservation of that memory. It's a hard road to follow, although God knows I've led the way. But others must follow, and you, Guzmán, have followed loyally. You and those like you, they remind the weak and the feckless. What is history, Guzmán, but memory? And the light of that memory must constantly shine upon those who would rather forget and slink back into the darkness. Once vanquished, the beaten must always remain so.'

Guzmán nodded. Across the room, Peralta was giving them furtive glances. Further away, Valverde glared at them.

'Loyalty has been at the heart of the Cause, Guzmán. Not all are as loyal as you. Even those who have done very well in our service, those who have most reason to remain loyal – even those at the highest level – some of them have started to forget who put them there and gave them what they have.'

Guzmán's mind raced. *Does he mean me? No, he wouldn't give me a speech. I'd be dealt with elsewhere. Maybe he wants someone taking care of – but then he wouldn't ask himself.*

'Let me be candid,' Franco said abruptly. 'Give me your opinion.'

'Of course, *Excelencia*,' Guzmán said.

'Valverde. *Capitán-General* of Madrid. Sterling war record. But can I trust him, *Comandante*? In your opinion?'

Guzmán was not one to sweat under pressure. Yet he felt beads of perspiration around his collar. *Shit. Do I mention the Dominicans? The pharmaceutical trade? The money? Especially the money.*

'I'm only a mere *comandante*, Excellency. It's not for me to assess the *Caudillo's* general staff.'

'Enough of that, Guzmán. It's your job, you know that. No false modesty. You've known me a long time. If I ask you something, it's because I want a reply.'

Not true, Guzmán thought. *Usually, you want the reply you thought of before asking.*

'*Capitán-General* Valverde is an honourable man—' he began.

'Yes or no, Guzmán.' Franco's impassive face hardly moved as he said the words.

'No.' Guzmán said, 'I wouldn't trust him. But I would say that, *Excelencia*. I hardly trust anyone. For me people are guilty until proven innocent.'

Franco's face twitched in a slight smile. 'That maxim has served you well, Guzmán. Yes. I think it's the way I view Valverde. He's always been one of those people whose ambitions are far in excess of their talents.'

Pots calling kettles, Guzmán thought. 'Lately, he's been very concerned about a gang of Dominicans,' he added.

'Dominicans?' Franco snapped.

'A bunch of criminals who arrived with the trade mission from the US. They seem unlikely businessmen to me. The general thinks they're trying to interfere with his interests.'

'Ah. I hope he isn't thinking of doing anything that might interfere with the cordial atmosphere of the trade talks?'

'Not that I'm aware of, *Excelencia*.'

'If he does, Guzmán, I'll want to know about it. We'd take a dim view of that.'

'Of course.'

'Has Valverde said anything about these talks? I know he strongly favours foreign investment. The problem is, I think he'd like that investment to be made to his own bank account.'

'I know he's a supporter of economic change and reform.'

Franco frowned. 'That's well known, although he's always careful to express his opinions moderately. I would be very interested if he starts to talk about political change.'

'The general did speak of the time when your stewardship of the nation would come to an end,' Guzmán said.

'Ah. And was he thinking of bringing it to an end himself?' Franco's mouth pursed.

'No, not that. Just that one day you would be gone and there would be others to take your place with different ideas.'

'Nothing more? Nothing about sedition or rebellion?'

'No, he said nothing of treachery. But he did add that I should choose my side in advance, *Excelencia*.'

'And did you, Guzmán?'

'I chose it long ago, *Excelencia*. The side of right. Your side. To the death.'

Franco smiled again. 'Of course. Excellent.' Looking beyond Guzmán he saw Carrero Blanco making subtle gestures with his watch. Clearly some appointment was being delayed by this impromptu chat with the *comandante*. Franco looked hard at Guzmán.

'These Dominicans. I want special surveillance on them.'

'*Muy bien*. Permanently, *Excelencia*?'

Franco's face betrayed a flicker of impatience. 'It's not a euphemism, Guzmán. Don't kill them. We need to know why they are here. If they're important to Valverde, they may be important to us.'

'But we could soon find out, *Excelencia*. We'll beat it out of them at the *comisaría*.' Guzmán could never see a reason for taking the long way around.

Franco shook his head. 'If they have come with the US trade delegation, Guzmán, then we must proceed carefully. We want to trade with the United States, not kill their citizens. Nothing must impede us in securing a trade agreement. Nothing. So make sure there is no trouble, *entiende?*'

Guzmán nodded. 'Surveillance it is, *Excelencia*.'

'Good. Well, it was a pleasure to see you again, *Comandante*. Remember what I said about kids – it's not too late to find yourself a good woman. But until you do,' he winked, 'remember what I always told the military cadets when I was in charge of the Military Academy. Always carry a condom.'

'As ever, wise advice, *Excelencia*. Thank you.'

'*De nada*, Guzmán,' Franco said pompously. 'In fact, I'll give you another bit of advice, do the football pools. I do. I enjoy them enormously. *Doña* Carmen often says I spend more time on them than affairs of state. You have to study form, you see. And you wouldn't believe the money you can win.' He winked. 'Until later, Guzmán.'

A slap on the arm and then Franco was walking across the room with Carrero Blanco, giving a regal wave as he went. Guzmán was watching him leave when Peralta appeared at his side, holding two glasses of wine. Guzmán took one without being asked and drank it. He thought for a second and then took the other glass and emptied that as well.

'I can hardly believe it,' Peralta half laughed, 'you and the *Caudillo*, chatting like bosom buddies. No wonder my uncle...' He stopped.

Guzmán's eyebrow raised in mock surprise. 'He worries that

Franco set me up in Madrid to keep an eye on him. I can't count the number of his own men he's had follow me round, trying to catch me plotting against him.'

'But if you are loyal to the *Caudillo*, how could my uncle dare touch you?'

'He wouldn't. Not publicly. But people have accidents. Until now, I hoped he was getting a little less paranoid, but things change...' He inclined his head, directing Peralta's gaze to a scowling Valverde, towering above two plump colonels, his uniform ablaze with medals. Guzmán raised his glass in salute and Valverde quickly turned back to his staff officers.

'Not a happy general, your uncle.'

'You're telling me,' Peralta sighed.

'Has he ever talked to you about his dealings in medicines?' Guzmán asked.

Peralta shook his head. 'No, but then he barely speaks to me anyway. All I know is what María tells me and that's very little. He's a director of the company which imports pharmaceuticals for hospitals – that's the extent of my knowledge. It seems a harmless sideline to me.'

Guzmán nodded. 'Harmless. Not been seriously ill lately, have you, *Teniente*?'

'No, thank God. No, I've been healthy all my life so far.'

'Do you like bullfighting?'

Peralta looked puzzled. 'Bullfighting? Well enough, I suppose. I rarely go. The general gets lots of complimentary tickets but none of them come my way. I listen to it on the radio when I can.'

'Do you remember Manolete?' Guzmán reached for two more drinks from a waiter's tray. He emptied the contents of one into the other and placed the empty glass on the tray.

'Manolete? Who doesn't? I was in my teens when he died but everyone said he was the greatest bullfighter who ever lived. They still show his fights sometimes at the cinema. He was sensational.'

'He was.' Guzmán nodded. 'It's a shame your uncle killed him.'

Peralta's jaw sagged. 'Are you joking?' he asked, already knowing Guzmán didn't joke.

'Not at all. Remember how he died after being gored at Linares?'

Peralta nodded: the photos of Manolete hanging from the bull's horn adorned most of the bars of Madrid.

'He died while they were sewing him up, *jefe*. He was gored in the femoral artery.'

'Not fatally.' Guzmán took a drink. 'He'd still be around today if it wasn't for your uncle's products.'

'What products?'

'Dried plasma,' Guzmán said. 'They needed to make it up there and then so they could give him a transfusion. If it had been untouched, things would have been fine. It wasn't and he was dead within minutes.'

'Untouched?' Peralta asked.

'What I mean is, just like a barman in a brothel, your uncle makes his products go further. Only instead of watering down the brandy, he adds something to the products to bulk them up.'

'And no one notices?'

'Of course they do but after that they frequently die.'

'And he does this with all the drugs he imports?'

'No. He can't risk a scandal. Some things he doesn't touch. Particularly drugs that are used on the bosses in the military or government ministers. You be careful next time you get a scratch, *Teniente*, that penicillin they give you might not be quite what you hoped.'

Peralta finished his drink. 'That's despicable.'

Guzmán smirked. 'Welcome to Spain, *señor*. Your uncle sells cut-price stuff to hospitals for the poor. The poor die. Only to be expected. That's what the poor do, isn't it? There's no fuss because no one really cares.'

'The poor might.'

'As I said, *Teniente*, this is Spain. No one gives a fuck about the poor.'

'But—' Peralta never finished his sentence because Guzmán

held up a great paw to silence him. Across the room Franco was bidding them all goodbye. A last regal wave and he was gone, leaving only the guests and their applause.

'You forgot to introduce me,' Peralta chided, hoping to lighten Guzmán's mood.

'I didn't forget,' Guzmán said, looking round for a waiter.

Franco's exit gave them licence to make inroads into the buffet. The catering staff exchanged a few knowing looks as the two policemen returned yet again to the table, but none were unwise enough to say anything. Guzmán ate because he was hungry and Peralta ate because he thought he might never see so much food in one place again. Roast chickens, mountains of chorizo, seafood vol-au-vents, each dish a revelation to a hungry man. Between mouthfuls of potato omelette, Peralta could even forget for a while the slaughter they had carried out only a few hours before. *That Guzmán carried out*, he reminded himself.

'I feel guilty you know,' Peralta said to Guzmán as they refilled their plates.

'Guilt? There's a strange thing to feel when you're stuffing your face,' Guzmán said.

'Yes, but I mean, María's at home with the kid and here I am making a pig of myself. She goes hungry sometimes to feed me and the little one.'

Guzmán laughed. 'Well take her something. One of these flunkeys could put you some stuff in a bag. I'm sure they're going to steal what's left at the end anyway. That's right, isn't it, my friend?'

The waiter looked round furtively. 'Certainly, sir. God helps them who help themselves, no?' And then, turning to Peralta, 'I'll make up a bag in the kitchen for the gentleman. Let me know when you're leaving, *señor*, and I'll bring it out for you.'

Certainly not, Peralta thought. *Take advantage of one's position when others are going hungry?* 'Thanks. I'll do that.'

'My name's Raoul, by the way, and if the gentleman should wish to show his appreciation by way of a small contribution...' Raoul smiled knowingly, rubbing his thumb and forefinger together.

'He wants a few pesetas,' Guzmán said. 'That right, Raoul?'

Raoul grinned. 'The gentleman is clearly a businessman. He knows how things work.'

Guzmán glared at the waiter. 'The gentleman is a policeman. And he understands the way things work only too well. Now piss off and bag up some of that food, Raoul.' Raoul was only too happy to follow Guzmán's order and slunk away, pale-faced, to the kitchens.

Guzmán looked at the *teniente*'s bulging cheeks and nodded approval. '*Hombre*. Get it down you while you can.'

'It means a lot to be able to eat all you want,' Peralta said. 'Did you ever go hungry?'

Guzmán bit into the pie in his hand. 'All the time. We never had enough food when I was a kid. My father was always out of work and my mother was too ugly to be a whore.'

Peralta looked to see if Guzmán was joking but Guzmán continued, 'We'd steal apples off the trees, eggs, the odd chicken. Like gypsies. In fact we'd steal off the gypsies if they had anything worth having.'

'*Jefe*, what about your new lady friend?' Peralta blurted, his face flushed with wine and food.

Guzmán looked at him blankly.

'The widow Martinez,' Peralta said. 'Take her some of this.' He beamed. 'A nice surprise. She'd be very impressed. That would keep you in her good books.'

Guzmán looked at him incredulously.

Peralta laughed. 'Christ, *jefe*, you're a one. Food's always a welcome gift. Everyone wants to eat.'

Guzmán still looked puzzled. 'I hadn't considered it, I must say.' He thought about it. 'This is your idea, *Teniente*. So if it goes wrong I'll blame you.'

Peralta nodded and went to tell Raoul to prepare another package. Raoul readily agreed, taking the opportunity to relieve Peralta of a few pesetas for his troubles.

The quiet murmur of the room was suddenly broken by

shouting and raised voices from the lobby. People running towards the main entrance. Guzmán reacted fast: most of the guests were straining their necks to see what was going on without wanting the discomfort of leaving their seats. But the noise sounded like trouble and trouble was Guzmán's speciality. He moved quickly and purposefully across the dance floor, tall and broad, drawn towards the sound of action. The *teniente* followed him, less purposeful, more angular and a good deal less threatening, his worn shoes slipping on the polished wooden floor.

Outside, the three policemen were refusing entrance to a group of swarthy, strangely dressed men. Peralta caught up with Guzmán. The *teniente* stared at the men in surprise.

'What are they wearing?' he muttered, taking in the peg-topped flapping trousers and exaggeratedly long jackets of the strangers.

'Zoot suits,' Guzmán said slowly. 'Younger *Yanquis* used to wear them during the war. I saw it on a newsreel. Some sort of fashion for young hoodlums and degenerates.'

The oddly dressed men were arguing loudly and vociferously as Guzmán and Peralta approached. Guzmán recognised them from Valverde's photographs. He could see the bald, bearded Melilla, the huge bulk and jug ears of the boxer, Sanchez. The languid wiry youth in a wide-brimmed hat and wearing sunglasses was Vasquez. As Guzmán studied them, Melilla started to push his way up the stairs. The others followed, jostling on the stairs behind Melilla who was now confronting the guards at the top of the staircase.

'Fuck you, man, fuck you.' Melilla was yelling abuse into the face of the policeman who had taken Guzmán and Peralta's weapons earlier. 'We got an invite, we're US citizens, man, we are *somebody*, not like you *nobodies*, so let us in, Don Jose. You don't want to mess with us.' He turned to grin at the others, a gold tooth glinting in the lamplight. The other Dominicans cackled encouragement.

'Sound like South Americans from the accent,' Peralta said quietly to Guzmán.

'To be precise, *Teniente*, I'd say the Dominican Republic,' Guzmán said. Peralta looked at him admiringly. He had so much to learn.

'Come on, we don't have all night, *señorito*.' The one with the sunglasses was practically face to face with the secret policeman. 'It's cold out here, man.'

'Yeah, where's the Spanish hospitality?' one of the others sniggered.

'You can't come in, this is a private reception,' the policeman said, uncertainly.

'That's where you're wrong, *señorito*,' the older one said, 'cos we're coming in and we got an invite from your very own Francine Franco himself. We're official, man.' Guzmán could see the man had an engraved invitation in his hand. He was also very drunk.

Suddenly Peralta stiffened. 'That one has a gun,' he muttered to Guzmán.

Guzmán instinctively reached under his left arm, only to caress the empty shoulder holster.

'Who's in charge here?' the older Dominican asked. 'Lemme speak to the *jefe*, the big *jefe*. I deal with the main man, don't waste my time with no hired helpers. Get me the organ grinder, not the monkey.' He grinned broadly, his gold front tooth twinkling.

'Yeah, I'd throw the man a banana but they ain't got no bananas in this country. They can't afford fruit, man,' the big boxer sneered before dissolving into intoxicated laughter.

'*Comandante* Guzmán. *Policía*,' Guzmán said loudly as he stepped toward the Dominicans.

The young man with the sunglasses and broad hat grinned mirthlessly up the stairs at Guzmán. 'Copper? Oh my, I'm gonna cry, man. The police is on us. Oh no.' He waved his hands, palms facing Guzmán.

'You're in a shitload of trouble, officer, if you don't let us in, man,' the older man said, this time his gold tooth flashing out of a snarl.

'I don't quite see how you work that out,' Guzmán said.

'Because there's six of us, man,' Goldtooth said. 'Why don't you find something else to do, while we make ourselves at home.'

More mirth. One of the other Dominicans burst into a loud cackle.

'See,' Goldtooth smiled threateningly, 'you be out of your depth here, man.' His left arm moved away from his side, drawing his jacket open to reveal a glimpse of the butt of a handgun stuck into his waistband.

Peralta was edging slowly forwards, trying to decide which of them he would try to grab if things turned ugly. He waited, hoping Guzmán would be able to resolve the situation or at least tell him what to do.

'Well, I do have other things to do,' Guzmán said in a conciliatory voice.

Peralta breathed more easily. Calm the situation, he thought. I remember this from the training at the *Academia*: defuse the situation, calm things down. Don't escalate the dispute.

Guzmán smiled, looking into Goldtooth's eyes. 'In fact I'm going to fuck your mother – once I've finished with your wife...' he paused, 'again.'

Goldtooth's eyes narrowed and he reached inside his jacket. There was a flurry of movement as the three policemen who had been on the door drew their weapons.

Goldtooth moved his hand from his belt. 'Hey, we're only here to party, Don Jose.'

Guzmán's fist smashed into the side of Goldtooth's face. The man flew backwards down the steps, sprawling amongst his companions. He lay motionless for a moment, the centre of a sudden whirl of activity as the Dominicans gathered around him, trying to get him to his feet, at the same time shouting curses up at Guzmán. Guzmán started down the steps towards them. Peralta followed.

'What the hell is going on?' It was Valverde, storming through the doorway, red-faced, riding boots clattering on the stone, medals glittering across his chest. Behind came him a gaggle of subordinates, also replete with rows of medals, although to a lesser extent than their general. At Valverde's side was a tall, middle-aged man in a well-cut suit, his dark hair short in a *Yanqui* crew cut. The man stepped past Guzmán and looked down the steps where Goldtooth was struggling to his feet, having staunched the flow of blood from his nose with a large silk handkerchief.

'What occurs here?' the man said in stilted Spanish.

'Ask him, man, he started it. All we want to do is party. And we are *invited*,' Goldtooth snarled, struggling to get at Guzmán. The other Dominicans restrained the incensed Goldtooth, his fury increased by Guzmán's mocking smile.

The man turned to Guzmán. 'I am Alfred Positano, US Trade Advisor to the Embassy. These men are part of the United States trade delegation. I can vouch for them. They are US citizens. I demand that you do not interfere with them.'

'These men have every right to be here, *Comandante*,' Valverde snapped, 'I want to know why they have been denied entrance. The *Caudillo* himself invited the delegation tonight.'

'They weren't invited to carry firearms,' Guzmán said, his eyes still locked on Goldtooth. The Dominican finally looked away and sneered under his breath to one of his companions.

'Weapons?' Valverde seemed surprised. 'No, that is of course out of the question. You must leave any weapons here, *señores*. The *comandante* is correct.'

A chorus of protest from the Dominicans melted into surly silence as the trade advisor said something to them. With a shrug, Goldtooth led the way, handing his pistol over before flouncing past Guzmán.

'We gonna meet again, man,' he hissed.

'I guarantee it,' Guzmán said without turning.

Now disarmed, the Dominicans swaggered through into the reception, their shouts and laughter echoing in the marble hallway.

'I trust we shall have no further trouble tonight?' the American said, looking first at Valverde and then more inquisitively at Guzmán.

'Please accept *Comandante* Guzmán's apologies for this misunderstanding,' Valverde said ingratiatingly.

The tall American nodded and went back into the building. Guzmán turned to Valverde. Three metres away, Peralta could see Guzmán's anger in his rigid posture and the big clenched fists.

'Armed, drunk inbreds coming into the same building as the *Caudillo*?' Guzmán spluttered. 'Have you taken leave of your senses?'

Now it was Valverde's turn to explode. 'How dare you talk to me like that, *Comandante*. I have a good mind to—'

'Enough.' Guzmán cut across him. Valverde's mouth opened in surprise at the discourtesy. 'I take it the *Caudillo*'s left the premises?' Guzmán addressed the question to one of the policemen on the door, further incensing the general. The man nodded and Guzmán turned back to Valverde. 'Now I know those lunatics can do no harm, I'll be on my way,' he said.

'This is intolerable,' Valverde growled in a low voice as the secret police returned to their positions on the door. 'You've gone too far. Those men were invited.'

'Those men were all carrying weapons,' Guzmán said coldly. 'I doubt the *Caudillo* intended to turn this reception into a Wild West show. Nor that you would permit it – since you're the host.'

'Franco had already left,' Valverde said icily. 'The Americans are very important to the *Caudillo* and are here to do business. It's unthinkable they intended any harm here. These *Yanquis* do things differently, that's all. You will have some respect, Guzmán, and you will obey orders. I saw you sucking up to Franco. Why the fuck he indulges you like that I don't know.' He lowered his voice. 'I want you to deal with those bastards on the street, you fool. Not in the middle of an official reception. Officially, we welcome them, Guzmán.'

'I could hardly let them carry arms in Franco's presence,' Guzmán said.

'Perhaps the *Caudillo* would take a different view of you if he knew how much cash you took from me,' Valverde sneered.

Guzmán inclined his head in a mocking bow. '*A sus ordenes, mi General.*'

Stepping back into the lobby, Guzmán retrieved his coat. He looked round for Peralta and saw him coming down the corridor holding two bulging bags of food.

'Nearly forgot,' Peralta grinned.

Guzmán walked to the door, standing to one side as Valverde came back in, tossing his cigar stub down the steps in a fury. He looked at Peralta in passing.

'Fucking clown. You can stay in that police station until you retire, you halfwit.'

Guzmán watched the general flounce back inside the building. He turned to the officer in charge of the door and asked for their weapons. 'So what was your plan for dealing with those Caribbean pimps?' Guzmán asked the officer.

The man looked uncomfortable. 'Sorry, sir. We'd no idea they'd be armed. But orders were to let them in.'

'Whose orders?' Guzmán lit a cigarette.

'The general, sir. A direct order.'

Guzmán tilted his head back, inhaling deeply. He nodded. '*Buenas noches, Capitán.*' Distracted, he threw his cigarette, underhand, into the mound of snow by the gate.

'Give me a cigarette, *Teniente*,' he snapped.

'I'm out of them, sir. Sorry.'

In the car Guzmán sank back into the leather seat, deep in thought.

'Where to, *jefe*?' the driver asked.

'Plaza Mayor,' Guzmán said, preoccupied.

'Sir, what about your date?' Peralta was sitting, cradling the two large bags of food.

'What?'

'Your date, sir, with your…lady friend. You said you were seeing her later.' He shook the bag as a reminder.

Guzmán's heavy eyes flickered. 'Ah yes. My lady friend.' He took the gunny sack from Peralta. Through the rough fabric he could feel pies, packages of sandwiches, paper bags full of pastries – even a bottle of something. Clearly Raoul had been satisfied with his tip. Or, more likely, had been concerned to satisfy the two policemen. Guzmán felt amused at how the notion of police aroused sudden respect. If he were to spell out what he actually did, how much more compliant would they be then?

'Lavapiés,' Guzmán told the driver. 'No, stop.'

The driver obeyed without question, pulling the car over to the side of the road.

'Sorry, *Teniente*,' Guzmán said, 'I don't have the time to drop you off. You'll have to get a tram or a cab. I'll see you in the morning.'

Guzmán sank back into his seat. Clearly the conversation was at an end. Peralta opened the car door and looked out uncertainly at the thick snow on the kerbside. He stepped from the car, grimacing as his feet sank deep into the snow.

'Sir, I don't suppose—'

The door slammed behind him.

Guzmán gave the address to the driver and the car glided away into the dim snow-light of Madrid.

Peralta began to walk, struggling to stay on his feet in the thick snow.

MADRID 1953, CALLE DE LA TRIBULETE

Señora Martinez opened the door. Framed in faint light from the room behind her, she was pale and her eyes were red.

'*Comandante.*'

'You didn't think I'd come?'

'No, not at all, I knew you would. Come in.'

Guzmán took off his hat and stepped onto the mat, stamping snow from his shoes. He put down the gunny sack. 'There's some food in here. From the reception. It's good stuff. I thought you might like it. You and the boy.'

'Thank you.' She was polite. Polite, he noted, not grateful.

'Franco's own chef made some of that.' Guzmán felt a sudden need to emphasise the importance of his gift.

'Then I look forward to eating it.' Her voice was soft. 'It will be the first time the *Caudillo* has provided anything for this family.'

Guzmán looked at her. Had she really just said that? In some circles it would be enough to count as sedition.

Señora Martinez gestured towards the armchair. 'Please sit down, *Comandante.*'

Guzmán took off his coat and handed it to her. He sat down. She remained at his side, holding his coat like a waitress. Guzmán raised an eyebrow. 'What?'

She pointed to the hat on his lap. 'Shall I take that?'

He handed it to her brusquely. She moved to the small hallway and hung up his hat and coat carefully. Guzmán watched the way her hips moved in the shabby dress. He was not encouraged.

Señora Martinez sat by the table, not far from Guzmán. She sat demurely, hands folded in her lap. Guzmán saw how chapped and raw her hands were.

'Is the boy in bed?' he asked.

'He's staying with a friend tonight.'

There was an awkward silence. The whole situation was awkward for *Señora* Martinez, but Guzmán too was uncomfortable. He found himself disconcerted by this tired, shabby woman who, for all her fearful acquiescence this afternoon, now looked at him without averting her gaze. Her eyes were pale blue, he noted. This was not how he had envisaged things, sitting in tense silence maintaining sitting-room formality. It was certainly nothing like the brothels he usually frequented. This was a proper woman. One who would expect small talk. He had met such women but now he was visiting one socially. He corrected himself. Almost socially.

'Would the *comandante* care for a drink?' *Señora* Martinez asked, maintaining her formal manner. 'I have some wine.'

'By all means,' Guzmán said, 'but, *por dios*, can't you address me as *tú*? Why so formal?'

Señora Martinez looked at Guzmán. Her eyes were the only part of her that did not seem faded or exhausted. 'I would prefer to use *usted, Comandante*, and I would prefer the *comandante* to do the same.'

'*Como usted quiere.*' Guzmán nodded, unable to break the icy barrier separating them. This was a new feeling for him. With anyone else he would have reacted differently. But this delicate woman interested him. That in itself was a novelty.

'A glass of wine. Yes, thank you, *Señora.*'

She went into the kitchen and returned with two glasses of red wine. Guzmán took one, thankful to have something to occupy himself with. He took a drink. The wine was cheap and sharp: in a restaurant Guzmán would have sent it back. He drank half the glass quickly.

'Do you work, *señora*?' he asked.

Señora Martinez took a sip of wine and placed her glass on a small mat on the table. Her actions were controlled and contained, enacted within her own world, a world apart from Guzmán's.

'Actually I have two jobs,' she said quietly. 'I work at a fishmonger's in the mornings and during the afternoon I help out at a grocery.'

No wonder she looks so tired, Guzmán thought.

He looked past her, noting the photograph of her husband had gone and in its place there was now a gaudy crucifix; Christ's wounds were highlighted in some sort of reflective paint, flickering in the weak light.

'It must be hard work?' Guzmán's thoughts were reverting to the Dominicans, wishing he had been able to deal with them properly on the steps of the *capitanía*.

'It's the only work I can get. People don't want to employ the widow of a...'

'Red?'

'Yes.' Her voice was sharp.

If she became any more brittle, Guzmán thought, she would shatter at the first touch. Not that he had any desire to touch her right now, he realised. 'But you found work anyway? That took some doing, *señora*.'

He saw tears welling in her pale eyes.

'It won't last, *Comandante*. They offer employment but then, when you start work, they begin to suggest you do things.' Her voice broke and she threw her head back, as if shaking those thoughts away. When she spoke again her voice was stronger.

'They expect things. The sort of things men make women do if they can. When their wives are out or away. They think a widow is always desperate for a man. And if they think you're a Red, they also think you're a whore.'

'I thought you Reds believed in free love, no marriage – that sort of thing?'

Her reaction startled him. Her pale eyes flashed, bright with anger, and she leaned forward, staring at him fiercely.

'*Jesús Cristo*, you call me a Red. *Bien*. Go ahead. They all do. Because of what my husband did. It's easy for you to judge, *Comandante*, like all men. When the war started, we'd been married a week. We lived here in Madrid. I had nothing to do with politics, and my husband very little. But Madrid was Republican. We saw the killings here, saw them kill the soldiers who rose up to support Franco. They burned the Montaña Barracks, slaughtered the garrison. There were patrols all over, seeking out those on the right. You were on their side or you weren't. Do you think we could have just said we wanted to stay out of it? Asked if it would it be all right if we didn't join in the war because we were on honeymoon? Do you?'

Her voice had risen. Guzmán saw the anger on her face. Had she reacted like that earlier in the day, he would have slapped her. Now he thought it admirable.

'You didn't want to support the Reds?' Guzmán said.

'I didn't want to support the war.' She looked fiercely at him. 'Do you know what I wanted? I wanted a proper honeymoon, but I never got it. My husband went straight into the militia. He decided it was for the best, that he should show willing. He marched off thinking France, America or Britain would soon step in, and then the fighting would soon be over.'

'And he never came back?'

'No. As far as I know, he was killed after being captured.'

'So many were, *señora*,' Guzmán said, speaking from experience. A lot of it.

'And so many were left behind, *Comandante*. Like me, and now with my poor sister's child to look after. And what are we? *Rojos*. So despicable people won't speak to us but not so despicable that men don't see us as easy meat, as women who will save them the cost of a whore. Men like...' She paused, suddenly aware she had said too much but nonetheless unable to curb her anger.

'Me,' Guzmán said, finishing his wine. It really was piss, he thought.

'You. Yes.'

She slumped in her chair, the anger draining from her. Her hands draped loosely in her lap and her face was pale and angular in the half light. Guzmán got up and walked across the room to the kitchen. He brought back the bottle of wine and filled their glasses, careful not to spill any. He placed the bottle on the table. *Señora* Martinez looked at him. 'Put it on a mat,' she said, 'you'll leave a mark.'

To his surprise, Guzmán did so. 'So you have to sleep with the grocer and the fishmonger to get work?' he asked.

'*Mierda*, do you really take me for someone who'd do that?' Once more the flame flickered in her mist-coloured eyes and her cheeks flushed with anger. A tendril of tawny hair fell across her forehead. Animated like that, Guzmán thought she was lovely. Anger was a marvellous thing.

'I was only asking,' he snapped. 'You were telling me. How do I know if you don't tell me?'

'I don't sleep with anyone,' *Señora* Martinez said, her voice was tired now. 'Not the grocer, not the fishmonger, not anyone. I haven't slept with anyone since my husband. And even then, he went away so soon...' Once more she struggled against incipient tears. And won, Guzmán noticed. He poured another drink. He inclined the bottle towards her glass. She shook her head.

'*Bueno*,' she said. 'You didn't come here to hear my life story, I'm sure. You made it clear what you wanted earlier today. Very clear.'

'I was angry then,' Guzmán said, defensively, 'your attitude annoyed me.'

Señora Martinez sat up straight in her chair. She stared at Guzmán. 'Listen, if I had to do this just to save myself, you could forget it. I'd rather go to prison. Or be shot. I wouldn't give in. But for the child...'

'I understand.'

She laughed. 'I very much doubt it, *Comandante*. If you understood, you wouldn't ask me to be your whore.'

'I wasn't expecting that,' Guzmán said. It was exactly what he had expected.

'No, of course not. You're not paying. In any case, you'll have to guide me, *Comandante*. I'm afraid my inexperience will be a great disappointment to you. But I'm sure the conquest of another Red will make up for that. So how do we begin? Do your whores lead you to the bedroom? Is that what you're waiting for?'

Guzmán was deeply uncomfortable now. Not only was *Señora* Martinez unsettling him but his concentration was slipping, his mind drifting back to the Dominicans. Giving this exhausted woman instructions in sex was the last thing he wanted to do.

'Firstly we'd have to agree a price,' he said, glancing over to his hat and coat hanging in the hall.

'You said if I... complied, you wouldn't take my nephew away. That was the price we agreed, I assume.'

'Yes.' Guzmán nodded. 'Then we'd have a drink.'

'Which we have.'

'And then,' Guzmán said, 'I'd watch you undress until you were naked.' *Although that would up the price considerably*, he recalled. And even then, many whores were reluctant to undress completely. Some of them were quite respectable.

Señora Martinez jerked as if she had been given an electric shock. '*Sinvergüenza. Desnuda?* Have you no shame, *Comandante?* Even my own husband never asked me that. You really have got a low opinion of me. It's too much.' Her head sank for a moment. 'Too much.' She took a deep breath.

'You asked me how the whores would do it. *Nada más.* I didn't mean to imply... besides, *señora*, no one could be naked in this apartment. It's freezing.'

'So how do you expect me to act as a whore for you, *Comandante?*'

Guzmán sighed. He had had enough of this. He got up from the chair. '*Señora*, you don't have to do anything. I can see now I was wrong about you. Misguided in the war, yes – but that was your husband's choice. And afterwards, I can see you did what you had to, in order to look after the child. I misjudged you.' It was a weak thing to say. But now, facing her, it was how he felt.

She stood up. Her face had softened a little, but only because she feared he was still a threat, he realised.

'Look, don't take my boy,' she said. 'You can do what you want. Anything. I'm sorry, I have a temper sometimes.'

'I've no intention of taking the boy.' Guzmán began to put on his coat. *Or sleeping with you*, he thought. *Bloody hell, I bet her husband shot himself rather than put up with her for a lifetime. And a temper as well? Hostia!*

'You won't take Roberto? You promise?'

'Absolutely, *señora. Le juro.*'

Now she was confused. 'I don't understand you, *Comandante.*'

'That makes two of us, *señora*.' Guzmán put on his hat and opened the door.

Her hand closed on his arm. 'You really mean it? About not taking Roberto?'

Guzmán turned, her hand still tight on his arm. It was not an unpleasant feeling. He had an idea. 'There's one thing I would ask, *señora.*'

Her face fell. 'Which is?'

'I'd like to see you again. All I ever see are policemen, prisoners and the occasional whore.' He noticed her expression. 'Socially. No obligation, I promise you. A meal, maybe the cinema?' He had said it. He felt a fool but he had said it. Now she would mock him. Fuck it, he'd tried.

She was standing close. Guzmán looked down at her, her pale face, the threadbare clothes, the defiant blue eyes now wide with surprise.

'Well, if it was really like that. I never get asked out. Not in a decent manner, anyway. If you mean it, that is?'

'I do, *señora.*' Guzmán handed her his card. 'Call me. When it suits you, of course.'

'Very well. I will, *Comandante.*'

'One more thing.' Guzmán took out his notebook and pencil. 'This grocer and the fishmonger, give me their addresses.'

'Why?' Her voice was suspicious again.

'Because,' Guzmán said, 'I'll see they won't bother you again with improper demands. In fact, *Señora* Martinez, they'll probably treat you as if you were a member of Franco's family after I've had a word.'

He wrote down the names and addresses in his notebook and stepped out into the cold darkness of the landing. *Señora* Martinez brushed past him, and switched on the miserable electric light. She smelled of soap.

'*Buena noches, Comandante.*'

The door closed before he could reply.

His feet echoed on the stone stairs as he made his way down to the street. *What the fuck happened?* he wondered. He had asked her out. A decent woman. On a date. *Hostia, all things are possible.* Across the street the lights of the Hispano-Suiza flashed as the driver saw Guzmán leave the building.

I could have made a fool of myself, he thought, still unsure as to whether he had left Alicia Martinez's apartment or she had got rid of him. *But she agreed.* The car quietly drifted to the kerbside, the powerful engine humming. He needed a drink. It was late, but not so late he couldn't find somewhere where he could drink enough to clear his mind of the formidable *Señora* Martinez.

MADRID 1953, PLAZA MAYOR

The car dropped Guzmán on the edge of the Plaza Mayor. It was late and only a couple of bars were still open, their windows glimmering pale defiance to the icy night. Guzmán watched the car drive off. He was angry. Angry because he had been brooding again about the Dominicans. He felt the rage run through him, pictured acts of violence in repeated sequences of intensifying ferocity until he felt his veins bulge as the anger pounded through him. He stopped by the statue of Felipe Tres in the centre of the cobbled square and looked round. Desolate and icy, the square was empty, with no sign of anyone following him. Guzmán's shoes crunched on the snow-covered cobbles as he headed for the nearest bar. The bar was dingy, almost empty, the air blurred by a fug of stale tobacco smoke. Two elderly men in heated discussion by a window. The barman was sitting behind the bar, his ear against a radio turned so low Guzmán could barely hear the martial music coming from it. He ordered a large brandy and sat nursing it. The old men's voices faded to a dull murmur as Guzmán began to think over the events of the day.

Something was troubling him and it wasn't – unlike for Peralta – killing fifteen men in cold blood. Things were happening. Things Guzmán sensed were wrong even though he was not sure why. Valverde was becoming a problem and Guzmán cursed himself for allowing the general to draw him further into his grubby world of patronage and bribery. On the other hand, he reflected, he had stashed the general's money away and there was no proof he had taken it. Taking a bribe alone wasn't going to bring him down – that depended on who the bribe came from, and what it was for. And he knew if Valverde fell from grace, those associated with him might also find themselves in a similar position, war hero or not.

And then there was *Señora* Martinez. How in hell had he thought she would be worth getting into bed? Jesus. No wonder her husband joined up so quickly. Probably wanted to get away while he still had his balls. Still, she was some woman when she got angry. She'd stood up to Guzmán better than most men ever did. When she talked to him, she looked him in the eye. That too had impressed him. And though she was no whore, she would have done what he wanted to save the boy. She wasn't a Red. Just a survivor. And a hard worker. Those were impressive credentials in his book, particularly for a woman. She interested him.

He stared into his brandy, occasionally shifting his gaze to the glittering collection of bottles on the shelves behind the bar. *Valencia – the original Scotch Whiskí*, read one label, in Spanish. Guzmán stared at it and then at the mirror behind. Outside, a man in a dark coat and hat walked slowly past the window. Guzmán lifted his glass and turned to offer a toast to the watcher in the shadows but he melted back into the night, stepping outside the weak pool of light radiating from the bar. *Fuck him*, Guzmán thought. Then the rage flared up and the urge to kill flowed through him, an urge too strong to resist. He had no wish to resist it.

He finished the brandy and threw a handful of coins onto the bar. He moved quickly, opening and closing the bar door behind him without making any noise. Outside, the columned walkway running around the outside of the square was empty.

Guzmán listened, his hand reaching inside his coat for the heavy automatic. He held the gun low by his side, and took a step forward towards the column in front of him, his slow careful footsteps sounding ridiculously loud in the silence. He swung the pistol up as he turned the corner of the column. Nothing. Guzmán looked again in the direction the man had been heading.

There was no one there.

He had no intention of sneaking from column to column around the entire square and decided to return to the bar. As he turned back, the light in the bar was suddenly extinguished.

Guzmán heard a metallic click somewhere in the darkness of the night-shadowed square and hurled himself to the ground, rolling behind the pillar as a blast of machine-gun fire tore across the spot where he had been standing a moment earlier. Glass shattered and the whine of ricochets echoed around the walkway. Guzmán edged closer to the column to try to see where the gunfire had come from. A second burst of fire rattled across the cobbles a metre away from his hiding place, throwing up a mist of stinging stone as the bullets ricocheted once more, their banshee whine echoing in the darkness.

Guzmán stood with his back to the column, straining to locate his attackers before he made his move. And he would make his move, he knew, because staying here only invited them to take up better positions. He ducked low, moving around the column, his pistol extended, covering the dark square. Nothing. He swivelled back, scanning the walkway on the far side of the square. The night was freezing, but for Guzmán nothing existed outside the immediate parameters of his senses, a world viewed through the sight of the large pistol as he searched the square for movement.

Behind the cover of the pillar, Guzmán scanned the walkway to left and right. If they were doing it properly, there would be at least three of them. One somewhere across the square to keep him pinned down and two more to slip round on the flanks. He decided to make a move. Lights had flickered on around the square after the initial burst of gunfire but they had gone off again quickly. No one wanted to get involved in something that was none of their business. Certainly no one had phoned the police – there would have been the bells of the patrol cars by now – meaning Guzmán could expect no help. Which was as it had always been, he reflected, wiping sweat from his heavy face.

Crouching low, Guzmán moved quickly to the next pillar. It only took a few seconds, running at a crouch with his automatic extended towards the darkened square. Nothing. His breath had quickened and he made himself take deep slow breaths as he prepared to continue his dash to the next pillar. Three pillars to go.

About thirty metres, and then he would reach the corner of the square. Working his way up that side, he would be able to reach the Calle Mayor and then make his way back down to the Puerta del Sol. He took another deep breath, straining to detect a sound that would indicate where they were. If they were still there. He moved again, crouching and aiming. To his left, the comforting reassurance of the bars and shops; ahead, the narrow walkway, striped by indistinct light. *No retreat, only the advance.* He passed one pillar and continued forward, legs aching from the constant crouching and kneeling, fighting to control his rage.

The gunfire was painfully loud and seemed to come from every direction. Windows to his left shattered, great shards of glass crashing on the stone floor of the walkway. Bullets ricocheted along the roof of the walkway, exploding against the darkened stones. Guzmán hit the ground and a red-hot pain tore across his leg just above the knee. He cursed as a second burst of machine-gun fire came from the direction of the statue in the centre of the square. A hail of bullets screamed less than a metre above Guzmán as he hugged the ground. The shooting stopped. Guzmán peered towards the dark mass of the statue and saw a slight movement in the darkness. He fired two shots, harsh whiplash cracks accompanied by the tinkling of the ejected cartridges.

Footsteps behind him.

Guzmán rolled onto his back, sitting up in a sudden swift motion, bringing his pistol to bear on the man coming around the corner of the square towards him. Guzmán fired, hitting him in the chest and sending him reeling back into a teetering stack of chairs outside a café. The chairs clattered noisily in all directions. The man lay where he fell.

Guzmán began moving quickly to the far corner of the square, still intent on reaching Calle Mayor. He heard movement and huddled behind the nearest pillar as a raking machine-gun blast carved across the stone, destroying the windows of the shops behind. Guzmán dived to the ground and fired three shots in the direction of the machine gun. There was an angry curse in the darkness and Guzmán heard something heavy and metallic hit the cobbles. As he lay on the icy stones, Guzmán saw a dim shape hobbling across the square and raised the Browning, steadying his right hand with his left to improve his aim. He squeezed the trigger.

'*Hijo de la gran puta.*' Guzman grunted.

There was no shot, just the sharp sound of the hammer on the empty chamber. The magazine was empty. Guzmán struggled to his feet, aware for the first time of the blood running down his leg. Barbed pain lanced through the wound as he tried to pursue the fleeing man. And then a bellowed curse as he lost his footing on a patch of ice and fell heavily to the ground. With no time to reload, Guzmán gripped the pistol by its barrel as a make-do bludgeon. The expected attack never came and as he hauled himself up, he heard footsteps fading in the darkness on the far side of the square.

Leaning against a pillar, he reloaded the automatic. The night was glassily silent. He heard only a faint ringing in his ears caused by the percussion of gunfire, and tasted the familiar astringent smell of cordite in the still air. Pistol first, he moved cautiously down the walkway towards the café where the dead man was lying. Where he should have been lying. In the shadows it was possible to make out the skeletal wreckage of the chairs but there was no trace of the dead man. Guzmán took out his lighter and snapped it into flame. The café doorway was illuminated in flickering light, turning the objects around him into vague monochrome etchings. Blood stains glinted black against the night-glazed flagstones. A large dark pool marked the spot where the man had fallen. Slick wavering tracks led away down the side of the square where someone had dragged him – he hadn't walked away by himself, Guzmán knew, given the amount of blood left behind. In the faint light, he saw the long shattered row of windows around the edge of the square.

They were good, Guzmán thought, as he made his way from the square down a series of side streets, pistol held by his side. Professional and daring as well. They had dragged the dead man away quickly and very quietly. Too quiet for his liking, since he had been unable to tell if they were Dominicans or not. Guzmán would have preferred that they were. But from the noise they had made earlier at Valverde's reception, he doubted if they could have stayed so silent during the attack. He looked round again, inhaling the thin sharp air, his breath a steaming halo in the pale street light.

The pain in his leg was very bad. How could a shard of glass hurt so much? It would slow him down, he thought angrily. He thought about returning to his *piso*. A few hours in bed and a couple of glasses of brandy would see him right. But it was possible they'd second guess that move and already be waiting there. Or they might be staking out the *comisaría* in case he went there. He felt a wave of rage, made worse by his hesitancy.

The *comisaría*. He made the decision as soon as he saw his leg, increasingly aware of the blood filling his shoe. He examined the wound. A deep bloody groove carved out of the flesh above his knee. It was more than a piece of glass, there was possibly a bullet in there. He used his handkerchief to staunch the bleeding. He needed to get back to the *comisaría* but he took his time in binding the wound with the handkerchief and then his tie. No use pressing on and hoping the bleeding would stop. He'd seen men in the war fighting on despite a gaping wound, unaware of their life's blood draining away. Guzmán felt his senses dulling. He was fucked if he was going to collapse. It was not that bad, he told himself. But it would slow him down and that made him vulnerable – and therefore angry: *Comandante* Guzmán was not a person to tolerate vulnerability – especially in himself. Señora *Martinez was vulnerable but she argued with me anyway.* His thoughts were becoming tangled. It was important to keep moving. If his legs would obey him.

Progress was slow. He was becoming light-headed. *If I could find a policeman,* he thought, *he could help. But there's never one about when you need it.* He laughed to himself. He paused by a street lamp and clung to it, looking back at the splattered trail he had left behind him in the snow. He took a deep breath of frozen air and continued on his way. A couple passed on the other side of the road, laughing. When Guzmán slipped and fell they turned, and were about to cross over to help when the woman saw the blood. She spoke to the man quietly and they turned again and walked quickly away towards Puerta del Sol, their anxious footsteps fading in the dark. Guzmán retrieved the big pistol from the icy pavement and stowed it in its holster, anxious not to drop it again in case it went off and put another more serious hole in him.

As he approached the *comisaría*, Guzmán had begun to notice flurries of light in his peripheral vision, frosted roses dancing across his line of sight. He was drenched in sweat and his leg had stiffened to the point where he had to drag it. The doors of the *comisaría* were only a metre away now, a metre of pain, of dizzying struggle to keep his balance. What was usually a short brisk walk had taken almost an hour. If the Dominicans were here, Guzmán thought, only vaguely lucid, he was finished. He looked down the narrow road. Saw nothing. Or was that the shape of a man in a black coat? Guzmán squinted, blinking the sweat from his eyes. *Take another step. You fat bastard, Guzmán, you could have run this distance when you were in the army. Peralta should be here. They would have shot him first. Someone will. He's with Alicia Martinez. Paying her with vol-aux-vents. Whores. It costs so much more if they're naked.*

'Not a bad woman really,' Guzmán slurred as the man in the dark coat started to come down the street. Guzmán heard his footsteps. Belatedly he began to fumble for the pistol but the ground must have shifted because there was a sudden impact and he found himself face down on the icy pavement. The footsteps continued.

'*Joder, jefe*, what the fuck have you been drinking?'

Someone rolled Guzmán onto his back. The sarge leaned over him, his voice suddenly concerned as he saw the blood.

'Probably a decent woman if you get to know her,' Guzmán said, his voice faint and distant. 'Admirable in her own way.' He tried to pull the Browning from its holster but his fingers had turned to rubber. 'Respectable women are hard to come by...'

The *sargento* was pushing open the door of the *comisaría*, his voice fading as Guzmán started to pass out. 'Give me a hand out here,' the sarge yelled. 'I think the *comandante* got shot by some woman.'

He knelt alongside Guzmán. 'You'll be all right in a minute, *Comandante.*'

Guzmán felt the world start to spin. He opened his eyes and saw the sarge kneeling at his side.

The sarge was looking at someone across the street. 'What are you looking at? Fuck off out of it before I arrest you.'

Guzmán's head lolled to one side and he saw the man in the black coat turn and walk briskly into the darkness. Then there was shouting, the sound of boots on stone and the cursing of the *sargento,* all suddenly giving way to a welcome dark silence.

The line of men lay waiting among the pine needles as the first Moors came through the narrow rocky lip that formed the entrance to the plateau. The kid saw one of the soldiers come forward into the long grass, alert, his bayonet fixed. The man stopped and called to his companions. Four of them followed cautiously, in single file. There was a brief discussion. One of them pointed upwards, towards the position where the men were hiding. The Moors started forward, again, dark faces shining with sweat, their uniforms dusty. They advanced cautiously, pausing to listen for any sound as they came.

The corporal fired first and the others immediately unleashed a sharp ragged volley, that was immediately accompanied by a rolling echo around the hill behind them. The nearest Moorish soldier fell backwards, his rifle clattering to the ground, his fez rolling along the stony path. The other Moors were mown down, scattered in a broken tangle of limbs, weapons and equipment. They lay, entwined in death, awkward and angular in their disarray, thin cordite smoke from the guns that killed them wafting across their bodies.

Shouts from below. The clattering of boots. A Moorish NCO ran up the stony path only to be hit by the crossfire from the Republicans above. Another of the African soldiers followed, stepping over his comrade's prone body, crouching but defiant, running forward shouting the praise names of God, cursing those who opposed him, his bayonet ready for the enemy above. The fusillade that struck him left a thin crimson mist hanging in the air, as his body rolled down the slope, raising small clouds of dust as it went.

The kid looked over to the corporal. The corporal grinned. They turned back, aiming their rifles at the narrow gap through which the Moors must come. The kid's mind was whirling. As long as they had

213

ammunition they could fend off the Moors all day – or at least until the enemy were able to get aircraft or artillery support. That would take time and by then it would be dark and new possibilities for escape would present themselves. As long as they had ammunition. The kid opened the pouch on his webbing belt and counted his remaining cartridges. There were five left.

CHAPTER NINE

MADRID 2009, CALLE DE LOS CUCHILLEROS

*J*oder.' Galindez sat on the edge of the bed; every movement provoked a firestorm of free-floating pain. She winced as she checked the bruises and grazes that were her souvenirs of the fight with Sancho. *You should see what the other guy looked like.* She tried lifting her right arm and groaned. *Shit, I am the other guy.*

Tali was making coffee in the kitchen. 'I'll help you with that, *querida*,' Galindez said, struggling to hold herself upright in the doorway.

'I can manage, Ana María. Go back to bed.' Tali steered Galindez into the bedroom. 'Stop being stubborn and lie down.'

Galindez slumped onto the bed and watched as Tali pulled the sheets over her. 'I'm not used to having things done for me.'

'I noticed.' Tali laughed. 'Last night you were telling me how to lock the door, put the salad back in the fridge and put the cat out. Then you slept for ten hours. Maybe a coffee will do you good.'

'I haven't got a cat,' Galindez called after her.

'Or a sense of humour, *mi vida.*' Tali came back from the kitchen with their coffee. 'And you talk in your sleep.' Sitting on the side of the bed, she examined the livid bruising around Galindez's right shoulder. 'How do you feel? And tell me the truth: don't give me any of that macho stuff.'

'Like I've been hit by a truck. How's that for honesty?'

'Be honest about this then: are we safe after what happened yesterday?'

'Of course. We can't let a loser like Sancho scare us, can we?'

Tali frowned. 'I am scared, Ana. It wouldn't have been so bad if

215

yesterday was just us being in the wrong place at the wrong time. But it wasn't. They were looking for us and Sancho was in on it. I don't think he's just some loser. He's dangerous.'

'That's true,' Galindez admitted. 'His fighting skills are on a different level to mine. I could hardly handle him.'

'No, Ana María, you couldn't handle him,' Tali said. 'I thought he was going to kill you.'

'He had a gun. Otherwise, I'd have beaten him senseless with that pool cue.'

Tali was unconvinced. 'It's a wonder he didn't shoot you. For some reason he hates you.'

'I did notice. And yet, at times when we were fighting, I thought he was holding back – as if he wanted to take me down a peg or two rather than just beat me senseless.'

'Maybe he wanted to humiliate you for standing up to him.'

Galindez nodded. 'He also said something about not messing with things that weren't my concern – and pushing the wrong buttons.'

'You think he meant entering the Guzmán password at work when you set the alarm off?'

'I think so. Maybe he wants to stop us finding out more about Guzmán. Remember that day at the university when he first attacked me? He said he was looking for "Guzmán's book".'

'So what do we do?'

'If he keeps this up, I'll report it. Have him arrested.'

'I'd like that. Will you do it? Please?'

'I promise.'

'You should stay in bed today,' Tali said. 'We can postpone the visit to Guzmán's HQ.'

'No, I want to go,' Galindez said, suddenly animated. She struggled to sit up and grimaced.

'Well, if you think you're up to it,' Tali said doubtfully. Galindez's expression told her she was. 'You get showered and dressed, Ana. I'll bring my car round to that little car park by the market – it'll save you a walk.'

Galindez found it strange having someone organise things for her. 'Yes, nurse,' she said.

The hot air was damp and heavy, pressed down under a sky bruised with storm clouds. Sitting on the low wall of the car park, Galindez wondered if Tali would arrive before the rain began. She pushed the letters she'd just retrieved from her mailbox into her bag. Scattered raindrops were beginning to pattern the dusty ground as Tali's car pulled up. Sliding carefully into the passenger seat, Galindez squirmed in discomfort as she pulled the seat belt across her bruised body. Tali heard her swear at the pain as she struggled to fasten it. She said nothing. It was clear Galindez wasn't one for being mothered.

'All set?' Tali asked.

'*Vamos.* Calle de Robles and step on it, my good woman.' Galindez smiled.

'You're in a good mood – considering.' Tali adjusted the mirror with considered precision before touching the St Christopher medal on the dashboard and then crossing herself and kissing her fingers. She sensed Galindez watching her. 'What?'

'Just observing your little ritual. It's cute.'

'Cute? It's prudent. You want to get there safely, don't you?'

'I trust your driving more than any ritual,' Galindez said.

Tali slowed as the car reached the main road. Traffic rolled past in an unbroken and unyielding line; no one remotely inclined to give way. She drummed her fingers on the wheel. 'I can do cute.' She launched the car into the gap left by a faster than average motorist. The driver behind her slammed on his brakes, loosing off an angry blast of disapproval with his horn.

'*Jesús Cristo,*' Galindez muttered. 'I only hope that ritual works.'

'Calle de Robles. Follow the M-30 and past the Planetarium, *verdad?*'

'*Exactamente.* Park in the first space you see. Those narrow streets are always full.'

'See, you're the sensible one, Ana María,' Tali said. 'I'm just cute.'

Appalling traffic, a slow procession of ill-tempered, overheated humanity. Drivers' arms hung from their windows, hands beating an impatient tempo on the hot metal; tempers on a hair trigger, sudden raging explosions of horns at every junction, screams of abuse at those perceived to be impeding the already funereal pace of the traffic. An hour passed. Galindez felt her shirt sticking to the seat. Tali seemed as cool and composed as she had been when they set off.

The sky turned darker. A distant murmur of thunder. Tali passed Galindez a bottle of water. The water tasted of warm plastic.

'You and Luisa seem to be getting on now,' Tali said, 'apart from the theoretical sparring.'

'She's been pretty good about us splitting up,' Galindez said. 'She even gave me a pair of ear studs as a break-up gift – they're lovely – look.' She held back her hair to let Tali see the small onyx studs. The car veered sideways and Tali reluctantly turned her attention back to the road, prompted by a chorus of blaring horns.

'Know what?' Galindez said. 'Luisa and I will never agree on the best way to write about Guzmán. Science versus hermeneutics, as she says.'

'She says it a bit too often for my liking.' Tali smiled. 'Even so, do you think there's any chance of a truce so Toni and I don't get too bored waiting for your arguments to end?'

'We do get carried away. But it's her fault. The idea was to approach this investigation from different angles. She'd do her textual thing while I tried to connect Guzmán to some of the killings after the war using more conventional methods. Instead, she insists on criticising my methods at every opportunity.' Galindez looked up, suddenly realising where they were. '*Mira*, that's Calle de Robles over there on the right – see the *farmacia* on the corner?'

Tali twisted the wheel and the tyres squealed as she cut across two lines of traffic, pulling in to the kerb and braking sharply, bringing them to a noisy halt. She turned to Galindez, self-conscious at her sudden recklessness. 'Sorry, Ana, did I scare you?'

'*Joder*. You terrified me. Do you always drive like this?'

'Pretty much.' Tali turned off the engine.

Galindez looked at her. 'It's funny, you don't look like the terror of the roads, *Señorita* Castillo. A case of still waters, I'd say.'

'It's always the quiet ones, Ana María.' Tali smiled.

'You can say that again. That's why I'm in such a good mood despite being black and blue.' Galindez slid across the seat. 'I mean, sending me that photograph. *Hostia*, it really got me steamed up.' She squeezed Tali's leg. 'Not that I'm complaining.'

Tali looked blankly at her. 'What photograph?'

'You know very well. It came in today's post just after you went to get the car. You must have known the effect it would have on me when I opened it.'

'Not really, Ana, because I didn't send you a photograph.'

'*Verdad*? What's this then?' Galindez pulled the manila envelope from her bag.

Tali looked at the handwritten label on the envelope. 'That's not my handwriting.' She slid a black and white print from the envelope and stared at the photograph. It was her. Under the shower, hands raised as she washed her hair. Definitely her. Her face captured in exquisitely sharp detail. Everything was.

'But...' Tali fumbled for words, her face pale. '*Dios mio*, Ana, I wouldn't let anyone take a photo of me naked. Is there a message?'

Galindez turned the photograph and examined the back. Nothing. She examined the envelope, turning it upside down. A small white card fell onto her lap. '*Mierda*. I never even checked the envelope. I was so sure it was from you.'

Tali picked up the card and stared at the written message. Her hand began to shake. '*Hostia*.'

Galindez took the card from her and read it:

I said I wanted to see them – Sancho.

'That bastard.' Galindez was flushed with anger. 'He must have planted a camera in your flat.' She chewed her lip. 'Another attempt to scare us.'

'In that case, it's worked.'

'I'm sure I'm right that he wants to stop us searching for Guzmán. *Dios mio*, Guzmán's still dangerous even after all these years.'

'That's great news, Ana María. Just as we're about to go into his *comisaría.*'

'We'll be fine.' Galindez got out of the car and carefully slung the bag holding her equipment over her aching shoulder. Across the main road, beyond the slow lines of traffic blurred by exhaust fumes, was the green cross of the *farmacia*. The building stood on the corner of a small, narrow street, high buildings on either side, their detail lost in shadow.

Crossing the choked main road was an exercise in risk-taking. Grabbing Tali's hand, Galindez dashed forward, darting across the lanes of traffic, pursued by the monstrous hooting of a refrigerated truck as it thundered past. They stopped to catch their breath on the corner by the *farmacia*. Galindez looked up and read the sign on the wall above the shop. 'Calle de Robles.'

The thunder was getting closer. High walls rose steeply around them. A few shops, a grocery, a fishmonger, a shop selling wool. 'Do people still knit?' Tali wondered. Probably not, since the shop appeared to have been closed for years, judging by the fashions on the faded knitting patterns, some time in the seventies. The windows were obscured by dust and the yellow cellophane sun-screen was pulled down inside. Pictures on the knitting patterns were almost bleached away; the shop a sort of desiccated relic.

Further along, the narrow road was bisected by another, much narrower street. To their right, an old building, a school or a seminary perhaps. Beyond that, a large church, strikingly unattractive, almost threatening, its sharp, uneven profile accentuated by dark, angular statues.

'*Mira.*' Tali pointed to the old building on the corner. Its great wooden doors were like those of a church and the bars on its windows seemed far thicker and more imposing than necessary. A sign above the door, in faded paint, *Policía Nacional*. A more recent sign pasted to the door: *Permanently Closed*.

'This is it,' Galindez said quietly.

'Hope so,' Tali said, producing a large key from her bag. 'I'd hate to think there were more like this. It's so ugly.'

'Is there a caretaker?'

'No.' Tali handed Galindez the key. 'We're on our own in there. And you know what? I can't believe it but I'm afraid of a building.'

The storm was almost above them now, the sky an ominous quilt of black cloud. Rumbling echoes shimmered along the cobbled street.

'A building can't hurt you.' Galindez put the key into the lock. The rusty metal protested loudly as she turned the key.

The door swung open. The air felt cold after the oppressive humidity of the street. Their eyes were not yet accustomed to the sudden change from the summer light and they stood hesitantly in the marble-floored vestibule, its dark panelled walls leading into darkness.

Galindez found an old light switch and pressed it. Weak lights flickered into life. '*Mierda*. It's like *la Familia Addams*,' she muttered.

A skeletal light vaguely illuminated the empty hallway. On their left, a wooden bench against the wall beneath a faded map of Madrid. At the far end of the hall, a small reception desk. Old, empty shelves, pigeon-holes for mail. Just an everyday office. *Except they tortured and killed people here*, Galindez thought. Behind the desk were glass-panelled office doors. To the right a set of wooden double doors. From the hand-drawn plan Toni had given her, Galindez knew those doors opened onto the corridor leading to the *comandante's* office and, ultimately, to the cells.

'What did Luisa say this building was before it was a police station?' Tali asked.

'A convent. Destroyed on the orders of the Inquisition. They built a seminary in the eighteenth century on top of the ruins.'

'Why would they destroy a convent?'

'Corruption, apparently.'

'What, the nuns were taking bribes?'

'No, moral corruption. They were all burned at the stake.'

'They did that outside, surely?'

'I hope so.' Galindez pulled out the plan and flattened it out on the dusty counter of the reception desk. '*Vamos a ver.*' The electric lights above gave off an absurdly weak light, smearing the plan with shadow.

Tali looked around nervously. Again.

'Come on, Tali. We may never get this place to ourselves after today,' Galindez said.

'That wouldn't be such a bad thing, would it?'

'You can't be that scared? We'd be crazy not to check it out now.'

The building reverberated as the storm outside intensified. Tali walked to the double doors and opened them. The corridor beyond was pitch-black and there was a strong smell of damp. Galindez moved the flashlight beam over the wall to help Tali find the switch. And then pale light twinkled unsteadily from a line of small bulbs in the ceiling.

'*Me cago en Dios,*' Tali whispered.

The corridor was some three metres wide and maybe two metres high. The floors were old stone, much older than the material used to construct the walls. There were a few more recent interventions here and there: light switches, patches of cement, a noticeboard. But those things had a dusty, dated quality, looking less like alterations than tentative additions the building had begun to reject. The corridor was cold and uninviting, Galindez thought, a strange place for what she wanted to say. But she felt safe here with no risk of being overheard or interrupted.

'Tali, I know it's probably the wrong time, but there's something I want to tell you.'

It wasn't easy. Galindez had never said this to anyone in her adult life. Had never wanted to and had never been able to. There hadn't been a right time with anyone else. But she'd not imagined the right time would be in the cold darkened corridor of an abandoned torture chamber with dust and cobwebs flickering in the pale beam of the flashlight and rolling angry thunder overhead. *But that's me*, Galindez thought, *when something has to be said, I have to say it.*

Tali shook her head. 'This isn't the place. Nothing good ever happened here. You can feel it. There's no room for love in this building. Let's finish the search and go.'

Galindez swallowed her disappointment. *I should have kept my mouth shut. What was I thinking of?*

'Look, Ana,' Tali said, 'things feel right when we're together. Leave it at that for now?'

'Sure,' Galindez said, grateful for the shadows hiding her disappointment.

They continued along the dim passageway. The flashlight shone on a door to their left, a few metres ahead. Galindez looked at the plan. 'That's it. Guzmán's office.'

A very ordinary door, Galindez thought, dark wood, with a large rusty lock. She noticed her hand was slick with sweat as she gripped the handle.

'What if it's locked?' Tali said, echoing Galindez's own concern.

The handle turned easily and the door opened.

Galindez fumbled for the light switch. A single electric bulb set in a khaki metal shade threw cadaverous light across a disappointingly bare room, empty except for a plain wooden desk.

'I don't like it.' Tali grimaced. 'I can imagine him here.'

'He's not here now though, is he? Let's check his desk.'

Galindez opened a drawer. It was lined with yellowing newspaper but otherwise was quite empty. Galindez picked up the newspaper and smoothed it on the desktop. '*ABC*. I'd expect Guzmán to read a right-wing paper.'

Tali examined the front page. 'Wednesday, June eighteenth, 1986.'

'What's the headline?' Galindez asked.

The front page was dominated by a black and white photograph

223

of a bullet-riddled car, its front door wide open, the driver slumped across the seat, one arm still on the steering wheel. The vague shape of another body was just visible on the back seat.

'ETA Provocation,' Tali read. *'Teniente Coronel* Carlos Vesteiro Pérez, *Comandante* Ricardo Sáenz de Ynestrillas and soldier-driver Francisco Casillas were murdered yesterday in Madrid by the terrorist group ETA in an attempt to destabilize the democratic system.'

'I wonder if Guzmán was still working here then?'

'Isn't it unlikely? After all, he disappeared in 1953.'

'I suppose. Though we can't be sure of anything without firm evidence.'

A search of the other drawers revealed nothing further. Meanwhile, Tali moved slowly around the empty room, examining the walls, peering at the stone floor. She stopped and knelt to examine something. 'Look at this, Ana María.'

Galindez left the desk and joined her, excited by the note of discovery in Tali's voice. 'Look there.' Tali ran her finger across the big flagstone beneath her. The stone was scarred by a deep, irregular fissure. 'Looks like it's split in two.' She touched the jagged incision in the broken stone. 'There might be something underneath.'

'Maybe.' Galindez pointed to the parallel patterns of scratches and gouges made by something heavy that led across the broken flagstone to the door. 'Clumsy removal men by the look of it. Moving something big like a filing cabinet. That's probably what broke the flagstone.'

Tali persisted, pulling at the stone, trying to lift it. 'Help me, Ana. I can't get a grip.'

Even with Galindez helping, the flagstone stayed put.

'There's probably nothing there,' Galindez said, 'and I can't get a proper grip with this bad arm anyway. We'd need a crowbar to lift this.'

She decided to examine the desk again. She lay on the floor and peered underneath.

'There's something under here.' She slid her arm under the desk, straining to reach the small object she'd seen.

'*Qué es*, Ana María?'

'Something's attached to the bottom of the desk. It's…' Galindez winced as she strained her injured shoulder. She paused. 'It feels horrible. I can't quite reach.' She withdrew her arm slowly, rolling away from the desk, exhaling heavily at the pain.

Tali knelt to examine the glutinous black smears on Galindez's hand. 'It looks like tar.'

Galindez tried again, this time using her other arm to reach under the desk. 'There's something under this sticky stuff. If I can get my nails under it I might be able to prise it off.' She struggled for a moment. 'Got it.' She rolled away from the desk.

Tali looked at the object in Galindez's hand. A crusted black viscous mass with a rusty piece of metal protruding from its centre. 'Look.' Galindez pointed to the crust. 'This is electrical tape. God knows how long it's been here.'

She took out a plastic evidence bag and sealed the gelatinous mess inside it. 'That's our first piece of evidence. Let's see if we can find any more.'

Leaving Guzmán's office they followed the passageway, passing several depressingly empty offices. 'Look in there.' Tali pointed to an open door on the right of the corridor.

Galindez saw a coffee urn rusting next to a cobwebbed sink. 'It looks like their mess room.'

Galindez pushed a corroded switch by the door, and the small light in the ceiling washed the room with a dirty grey glow. A sink, a small stove, empty cupboards, a cup and plate on one of the tables, all thickly furred with dust and cobwebs. Galindez started examining the fly-blown papers pinned to the noticeboard with rusty drawing pins. Messages and memos relating to expense claims and holidays. She lifted some of the papers with her gloved finger, finding other, older messages underneath. And then she saw it.

'Tali. *Ven aqui. Rapida.*' Her voice was taut with excitement. '*Mira.*'

A typewritten notice, signed in a strong, broad hand, the ink faded to an ethereal blue.

```
Important Notice - 16th January
All leave cancelled until further notice. No
exceptions will be granted. Officers and men
will gather in the mess room at 18:00hrs for
further instructions.
Comandante L. Guzmán, Officer Commanding
```

And his signature. Guzmán.

'*Puta madre*, it's him.'

'But January of what year?' Galindez said, in frustration. 'God, it's like he's taunting us.'

'*Venga*, Ana María,' Tali said. 'You wanted to find something. Christ, it's his autograph.'

For a moment, Galindez stared at the paper, willing it to give up its secrets. It didn't and she opened her shoulder bag, bringing out another plastic evidence bag.

Further along the corridor, they halted at a large heavy door, the studded wooden panels reinforced by diagonal iron bands.

Galindez looked at the plan of the building. 'This is the door to the cells.'

The door swung open on dark greasy hinges. A damp unpleasant odour drifted up from below.

'What's that smell, Ana?'

'Drains, I think.' Galindez's flashlight cut through the darkness beyond the old door. A flight of stone steps led down into a narrow corridor. Steps worn smooth by centuries of passing feet.

They went down into the passageway below. It was narrow and crypt-like, its curved roof almost too low even for Galindez to walk upright, the dark rough stonework of the walls punctuated by olive-coloured doors, eight cells on each side. At the end of the corridor was another great door strengthened with bands of iron, a door clearly even older and stronger than the one they'd just come through. This door seemed crude and primitive: the wood seemed to strain against the bands.

'What's behind that door?' Tali whispered.

'The vaults.'

Tali found the light switch and the low short corridor was latticed with sinister sharp-angled shadows from the miserable glimmer.

'This must have been one of the original dungeons,' Galindez said. 'Guzmán and his men just adapted it by fitting these modern doors.'

The cell doors were made of thick metal. Galindez pushed one. It was unlocked.

The flashlight played on the inside of the cell and over the low arched ceiling, the beam glinting on the damp green sheen of the stonework. No bed, no sign of occupation.

'Let's get a closer look, I don't want to miss anything.'

'What are you looking for, Ana María?'

'Prisoners sometimes leave graffiti,' Galindez said, running her hand over the stonework. 'I can't see anything. It's hard stone. Maybe it was difficult to make a mark or maybe they weren't here long enough to scratch anything.'

'That's a comforting thought,' Tali said gloomily.

Galindez began examining the other cells.

'I've still got a bad feeling about this place,' Tali said quietly.

'Just this last cell and then we're done, all right?'

Tali muttered reluctant assent as Galindez pushed open the cell door. The smell hit them at once. Tali stood behind Galindez, peering over her shoulder. 'Something bad happened here,' Galindez muttered. 'It feels wrong.'

'What do you mean? It's haunted? Come on, don't spook me any further, Ana,' Tali said. 'You've got a Ph.D. in forensic science. You know places aren't haunted.' Yet she too sensed the malevolent atmosphere, its mixture of malicious aggression and wretched despair.

'I think maybe they saved this cell for the people who suffered the most,' Galindez said. 'It smells of fear. And shit.'

It was true. There was a faint faecal odour. Tali suggested it was probably due to ancient plumbing.

'There are no drains down here, Tali. This place must be steeped in human waste.'

'Even so, that's not the same as being haunted.'

'Oh yes it is,' Galindez said. 'It's a physical trace of all the people who died here.'

Tali looked towards the ancient door at the end of the corridor. '*Madre de Dios*,' her eyes glinted in the sullen light, 'what if they're still down there?'

The building trembled under the sustained violence of the storm. The sky was suddenly torn apart by a terrific echoing clap of thunder. They flinched. And with the noise of the storm came unwelcome insight.

'I think they kept prisoners in this cell so they were near to the door to the vaults,' Galindez said quietly. 'They wouldn't go through the door willingly because they knew something horrible was waiting for them down there – so they were kept here to make it easier to force them down into the vaults when their time came.'

'*Joder*, you're really creeping me out. Let's go,' Tali said. Then she saw Galindez's face. 'Ana?'

Galindez heard her but said nothing. Could say nothing. It was as if her thoughts had congealed, thickened by the oppressive air of this dismal repository of pain and suffering. Coherent thought was replaced by echoing screams of terror, the sounds of desperate futile struggles to resist being dragged towards the ancient door, the noise of beatings and more screaming, screams that were nothing compared to those that came up from the vaults as the door opened.

'*Mira*, I'm shit scared, Ana. Can we go and discuss this somewhere else? Like several kilometres away?' Tali pushed Galindez in frustration. 'Ana, what's up with you? Are you in a trance? *Puta madre*, Ana, *por Dios, coño. Que cojones haces?*' Her voice was sharp with anxiety.

Galindez felt the screaming fading, her thoughts returning to normal, time suddenly restored. *What was that?* 'Sorry, I was dreaming. I'll check this last cell and we'll go. Promise.'

'Are you sure you're all right, Ana María?'

'Of course.' Shaken, Galindez began to explore the rough stone of the cell with her fingertips. The beam of the flashlight suddenly picked out a line of letters. Tali crouched next to her, training the flashlight onto the wall. And then she crossed herself.

The letters were quite large. They must have taken some time to carve.

I AM IN HELL, AND WORSE TO COMME BELOW.

PRAYE FOR ME. S.VILAR 7 SEPTIEMBRE 1741.

Tali's voice trembled. 'Fuck. This is freaking me out.'

'There's more.'

'What does it say?' Tali sounded really worried now.

'It's a series of crosses. Look.'

Tali peered at the irregular line of rough crosses.

'These weren't all carved at the same time.' Galindez said. 'I think he was recording something.'

'You mean like how many days he was kept here?'

Galindez shook her head. 'He wouldn't have known: there's no daylight in these cells.'

'You're right,' Tali agreed, 'maybe he was counting how many times they took him down into the vaults?'

'Maybe,' Galindez said, 'and look how many there are. If each cross represents a session of being tortured, he'd have been in a terrible state at the end.' She photographed the inscription before continuing the search. Tali was silent now. The graffiti had frightened her badly. That and Galindez's behaviour a few minutes earlier. Further along, Galindez found scratches, as if someone had begun to carve something into the stone but had been interrupted.

'Here's another one.' She shone the light onto faint words etched in the damp stone. A name and a date.

ALICIA MARTINEZ 17-1-1953

'Christ. A woman,' Galindez said. 'Maybe she was one of Guzmán's prisoners. How awful that must have been.'

The camera flash bleached the darkened cell momentarily. The dark returned.

Outside the cell, Tali leaned against the corridor wall. 'Sorry. I'm feeling a bit weird. I'll be fine in a second.' She rested against the wall, running a hand over her face. Tilting back her head, she took deep breaths, trying to stay calm. As she looked up, she saw the stone arch over the ancient door. '*Puta madre*. Look at that.'

The lintel over the ancient doorway was alive with carvings. Small, delicate, time-worn filigrees of menace and hate: bodies being torn apart, impalings, hangings, corpses with no heads, skulls with eyes being gouged out. Taloned hands grasped serrated blades buried in the twisting bodies of their victims. Spectacular, impossibly violent rape, insanely bloody slaughter. As Galindez focused the camera on the carvings, Tali was already making her way back up the corridor.

'There are more of them over the arch at this end as well,' she called.

Galindez photographed the carvings while Tali waited unhappily at the top of the stairs. '*Ay*, Ana María, *no puedo más*,' she said plaintively.

'I don't think I can take much more either,' Galindez agreed. 'Let's go.'

Outside, Galindez turned the big key in the lock of the outer door of the *comisaría*. She savoured being back in the real world, in the bruised light and pressing heat of the passing summer storm. Tali waited across the street. Further away they could hear the distant rumble of traffic from the M-30.

'*Mierda*, we forgot to turn out the lights,' Galindez said, wondering if it was worth making another journey in there, to restore the malevolent building back to the silence and the dark.

'Leave them.' Tali's voice was stronger and more confident in the daylight. 'Let them sue us.'

Guzmán felt corpses pulling him into the stinking marsh. All around him, the bee-hum of bullets, the crack of small-arms fire, smoke, the moans of the wounded and the dying. Men screaming for their mothers, their wives, a priest. Begging to die, the voices of pain broke in waves of ceaseless torment. He heard the roaring of the dead, ancient voices calling his name, spectral hands clinging to him, trying to drag him down. 'Guzmán, Guzmán.'

'I think he's coming round now.'

Light. White light. He opened his eyes. The *sargento* was shining a torch into his face.

'Put that fucking light out.'

'Looks like you're all right then, sir.'

Guzmán was lying on a table in the mess room. Beneath him was a dirty sheet bearing some impressive bloodstains. They had removed his trousers: he saw a thick bandage around his knee. Then he felt the pain. '*Puta madre.*' He sank back onto the table. *Sargento,*' Guzmán barked.

'*A sus ordenes, mi Comandante.*'

'Not now, *Sargento*. You're not on parade. Who saw to my leg?'

The *sargento* nodded towards a man standing just outside the thin pool of light from the lamp above Guzmán's makeshift operating table. A spectral figure dressed in black, his thin cadaverous face accentuated by wire-rimmed spectacles.

'*Herr* Dr Liebermann. I should have known. Who else?' Guzmán growled.

The man snapped to attention with a sharp click of his heels.

231

'*A sus ordenes, Comandante.* You were one of the few members of this unit I haven't had the pleasure of attending to – until now.'

'No half-price abortions tonight then?' Guzmán asked.

Liebermann stiffened. 'I have interrupted a reunion dinner with several former members of the Condor Legion to attend to you, *Comandante* Guzmán, and you insult my professional integrity?'

Guzmán shrugged. 'As a matter of fact, yes. But if you're too offended, *Herr Doktor*, I think the British or Americans are still keen to offer you suitable accommodation – just like they did with your colleagues at Nuremberg.'

Liebermann's face twitched. He knew it was better not to offend those who had provided him with protection since his flight from the crumbling Reich. He knew also it was sensible not to offend Guzmán because of what Guzmán was capable of doing to him physically. 'I do my best as police surgeon, *Comandante* Guzmán,' he said, his clipped tones distorting the Spanish words. 'Mock me if you wish, but no one has ever questioned my skill as a doctor.'

Guzmán sat up and slid his legs over the edge of the table. He tried to put his weight on his injured leg and winced.

'You forget, *Herr Doktor*, I saw the evidence. The Allies sent us copies when they were searching for you.' Guzmán swore as he tested the leg again. He slumped back on the table, grimacing in pain.

'If I may suggest, *Comandante*, a couple of days' rest are needed to get over the shock of losing so much blood. You were lucky, the bullet went straight through the flesh. Any lower and you would be limping for a very long time.' Liebermann paused for a moment to see if Guzmán would thank him. Guzmán did not. 'I must advise you,' Liebermann continued, 'despite the wound, a contributing factor to your collapse was the consumption of a considerable quantity of alcohol.'

'Nonsense,' Guzmán snorted. 'Alcohol has a medicinal value.'

The doctor closed his medical bag, nodding. 'As you please, *Herr Comandante*. However, the fact I was able to clean and dress the wound without you waking does seem to support rather than contradict my hypothesis. Especially since I used no anaesthetic.'

'I'm a heavy sleeper,' Guzmán muttered.

'I bid you good morning, *Comandante*. I shall present my bill in the usual manner.'

'You can present it up your arse, Liebermann, whether we pay it is another matter.'

The doctor left the room with a reptilian grace, moving backwards to the door where he exited with a final click of his heels, still moving backwards as the door closed on him. Guzmán stared after him with distaste.

'Did you watch him while he did it?'

The *sargento* nodded. 'Yes, it all seemed above board, *jefe*. Hey, I knew you were pissed, boss. Was it on the *Caudillo*'s booze?'

'I was shot, you insubordinate bastard,' Guzmán snapped. '*Vamos*, there are things to be done. Where are my trousers?'

'That was a problem, *jefe*. You're not a light bloke. Hard to manoeuvre around. He cut them off.'

'Cut them? *Mierda*, they were pure wool. Fucking Nazis.'

'There's some clothes in the storeroom, *jefe*.'

'Fuck that, those are prisoners' clothes. There's a suit in my office behind the door. Bring me that.'

The *sargento* moved towards the door.

'*Espera*. Where's my pistol?'

'In your office, *jefe*, on the desk.'

'Right, bring it to me when you get the suit.'

'What do you want with your gun?' the *sargento* asked curiously. 'You need to stay in bed, the doc says.'

'I want to blow your fucking head off.'

The *sargento* grinned. 'Glad you're feeling better, *jefe*.'

Dressed and back in his office, Guzmán sat at his desk, occasionally wincing with pain. Peralta waited patiently, watching the *comandante* doodle idly on his blotter.

'And you didn't recognise any of them, sir?' Peralta asked.

Guzmán looked up wearily. 'I didn't *see* any of them, *Teniente*. Only the one I shot and that wasn't for long.'

Peralta shook his head. 'It doesn't add up, sir. The Dominicans didn't seem to have the discipline to carry out an attack like that in silence.'

'I don't care, they're going to wind up dead if I have my way,' Guzmán spat.

'Surely you mean if they're guilty...' Peralta's voice faltered under Guzmán's withering look.

'Dead, Acting *Teniente*. Dead as a fucking doornail. They come over here and fuck with us and you talk about establishing guilt? This isn't a philosophical discussion. Christ, you'd have lasted about five minutes in the *Guerra Civil*. Now, what information do we have? Or have you spent the last three hours playing with yourself like everyone else in this crappy excuse for a police station?'

Peralta opened his notebook. Guzmán let out an exasperated sigh.

'No gunshot wounds reported at any of the hospitals in the Madrid region,' Peralta began. 'No reports of medical practitioners being approached to treat any such victim. Whoever it was, they aren't being treated in the city.'

Guzmán snorted. 'There's a reason for that, *Teniente*. The guy I shot was dead when he hit the ground. We're looking for a body. And they're much easier to dispose of.'

'There's been quite a commotion from local businesses. Almost half the windows of the bars on the Plaza Mayor were shot out in the attack. Many owned by Falange members.'

'They'll be wanting compensation. Fuck them.'

Peralta nodded. 'They've already begun, sir. In fact, the *capitán-general's* office telephoned an hour ago. They need a report for General Valverde immediately.'

Guzmán frowned. 'Can't bear to call him uncle, can you? Well, we don't want him interfering – he'll cause all sorts of problems if he starts meddling. This is a secret unit and we don't want anyone's attention and anyway, someone already has it in for me: this was a planned attack. There was only one reason why they didn't get me.'

Peralta looked up from his notebook. 'And that was?'

Guzmán smiled, his face unhealthily pale. 'I was better than they were.' He banged his big fist on the desk, causing Peralta to jerk upright in his seat. 'If I could get the drop on them in an ambush, I can fucking well take them down,' Guzmán shouted. 'Now, the question is, was it the Dominicans? Because if it was...' He crashed his fist onto the desk again. 'I'll have them.'

'Nothing suggests it was them, sir,' Peralta said, turning the page of his notebook.

'Is that conclusion based on evidence or did you feel it in your water, *Teniente*?'

Peralta he found the page he'd been looking for. Guzmán braced himself for more of the *teniente*'s insights by lighting a cigarette. Peralta looked hopefully at Guzmán's packet of Ducados. Guzmán ignored him, inhaling the black tobacco smoke deeply.

Peralta began to read. 'Several sightings of them, mainly from informers. They went to a bar on Calle Toledo, sleazy place, called Bar Dominicana. My sources tell me it's a front for all manner of illegal activities, including prostitution.'

'Did you pay them for that information?'

'Yes. Of course, *Comandante*.'

'I could have told you all that for nothing,' Guzmán said coldly.

'They ran up a large bill and started an argument about it. There was some pushing and shoving before they agreed to pay. Then they asked the owner to call them a cab and drove to the Hotel Tres Reyes. By that time we had men following them. They entered the hotel and stayed there until this morning when they left to go on a tour of a local irrigation project with several members of the American Embassy staff.'

'Including Positano?'

'*Señor* Positano was one of the party, yes.'

'How did we get the information from the informers so quickly?'

Peralta smiled modestly. 'After you dropped me off last night, I came back here and got the sarge to make some calls. I also used some informants I had in the *policía armada*.'

'And was Positano with the greasers all last night?'

Peralta shook his head. 'He was at the reception until it ended. He took a taxi back to his hotel, had a drink at the bar and then went back to his room with a whore.'

'And this is from your informers?'

'I followed him myself.'

Guzmán was surprised.

'Well done, *Teniente*. And I thought you were homeward bound for a warm bed.'

'The snow prevented me getting home,' Peralta said, running a hand over his stubble. 'It was easier to walk here and do some work.'

Guzmán stood up, growling a barrage of obscenities at his injured knee.

'Does it still hurt?'

'No,' Guzmán growled, limping over to the filing cabinet. 'I'm just worrying about how our Lord suffered on the cross. *Hostia*. What do you think, you cretin?' He tugged open a drawer and pulled out Valverde's bottle of Carlos Primero.

'Your uncle gave me this. It has certain medicinal properties which I'm in need of.'

'Sir, I don't think...' Peralta dried up as Guzmán bore down on him with the brandy.

'You don't think what, *Teniente*?'

'I don't think you should be drinking alone, sir.' Peralta said hastily.

Guzmán eased himself into his chair. 'Quite right, *Teniente*. You know I disliked you from the word go. But you have some qualities, even if you are a sanctimonious, God-bothering, oily simpleton with no fucking humour and the imagination of a schoolgirl.'

Peralta considered protesting. Instead, he kept quiet. Keeping his mouth shut would clearly be a key skill in working for Guzmán.

'Get two mugs, *Teniente*, some coffee and get the sarge. We need to plan what we do next.'

The *teniente* obeyed. Guzmán heard Peralta's footsteps on the flagstones, the crash of the door of the mess. Every sound in the building told Guzmán something. The *comisaría* was home. He knew every nook and cranny, every creak and groan of the building and what lay beneath. There was scarcely a room where he hadn't hurt or injured someone in the line of duty. And sometimes outside it as well. His leg ached badly and he would have to get some sleep soon. But not before he had a plan. Once you had a plan everything else fell into place. The plan worked or it didn't. That narrowed events down to two possible outcomes and with those in mind, he could work to make certain he got the result he wanted. Guzmán hated uncertainty.

A knock at the door.

'It's me, sir.' The *sargento* appeared even more dirty and unkempt in the pallid electric light of the office.

'Did you bring a mug?'

'Do I need one, *jefe*?'

'Didn't Peralta tell you I wanted to see you?'

'The *teniente*? Nah, *jefe*. I've just come from reception. There's someone here for you.' The *sargento*'s ravaged face broke into a leer. 'A woman. Fair-haired, nice tits too.'

'It will be your sister. I'm going to have her over my desk.'

The *sargento* scowled. 'No need to be like that, *jefe*, not when I'm bringing good news like this. She's not a whore, that's all I meant.'

'Really? And how often can you say that about a woman round here, *sargento*?' Guzmán laughed. 'Tell Peralta I'll see him when I'm done with her. We've some work to do later.'

'*A sus ordenes, mi Comandante.*' The sarge retreated into the corridor.

Guzmán ran a hand through his hair and, as an afterthought, stowed the bottle away in his desk drawer. He had just closed the drawer when the door opened and the sarge showed Alicia Martinez into the room. She wore a faded blue coat. Guzmán noted the worn fabric had been mended in several places. Her boots had also seen better days. *Señora* Martinez's cheeks were pink from the cold and she was shivering. She clasped her hands in front of her, defensively. Guzmán saw how chapped they were.

'*Señora* Martinez.' Guzmán tried to stand but his leg gave way, causing him to fall back into his chair amidst a flurry of oaths. Trying to regain his composure, he waved a hand at the empty chair where Peralta had been sitting. She sat, arranging herself with calm delicacy. Guzmán watched her with admiration.

A knock at the door announced the sarge who staggered in with a tray bearing a pot of coffee and two cups and saucers Guzmán didn't recognise. In fact, he had never seen cups as clean in the *comisaría* before.

'Your coffee, *Comandante*.' The sarge placed the tray on Guzmán's desk, stepped back and saluted. A real salute. Guzmán wondered how long it had been since he had done that.

'That will be all, *Sargento*.'

'*A sus ordenes, mi Comandante.*' The sarge almost bowed as he left.

Guzmán looked at the coffee. 'Would you care for a cup?'

'Perhaps I should pour it, *Comandante*?'

'You're my guest, why would I let you do that?' *This is how gentlemen talk to women. Peralta would approve.*

'Your leg's bleeding,' she said, 'what on earth happened?'

It was true. A small pool of blood had formed around Guzmán's foot. He glared at it, annoyed both by the attention it drew to his fallibility and also because the trousers to yet another suit were now spoiled. He pressed down on the bulky bandage beneath his trouser leg.

'There was some trouble last night. I got a minor injury. It's nothing.'

She looked unconvinced. 'If you say so. It doesn't look minor to me. At least let me pour the coffee.'

He watched as she filled their cups. *She moves gracefully. They do things differently, these respectable women.*

'You wouldn't like a drop of brandy in it, would you?' Guzmán asked in an inspired moment. She would refuse of course, but his offer would mean he could have one.

'Brandy?' she asked, uncertainly. *'Gracias, Comandante.* Just a drop.'

Guzmán poured a large shot of brandy into her cup. She stirred it, then held the cup to her nose for a moment to savour the aroma before she drank. 'That's so warming. I got frozen stiff coming here.'

'I'm surprised to see you.' Guzmán swallowed his coffee in one large mouthful before filling his cup with brandy. 'I imagine you were glad to see the back of me last night.'

She frowned. 'Not entirely, *Comandante.* You were quite pleasant by the time you left. I very much appreciated your offer to… to have a word with my employers.'

'De nada, señora. It's nothing. I can't stand bullies. Or cowards.'

'Nor can I,' she said and Guzmán wondered if she had been smiling when she said it. Perhaps not, he decided.

She sipped her coffee. For someone who looked poor, she had an attractive way of moving. It was not sexual, in the way the gypsy whores moved, but elegant. Elegant and capable.

'By the way, I have something for you, *Comandante.'*

'Oh?' Guzmán said, surprised. 'It isn't my birthday, *señora.'*

'There's no need to be sarcastic, *Comandante.* It's a letter. Some welcome news, that's what the man said.'

'The man?'

'The man who called this morning. A well-dressed gentleman. Dressed as if he were going to a funeral.'

He will be if he's the one who's been following me, Guzmán thought.

'He came to your apartment?'

'Yes, at about nine o'clock.'

Guzmán poured a second cup of brandy and offered her the bottle. She shook her head, only relenting when he insisted. It amused him to see how her cheeks glowed by the time she'd finished her coffee.

'The gentleman said he was an old family friend. From the old days before the war.'

'Ah. The old days.' Guzmán was tired and his leg hurt. But anything from his past always needed to be treated with suspicion. This wasn't a time to take things easy. Taking it easy could cost you, he thought. He sat up in his chair, wincing at the pain.

'And his name was?'

'He didn't say. He said he had been asked to find you some time ago, but no one knew where you were. By coincidence he came across your name in a newspaper article. You won a medal, apparently.'

'Apparently I did.'

'For rudeness, I imagine.'

Guzmán stared at Alicia Martinez, with her shabby coat, her chapped hands and her glowing cheeks. He looked into her pale eyes, eyes that looked as if they had been coloured with pain for most of her life. And yet her eyes were more alive than any he had ever seen, even though they were losing focus as she struggled to concentrate when he spoke. *One more drink and she'll be on the floor.*

'Another drink?' he inquired gently.

'No thank you, I think I've had quite enough. I don't drink much as a rule.'

'Nor do I, *señora.*'

She almost smiled, Guzmán thought, *perhaps I really can be charming if I try.*

'So did our mystery *señor* say how he found out where I was?'

'He said he telephoned the *policía* and they gave him the address of this *comisaría.*'

'How strange. In the Special Brigade, we tend not to give out such details.'

'You think he was lying?'

He was amused by her surprise. But then, she wasn't part of the job. Sometimes he forgot there was a world out there that didn't revolve around issues of internal security.

'And you're certain he never mentioned his name to you?

'No.' She chewed her lip. 'And I didn't ask. I thought he might be one of your lot.'

'Our lot?' Guzmán asked.

'*La Policía Secreta*,' Señora Martinez said. 'I didn't want to get into more trouble.'

'You aren't in any trouble with my lot, *señora*. I thought I made that clear last night.' Guzmán smiled. 'You said he gave you something for me?'

'I have it here.' She rummaged in her handbag and took out a brown envelope. He took it, again noticing her chapped hands. *Clearly a hard worker, this woman. Two jobs.* Hostia: *admirable. And not a real Red after all.* Then he noticed.

'You've taken off your wedding ring.'

She blushed. *When was the last time I was with a woman who blushes?* he wondered, unable to recall if he ever had. He felt a sudden strange intimacy, strange because intimacy was alien to Guzmán's life.

'I had to – it's embarrassing…'

'You pawned it?'

She nodded. Her pale eyes hinted at tears. *She really is quite attractive. For her age, anyway.*

'Hard times call for measures to match.' He looked at the envelope and saw his name, written in a thin, spidery hand.

'Did this gentleman say anything else?'

'He just said it was for *Comandante* Guzmán and that you'd be pleased to receive it.'

'Did he say why he was delivering the note to you? After all, I only met you yesterday. No one who knows me would use you as my contact address.'

She looked puzzled. 'I can't explain that, *Comandante*. I assumed he knew you'd be at my flat last night and thought you'd still be there in the morning. I seem to remember that was your original intention. I thought you must have told him you would be there.' The reproach in her voice was clear. 'Before you changed your mind.'

'I told no one, *señora*. Not about my plans nor how they changed.'

241

'I'm very glad to hear it, *Comandante.* '

Mierda, Guzmán thought, *this woman has an answer for everything. And more. She'd be a better assistant than Peralta. At least I can win an argument with him.*

'Well.' He looked at the envelope and then back at her. 'Shall I take a look?'

She almost smiled. 'Yes, I hate a mystery. Don't you?'

'Of course. Policemen detest mysteries. *Vamos a ver.*'

His finger tore under the seal of the envelope, ripping the coarse brown paper open. Inside was a small folded piece of foolscap. He read it without speaking.

Alicia Martinez waited.

Guzmán stared at the paper.

'Is it good news?' The brandy had made her bold.

Guzmán's expression made her sit back in her chair, suddenly frightened.

'What on earth is it, *Comandante*?'

Guzmán got up, heedless of the pain in his leg and the blood trickling into his shoe.

'Thank you for this, *Señora* Martinez. I appreciate it. If this man contacts you again, please telephone me immediately. You still have my card?'

She nodded, a mixture of curiosity and trepidation on her glowing face. 'I hope I haven't brought bad news?'

'No. Not at all. But you need to go now. I have things to do. I'm very busy. My apologies. Thank you for your assistance.'

Startled, she moved clumsily to the door. Guzmán was staring at the scrap of paper again. He looked up.

'I... *adíos, Comandante.*' She fumbled with the door handle.

'Wait...' Guzmán said. 'Take this.' He held out the bottle of Carlos Primero to her. It was almost half empty, but it was very expensive: if she didn't drink it she could sell it.

'*Gracias.*' She looked puzzled. But she took the bottle, he noticed, and placed it in the depths of her tattered bag.

'And this.' He held out several banknotes.

'What do you think I am?' she snapped. 'I can't take money from you.'

'Take it and get your wedding ring back. I order you to, *señora*.' He paused. 'I mean, I'd like you to. To let me be of some assistance. I don't want the money back. Think of it as being for services rendered.'

'Services?' Her cheeks were burning now. He liked to see her angry.

'You brought me this.' He held up the paper.

She relaxed a little. 'You still haven't told me what it says.'

Guzmán smiled. 'That's right. And the money should buy your silence. That's all it is, a little bribe, *una propina*, not to talk about it. *Nada más.*'

'If you say so. Thank you.' She opened her purse and put the money into it.

'It's American money,' Guzmán said. 'You'll need to change it. You'll get a good deal. Do you know where to go?'

She nodded.

'Then thank you for coming. Turn right outside and go through the doors at the end of the corridor.' Guzmán sat back down at his desk. He heard her footsteps diminishing in the corridor and then the sudden bang of the swing doors. Guzmán smoothed the foolscap paper on the desk. He looked at it again and again, as if the intensity of his stare would somehow reveal something about the writer. The handwriting was feeble, almost childish. There was no address, nothing to identify where the note had come from. He read it once more:

Sunday 11th January 1953

Querido *Leopoldo*,
After all these years, I learned you're alive. God and his blessed mother have guided me to you. I'm coming to Madrid in the next few days and will contact you when I arrive.
Hasta muy pronto,
Un abrazito muy fuerte,
Mother.

Alicia Martinez pulled her coat tighter at the collar in anticipation of the raw cold outside the door. The sarge watched her as she passed the reception desk, studying the movement of her hips. She'd never make a whore, he thought. *'Buenas tardes, señora.'*

'Buenas tardes.' She didn't look back.

The big door swung open. Outside, it was snowing and the afternoon light had already started to dim. In the brief moment before the door closed, the sarge saw her breath hanging in the cold air. Then she was gone. The sarge took out a cigarette and, as he lit it, he heard Guzmán roar his name. He cursed, inhaling deeply before grinding out the cigarette on the stone floor.

MADRID 1953, BAR FLORES, AVENIDA DE MONTE IGUELDO

The afternoon light had faded by the time Guzmán led Peralta and the *sargento* into Bar Flores. Peralta had wondered about the wisdom of planning their strategy in a public place but Guzmán insisted they conduct the discussion somewhere that served alcohol. They sat at a table by the dirty window, looking out into the darkening street. A number of customers stood at the bar with a few more at the tables at the back of the room, all swathed in black tobacco smoke. The waiter brought their beer. Guzmán was at once annoyed by the beer, deciding it an unsuitable drink for a winter's day. Once annoyed, he raged for several few minutes about the traitors and turncoats who abounded in the police and armed forces. He unleashed his diatribe with venom, poking the sarge in the chest at one point as a means of emphasising the fact that such treachery deserved sudden and massively violent intervention to put an end to it.

'Fuck's sake, *jefe,*' the *sargento* protested, 'I haven't been grassing you up. Lay off. Pick on him,' he nodded at Peralta, 'he's the one with connections at the top.'

'I wish,' Peralta said. 'My clout with General Valverde is precisely nil. It's hard to imagine him disliking anyone quite as much as he does me.'

'I can understand that,' the sarge sneered.

'That may have changed, *Teniente*, after the phone call I got from him,' Guzmán said. 'He's mightily pissed off. Unfortunately, so is Carrero Blanco's office.'

'You're in the shit, *jefe*.' the sarge said.

'I think you will find the actual expression is *we* are in the shit,' Guzmán said, 'all for one and one for all, no?'

'I never shot up the Plaza Mayor,' the sarge said glumly.

'I wish it had been you who was shooting at me,' Guzmán said. 'Then I could have killed you and shut you up for good.'

Peralta sighed. 'This isn't getting us anywhere, sir.'

Guzmán looked at him for a moment and then nodded. 'For once, *Teniente*, you're correct. *Muy bien*, let's try and work out what's going on.' He looked across the table. 'Sarge?'

The *sargento* leaned back self-importantly. 'Well, in my opinion...'

'No,' Guzmán interrupted, 'I don't want your opinion. Get the drinks in.'

The sarge sullenly waved at the waiter.

'Right. Notebook out, Peralta. Make some more of your excellent and lengthy notes,' Guzmán said. 'Start with the Dominicans.'

'An odd lot,' Peralta observed. 'They don't seem like members of a trade delegation at all. Not least since they have such weighty criminal records.'

'I agree, they're dangerous,' Guzmán said. 'And yet the US ambassador and that bloke with the Italian name vouch for them. A bunch of thugs and yet with highly respectable friends. Why?'

'Maybe the Yanks thought it would be tough over here, so they brought a bit of hired muscle?' the *sargento* said, taking the glasses of beer from the waiter. Guzmán paused and waited until the man had retreated to the bar.

'I agree,' Peralta said, adding to his pencilled notes.

'Too simple.' Guzmán shook his head. 'They could bring soldiers in plain clothes, or police or secret service – like those goons they have at the embassy. They want to do business, not have the entire delegation arrested. You'd think they'd want to keep a low profile.'

'Those greasers certainly aren't keeping a low profile,' Peralta said, still writing.

'So that's one question,' Guzmán said, gulping down his beer and then calling for the waiter to bring more. He paused to wipe froth from his mouth. 'Second question. Who shot at me last night?'

'Well, *jefe*,' the *sargento* grinned, showing more of his devastated teeth, 'we could make a list of all the people who might want you dead. Mind you, I don't think the *teniente* there has enough paper to write them all down.'

Peralta thought about smiling but decided against it.

'And they don't seem like blokes who'd fuck up a simple ambush,' the sarge said.

'That's reassuring.' Guzmán said. 'Next, who the hell is following us around?'

'Someone's been following us?' Peralta asked in surprise.

'The bloke in the black coat you mean?' the sarge said.

'You noticed him then?'

'I noticed him right away,' the sarge said. 'I thought he was probably another one of Valverde's lads, spying on us.'

'I wondered about that,' Guzmán said, 'but then *Señora* Martinez came by yesterday and she'd a visit from him. Just how he knew she had any connection to me is puzzling. When we arrested *el Profesor*, you came out of her building after me, Sarge. Did you see anything?'

'Didn't see no one.' The sarge shook his head. 'I poked around in the mailboxes but there was nothing interesting. Then I heard you shouting for me.'

'Someone must have seen me there,' Guzmán said.

'Jealous boyfriend?' the sarge smirked.

'One more like that and I'll fucking hurt you,' Guzmán snarled. 'I hardly know the woman and someone gives her a message for me. Very odd.'

'What message?' Peralta scribbled notes furiously.

'A message from my mother. She's coming to see me. Soon.'

'Nice.' The sarge grinned. 'A visit from *Mamá*. Maybe she'll bake a cake, *jefe*.'

Guzmán's big fist smashed into the sarge's forehead. The sarge flew backwards in an arc of beer, hitting the floor with a loud crash that silenced the café. Guzmán glared at those customers daring to show an interest. They rapidly returned to minding their own business.

'*Señores*,' the manager came around from behind the bar, 'I will not have this behaviour in my bar. It is uncivilised. It's—'

Guzmán turned, lifting his coat away from the big automatic in its holster beneath his left arm. He let the manager look at the weapon for a moment.

'*Policía*,' Guzmán growled. 'Are you interrupting us in the pursuit of our duty?'

The man backed away, mumbling apologies. Guzmán called after him, ordering a bottle of wine and some tapas. The manager scurried behind the bar purposefully. Life returned to the café. The sarge dusted himself off and sat down, dripping beer.

'No more lip, *Sargento*. *Me entiendes*?'

'*Lo siento, jefe*. I didn't mean any harm.'

'I did,' Guzmán said. 'But the question is, who's this man in black who passes a message from my mother to a woman I've only just met?'

'Aren't you in touch with your mother, sir?' Peralta asked.

'My mother died in the Civil War,' Guzmán said. 'So it's unlikely she's going to go to the trouble of sending messages through some third party who just happens to be following me around. I want to know if this is linked to those Dominicans.'

'Well, we know where the Dominicans were the other night,' Peralta said, brightly. 'Maybe they'll go again – a taste of home, familiar territory.'

Guzmán nodded. 'Bar Dominicana. We'll pay them a call. *Qué hora es*?'

'Six thirty.' Peralta moved to one side as the manager arrived with a bottle of his best wine and plates of omelette and sliced ham. He returned to the kitchen to bring them more food: sausages, anchovies, stuffed peppers filled with spiced pork.

'The night is still young, *señores*,' Guzmán said, taking a large bite of one of the peppers. 'Excellent,' he nodded appreciatively to the manager, 'we'll come here more often.'

MADRID 1953, BAR DOMINICANA, CALLE DE TOLEDO

There were plenty of lowlife bars in Madrid, Peralta knew, but the Bar Dominicana looked far, far worse than any he had previously encountered. The bar's front windows were filthy, emblazoned with its name in large peeling letters. This was a place that reeked of trouble and they were still metres away from it. And, Peralta reflected, trouble was highly likely, since Guzmán had spent the last three hours drinking continuously. At Bar Flores, Peralta had been unable to look the owner in the eye when Guzmán refused to pay the bill when they left. In fact, now he thought of it, Peralta realised it was Guzmán's drunkenness that worried him the most. A big, violent man was worrying enough when drunk. Such a man armed with a powerful automatic pistol was even more so.

Though badly lit, the street was still not dark enough to hide the motley collection of prostitutes and beggars loitering in the grimy doorways of rundown buildings, each of which seemed to emanate the smell of cabbage and shit. Mainly shit, Peralta noted. As they approached the door, the sarge wandered off to bargain with a tall, bulky prostitute. While they argued loudly about her prices, Guzmán and Peralta entered the bar. And that, Peralta thought morosely, was their plan. What there was of a plan. The sarge would enter later and pretend not to know them. The rest was down to improvisation and intuition.

The smell inside was rank, a fetid stew of body odours, cooking, drink, cigarettes and dirt. Peralta looked around in disgust. At the back was a long zinc-topped bar. Tables and chairs – none of which matched or were even vaguely coordinated – were strewn around in an unsuccessful attempt to create the impression of a café. Against a wall in the back corner was a small stage and a piano. The entire place looked like one of the houses Peralta had seen as a kid where a bomb had fallen, killing everyone in the house and churning the occupants and their goods into bloodied chaos. This place, however, lacked the tragic presence by which the bombed houses evoked pity. Here, he felt only disgust.

The customers looked them over with casual brooding resentment since Guzmán and Peralta's clothes marked them out as possible policemen. Peralta met the eye of anyone who looked at him, noting with satisfaction they soon looked away. Guzmán also faced down some of the hostile looks, looks which became even more hostile when he lurched against a table and spilt the drinks of a ragged couple holding an intense and highly intimate discussion. To Peralta, they resembled a pair of harpies escaped from Goya's *caprichos*. Guzmán ignored their wailed protests and made his way to the bar where an elderly woman with a painted face was serving. Fat and dissolute, Peralta thought she must be a failed prostitute fallen from hard times to harder ones and probably still travelling downwards.

'*Buenas tardes, señores.*'

Her voice was deep with a Caribbean accent. Peralta guessed she must be in her sixties but was disinclined to study her more closely because of the cluster of cold sores she sported around the lurid gash of her painted mouth. Her eyebrows had clearly been shaved off and then redrawn with a pencil some five centimetres above her eyes, giving her the look of a decaying clown. Guzmán leaned on the bar.

'Mmm, big boy, what can I do for you?' the woman's voice was husky with smoke, drink and quite probably a whole genealogy of vice besides.

Guzmán lit a cigarette, offering one to Peralta in a moment of generosity. Peralta lit Guzmán's cigarette and then his own. The woman watched them.

'Got a smoke for a lady?' She placed one large, chubby hand on her hip.

'Of course.' Guzmán exhaled a cloud of smoke. 'If you can find a lady in this place.'

The painted face distorted for a moment and then cracked in a lopsided smile, revealing an incomplete set of brown teeth. Peralta looked away.

'You a funny guy. You make a joke with Mamacita? Oh you so cruel, pretty boy. But mess with Mamacita and you gonna get hurt.'

Guzmán looked at Mamacita, the cigarette hung from his lips, a wisp of smoke rising slowly. Peralta realised Mamacita had just done something incredibly stupid: she had threatened Guzmán. Even in fun, it was a big mistake and with a drunken Guzmán, it could end very badly. Peralta saw Guzmán's right fist clench, ready.

'Say something, big boy? Why you here? Why you come to Mamacita if you going to be bad like that? You so rude, *chico*. Why you here? You on business?' The ruined face creased into another hideous smile. 'You want business? You want girls, right? Yeah, that's what you want. 'C'mon, big boy what's your business?'

Guzmán stared at the frightful face confronting him. Peralta placed a hand on his arm. Guzmán tensed.

'Come on, Leo,' Peralta said with exaggerated bonhomie, 'relax and enjoy yourself. We don't want this lady calling the police on our account now, do we?'

Guzmán shrugged, recognising the *teniente*'s effort to defuse the tension – which was just as well, Peralta thought, since otherwise it could have turned very nasty for him.

'We've been on a long trip,' Peralta said, gushing with improvised jollity. 'We just want to have some fun. My friend's a bit tired, that's all.'

'Bit tired.' Guzmán echoed, relaxing his fists.

'A bottle of house red please, *señora*.' Peralta smiled.

The fat woman shrugged. 'OK, gents, I thought maybe you were being a bit rude and I don't like that. But paying customers...' she gave them an evil grin, 'I like them.'

As she waddled away, Guzmán turned to Peralta.

'Nice work there, Peralta. I was getting steamed up seeing that fat hag. Makes me squeamish. I never understand why men like that do it.'

'Men?' Peralta said.

'Ever the choirboy eh? Penny dropped now?'

Peralta nodded uncertainly. 'Christ.'

Mamacita returned with a bottle and two glasses. Guzmán watched as she poured it.

'Is that an Albanian red, *señora*?'

'Albania? This is from Burgos. Albanians are all cowards and goat herders,' Mamacita said, evidently well informed on small Balkan countries.

'You're not from Burgos by any chance, *señora*?' Guzmán was laying on the charm now, Peralta noted with sudden unease. Guzmán being superficially pleasant was a disturbing experience.

Mamacita quivered. 'No, no, big boy. No, Mamacita comes from the Dominican Republic. An island of dreams, long beaches, palm trees. Long, long time I been here, since the war.'

Guzmán took a drink. Peralta noticed his face twitch momentarily and then took a swig himself. The wine was like a badly kept vinegar.

'Where in the Republic exactly?' Guzmán asked.

'Say, you not a copper, big boy? You not a bad old policeman come to shut Mamacita down? *Vaya*, that would be just too bad.' She clutched at her bosom, and then, finding the padding in the front of the dress had shifted, vigorously rearranged it. 'Mamacita from Puerto Plata. Nice place. Bad people. People don't like Mamacita. Mamacita can't be Mamacita there, know what I mean, big boy?'

'Do we really look like police?' Guzmán asked.

'I guess not. What do you two boys do?'

'Salesmen.' Guzmán looked at Peralta and the *teniente* nodded quickly in agreement.

'You sell stuff, big boy? And you, pretty boy...' she beamed raggedly at Peralta, 'you gonna sell me something? Cos I got things I can sell you, handsome.'

Much to Guzmán's amusement, Peralta was lost for words.

'We'll see about that later.' Guzmán said. 'I'm worn out, *señora*, we're going to go and take a seat.' He indicated an empty table near the stage.

'You go on over, boys.' Mamacita smiled. 'Just keep on spending. You want to buy more fun, I can help there too.'

'She means whores,' Peralta said, as they sat down at the filthy table. The ashtray was overflowing and after a moment's thought, Guzmán emptied it onto the floor.

'Whores, eh? You surprise me, *Teniente*.'

'Better not use my rank.' Peralta leaned forwards across the table.

Guzmán nodded. 'Good thinking, Francisco.'

'Thanks.'

'That's quite all right. *Francisco.*'

'You're overdoing it now.'

'I think since we're such good chums, I think I'll call you Paco. *Paquito.*'

'My wife does.'

'That's not what she'll call you if she finds out you were in here.' Guzmán chuckled.

The Bar Dominicana was getting busy. The clientele seemed largely to be from the neighbourhood – and therefore a bunch of losers, Guzmán noted. Peralta, with the experience of his training in police college, argued they were typical criminal types, going on the evidence of their physical condition and degenerate bearing. The argument ended as did so many of their arguments, with Guzmán ordering the *teniente* to get another round of drinks. Peralta doubted he could stomach more of the house wine and opted for a bottle of brandy – much to Mamacita's delight as she blatantly overcharged him. Guzmán also reacted favourably when he saw it.

'Excellent, Paco. Sit down and pour, the stripper's just coming on.'

As soon as the first dancer appeared, Peralta regretted sitting so near to the stage. Thin, undernourished and wan, the girl wore a dress that looked as if it were about to fall apart. Not that it did, since within a few moments of the fat sweating pianist beginning his heavy-handed accompaniment, she was taking it off. Or would have if she had been able to undo the zip at the rear. Panic-stricken, she struggled with the zip, beset by an avalanche of cat calls and insulting comments about what she would look like when she finally got the dress off. Some of the loudest of these came from Guzmán.

Peralta squirmed in helpless embarrassment as the girl finally removed her dress and began to take off her grimy underwear. He looked away. Across the room, he saw a familiar face.

'Shit.' Peralta sat lower in his seat, trying not to make eye contact.

Guzmán tensed. 'Who is it?'

'Tomás Capuchón,' Peralta said. 'One of my informers at the *policía armada*.'

'Has he seen you?'

'I don't think so. He's over there with a couple of blokes. No one I know.'

'Try and get him alone,' Guzmán said. 'If he comes here he may know our greasy friends. I think you should have a little chat.'

'I'll wait till he goes to the toilet,' Peralta said, 'and then grab him.'

'Well, remember to grab him by the arm.' Guzmán smirked.

The girl was naked now apart from her tattered shoes and was attempting an awkward, uncoordinated dance to the accompaniment of a barrage of obscenities. Peralta felt degraded. When he got home he would have to scrub the smell of this place from his skin. At one point, he looked at the girl on stage and she met his eye. Peralta shrivelled into his seat, ashamed. Confession would be even more lengthy than usual this week.

'This is a disgrace,' he yelled into Guzmán's ear.

'You're right, she's ugly as sin,' Guzmán said through a cloud of brandy fumes before starting to barrack the stripper again.

'There he goes.' Guzmán nudged Peralta, nodding towards Tomás Capuchón as he went through the door at the side of the bar. Peralta got up and followed him.

The corridor leading to the toilets was as grim as the rest of the Bar Dominicana, although the lighting was worse. A single filthy bulb swung from a wire running haphazardly across the ceiling and down one of the mildewed walls. From the bar Peralta heard the muffled braying of the crowd. He followed the corridor and turned a corner. On either side was a battered toilet door. Peralta pushed open the door marked *Caballeros*. The smell hit him at once; it came from a cubical where the cracked toilet brimmed with a fetid growth of shit and newspaper. Capuchón was pissing into a battered urinal. Peralta stood behind him.

'Won't be a minute,' Capuchón said without looking round.

'Take all the time you want, Tomás,' Peralta said, 'I'm only here for a chat.'

The man turned his head. 'Oh, it's you, *Sargento* Peralta.'

'It's *teniente* now, Capuchón.' The man's thin face and protruding front teeth gave him the look of a rat, Peralta thought.

'Still at the same *comisaría*, *Teniente*?'

'No, I transferred. I'm at Calle de Robles now.'

The address had an immediate effect. Capuchón turned. He looked worried.

'The *Brigada Especial*? They're a rough lot, *Teniente*. You keep bad company, I must say.'

Peralta moved closer. 'Never mind your opinion of the forces of law and order, *amigo*, I think you can help me. In fact, Tomás, you'd better help me or you may find yourself paying us a visit at Calle de Robles. Then you can tell my friends there just what bad company they are.'

Peralta saw concern in Capuchón's face. Not the level of concern Guzmán might inspire, but at least he was making an impact.

'No need for that, *Teniente*. Just tell me what you want and I'll be glad to help you. You know me, always willing to help the police. I fought against the Reds in the war you know, I'm one of you lot really.'

'That's a real comfort to us, I'm sure, Tomasito. But I want to know about some Dominicans. They've come to Madrid with a trade delegation. Or so they say.'

Capuchón went pale. His eyes flickered from Peralta to the door. 'Sorry. Can't help.'

The words spluttered out as he tried to push past Peralta. Peralta slammed his hand against the man's chest, pushing him back. For a second Capuchón looked as if he would fall into the urinal but he managed to steady himself by clutching the filthy washbasin. Panting, he stood at bay, darting frantic glances at the door. He was sweating.

'What the hell's wrong with you?' Peralta snapped. 'Christ, they're a only bunch of foreign hoodlums.'

'Yeah? Well that's fine for you to say, *Teniente*, but I don't know anything about them. So I can't help you. Would if I could but I can't. I'd better go.' His voice cracked as he tried once more to push past Peralta to the door. Once more Peralta stopped him in his tracks, this time with a sharp punch to Capuchón's midriff.

Capuchón sank to his knees. 'Let me go. You don't know what you're messing with.'

'I'm going to mess with you, Tomás. Or rather my *jefe* is. *Comandante* Guzmán. Ever heard of him? I thought so. He's got an interest in these Dominicans and unfortunately for you, he lacks my patience. Come on, let's be having you.'

Capuchón started babbling. '*Bueno*, I'll do it. But these people are dangerous, I mean really dangerous, *Teniente*. I'll help you, but if I do, I'll need your help to get away from Madrid.'

'That's easily done, Tomás. But I need to know more about what they're doing here. You help me, I help you. That's how it works, you know that. Now, let's take the air for a minute.'

Peralta guided Capuchón out into the corridor. A fire exit opened onto a courtyard strewn with abandoned boxes and machinery. What light there was came through the dirty windows of the apartments above.

Peralta reached into his pocket for his cigarettes, surprised to find he had none. 'Got a smoke for me, Tommy?'

Capuchón held out the carton and Peralta took a cigarette and lit it.

'American cigarettes, Tomás? Ducados not good enough for you now?' Peralta inhaled deeply

'They're not hard to find, *Teniente*. You can get anything on the black market.'

'I want information,' Peralta said, 'and they don't have that for sale on *el estraperlo*, so tell me about the Dominicans.'

Capuchón shuffled uncomfortably. '*Bueno*. They're setting up some sort of business.'

'Business?'

'I don't know what, *Teniente* – honest. They've bought some properties and they're buying up people as well – putting them on the payroll. Pimps, whores, pickpockets, fences. They offer money up front to work for them.'

'Doing what?'

'Whatever they say. These are hard guys, *Teniente*. They don't mess about. If they buy you, they buy you. One bloke down the road, he crossed them. They cut him up bad.'

'How bad?'

'Dead. That bad. They say it was nasty.'

'Who says?'

'People on the street. The Dominicans took him to the old bodega near the church of San Rafael. It's been abandoned since the war. They gave him a hard time and then...' He drew his hand across his throat.

'How long since this happened?' Peralta asked.

'*Tres dias*. Far as I know he's still there.'

Peralta took out his notebook.

'You said they were buying property. Give me some addresses.'

Capuchón reeled off a list of bars, cafés and brothels, pausing to allow Peralta to catch up. Finally, the *teniente* put away his pencil.

'This is helpful, Tomás. *Comandante* Guzmán will be impressed.'

'All I want is to be helpful, *Teniente*.'

Peralta held out a hundred peseta note. Capuchón pocketed the bill quickly.

'One more thing,' Capuchón said, looking around the darkened courtyard. 'This place is theirs. It's the first place they bought. They threatened Mamacita into selling and then hired her to run it for them. You be careful.'

'Oh? And why would that be?'

'They'll know you're here. And if they know you're *poli*, things could get nasty.'

Peralta thought of Guzmán's big Browning and his desire to use it on the Dominicans.

'They could indeed, Tomás. Are they here tonight?'

'Not as far as I know.'

'Make yourself scarce then.'

'I wouldn't mess with them, *Teniente*. Seriously.'

'Let us worry about that. But I want you to call in to the *comisaría* in a few days and update me with anything you've heard. And make sure you do, Tommy, won't you? You don't want *Comandante* Guzmán having to come and fetch you. You really don't. Now, *vete. Y buenas noches.*'

'*Muy buenas, Teniente.*' Capuchón moved stealthily across the courtyard and disappeared into the murk of an alley on the far side.

Returning to the bar, Peralta felt the smoky warmth sweep over him as he came through the door. The air was drenched with the scent of unwashed bodies. There were fewer people than before, although the noise was just as intense. Guzmán was loudly heckling a juggler, succeeding spectacularly in putting the man off. The clubs crashed to the stage floor and the glowering juggler hurriedly left the stage. Peralta noticed the sarge nursing a drink at a table nearby, a picture of dissolution, indistinguishable from the bar's regulars.

'Complete rubbish.' Guzmán indicated the departing juggler. 'I could do better.'

'I've got some news,' Peralta announced, pleased to be able to return to the job in hand. His idea of a good night out didn't involve strippers, transvestite barmaids or jugglers.

Five minutes later, Peralta and the sarge were struggling to keep up with Guzmán as he hurried down the frozen street.

'*Jefe*, slow down a minute.' The sarge was gasping noisily for breath.

Guzmán slowed slightly.

'Unfit, *Sargento*, that's you. Too much time with the whores. What's your excuse, *Teniente*?'

'Don't worry about me,' Peralta said, turning his collar up against the cold. 'Although it might be easier to take a taxi.'

'Find one and we'll take it,' Guzmán snapped. 'We need to have a look at that bodega. Any evidence on those *hijos de puta* and we can take them, American trade delegation or no.'

'The bloke there is dead, *jefe*,' the sarge moaned, 'he'll keep for a few more minutes, we don't have to run there.'

'Keen as ever,' Guzmán growled. 'Just keep up, man.'

'There's a taxi.' Peralta raised his arm as a cab spluttered towards them.

'*Gracias* blessed Virgin for answering my prayer,' the sarge wheezed.

'You couldn't spell God, *Sargento*, let alone pray to his mother.' Guzmán laughed.

MADRID 1953, PLAZA DE SAN RAFAEL

The church of San Rafael loomed across the silent cobbled square, the spire of the church skeletal and menacing, etched black against the faint city light.

'That's it.' Peralta pointed to a decrepit storefront on one side of the church. It was clearly abandoned: peeling walls, boarded up windows, the sign faded from years of neglect.

Guzmán led the way, hugging the shadows as he moved towards the bodega.

The sarge rattled a rusty padlock on the barred doorway. 'All locked up at the front.'

'There's an alleyway down the side,' Peralta said. 'We can try round the back.'

The alley was no more than the space between the bodega and the next building. They entered it in single file. Guzmán led the way, his pistol extended before him. They emerged into a small yard littered with debris and bordered with piles of shattered bricks and masonry. Guzmán walked to the rear of the bodega and used his lighter to examine one of the windows. The wooden slats nailed over the window were askew and when Guzmán pulled one, it came away in his hand. Quickly, he stripped away the remaining slats to reveal the gaping window, its glass long gone.

'Someone's been here, all right,' Guzmán said, holstering his pistol. 'In you go, Sarge. *Teniente*, give the *sargento* a leg up.'

Peralta crouched, bracing himself as the sarge placed a foot in his cupped hands and then the *teniente* lifted him unsteadily, struggling to support his weight. The *sargento* grabbed hold of the window ledge and with some difficulty pulled himself in. A dull thud was followed by a few obscenities before the sarge reappeared and beckoned them to follow. Guzmán hauled himself up and then pulled Peralta up after him. Dusty and panting from the sudden exertion, they found themselves in the wreckage of a large storeroom, shelves filled with ancient bottles, the labels now obscured by dust.

Guzmán snapped open his lighter. Moving carefully across the room, he found the light switch and tried it without success. Holding the lighter aloft, he moved towards the dark outline of a large table. 'Now we're talking.' The struggling lighter flame illuminated old papers and ledgers scattered across the table top and, more importantly, a bundle of old candles. Guzmán lit several candles, nuancing the room with sickly irregular light and sending deep, dancing shadows over the skeletal ruins of the abandoned building.

'There was heavy fighting around here in the War,' Guzmán said. 'They probably shut up shop in a hurry and never came back.'

'What's that smell?' Peralta asked. Against the background odour of dust, damp wood and accumulated neglect was the odour of something rotting. Guzmán and the sarge recognised it at once.

'Looks like your informant was correct, *Teniente.*' Guzmán transferred the candle to his left hand as he reached into his coat for the Browning.

'It's got to be a corpse,' the sarge said, drawing his pistol.

They moved slowly, the floorboards groaning as Guzmán led the others to the front of the building. Passing through a doorway, the door hanging raggedly from one hinge, they entered what must have been the bar. There was little of it left. What remained of the tables and chairs were smashed and piled in small heaps.

'Broken up for firewood,' Guzmán said, now holding the candle up towards the pool of darkness on the far side of the room. They could make out the bulk of the old bar, the bottles and glasses shrouded in thick layers of cobwebs. Behind the bar was an ancient mirror, flanked by shelves now empty but for an extensive lacework of cobwebs, frosted with the accumulated dust of the fourteen years since the war ended. There was something more recent on the bar. Guzmán lifted his candle higher. Peralta gagged, trying not to retch as the smell became overpowering.

'Fuck.' The sarge held his candle over the thing on the bar. The dancing light enabled them to see what was there, unfortunately for Peralta.

Guzmán moved closer. Even he was taken aback as he looked down on the pile of flesh that had once been a person. '*Hostia,*' he muttered, 'it looks like they filleted him. Look, they cut off the arms and legs, and piled them up here. No head though.' He leaned forward over the bar, holding the candle up again. 'Ah, there it is. Must've rolled down there when the rats started on it.'

Peralta felt sweat run down his face as he struggled not to throw up. The sarge's curiosity had now taken over, and he leaned over the pile of flesh on the bar top and whistled.

'Real butcher's job. *Mierda*. I've never seen anything like it. They opened up his belly as well.'

'Yes,' Guzmán agreed, 'bait for the rats probably – trying to speed things up.'

Peralta moved away from the bar, hoping he might be able to contain the urge to vomit. He turned, scanning the room with his candle. Heaps of firewood. And a chair. Peralta lifted the candle, illuminating the dark shape in the chair. He called to the others, his words suddenly cut off by a stream of steaming puke.

Guzmán and the sarge ran to where Peralta was kneeling, spitting bile. They lifted their candles, illuminating the chair. Someone was sitting in it. It was Tomás Capuchón. He was sitting casually, legs crossed as if there for an evening drink. Someone had cut off his head and placed it in his lap. In his mouth was a crumpled hundred-peseta note.

The Moors were becoming cautious, crawling up the rocky path and trying to snipe from the lip of the plateau. For a while this tactic failed miserably: the defenders opened fire the moment a head appeared at the top of the steep defile. Now and again one of the Moors would come running up the stony path, enraged, intent on reaching them with the bayonet. They died almost instantly. A couple tried to throw grenades but were shot as soon as they left the shelter of the ravine. The grenades tumbled back down the pathway and there were screams and shouts from those behind as they tried to avoid the resulting explosion. The Moors had expected to end this by now, their pursuit had been that of victors: intent on the vengeance which normally followed their triumph in battle – the herding together of the conquered prisoners, the protests, the pleading, the screams as the killing began. This resistance had not been expected and it angered the Moors greatly.

The kid looked at the corporal who winked in an attempt at reassurance. The kid peered down the sight of his rifle at the narrow entrance to the plateau. When a dark head appeared he squeezed the trigger. A hollow click told him the magazine was empty. A few shots from those men who still had bullets drove the Moors back yet again. Now, there was angry shouting from below. Lying in the grass above, the kid could hear them shouting a name again and again, 'Guzmán... Guzmán... Guzmán...'

CHAPTER ELEVEN

Another day of unrelenting heat. A clear blue sky dotted with occasional candyfloss clouds. The radio warned that traffic was getting heavy along the A-6. Galindez was only too aware of that, as her car crawled in the traffic towards the Institute of History and Military Culture. Finally, the traffic began to pick up speed as she passed the Arch of Victory and the green and leafy Parque de la Bombilla. The austere lines of the Air Force Headquarters ahead marked her turn-off and a few hundred metres later, she entered the parking lot of the Military Institute. A security guard checked her pass. She guessed he was probably wondering how a young woman like her had such high-level clearance. Uncle Ramiro's doing, of course. She parked the car and got out, looking round for signs to the archive. The five old tan and grey barracks of the institute loomed over her.

'Dr Galindez?' She turned quickly. She hadn't even heard the man walking towards her. Clean cut. Smart suit, well-polished shoes. 'Diego Aguilar, *mi honor es mi divisa.*'

The motto of the *guardia civil.* 'You're with the Job?'

'Special operations. I'm keeping an eye on you. On behalf of a relative.'

The penny dropped. '*Tio* Ramiro?' She relaxed.

'I always refer to your uncle by his rank,' Diego said.

'How long have I been under surveillance?' Galindez asked.

'A few days.'

'Why? I didn't say anything to Uncle Ramiro.'

263

'You didn't need to.' Diego looked at her impassively. 'You tried to access restricted information using the database at HQ. I imagine you remember that?'

'It was a coincidence,' Galindez said, irritated by Diego's air of disapproval. 'I entered variations of a name into a search and it set off the alarm. That was all.' *And Mendez was supposed to fix all that*, she recalled.

'A coincidence? Yes, of course.' Diego gave her a doubtful look. 'But we think there are others who're also aware you entered that password. People outside the *guardia*.' He looked at her coldly. 'Bad guys. With an interest in our sensitive material. And now it's likely they think you have access to that material. It could cause trouble for you.'

'Actually, there's been some trouble already.'

'*Ya lo se*. I saw the fracas in the Plaza Mayor, although I lost sight of you and your companion when it all kicked off. There was a skinhead; big guy, facial jewellery. He was directing things.'

'He's called Sancho.' Galindez filled Diego in on Sancho's assault on her at the university and her fight with him after the incident in the Plaza Mayor. When Galindez mentioned Sancho's interest in Guzmán's book, Diego was puzzled.

'I'm not aware of any book.' Diego said. 'But I do know about Sancho. He's dangerous. Convictions for racist attacks and a member of several ultra-right-wing groups. Steer clear of him.'

'I'll try,' Galindez said, clenching her fist at the thought of meeting Sancho again.

Diego looked at his watch. '*Vaya*, I'd best get going. Good to meet you, Dr Galindez. I thought you'd feel safer knowing I was around.'

'Is it OK to mention you to Tali?'

'That would be *Señorita* Castillo?' Diego consulted a page in his notebook. 'The attractive blonde woman I've seen you with?'

'She's my partner.'

'*Bueno*.' Diego raised an eyebrow just enough to annoy Galindez. 'That's something I don't think your uncle knows.'

'That's the way I'd like to keep it.'

'As you wish.' Diego handed Galindez a slip of paper with his mobile number on it. 'Any trouble, just call me. We can have people with you in minutes.' He climbed into his car.

'*Muy agredecida.*'

'You don't have to be grateful, you're *guardia*. We look after our own.'

His car slid away into the wavering heat, the lines of the vehicle warping in surreal distortion as it turned onto the main road. *Armed protection.* Galindez's relief was diluted by her annoyance at Diego's high-handed attitude. *Whatever*, she told herself, *it's not the first time. I've had worse.*

Galindez called Tali and gave her Diego's number. With Tali suitably reassured, Galindez decided it was time to start work in the archive.

The institute had the weathered formality of an old soldier, a stern but reassuring presence as she walked across the courtyard to reception. The receptionist asked Galindez to sign in before leading her down a tiled corridor to a small office, its faded furnishings at least a couple of centuries old. The director of the archive rose from his seat, greeting Galindez in his most formal manner.

'*Encantado*, Dr Galindez.'

'*Igualmente.*'

The director examined her security pass. 'With this level of clearance,' he smiled, 'you have unrestricted access to the material here, Dr Galindez. Although there are certain problems.'

'Problems?'

'The contents are in a state of disarray,' the director said, apologetically. 'The material was brought here during the transition to democracy. Things were done hurriedly and a lot of material went missing. Everything's a mess, I'm afraid.'

'No problem. I'm happy to look for myself and see what I can find.'

'*Bueno.* I'm afraid access is all we can offer, Dr Galindez. We just don't have enough staff any more. To tell the truth, I'm not sure why we keep this archive at all.' He sighed. 'Although, since I'm retiring in a few months, I needn't worry about that. It will be a shame to leave it in such a state because it's an impressive collection in its own way – if you can find what you're looking for.'

'I look forward to the challenge,' Galindez said.

'*Perfecto*. You'd make a good librarian with that attitude. Now, if you'll follow me.'

He led Galindez down the corridor to a large oak door with brass fittings. Opening the door, he stepped back to let Galindez enter.

A short wooden staircase led down into the archive. Galindez looked around. It was just an old library, she thought. An old library where they dumped all this material when it was decided Spain would remain silent about the years of the dictatorship in return for the introduction of democracy. The archive was far from inspiring. The only windows were set around the high ceiling and the smoky leaded glass distorted the sunlight, diluting it into uncertain pale strands that striped the rows of dark wooden shelves. At this end of the library were round tables, with small reading lamps and leather-bound blotting pads arranged neatly alongside old copper inkwells. A few leather armchairs on each side of the archive gave the place the appearance of a gentleman's club. Actually, Galindez thought, from the look of the other users of the library shuffling through the half-light, that was what it was. Which explained the looks some of the elderly patrons of the archive were giving her.

'Help yourself to a desk,' the director said. 'There's no internet connection, I'm afraid. But there are pencils and paper in the drawers of each desk. Do you have everything you need for your work?'

Galindez patted her shoulder bag. 'I've come prepared.'

'*Bueno*. If you find something interesting and need a copy, I'll try and arrange it – although it will take a few days and we'd have to charge.'

'That's very kind. *Gracias.*' Galindez wondered if the copies would be made by hand.

'If you wish, I can show you the layout of the archive, Dr Galindez?'

Before she could answer, the receptionist appeared in the doorway behind them.

'*Lo siento, Señor* Director, I have *Coronel* Cabrera on the phone for you.'

He raised his hand in apology. 'I'll have to take that I'm afraid.'

'No problem, I'll be fine.'

With the director gone, Galindez sank into an armchair, away from the dusty old men working at the tables. As she checked her notebook, a middle-aged man wearing a drab brown work-coat approached.

'Dr Galindez? I'm Agustín Benitez. I believe you want to know about the archive?'

'*Encantada.*' Clearly the director felt guilty for leaving her so abruptly and had sent Benitez to help her.

The man's handshake was clammy. His appearance suggested to Galindez that he'd spent too much time in the mildewed twilight around them: thinning, badly cut hair, heavy brows, wide fleshy lips and the unblinking stare of a toad.

'This place doesn't seem terribly well guarded for a secret archive.'

'It's not top secret stuff,' Benitez said. 'Didn't the director tell you the state it's in?'

'He did. Is it really that bad?'

Benitez laughed. 'A complete mess. When the material was brought here, they were in a hurry to get rid of it. A lot of people had something to hide back then. And on top of all the other problems there were *los Centinelas.*'

'The Sentinels? Who were they?'

He stared. 'I thought you were from the *universidad*? An historian?'

'I'm a forensic scientist.' Galindez didn't like Benitez's attitude. *Maybe the archive makes people crabby.*

'A military historian would have known. We get a lot here. Real experts.'

Benitez was both creepy and irritating – a bad combination in someone who was supposed to be helping her. 'Perhaps you could complete my education, *Señor* Benitez?'

'By all means. Clearly someone ought to. *Los Centinelas* were a group of high-ranking officers in the armed forces, the *guardia* and the police, dedicated to protecting Franco during the Civil War. After the war ended, they continued engaging in various activities on his behalf – discrediting critics of the regime, assassinations, that sort of thing.'

'Weren't those activities part of their job descriptions anyway? Or was being a *centinela* a way of enhancing their career prospects?'

'Joke about it if you wish, *señorita*. They met in secret, wore a special ring and regularly swore oaths to the Church and Franco. And they did any dirty work required of them without question.'

'A special ring?'

'A symbol of membership, made from gold brought from the New World by the *conquistadores*.'

Galindez nodded. 'So really, *los Centinelas* were like the Rotary Club – only better armed and more violent. You said this was after the war ended. When did they cease their activities?'

'They never stopped,' Benitez said quietly. 'The *Centinelas* continue to this day, so I'm told. They were very active during the transition to democracy in the late seventies – that's when many of our files went missing.'

'And no one tried to stop them?'

'No one wanted to stop them. The military weren't committed to the transition. Many of them were actively hostile to democracy.'

'And do these *Centinelas* still take things from the archive?'

'We think so,' Agustín said. 'It's difficult to be certain – they'd hardly tell us. But every now and then documents go missing. The state of this place, we probably don't know the half of it.'

'*Bien*. If I see someone in a gold ring carrying away your files, I'll give you a shout.'

'This is no laughing matter, *señorita*. It never hurts to remember the way things were not so long ago – so we don't take things today for granted.'

'*Hombre*, I was only joking,' Galindez said, irritated. 'But while you're here, I'm looking for material relating to police operations in 1953. Can you point me in the right direction?'

'Of course. The archive is organised into blocks. Each covers about five years. It runs from the late twenties through to the early eighties. The fifties you'll find down in the first two sections at the far end. But as to whether you'll find what you're looking for,' he shrugged, 'I can't say. It's like doing *El Gordo*. Maybe you win, maybe you don't.'

'I don't do the lottery, *Señor* Benitez.' Agustín was really starting to annoy Galindez. 'I'll see what I can find. Thanks for your help.'

'I hope you find what you're looking for,' he said, stuffily. '*Sí Dios quiere.*'

'To be frank, I rely on attention to detail rather than God's will. *Buenos dias.*' Galindez stood up, wondering what it was about Benitez that pissed her off so much. Whatever it was, she thought, it worked. And from his expression, it was mutual.

With Benitez gone, Galindez left her notebooks on one of the round tables before heading into the gloomy warren of shelves. Intermittent beams of struggling sunlight played over the dingy contents of the archive. It was surprisingly cold. A sweater would have been a good idea, she realised, even though they'd forecast a high of thirty-one degrees today for Madrid. And all around her, the files, cartons, boxes, stacks of paper – the detritus of mass bureaucracy. So many files. Some with typed labels, now almost faded away, others illegible, obscured by dust and latticed cobwebs. How appropriate, Galindez thought, the dark bureaucratic memory of Franco's rule consigned to slow decay among the whispering shadows.

Occasional faint lights illuminated sections of the archive with an insipid pallor. Galindez noticed a label: 1935 – *Guardia Civil*. Idly, she pulled out the file. Grey dust clung to her fingers. Inside, she found a series of memoranda, invoices and letters, relating to the cost of supplying rural *comisarías* around Málaga. Routine logistical inscriptions from a time long gone. Galindez slid the folder back into place alongside a file labelled *Addresses of Prominent Jews and Freemasons in Madrid: A–E. 1938*. The files seemed to be in almost random order – worse, it was beginning to feel as if all the material had been shuffled into this chaotic state in order to frustrate those seeking something specific. Galindez realised she could spend months in this dismal light, hemmed in by cloistered silence and breathing air infused with the smell of old men and ageing paper and still not find anything. *Joder.*

She reached the far end of the archive. There was a gap of two metres between the end of the rows of shelves and the far wall. Several doors in the wall. *Privado: Solo Empleados.* Another marked *Hombres.* Naturally, she thought, there was a men's toilet but no door marked *Mujeres.* The archive belonged to a time when women were invisible in so much of Spanish life. A third door was marked *Sala de Emergencia.* God, if that was the only emergency exit, she smiled to herself, all those ancient scholars at the other end would be in real trouble if they had to evacuate the place in a hurry.

Her thoughts were interrupted by the tattered sign on the penultimate row of shelves in the far corner. '*1950–1954.*' She felt a little better now: at least it was the right time period. Nothing for it but to examine everything with a label. That was going to take a while, she was certain. But once she started something, Galindez would see it through. She remembered *Profesora* Suarez's comment about her when she was finishing her doctorate: *Ana María has a dogged persistence in her approach to work that is both unusual and rewarding in someone of her age.* *Tío* Ramiro thought it was an insult until Carmen calmed him down and explained what the *profesora* meant.

Galindez read the labels on the nearest files: *Report on Trade Union Activities in Barcelona 1952.* Another: *Arrests of Subversive Elements by undercover officers 1951–53, Madrid.* Many files weren't labelled. Examining a few, Galindez realised that although

270

some might be potentially useful, others should have been consigned to the waste bin sixty years ago. Even when she found sections that might have something of interest, a search like this took considerable time. Her back ached from constant bending to check material on the lower shelves. And then she saw it, a large box file with a yellowing label. Faded typewritten words: *Office of the Capitán-General of Madrid: Correspondence Concerning Comandante Guzmán 1951–52*. Galindez stared at the label, feeling the same excited anticipation she used to have opening her Christmas presents from *Tia* Carmen – although those were usually pieces of scientific equipment. Something related to Guzmán at last. And down to her persistence, not *Señor* Benitez's reliance on divine will.

Galindez had just started to open the file when she became aware of someone coming down the aisle in her direction. A man in a dark suit, his face half hidden by shadow. She guessed he must be quite old, since he bent forwards and was walking unsteadily, clutching from time to time at a shelf for support. A sudden thought chilled her. *Shit.* What if he was looking for this file? Galindez had a sudden vision of him being some high-ranking librarian or administrator about to announce the file was not available for some reason. *Just my luck. That'll teach me to mock Benitez.*

Galindez made a snap decision and replaced the file, pushing it to the very back of the shelf, leaving a space in front of it. Anyone glancing down as they passed would only see the empty space. That done, she walked calmly around the end of the row, and turned into the next aisle. Pushing aside a couple of boxes of papers, Galindez was able to peer through the gap to the shelf where she had just concealed the Guzmán file. The old man was getting nearer: she could hear his laboured breathing. Maybe he just needed the toilet – it was a cruelly long journey for the old men who used the archive. Whatever his need, the man suddenly came into her limited field of vision as she peered through the gap between the files. He paused – *hijo de puta* – he paused right by the

271

spot where, half a metre below him, Galindez had left the file. And then, she saw him bend and she heard the noise of something moving on a shelf. *Fuck. Don't let him find my file.* The man straightened up, his hand grasping the shelf for support. Galindez felt relieved: he wasn't holding the file. *Now go away, señor.* The man lurched to the end of the row and turned right, in the direction of the emergency exit. Galindez exhaled, realising she had been holding her breath until the man passed her hiding place. As she prepared to retrieve the file, there was a sudden flurry of activity out of her line of sight.

Leaning round the end of the row, she saw the old man struggling, his arms pinioned by two men in suits. He wasn't putting up much of a fight. Two fit men against one old man wasn't fair, she decided, whatever he'd done. She tensed, preparing to step in. Then one of them said, '*Policía.*' Galindez drew back behind the shelf. Police – the old man must have done something then. She hazarded another cautious look around the end of the aisle and saw the men bundle the old man through the emergency door. She knew that was the way to do it: make the arrest, then straight out of the nearest exit and into the squad car. And then a sinking feeling: *Did he take the Guzmán file? Shit, what if that's why the police were after him?* Or maybe he was one of those oddballs who rob libraries for years, filling their grubby homes to overflowing with their stolen collections?

With a resigned sigh, Galindez returned to the shelf where she had hidden the Guzmán file. The empty space on the shelf was now taken up by something in a plastic carrier bag. She picked the bag up. It was heavy: inside were several fat cardboard files bound together with string. She checked the back of the shelf. The Guzmán file was just where she left it. As she reached for the file, Galindez became curious about just what the old guy had been up to. If there was anything of importance in the files he'd left here, maybe she should hand them over to the police. It was worth a look. She put the Guzmán folder into the plastic bag alongside the other files and went back to the far end of the archive. The old men in the leather chairs and at the tables were all engrossed in their old documents. No one looked at her – except one old boy and he wasn't looking at what she was carrying anyway.

A lengthy queue of elderly scholars snaked back along the corridor leading to the director's office. Galindez found to her chagrin that they were all waiting to request copies of various papers. *Mierda.* Not one accessible photocopier. She looked down the line, counting at least thirty people. And the line wasn't moving. The bag of files was heavy and she didn't even know what she wanted copying. In the university library she'd have copied everything just to be safe. How long would it take them here to copy the mass of papers she was carrying? And worse, what if they refused to copy the Guzmán file? She needed something on him and this was the first evidence she'd come across, other than his diary.

A very un-Galindez-like thought occurred. Why not just borrow the file on Guzmán, copy what she needed and return it later? No one knew it existed anyway. Galindez recognised she was rationalising her intended behaviour like most criminals did. *But I'm not a criminal. I'll just bend the rules this once, it would save so much time. Christ, I never even had an overdue library book at uni.* She would return the files in a couple of days and no one would ever be any the wiser. *Hostia*, probably no one would even look at them again.

She made her way back to the reception desk. The receptionist was talking on the phone. Galindez signed out in the visitors' book and strolled to her car, stowing the carrier bag in the boot. She was about to start the engine when she noticed her left palm was wet. She'd been carrying a heavy bag on a very hot day: no wonder her hand was sweaty, she thought. She looked down. It wasn't sweat on her hand. It was blood. Fresh blood. Galindez got out of the car and opened the boot. It was clear now where the blood came from: the carrier bag was smeared with it around the handle. The old guy must have cut himself. Taking a tissue from her bag, Galindez wiped the blood from her hand before driving away.

CHAPTER TWELVE

/ This has got to stop. It's humiliating. It lowers morale and it makes you look ridiculous. It has to end. Understood? *Me entiende, Teniente?'*

Guzmán was sprawled in his office chair while Peralta stood uneasily in front of the *comandante*'s desk. Peralta looked at Guzmán shamefacedly.

'Of course I understand, sir, I can't help it. It's just—'

'Enough. You simply can't go round spewing up every time you see a dead body. It's ridiculous. How would you go on if you had to take a few Reds out one night and shoot them? You can't aim straight if you're throwing up right, left and centre, can you?'

'I apologise, *mi Comandante*. It won't happen again.'

'Don't let it, Peralta. I haven't told anyone but the sarge will. And then the lower ranks will have nothing else to talk about. Don't give them the means to undermine you. If this becomes a problem, *Teniente*, it's *your* problem. Understand?'

'*Si, mi comandante,*' Peralta said miserably. Guzmán dismissed him.

Peralta had slept little that night, trying to think through what was happening, trying to get a grip on the facts the way they had showed him at the academy. It wasn't working.

Guzmán called Peralta and the sarge into his office at midday. There were two blackboards set on easels at the far end of the room next to his filing cabinet.

The sarge looked at the blackboards quizzically. 'We going to be doing drawing?' he asked. 'I can do a doggie or a horsey if

274

you like, *jefe.*' He looked round at Peralta. 'I ain't drawing you though.'

'You'll be drawing this blackboard out of your arse in a minute.' Guzmán was writing on the left-hand side board. A name: *Valverde.* Then another, *Positano.* The sarge glowered at Guzmán but he glowered in silence.

'Right,' Guzmán said. 'This is what we have so far. The general – sorry, *Teniente* – *Tio* Valverde, is worried about these Dominicans moving in on his pharmaceutical interests. So he asked me to check them out and mark their cards.'

'Seems fair,' the sarge said, 'you do him a favour and then he owes you one.'

'True enough,' Guzmán agreed, leaving out the matter of Valverde's bribe, 'but doesn't it strike you as odd? Franco gave him the monopoly over the importation of medicines into Spain and it makes him wealthy. Fair enough, that's how it's done. But why should a bunch of creeps from the Caribbean with a track record as long as your arm pose any threat to the *Capitán-General* of Madrid? Valverde wants it all done on the quiet and even Franco doesn't want us to bother them. Normally, they wouldn't think twice about taking them out of circulation. One word to us and that'd be it.'

'Is it fear of offending the Americans?' Peralta asked.

'Must be,' Guzmán said. 'Maybe there's more to the trade deal with the *Yanquis* than we know. We need more information. This is useless, trying to guess what they're up to. *Teniente*, you contact Exterior Intelligence Services and see what they've got on *Señor* Positano. You could also try the Diplomatic Corps, see if we can get any information from the police in *Los Estados Unidos*. There must be something our people over there can dig up. We've got enough spies there, for God's sake.'

'They're a friendly country,' Peralta said, 'more or less. Surely we wouldn't...'

Guzmán stared hard at Peralta and gave an exaggerated sigh. Peralta shut up.

'You, *Sargento*, lean on the collection of lowlife scum you use as informers and get me the news on the street. You could probably start with your family, I imagine.'

'And you, sir?' Peralta asked.

'I'll be minding my own fucking business and doing my job – part of which consists of telling you what to do, *Teniente* – thanks for asking.'

When they had gone, Guzmán lit another cigarette. He began to pace the room. From time to time he scrawled on one of the boards. Standing back, he looked at the tangle of names, thoughts and connections assembled on the dusty wood. There was nothing that made sense. He picked up the eraser and ran it over the board. Maybe a coffee would help, *a real coffee*, he decided. He pulled on his overcoat and strolled down the corridor to the reception hall.

The corporal behind the desk saluted. '*A sus ordenes, mi Comandante*. I have a communication for you. Just arrived.'

The man pushed an envelope across the desk. Guzmán looked at the spidery writing.

'Who brought this, *Cabo*?'

'Can't say, sir. Someone left it when I popped into the office. Sorry, sir.'

'If someone can wander in and leave an envelope without being seen, *Cabo*, they could wander in and leave a bomb. And if you leave the desk unattended again, you'll think one has gone off under you and I won't be addressing you as *Cabo* either, because you'll be back in the ranks. Do I make myself clear?'

'*Perfectamente, mi Comandante.*'

Guzmán snorted and walked to the door. A flicker of anger pulsed through him. He turned. The corporal snapped to attention.

'You stupid fuck,' Guzmán spat. '*Que coño eres.*'

The corporal swallowed, remaining at attention until Guzmán was outside in Calle de Robles. Even then, another minute passed before the corporal felt safe enough to curse the *comandante*.

The sky was a heavy grey. The piles of snow along the sides of the streets were still frozen. No hint of the sun behind the opaque quilt of cloud. Guzmán was angry. Things were not supposed to be like this. The Special Brigade wasn't set up to do ordinary police work. Still, they would have to try, because otherwise Guzmán was going to lose credibility with the *Caudillo* and he couldn't let that happen.

Guzmán crossed the road and entered the smoky fug of a café. He sat on a stool at the end of the zinc-topped counter, with a good view of the street. A horse and cart clattered past. Guzmán ordered coffee and brandy, watching distractedly as a woman came running out to scoop the steaming horseshit into a bucket. Once the barman had served him, Guzmán took the envelope from his pocket.

Comandante Leopoldo Guzmán, Comisaría, Calle de Robles no13, Madrid.

No stamp, no postmark and delivered by hand. Guzmán slipped his finger under the seal and ripped open the letter, extracting a single folded piece of thin writing paper. A short message, in the same thin spidery hand as before.

Guzmán glowered at it.

Thursday 15th January 1953

Mi querido *Leo,*

I've arrived in Madrid at last. I'm staying at a Hotel called the Alameda. Will you meet me tomorrow in the Retiro Park at three by the fountain on the Paseo de México? After all these years I so look forward to seeing you once more and hearing your voice.

Abrazos, *Mother.*

Guzmán put the letter in his pocket. What the hell was going on? *Señora* Guzmán was long dead, killed along with her husband during the attack on their village. Someone was taking the piss. Not for much longer. Guzmán tipped his brandy into the coffee and drank it in one swallow. He stood up, about to leave a handful of coins on the counter. He changed his mind and walked out into the brittle cold. A taxi idled down the street and Guzmán flagged it down.

'Hotel Alameda.' He told the driver. '*Rapido.*'

MADRID 1953, COMISARÍA, CALLE DE ROBLES

Peralta returned to the *comisaría* around midday. His enthusiasm for telling Guzmán what he had found out diminished rapidly when he reached the desk.

'General Valverde, *Teniente*,' the *cabo* said as he saluted. 'He's in the *comandante*'s office. You're to report to him at once, sir.'

Peralta clattered down the cold stone corridor to Guzmán's office. Valverde was standing by the blackboards. Peralta noticed Guzmán had erased the diagrams and scrawled comments. It made him feel vaguely guilty.

'Has Guzmán taken up drawing?' Valverde asked. He walked over to the desk and settled himself in Guzmán's chair.

'Just outlines of the investigation, sir.'

Valverde looked up at Peralta and gestured for him to sit down. 'And how is the investigation going, *Teniente*?'

Peralta paused for a moment. 'Our enquiries are going well, sir.'

Valverde snorted contemptuously. 'And your enquiries centre on what exactly, *Teniente*?'

Peralta hesitated, trying to think of what he should say – and what he should not.

The general's cheeks reddened. He stared at Peralta, his moustache quivering. '*Puta madre, Teniente*, we're all after the same thing here. How dare you even consider not keeping me informed?'

'I haven't reported to *Comandante* Guzmán yet, General.'

'Ah,' the general became more conciliatory, 'and you're hesitating to report to me because it would be disrespectful to *Comandante* Guzmán?'

'*Exactamente, mi General.*'

278

Valverde laughed. 'It's admirable you are so loyal to a man who is one step away from being a certifiable psychopath. As your uncle *and* as your senior officer, however, I would advise you to choose your loyalties very carefully.'

'I'm not sure I understand, sir.'

Valverde sighed, as if talking to a young child. '*Teniente* Peralta – and by the way, I have confirmed the rank, against *Comandante* Guzmán's most strident protests.'

'I'm most grateful to the general,' Peralta said.

'So you fucking should be,' Valverde snapped. 'If I've not showed you any preferment, *Teniente*, it's because I've been waiting for you to prove yourself. And you haven't. I must tell you, boy, when my niece said she wanted to marry you, I thought you'd got her pregnant, which would have presented me with the dismal choice of shooting you or having you marry into the family. And to be honest, shooting you would have been my preferred option.'

Peralta flushed. 'I must protest—'

Valverde cut him short. 'No matter. My niece loves you. And you're clearly a hard worker. I think you've a lot of potential – no matter what *Comandante* Guzmán says.'

'*Comandante* Guzmán is my immediate superior. He's entitled to point out my faults in order to help me—'

Valverde silenced Peralta with an upraised hand. 'Please, *Teniente* – or Francisco, if I may?'

'I would prefer my rank in this setting, *mi General*.'

'As you wish. But please, don't feel you have to profess any loyalty to Guzmán. His loyalties are to himself and the *Caudillo*. Undoubtedly in that order. But perhaps you'd know more about that than me?'

'As far as I know, *Comandante* Guzmán's conduct has been impeccable. As for his devotion to duty, I assure you he has never expressed anything but the most loyal support for the *Caudillo* and for Spain,' Peralta said, bristling indignantly.

'You're a fool,' Valverde snapped. 'A fool to believe that about Guzmán.'

'Perhaps there's something the general knows which I don't?'

'There's undoubtedly a lot I know that you don't, you little fuck.' Valverde's face became even more florid than usual.

'Then perhaps the general will excuse me?'

'For God's sake, man, I'm trying to help you.'

'My apologies, *mi General*, but I'm afraid I don't understand in what way the general is trying to help me.'

Valverde took a deep breath, making an effort to calm himself down.

'*Teniente*, I speak to you as a brother officer and as your uncle by marriage. You're a decent man, but decency isn't a necessary requirement for someone engaged in this line of work. Guzmán has survived so long because he has no scruples. None. Whatever the *Caudillo* asks of him, he does. And the *Caudillo* has asked a lot.'

'But is that wrong, sir? Surely we must all do that?'

'We do. But Guzmán abuses it. He's almost completely unaccountable. I have little control over his activities. There's always the possibility he'll go over my head in some matter to the *Caudillo* himself. Worse, if he did, Franco would listen to him. This is an insufferable insult for me: The *Capitán-General* of Madrid, undermined by having Franco's spy camped on my doorstep.'

Valverde's colour was rising again. 'This is not the way a modern state conducts itself, employing a brute like Guzmán as the Head of State's personal assassin,' he muttered. 'It was how things were done in the war. But the war is over, *Teniente*. And Spain has to adapt to that.'

'I don't understand.'

'It's simple. Franco and his ministers still think along the same lines that won them the war. But change is needed now. People tire of doing without while the rest of the world prospers. No one trades with us. No one will equip the army. And why? Because they see us as a nation of fascists, run by a military government brought to power with the help of the Nazis.'

'We are run by a military government,' Peralta said. 'Every minister was a member of the armed forces.'

'No. We're ruled by *Generalísimo* Franco. Not a government. Not the army. Him.'

'But he saved us from the Reds, the Communists and atheists, the Freemasons...'

'And that's all done and dusted now. The world is changing. There'll be no room soon for a country run by force of arms. Apart from Russia – and one day the Yankees will sort them out with their hydrogen bombs. We have to worry about the here and now, and how Spain can become great again, rather than being a poor relation to the rest of Europe. And as long as we're run by one man, that's what we'll be.'

Peralta frowned.

'For Christ's sake, *Teniente*, don't look at me like that. I'm not preaching rebellion. I'm talking about a point in the future when there will have to be change. There doesn't have to be violence but there has to be a plan.'

'A plot, you mean?'

'I mean a plan for running the country, not to depose the *Caudillo*. God, he'd probably welcome it if it meant he could step back from having to deal with every last issue himself. I'm talking about Franco as Head of State – but with a more representative government, one that would be more professional than what we have now.'

Peralta shook his head. 'I don't like it. It sounds like treachery to me.'

Valverde struggled to keep his temper. 'Nonsense. Governments reorganise all the time. That's all it is, a reorganisation. Moving talented people to where they can do the most good. You have a talent for police work. You'd benefit from such a reorganisation. As would Spain. At least consider it.'

It was hard to deal with, Peralta thought. If someone talked like this in public, they'd be arrested. Rightly. 'I need time. I can't say just yes or no to something this important.'

'You don't have much time, so make your mind up quickly, for once in your life. I need capable men for the task ahead.'

'What would I have to do?' Peralta asked.

'*Muy sencillo.* We need to know what Guzmán is up to, who he talks to, what he's thinking. He trusts you because he thinks you're stupid. He thinks in a couple of months he'll get you transferred so he can go back to his own way of doing things without having to worry about you. So repay him in kind: keep me informed of everything he does, everything he says, the calls he makes, the letters he sends. And communicate it to me at once.'

Peralta nodded. He felt a bead of sweat on his receding hairline. His heart was hammering. 'And if I did?'

Valverde smirked, the look of a man used to getting his way and about to get it again.

'For a start we'll triple the salary you get here. Paid straight into your bank account. You can keep your wife in comfort – as a real man should. And you'll be helping Spain. A Spain great, united and free. At last.'

Peralta felt himself shaking.

'Guzmán wants rid of you,' Valverde said. 'He's a dangerous man as you've already seen. Make use of him to do your patriotic duty – and give yourself a hand up at the same time.'

Something bitter burned in Peralta's throat. He nodded weakly.

'Be part of this,' Valverde said in a low voice. 'Be part of this or you will be against it. And make no mistake, this will happen, and when it does, if you were not for us before, you'll be against us then. And those who were against – like Guzmán – will be dealt with. Once and for all.'

Peralta nodded his understanding.

Valverde got to his feet. 'Then you'll do it, *Teniente*?'

Peralta looked up at the ruddy face, the bristling moustache and the icy eyes of the man whose own troops called him the Butcher of Badajoz.

'I'll do it.'

'Excellent.' Valverde walked to the door. 'Keep in touch. You know what I need.'

The general's boots echoed down the stone corridor and

Peralta heard the doors close behind him. Then he ran out into the corridor, clutching his hand over his mouth until he made it to the safety of the toilet. Luckily, there was no one around to hear his retching.

'Hotel Alameda, *señor.*'

Guzmán looked up. He had been concentrating on the Dominicans again. He knew that if he had enough time to mull things over he would reach some sudden epiphany where the logic behind the events of the last few days would become clear to him. He knew this, not because it had happened before, but because he had seen it at the cinema. But then he'd also seen those films where men brooded over women. He thought them worthless at the time. Now, they seemed more of a warning, given the frequency with which thoughts of *Señora* Martinez diverted his thinking away from official matters.

He got out of the taxi and gave the driver a handful of change. The man took it without comment, knowing if he had been short-changed, it would be better not to dispute it with a man of Guzmán's build.

The Hotel Alameda was a tall nineteenth-century building that had clearly seen better days. The first two floors of the building were private apartments and Guzmán watched them go past through the bars of the antique lift. The elderly lift attendant peered at him. Guzmán saw one of the man's eyes was clouded by a cataract.

'The gentleman has no luggage?' the attendant asked.

'The gentleman is not staying here.'

The gates clanked open at the third floor. A threadbare carpet led down a narrow dark hallway towards a small reception desk. The place smelled of damp. *So,* Guzmán thought, *this is the kind of place my mother stays.*

The woman behind the desk looked up at him. Blousy and overweight, she reminded Guzmán of the madam of a brothel, quite possibly an accurate job description, given the general state of decline apparent in the hotel's furnishings.

'Do you have a reservation?' the woman asked without interest.

Guzmán held up his identity card. '*Policía*. Do you have a *Señora* Guzmán here?'

The woman shrugged. Guzmán stared at her.

'I'll see.' She opened the register and squinted at the names on the yellowed paper.

'*Si, señor. Señora* Guzmán, booked in for three days from today. She arrived earlier this morning. Old lady. Room thirty-eight. Do you want me to give her a knock?'

'Just point me to her room – I'm a relative. I'll surprise her.'

The woman pointed back the way he had come. 'Past the lift and then turn right. It's at the end of the corridor.'

Guzmán turned to follow her directions.

'So what relation are you to the lady?' The woman leaned forward on the desk.

Guzmán turned. 'I suggest, *señora*, you mind your business and I'll mind mine. If I develop an interest in your business it might be very unpleasant for you. *Me entiende, señora?*'

The woman blanched. 'It's *señorita* actually.'

'That doesn't surprise me at all.'

Guzmán walked down the corridor, past the caged lift shaft. Somewhere below he heard the metallic groaning of the lift mechanism. He decided he would take the stairs when he left.

The place was silent, no sound of the residents penetrated the solid-looking doors with their large metal numbers. Guzmán looked back to check no one was following him. He pulled the Browning from its holster. If the Dominicans were in there, they might open fire at once. He crushed himself to the right of the door, against the wall, and knocked. No answer. He knocked again. Nothing. Guzmán placed a hand against the door, testing its resistance as he pressed on it. Then, stepping back, he kicked the door just below its handle. The lock yielded with an unhealthy crack and the door opened inwards. Guzmán stepped into the room, pistol raised.

The room was as dilapidated as he expected, given what he had seen so far of the state of the Hotel Alameda. A bed to the right, a chair and a dressing table by the window. Cold winter light glinted through grimy net curtains. There was a faint smell of lavender. A suitcase lay open on the bed. Women's clothes. From the look of them, an old woman. Guzmán rummaged through the case with a practised hand. No weapons. No cash. A copy of a knitting magazine, a ball of wool. Something cold and glassy. He pulled out a framed photograph. A young man in uniform looked blankly at the camera.

'*Ay, Mamá*, I was so young.' Guzmán slipped the picture inside his coat. He searched the drawers of the small bedside table, finding an old Bible with a faded inscription forbidding its removal from the hotel. Guzmán flicked through its pages but there was nothing hidden in it. Out in the street he heard a car horn. There was nothing to keep him here, he decided, and moved swiftly out of the room, pulling the door closed behind him and then, sheathing the big pistol, he returned to the reception desk.

'You find her?' the receptionist asked sullenly.

'No, she's out. Did you see her today?'

'Earlier on. What an old dear with her white hair. All in black. In mourning, I expect?'

'I expect so.' Guzmán turned towards the stairs.

'Do you want me to tell her who called?'

'No.' Guzmán went down the stairs, passing the lift as it shuddered upwards. He looked in but the only passenger was a fat middle-aged man with a collection of bags and suitcases at his feet.

Outside, the air was sharp. Guzmán looked around at the miscellany of rundown buildings. A beggar on the other side of the road slumped against a wall. It was time for a drink. Guzmán crossed the road, ignoring the beggar's pleas, and entered a narrow side street. He paused at the window of an art dealer, paying close attention to several religious themed paintings. Out of the corner of his eye he saw the man following him, ducking into doorways, idly loitering, suddenly perusing his newspaper. One thing was clear, Guzmán thought, this wasn't someone accustomed to surveillance work. The first time Guzmán looked at him, the man should have abandoned his pursuit and let a back-up take over.

Pausing again, Guzmán examined some fading tomes in a second-hand bookshop. Further down the street, Guzmán saw a man apparently studying the contents of a shop window. Maybe he was the back-up. Yet neither the man ahead nor the one following seemed aware of each other. Guzmán would have expected more movement, a sudden entry into a shop or maybe suddenly engaging a passer-by in conversation. Guzmán continued his study of the ancient books, constantly moving his gaze between the man behind and the man in front.

The man behind now walked towards him. Guzmán looked to his right: the other man was walking away in the other direction. Maybe he wasn't part of the surveillance team, then. Behind him, he heard the man in the black coat getting nearer. Guzmán stopped and surveyed the contents of a milliner's window. A handwritten sign was propped behind the neat arrangement of sombre headwear: *The Reds didn't wear hats.* Guzmán smiled to himself at the ingenuity of linking millinery to patriotism. Behind him, the footsteps were getting closer. A quick glance down the street was enough: the man in front was over a hundred metres away, and then disappeared round the corner. He was not part of this, then.

Guzmán admired a dark fedora for a moment. Maybe he would try it on later. The shop owner might decide to donate it to a servant of the State, if he knew what was good for him. The man in black was six metres away now and Guzmán turned to face him. Black overcoat, hat, this was the one who had been outside the *comisaría*, Guzmán was sure. The man smiled, as if approaching an old friend. Both the man's hands were visible and there was no weapon. Guzmán kept his right hand inside his coat. It would be the work of a moment to bring out the Browning and shoot the man in the face if necessary.

'*Comandante* Guzmán, I presume.' The man looked gaunt, his eyes were dark-shadowed and there was a trace of stubble. He advanced with his arm extended, ready to shake hands. Guzmán relaxed his hold on the pistol and seized the man's wrist, twisting his arm behind his back and pushing him into a doorway. The man didn't struggle. Crushed between Guzmán and a locked door and with his arm held almost at breaking point, he was helpless.

'Please, there's no need… My arm, please, *Comandante* Guzmán… I can explain.'

'You'll need to. Otherwise I'll break it. And every other bone in your body after that.'

The man was clearly frightened and there had been no resistance. Nonetheless, Guzmán kept him pinioned while he searched the man's pockets and patted him down for a hidden weapon.

'*Comandante*, I can explain, I mean no harm.'

'All right. I'll let go of your arm now. If you try anything, I'll cripple you for life.'

Guzmán released him. He was no threat: Guzmán could tell from the fear in his eyes.

'You're lucky I didn't shoot you,' he said, 'I don't like being followed.'

'*Comandante* Guzmán. Permit me. My name is Teodoro Lopez. Perhaps you would allow me to buy you a drink?'

The man indicated a small bar across the street. Guzmán's first thought was of an ambush. But the man was too shaken. No one was such a good actor.

'Normally I wouldn't drink on duty,' Guzmán said, 'but as you're offering, and as you've some explaining to do, I accept.'

He let Lopez enter the bar first. It was almost empty. A couple of elderly workmen near the door carried on their conversation without even looking up. The barman was clearly pleased to see them and no wonder, thought Guzmán, the two workmen looked as if they had been nursing the same drinks all morning. He chose a table in the corner of the room and sat with his back to the wall. Lopez ordered coffee. Guzmán asked for a large brandy. The bar was clean and warm and Guzmán shouted a request for a portion of *tortilla* to the barman.

'The cold weather gives one an appetite.' Lopez smiled.

'You seem remarkably cheerful for someone who just came this close to having his head blown off. If you followed me at night like that you'd be dead now,' Guzmán said.

Lopez looked suitably disconcerted. 'Surely you wouldn't be quite so precipitate, *señor?*'

'I would,' Guzmán said. 'You can shoot who you like in my job. It's one of the perks.'

Lopez tried to regain his composure. 'I'm no threat to you, *Comandante.*'

'I can see that for myself, *Señor* Lopez. That's why you're still breathing.'

'In fact I have news, *Comandante,* news I'm sure you will be pleased to hear.'

'Really? They say no news is good news,' Guzmán said. He drank his brandy in one swallow and handed the barman the empty glass. 'Fill her up.'

'I am, *Comandante* Guzmán, something of a detective myself,' Lopez said.

'I didn't say I was a detective.'

'Ah. An erroneous assumption. I apologise. In my case, I am, in fact, an investigator.'

'Spain's full of them.' Guzmán smiled, taking the refilled glass from the barman. 'We invented the Inquisition, didn't we?' This time he took a sip and put the glass down. The barman retreated behind the zinc-topped bar, hopes of a sudden upturn in sales dashed.

'So what do you investigate, *Señor* Lopez? And for who?'

Lopez coughed. 'I usually deal with cases of, shall we say, marital infidelity.'

Guzmán choked on his brandy. 'You're a private investigator?'

Lopez was put out by Guzmán's sudden mirth. 'I can assure you, *Comandante*, my clients usually don't consider their situation at all amusing.'

'Well, possibly not, *Señor* Lopez but your profession – if we can call it that – nearly got you killed today. And I can assure you I haven't been carrying on with anyone's wife. Is that why you have been following me?'

'I have on several occasions been in the vicinity of your work, *Comandante*. Merely so I could ascertain your identity and approach you.'

'A knicker-sniffer?' Guzmán chuckled. 'You certainly had me fooled. *Coño, un huele bragas.*' He leaned forward aggressively. 'And to think I was wondering whether to kill you.'

'There was no intention to deceive,' Lopez said, suddenly worried. 'However, while investigating on behalf of my client, I did find contact between you and a widowed lady.'

Guzmán placed his glass slowly on the table, his sense of humour gone, his hand balling into a fist. '*Señora* Martinez?' His voice was ice and gravel.

'The very same. She seems a very respectable woman.'

'I don't need your opinion on that.' Guzmán snapped. 'In any case, she's a widow. But what has any of this to do with you?'

Lopez gave Guzmán a faint smile, which was a mistake. Guzmán grasped him by his collar. 'I'm glad you find it funny, Lopez, because I'll find it even funnier when I'm beating the shit out of you at the *comisaría*. If you survive the journey there, that is.'

Lopez waited for Guzmán to release him. Sweat dribbled down his forehead. 'It was my understanding the *comandante* is a friend of this lady. My client therefore asked me to contact *Señora* Martinez with a view to gaining her assistance in re-establishing relations with you. A gentle intermediary, shall we say. In case you were inclined not to meet him.'

'Your client being who exactly?' Guzmán interrupted.

'Your cousin Juan.'

'My cousin Juan?'

'Juan Martin Balaguer. Your cousin.'

'You assume I have a cousin Juan?'

Lopez looked puzzled. 'He saw an article about your wartime act of heroism in the newspaper and wondered if you were the relative he was looking for. He had made most of the enquiries by the time he engaged me. All that remained was to ascertain your exact whereabouts and make contact.'

'Why didn't you write a letter?'

Lopez shrugged. 'I was told it was important I make contact with you in person.'

'Just to tell me of the existence of a cousin Juan who I don't even remember?'

'No, no, *Comandante*. To give you the good news of your mother. That the lady is still alive.'

'She died in the war. Almost all the family did. The village was attacked by the Reds and they were killed. I know this, *Señor* Lopez, because I had enquiries made myself, thorough ones.'

'Of course,' Lopez nodded vigorously, 'but in times of war people are scattered, seek shelter and then afterwards,' he raised his hands, 'afterwards, communication may difficult. Impossible. You thought your mother dead and she thought the same about you.'

Most liars would betray themselves when confronted with Guzmán, yet Lopez's naivety seemed genuine enough. Guzmán rolled the last mouthful of brandy around his glass.

'You say Cousin Juan made most of the enquiries?'

'Indeed.'

'And to who did he make them? Ringing up the secret police and asking if they have a certain person there is usually enough to attract our close attention.'

'At first *Señor* Balaguer contacted the newspaper. The local press had reproduced an article from a Madrid daily. They suggested he contact the *capitán-general's* office; given the nature of your fame, it was presumed they would know of you. And of course they did.'

'And they told him where I worked.'

'After some discussion, I believe.'

'I'll bet. And how did you become aware of my "friendship" with *Señora* Martinez?'

'*Señor* Balaguer knew of it – I assume from his dealings with the *capitán-general's* office. Accordingly I went there under the impression she would be pleased to convey the message from *Señora* Guzmán to you.'

Guzmán looked hard at Lopez. 'There are telephones in Spain. Why didn't my mother call me? Or Cousin Juan, since he's so keen to track me down?'

'*Comandante*, I'm only paid a modest sum for my services. I am no more than a conduit for my clients' wishes.'

Guzmán smiled. '*Bien*, *Señor* Lopez, I think I need to know more about your clients.'

'But of course, *Comandante*. They're anxious to meet you. An anxiety, I would add, aggravated by the length of time you've been separated.'

Guzmán nodded. 'It's been a very long time, *Señor* Lopez. I'll make contact with them as soon as possible.'

'So many memories,' Lopez nodded, 'so much to talk about.'

'Absolutely,' Guzmán agreed. 'I look forward to it.'

MADRID 1953, COMISARÍA, CALLE DE ROBLES

Peralta hoped coffee would wash the taste of bile away. Something was wrong. There was blood when he puked and the pain in his stomach was almost constant. He increasingly feared for his wife and child, worried the pain in his stomach was something serious. The thought of her alone, adrift amongst her vile relatives – especially the general – brought him to the verge of tears. He knew bitterness was futile, the priests said so often enough, even though they still endorsed the continued persecution of those who had fought for the Republic. But it was hard not to feel bitter when the pain returned, intense agonising shards, flickering deep in his belly.

Peralta walked unsteadily down the corridor, past Guzmán's office and out into the reception hall. The *sargento* was writing in the day book. Behind him, in the big office, twenty officers were working on the daily business of the *comisaría*. Making phone calls, amassing information, compiling lists of who had done what and who said so. The everyday appearance of the office belied its true purpose: it seemed normal, with the bustle of men in their shirtsleeves, the chattering typewriters, reams of paper being filed into coloured dossiers. Yet here, Peralta knew, their job was people. People who the regime would not forget, nor forgive. In those stacked filing cabinets were thousands of cross-referenced cards, the memory of Franco's regime, holding details of enemies: real, potential and imagined. Neatly catalogued, awaiting the arbitrary violence of deferred vengeance.

The *sargento* looked up and grinned. 'Afternoon, *Teniente*. All well? Can I get you anything?'

Peralta patted his stomach. 'Pain in my guts. I'll be all right in a minute.'

'Too much booze at the Bar Dominicana? The *jefe* likes to let rip when he's out on a job. It can be hard to keep up if you're not a big drinker.'

Peralta knew it wasn't drink that was hurting. 'Can I ask you something, *Sargento*?'

'Course you can, sir, that's why I'm here. To be of use. Even to you, *Teniente*.'

'How much do you trust *Comandante* Guzmán?'

The sarge's face darkened. 'That's a funny thing to ask. I'd trust the *comandante* with my life. He can be a bad bastard, but trust him? I'm surprised you're asking, frankly, sir.'

'I just need to know. I need to know I can trust him.'

The sarge leaned across the desk. He looked at Peralta contemptuously. 'We all trust the *comandante*, *Teniente*. If there's trouble he wouldn't ever let you down. But while we're on the subject, what me and some of the blokes have been wondering is whether we can trust you?'

'That's outrageous, *Sargento*—' Peralta clutched his stomach at a fresh spasm of pain.

'You'd better go back to your office, *Teniente*, if you think you can make it.'

Peralta nodded.

'Sir?' the sarge called. Peralta turned.

'If it helps, *Teniente*, I'm sure we can trust you.'

'*Gracias.*' Peralta pulled open the door and stepped into the icy corridor.

'As far as I can fucking throw you, *puto*,' the sarge spat, watching the door close behind *Teniente* Peralta.

MADRID 1953, PARQUE DEL BUEN RETIRO

The Retiro park was hazy with a mist that drifted across the lawns and paths, draping the trees in quiet melancholy, erasing the outlines of the familiar gates and statues with a milky opacity. Guzmán looked at his watch. His appointment with *Mamá* was getting closer. Whether she would turn up, he very much doubted. This had to be a set-up. But by who? he wondered, lighting a cigarette. If it were Valverde, why the elaborate pretence and the charade of the long-lost cousin? If it was Franco, it would be done immediately, without any messing around.

Whoever was behind it all, Guzmán was happy to take them on. He had always thought there would be a day like this, a sea change when things finally turned against him. He had neither feared it nor worried about it. If it had come, too bad. Let them all come. People had come after him before: he'd killed them. That was what he did best. He exhaled smoke, watching it blend into the folds of mist around him. The park was deserted, frozen and vague in ghostly clinging mist. He looked around carefully, finding no sign of an observer tailing him while others moved into position.

No sign of a group, ready to rush him and overpower him. No sign of anyone. He paused by a clump of trees and peered through the damp shifting haze. Then, slowly, he stepped back into the trees, melting into the mist-shrouded branches. He waited.

He heard a couple pass within a metre of him, arms around each other, talking softly, laughing in their shared discomfort of the cold. Guzmán heard them talk without fully understanding, annoyed by their intimacy. The way the woman leaned against her man, her face raised to his. Just like in the romantic films at the cinema. How could people love in a society like this? He had always thought survival was all. And love was a weakness. Certainly so many of his victims had been broken all the more quickly once their loved ones were brought into the interrogation room. For a fleeting moment he tried to imagine *Señora* Martinez leaning against him, her face angled up to him, her pale eyes closing as he lowered his mouth to hers. Could almost imagine the taste of her. He recoiled from the thought. *Absurd. Fucking absurd. Daydreaming like a schoolgirl. Those films were lies.* Romantic dreams were drivel, like believing in fairies or trolls. He was standing amongst dripping shrivelled trees, soaked by heavy mist, ankle-deep in snow, checking the action of his automatic pistol. This was his world. This was what he knew. This was what he did.

He eased the gun back into its holster and reached into an inside pocket, bringing out the big combat knife he had carried since the war. It gleamed in the chill afternoon air, the edge honed to wicked sharpness. There was something liberating about the knife. Something about reducing the space between killer and victim, creating a more tactile shared experience for both parties, even though, of course, the satisfaction of the act could never be shared equally.

It was five to three. Guzmán checked the pistol again. A gunshot in the Retiro would draw onlookers immediately and he wanted to avoid that if possible. Guzmán wanted no interference while he did his job. And no witnesses. He held the knife against his thigh. In the mist no one would see it until he was close enough to use it.

Often they might never see it until it was leaving their body and, by then, they had no real interest in the things of this world. Ahead of him, he saw the fountain at the end of Paseo de México. Beyond it, the ice-covered waters of the lake. Guzmán felt the slow rage beginning to burn, caustic in its gradual ascendancy over reason. He was ready.

He walked slowly past a statue of a nobleman with helmet and spear, caked in bird shit. An appropriate end, he thought, for the self-seeking, vainglorious bastards who strutted through history, dribbling in their moment of glory before obscurity beckoned them to return. No one and nothing transcended death. Life was just an opportunity to defer oblivion. When his time came, the blackness would rise around him and there would be no more dreams filled with screaming and the sharp scrabbling of rotting claws.

Guzmán stopped, listening intently, focusing as he breathed the frozen air, alert for the slight noises men make as they try to lie silent in ambush. He tensed as he heard a noise. Slow footsteps. A figure emerging from the mist, faint and indeterminate. Guzmán paused. He had thought they might come in a group, or that gunmen might be positioned in the bushes or behind trees. But not this. This truly was a surprise.

The old woman came slowly forward. She wore a black coat, a black hat, white hair. Her bag clutched close to her side. A typical Spanish old lady, dressed up in her finest for a visit to the capital. To see Guzmán once more. After all these years. Her breath misty in the thin air. He walked towards her, straining for sounds from the shadows. Heard nothing. Nothing, except the tip tap of the old woman's heels on the path as she walked, peering through thick spectacles.

'Leo?' She stopped, an antique mole, squinting in the fading afternoon, trying to make out his face. '*Eres tú?*' She looked into his eyes. He looked back.

'*Holá, Mamá.*'

Guzmán stepped forward, the knife bright and gleaming in his

295

hand as it travelled in an upward arc from where he had held it unseen against his leg. It was possible she might have seen its deadly trajectory as he drove it home with all of his vast strength, but the knife entered under the sternum and tore into her heart before she could express any surprise. She fell backwards, a rag doll in shattered motion and Guzmán knew she was dead. The thick glasses tinkled on the frosty path. Her bag spilled open at her side. Guzmán wiped the blade on the black coat and took the woman's bag. Inside her coat pocket he found a small worn purse and took that as well. He grabbed the woman's ankles and dragged her off the path and into the shadows of the bushes. He returned, collected her hat and a shoe and placed them with the body.

Within moments he was back among the mist and the trees, working his way to the park exit. It was cold and he saw no one until he left the entrance and crossed the main road, blending in with shoppers and office workers before cutting down a narrow, high-walled alleyway. Soon, he was walking through familiar back streets toward the *comisaría*. The adrenaline surge that earlier had burned through him was now drained away. He felt tired and hungry. There was a sense of disappointment. Guzmán had been expecting an ambush, not a visit from *Mamá* Guzmán, for fuck's sake. That meant his evaluation of events had been wrong. Scowling, he pulled out a battered packet of Ducados, put one into his mouth and lit the black tobacco, inhaling deeply. *When the plan doesn't work, find a new plan.* Had it been Franco who said that? Time and history obscured the authorship of ideas and Guzmán now faced a present in which ideas – whoever they came from – were not working. That meant change, and change, Guzmán knew, as he passed the ominously skeletal church at the end of Calle de Robles, change was disturbing. At least for those upon whom it was imposed. When he reached the *comisaría*, the sarge was at the desk as always, waiting for him. There was usually something the sarge needed to tell him. Sometimes he had news or a message and today was no exception. Today, the sarge told Guzmán that Peralta was a traitor.

MADRID 1953, COMISARÍA, CALLE DE ROBLES

Peralta had been sitting in his cramped office most of the afternoon making telephone calls and writing his usual copious notes. His conversations with the various intelligence services were providing useful information and the investigation was progressing, he thought. But progress was blighted by the constant pain in his belly. It felt as if some strange creature nestled within his gut, tearing into his innards with nagging claws, the pain radiating in complex, excruciating patterns. At times the pain dimmed, but it never went away. At five o'clock the sarge knocked on Peralta's door to let him know Guzmán was waiting for him in the vaults.

Peralta followed the sarge down the flight of steps to the cells. The stone corridor running between the cells was lit only by a menacing grey glow from the anaemic lights. Peralta noticed the roughness of stone in the walls and ceiling, very much different to that of the building above them. Older. More coarse.

'The Inquisition used to use these cells,' the sarge said cheerfully as they walked down the ancient corridor. 'Long before we moved in, of course.'

They reached the old iron banded door at the end of the corridor. The door was usually locked and bolted. It was open.

'Steps ahead, sir.' The sarge waited for Peralta to go through the door to the vaults.

The lighting was worse than in the corridor as they descended a rough-hewn spiral staircase hacked into the subterranean rock. The walls were damp to the touch as Peralta steadied himself, suddenly afflicted by vertigo. They descended for what he thought must have been fifteen metres. It was impossible to gauge accurately since they were descending into darkness and the solitary electric light above the door was now faint and far above them. The steps ended. Peralta had the impression of being in a large hall, their footsteps echoed around them in recurring waves and there was the steady dripping of water. In the distance was the faint sound of running water. It sounded like a river.

Peralta stopped. 'How are we going to see, *Sargento*?'

He waited for a reply. The *sargento* must be there. He was no more capable than Peralta of seeing in the dark. For a moment Peralta wondered if he was going to be abandoned. Maybe this was a game the sarge played on newcomers. But he didn't seem to be one for games.

A light came on. Dazzling, almost painful, it cut through the darkness, picking out Peralta in its beam. The *teniente* held up his hand to shield his eyes. To his side he saw wet stone walls and above, the curving stone ceiling ribbed, skeletal, like some underground church, its buttresses distorted by Peralta's inflated shadow.

'Stay there, *Teniente*.' Guzmán's voice came from behind the beam of the powerful searchlight. The sarge moved past him, hunched shadow and menace as he strode to take his place behind the light with his *jefe*.

'What's going on?' Peralta called, suddenly uneasy.

'That's what I'd like to know,' Guzmán said, suddenly killing the light. The darkness was total, like being blind.

'Give him a clue.' It was the sarge, the sibilant menace in his voice reinforced by a cascade of whispering echoes rippling away into the dripping blackness.

'*Paciencia, Sargento*. There's no rush.'

Peralta's voice echoed against in the dank silence. 'Why exactly are we playing silly buggers down here, *Comandante*? Surely we've better things to do?'

'We've got better things to do.' The sarge again, an inflection of malice in his voice.

'I think you've got something to tell me,' Guzmán said.

Something is wrong here, Peralta thought. 'If I've done something, I have the right to know what it is.' His tone of indignation sounded weak.

The light blazed on again, forcing the *teniente* to shield his eyes once more. Through his fingers he could see the vague illusory outline of the two men, intangible shadows obscured by the light. But this was no illusion: they were very real.

'For Christ's sake, what are you playing at? I can't see.'

'That's the least of your problems.' The sarge sounded angry.

'I still don't know what the problem is,' Peralta said.

'Well, *Teniente*,' Guzmán's voice echoed around the damp walls and ceiling, making it seem as if he were speaking from every corner at once, 'perhaps you'd like to tell us how you spent your day?'

'Is that it?' Peralta was incredulous. 'You think I've been skiving? You bring me down to this dungeon and treat me like a suspect because you think I've been taking it easy?'

'This place has a long history of questioning,' Guzmán said. 'The Inquisition worked here. We think there was probably something going on before that. Something nasty. It's a good place to come when we need to work undisturbed.'

'No one comes down here uninvited,' the *sargento* hissed. 'And very few leave.'

'None so far,' Guzmán corrected him.

'True enough, *jefe*. See, *Teniente*, once you're down here, you're in big trouble. Such big trouble it's very hard to get out of it. In fact, it's so hard to get out of, really the only thing you can do is to cut a deal with us.'

'A deal?' Peralta was still trying to grasp what was going on. 'What deal?'

'There are worse things than dying,' the sarge said icily.

'What?' Peralta's voice was high and incredulous.

The light went out. Shimmering echoes. The slow dripping of water. Distant scuffling.

'Put that bloody light on.' Peralta tried to assert himself, to regain some sense of control. Tried to stop shaking. He failed.

'Tell us about your day,' Guzmán said.

Peralta heard someone moving in the dark, someone moving towards him.

'The *comandante* asked you a question.' The sarge's voice was very close, his breathing laboured and heavy with anger.

Guzmán's tone was almost conversational. 'You need to answer,

Teniente, or the sarge will break both your legs at the knees. And then your arms as well. You'll do a great deal of screaming and we'll leave you for a few hours to get used to the pain of being a cripple. Then it will turn nasty.'

Peralta shivered. He was sweating profusely. *'Comandante,* this is no way to treat an officer under your command.'

'Say the word, sir.' The sarge sounded even nearer. Peralta heard his breathing. And the sound of metal dragging on stone.

'Teniente, the *sargento's* itching to do some real physical damage to you. It would be best if you just follow my advice and tell us what you've been doing today. Otherwise, this is going to turn ugly. The sarge can do a lot of damage with that crowbar he's carrying.'

Peralta tried to maintain his dignity. 'I spent the morning liaising with External Intelligence Services, checking on the Dominicans and *Señor* Positano. I'm waiting for them to get back to me about Positano. They came up with something I thought was of interest. This Ernesto Melilla – the one with the gold tooth...'

The sarge shuffled impatiently in the dark.

'Siga,' Guzmán said.

'Melilla was in this country in March last year.' Peralta's mouth was dry. 'We think it was him anyway – the date of birth on his passport matches the criminal records General Valverde gave you.'

'It's possible. But even so, what does that tell us?' Guzmán said.

'The thing is, sir, on his last visit his passport stated he was a *teniente coronel* in the Dominican Army.'

'If it was the same man, that is,' Guzmán said. 'A crook with a record as long as your arm holding a military position? No, *Teniente,* that doesn't sound right.'

'Tell the *comandante* what else you did,' the sarge muttered.

'As I said, I left enquiries about Positano at Exterior Intelligence and returned to the *comisaría* around midday. General Valverde was waiting for me.'

'Ah, yes, your uncle,' Guzmán said casually. 'And how was he?'

'Charming as ever,' Peralta said. 'Particularly interested in what you were up to, sir.'

'He always is,' Guzmán said. 'And?'

'He then tried to implicate me in an act of treachery and asked me to spy on you.'

'He admits it,' the sarge spat. 'Let me loosen him up a bit, *jefe*. Break something.'

'Keep quiet,' Guzmán snapped. 'He wanted you to spy on me. What did you say to that, *Teniente*?'

'Naturally, I agreed.' Peralta heard the *sargento*'s muttered curse behind him.

'And what would you get for this service to the general?' Guzmán asked.

'Money. Possibly your job.'

'Traitor's gold, more like,' the sarge snarled.

'One more thing,' Guzmán said, 'before the pain starts. And a word of warning: if it starts, *Teniente*, it only ends when you die.'

'That could take days down here.' The sarge sounded happier now.

'Why didn't tell me about Valverde?' Guzmán asked. 'Did you think no one would notice the *capitán-general* of Madrid rolling up to see a junior officer in the absence of his commanding officer? A junior officer related by marriage to the general?'

'*Con permiso, Comandante*,' Peralta said stiffly, braced for the *sargento*'s attack, 'I thought if I refused the general's offer, it would put him on the defensive. Agreeing to spy on you ensures that you can decide what information he receives.'

'That would be a real act of loyalty,' Guzmán agreed. 'I'd be more convinced if you'd let me know the minute I came back.'

'I didn't even know you were back,' Peralta retorted. 'However, the details of my inquiries on the Dominicans and my conversation with the general are typed up and in a red folder in the tray on your desk.'

'Is that true?' Guzmán asked the sarge.

'How the fuck do I know, *jefe*? I just listened in to the conversation like you told me.'

'The room's bugged?' Peralta asked in surprise.

'Oh yes,' the sarge said, 'we recorded every traitorous word you said, *pendejo.*'

'*Sargento*, refrain from insulting the *teniente* for a moment,' Guzmán ordered. 'And go and see if the report's there as he says.'

The light flared back into life, blinding Peralta again. He turned away, only to see the *sargento*, a metre away, his face twisted in anger, making him even uglier than seemed possible. In his hands was a rusty iron bar.

'Hang on,' Guzmán said. 'I can't trust the sarge not to throw the report in the bin just so he can have some fun.' There was a growl of protest from the *sargento* but Guzmán ignored it. 'You really wrote it all up?' he asked Peralta.

'Of course I did, *Comandante*. You can check for yourself.'

'Don't trust him,' the sarge protested. 'He's bluffing.'

'No,' Guzmán said, 'I think the *teniente*'s telling the truth. No one could fake such fucking pompous outrage.'

The searchlight went out and darkness returned. Guzmán snapped on an electric torch. The beam was thin and weak but enough to guide them back to the stone stairway. Peralta followed Guzmán, aware of the sarge panting at his heels, his breath fetid, like some street dog. Peralta was still shaking as he stepped through the ancient doorway into the low corridor. He felt comforted by the fact that the report was where he'd said, on Guzmán's desk.

'There's a river down there,' the sarge said in a low voice. 'You'd have gone in it. They all do. No one ever came down here and went back up. Except us.'

'Sarge, give it a rest,' Guzmán snapped. 'It's just hard for you to deal with an honest man when you meet one.'

'As if there's any such thing,' the *sargento* snorted. 'Not in this fucking country.'

The firing slowed to a sporadic crackle. Desultory shots kept the oncoming Moors pinned down around the lip of the plateau, but they were gaining ground, scrambling up the rocky pathway, crouching as the bullets whined around them and returning fire while their comrades began crawling forwards through the grass. The Moors were veterans with years of experience of colonial war in Africa and they knew how to fight. The men who opposed them were largely volunteers, experienced but hardly professional, their spirits weakened by continuous defeats at the hands of the Fascists. For a while they felt secure with the African troops pinned down by their fire. Now, as the ammunition ran out and the Moors inched towards them, they began to feel the terror again. The terror of approaching death.

The kid saw what was happening. Those who panicked, who turned and ran to the welcoming shelter of the trees, made good targets. They were cut down by the fire of the Moors, pitching backwards and rolling in the dusty grass. The Moors' aim was deadly and there were very few wounded. That was just as well, since any wounded would soon face the bloody wrath of their enemies and none would die quickly or without suffering.

The kid began to crawl up the slope, pushing his rifle along in front of him. It was hard work and the scrubby ground was sharp beneath him. But he pressed low to the ground, keeping his head down as bullets whined above. He paused, sweat running freely down his face. To his right he saw the corporal moving in a similar manner, careful to remain hidden in the grass. Progress was slow and the screams from behind them were unsettling. The kid rolled on his side and looked back.

Freed from the terrible fire that had kept them pinned down, the Moors advanced past the pile of their comrades' bodies, rushing forward to engage the Republicans. Those men who could not flee were helpless against the long bayonets. It was hard for the wounded: there was no hope of putting up effective resistance and even less of surrendering. Many died under the long knives of the Moors. It was grim work and the kid heard them die, heard their shouts and screams for help to God, their friends, their mothers. One man managed a 'Viva La Republica!' before his screams told the kid he too had met the vengeance of the Moorish troops.

The kid continued to crawl. There would be no escape, he realised, even in the shelter of the trees. Without ammunition and with little likelihood of climbing down off the mountain without encountering more Fascist troops, they were trapped. As he finally struggled into the bushes that littered the treeline, the kid knew it was finished. He turned to look back down the hillside. A busy tangle of African troops moved around the corpses of their slaughtered enemies. It had been said they took body parts as trophies. The kid saw now that it was true. There were some twenty Moors and a large number of bodies around the entrance to the plateau. And there were more bodies below, he knew that. The death toll among their pursuers was high, although he took little satisfaction from that: there were still plenty left. Glancing through the trees he saw the corporal and four other men. These were not good odds and they had few options left. There was little they could do but wait for their enemies to come up after them and to reveal to them the manner of their death.

CHAPTER THIRTEEN

The stone walls of the small bar softly echoed with the murmur of early morning conversation, punctuated by the aroma of mushrooms and garlic from the grill. Tali sat at a table in the corner, waiting as Galindez brought over the stone jug of wine and two small plates teeming with mushrooms and roundels of bread. Tali heaped a piece of bread with mushrooms and took a bite. She gasped, fanning her mouth with her hand before gulping down a mouthful of the cold red wine.

'*Cuidada*, they're really hot,' Galindez said.

'Now you tell me. But they're so good it's hard to wait.'

Galindez sipped her Coke and watched people passing by the open door. Eight thirty, and the city was bustling with crowds on their way to work. The dazzling glare promised another tortuous day.

'I wonder how Mendez and the tech team are getting on at your place?' Galindez said. 'There's two of them with a load of devices straight out of *Star Wars*. Whatever type of equipment Sancho planted, they'll find it. They checked my flat in a couple of hours when I was at the archive.'

'Well, I hope they find that bug or whatever it is. I'm not used to having an uninvited audience in my shower, especially not a creep like Sancho.' Tali wolfed down a last mouthful of mushrooms and finished her wine.

'About what I said last night...' Galindez said, quietly.

'I told you it would sound better outside Guzmán's HQ.'

'You were right.'

'Even if you hadn't told me how you felt about me, I would have known. Know why?'

Galindez shook her head.

'You never once suggested opening the files from the archive.' Tali laughed. 'I knew it must be the real thing if I was more important than Guzmán.'

'Well, I was distracted.' Galindez smiled.

'So you think Mendez will be done by tonight?'

'Yes. And Mendez always does a thorough job.' Galindez poured the last of the wine into Tali's glass. '*Bueno*. We've got a whole day to work through those files. Drink up and let's go and get started.'

Tali emptied her glass and walked to the door, Galindez started to follow her.

'*Oyes tú*,' the barman called. '*Adónde vas?* Going without paying? You'll ruin me, *señorita*.'

Flustered, Galindez returned to the bar, rummaging for change. As ever, her purse had too much crammed in it to find what she was looking for. Her ID card fell onto the counter. 'Sorry, I'm all fingers and thumbs, today.' She realised she hadn't enough money on her.

'Leave it, *señorita*,' the man said. 'I can see you're in a hurry.'

'I live in the flat upstairs,' Galindez said, embarrassed. 'Can I pay you next time?'

'On the house, *señorita*. A couple of pretty girls brighten the place up anyway.'

She thanked him and hurried out into the cobbled street.

The other barman looked at his colleague, puzzled. 'Who're you giving freebies to?'

'That little brunette who lives in one of the apartments *arriba*. I saw her ID card: she's *guardia civil*. Would never have guessed that. Good customer relations, no? Never hurts to have them on your side.'

*

306

Galindez read the text from Mendez:

Finished at Natalia's. Micro camera in bathroom – removed.
Radio microphone in landline phone – removed. Radio
microphone under bed – removed. Let's do lunch sometime
Ana María?- Mendez.

'Sounds like Sancho wired up every room.' Tali said.

'Well, you're free of eavesdroppers now.' Galindez placed the plastic bag containing the files on the desk by the window and waited while Tali made coffee.

'What will you say in your contribution to Luisa's report on Guzmán?' Tali asked.

'I'll start by examining those bodies from the mine. In fact, I might go back to Las Peñas for another look around. And there could be material in his diary I can use to develop a profile of him.'

Tali sipped her coffee. 'What do you make of the diary so far?'

'It's puzzling. He seems a very conventional child to begin with, church-goer, choir, music lessons. You'd think he would have been popular. It's clear his parents were abusive, he'd be taken into care today without doubt. And it's not just his parents. By the time he hits puberty, all the villagers seem to have turned against him. In a couple of cases they physically attack him.'

'I noticed that. And without obvious reason.'

'*Precisamente*. Then the war comes and that's when his career takes off. There's one thing that strikes me. The handwriting: have you noticed how it changes when the war starts? It gets much stronger and angrier.'

'It's not my field, Ana.'

'Nor mine, but the difference is definitely there. It makes me think he underwent a profound change – although I suppose that's not surprising – he must have seen a lot of action. And prolonged exposure to wartime violence would have had an impact on him and his men.'

'You mean they would have remained violent?'

'I mean they didn't need to alter their behaviour very much. Men used to intense combat in a civil war would take a while to settle down into normal society again at the best of times. But they didn't have to: Guzmán and those like him were used to terrorise the population and to eliminate enemies of the regime. For them, the war didn't end.'

'So you don't buy Luisa's theory about him being a mere cog in the machinery of Franco's dictatorship?'

'You know what Luisa and I are like. It would be unusual if we agreed on anything – I certainly don't think Guzmán was just another narrative to be deconstructed. People are far more complex than Luisa depicts them. I wonder what her motivation is sometimes – it feels like she's making excuses for the people who carried out Franco's orders.'

'You could be right. She likes to be seen as radical and controversial.'

'Well, enough of her. *Vamos*. Let's see what's in these files I borrowed.'

'There's a euphemism if ever I heard one,' Tali said pointedly.

'They're not stolen,' Galindez muttered. 'It's just more convenient for us to go through them here. I'll put them back where I found them in a couple of days and no one will be any the wiser.'

She took the files from the plastic bag. First the old man's files, roughly tied with string. Below them, the file bearing Guzmán's name marked *Cuartel del Capitán General de Madrid*. She opened it, taking out a yellowing letter with the crest of the military governor's office. This was more like it, back on Guzmán's trail.

'Shall I open this one?' Tali lifted the old man's file by its string. 'Go ahead.'

Tali cut the string and opened a folder. She began skimming through the papers. She frowned. 'Sorry, Ana. These all seem to be from the seventies.'

'Well, at least there's a reference to Guzmán in this one. Look.'

Tali pulled her chair closer as Galindez read excerpts from the letter: *rank insubordination... discourtesy... conduct not becoming a senior officer...*

'He was a killer,' Tali said incredulously, 'and someone's complaining he's rude?'

Galindez turned to the next letter. She gave a heavy sigh. 'Guzmán's paperwork isn't up to date and his men appear slovenly.'

'Who wrote that?'

'The Military Governor of the Madrid Region, General Antonio Valverde.'

'Bit of a *llorón* then, our Antonio?'

'A complete whinger from the look of it. Guzmán did this, Guzmán did that, failed to acknowledge my authority, made arrests without consultation and so on and so forth. *Mierda*, Guzmán even had the water pipes repaired without authorisation.'

'Wait till we catch him,' Tali smiled, 'the first charge will be paying unauthorised plumbers' fees. They'll extradite him to the Hague for that.'

'*Mierda*, Tali. I hoped this would give us more insight into Guzmán and his activities. All it tells us is that he was rude, a bad communicator and couldn't even enforce a proper dress code among his staff.'

'Try another,' Tali suggested.

'OK, let's see.' Galindez began to read the next letter.

'Ana? What is it?' Tali asked, noticing the intensity of her expression.

'General Valverde suspects Guzmán of keeping a record of his activities.'

'Does it give details?'

'There's a fair bit of toadying: "my unpleasant duty to report... reluctantly I have to bring to your Excellency's attention..." Christ, Valverde was really trying to drop Guzmán in the shit. There's more. "It is my belief that Comandante Guzmán has been keeping unauthorised records of operations and activities officially designated as secret."'

Tali peered over her shoulder. 'What's that handwritten note in the margin?'

'Someone called Gutierrez. I don't know who he was. It says "no further action required". Interesting. This suggests that Guzmán wasn't quite the blue-eyed boy in Franco's set-up. In fact, it looks like Valverde was out to blacken Guzmán's name.'

'It seems very petty.'

'Tell you what,' Galindez said, warming to her theme, 'if Valverde did undermine Guzmán's position with Franco, it might explain why Guzmán disappeared in 1953.'

'What about these other papers? Want to read them while I put Valverde's complaints into chronological order?'

'OK. That sounds like a plan, *Señorita* Castillo.'

Galindez idly began to skim the papers from the seventies. They weren't quite as anodyne as she'd thought. Five minutes later, she was avidly reading them. After twenty minutes she looked up. 'Tali, you need to see these.'

'*Qué pasa?*' Tali asked, surprised by the concern in Galindez's voice.

'I think we're in trouble,' Galindez said. 'Big trouble.'

Tali looked over Galindez's shoulder at the documents on the desk. 'Is this to do with Guzmán?'

'No, it's an invoice for four Ingram M10 machine guns. By a *guardia civil* special operations unit.'

'So what, Ana? They're armed. They bought guns – is that such a big deal?'

'You'll see in a minute. Look at this memo, from someone calling himself Xerxes.'

'And addressed to "those who should know". That's a bit mysterious, isn't it?'

'Read it, Tali.'

'"January twenty-fifth,1977: the operation at 77 Calle de Atocha was successful. Tactical Leader reports Tiburón proved himself useful and that the involvement of the *guardia* was invaluable in attaining our goals. The Reds in the building were

310

engaged, one was killed immediately, the rest were put against a wall and given our response to their demands for democracy.'"

'You know what he's talking about, don't you?' Galindez said.

'It's the Atocha massacre, isn't it? Fascist terrorists killed someone in an office?'

'They killed five people,' Galindez said. 'Right-wing gunmen went to an advice centre on Calle Atocha and killed four lawyers and a law student. There was a pregnant woman. They shot her as well.'

'I remember. My dad's a lawyer, he told me about it after we did it in history class. Didn't the killers want to derail the transition to democracy?'

'That's right,' Galindez said, 'they hoped the funerals would spark left-wing riots so the military would step in and take over governing the country again.'

Tali looked at Galindez in alarm. '*Joder*, Ana María, so it wasn't just terrorists: according to that memo the *guardia civil* were involved.'

'Seems so,' Galindez agreed. 'That will cause some problems when it hits the fan. Now look at this.' She slid another memo across the table. It was dated 27 January 1977.

```
We have now decided the action at Atocha will
be blamed on the group known as Alianza
Apostólica Anti-Communista. Their political
motivation and background make them ideal
suspects. Their arrest will generate
considerable sympathy and their trial will
detract from our involvement. Coming so soon
after the other killings, this is bound to
incense the Reds and create further
opportunities for action against them.

In recognition of their actions, Tactical
Leader and Tiburón are promoted with
```

```
immediate effect. They remain willing to
assist in further actions as necessary. The
Ingram M10s used in the operation have been
destroyed and all documentation pertaining to
this operation is being collected by Los
Centinelas for disposal.
```

Viva España! Arriba España! Xerxes.

'*Los Centinelas,*' Galindez muttered. 'The ones Agustín Benitez told me about at the archive.'

'And they slipped up, didn't they?' Tali said. 'The memo says they destroyed all the documentation – but they didn't.' She paused. '*Mierda*. These might be the only copies in existence.'

'In which case, they'd want this material very badly if they knew it still existed. Thank God they don't know we've got it. I think we'd better read the rest of these files,' Galindez said.

Three hours passed. Three hours of reading and note-taking, punctuated by sudden exclamations of surprise. Three hours of Spanish history being unravelled and rewoven by these impersonal, typewritten communications in which the only emotional reference point was the call to arms from the Civil War – *Arriba España* – at the end of each memo. Three hours of entering names, dates and events into Google – discovering new, subterranean layers of history in the dusty documents. Finding beneath conventional versions of events, other, darker accounts, strewn with violent nuances and complexities. The revelation of previously unknown actors and motives behind apparent accidents and suicides. And other, less subtle operations, the assassinations and attacks, all with full details of the Sentinels' involvement. Apparently disparate events now remorselessly converged into a deliberate pattern of provocative action aimed at destroying Spain's emergent and fragile democracy. And disturbingly, the growing realisation of the value of these documents to *los Centinelas*.

'They upped their game after the Atocha killings,' Galindez said, watching Tali labelling various piles of papers. 'When they failed to provoke public disorder they went for something bigger.'

'You can't get much bigger than a military coup,' Tali agreed. 'This material relates to *Operación Galaxia* in 1978.'

'That didn't get far.' Galindez pushed more papers towards her. 'All three of the main conspirators were arrested while they were planning it.'

'Assuming they were the main conspirators.'

'True. There were three people in charge of the operation: a *guardia* lieutenant colonel, an army commandant and a colonel whose name was never revealed. This memo from December 1978 shows Xerxes didn't think much of them:'

```
To all who should know:
Galaxia has been aborted. Those entrusted with
its organisation have behaved like clowns,
meeting in public places and making arrest
ever more likely. In order to avoid being
compromised, Tactical Leader gave relevant
information to the security services and all
were arrested. Tejero and Ynestrillas face
court martial in due course. Tactical Leader
has naturally been cleared by the security
services and will not be named in any
proceedings.
```

'The one they call Tactical Leader betrayed the other conspirators to keep himself safe,' Galindez continued, 'and the two who were arrested never talked. No wonder: blowing the whistle on *los Centinelas* would be far too dangerous.'

'And then their final attempt in 1982.' Tali placed a label on top of the pile: *23F*. 'Twenty-third of February and Lieutenant Colonel Tejero takes over the parliament building and holds the politicians inside hostage. That coup nearly came off.'

'Nearly,' Galindez agreed. 'Until the King stepped in and brought the army back onside. Look at this last memo following the collapse of the *23F* coup attempt:'

It has been agreed unanimously that further
military action is undesirable. Tejero's
involvement in this ludicrous action – for
which we gave no permission – means he is no
longer reliable. In due course he will be
sentenced in a civil court. He is of little
consequence. We also note the unauthorised
involvement of Ynestrillas. *Los Centinelas*
previously warned him not to involve himself
in any action such as this. He cannot be
forgiven. He will be assigned to Tiburón when
the time is right.

Politicians of all sides agreed to the
so-called Pact of Oblivion: past events which
the Reds and their supporters called crimes
were to be forgotten in return for our
acquiescence to the introduction of democracy.
It is important they continue to believe we
still adhere to that charade.

For the present we must remain silent,
observing and preparing. But we shall not
forget and there will be no lasting pact. The
betrayal of the *Caudillo* will be avenged and
Spain will rise again, *Una, Grande y Libre*.
The Reds may forget. We will not, and when our
vengeance comes, there will be no mercy and no
forgiveness.

When further action is appropriate, we will
notify you. Until then, all communications
must go through Guzmán. We recognise some of

you find Guzmán difficult and unreliable but
for the moment, there is no alternative.

Arriba España. Xerxes.

'Guzmán. *Joder*,' Galindez said, excited now. 'So he was still alive and heavily involved in plots to subvert democracy.' She looked at the memo again. '*Mierda*, perhaps he was a *centinela* himself.'

'They also say Guzmán was difficult and unreliable. Do you think that was because he didn't support the attempted coups?' Tali asked.

'No, he must have been heavily involved if they all had to go through him, surely? Let's check and see if there's any further mention of him in these papers.'

Tali shuffled through the memos impatiently, skimming the contents, reading out the names of several politicians still in office as well as artists and intellectuals who had pledged support for the coup. Other documents revealed the addresses of safe houses and contact numbers. Most chilling of all was a thick wad of names and addresses of those *los Centinelas* intended to execute once the coup was under way. But no further mention of Guzmán. And no more plots; 23 February 1982 seemed to signal an end to *los Centinelas'* activities.

'Perhaps they gave up?' Tali wondered. 'The *Pacto de Oblivio* worked as it was intended to: it forced them to accept democracy.'

'Maybe not.' Galindez looked again at the last memo. 'Xerxes ends by suggesting they went along with the pact to take the heat off them after the failed *23F* coup. But he clearly didn't plan to honour the pact – quite the reverse. They thought they'd bide their time before having another go.'

'But surely they can't still be waiting thirty-odd years later? Democracy's well established now.'

'A lot of people back then were willing to support violence to prevent the introduction of democracy,' Galindez said. 'And we've got the names here of hundreds of people involved – many of them still in important public positions. This is political dynamite.'

'It's dynamite all right,' Tali frowned, 'and we're sitting on it.'

Something was nagging at Galindez's memory. 'Tali, that last memo said Ynestrillas was not forgiven – he was assigned to Tiburón. What do you suppose that meant?'

'I don't know, but his name rings a bell.'

'*Hostia.* Of course it does. He was the guy on the cover of that old newspaper we found in Guzmán's office.'

'You're right. Let's see exactly what happened.' Tali went over to Galindez's laptop and entered the name into Google. 'It's the same person all right – *Comandante* Ynestrillas. Assassinated in Madrid in 1986 by ETA along with two colleagues. Here's the same photo of their bodies.'

'And the memo from Xerxes says Ynestrillas was assigned to Tiburón. So maybe it wasn't a terrorist killing. Perhaps this Tiburón did it? *Puta madre*, Tali, what if this Tiburón was Guzmán?'

Tali looked hard at Galindez. '*Hostia*, this just gets worse, Ana María. They murdered a senior army officer in broad daylight to keep him quiet. If they could do that, what would they do if they knew we'd got this information?' She slumped onto the sofa. 'We've got to do something with these papers. They incriminate too many important people. We don't want to be the only ones who know about this.'

'I can't just give them back,' Galindez said, shifting uncomfortably in her seat.

'Why not? Say you picked them up by accident – that's more or less the truth.'

'Even if I give them back to the archive how do we know the *centinelas* won't find out? They'd guess we'd read them. We'd still be a target. Besides...'

'What?'

Galindez knew Tali was going to be angry. 'I can't give them back. I'll lose my job. I took restricted papers using a high-level security clearance. It would get Uncle Ramiro into trouble and there'd be an inquiry. I'd be fired. Christ, I might even go to prison.'

'So you'd rather be hunted and killed by a secret fascist group, Ana?' Tali's anger burned in her cheeks. 'Sorry if I don't sound all that supportive.'

'But if I wreck my career...'

'We'll still be alive, for fuck's sake. You'd find another job.'

'Yes, probably at Superprecios stacking shelves and watching *Dora La Exploradora* on afternoon TV. There's got to be a better way.'

Tali sighed. 'Isn't there someone who'd know what to do with these papers?'

'It would have to be someone powerful – someone they couldn't get at.'

'Your Uncle Ramiro?'

'No. He'd arrest me himself. He's old school.'

'You think of someone then.' Tali pushed a pile of newspapers to one side and Galindez sprawled next to her on the sofa. She saw the copy of *El Pais* on the top.

Tali noticed the silence. 'What?'

Galindez pursed her lips. '*Mira.*' The newspaper's front page was taken up with a colour photo of a well-dressed man with an immaculate coiffured mass of grey hair. 'What about him?' Galindez said, pointing to the headline: *Top Judge Tries to Seize Franco's Assets.*

'Bernadino Delgado? The judge who tried to have Tony Blair arrested for war crimes when he changed planes in Madrid?'

'That's him. A massive publicity hound, always picking fights with government and big business and bringing high-profile prosecutions...'

Tali hugged her. 'And he's staunchly anti-Franco and anti-fascist. *Hostia.* That's brilliant. The *centinelas* would have more to worry about than us after that.'

'Yes, he'd give the names of everyone in those documents to the media in a heartbeat. The *centinelas* couldn't keep that quiet.'

'That's the plan then?'

'Definitely. We'll give the papers to the judge and let him deal with them.' Galindez reached into the pocket of her jeans for a tissue.

'Did you cut yourself?' Tali asked, noticing the crumpled tissue smeared with dark, congealed blood.

CHAPTER FOURTEEN

The temperature had fallen again and the cold animated the city. People moved quickly and purposefully, limiting the time they spent in the chill air. Guzmán and Peralta crossed the road, dodging through the traffic, Guzmán returning cat calls from irate drivers as he went. They entered the café.

'You look like you could do with something to eat,' Guzmán said.

'I'm not sure about that, seeing as how you were ready to kill me a little while ago.'

Guzmán looked up, his heavy-hooded eyes expressionless. 'To be accurate, *Teniente*, it was the *sargento* who was going to kill you.'

'He doesn't do anything unless you tell him to.'

'I'd like to think so, though I have my doubts. But since he's not going to kill you, can't you give it a rest now? *Hostia*, I've never known anyone complain so much.'

Peralta decided to try and restore some normality to the situation. 'Have you and the sarge worked together for long?' he asked.

'Long enough. I met him in 1939. I'd just been promoted to *capitán*. I was given a special assignment. Franco had taken an interest in me and he kept putting me on special details. Seeing if I was up to the job.'

'What job?'

'The one I've had ever since. This job,' Guzmán said, beckoning the waiter. 'Plate of eggs. Coffee, and a large brandy.'

'Plate of eggs and coffee.' Peralta couldn't face brandy, despite

319

what had happened earlier beneath the *comisaría*. His stomach wouldn't take it.

Guzmán lit a cigarette. Seeing the *teniente's* expression, he offered one to Peralta. 'You can always buy yourself some. We do pay you, you know.'

'I know. I keep forgetting. What was this special job? Or can't you say?'

'It was the summer of 1939,' Guzmán said. 'I'd got the medal two years earlier. After that, Valverde and then Franco kept me on as a sort of errand boy attached to their staff. I didn't care, I was a kid. But after a few months, they started putting things my way. Naturally, I always accepted. There wasn't really a choice.'

'What sort of jobs?' Peralta asked.

'Coffee making.' Guzmán smiled. The waiter brought their drinks.

'Making coffee?'

'*Puta Madre, coño*, don't you remember the War? When old General Queipo de Llano was commander of Andalucía? The radio crackling every night with his broadcasts about how they'd captured Republican women – "Now the Reds' women know we are real men," he'd say. And radio calls from his men out in the field: "We've captured a *Señor* Fulano, what are your orders, *mi General?*"'

'And what were his orders?'

'That's the point. He never said "shoot them in the back" or "rape their women and then kill the lot of them and burn them in a pit". No, he'd say "give them coffee, plenty of coffee". Guzmán laughed.

'You find that funny?'

'Of course, it made us laugh. And that's why we said it ourselves, see? *Dales café*. And then the bullet. It's what he ordered when they arrested that *maricón*, Lorca. *Que le den café, mucho café*. And of course they did. Bang. Well, two shots, that's what Queipo said. One for being queer and one for being Red. You don't know your history too well, do you, *Teniente?*'

Peralta decided to suffer Guzmán's patronising without complaint.

'Anyway, you're getting me off the subject,' Guzmán grumbled. 'It's summer 1939. The war's over. There were thousands of Red prisoners everywhere. A lot of them women. Members of various militant groups.'

Peralta nodded.

'So, a *guardia civil capitán*, Gabaldón, gets killed by some resistance group,' Guzmán continued. 'The bosses can't let it go unpunished, so they bring a load of prisoners to trial early, including a bunch of young women. Later on, the youngest ones came to be known as *Las Trece Rojas Rosas*. Because there were thirteen of them, see? And because they were Reds. The judge considers the case and sentences them all to death.'

'How old were you?' Peralta asked.

'Nineteen. Because of the medal they'd made me a *teniente* and I was going to be up for *capitán* if I played my cards right.'

'And you shot thirteen women?' Peralta looked at Guzmán in horror.

'Not at all. They sent me to observe. To see if I was tough. As if I'd never seen anyone killed before.'

'What was that like?' Peralta asked. 'Seeing them shoot women?'

Guzmán looked at him blankly. 'There were men as well – they shot about fifty-six in all, did them in two groups. I just kept out of the way and watched as I was told to. It was a strain on the nerves for some of the firing squad though.'

'But not for you.'

'*Hombre*,' Guzmán said, 'I'd seen worse. In any case, it's not difficult watching. Know why?'

'No, I don't think I do.'

'Because in battle the other side have a chance of shooting back. If you get a job where all you do is stand there while someone else does all the work, you can hardly argue, can you?'

Peralta looked at Guzmán, appalled. 'They were kids. How could you approve of something like that? It was unnecessary.'

Guzmán glowered. 'Yes, it was unnecessary, *Teniente*, and no, I didn't approve and it wasn't very pleasant, although they died

321

very bravely – for all the good that does anyone. But no one asked my opinion – just like I'm not asking for yours now. My point is, in this work you do what you're told. And if it doesn't involve any effort on your part, you make the most of it – and you don't belly ache, for fuck's sake.' Guzmán turned and angrily shouted for the waiter to bring him a brandy. 'Anyway, to answer your question,' he continued, more calmly, 'that was when I met the sarge.'

'He was part of the firing squad?' Peralta watched his cigarette go out in the ashtray.

'Yes. He'd not long been released from the lunatic asylum.'

Peralta laughed. 'I can imagine.'

Guzmán scowled. 'He'd been in there for most of the war. It was run by Reds – so naturally when our lot won, we let him out.'

'They'd locked him up even though he wasn't mad?'

Guzmán sighed. 'Do keep up, *Teniente*. They'd locked him up because he *was* mad. But, since he was on our side, we decided he wasn't quite so mad after all. He's been very useful over the years.'

'And you were going to let him loose on me?' Peralta snapped.

'Christ, are you still sulking about that?' Guzmán lit another cigarette. Outside the window a beggar staggered across the road, indifferent to the world and the world completely indifferent to him. 'It's not like it was personal.'

'That doesn't make me feel any better.'

Guzmán snorted. 'I had to know I could trust you. Valverde hates me with a passion. And you are his nephew, after all.'

'Only by marriage.'

'Nonetheless. He's tried for years to get someone into the *comisaría* to spy on me. I have to be very careful.'

'Well, he didn't convince me to do it.'

'I had a hunch he wouldn't. But hunches don't keep you alive. Attention to detail does.'

'Well, you certainly attend to detail, *jefe*,' Peralta muttered.

They paused as the waiter brought their food. Guzmán looked at the egg on his plate. 'What's this?'

'Plate of fried eggs, sir, as you gentlemen ordered.'

'Correct me if I'm wrong, but this is one egg.'

'*Si, señor*. But technically, it's a plate of eggs. The instructions of 1939 state clearly that, in the home or in restaurants and cafés, the dish known as a plate of eggs shall consist of one egg.'

'Actually, sir, that's quite correct,' Peralta said.

'*Joder.*' Guzmán's look sent the waiter scurrying away. 'You were saying I attend to detail. Do you?'

'Of course. It's a necessary function of police work.'

'Well, there's something coming up that will require attention to detail,' Guzmán said.

'*A sus ordenes, mi Comandante*. I hope the *comandante* will think it appropriate to assign this task to me. That way, you can be certain of my loyalty.'

Guzmán sighed. 'You really are the most pompous prick, *Teniente*.'

'Even so, sir.'

'You've got to learn how things are done,' Guzmán said. 'You have to pull your weight and that isn't always easy in this unit. So I want you to work with the sarge for a while.'

Peralta had a sinking feeling. 'Doing what exactly, sir?'

'Whatever I tell you,' Guzmán said.

Peralta nodded unhappily. Every value he'd ever had seemed to be inverted or distorted by Guzmán on a daily basis. Yet there was no alternative – unless he were to follow his conscience and resign, which would mean poverty, and that was unthinkable. '*A sus ordenes, mi Comandante.*'

MADRID 1953, COMISARÍA, CALLE DE ROBLES

'The question is,' Guzmán said, putting his feet on his desk, 'how come some mystery man gives *Señora* Martinez a letter from my dead mother?'

'She's got to be involved,' the sarge said.

'Maybe not,' Peralta said. 'The man saw the *comandante* go up to her *piso*. So he decided to use her to pass on the letter.'

'*Imposible*.' Guzmán made himself more comfortable. 'How could he have known I'd visit her? We raided the house next door – she wasn't on our list.'

Peralta frowned. 'If someone's been watching us, they could have decided to use her as a go-between.'

'Bollocks. If my dear old *mamá* wanted to contact me – even with the slight problem of her being dead, *qué en paz descanse*, why the fuck would she get some anonymous bloke to take a letter to a woman I met hours before?'

The sarge nodded. 'As you say, *Señora* Martinez didn't know you'd turn up on her doorstep. So she couldn't have planned anything in advance.'

'The only ones who knew we were going to that address were us.' Guzmán was getting angry. 'And frankly, whose doorstep I turn up on, *Sargento*,' Guzmán's voice rose, 'is no fucking business of yours, *me entiendes*?'

He exhaled a cloud of smoke, deep in thought. 'They want me to think my dead relatives are alive,' he said finally. 'Why?'

'The Dominicans?' Peralta said. 'Setting up an ambush. When you turn up to see these long-lost relatives, they'll make a move.'

'Possibly.' Guzmán nodded. 'Although they haven't acted with a great deal of subtlety so far. *Hostia*, if it is them I'm going to be fucking angry. We still don't even know for sure yet what they're up to.'

'Maybe they want to set up supply chains to other countries from here?' Peralta said. 'Spain's the gateway into Europe for drug smuggling. Perhaps the Dominicans want to take advantage of that? Bypass Marseille, perhaps? Cut out the French.'

Guzmán nodded. 'It makes sense. They could easily handle the local talent if things got rough.' He blew a dense cloud of smoke towards Peralta. 'We'll have to be careful with this investigation,' he grumbled. 'Franco said to lay off but Valverde wants us to protect his bent business from the Dominicans. We're caught in the middle.'

Peralta stood up. 'I'll see how my enquiries are going. I've asked for help from the Exterior Intelligence and Counter Intelligence Services. They're treating it as a priority.'

'Excellent. Let me know what you come up with,' Guzmán said.

Peralta pulled on his coat. The walk over to Exterior Intelligence would be a welcome change from the claustrophobia of the *comisaría*. In fact, just being able to leave the *comisaría* was comforting after what had happened. His colleagues had been on the verge of killing him and he was still shaken by the experience. *They put the bodies in a river? What would they have told his wife? Would she have got a pension?*

He stepped out into the thin, sharp winter air. Out of the *comisaría*. The problem was, he thought sadly, he would have to come back again.

MADRID 1953, SERVICIOS DE INTELIGENCIA EXTERIOR Y
CONTRAINTELIGENCIA

The short walk was still long enough to have Peralta shivering by the time he arrived. He no longer walked the street observing passers-by. It was those he might not see that worried him. He began to spend time looking in shop windows, suddenly turning back the way he'd come, hoping to spot anyone following. No one was. It occurred to him that he maybe wasn't important enough to shadow as they had Guzmán and the Sarge. He found that troubling.

At the offices of *Servicios de Inteligencia Exterior y Contra Inteligencia*, Peralta waited patiently while the soldiers on duty checked his identity. Climbing the ornate staircase to the American Section he passed into a world of dark, dusty offices filled with filing cabinets and huge shelves of files and dossiers. He followed a narrow corridor of endless doors, each opening onto varying numbers of intelligence personnel, translators and the occasional spy.

Halfway down, Peralta found the place he was looking for. He knocked and entered. A man sat at an ancient wooden desk, his plump figure framed by piles of newspapers, journals, books, letters and telegrams. The room was almost in darkness, a small lamp on the desk providing a patch of feeble light in the midst of the chaotic paperwork. Behind the man was an ornate window with glass so filthy it was hard to imagine daylight could penetrate it even in the brightest summer.

'Francisco, *coño*! When you phoned the other day I couldn't believe how long it's been since I last saw you.'

The man got to his feet and came out from behind his desk to hug Peralta against his corpulent body. Peralta slapped him on his broad shoulders.

'Jaime. It's been too long. How are you?'

Jaime laughed, wheezing with the sudden exertion of the welcome.

'The same. Buried in paper. But it's a living and a pension. What more can you ask?'

Peralta pulled up a chair, removing a pile of yellowing periodicals and depositing them on the threadbare carpet.

'So how's life in the *Brigada Especial*?' Jaime asked, suddenly serious.

'Secret.' Peralta laughed.

'Seriously, Paquito. When I heard you were there, I almost crossed myself. Me, a committed atheist.'

Peralta looked round furtively at the door.

'What's the matter? You don't think anyone's going to be listening to our conversation, do you? This must be the safest place in Madrid to talk. You don't think anyone would be spying on...'

Peralta's face made it clear that was exactly what he was thinking. When Jaime spoke again, it was in a low, conspiratorial tone.

'So it really is like that where you are? Cloak and dagger stuff?'

Peralta looked at him and nodded. 'You never know who's listening – truly.'

'You're not in... *we're* not in any danger, are we?' Jaime asked anxiously.

Peralta shrugged. 'You can never be sure.'

Jaime dabbed his big wide face with a handkerchief. 'This all sounds a bit worrying, Paquito. I hope you aren't involved in anything out of your depth?'

'Jaime,' Peralta said, 'I've never been so out of my depth. Or so frightened. And the trouble is,' he added, 'the most frightening ones are those I work with.'

'And this query?' Jaime indicated the papers on his desk. 'This *Señor* Positano? Is he a threat?'

'I was hoping you'd tell me,' Peralta smiled. 'He's of interest to us, but we know nothing about him, other than he keeps some bad company. Which is why it's so useful to have an old friend like you working here. At school you were always buried in the dustiest books. Spending all day checking up on details and facts – this must be your idea of heaven.'

Jaime grinned and reached across the desk, gathering a handful of papers. 'I love it here, although I never know why I'm doing something. I just track down the information required, it goes off to the military or the police and that's it. The same with your request – I don't know why you want it and I couldn't care less – although after what you've said about your job I'm starting to wonder if the Russian army is lurking out in the corridor.'

Peralta laughed. 'I don't think you need worry about the Russians right now. We deal with domestic security, they're not our concern.'

Jaime sucked at his lower lip. '*Are* you going to tell me what this is all about?'

'No.' Peralta's tone was emphatic.

Jaime sighed. '*Bueno*. I won't ask again. But I do worry, Paco. You know you said it was OK to use your boss's name?'

'Of course.'

'Well I did. And that's when I first started to worry about you.'

'Why? Just because I said to mention Guzmán was in charge of the investigation?'

'We deal with the different branches of the security services all the time. I often have to say who I want materials for. Bureaucracy is the way we do things here, Paco. Things don't work all that quickly.'

'It's always the same,' Peralta agreed with a smile, 'Bloody pen-pushers.'

'Last time I called the States for some information, it was for General Valverde,' Jaime said. 'They took a week to get back to me.'

'So they're slow,' Peralta said, 'what's your point?'

Jaime wiped his sweaty face with his handkerchief, 'The point is, when I mentioned *Comandante* Guzmán's name, they called me back within the hour. And then someone else called from Military Intelligence to check I'd got what I wanted and was satisfied with the information.'

'*Comandante* Guzmán is very well connected,' Peralta said.

Jaime wiped away another bead of sweat. 'Well, tell me if this is helpful, because it feels as if he isn't someone a person would want to get on the wrong side of.'

'That's true,' Peralta agreed. 'But you've nothing to worry about, honestly.'

'This Positano gentleman,' Jaime began, 'what do you know about him?'

Peralta shrugged. 'He's the leader of the trade delegation to Spain, so I assume he's someone important in one of their governmental departments.'

Jaime nodded. 'Senior Trade Adviser, to be exact. Since 1946.'

'So he's got a good job. Any background information?'

'There's his army record. Purple Heart, wounded during the invasion of Italy. Congressional Medal of Honour. A brave man.'

'You don't have a cigarette by any chance?' Peralta asked.

'*Mierda*, Paco, you've still got the same habit as when you were fifteen. You could buy cigarettes you know, instead of cadging them from other people.'

'So my boss tells me.' Peralta smiled.

Jaime reached into his desk drawer and brought out a crumpled pack of Chesterfields. He offered the packet to Peralta who took two with a grin, putting one into his top pocket for later.

'I suppose you want a light as well?' Jaime retrieved a box of wax matches from his drawer and pushed them across the desk to Peralta. 'I presume you can light it yourself?'

Peralta hunched forward as he lit the cigarette. Jaime slid a glass ashtray towards him. 'Be careful. You're in a building full of paper.'

'I'll be careful. Now, you were saying about Positano?'

'He's been employed as a government trade adviser since he left the army in 1946.'

'So nothing terribly interesting? He had a good war and then got a good job afterwards? Sounds like Spain.'

'I found his place of birth. Born Positano, Italy, 1915.' Jaime read from the paper in front of him. 'It's near Naples. He arrived in the US in 1934.' His plump finger moved down the typewritten page. 'He was arrested the following year on suspicion of murder in Chicago.'

'Murder? Are you sure?'

'Shall I read you what the paper said? I had to take this down over the phone, it will have cost the State a fortune.'

'Money well spent if it helps us.' Peralta blew a cloud of thick tobacco smoke across the desk. Jaime frowned at him, the faint light twinkling on his balding round head, his eyes small and glinting behind the thick spectacles. 'Sorry.' Peralta waved smoke away with his hand.

'"Italian-born youth charged with homicide",' Jaime read. '"Alfredo Positano, aged twenty, born Naples, Italy and resident in the United States was today arrested and charged with four counts of murder following the shooting earlier this year on February 14 known as the St Valentine's Day Massacre. Police sources claim Positano was a member of the Capone organisation."'

'A gangster?' Peralta said. 'What happened?'

'The case disappeared. One of our men tried his damnedest to find out. It wasn't even on file at the Chicago police station where he was arrested.'

'That proves nothing,' Peralta said. 'Many of our records were lost in the Crusade against the Reds. It happens.'

Jaime nodded. 'But our man also looked at a couple of other serious cases reported in that same day's newspaper. Both were mentioned in the next week's edition and both cases were still on file with the Chicago police. The official records of Positano's case vanished.'

'You should be in the police yourself.' Peralta grinned. 'That's excellent work.'

'I know,' Jaime said. 'Unfortunately that's all I could get.'

'Can I take that folder?'

'Don't lose it. It's the only one there is. We hate to have to repeat inquiries; our people might get noticed if they become too visible.'

'I'll be very careful,' Peralta promised.

Jaime began putting the papers back into their cardboard folder.

'Listen, you must come and see us, Jaime. You still haven't seen the baby,' Peralta said.

Jaime looked up, his eyes sad behind the thick prisms of his glasses. 'Probably not a good idea, eh? After last time. Your wedding.'

It was Peralta's turn to look sad. 'She didn't mean it, Jaime.'

'Yes she did. And you backed her up.'

'I'm her husband. Naturally I had to.'

'I suppose so.'

Peralta looked at him angrily. 'Actually, if you're going to bring up the subject, it's hardly normal behaviour, is it? Christ almighty, the Bible says it's an abomination, Jaime. I ignored it when we were younger, no matter what others said about you. But you know as well as I do you have to keep those things quiet.'

'Don't you mean hidden?'

'Hidden. Yes. Bloody well hidden. Jesus, you could lose your job here, man. A good job with a pension. Just because you're a...'

'*Maricón*? Because I want to love someone like everybody else does?'

'Because you don't want to love someone like everyone else does. You want something that's against the laws of man and God. You can't get away with it for ever. *Hombre*, this is a Catholic country. Laws, Jaime. Laws and rules. And you're breaking them.'

'Spoken like a policeman.'

'I am a policeman,' Peralta said, gathering up the folder from the desk. 'I swore an oath to protect public morality.'

'So if one day I'm with a friend, in the Retiro after dark or down by the banks of the Manzanares, away from prying eyes, not hurting anyone and you and your *Comandante* Guzmán come along, I suppose you'd arrest me?'

'I might,' Peralta said, 'though I doubt *Comandante* Guzmán would.'

'What? He's more tolerant than you, is he?'

'No. He'd kill you. He'd take out his pistol and shoot both of you. And you know what? No one would turn a hair.'

'Some company you keep,' Jaime spluttered. 'I hope you're proud of yourself, going round keeping us *maricónes* off the street. You're no better than those bastards who shot Lorca.'

Peralta raised a finger to his mouth, 'Hush, Jaime. For Christ's sake, Lorca wasn't just a *marica*, he was a Red.'

'He was a genius and men like you and Guzmán shot him.' Jaime's eyes were blazing. 'Have you got your gun? Are you carrying it now?'

Peralta frowned. 'What?'

'Your gun. Show it to me. Let me see it. Let's see what makes you so tough, Paco.'

'Don't be stupid, Jaime.' Peralta took a step towards the door but Jaime followed him.

'Show me. Show me or I'll shout so the whole building will hear that I'm queer and I'll tell them you are too.' His voice was far too loud now. Peralta could hear someone complaining through the thin wall from the next office.

Peralta sighed and pulled aside his coat and jacket. The revolver hung in the leather holster under his left arm.

'Let me see it.' Jaime stared, fascinated, at the gun.

Peralta drew the pistol from its holster. The metal glistened, dark and oily. He held the weapon in the flat of his hand towards Jaime. 'That's all it is,' he said flatly. 'Small-calibre service revolver. We all carry one like it.' *Except Guzmán*, he thought, *he carries a small cannon around with him.*

'Give it to me,' Jaime said.

'Why? What good would that do you?'

'So I can make you feel how I feel all the time. Vulnerable, afraid, always worrying about what might happen. That anyone could hurt you or harm you. Let me show you how that feels.'

Jaime lunged forward, grabbing at the pistol. Peralta moved backwards and Jaime stumbled to the floor, still scrambling towards him, an absurd ball of a man, attacking on his knees. Peralta's hand curled around his pistol. He took a step back and then smashed the butt of the gun across Jaime's head. Jaime cried out and sank back, his face covered in blood from the wound in his scalp. He began to sob. Peralta put the gun back in its holster.

The door opened and a man with the faded, undernourished look of a civil servant peered in hesitantly. '*Qué pasa?*' he demanded, looking down at Jaime.

Jaime said nothing and continued sobbing, dabbing ineffectually at the wound on his head with his handkerchief. Peralta reached inside his jacket and pulled out his identity card. '*Policía*. Mind your own business.'

The man stepped backwards but did not leave. Outside two more civil servants were peering in through the open door.

Peralta held his identity card towards them. 'You're friends of this gentleman?'

'We're his colleagues,' one said. 'What has he done to deserve this? I must protest.'

Peralta took a step towards the man. 'And I wonder whether you have the same taste in little boys as your colleague. Because if you have, I'll arrest you as well.'

Cowed by Peralta's threat, the men moved back into the corridor. Peralta guessed that they knew, the way he had always known about Jaime. An implicit knowledge, ignored until events forced it into the open. He went into the corridor. The men shuffled in fear and humiliation, powerless in the face of the *teniente*'s authority. He walked past them, along the corridor. Behind him, he heard loud sobbing from Jaime's office. The staircase leading down into the marbled entrance hall echoed with his footsteps. By the time he reached the lobby, the sound of weeping had stopped.

Peralta took the stairs to the street two at a time, suddenly feeling alert and alive as he began to walk briskly back to the *comisaría*. *Jaime went too far*, he thought. *Took advantage of the fact that I never said anything about his perversion.* He walked slowly, justifying to himself what he had done. *He asked for it.* Jaime should never have tried to implicate him publicly in his sordid secret. And he'd never liked *Señora* Peralta anyway. *She was right all along.* Jaime deserved all he got. It hadn't been easy, but Peralta had asserted himself, shown him some things would not be tolerated. And those pen-pushers in the corridor had backed off, because they saw the power he had. *Guzmán said I would never get used to this work.* Peralta knew he had done what was necessary. Had been right to do it. *Good job, Teniente.* He stopped for a moment. Not because the last phrase in his head didn't sound right but because it wasn't his own voice congratulating him. It was Guzmán's.

The air was icy cold, the sky heavy with dark cloud. Peralta stopped at a tobacconist's and bought a pack of cigarettes. Flakes of snow fell and the city began to darken. There were worse things than darkness, he thought, inhaling the thick smoke. It was what was in the darkness that mattered. Snow fell heavily but he whistled as he walked back to the *comisaría*. He was still whistling when he entered the building and the sarge greeted him with the news about the bodies.

MADRID 1953, COMISARÍA, CALLE DE ROBLES

Guzmán looked up from his desk. 'You took your time.'

'I was at *Inteligencia Exterior.* Positano's file.' Peralta held up the cardboard folder.

'I know you were, *Teniente*. I just had a phone call from the Ministry. Apparently you beat one of their civil servants half unconscious with your pistol. I find that hard to believe since you don't normally pay such close attention to detail in your work.'

'It's true, *jefe*. There was some trouble.'

'Which was?'

'Do I have to say?' Peralta asked. 'He's a friend. Was a friend.'

'I thought we'd established we can have no secrets here,' Guzmán said evenly. 'To be more precise, *you* can have no secrets here.'

Peralta sighed. 'He's a *maricón*. He used to keep it quiet but was irritated because my wife wouldn't have him to the wedding.'

'I admire her intolerance,' Guzmán said, 'though I do question your choice of friends.'

'We were at school together,' Peralta said simply. 'I hadn't seen him in years.'

'And you beat his brains out at your reunion?' Guzmán asked, amused. 'What was it, some sort of lovers' tiff?'

'I resent that.' Peralta drew his gaunt frame up to his full height, a gesture which failed to impress Guzmán. 'I had nothing to do with his sordid lifestyle – although, as I say, he kept it quiet. But he confronted me with it today. He insulted my wife and he insulted Spain. I felt justified in defending my honour.'

Guzmán grinned. 'Well, good for you, *Teniente*. I can see I've underrated you. You'd better have a seat, all this exercise may be bad for your constitution. Actually, we've had a bit of a shock here as well.'

'The sarge said as much when I came in.'

'What did he say? Out of interest.'

'His exact words? "Christ, *Teniente*, we've got twenty stiffs on our hands and the boss is going fucking crazy."'

'That's about the size of it.' Guzmán nodded. 'All over Madrid, bodies have been turning up faster than in a Haitian cemetery on a Saturday night. Valverde's running around like a blue-arsed fly and screaming for action. Must be getting it in the neck from above.'

'What's going on? How were they killed?'

'That's the beauty of it,' Guzmán said, his face returning to its usual brooding severity. 'We don't bloody know. They're just dead. Young and old, poor, middle class. It's been a devil to keep quiet.'

'How can they just be dead?' Peralta asked.

Guzmán shook his head. 'God knows. But *Herr* Dr Liebermann is in the mess room having a look at a couple.'

'You put the bodies in the mess?' Peralta said. 'We eat in there.'

'Don't worry about it,' Guzmán said, standing up, 'they only take up a couple of tables and they won't eat much.'

Liebermann looked up as Guzmán and Peralta entered the mess. He peered at them through his thin, wire-rimmed spectacles.

'Ah, *Comandante. Teniente* Peralta, *Guten Abend.*'

'Speak like a Christian,' Guzmán snapped. The German gave him a stealthy look of hate before bending again over the corpse on the table. Peralta stepped nearer to get a better view. A youngish woman, hair the colour of straw. Peralta could see she was middle class from her jewellery. Liebermann was struggling to pull the woman into a sitting position and looked to Guzmán, expecting help. Guzmán didn't move.

'I don't think she wants to go with you, *Herr Doktor.*' Guzmán pronounced the German words with exaggerated distaste.

Liebermann held the woman's shoulders, trying to wrestle her into a sitting position.

'Please, *Herr Comandante,*' he said in his clipped Spanish, 'I need to remove her blouse. It shouldn't be difficult, rigor mortis hasn't set in yet.'

'Take her blouse off? We're paying you for this,' Guzmán said, 'and you want to play with her tits? You should pay us, *Herr Doktor.*'

Peralta could see Liebermann was incensed. The more he rose to the bait, the more Guzmán would enjoy it.

'Let me help you.' Peralta moved forwards to take hold of the woman's shoulder but Liebermann waved his free hand.

'I've got her weight now. Just undo the blouse.'

'*Venga, Teniente,*' Guzmán said, 'you must've done that before surely?'

Peralta undid the bone buttons of the woman's blouse. They were large and difficult to pull from the buttonholes.

'*Rapido, Teniente,*' Guzmán heckled, 'what's up – first-night nerves?'

Peralta finally unfastened the last button and yanked the woman's blouse from the waistband of her skirt. He then pulled back the blouse over one shoulder while Liebermann held the other. The woman's head fell back into the space between the two men. With some effort, Peralta inclined her towards Liebermann while he pulled the woman's arm free from the sleeve and then Liebermann did the same at his side. They lay the woman back down on the table, now suddenly exposed, her black brassiere a stark final defence of her modesty.

'Well, let's have that off then,' Guzmán said cheerfully.

Liebermann looked at him coldly. 'That will not be necessary, *Herr Comandante.* It is her armpit I wish to examine.'

Guzmán turned to Peralta and winked. 'That's the Germans for you,' he grinned, 'go straight for the weird stuff.'

Liebermann lifted the woman's arm. He poked at the thick tuft of hair, pulling the skin taut, probing. 'There,' he said with an air of martyred vindication.

Guzmán leaned forwards. 'She's got spots under her arms,' he said uninterestedly.

'They aren't spots, though, are they, Dr Liebermann?' Peralta asked.

Liebermann smiled cadaverously. 'You are correct, *Teniente*. They are needle marks. This lady has been injecting something. And, if I may conjecture, *Herr Comandante?*'

Guzmán had been admiring the pearl and silver necklace the woman was wearing and looked up distractedly. 'Do what you like, doctor, as long as you pronounce it correctly.'

Liebermann sighed again. 'I suggest that, from the number of needle marks, this lady was addicted to whatever it was she injected. Morphine, I imagine. And,' his voice became more pompous, 'I would further suggest we will find the other bodies you have encountered will exhibit a similar cause of death. These injections, *Comandante*, they use parts of the body where they can't be seen – the armpit, between the toes even.'

Guzmán stepped back from the weak pool of light illuminating the half-naked corpse. 'You know, doctor, if you'd brought the same level of expertise to your tactics at Stalingrad, they'd be speaking German in London and Paris by now and you'd still be sewing children's heads onto gypsies in one of your camps.' Guzmán strode to the door and left the room.

Peralta nodded to the German. 'Thank you, doctor, you've been a great help.'

'And you, *Herr Teniente*, are a gentleman,' Liebermann said, bringing his heels together with a sharp click as Peralta hurriedly followed his boss back to his cheerless office. Liebermann sighed and turned back to the dead woman. This was what he liked. Someone who couldn't mock him, who could not resist his intimate explorations. It brought back memories of happier times, he thought, lifting his scalpel. The times in the camps. Though when they were alive it had been so much more interesting. He sighed again. *Beggars can't be choosers.* Then he began to cut.

The kid ran, following the corporal through the trees. Both still carried their rifles, although the effort was slowing them down. Five of them still alive. The kid felt sweat run down his face from his sodden scalp. His clothes were soaked, chafing at every move. The heat was unbearable but the thought of the Moors' long knives kept him moving.

Some way ahead, the others had stopped running. The corporal caught up with them and a rapid argument began as to whether to continue their hopeless flight or attempt to surrender. The corporal thought they should continue upwards. These men had known him for well over a year, yet now they looked at him as if they had never seen him before, and in their eyes he saw something he had seen in prisoners' eyes when they were about to be executed. A void, an emptiness as the brain refused to allow the eyes to see any more horror, and reason bridled against the ghastly imminence of death. They were the eyes of the dead.

The corporal checked the magazine of his rifle. Three bullets left. He removed one and gave it to the kid. Of the other men, only one still had a rifle. Another man had lost his weapon and his fear was so great he could not stand still, his feet moving in involuntary anticipation of further flight. The corporal went through the man's pockets and found several bullets which he shared with the kid.

The ground rose ever more steeply ahead of them. It was clear they would soon find themselves trapped against the sheer slope of the hillside above them. This was as far as they could go. In their condition they could not climb the cliffs looming above. Now flight was no longer possible, they prepared for a final confrontation with the Moors. One of the men unwrapped a rolled-up groundsheet and

338

brought out a tommy gun, its round magazine slick with oil. He had carried it all this way without using it, saving it until the time arrived when he could deploy it to its best advantage. He and the corporal had been regular soldiers and they now set out their battle plan. The kid was placed in bushes far over to the right. The corporal took up position in the centre, amongst scrub that would afford him cover until the Moors got near. The two others were placed on the left, the one without a weapon was now clutching the corporal's bayonet. The kid knew he would never be able to use it if the Moors got close. The tommy gunner crawled further into the deep coarse grasses and shrubs amongst the trees, seeking a suitable spot somewhere between the two men on the left and the corporal.

The kid lay in the dry grass and waited. He placed two grenades in front of him. When he had fired the five bullets he now possessed, he would throw one of the grenades. The other he would use on himself. He had seen it done before: remove the pin and hold the deadly canister to the side of his head. Death might be inevitable, but at least he would cheat the Moors of the manner in which it was done.

There were shouts amongst the trees below them. And again he heard the harsh voices of the Moors calling 'Guzmán'. Whoever Guzmán was, he was coming.

CHAPTER FIFTEEN

Galindez strolled slowly towards the Faculty of Modern History. Buildings and trees rippled in the torrid, wavering air, shapes and colours merging in fluid patterns. The humidity was getting to her: she felt a headache coming on. The stone steps leading to the entrance reflected the remorseless heat against her bare legs. At the top of the steps she paused as a barb of sharp pain flickered behind her eyes. *Bloody heat. It's giving me a migraine.* Thankfully, inside the building it was cool and quiet. A low murmur of distant voices. Luisa was sitting in her office by the open window, looking out over the sweltering campus. Hearing Galindez in the doorway, she turned.

'*Holá, Ana. Que calor, verdad?*'

'Yes, it's murder. Thirty-three degrees today,' Galindez said, settling into a chair.

'And how's your investigation going?'

'Slowly. At the moment, I'm putting names from the diary into our database to match them with lists of people who went missing in the war. It's very hit and miss: even if we can match the name, there's often no surviving relative for me to get a DNA sample to confirm the identity. It'll take a while: there are twenty-three sites identified in his diary.'

'And you're going to excavate all of them?' Luisa's smile was softly mocking. 'I hope the *guardia*'s paying.'

'Of course not. We don't have the resources, though I may be able to get permission to open up one or two sites – we'll see. I'm also going to do an examination of the remains from Las Peñas in a day or two when there's a laboratory available.'

Luisa nodded. 'So you've come up with very little, really, Ana María.'

'Which is why I'm doing the tests on the skeletons,' Galindez said, annoyed by Luisa's patronising tone.

'You must do as you see fit, Ana.'

Luisa was insufferably smug this morning, Galindez thought. 'I expect you've made more progress, Luisa?'

'Oh yes. What with the Freudian discourse analysis on the early diary entries and the intertextual exposition of the later material, we've built up a mass of narrative data. Later on, we'll merge that with the stories of survivors, biographical accounts and so forth. Toni refers to it in his thesis as "revoicing".'

'I'm sure he does, Luisa. You're his Ph.D. supervisor, after all.'

Luisa frowned. 'Ana, why so hostile? You've a free hand here to do what you like for this report. You don't get that in the *guardia*. Try to be a bit more amenable to the ideas of others.'

'That cuts both ways. For example, if I write a forensic paper on Guzmán, will you include it in the report?'

Luisa cast a glance over Galindez's legs. She pulled her chair closer. Uncomfortably close. 'It's an excellent idea,' she said, 'parallel narratives, separated by epistemological divergence. It's nice having that kind of tension. Though my approach will be altogether more populist.'

'Really?' It was difficult for Galindez to imagine Luisa descending from the theoretical clouds long enough to be populist.

'Definitely. I want to bring the experiences that shaped Guzmán to a wider public. Not just an academic audience, but Spain as a whole: *Guzmán – My War Within*. That's the working title. An account of how a sensitive and talented young man ends up in charge of policing Franco's defeated enemies. There's a big market for work of this kind. People want to share those experiences in all their raw detail. I think I'll be able to help them share what Guzmán suffered. Connect his suffering to Spanish society in general. Make connections.'

'Oh come on, that's just adding insult to injury,' Galindez said. 'At the very least, Guzmán was orchestrating people's suffering – even if he didn't actually harm anyone himself as you clearly believe. Portraying him as a victim is going to upset a lot of people, surely?'

'You're missing the point.' Luisa smiled. 'The Pact of Oblivion silenced so many voices in this country. Now, those voices are crying out to be heard. In fact, I've found that many people from families who supported Franco feel their experiences were silenced once democracy was established. I think there's a big market – sorry, audience – among them as well. People don't want to feel guilty for what their parents or grandparents did in the war. Nor should they. I can help them see how behaviour in the war can be explained in terms of the wider context. Let them know they needn't feel guilty.'

'Using textual analysis, of course?'

'Correct, Ana María,' Luisa said, as if Galindez had just answered a question in class.

Galindez was starting to understand Luisa's plan: aim at volume sales rather than academic consumption. Break out from the confines of research work and start shifting books. *Mierda*, a memoir of misery, exploiting the suffering of the Civil War alongside a ludicrously sanitised portrait of Guzmán. Worse still, Luisa was providing a means for those who supported the dictatorship to reinvent themselves as victims. A fabrication, Galindez thought angrily, *no scientific evidence at all.*

She calmed herself, realising that while Luisa improvised her account of Guzmán's secretive life, Galindez could continue with her own work, focusing not only on the bodies from the mine but also pursuing Guzmán's involvement in the attempted coups in the seventies. Luisa didn't yet know about the *Centinelas* material. She would find out about it later, Galindez decided. Much later.

'The Guzmán report will be submitted to the European Union Education Commissioner you know,' Luisa said. 'As part of the bid we're making for funding for the new Research Centre: The

International Centre for Intertextual Historical Studies. The university is very excited about it, given that the funding amounts to several million euros.'

Now Galindez understood why Luisa was so pleased with herself. 'Who's going to be in charge of the centre, Luisa?' She asked, already sure of the answer.

'I've given tentative acceptance.' Luisa beamed.

Galindez congratulated her half-heartedly.

'You know, Ana,' Luisa said, 'I do miss you. I miss touching you.' Her hand slid over Galindez's knee. 'Your skin fascinates me.' Her hand moved higher, settling on her thigh.

Galindez's first thought was to push her away. But it was suddenly impossible to think. A dark band of pain slid across her consciousness. Where her thoughts were clear and precise a moment ago, there was now a dull, painful fog. She tried to protest, but instead of words, she found herself frozen in submissive confusion, thoughts and words failing to align themselves in meaningful patterns. Luisa's hand moved up her leg towards the hem of her skirt. Rigid, unable to form the words to stop her, Galindez found herself spectator to her own unwanted seduction.

'I thought so,' Luisa said. 'You just wanted me to make the first move.' Galindez struggled to speak. All she had to do was tell Luisa to stop, yet her voice was hesitant, stammering unsuccessful attempts at protest. Luisa placed her finger on Galindez's lips. 'I know what you want, Ana María.' Her hand slid under her skirt and Galindez felt the enervating miasma grow as Luisa's hand moved like a slow rising flame on her thigh, her finger tracing random, teasing patterns.

'No.' Galindez's voice was slow and confused as she struggled to her feet, snatching up her bag as she staggered to the door.

'Don't be silly,' Luisa said softly. 'What's the problem?'

Galindez couldn't say, because she didn't know, couldn't explain. She had no language for this. She walked unsteadily from the room and down the corridor. Outside, the mental haze began to lift, the raw heat of the day suddenly seemed cleansing. But something was wrong, she thought. She leaned against the wall outside the faculty entrance, keeping in the shade. *I forgot Belén's email, then the episode in the* comisaría *and now this. What's wrong with me?* The trouble was, she knew. The doctors had said it might happen. For eighteen years, she'd believed it wouldn't.

MADRID 2009, CALLE DE LA RIBERA DE CURTIDORES

Galindez and Tali strolled leisurely down the cobbled hill, window shopping and dawdling in the lazy afternoon heat. Shop blinds were tightly drawn against the glare. Outside the Bar Almeja, a few customers braved the fierce sun, lounging at tables crammed into a diminishing area of shadow. Further along, an African drummer beat out a low, tumbling rhythm, bouncing percussive echoes off the high walls around him.

At a stall a man was frying *churros*, pouring lines of batter into the deep hot fat until they were brown before covering them with sugar and salt. The smell of frying filled the warm afternoon air. Tali bought a paper cone full of steaming churros and bit into one with relish.

'*Quieres?*' She rattled the cone, showering sugar onto the pavement.

'Not really. I eat less calories in a week than you've got in that bag,' Galindez said.

'They remind me of childhood. The taste makes me feel like a little kid again.'

Galindez felt a sudden sadness. *I can't remember what childhood tastes like.* 'Go on, then, just one.' The *churro* was hot, salty and sweet. And very greasy.

'Want some hot chocolate to dip them in?' Tali asked. 'Go the whole hog?'

'I'm fine. You go ahead.'

Tali bought a plastic cup of thick warm chocolate and dipped a churro into it. After a moment Galindez followed her example.

'The Galindez willpower at work,' Tali laughed, wiping chocolate from her lips.

'I know. I'm just a slave to my desires. *Mira*. Look over there. It's a fortune-teller. You don't see many of those. Let's take a look.'

The dirty shop window was almost empty but for a shelf covered with a piece of ancient black velvet. In the middle of the velvet was a large glass ball. A handwritten card was propped against the ball:

Aurelia, Genuine Gypsy from Jerez – Fortunes told – Tarot and palm readings – Love potions – Husbands and Wives found – Luck restored

'It's all nonsense, isn't it?' Tali snatched the last churro.

'Scientifically speaking, it is. To be honest, I'm intrigued by them.'

'Really? Go in then, Ana. My treat.' Tali opened the door. Inside, the shop was dark. It smelled of damp and dust. '*Holá, señora*,' she said to someone inside. 'How much for reading my friend's palm?'

A cracked dry voice told her it was fifteen euros.

Tali stepped into the darkened shop and paid. '*Venga*, Ana María. In you go. I'll wait by the *churro* stand.'

Inside, the small room was draped in dark cloth embroidered with the moon and stars in silver thread. It was cold after the heat outside. An old lantern gave off a strong smell of paraffin. As her eyes accustomed themselves to the gloom, Galindez saw an old woman dressed in black, sitting at a table. She smelled of smoke and roses. Outside, the faint drumming pulsed hypnotically.

'*Muy buenas, señora*.' Galindez could still taste *churros* on her lips.

'*Muy buenas, hija*. Come nearer, *princesa*, I don't bite.' The old woman took Galindez's hand in hers, her sharp nail tracing the lines on her palm.

'Odd things are happening,' Galindez said. 'I want to know how they'll turn out.'

The gypsy sighed. 'We all want that, *hija. A ver.*' She bent closer.

'I see a man. Is there a man in your life, *guapa*?' She saw Galindez's amused surprise. 'No? This man wants you. He knows you're looking for him. He's a writer, isn't he? I see him sitting at a desk, writing in a book. The book you're looking for.'

Suddenly, with a cry, the gypsy released Galindez's hand as if it were red hot. She struggled to her feet, crossing herself. '*Qué te vayas. Fuera. Por Dios.* I can't see any more. Go.'

'*Puta madre*, you're supposed to tell me I'll meet someone nice, have six kids and live happily ever after,' Galindez snapped. She was angry: she'd only come in for a bit of fun, not to be spooked by this old witch.

The old woman grabbed her arm. 'Here, I can't take this.' She handed Galindez the money Tali had given her. 'Now go, *chica*. And be careful.'

Galindez opened the door, glad to see bright sunlight again. And then, curious, she turned back. 'Why can't you tell my future, *señora*?'

The old gypsy sank back into the seat behind the table, her face lost in deep shadow. 'You don't have a future, *chica. Dios mio*, you only have the past.'

The door slammed behind as Galindez stepped back into the street. She heard the sound of the lock turning. Across the road, Tali waited in a pool of sunshine, listening to the African drummer. 'Well, what did she say?' She looked in surprise as Galindez handed her the money back.

'It was rubbish. *Joder,* some fortune-teller she is – she nearly frightened me to death. Never again.' Galindez plucked a five-euro note from Tali's hand. 'I think I need more *churros*.'

CHAPTER SIXTEEN

ierda. There are bodies all over the city.' Guzmán put down the telephone.

'How many, *jefe*?'

'Forty-five so far.' Guzmán said, looking absently across the room.

'Forty-five?' Peralta was shocked. 'This is a massacre.'

'There's certainly going to be trouble,' Guzmán said, annoyed. He got up and walked to the door. Peralta followed him across the corridor into the mess room. Inside, twenty uniformed policemen were cleaning rifles, opening cases of ammunition and placing cartridges into rucksacks. The tables were strewn with the detritus of combat: bayonets, pistols, a pair of metal knuckledusters studded with long spikes. The men worked methodically, cheerful and boisterous, the promise of action invigorating them.

At the centre of the hubbub was the sarge, grinning as he packed a satchel with hand grenades. He saw Guzmán and saluted. Guzmán returned it by giving the *sargento* the finger. He then took out a packet of Ducados and lit one. Peralta looked longingly at the cigarettes and Guzmán absently passed him the packet, belatedly realising his mistake.

'They sell them. You give them money, they give you cigarettes. It works every time.' Guzmán's words were punctuated by clouds of acrid smoke.

Peralta nodded. 'Sorry, boss, I thought I had some.' Guzmán sighed and turned away. Tapping the loose black tobacco back into the end of the cigarette, Peralta lit it, taking a deep drag until the tobacco burned evenly. As the coarse smoke hit his lungs, he coughed, thus failing to see Guzmán as he mouthed something to the sarge. The sarge guffawed and without warning tossed a hand grenade to Peralta. Alarmed, the *teniente* caught it, snatching it out of the air with two hands before gingerly placing it on the table.

'Hope you put the pin back, *Teniente*,' the sarge cackled. Peralta looked in horror at the green-grey ball of metal.

'Very funny, *Sargento*.' He tried to affect a more nonchalant air and failed. Throwing explosives around a crowded mess room was not his idea of entertainment, although from the smirks and sniggers, Peralta could see he was alone in thinking that. He returned to his cigarette, inhaling the smoke gratefully. Guzmán was looking at the table of weapons, lost in silent meditation. Peralta waited.

'Ever think about what makes this country tick?' Guzmán asked.

'What it runs on, you mean? Like petrol? Oil? '

Guzmán looked at him. 'Power.'

'Power? That's what I said, *jefe*, petrol and oil—'

'No. Power. As in the army, the navy, the air force, the police, the *guardia civil*. Franco. Us. *Coño*, can't you see?'

'Well yes, of course, I understand,' Peralta said, not understanding.

Guzmán looked at him, unconvinced. 'You speak to an informant, some bootblack on Calle Durango. He tells you shit. He's clearly lying. What would you do?'

'What any good policeman would,' Peralta said. 'Give him a slap. Maybe a kick up the rear.'

'And why would you?'

Peralta frowned, annoyed at Guzmán's tone. 'So he would know he couldn't mess me about. And so anyone he talked to would know that I do my job right.'

Guzmán nodded approvingly. 'Exactly. And what is it we do here?'

Peralta thought for a moment. There were many ways of

describing it: protection of the State, upholding public order and morality, the maintenance of Christian society. He looked at Guzmán. Guzmán's face was impassive.

'We kill people,' Peralta said. 'To order.'

Guzmán beamed happily. 'We do, *Teniente*. We do it properly. And we do it for the State. The State's built on scaffolding and people like us are that scaffolding. And to keep everything held up and stop it falling down, we have to do things right. That's what keeps the pay cheque coming, no?'

'What we do is about more than money,' Peralta said.

'We all have a price,' Guzmán smirked, 'don't we?'

Peralta was not convinced. 'Possibly.'

'So if Carrero asked you to take it up the arse, would you? For money. Say enough to buy a house.'

Peralta flushed. 'Of course not. Not for any money. And I didn't even know the *almirante* was queer.'

'He isn't. But who knows, he might try it one day. What if he said he'd kill your kid?'

Peralta was unhappy with this turn in their conversation. But it was Guzmán who decided their topics of conversation. Always.

'I'd kill him first. There are limits,' Peralta said.

'You're in a cell and he has your kid. Maybe your wife too. They've repeatedly raped her in the next cell so you can hear. Now he says unless you take it up the arse, they kill the kid. Slowly. All you could do is beat on the walls like a lunatic while you heard every scream. What then?'

'When you put it that way, a man would have little choice but to give in.'

'*Maricón*.' Guzmán laughed. 'See, you're a whore as well. We just needed to establish your price, didn't we?'

Peralta chewed his lip and stayed silent.

'*Muy bien*. So we agree,' Guzmán said. 'Think about Franco for a minute. His rule depends on some things being predictable. People go hungry but there's about enough for most of those who deserve it. So people can be fairly certain they'll eat each day. Well,

349

most of them. We also have to have the certainty that life will carry on in certain ways. That Reds, fairies, Communists, Freemasons and Liberals will all be dealt with.'

'Order, you mean.'

'Exactly. Order. So everyone knows what's what. That there's a line.'

'And you don't cross that line.'

Guzmán grinned. 'It's the same as with your bootblack informant who messes you about – you let him go so far and no further.'

'We don't know who's crossing the line, though. I mean, who'd want to kill forty-odd people?'

Guzmán sighed. 'We have a pretty good idea *who*. Our Caribbean pals.'

'But we don't know why.'

'The point is,' Guzmán said, exasperated, 'that it's going to draw attention. Even if it's kept out of the papers, it makes Valverde look weak and threatens his shady dealing in drugs. Makes other criminals wonder if maybe they should sell a bit of stuff – given that people are avoiding the general's businesses for fear of dying. But worse, it makes the *Caudillo* look weak. It makes society look weak. *Our* society. Instead of fearing that knock on the door at night and having the sarge and me waiting on the mat when they open the door, they're going to start thinking maybe another way would be better.'

'Like Communism?'

'Of course. They'll start thinking they're free to look at alternatives. Thinking new ideas, foreign ideas, *joder*, even thinking about democracy, and where will we be then?'

'Out of work for a start,' Peralta said glumly.

The sarge walked past, cradling a rifle across his forearms.

'We'd be on trial, wouldn't we, *jefe*?' He looked at Guzmán for support. 'Like all those Nazi *pendejos*. The ones that didn't take poison, that is. Would you take poison, *jefe*?'

Guzmán shrugged. 'Hard to say. If it was the rope, maybe not. Hanging's quite quick. You get a good meal first.'

'That's right, *jefe*. A condemned man can have anything he wants.'

'I don't seem to remember you doing much cooking for any of those Reds you killed,' Guzmán sneered. 'It was all we could do to make you do it quickly.' He looked over at Peralta to see if he was suitably disgusted. He was.

Guzmán picked up the hand grenade from the table. 'Sarge, you weren't seriously thinking of taking this on our trip to the Bar Dominicana?'

The *sargento* shrugged. 'Best to be prepared, sir.'

'Even so,' Guzmán said, 'that might just be a bit excessive.' He handed the grenade back to the Sarge. 'Better leave that for another day.'

The sarge moodily collected the satchel of grenades and trudged into the armoury.

'Shame to spoil his fun,' Guzmán said, 'but he can get carried away.'

'I can imagine,' Peralta said.

'Enough of him,' Guzmán said, becoming more animated. 'We've got to find out who did this. All these bodies are going to cause a fuss. Even if we suppress the news of it, those upstairs will be getting jumpy. And we don't want them interfering.'

'You think they will?'

'Almost certainly,' Guzmán said. 'The question is how long we've got before they find out.' He paused as the doors to the reception hall crashed open. '*Mierda*, it's happened already.'

They recognised Carrero Blanco at once. He stormed towards them, his overcoat flapping, the buttons and badges of his admiral's uniform twinkling under the faint lights.

'*Almirante*.' Guzmán snapped to attention and saluted smartly. Peralta struggled to do the same – without experience in the army his military bearing was at best sloppy.

'*Joder*, Guzmán, what the hell is going on, man? There are corpses all over the city,' Carrero Blanco barked.

'We're well aware of it, *Almirante*,' Guzmán said. 'Perhaps you'd like to step into my office to appraise the situation?'

351

Carrero Blanco nodded and waited for Guzmán to open the door for him. Inside the office, he sat at Guzmán's desk – just as Guzmán had expected. *They all do that. Like dogs pissing on a tree.* Guzmán took the other chair. Carrero Blanco was taking off his heavy leather gloves, his peaked cap placed in the middle of the desk. Peralta paused in the doorway.

'Not you,' the admiral said coldly. 'You're one of the Valverde clan, no?'

'Only by marriage, sir,' Peralta said, standing to attention.

'Get out,' Carrero Blanco snapped. 'I want to speak with the *comandante.*'

'*A sus ordenes, mí Almirante.*' Peralta executed a clumsy salute and stepped backwards into the corridor, pulling the door closed as he went.

He turned and was startled to find the sarge half a metre behind him. '*Jesus Cristo, hombre,* don't you know not to sneak up on someone like that?'

The sarge's mouth split into his ghastly grin, exposing the broken remnants of his teeth. 'Sorry, *Teniente,* I was trying to tell the *comandante* that *Almirante* Carrero Blanco had arrived but the *almirante* pushed me out of the way before I got the chance. Is he with the boss now?'

'He's with *Comandante* Guzmán, yes.'

'About the bodies, I suppose?'

'I imagine so. Any more news on them?'

'There's forty-nine now. I expect there'll be a few more who no one's noticed yet.'

'And what do you make of it?'

The sarge looked at Peralta contemptuously. 'Not difficult, is it?'

'Then perhaps you'd explain anyway, *Sargento?*'

'I'd say someone's brought a load of dope into Madrid hoping to get rich quick. Likely got it in Barcelona, since the place is full of drugs. Then they cut it to make it go further. As long as the colour looks about right, the dope fiends will buy it.'

'So you don't think it's linked to the Dominicans? We know they've been muscling in on the local drugs trade.'

The sarge shrugged. 'Be a bit odd, that. If you're dealing drugs you want your customers to come back, not die. Cutting a big consignment is a risky business – for the buyers. A bag of bad shit, sold off in little parcels, it's like a shotgun. You pull the trigger and there's a mess all over the fucking place.' He paused. 'Sir.'

Peralta bit his lip. 'You've made a list of the names and addresses of the victims?'

The sarge shrugged. 'Of course. Some of these people have families who'll need to know.'

'And what are we going to tell them?'

'That there's been a mystery virus. That's what the *comandante* said. We've already contacted the press to let them know what they can print. Thirty dead will be the official figure. They'll be buried immediately – because of the risk of infection. The coffins will be sealed at the hospitals as well.'

Peralta rummaged unsuccessfully in his pocket for a cigarette. 'That doesn't get us any nearer to explaining why anyone would do this.'

The sarge watched Peralta continue his hunt for a cigarette for a moment before wearily pulling a crumpled packet from his pocket. 'Here you go, *Teniente*.' Peralta took the cigarette and waited for a light.

'It's easily explained,' the sarge said. 'The more you cut the dope, the more money it makes. But the more junkies you kill, the more attention you get – and drug dealers usually don't want attention – especially from the likes of us.'

The sarge found the remnants of a box of wax *cerillas* and managed to strike one into flame.

Peralta breathed in the strong smoke gratefully. 'I think there are two possibilities, *Sargento*. The first is as you say, someone cut their supply with something to make it go further and they accidentally overdid it. The other possibility is that they did it deliberately.'

'They'd be bad bastards if they did that, *Teniente*. But why do that?'

Peralta took a drag on his cigarette in what he hoped was an enigmatic pause. 'Think about it. There's only one real competitor for the Dominicans in Madrid.'

The sarge grunted. 'Valverde. But the general sells most of his supplies through *farmacias* to legal addicts. If these stiffs we've been bringing in are legals, that'd mean that Valverde's supplies had been got at.'

'What better way to discredit the competition, *Sargento*? If people don't feel safe with legal sources of drugs, they'll turn to other outlets.'

'Like those Caribbean greasers,' the sarge said.

'Exactly. Which means that Valverde will need to take action to protect his business.'

'And that will mean the *comandante* will get his way,' the sarge leered, exposing more of his devastated teeth, 'which is always a good thing, for us, as well as him.'

'I'll speak to him about this as soon as he's finished with the *almirante*,' Peralta said. 'I imagine he'll be interested to hear our conclusions.'

The sarge started to walk towards the mess. 'I shouldn't get too excited, *Teniente*.'

'Why's that, *Sargento*?'

The sarge turned and looked mockingly at him. 'Because I had this conversation with him about an hour ago, sir, and he reached the same conclusion then.'

Guzmán stood stiffly to attention as Carrero Blanco shouted abuse at him. It was becoming quite a dressing down.

'Guzmán, what the hell's going on? Over forty-five people dead. The *Caudillo*'s incandescent. We've had to double the number of censors to keep this out of the foreign press.'

'With respect, *mi Almirante*, this is a situation we could not have anticipated.'

The admiral continued his tirade. 'You won't be anticipating anything soon, Guzmán, because you'll be out on your ear with no job and no pension. We didn't give you the job you have just to amuse you, *entiende*? We simply can't have something like this happen. Especially now. The *Caudillo* gives a major speech in two days and he wants to welcome the Americans to the new Spain. The new Spain, Guzmán, one where there are no corpses in the streets. Certainly not forty-odd of them.'

Guzmán felt the urge to punch Carrero Blanco senseless. But he needed to keep control. *Sometimes you have to eat shit. But you should never get used to the taste of it.*

The admiral calmed down a little. 'So what the fuck happened, Guzmán? Do we know?'

'We do, *Almirante*. These people were all addicts, poisoned by contaminated drugs.'

'Poisoned?'

'Definitely, though we don't know if it was deliberate or not yet.'

Carrero stared at him. 'We know who controls the supply of drugs in this city, *Comandante*. General Valverde. You surely don't think he'd poison his own customers?'

'I doubt it, *mi almirante*. There are more likely suspects. The Dominicans. We know they're involved in the drugs trade.'

'*Cuidado*, Guzmán,' Carrero said. 'Take great care before you do anything we – meaning you – would regret. We don't want to upset the *Yanquis*. We need these bloody Americans, Guzmán. If we don't get them to part with some money, the country will be bankrupt within the year. I'll tell you now, the *Caudillo* has already instructed the trade negotiators how to deal with these *Yanquis*: agree to anything, let them walk all over you and then take their money. Is there anything there you don't understand?' His expression indicated it was a rhetorical question.

'Yes.' Guzmán never liked rhetoric.

'What?' The admiral sighed.

'I don't understand why we have to let a bunch of Caribbean criminals parade around the capital flaunting the law. The *Yanquis* could sort out the trade agreement without them. They're criminals and I'm certain they've had a hand in this heroin business. Say the word and I'll round them up.'

Carrero stared at him hard. 'Listen, Guzmán. You wouldn't be where you are without keeping on top of things like this. Your instinct for the job is a great asset. But just as important, you've avoided doing anything that would annoy the *Caudillo*. Others have had his trust besides you – the difference being they forgot if you cross him, there's rarely a second chance. You sit near the fire or you're out in the cold. Simple as that.'

And you can teach my grandmother to suck eggs, Guzmán thought. 'I must stress these Dominicans have already engaged in criminal acts, they're suspects in a murder case involving one of our informers and—'

'Enough.' Carrero Blanco waved a leather-gloved hand. 'They may well be criminals, Guzmán. The world's full of criminals – look at the army or the Church and Christ Almighty, don't even start me off about politicians. *Fíjate coño*, a few dead junkies don't matter, do they? How many did we shoot in the *Guerra Civil*? The fucking streets were full of dead. We didn't care then and we don't care now. Junkies take that filth, ruin their lives and lose their immortal souls: they're scum. Good riddance. But the *norteamericanos* don't want to see people lying dead in the streets of Madrid. Not while they're here, anyway. They prefer such things to occur out of sight. Find out who sold these drugs. If it's the Dominicans, arrest them quietly and discreetly *after the fucking trade talks are over, not before. When we tell you to.* You do understand what I just said, don't you, *Comandante*?'

'I understand perfectly, *mi Almirante*.'

Carrero frowned. 'I hope so, Guzmán. Because if the *Yanquis* think we aren't in control of our own capital, they might think twice about trading with us. And if that happens, you'll be the one who's blamed.'

'And if the poisoned drugs were linked to General Valverde's businesses?'

'A good question,' Carrero said. 'A couple of months ago I'd have said it would damage his standing, even hasten his retirement. But his influence with the *Caudillo* has grown lately. He's been working with a number of economists and businessmen developing strategies for economic growth.'

'And the *Caudillo* takes him seriously?' Guzmán scoffed.

'Unfortunately yes.' Carrero frowned. 'The *Caudillo* believes his ideas could enrich Spain in the years to come.'

'I see.' Guzmán was incredulous. *Enrich Spain. Enrich Franco, more like.*

'The instructions remain the same, Guzmán. Keep an eye on him. But try not to infuriate him any more than usual. You never know, the way he's going, he might end up commanding you one day.'

Guzmán moved ahead of the admiral to open the door.

'One more thing, Guzmán.' The admiral gestured imperiously for Guzmán to leave the door closed. He reached into his leather coat and took out a piece of paper. 'Deal with this individual, will you?'

Guzmán took the paper and looked at the name and address. 'No one I know.' He shrugged.

'That's not important,' Carrero Blanco said, with a hint of irritation. 'What is important is that the *Caudillo* wishes you to deal with him as you've dealt with so many enemies of Spain.'

'What charges?' Guzmán asked. 'Shall I bring him here or—'

The admiral interrupted with undisguised impatience. '*Mierda*, Guzmán, when did you become so fond of bureaucracy? Never mind what he's done. You're not his fucking lawyer. He's guilty and he needs to be dealt with. And, for reasons which scarcely concern you, it suits us,' he paused before correcting himself, 'it suits the *Caudillo* that you deal with him at his home. It's a warning. The people it's meant for will understand.'

Guzmán nodded. 'Consider it done.'

Carrero Blanco smiled. 'I do, Guzmán, I do. And Guzmán, if there's anyone with this person, then they are as guilty as he is. *Entendido*?'

'*A sus ordenes, mi Almirante.*'

'Always a pleasure, Guzmán.' Carrero gestured for Guzmán to open the door. He emerged from Guzmán's office and stamped down the corridor, flanked by his bodyguards. Once he had gone through the swing doors, Guzmán looked round for Peralta. It was time to begin work.

MADRID 1953, CALLE CIPRIANO SANCHO

'Who's driving, *jefe?*' the *sargento* asked, opening the door of the truck.

Guzmán gave him a hard look. 'Here's a clue, *Sargento*: it's not going to be me.'

'*A sus ordenes.*' The *sargento* moved round to the driver's door and climbed in. Peralta squeezed into the middle of the front seat, pressed between Guzmán on one side and the handbrake and the sarge on the other. Guzmán lit a Ducado and began to fill the cab with thick pungent smoke.

'I don't suppose...' Peralta began.

'*Hostia*, buy some. I've told you before. I'm not a charity, *Teniente.*'

The engine grumbled into life and the sarge reversed the truck. Reaching into his coat, he produced a battered packet of Lucky Strike. 'Here, *Teniente*, have one of mine. *Again.*'

Peralta took one, eyebrows raised at the sarge's new-found generosity.

'You've done it now,' Guzmán said gloomily, 'he'll never buy a packet. You'll have to get a crateful on the black market, Sarge. That'll keep the *teniente* going.'

'I'll buy some I promise,' Peralta said, knowing it was unlikely.

'You can owe me, *Teniente.*' The sarge grinned, his rotting teeth less visible in the darkness. He spun the wheel sharply and drove out into the main road.

'You know there's something I wanted to ask you.' Peralta

turned to Guzmán who was leaning against the cab door, eyes closed.

'Just so long as you don't keep me awake,' Guzmán growled.

'What do you know about the St Valentine's Day Massacre?'

'Sounds fun,' the sarge said, turning to join in the conversation. 'Was that one of our massacres? Where the Reds burned those priests alive? Or where—'

'*Yanqui* gangsters,' Guzmán interrupted. 'Pretending to be police. They arrested some of their rivals and then shot them.'

'Some people,' the sarge said with mock disapproval.

'Who cares anyway?' Guzmán said. 'Degenerate *Yanqui* criminals go round shooting one another – big deal. Why do you ask?'

'Positano,' Peralta said. 'He was arrested for murder as a young man. Got off, no one knows why and his arrest records have disappeared. Then he turns up in the war and gets a prestigious medal.'

'Didn't we all,' Guzmán muttered.

'What if he still has links to the Mob?'

'Keep going, *Teniente*,' Guzmán said, suddenly interested.

'*Pues*, suppose he was in the Mob but then gets called up to the army. He does all right in the military and then after the war he's offered a good job with their Department of Trade.'

'But he still keeps his links to the Mob?' the sarge added. '*Qué bueno*. He'd be worth a fortune to them.'

'Excellent, *Teniente*,' Guzmán said, the tip of his cigarette glowing red in the darkness of the cab. 'Positano scouts out opportunities for his gangster friends while on official business and the Dominicans provide the muscle to back him up. I think we're making progress here, *señores*.'

The truck slowed down.

'That's the street you wanted, *jefe*.' The sarge pointed to a narrow side street. A single lamp threw thin grey light onto the trampled snow.

Guzmán took out the paper and examined it in the flickering glow of his cigarette lighter. 'This is it, all right.'

'Mind if I do it, sir?' the sarge asked. 'Been a while since I did a visit like this.'

'Be my guest, Sargento,' Guzmán said. 'Want my friend to help?'

The sarge nodded and Guzmán slid the Browning from its holster and handed it to him.

Opening the truck door, the sarge climbed down into the icy street, pushing the pistol into his belt. Freezing air flooded into the cab. Guzmán turned to Peralta.

'Off you go, *Teniente*, I think you should accompany the sarge on this little errand.'

'What about you, *jefe*?' The sarge smirked.

'I'll stay here,' Guzmán said. 'I promise not to talk to any strangers.' He leaned towards the open door. 'By the way, Sarge.'

'*Sí, mi Comandante?*'

'*Dales café, Sargento,*' Guzmán said, '*mucho café.*' He slammed the truck door closed.

'What was that the boss said?' Peralta asked as they began to walk down the street.

The sarge shrugged. 'Shop talk.'

The street was silent. Miserable houses, clusters of dilapidated apartments. The plaster on the buildings peeling away from the bricks, weather-worn paint hanging off the doors, dull light glinting through curtains and blinds. A normal Spanish street, Peralta thought.

'Who are we after, *Sargento*?'

The sarge shrugged. 'Just a name, *Teniente*, that's all I have.'

'He must have done something?' Peralta persisted.

'You'd think so.' The sarge looked at the numbers of the houses. 'Here we are.' He examined the names on the cluster of doorbells, 'Are we likely to have any trouble here?'

'No. No trouble, *Teniente*. We're just delivering a warning,' the sarge said, pushing one of the doorbells. A harsh ring sounded somewhere above and they heard a door open. Footsteps on the stairs. Peralta pushed the front door and they stepped into a bare entrance hall, with a series of ancient metal mailboxes. At the far end of the hall, wooden stairs climbed up into shadow. A man emerged from the shadow, descending the stairs into the pale light of the hallway.

'*Señor* Roberto Flores del Rio?' the sarge asked, politely.

'That's me.' The man adjusted his thick spectacles. 'How can I help you?'

'Roberto? *Quien es?*' A woman's voice. Hurried footsteps on the stairs. A moment later there were two of them. Plump and middle aged. Peralta sensed their fear. He waited for the sarge to make the arrest.

'What do you gentlemen want?' the man asked. His wife moved behind him.

'Nothing to be alarmed about,' Peralta said reassuringly, holding up his identity card. 'We're police officers. We want to talk to—'

Without warning, the sarge shoved past Peralta, unbalancing him. The *teniente's* cheap shoes slipped on the smooth wooden floor and he fell, clawing at the wall for support. As Peralta fell, the sarge lifted the pistol and fired straight into the man's face. The blast threw the man backwards onto the stairs and his body slid brokenly down to the hall floor, his head resting in a growing slick of blood, glinting black in the half light. The woman stood motionless, her eyes wide, her mouth open but strangely silent, her face covered with a speckled mask of her husband's blood.

Gasping and confused, Peralta tried unsuccessfully to struggle to his feet. He gaped at the sarge, seeing his right arm extended towards the woman, his gloved hand gripping the big automatic. Taking aim.

The deafening blast made Peralta cry out. The woman fell across her husband's body, hands clasped to the wound in her chest. The *sargento* stepped forwards and shot her repeatedly at point-blank range, the woman's body shuddering at each blast, the hallway ringing with the percussive explosions. The air stank of gun smoke and burned clothing. And blood.

The *sargento* turned to the door, grabbing the lieutenant by the arm and hauling him to his feet.

'*Anda, Teniente*, we're done here. *Vamonos.*'

Peralta followed, stumbling on the icy pavement. He tried to speak.

'Just keep going, *Teniente*,' the sarge said. 'Let's get back to the truck.'

'I can't hear you,' Peralta spluttered as he staggered after the sarge.

They reached the vehicle and Guzmán lent a grudging hand in dragging the resistant *teniente* into the cab.

'Drive, *Sargento*.' Guzmán took his pistol from the sarge and began to reload it.

Peralta shivered with shock, lodged between the two men. They ignored him.

'Coffee for two,' Guzmán said. 'And you used a full clip, Sarge?"

'You said the *almirante* made a big thing about them deserving it so I put the lot into them.' The sarge smiled. 'With all that lead, they'll need an extra pallbearer for the coffins.'

Peralta's head jerked as the conversation fluttered around him, trying to keep his undamaged ear towards whoever was speaking. 'You shot them,' he stammered.

'What a detective. No wonder you joined the police, *Teniente*.' The sarge cackled. Even Guzmán laughed.

'He shot them *technically*, Peralta,' Guzmán said. 'Their deaths had already been decided on. All we do, *Teniente*, is follow orders. It's what keeps the pay cheque coming.'

'You can say that again.' The sarge nodded.

MADRID 1953, CALLE JOSE DELGADO

At one o'clock, Alicia Martinez left the fishmonger's shop, her work over for the day. It was cold, the buildings in the street imprecise in the pale mist as she made her way to the bus stop. In her bag was a large bream, a present from the fishmonger. Since *Comandante* Guzmán had spoken to her employers they had treated her with remarkable courtesy. He was clearly more important than she'd first thought. And more reasonable too. What had begun as an ugly episode had actually ended quite pleasantly. Surprising how things turn out, she thought: having an admirer. A potential admirer at least. He found her attractive, that was clear, despite him being horrible to her at first. Yet he'd behaved quite properly after that. The thought made her smile. *Me. Thinking about a man. A policeman.* So much had happened in the last few days to make her think, especially given the deadly monotony of day-to-day survival she had become accustomed to since the war. She still loved her husband, but he was gone now and she had no one. No one but little Roberto. It had never occurred to her that life might change from its constant daily drudgery but the *comandante* had introduced new complexity into her life. The possibility of change.

A car glided past, slowed, stopped. Head down against the cold wind, she hardly noticed the car door slam, nor the footsteps on the snow behind her. A blow to the head sent her sprawling on the cold pavement, her basket spilling the bream into the snow. She struggled to her knees, dazed, looking up at the man towering over her, now dragging her to her feet. And then he seized her by the hair, forcing her towards the waiting car. She saw the open door, tried to struggle as she was bundled into the back seat, the man using his weight to pin her down. She squirmed, tried to reason with him, to get him to explain what was happening. She heard the sound of liquid in a container, the cap being removed and a sickening smell as a rough cloth suddenly covered her mouth and nose. Then she was fighting for breath, struggling under the man's weight. She tried to call out but only drew in thick cloying fumes from the cloth, still struggling as the light began to give way to a deepening fog that clouded her thoughts. Alicia Martinez heard the men's voices, distant, receding.

'Her basket,' one said.

'*Hostia*, she's got more than a basket to worry about when she wakes up.'

The engine started noisily. And then the darkness took her. For a while at least.

'Guzmán.' The Moor's voice was sharp and insistent. The kid lay in the dry grass, trying to contain his urge to gasp for air, knowing if he gave in, they might hear him. And then the Moors stopped shouting and fell silent. They were coming. He could hear one of the African soldiers approaching, could tell from the measured sound of the man's boots on the desiccated soil how careful he was, suspecting an ambush, but coming on anyway, unafraid. The Moors had spread out, increasing the distance between them, making it less likely they could be cut down by one burst of fire. They were good soldiers, trained in a harsh land into the brutal ways of their masters and accustomed to ruthless and merciless warfare. This was ideal territory for them.

The kid lay motionless, the world diminished to the haze of dried grass and shrubs he saw through the sight of his rifle. Nothing stirred. Sweat ran down his cheeks. The footsteps stopped. Now there was a painful silence, a silence that stretched the kid's nerves more than the screams of the dying ever had. The grass moved. A shadow emerged through the parched undergrowth. The kid saw the uniform, the ammunition pouches, the long rifle with its wicked bayonet. He remained still, his rifle pointed at the man's belly. To raise his aim would require movement and that would give him away. Instead he waited, sweat streaming down his face, the rifle unsteady in his shaking hands. The African looked round, slowly checking for signs of the enemy before he advanced, one slow measured step after the other. Over to the kid's left someone shouted. The Moor's head snapped round towards the sound and the kid lifted the rifle and shot the Moor in the chest, the report painfully loud, the recoil of the rifle hard against his shoulder. The Moor fell, his rifle clattering to

365

the ground, smoke coming from the charred hole in his body. He lay
on his back and did not move. Nor would he, the kid knew.

There was more shouting. Two shots. A long, anguished scream.
The sound of someone suffering, suffering while knowing that,
although the suffering would end in death, death would be some
time in coming. The screaming stopped and then started again,
rising and falling, a demented fugue conducted by the men with the
long knives. And now shouts in Spanish and Arabic. The sound of
men running.

The kid kept low, crawling through the scrub, finding a spot
between two stunted trees where he could hide. Across the parched
hillside, five of the African soldiers were gathered around something
on the ground. One of them raised his rifle and thrust it downwards.
They were bayoneting someone. Two people – the soldier who had
lost his rifle and his mate. It took them some time to die. The kid
watched it all. When the men were finally dead, he saw the Moors
hacking at the corpses, lifting grim trophies in bloody hands. And
then, a shout. The kid saw them turn and look back. One of them
waved, beckoning. Guzmán had arrived.

CHAPTER SEVENTEEN

*Q*ue coño es este?' Galindez threw the newspaper angrily onto the breakfast table.

Tali looked up. 'Is that Luisa's piece about the new research centre?'

'Bloody right it is. You know what? She criticises my contribution to the Guzmán project. Listen:

This contribution from a member of the guardia civil represents – textually speaking – an example of the Guardia's historical role of repression and control. History and historical memory do not lie within the conceptual calculus of mainstream science. In reconstructing the historical narrative of those found in these unmarked graves the tenets of positivist science do not obtain. We read this forensic report with its obsessive attention to detail, its analytic passion obscured or, perhaps, repressed by its reliance on cold, scientific detachment. As if the author were trying to detach herself from a scene so intense it must be buried in calculus and calibration; operationalising suffering into a two-dimensional sketch, an always provisional account of the technical and the probable.

Nowhere in this mass of forensic detail do we approach anything resembling a coherent emotional narrative, nor does it deploy the necessary experiential vocabularies of cruelty and suffering needed to articulate lived human experience. Science will not – cannot – do this for us. The reconstruction and reformulation of life using restrictive

367

pathologised understandings is limited. In short, we must restore the palimpsest.'

'Palimpsest?' Tali shook her head. '*Dios mio.* That's from an essay by Derrida.'

'You've read it?'

'Some of it. Luisa's very into his work. What you do is well outside her field of interest. Strange really, that she wanted you to join the team.'

'She said she wanted my scientific expertise,' Galindez said, suddenly defensive.

Tali laughed. 'She wanted *you.* And she got you for a while, *mi corazón*, even though it meant letting you stay on the investigation after you split up with her.'

'But we agreed to differ. She's been writing her part of the report knowing I was taking a different approach. Yet not only does she slag me off in this article, it's also a blatant advertisement for her forthcoming book on the suffering of young Guzmán – how society is responsible for his deeds. She's not only damning my contribution before it's even finished, she's making it look as if it's the *guardia civil* who've written it to silence her and prevent her... what the fuck does she call it? Revoicing the victims. *Dios mio,* at least you can identify the arguments in my work, not like her wordy, lit-crit crap. Uncle Ramiro will go nuts if we get a load of bad press as a result of this.'

'She set you up.' Tali poured more coffee. 'She wanted your expertise so she could bounce her intertextual work off it and make you seem as if you were censoring her attempts to stand up for victims everywhere.'

'Well, it's very negative. And sneaky.' Galindez slumped back into her chair. 'And she's used this piece to support the university's bid for European Union funds for the Centre for Textual Studies. With her at its head, of course.'

'Ana María Galindez meet Luisa Ordoñez.' Tali laughed. 'She's a sharp operator, *cariña*. Stand too close to the flame and you get burned, no?'

'It makes me look an idiot and it'll confirm all Uncle Ramiro's prejudices about women and forensic scientists. I'll probably be demoted to coffee lady – no, make that assistant coffee lady.'

'You haven't completed your work on the Las Peñas killings yet, *mi amor.*'

'True. Hopefully, I'll come up with something to challenge Luisa's picture of Guzmán as a victim of circumstance.'

'There's a quotation in his diary about that, isn't there?'

'Yes, that line from Ortega y Gasset: "I am me and my circumstances." It worries me.'

'*Por qué?*' Tali perched on the arm of Galindez's chair and smoothed her hair.

'Because it sounds like something a thoughtful man might write in his diary when his conscience was troubling him,' Galindez said. 'Luisa will no doubt claim it supports her argument. *And* there was that memo in the *Centinelas*' file, saying Guzmán was difficult and unreliable. Fuck, what if he actually was against the attempted coups?'

'I can't imagine Guzmán was on the side of the angels. Keep working on it.' Tali said. 'After all, what was it your teacher said? That you were revoltingly dogmatic?'

'You cow,' Galindez smiled, 'she said refreshingly dogged.'

'Made you laugh, Ana María.'

'You always do.'

'So don't take things so seriously, *mi vida*, just stick with it. It's what you do best.'

'I'll get started once I've had another coffee,' Galindez said, pouring a refill. 'Anything in the papers?'

Tali pushed the newspaper across the table towards her. 'They found an undercover *poli* dead yesterday.'

'A cop? *Nacional* or *Guardia?*'

'*Nacional.* Shot dead at the Campo del Moro.'

Galindez skimmed the piece. 'Undercover agent… dangerous operation, colleagues paid tribute to Enrique Bolin, 39, married, two daughters. God, it's sad when this happens.'

'Still glad you didn't go into uniform?'

'*Absolutamente*. It wasn't for me.' The photograph accompanying the article showed a familiar crime scene, the English-style formal gardens of the Campo in the background and in the foreground, a knot of forensic officers in white coveralls. Behind them, several men, clearly plain-clothes officers. At the centre of the tableau was the body, covered by a plastic sheet. In line with the law, the faces of all the policemen were obscured by small pixellated boxes. Below the piece was a small photograph of the dead man.

'Ana, *qué te pasa*? You've gone white.'

'This is the man who hid the *Centinelas*' memos in the archive,' Galindez said, clearly shaken. 'The guy whose blood was on the plastic bag containing the files. I sent the bloodied tissue to Mendez for DNA analysis.'

'But you said he was an old guy.'

'Because he walked kind of doubled up. He must have been injured. Oh my God, I just watched while they grabbed him. When I heard someone say "Policía", I thought it was the other guys who were police. Shit, this is terrible. I could have helped him. I should have helped him.'

'It gets worse, *querida*.' Tali pointed to the photo of the policemen with their pixillated faces. 'They can't hide the identity of this one, can they?' Despite the attempt at anonymising the image, Galindez recognised the man immediately. Sancho.

'*Puta madre*. Sancho's a cop? That means that we can't even rely on the police if we need help. The *Centinelas* have infiltrated them.'

Tali came out of the bathroom. She was wearing her hair up. 'What do you think?'

'It looks great like that,' Galindez said.

'I borrowed your black studs, hope you don't mind?'

'No, you wear them if you want. They look good on you.'

Tali looked in the mirror. 'Maybe not. I think something lighter would go better with my hair. Thanks anyway.'

She took out the studs and went back into the bathroom. When she came out again, she saw Galindez's expression. 'What's up, *querida*?'

Galindez shrugged. 'I'm worried about Sancho, I worry about not finding more evidence about Guzmán and—'

'God you're a terrible liar.' Tali shook her head in disbelief. 'What's really upsetting you?'

Tali was taken aback by Galindez's sudden rush to embrace her, an unexpected need for affirmation and support that surprised them both.

She buried her face in Galindez's hair. Light kisses, warm breath. The gentle pressure of her body. Her soft voice, '*Qué cariñita? Qué te pasa mi amor? Qué te pasa?*'

'Something happened with Luisa. Something weird.' Galindez shook her head, trying to make the memory go away.

'What did she do?'

'She came on to me. It wasn't so bad. But it was what I did that frightens me.'

'Jesus, what, exactly?' Tali asked. 'You didn't hit her, did you?'

'No, nothing like that. I froze. I'd started with a headache a little while before and then this happened. My mind just clogged up and stopped. I sat there like I was watching a movie, completely distanced from it. She started making a pass at me. She was stroking my leg and for a minute or two I couldn't stop her. Finally, I managed to get up and leave. But it was so hard to break away – as if I was hypnotised…' she paused, 'or I'd lost my mind.'

'And were you OK after that?'

'It passed off pretty quickly. But it felt as if I'd lost my mind – I couldn't think at all.'

'You went a bit funny in the *comisaría* as well – *recuerdas*? Have you had anything like this before?'

'Never,' Galindez lied. If she mentioned the possibility of her amnesia recurring, Tali would insist on her seeing a doctor. She didn't have time for that. Didn't have time for them. Not after what they did when *Papá* died.

Tali hugged her. '*Dios mio*, Ana María. You've been under so much stress lately, maybe it's that?'

'It must be. But it's scary. Normally I have this feeling I have to keep going, no matter what. I was like that with all my studies: I felt if I took a day off I'd never catch up again. Same at work. I never like feeling out of control.'

'Did you think I hadn't noticed, *mi vida*?' Tali said. 'Come on, there's so much positive stuff to focus on. Apply some of your repulsive drudgery.'

'You know what? This is the happiest I've ever been – despite all that's been happening.'

'Well, as long as I'm good for something, Dr Galindez.' Tali moved closer.

'Don't,' Galindez groaned, pulling back. 'We've got to take those documents to Judge Delgado's office.'

Tali sighed. 'OK. But you'll have to make it up to me, Ana.'

'Or we could wait until it gets dark before we deliver them,' Galindez said. 'It might be safer.'

'See, you're still the clever one.'

Outside there was a faint rumble of thunder. A few minutes later the rain began.

The evening sky was bruised by rain clouds. The windows of the elegant offices and shops of Calle de Serrano glimmered with halos of soft light distorted by the hazy curtain of rain. A few chic pedestrians hurried by, hunched under umbrellas, paying little attention to the two women standing in a doorway, waiting for the rain to ease.

The night was filled with the sound of rain. Noisy cascades poured from roofs and balconies, awnings bulged and sagged, overflowing noisily into the street below. Walking up the rain-washed road, they paused, feigning interest in the glittering windows of Cartier while Galindez scanned the street for any sign of them being followed. Satisfied they were alone, they continued on their way in silence, subdued by the steady rhythm of the rain.

Judge Delgado's office was set amid a group of similar, expensive office buildings, its only notable feature the reinforced nightsafe by the door. That and the ten-centimetre-thick bulletproof glass of the windows. Galindez pulled the plastic bag containing the files from under her coat. She passed it to Tali and stood guard while Tali tried to slide the flap of the nightsafe open.

'Stop.'

A familiar voice somewhere in the shadows across the road. Galindez looked up, the water streaming down her face, stinging her eyes. She saw only the blurred lights of shops, all detail lost in the screen of rain.

Illuminated by the twinkling lights of a stylish fashion emporium was Sancho, rain streaming from his shaved head. Behind him, another figure. Galindez recognised the pasty features of Agustín Benitez, the man from the archives. Agustín looked across the road at Galindez and said something to Sancho. They came forwards. Above the drumming of the rain, Galindez heard Tali's breathing, rapid with fear.

Adrenalin burned in her veins as Galindez stepped forward, placing herself between Sancho and Tali, her fists clenched. Sancho reacted angrily. He muttered something to Benitez and shook his head at the reply. He came nearer, splashing through the water streaming down the road. Two metres away from Galindez, he stopped.

'Come any nearer, Sancho, and this time I'm really going to hurt you,' Galindez said in a low voice. She wiped wet hair away from her face, revealing the dark violence in her eyes.

'You don't know what you're dealing with,' Sancho said quietly. 'You're way out of your depth and you don't have a fucking clue.' He took another pace forward. Galindez tensed. The next step he took would trigger her attack.

'That's close enough. Keep away from her.'

Diego Aguilar was standing ten metres up the road, his pistol in a two-handed grip, aimed at Sancho. 'I'll shoot if I have to. Back away.'

Sancho looked at Diego venomously. '*Hijo de la gran puta. Look who it is. Mess me about and I'll fuck you up, puto.*'

Diego shrugged. 'I don't think so. That's not an opinion: my friends agree with me.'

Three men in black combat gear holding automatic rifles emerged from the shadows behind Diego. Sancho cursed angrily. Benitez shrugged and Galindez heard him telling Sancho to be cool.

'Drop the file in the night safe,' Galindez whispered to Tali.

Sancho heard her. 'No. Do not let her put that file in there, Galindez. Don't—'

He took half a step forward and Galindez moved towards him, both fists raised.

Tali let the flap close and the package slid into the steel-plated safety of the safe.

Sancho shouted in exasperation and punched the palm of his hand. There was a muttered argument with Agustín for a moment and then the two of them splashed away down through the grey rain. Streaming water infused with surreal neon reflections lacquered the black surface of the road as Sancho and Agustín turned the corner. Then they were gone.

'We did it.' Tali's voice trembled.

'Go that way,' Diego called, pointing in the opposite direction to Sancho and Agustín Benitez, 'I'll make sure those two don't follow you.'

'Thanks, Diego. I owe you one.' Galindez walked past him, one arm around Tali's shoulders. Diego looked at them impassively. 'We look after our own, Dr Galindez.'

Galindez and Tali kept walking. The rain was easing now and they could hear the distant pulse of traffic again. The silence after the prolonged rain was strangely unsettling.

'What's Diego's problem?' Tali asked, once they were out of earshot.

Galindez shrugged. 'I've got a feeling it's me.'

CHAPTER EIGHTEEN

MADRID 1953.

Alicia Martinez opened her eyes. It was dark. A sharp, piercing pain lanced through her head and she felt an urge to vomit. Her senses came back slowly, and as they did so, fear began to surge through her, her terror made all the worse as she began to remember the violence of her abduction. She was lying in pitch darkness on damp cobblestones. She remembered the men and the car, the sickly smell of the chloroform. It was hard to think. She moaned, feeling handcuffs tight against her wrists. It was difficult to sit up with her hands pinioned behind her. She struggled to her knees, uncertain where she was. Then footsteps, the sound of a key turning in a lock.

The door opened, flooding the cell with a sickly light. Weak though it was, the light was too much for her eyes, making the pain in her head throb with malicious intensity. She had never known her heart beat so hard, not even during the shelling of Madrid at its worst. She opened her eyes. They waited in the doorway, black outlines in the pallid light from the corridor. *Señora* Martinez wanted to demand an explanation but her tongue felt too thick and dry to speak. She tried to stand, staggering drunkenly as one of them seized her by the arm. Her hands were numb with cold and pain. She realised her shoes were missing, the awareness provoking a sudden sense of loss as she felt the damp cold stones beneath her feet. The man turned the key in the handcuffs, the blood flowing painfully into her hands as he removed the cuffs.

'Don't say anything yet, *señora*,' the one at the door said. 'Just listen. I'm going to ask you some questions. I want you to answer them. If you don't tell us the truth, things will go very badly for you. *Entiende?*'

She was shaking. Strangely, despite the cold, she was sweating heavily. She couldn't see his face, just his angular outline in the ghost-light from outside the room. The other man was an ominous presence behind her, forbidding her to turn round, ordering her to address the man in the door.

'We want to know who gave you a letter to deliver to Guzmán,' the man said.

Señora Martinez was happy to tell them and told them repeatedly, first calmly and then later, in a voice verging on hysteria, about the man in the black coat and hat. About the letter. The money he had paid her. How she met the *comandante* when he arrested her neighbours. She told them in detail, though she omitted his attempt to force her to go to bed with him.

'There's something you aren't telling us,' the man at the door said. 'You must cooperate, *señora*. Otherwise things will get worse.'

Alicia Martinez hung her head, struggling not to cry. She had told them everything they needed to know. Why couldn't they believe her? She tried to speak again but couldn't.

'Right.' The exasperated voice of the one standing close behind her. Too close. She could smell him: sweat and tobacco. 'Before we begin, *puta*, you're not dressed properly for this.'

Her shaking became more violent. The man called her *tú*, as if addressing a child.

'Come on, *pendeja*,' the man spat. 'Get undressed. *Rápida, puta*. Don't keep us waiting. Get your kit off and throw it over there by the door.'

Alicia Martinez felt her world sliding into nightmare. Sweat dribbled down her face, her clothes were soaked with her fear. Disbelief turned to a debilitating terror as the man slapped her in the face. Shocked, she tried to protest but all that came was a low moan of fear and pain. He slapped her again. Another couple of slaps and she began to beg. He pulled her around the cell by her hair, pushing her into the wall, shoving her towards the door and then dragging her back by her hair into the darkness. She began to scream.

The man released her and she slumped against the wall. She heard his ragged breathing. The one at the door said nothing, waiting impassively as the man began to hit her, striking her first in the stomach, then a punch to her breast. A blow to her ribs. Backhanded slaps to her face. Tears and snot poured from her nose and she gasped for breath, feeling the strange dryness of her tongue as she did so. The man continued shouting, cursing her, striking her with hard, sudden blows. Her world was collapsing. Her world. A world of routine and work but at least one in which she made choices and decisions. Here, she was trapped in an uncertain world of pain and humiliation. There was nowhere else but this damp patch of stone on which she stood. Nowhere to hide from the blows raining down on her, the insults ever more obscene and threatening. He was the one who told her what happened in this world. What she must do. And now, he was shouting, she had to remove her clothes. Shouting it again and again, each time reinforcing the order with a slap or a punch. She cowered against the wall. The man lifted his hand to strike her again. She could take no more. She began to undress.

She was dizzy, her head ached and nothing made sense any longer. They had left her sprawled on the damp stone floor while they went for a smoke. She had names for them now: Slapping Man and Watching Man. And they had only just begun. Slapping Man had said so. 'Don't go away, *pendeja*, we're coming back and when we do, we'll really get started.'

Señora Martinez crouched in the far corner of the cell. She was dressed only in her slip. Her other clothes were strewn around the floor: Slapping Man had even made her take off her stockings, laughing as she struggled to do so, giving her a running commentary of what he was going to do to her once she had confessed.

She could see no way out. Beatings, rape, even death. No one knew she was here. Nor would they. In this country, people could just disappear off the face of the earth. She had no idea who these men were. She knew nothing except their interest in the *comandante*. Why did she ever take that letter? What a fool she'd been. If only she could warn him. Let him know about these people. Her mind boiled, overloaded with thoughts, balancing on the edge of incoherent hysteria. Too many thoughts. To think, earlier she had been daydreaming like a schoolgirl about the *comandante*'s offer to take her out. She would have accepted. God, if only he knew where she was, he would help her. Tears ran lazily down her cheeks. They were going to come back, take away the rest of her clothes and then hurt her again. And no one would know. Not the *comandante*, not Roberto, *nadie*.

She felt the stone wall against her back. Maybe she could leave a trace behind. Some evidence that she once existed. But she had nothing to make a mark on the stone with. She rubbed her hands together for warmth, felt her wedding ring. The one she had reclaimed from the pawn shop with the *comandante*'s money. She slid the ring off and turned to the wall. It was too dark to see so she had to work carefully. Just her name. Her name and the date. The memory of a person inscribed in stone. When she had finished, she traced the letters with her fingertips. It was a small sense of achievement and it lasted until she heard them coming back.

"*Señora*, is there anything else you want to tell us about the man who asked you to give the letter to the *comandante*? Perhaps you forgot something before?' Watching Man asked.

'Please, please stop.' She was almost hysterical, sitting in the corner, her knees drawn up to her chest, eyes swollen and red, her nose running and her limbs shaking uncontrollably. 'Please. I have to get home for Roberto.' She gasped for breath. 'I told you, the man came and asked me to give a letter to *Comandante* Guzmán. He gave me money.' Her hands clasped in supplication. 'I took the money. I'm poor. I did nothing wrong. You can have the money. All of it. It's at home. I'll get it for you. I promise.' Her voice broke under the weight of her fear. What more could she do? She'd told them the same details each time. The same details she had told them willingly even before Slapping Man began to work on her.

'You won't be going home,' Slapping Man snarled, confirming her worst fear. 'Ever.' He poked her with his boot, trying to push the hem of her slip higher up her thigh. 'Know what we've got outside the door for you?'

'No.'

'Castor oil,' he gloated. 'Litre bottles of it.'

Señora Martinez continued to cry, her shoulders heaving with the exertion.

'When you've drunk one of those,' the man said, 'you'll have this cell awash with shit in ten minutes. And then we'll give you another. Before that though, *puta*, I think we'd better have your *bragas* off.' He reached down and lifted the hem of her slip, reaching up to grasp the waistband of her pants.

'No, don't. Please.' Her voice was incoherent with fear, as if she no longer possessed an adequate vocabulary of protest. In any case she now knew they would take no notice of what she said until she confessed. And maybe not even then.

'And we've got the bucket.' Slapping Man was still struggling to pull off her pants. Alicia Martinez doubled up on the cell floor, desperately clutching her underwear with both hands. 'The bucket,' Slapping Man said, pulling again, dragging her a metre along the cell floor, while she vainly struggled to keep her pants on. But he was stronger than her and he finally wrestled her pants down and dragged them over her resisting legs, throwing them towards the door. 'We call it the *baño*. Not because it's a real bath, but because it's full of water. We'll hold your head under, you bitch, and you'll tell us anything we want to know. Anything. You'll see. I'll hold your head and this gentleman will hold your feet. They say it's like dying. Only worse.'

Señora Martinez was approaching hysteria, shaking her head uncontrollably, trying to make them see, to understand her innocence but her powers of communication had broken down in the face of this last onslaught.

'We'll have that off as well.' Slapping Man tried to slide the strap of her slip down. She flinched, huddling into the corner, trying to press herself into the cold stone. He reached forward and flicked the strap from her shoulder. She hunched, arms clutching her chest to hold the material in place, whimpering.

Slapping Man was panting now. 'Take it off or I'll do it for you.' He reached out again, reaching for the strap, engrossed in his work. So engrossed that he was unaware of Guzmán in the doorway, pushing Peralta aside and striding into the cell. By the time the sarge looked round, Guzmán's fist was already swinging towards him. There was a sharp crack and the sarge's head snapped back as he fell, hitting the wall before sliding unconscious to the floor.

'What the hell is going on here, *Teniente*?' Guzmán shouted, rounding on Peralta, eyes blazing. 'I'll have you both arrested for this.'

'They will be severely punished, *Señora*,' Guzmán repeated in his most conciliatory voice. He was sitting next to Alicia Martinez, as she shivered by the stove in his office. Consoling people was not the strong point of a man whose usual professional vocabulary was one of pain and death. On a personal level, consolation had never really been required of him and he had never needed to offer it. Until now.

He was pleased. Pleased because she was grateful. Guzmán had saved her. She had said so. There were a lot of tears and when he offered her his handkerchief, she took it gratefully. Her eyes were puffed up – but only from tears: the *sargento* had been careful not to land too many blows on her face.

'No need to cry now,' Guzmán said. 'They won't hurt you any more. I promise you.'

'I can't help it,' she sniffed, 'they, he...' Her voice broke in an anguished sob of pain. 'He would have...' She was unable to finish. Luckily for her, she had only a vague grasp of what the *sargento* might have done had he been given the word.

'A disgrace,' Guzmán said. 'Spanish men behaving like that. Incredible.' Lying was much more his forte. Lies could be presented much more easily than the truth. And usually to better effect.

She turned to him, her eyes flashing angrily. 'How could they have thought I had done anything wrong, *Comandante*?'

'These are hard men, *señora*,' Guzmán said. 'Their jobs coarsen them. They treat decent people as if they were criminals. It's all the same to them: guilty until proven innocent.'

'But what they did...' Her voice faltered. 'They wouldn't even believe me when I told them the truth.'

Of course not, Guzmán thought. It was only when a person was riddled with fear that truth could be properly ascertained. Only when you looked into their eyes and saw whether or not they were lying, whether they needed to be taken down another level into the nightmare world of pain Guzmán and his men routinely introduced their prisoners to. Luckily for *Señora* Martinez, it had not been necessary to take her very far down that route.

'I assure you they'll be punished,' he said.

'I don't care about that,' Alicia Martinez said. She was still shaking. 'It's that they did this to me without even giving me a chance to answer their questions.' She looked up at him. 'Did you know they were going to arrest me?'

It had taken her a while to think of that, Guzmán thought. 'Of course not. I swear on the Blessed Virgin, *señora*. Those two were supposed to be investigating your neighbours, the ones we arrested the other day. They decided to interrogate you without consulting me. If I'd been here when they brought you in I could have prevented it. I'll tell you this,' he raised his voice angrily, 'I will never let them forget how low their actions have been. Never. And I'll make sure they spend the rest of their careers sitting at a desk, not molesting innocent women.'

'Well, they deserve that,' *Señora* Martinez said, somewhat placated. 'What's so awful is how they planned it – drugging me like that. So calculated.'

'They're the sort of people we have in this job,' Guzmán said.

'I'm afraid we aren't picked for our etiquette or table manners, *señora.*'

She smiled for the first time since he had helped her dress in the cell, waiting while Peralta dragged the semi-conscious *sargento* down the corridor. Guzmán would not forget that moment, when *Señora* Martinez had placed her arm around his waist for support and hidden her face against his chest.

'I can't look at them.' Her voice quavered.

Guzmán had guided her from the cell, shielding her from the sight of Peralta as he knelt over the sarge, trying to rouse him. It had been a strange feeling for Guzmán, his big arm around her narrow shoulders, her tears soaking into his shirt. For a moment he had wondered whether he should attack Peralta, to further demonstrate his outrage to *Señora* Martinez but decided against it.

'I'll take you home,' Guzmán said. 'Then I'll deal with those two.'

'You've been very kind, *Comandante.* I just feel so... ashamed.'

'You did nothing wrong, *señora.*'

'It's what they might have done to me. I feel dirty.'

'Listen,' Guzmán said, 'I'll arrange a car. I'll drive you myself. And I'll make sure those two are out of the way until we've left the building. You won't have to see them again.'

She looked at him gratefully and reached out her hand and placed it on his. Guzmán sat motionless and tense, looking down at her pale flesh contrasted with his hairy fist, as surprised by this moment of intimacy as he was confused.

'Thank you,' Alicia Martinez said.

Peralta slumped at a table in the mess, watching detachedly while the sarge applied a damp cloth to the swelling above his eye.

'*Mierda*, that was some punch he gave me,' the sarge said.

'You're lucky he didn't kill you. Or both of us, he was so angry,' Peralta muttered.

'*Vaya.* He's not angry. We was only doing what he ordered.'

Guzmán entered.

Peralta jumped to his feet. 'What the hell is going on?' he shouted. 'We interrogate that woman and then you come in and punch the sarge and shove me out of the way screaming what bastards we are.'

'Well you are,' Guzmán said. 'Doing that to a woman. Luckily she doesn't want to make a complaint.'

'Complaint?' Peralta's voice rose in disbelief.

'Calm down, *Teniente*.' The sarge exposed his rotting teeth in a broad grin. 'We did the dirty work and the *comandante* comes out smelling of roses. He had to make it right with the lady.'

'That's the size of it,' Guzmán said, peeling off several banknotes from the roll in his hand. 'Here.' He threw them on the table towards the sarge. 'That should pay for the slight discomfort. Although to be honest I can't imagine it would make much difference. You'd still be crazy.'

The sarge grabbed the money and shoved it into his pocket. '*Gracias, jefe*. If you need us to work on her some more...'

'Don't push it,' Guzmán growled. '*Teniente*, you managed that job quite well.'

'It made me feel dirty.' Peralta was choked with anger. 'I'm ashamed.'

'The sarge did it carefully,' Guzmán said. 'You were just the straight man and you did fine. And the important thing is that she's off the hook. So now everyone's happy.'

'Especially me,' the sarge added.

Guzmán smiled. 'Mind you, she thinks you were the bad bastard, *Teniente*. All that silent watching. A bit creepy, she said.'

'It was wrong,' Peralta said, glowering at the sarge's obvious relish of the situation.

'*Bueno*, I'm going to drive her home,' Guzmán said. 'I need a car. What have we got tonight?'

'There's the black SEAT out the back,' Peralta said.

'The one you used to pick her up?'

'That's the one, sir.'

'The one that will stink of the chloroform you used on her?'

Guzmán snorted. '*Puta madre, Teniente*, I thought you were the sensitive type?'

'There's the Buick. That's a nice car.'

'You're right, Sarge. Go and get me the keys. And *Sargento*?'

'*Jefe*?'

'Don't go in my office,' Guzmán said in a low voice.

'*A sus ordenes.*'

The sarge ambled out of the door. Peralta sat at the table, not looking at Guzmán.

'What's your problem now, *Teniente*?' Guzmán asked, without interest.

'We could have questioned her without any of this,' Peralta said, angrily. 'You said you had feelings for her and you allowed that maniac to strip her and made me join in. You disgust me. You're—'

Guzmán moved far more quickly than the *teniente* expected and seized him by the throat, propelling him backwards off the chair. Peralta tried to breathe but all he could manage was a laboured rasp as Guzmán pinned him against the wall.

'Speak to me like that again and I'll kill you. *Me entiendes, Teniente*?'

Guzmán released his grip and Peralta slid to the floor, spluttering for air.

'I understand perfectly,' he croaked.

'No you don't,' Guzmán snapped. 'You don't fucking understand anything. You did the job. You obeyed orders. And now she isn't a suspect, I don't have to worry about her. This is the way these things are done, *Teniente*. If you wanted to join the Boy Scouts you should have said so. You're with the grown-ups, now, Peralta. Remember that. And here,' Guzmán pulled a few dollar bills from his pocket and threw them on the table, 'now you know what it's really like in this squad, you get the same perks as the others.'

The sarge returned with the car keys. Guzmán snatched them from him and went back to his office.

'What's that?' The sarge pointed to the crumpled notes on the table.

Peralta shrugged. 'The *comandante* left it. I don't want it.'

The sarge grabbed the cash and tucked it away. 'My lucky day today, *Teniente.*'

'Good for you.' Peralta clutched his stomach as he felt a sudden barb of pain.

MADRID 1953, CALLE DE LA TRIBULETE

Guzmán walked with *Señora* Martinez to the doorway of her building. She had been quiet during the drive. Not surprising, Guzmán thought, she was probably exhausted after the workout the sarge had given her. Even so, she had talked with him about the boy and her hopes for his future. She was a bright woman. Aware of the constraints of her own life and content to try to improve the chances for her nephew whilst resigned to the tedium of her own marginal existence. Guzmán approved of such realism.

She paused at the door. 'Thank you for the lift, *Comandante.* Would you like a drink?'

That was a surprise. He thought she would want to get into her flat and lock the door.

'We have a job on tonight,' he said, looking at his watch. He hoped he saw a look of disappointment in her eyes. 'I have to be at the *comisaría* by midnight. But a drink would be much appreciated, *señora.* Thank you.'

The stairs were dark. There was a faint smell of damp. Overtones of chorizo, garlic and onions. Guzmán waited as *Señora* Martinez unlocked the door. Entering the small apartment, he felt clumsy and awkward. He rarely made social visits. On official duties, it was different: he was in charge. Here, he was like a bull outside its own pasture: defensive and wary.

'*Tinto, Comandante?*'

He nodded. *Señora* Martinez poured the red wine into cheap glasses.

'If you want to pick up the boy,' Guzmán said, 'I'd be happy to drive you.'

'It's only round the corner. There's no need. But thank you. In fact, *Comandante*,' she looked at him, her pale eyes luminous in the weak light, 'thank you for everything. For saving me from those men.'

Guzmán could handle polite conversation when he had to, he could handle social niceties and even small talk if necessary. He could conduct himself in the detached, formal manner polite company demanded. Which was why it seemed so strange when, as *Señora* Martinez came nearer to him, he reached out his hand to stroke her face, tracing the sharp line of her cheekbones and then following the soft curve of her mouth. She didn't flinch as he had feared. Instead, her eyes closed and she stood while his hand moved over her face, across the arc of her eyebrows, along her hairline. His fingers brushed through her hair. He felt her relaxing. Trusting. She placed a hand against his chest. He could feel the heat of her palm pressing gently against him.

And then the moment broke. He broke it. His hand moved from her cheek, glided down her throat and settled on her breast. Her eyes flickered open. She pressed her hand against his chest, pushing him away. 'Not now. Not after what happened today.'

For a moment, he felt stirrings of rage. If he wanted, he could have her now and no one in this world would stop him. Just as he could have allowed the sarge to work on her all night, until by morning she would have been ready to do anything he wanted. But those were just possibilities. The truth was, Guzmán liked allowing her this control. Liked her to think she could draw the line, could tell him when he was going too far. It was a game, a gift from him to her. It was also her gift to him. She thought if she drew the line, he would respond. Would behave like a decent man. And he could – if he chose. He had observed how others did it. He had learned things that way before.

'I'm sorry, *señora*.' He took his hand away. The air was strangely thick around him. He was excited.

'I didn't mean to give you the impression...' she began.

'You gave no impression, *señora*,' Guzmán said. 'I behaved badly and I apologise.' He moved towards the door and put on his hat. He lingered in the doorway for a moment.

'You must think me ungrateful,' *Señora* Martinez said. 'After what you did for me. But I can't...'

'Not at all,' Guzmán said, 'you've nothing to be grateful to me for.'

She stood at the door and watched him go.

At the top of the stairs he turned. 'When you're feeling better, do you think we might still go out somewhere?'

Alicia Martinez smiled. It was the first time she had smiled since Guzmán's men dragged her into the car. 'That would be nice, *Comandante*. Of course.'

MADRID 1953, COMISARÍA, CALLE DE ROBLES

'You'll be wanting to know about tonight, I imagine, *Teniente*.'

Peralta looked up, annoyed at Guzmán's tone. 'I await your orders, *mi Comandante*.'

Guzmán nodded approvingly. 'As you should, *Teniente*. I hope I can count on you if there's any trouble?'

'*Absolutamente, mi Comandante*.'

'I hope so,' Guzmán said. 'It could turn rough down there.'

'I won't let you down, sir.'

Guzmán nodded. 'Good. I'm sure you'll be fine. Anyway, a bit of action will toughen you up. You need to be hard in the Special Brigade. Especially up here.' He tapped his forehead. 'Although it also helps if you can punch as well. And that's true, *Teniente*, whether you're arresting them or getting information out of them.'

'There are other ways to get information without brutality,' Peralta protested.

'But they're not reliable. Sometimes you have to be a bit rough. The main thing is to get to the truth.'

'Like with *Señora* Martinez?'

Guzmán scowled. *'Joder, coño.* Don't start. We've discussed that. She's in the clear. And don't take that tone of voice with me, *Teniente.* What we do, we're doing for Spain.'

'For Franco, you mean.'

'For Franco,' Guzmán agreed. 'He is the State. And running the State depends on things being predictable as I've told you already.'

'But things aren't predictable, are they?' Peralta said. 'We couldn't have predicted someone poisoning a consignment of heroin, could we?'

'No, but the motive behind it is obvious,' Guzmán said. 'They're doing it for Positano. Ruin Valverde's business and then take over. And who'll supply the stuff they'd sell? Positano's chums in the Mob.'

Peralta nodded, but Guzmán hadn't finished. 'I couldn't give a fuck about Valverde's business interests but this is going to draw attention and that's the last thing we want. If it gets Spain a bad press abroad, that will piss off Franco mightily. Questions will be asked and it will end up being us who have to answer them. And then people may begin to wonder if we're still up to the job. We need to get these Dominicans off the streets before things get uncomfortable for us.' Guzmán glared at Peralta. 'By us, I mean me.'

'Maybe we'll be able to do that tonight, *jefe,'* Peralta said. 'If we're lucky.'

Guzmán smiled. *'Puta madre,* I hope so, *Teniente.* I could do with some good luck.'

MADRID 1953, BAR DOMINICANA, CALLE DE TOLEDO

A light snow was falling as the truck stopped at the end of the street. The sarge turned off the engine. Peralta slumped between Guzmán and the sarge, sucking on a cigarette. In the pale light of the distant street lamp he looked even more grey and cadaverous. From time to time, he clutched at his stomach. Guzmán checked his pistol and holstered it.

'I hope you aren't going to be sick,' Guzmán said. 'I've already told you about that.'

'Something wrong with my belly, that's all. Rich food or something,' Peralta said, miserably.

'That's good, *Teniente*,' Guzmán opened the cab door, 'because I'd hate you to miss any of the action.'

Peralta slid across the seat and followed Guzmán into the freezing night. Fifteen *guardia civiles* were getting out of the back of the truck, threatening and angular in their cloaks and tricorne hats. Guzmán spoke to them quietly, describing the layout of Bar Dominicana, showing them the side alley leading to the courtyard at the back.

'Five minutes, *Cabo*, then come in and secure the place,' Guzmán told the corporal.

'*Vamonos, señores.*' Guzmán strode down the street, Peralta half running to keep up with him, while the sarge strolled nonchalantly behind, whistling softly through the gaps in his remaining teeth.

As they neared the entrance, Guzmán turned to repeat their orders.

'I'll speak to Mamacita at the bar, Sarge you go out the back, make sure the door's open for the *guardia civiles*. *Teniente*, you check upstairs. When the uniforms come crashing in, there will be a sudden rush as the whores and their customers try to do a runner. If any of them try to get away...' he raised his hand, index finger outstretched, 'stop them.'

The sarge sniggered, clearly happy. Peralta remained miserable.

'Better dead than Red,' the sarge called as Guzmán pushed open the door and entered. The door closed, cutting off the brief murmur of a piano above a background of voices and clinking glasses. The sarge counted ten and followed him.

Peralta waited, anxious and numb from the brittle cold. He began to count but gave up. He pushed the door and stepped into the Bar Dominicana.

The place stank. The air was humid and drenched in the smell of sweat, the ceiling wreathed in pungent clouds of black tobacco smoke. Another burst of sharp pain flickered in Peralta's stomach as he moved through the crowded bar towards the rear exit. Guzmán was already at the bar, pushing through the throng of customers. Behind the bar, the faded ruin that was Mamacita was holding court, sloshing a variety of coloured drinks into glasses, shouting obscenities and putting on a performance that eclipsed the pianist's stumbling attempts.

Peralta shoved through the tipsy crowd to the door at the back of the club. He pushed open the door and stepped into the empty hallway. He heard the faint sound of a door banging, probably the sarge opening the back door for the *guardia*. The hubbub of the bar faded as Peralta made his way up the stairs. A floorboard creaked and he hesitated before continuing upwards. At the top of the stairs was a long corridor with doors on either side. Long ago this had been a hotel: Peralta saw faded fire regulations on the wall, dating from the turn of the century. From one of the rooms down the corridor he heard laughter. A door opened and a fat man emerged, hurriedly pulling on his jacket. The man ambled down the corridor, carefully avoiding eye contact. As he hurried past Peralta he spoke quietly, 'If it's Carmela you've come to see, be careful. She's in a hell of a mood.'

The fat man shuffled down the stairs and Peralta heard the noise of the bar for a moment as the man opened the door. Somewhere down the corridor, there was a man's groan followed by a woman's laughter. Peralta walked slowly and carefully, listening to the noises of corporeal indulgence. It made him feel strangely sad. Not cynical, like Guzmán, but genuinely sad. He would mention it at his next confession.

'*Oye, coño*, who the hell are you? What're you doing sneaking around here?' The voice was sharp, confident and came from behind him.

Peralta whirled round. He knew that face. It was the fat Dominican. His suit was outrageously tailored, the colour too bright not to stand out against the sepia blandness of Spanish life. 'Who're you, *hombre*? You deaf?' His Spanish was heavily inflected by traces of the Caribbean and his face was angry and shining with sweat. He was very drunk.

Peralta was only about two metres away from him. He felt unsure about trying to draw his pistol. The big man looked like he could move faster than he could.

'I'm looking to buy some stuff,' Peralta said.

'Oh? And who said you could get anything here?'

'A friend,' Peralta said quickly. 'Fat guy, civil servant, balding, a *maricón*.'

The man looked unconvinced.

'Mamacita said any friend of his was all right by her,' Peralta added, suddenly inspired, 'she told me to come straight up.'

The man relaxed and grinned. 'If Mamacita sent you up here, *caballero*, that's cool. *Qué quieres*? Stuff just for yourself or you planning to have a party?'

'Just for me. *Morfina*. I use it for the pain in my leg.'

The man grinned. 'Yeah. No doubt. Old war wound maybe? That's what they all say, *señor mio*, but that's cool. We just sell it, we're not your *mamá*. You shoot up all week and twice on Sunday if you want. No one here's going to say a thing.'

'That sounds good to me.'

The man turned towards the half-open door. 'If you got the money, that is? Because if not, then you a time-waster man. No time for time-wasters here, brother. No time at all.'

'I can pay,' Peralta said, listening for the sound of the *guardia civil* arriving downstairs. Once the raid began it would be easier to reach his weapon.

'You pay twice, man,' the big Dominican grinned, 'once in cash and once with your immortal soul. But all I need from you, brother, is your cash.' He laughed loudly and pushed open the door. 'Come on, it's all here, man, whatever you need, whenever you need it.' The man entered the room, turning his back on Peralta. Quickly, Peralta reached inside his jacket, pulled out his pistol and transferred it to his overcoat pocket as he followed the Dominican through the door.

The room was surprisingly warm. Peralta saw a wood-stove in one corner, its light welcoming and cheerful, a distinct contrast to the atmosphere as he looked across the green baize of a large card table at four unsmiling faces. Peralta nodded, mumbling good evening. No one replied. He scanned the faces. None of them were the Dominicans in the photographs at the *comisaría*. That was a relief.

'Who are you?' A thin-faced bald man with round glasses peered at him intently.

The big Dominican cut in. 'Mamacita says he's cool. Civil servant. Wants *morfina*. For his leg.' He guffawed.

The thin man didn't laugh. 'This isn't a pharmacy. It will cost you. Got any money?'

Peralta nodded, feeling himself start to sweat. The four men at the card table continued to stare. The big Dominican frowned at Peralta. 'Don't I know you?'

'I've been here before,' Peralta said. 'With my friend.'

'Oh yes?' The Dominican scrutinised him. 'Yeah, I knew I'd seen you before.'

Peralta thought the man was putting too much effort into trying to remember him. His right hand closed tightly on his pistol.

The Dominican's face changed, the smile was gone now. 'Course I seen you before.' His voice was icy. 'Now I remember you, *pendejo.*'

Guzmán stood at the bar, allowing himself to be jostled by the lowlifes dancing attendance upon Mamacita. Up close she – or more accurately he – was a study in ruin: the make-up applied inaccurately and too thickly, the effect of the vivid blusher spoiled by his thick stubble, the mouth a careless gash of colour around ruined teeth. She paused from pouring cheap champagne into the collection of glasses on the filthy bar. Her eyes narrowed in recognition from beneath the shadow of her cheap wig. She was, Guzmán noted, steaming drunk.

'Oh no. Not *Señor* Policeman again.' Her voice was too loud, alerting the customers in the vicinity. 'Can't you leave a girl alone, copper? Police.' She began to shout, this time in a much louder voice. Guzmán suddenly realised it wasn't the decaying bunch of losers around him that she was trying to alert. He snatched up a bottle from the zinc counter and leaned quickly across the bar, smashing it over Mamacita's head, knocking her backwards into the shelves. She slid to the floor in an exploding shower of cheap liquor bottles and dirty glasses as the shelves collapsed around her. Customers began heading for the exit. Guzmán drew his pistol and fired once into the ceiling. A rain of plaster and debris showered down.

'Police. Everyone stay where they are,' Guzmán shouted. The rear door burst open and the *guardia civiles* crashed in, bayonets fixed – a little excessive, Guzmán thought, even for men under his command.

'Two men on that front door,' Guzmán instructed. 'Get these people sat down until we get a truck to take them away.'

The *guardia civiles* herded the shabby clientele of the Bar Dominicana into the centre of the dance floor. They stood, skeletally malnourished, meekly obeying the shouted orders of the *guardia*. The sarge, no less dissolute than his prisoners, grinned a broken smile at Guzmán.

'Everything's under control, *jefe*. Where's the *teniente*?'

A series of shots came from upstairs. Guzmán ran towards the rear door yelling to the sarge to follow.

From downstairs came the sound of shouting and the crashing of tables and chairs being overturned. Then there was a gunshot and muffled sounds of chaos. Someone was shouting outside the door. For Peralta, time slowed, his focus becoming clearer as thought was overtaken by action. The Dominican turned to the door, reaching inside his jacket. Peralta pulled the revolver from his pocket and aimed it. The thin man shouted out a warning as Peralta fired, trying to shoot the Dominican in the chest. He would

393

have succeeded if his aim had been better; instead, the bullet hit the man just below his Adam's apple. The Dominican crashed against the wall and slid down it in a spray of arterial blood, his gun clattering on the floor while he clutched at his throat, trying in vain to arrest the haemorrhage that was now choking him.

The men behind the card table leaped to their feet, heading for the window, the table toppling towards Peralta in a flurry of cards and cash. Peralta fired as the first one struggled to open the sash window. The bullet hit the man in the back of the head and he fell forward against the window before slumping to the floor, the bloodied glass shattering noisily around him. Peralta fired at the three others as they vacillated for a moment, fatally indecisive as to whether to escape through the shattered window or turn on their attacker. Two of the men went down, but the thin man remained for a second, trembling – whether it was rage or fear, Peralta would never know. The man faced him, eyes ludicrously wild through his round spectacles and Peralta shot him twice in the chest, the impact throwing him back against the wall, still struggling to stay on his feet. Peralta took a step forward as the man sagged, hands clasped across the growing stain on his chest. Peralta aimed slightly above the man's hands and fired again. The shot was harsh and final. The man's hands fell from his chest and he dropped heavily to the floor. Peralta's ears were ringing and the lieutenant briefly wondered if he might have been deafened. With luck, it would be grounds for retirement.

The door crashed open and Guzmán stepped into the room, pistol raised. He walked slowly, taking in the sprawled bodies, shaking his head at the blood.

'*Coño*,' he laughed, 'I can't take you anywhere.'

Peralta stared at the dead Dominican sitting on the floor, his back to the wall, a long thick smear of gore on the shabby wallpaper marking his descent. Around him was a growing pool of blood.

'They thought they could escape,' Peralta said, looking round at the carnage.

'Well, they got that wrong,' Guzmán chuckled, lighting a

cigarette. As an afterthought he passed the cigarette to Peralta and lit another. 'You might be able to buy some downstairs before we leave,' he added.

The sarge appeared at the door. '*Hostia*, you got them then, *jefe*?'

Guzmán snorted. 'I got no one, *Sargento*. The *teniente* did this all by himself. And luckily these don't look like our Dominican friends, except...'

He bent forward over the big corpse by the door. 'Fuck.'

The sarge moved closer to get a better look. 'He's one of them all right.'

Guzmán sighed. 'Nice work, *Teniente*. The Head of State orders us not to go near these bastards and you almost shoot the head off one of them. Where did you learn to shoot people in the neck, by the way?'

'You did that on purpose?' The sarge was momentarily impressed until he saw Guzmán's face. 'Nah, thought not.'

Peralta put his pistol back in its holster. He seemed to be withering in front of them. His shoulders were hunched, his thin frame melting into the layers of shabby clothes.

'He tried to pull a gun.' Peralta's voice was faint. 'Then they tried to escape.'

'Well, it's done now,' Guzmán said, looking round at the dead men. '*Sargento*?'

'*A sus ordenes.*' The pile of corpses had cheered the *sargento* up enormously.

'*Teniente* Peralta entered the room and was obliged to shoot three desperate criminals. That clear?'

The sarge shook his head. 'There are four of them, *jefe*.'

Guzmán sighed. '*Imbécil.* There are *three*, count them again. And get rid of this.' He kicked the dead Dominican's leg. 'Get his wallet, any identification and destroy it. Get rid of his clothes and get rid of the body. Somewhere where it won't be found for a long time.'

'Understood, *Comandante*.'

'And you,' Guzmán turned to Peralta, 'had better come with me.'

Downstairs, the bar was milling with *guardia civiles*, checking identity documents, poking frightened customers with their rifle butts as they herded them against the bandstand. 'Anything?' Guzmán asked indifferently.

'A couple of lowlifes we've been looking for, a few small-time thieves, nothing more.' The corporal sounded disappointed. 'The men with the whores were here because it's cheap. And you can see why.' He nodded over to a small group of women sitting around a table smoking. They were in various stages of undress, their dressing gowns and nightdresses even more tawdry under the baleful lights of the Bar Dominicana.

One woman looked over at Guzmán, her face a mask of thick make-up. 'When can we get back to work, officer?'

Guzmán lit a cigarette. 'When I say, *señorita*. Think of it as a little coffee break and enjoy being upright for a few minutes. We'll need you to answer a few questions.'

The woman swore, although she took care Guzmán didn't hear.

Guzmán looked at Mamacita, sitting bedraggled and handcuffed, the wig askew, quietly weeping, lines of mascara running down his face and mixing with his stubble.

'Take it back to the *comisaría*,' Guzmán told the corporal, 'and, while you're at it, anyone else who seems even the slightest bit suspect.'

The corporal saluted and barked orders at his men. A truck was waiting outside and the prisoners were led to it. Guzmán walked over to the ramshackle bar, reaching for an unopened bottle of brandy. He took off the top and drank from the bottle before handing it to Peralta. The lieutenant swigged the brandy gratefully, but then choked and spluttered most of it onto the floor.

'It's a bit rough.' Guzmán smirked.

He motioned for Peralta to sit down at one of the filthy tables. Peralta sat with his head down, morose, periodically tugging at the brandy. Guzmán took the bottle from him.

'You did well, *Teniente*,' he said. 'You were in a tight spot and you did what you had to. No one can ask for more.'

Peralta shook his head. 'I let you down, *jefe*. I should have kept them covered, called for help so we could have interrogated them.'

'In which case you'd be dead now,' Guzmán said. 'You did the right thing. You stayed alive.'

'But you said *Almirante* Carrero Blanco ordered us not to touch them under any circumstances,' Peralta muttered.

'And no one has.' Guzmán smiled. 'You shot three criminals in the execution of your duty. There was no Dominican here, *Teniente*, do you understand? There was no fucking Dominican.'

'I understand, sir.' Peralta looked grey and much older.

Guzmán and Peralta sat, drinking brandy, watched by the hostile whores, while the *guardia civiles* carried out the bodies wrapped in sheets and laid them by the front door to await a truck. Peralta noted there were only three bodies. From the rear of the building he heard the low rumble of an engine.

'The sarge will do a good job,' Guzmán said. 'He's had lots of practice.'

'I've never killed anyone before,' Peralta said quietly.

'Well, there you are,' Guzmán was suddenly cheerful, 'you've got an interesting story to tell the wife when you get home.'

Peralta thought about it for a moment and reached for the brandy again.

The sarge ambled back into the bar. 'Whenever you're ready, *mi Comandante*.'

Guzmán stood up and took a last mouthful of brandy. He looked at the bottle, scrutinising the label and then hurled it into the mirror behind the bar. Peralta flinched at the impact and leaped to his feet. His nerves were going. The whores appeared much less startled at Guzmán's behaviour. The one who had spoken earlier got to her feet.

'*Oiga*, leave us somewhere to work. Have some respect.'

'Respect? For you? Of course, *señorita*,' Guzmán snarled. 'We'll leave you alone for now, although you may see us again in due course.'

'Well, let's hope you're paying customers next time, *señor*,' the woman laughed.

Guzmán looked icily at her. '*Mujer*, if I was paying you, I'd expect change from a duro. Keep quiet, you bag of shit, and hope you don't find yourself in one of our cells, *puta*, because if you do, you'll wish you'd never been fucking born.'

The woman swallowed hard and stayed quiet. Guzmán followed the remaining *guardia civiles* outside to the truck. The vehicle's engine spluttered black fumes into the night. The cold air stank of petrol. There was laughing and joking as the men lined up to get aboard. Up the road, perhaps fifty metres away, was another truck, cloth-topped, military-looking.

'That one of ours?' Guzmán asked the sarge.

The sarge peered at the truck. 'Don't think so. We only had this one and the one from the *comisaría* for the prisoners. Anyway, we'll soon find out, look, he's reversing.'

The truck had started its engine and was slowly coming down the street towards them.

'Looks like they've been having a fag while we did the hard work,' the sarge muttered.

'*Cabrónes*, we could have been finished here if they'd lent a hand,' Guzmán said.

The truck came closer. Guzmán, Peralta and the sarge waited, interested to see which branch of the police or the military had turned up so late. The truck stopped about twelve metres away and the canvas awning over the back fluttered open. In the dim light Guzmán saw dark shapes crouched over some kind of machinery. Then the driver of Guzmán's truck put on his lights and the rear of the reversing vehicle was vividly illuminated as the light picked out men crouching over a heavy machine gun on a tripod, one of them holding a long ammunition belt. Guzmán saw a shadowed face and the glitter of a gold-toothed grin before the thin night air was torn apart by machine-gun fire.

The kid flattened himself against the rough bark of the tree. Three more African soldiers emerged from the long grass to join their comrades gathered around the bodies of the men they had just butchered. Of the Moors pursuing the fleeing Republicans, there were now nine left. Nine against three. Those odds were bad enough, but as the kid knew only too well, the enemy were better trained and battle-hardened. And eager to kill. Another figure appeared, carrying a large pack, moving slowly through the dusty shrubs. The kid remained motionless behind the safety of the tree, waiting, not raising his rifle yet, in case it attracted attention, even a hundred metres away.

The burning afternoon enforced a dazed torpor on the arid landscape. Suddenly, an unexpected moment of action took the kid by surprise. The corporal stood up from his hiding place in the long dry grass some six metres from the Moors. He had the advantage of surprise, and the gunshot echoed around the jagged slopes of the hillside as one of the Moors fell lifeless to the dry ground. The corporal struggled to work the bolt of the rifle, ejecting the cartridge and bringing the rifle up again, but this time more slowly as a volley of shots from the remaining Moors tore into him. Staggering, the corporal fired from the hip before falling to the ground, a small dust cloud rising around his body. His last shot had struck home – though not fatally – one of the Moors lurched drunkenly and dropped his weapon, clutching his belly as he fell. The rest closed ranks as they bore down on the corporal. Men grouped together made a good target. Resting his rifle on a branch, the kid squinted down the sight.

The Moors had reached the corporal. They were shouting and mocking, trying to determine if he was dead or merely pretending.

They would not know. The man with the tommy gun suddenly rose up behind them, the gunfire a deep metallic stammer raking the group of Africans only a metre or so away. The tommy gunner leaped forward, still firing into the bodies on the ground. He stopped, the kid saw him straining his neck forward to look for movement. There was. The wounded Moor struggled to his feet and shot the machine gunner, who fell as if pulled by an unseen cord. The brief silence was broken by the sharp crack of the kid's rifle. The Moor crumpled to the ground. The echo died away and the silence that followed was strange and artificial.

The kid struggled to control his breathing. Sheltered by the wizened tree, he was now the last one. But how many of the Moors were still alive? Cautiously, he edged his head around the tree trunk. He could make out several dark shapes on the ground. And then he saw the man he had just shot stand for a moment before falling again. Heard him call out. 'Guzmán. I'm hit.'

From the deep scrub the kid saw the figure with the big pack begin to run across the dry ground, quickly dropping to his knees as he reached the wounded Moor.

The kid had choices to make. Lowering himself to the ground, he began to drag himself forwards with his elbows, the heavy rifle gripped in both hands. Crawling like this in such heat was torture and he made progress slowly. Sweat stung his eyes and he paused repeatedly to wipe it away, listening for the sound of someone coming to the aid of the two men ahead of him. No one came.

CHAPTER NINETEEN

This afternoon there was a queue waiting to pass through the scanner, some conference on global policing on the fifth floor. Galindez waited in line with Tali, discussing cross-national similarities between police officers. Finally, with the crowd of visiting cops dispatched up to the conference centre, they were able to take the lift to the forensic department.

'I feel a lot safer here after what happened last night.' Tali said. 'Sancho must have followed us to the judge's office from your flat.'

'And we know now Sancho and Agustín are working together – which also means the *Centinelas* know I was at the archive. Sancho seemed very keen to stop us depositing the documents in Judge Delgado's night safe – so he probably had an idea what was in them.'

'I reckon those two are enforcers for the *Centinelas*.'

'It looks like it, although I'm sure it wasn't them who grabbed the cop in the archive.'

'No offence, Ana, but you were sure the guy in the archive was an old man. Now it turns out he was only thirty-nine.'

'It was the way he was bent almost double – he must have been wounded and was trying to escape through the exit at the back of the archive. If I hadn't been so preoccupied with the Guzmán file, I might have realised what was happening and been able to help him. *Mierda*, a fine witness I'd make.'

'*Tranquila*,' Tali said. 'It's not your fault.'

Leaving the lift, Tali followed Galindez down the corridor and into the tiny cubicle of her office, watching as Galindez logged onto the network.

'There's an email here from Mendez. It's the result of the DNA analysis.'

From: Mendez.M.C.@guardiacivil.es

To: Galindez.A.M.@guardiacivil.es

Subject: re: Request for DNA Check

Ana María, DNA match established. Details of match:

Subinspector Enrique Bolin, Policía Nacional, dob.25/10/1970. d.14/08/2009.

Ana – this guy turned up dead two days ago, where the hell did you get this sample?

Mendez.

'This confirms that Bolin was definitely that poor guy I saw hide the file in the archive,' Galindez said.

'Stop beating yourself up, Ana. You couldn't have known what was going on.'

Unconvinced, Galindez deleted Mendez's email and opened the database. 'Let's see what we can find. They update the information every week. New sources of documents turn up all the time – births, arrests, intelligence reports, that kind of thing. Thank God for bureaucracy.'

'How about killings in *la Guerra Civil*?' Tali asked.

A man's voice came from behind her. 'That depends on whether the killing was recorded. In *la contienda* they often didn't bother with such niceties.'

Galindez straightened. '*Capitán* Fuentes, I was just demonstrating the new database.'

Fuentes, short-clipped grey hair, tanned, stern military face. A big smile for Tali. He was holding a large manila envelope.

'Pleased to meet you, *Señorita*…?'

'Natalia Castillo.' Tali smiled. '*Mucha gusta.*' Galindez noticed Fuentes' surprise as he shook her hand. She remembered Tali's strong grip from their first meeting.

'Do you work for us?' Fuentes asked.

'I work at the university,' Tali said. 'The Guzmán investigation.'

'Of course.' Fuentes nodded. 'Well, we're very keen to participate in these inter-agency projects. Sorry, is it *Profesora* Castillo or doctor?'

Tali shrugged. 'Nothing quite so grand, I'm afraid, just plain old *señorita.*'

Fuentes gave her his most charming smile. 'I say something similar when people think I should be a *coronel* at my age. But we're all part of a team, that's the main thing, no?' He grinned. And you're lucky having Ana María on your team. We're very proud of her work so far. I know she gets fed up working on war graves but that's going to change when she gets her transfer to the profiling section. I keep telling her, just be patient. As long as the pay cheque keeps coming in, that's the main thing.'

'That's what Ana María always says.' Tali gave Galindez a wicked smile. Galindez frowned and drew her index finger across her throat.

'She would.' Fuentes nodded, not noticing Galindez's discomfort. 'She's from a *guardia* family. Her father was one of the best. He set the bar very high for the rest of us.'

Galindez squirmed, sensing the inevitable direction of the conversation. Annoyingly, she was correct.

'You knew Ana's father then?' Tali asked, breaking another of Galindez's many invisible rules – never to enter into discussion about other people's relationship with *Papá*.

It was always so predictable, Galindez thought: *Miguel Galindez? Salt of the earth,* guardia *through and through, tough as they come.* Clichéd variations on a theme, frequently with a hidden subtext: *A shame about the daughter – she can't even remember him.* As if she could help it.

'Back in the day,' Fuentes said, 'I worked with both Ana's uncle and her father. Mind you, Natalia,' he gave Tali his most charming smile, 'back then, I was young and I had more hair.'

'What was Ana's dad like?' Tali asked.

'A bit older than me,' Fuentes said, 'and very tough. He knew the rules and he made sure the men kept to them.'

Fuentes was being so affable, Galindez couldn't help joining in. 'That sounds familiar. *Tia* Carmen said if I didn't lace my shoes up correctly, *Papá* would make me undo them and start again.'

'That was Miguel,' Fuentes agreed. 'The men liked him because he'd never ask them to do anything he wouldn't do himself. If we made an arrest, no matter how big the guy was, your dad went in first.'

'So all three of you worked in the same unit?' Tali asked.

'No. They'd both just been promoted when I joined. That would have been the late seventies. They were in the Tactical Unit – public order, counter-terrorism, that sort of thing. I was still learning the ropes while they were sorting out demonstrations.'

Galindez laughed. 'I can't imagine Uncle Ramiro running around with a baton, chasing demonstrators.'

'We all did back then, Ana. But Ramiro was a very bright officer. He never stayed in any post for long. I suppose because his father was a general, Ramiro wanted to do as well as him. When you look at his career now, he's done better.'

'With the Afghanistan job, you mean?' Galindez said.

Fuentes raised his eyebrows. '*Joder*, the rumour's true then?'

'Uncle Ramiro mentioned it last week. I thought everyone knew.'

'You see how it is, Natalia?' Fuentes grinned. 'I'm in charge of this department but the real power lies with Ana María – the girl with a general for an uncle. She knows what's going on.'

Tali raised her eyebrows. 'You might think so, *Capitán*.'

Laughing, Fuentes walked to the doorway and paused. 'Nice to meet you, *Señorita* Castillo. I'll catch you later, Ana María. Oh, and here,' he passed her the envelope, 'Dr Del Rio sent this up for you. The results of a handwriting analysis you requested.'

Tali looked at Galindez questioningly.

'The Guzmán diary.'

'Ah, the dreaded Guzmán,' Fuentes said. 'I'll leave him to you.'

Galindez peered at the computer screen. Her eyes were dry and the words on the screen were starting to blur. Through the windows, the shimmering lights of Madrid formed abstract patterns in the summer night, the precision and geometry of buildings vague in the iridescent darkness. Tali was sleeping, her face hidden in her folded arms. Galindez ran a hand softly across her hair. She didn't stir.

The screen was blank. The database hadn't provided a single match for any of the names listed in Guzmán's diary. But, Galindez realised, those people probably never had any further record kept on them, once Guzmán's unit had come for them. They disappeared into thin air. She chewed her lip. Not thin air. They disappeared into hidden graves or sites like the abandoned mine at Las Peñas. What she needed were the names of people who had existed officially, whose lives had generated documents and records.

She remembered that first afternoon at the university in Seminar Room B. The photograph of Guzmán. Sullen eyes under dark angry brows. And there was the other man with him, thin-faced *Teniente* Peralta. She entered Peralta's name into the search engine. The numbers at the top of the screen spun and two hyperlinks suddenly appeared. Not one hit in hours and now this.

'Tali.' No response. 'Natalia. *Querida.*'

Tali looked up, eyes struggling to focus. 'I fell asleep. Sorry.'

'Look, I got two hits on *Teniente* Peralta.' Galindez selected the first link:

Name: Peralta, Francisco Luis
Subject: *Capitán, Policía Armada, Brigada Especial*
Entry from: Police archive c.1952–1954 (no specific date) Record of award of Police Medal for Gallantry: 'Exceptional Bravery in the Line of Duty' – No details

'So he was brave,' Tali said. 'Good for him. *Muy bueno.*'

'Trouble is, there's no further information.' Galindez frowned. 'But Peralta got his medal around during the time Guzmán disappeared. Christ, maybe he got the medal for making Guzmán disappear. Perhaps we can follow that up?'

'Let's do it when I'm conscious. Can't we go home? Please?'

'Just let me look at this other entry for Peralta. Then we'll go, I promise.'

<u>Name:</u>	Peralta, Roberto Martinez d.o.b 12/6/1946
<u>Title:</u>	Child. Adopted
<u>Adoptive Parents:</u>	*Capitán* Francisco Peralta, police officer and María Cristina Peralta y Valverde, housewife. Real mother unknown.
<u>Entry from:</u>	Adoption records. June 1953

'And?' Tali was exhausted and impatient.

'*Teniente* Peralta adopted a seven-year-old child. Called Martinez. Don't you see? The boy could have been the son of the woman whose name was scratched on the wall at the *comisaría* – Alicia Martinez.'

'Martinez is a common name.' Tali didn't sound convinced.

'There has to be some link,' Galindez muttered.

'You mean some link to Guzmán?'

'Of course. *Teniente* Peralta became *Capitán* Peralta. He was promoted. Something happened: he got a medal, promotion. Why?'

'Lots of things happened in the fifties, Ana. Guzmán wasn't behind all of them. He was just one man. *Nada más.*' Tali sighed.

'He was a very powerful man,' Galindez said. 'What he was doing – like many others – was keeping a dictator in power. A dictator who had supported Hitler, for God's sake. Yet if Luisa has her way, Guzmán will go down in history as some sort of victim. I can't believe he's as innocent as she makes out.'

'This isn't just about you proving Luisa wrong,' Tali said angrily.

'*Hostia*, you found material that's a lot more dangerous to us than Guzmán, Ana María. The *Centinelas'* files named hundreds of people who would have supported a military coup. Not to mention the people they were going to kill if the coup succeeded. Even though we've given the files to Judge Delgado, they may still come after us. We need to think about the present as well as the past. Don't get so hung up on Guzmán. You're getting obsessed, *mi amor*. Leave it.'

'*Obsesionada*? Maybe I am. But don't forget the *Centinelas* said they were using Guzmán in the build-up to those attempted coups. He was working for them, helping with their plans to undermine democracy.'

'Well, the *Centinelas* will be exposed anyway once the judge publicises all those names in the files,' Tali said.

'Don't you see?' Galindez continued. 'The past and the present both involve Guzmán. I can use him to denounce the *Centinelas'* terror attacks in the seventies and eighties and to demolish Luisa's arguments. She can't argue he was just a victim of circumstance if I can show he was involved in murder and treason.'

Tali sighed. 'Aren't you pinning all your hopes on just one man? Luisa says he's innocent, you say he's guilty. Life isn't always so clear cut. Maybe Guzmán isn't the key to everything.'

Some of Galindez's energy started to drain away. 'That's what worries me.'

'You're still worried about the line in the diary, aren't you? The quote from Ortega y Gasset.'

'*Exactamente*. What if I'm wrong and Guzmán had a conscience after all?'

'It's possible. But surely if even the *Centinelas* thought he was difficult and unreliable, it isn't all that likely he was the strong sensitive type, is it?'

'I'm sure he was the opposite. I want people to know exactly what Guzmán did. What the *Centinelas* did. I want people to have closure.'

'Are you sure this isn't about you looking for closure, Ana María?'

'I want to know what happened to Guzmán. And to Alicia Martinez – so she's not forgotten, not just a name scratched on a cell wall.'

Tali groaned with exasperation. 'Stop being so emotional. And stop worrying about proving Luisa wrong. Just do your investigation the way you think is best. You're the one who believes in the value of solid evidence. You've got to come up with some, *querida*.'

'You're right. I've still got the bodies from Las Peñas to examine.'

'Fine. But, *por el amor de Dios*, Ana María, do it another day.'

The screen went blank as Galindez logged out. The manila folder waited unopened on her desk. Guzmán and *Teniente* Peralta could wait, she decided. But something else couldn't.

'Give me five minutes? I've got to pop downstairs to see someone.'

Tali shrugged. 'Wake me when you're done.'

The lift murmured quietly as it descended. The crime lab was in half light. Galindez walked through the familiar banks of equipment, passing shelves laden with bottles, jars, test tubes – the sterile paraphernalia of science. A light came from a table at the far end of the room where a woman in uniform was dusting items for fingerprints. She stood up as Galindez approached. A tall woman – almost 1.8 metres, high cheekbones, dark skin – the best of her Dominican mother and gypsy father. A sergeant's badge on her sleeve.

'*Holá*.' A soft low voice. 'How are you, Ana?'

'*Bien*.' Galindez thought she might as well lie. She was getting lots of practice lately.

'No more trouble with hidden cameras in your girlfriend's bathroom?'

'No, you did a good job,' Galindez said. 'Listen, I'm in a bit of trouble. That's why I need this favour.'

'Can't you tell me what's going on? Maybe I can help...'

'No. This is something I have to do, Sarge. I can't involve anyone else.'

The sergeant went to a locker and brought out something bulky, wrapped in a towel. She placed the bundle on the table. 'You're sure you want this?' Galindez's look told her she did. The sergeant lifted the corners of the towel, uncovering a dark object nestling dull and oily on the white cotton. 'Glock Nineteen. Fifteen-round magazine. The gun's clean. No serial number. Will that do you?'

Galindez lifted the pistol, feeling its weight. 'It's great, *gracias.*'

The sergeant looked at her. 'Be careful, Ana María. Whoever these people are, they're not amateurs and, from what you told me on the phone, everywhere you've gone, they already knew in advance. There's only two of you and they knew. See what I'm saying?'

'I do.' Galindez tucked the pistol into her waistband, covering it with her shirt. '*Gracias*, Mendez. I owe you one.'

'You know how it is, Ana María,' Mendez said. 'We look after own.'

Outside, there was a band of light on the horizon. Tali leaned against Galindez in the cab, dozing fitfully. Galindez wanted to tell her that if things hit the fan, she could handle it. But maybe it wouldn't come to that, she thought. Maybe.

The cab stopped outside Tali's building. She'd slept all the way. Galindez had spent the journey fretting about what Mendez said. Tali opened the door to her apartment and flicked the light on. The room was still scattered with some of the equipment Mendez left after searching the place for bugs.

'I'm wrecked,' Tali said, 'do you want a drink or shall we go to bed?'

Galindez found it difficult to speak, knowing that once she'd said what she was about to, she couldn't take it back. 'Sit down, Tali.' Her voice had an edge to it.

Tali sat on the edge of the sofa. '*Pasa algo?*'

'*Sí*. I'm worried. Everywhere we've been since starting this investigation, someone – whoever someone is; Sancho, the *Centinelas* or whatever – always seems to know where we'll be.'

'Is that surprising? We know they've been following us.'

'But they didn't need to follow us, *they knew*. So how did they know?'

Sudden understanding flashed in Tali's eyes. '*Qué coño dices?* You think it's me? *Puta madre*, Ana, you think I've betrayed you to them?'

'It wouldn't be difficult. You wouldn't even have had to talk to them. You could carry a tracking device – they're tiny.'

Tali stood up angrily, 'Do you want to search me? Go ahead.'

'I don't need to.' Galindez went over to the boxes Mendez had left and opened one, taking out a small scanner. 'This will pick up a tracker six metres away.'

Tali's face was a mixture of hurt and anger. 'Do it then. All I've ever wanted was to help you on this project.' Her fists clenched.

'I can't carry on if I suspect you,' Galindez said. 'God knows I don't want to, yet there's only you it could be.'

Galindez felt her hand tremble slightly as the small scanner came to life. The machine twittered softly and a red light started to flash as she pointed the scanner at Tali.

'Well?' Tali snapped.

'It's detected a bug. But the noise should increase when I point it at you.'

'There's nothing to detect.' Tali frowned. 'Or maybe you want to cut me open to see if I swallowed it? Would that satisfy you?'

'I'm sorry.' Galindez turned the scanner away from her. 'I didn't want to believe it. Jesus, Tali, I'm being paranoid and stupid. I'm sorry. But look, the machine is definitely picking something up.' She turned the scanner in her hands, trying to see if there was another control to adjust. The machine gave a high-pitched screech and a yellow light alternated with the red. 'That's odd.' She frowned.

'Ana,' Tali said, 'it went off when it was pointing at you. Aim it at me again.'

Galindez turned the scanner towards Tali. The noise diminished and the yellow light went out. Galindez pointed the machine back to herself. The screeching and flashing began again.

'Oh my God. It's me. *Mierda*, can you forgive me?'

'It's understandable,' Tali said sadly. 'When you can't trust anyone, everyone's a suspect.' She took the scanner from Galindez. 'Come on, let's find it. What do I do?'

'Just press that button and point the machine at me. No, wait. We need to find exactly where it is. It's got to be hidden in my clothes. You'll have to scan them individually.'

Galindez undressed, taking off an item of clothing and passing it for Tali to run the scanner over it. Each time, the machine didn't respond. The noise and lights only increased when the scanner was aimed at Galindez.

Galindez paused, shivering slightly. She unfastened her bra. 'Here, maybe it's hidden in the wiring.'

Once more, nothing happened. The noise diminished, then screeched once more when Tali turned the scanner back toward Galindez. 'Christ, Ana, where the hell is it?'

'This is crazy.' Galindez stepped out of her pants. Tali took them from her. There was no reaction from the scanner.

'Try my watch – that's all that's left.' Nothing happened.

'No other jewellery?' Tali asked. 'No, I can see you haven't.'

'Only these studs in my ears.' Galindez took one out and handed it to her. The machine stayed silent. Galindez removed the other stud. The machine suddenly erupted as Tali passed the scanner over the stud, squawking and flashing in robotic excitement.

She turned off the scanner. 'That's it. Remind me, where did you get those?'

It was hard for Galindez to think, naked and miserably guilty at having suspected Tali. And then she remembered. The break-up gift. 'They were a present from Luisa.'

'*Joder*, that's right. So she's involved with the *Centinelas*?'

'I'd never have thought it,' Galindez said. 'She's always got her head buried in her theoretical work. But she's determined to prove the innocence of a lot of people who were involved in atrocities. Maybe that's it, she's trying to whitewash the Franco years for the *Centinelas.*'

'And her rivalry with you would give her extra motivation,' Tali said. 'You've been intruding on her favourite subject: *Comandante* Guzmán.'

'*Absolutamente.* So she's been trying to track me. *Dios mio,* that gives me the creeps. She could have followed me all over Madrid. She's been huddled over a computer map, knowing if I was at work or the archives or...'

'Or even at my place.' Tali nodded. 'Are you going to have it out with her?'

'Eventually. But I can play games too: she can only track this bugged stud, not me. So, if the stud ends up in a bus or under the seat of a taxi, it might take a while before she realises what's happened.'

'I like it, Ana. Hey, you realise she'll know you're here tonight?'

'I guess so. Probably wondering what we're up to.'

'In that case, it would be a shame to disappoint her. And besides,' Tali pulled Galindez towards her, 'you've got some making up to do to me, Dr Galindez – after those wild accusations.'

'Well, *Tia* Carmen always said never go to bed on an argument.'

'She was right – and we don't have to worry about being spied on now.'

Outside, the light of the pale dawn dappled the street, spilling over the dirty car parked across from the entrance to Tali's building. The driver checked his watch and lit another cigarette. He turned the volume control on the car radio, hearing a swirl of white noise and then above it, the sounds of movement and of voices in muffled intimacy.

The man opened the glove compartment and slid out an iPad. The screen blinked into life on his touch as he operated the software to activate the camera in Tali's apartment. The small screen filled with a grey, clear picture, produced by the combination of light-enhancing technology and Chinese military-grade microcomponents used in the hidden camera. Almost undetectable and incredibly small, the camera had lain dormant while Mendez and her team searched the apartment and removed the equipment they found planted there. The equipment they were intended to find. He watched the two women with little interest. It was nothing he hadn't seen them do before. If it had been down to him, he wouldn't have bothered with such extensive surveillance. But it wasn't down to him, so he did what he was told. In his rear-view mirror he saw another vehicle draw up behind him and flash its lights. He ran a hand over his face, feeling the stubble and the sharp edges of his piercings. He started the engine and drove off, leaving the other car to slide into position to continue the surveillance.

CHAPTER TWENTY

MADRID 1953, BAR DOMINICANA, CALLE DE TOLEDO

Guzmán hurled himself to the ground as the machine gun opened up. Bullets exploded around him and he heard their impact on glass, metal and flesh. Shouts and screams competed with shrieking ricochets. Under the truck, Guzmán crawled towards the cab, while overhead the vehicle shuddered as it was riddled by the heavy-calibre machine-gun fire. A pause in the firing – maybe a jam in the belt or perhaps they were reloading. Directly above him, the truck's engine noisily leaked steam in a dozen places, oil and fuel lazily slopping onto the icy ground. Guzmán pulled himself out from under the front. Now the vehicle was between him and the machine gun. Crouching, he looked up into the cab and saw the driver, slumped over the steering wheel, the windscreen a spiderweb of bullet holes spattered with his blood.

A rifle shot exploded from across the street. Guzmán turned and saw the body of a civil guard in a doorway, enveloped in his cape, a colleague standing over him firing repeatedly at the machine gunner. Then the machine gun erupted again and the man disappeared as a storm of bullets hurled him through the glass door of the shop. A rattle of rifle shots. Those *guardia* who had not been cut down by the burst were now returning fire, an act which brought yet another sweep of the big gun, its hail of bullets shattering windows and tearing through anything and anyone in their way.

Guzmán crouched low. A blast of gunfire tore through the vehicle, showering him with shards of glass and metal. He took a look down the side of the truck. The pavement was littered with

414

dead *guardia civiles*. Scattered equipment and tricorne hats were strewn crazily in the snow. The window of the Bar Dominicana was destroyed and Guzmán caught a glimpse of the whores fleeing to the back of the room. Something moved amongst the corpses heaped around the café's doorway. Peralta. Guzmán was surprised. He thought the *teniente* had been killed outright. Peralta was lying behind two corpses, pistol clutched in both hands, firing careful shots at the machine gun. His aim was woeful and Guzmán knew that once the machine gunner saw Peralta's muzzle flash he would turn his attention to him.

Crawling would have only made Guzmán an easy target so he ran, firing as he went. He jumped over the first corpse and fired into the rear of the truck ahead, seeing the man with the machine gun belt topple backwards into the truck.

'Fire at the gun.' Guzmán's voice echoed loud in the darkness. He saw Goldtooth struggling to free a jammed cartridge from the machine gun. The remaining *guardia* across the street commenced a rapid fire on the truck, the bullets exploding windows and lights, screaming off metal into the night. Guzmán stood, firing fast and steady at Goldtooth. Bullets whined around him but Goldtooth stayed on his feet, still trying to free the jam. Suddenly and noisily, the truck changed gear and lurched forward. Guzmán ran after it, trying to get a glimpse of someone to aim at. The truck accelerated and Guzmán fired his last shot straight at the running board. With a screech of tyres, the vehicle rounded the corner at the end of the street and was gone.

Guzmán turned back to the piles of bodies behind him. Peralta was on his feet, reloading his revolver with a ponderous attention that infuriated Guzmán.

'*Teniente*, call the *comisaría* for medical help and reinforcements. *Rapido.*'

He began examining the fallen *guardia* for signs of life. It was messy work but he had done it many times before. By the time he had finished there were thirteen dead and three badly wounded. Only four were left on their feet.

415

Guzmán found the sarge lying with his head against a kerb stone. A dead *guardia civil* lay across the sarge's legs. They must have been cut down as they tried to make for the relative safety of a shop doorway.

'Ambulances are on their way.' It was Peralta. The *teniente* knelt beside Guzmán and helped roll the dead *guardia* off the sarge.

'Poor sod,' Guzmán said, 'he'll be missed.' He paused. 'Though I don't know who by.'

'I don't think he's dead, sir,' Peralta said, feeling a pulse in the sarge's neck. The sarge groaned and his eyes rolled open.

'You lucky bastard,' Guzmán said.

'Like a black cat, me.' The sarge struggled to sit up. 'What hit me?'

Guzmán checked him cursorily. 'It ought to have been about twenty fifty-calibre bullets, *Sargento*, judging from the bloke who fell on you. He took your share.'

'Glad to hear it.' The sarge put a hand to his head gingerly and brought it away covered in blood. 'But I cracked my bloody head open.'

'No damage done, then,' Guzmán said, losing interest. He turned to Peralta. 'Come on, we can get a quick drink if there's anything left of that bar.'

MADRID 1953, COMISARÍA, CALLE DE ROBLES

'Immediately, yes.' Carrero Blanco's voice was curt. 'Get over here to the office of the *capitán-general* as soon as you can. General Valverde has offered me the use of his office. I'll expect you within the hour.'

Guzmán hung up the phone. He was unshaven and bleary eyed.

'Upstairs?' Peralta asked.

'The top.' Guzmán slurped his coffee. 'An immediate meeting. I'll get a shave and you can drive me. Then take the car and go home for a few hours.'

'I'd rather do something useful,' Peralta said. Guzmán frowned. 'Although, I could do with a bit of sleep, sir,' Peralta added quickly.

'You'll need it.'

The wind moaned through the streets in spiteful gusts. No more snow had fallen, but it was bitterly cold, the winter turning the city to a faded charcoal sketch.

Peralta negotiated the busy streets carefully while Guzmán sprawled in the back seat.

'Just don't worry,' Guzmán said again, annoyed at having to repeat himself in the face of Peralta's continuous fretting. 'You shot all three in self-defence. That isn't too much to remember, is it? The sarge and I will say the same thing – although it's unlikely anyone will ask after what happened to the *guardia civiles* last night.'

'What do you think the newspapers will say, *jefe*?'

'They'll say you drove into that tramcar and killed us both. Look out, *coño*.'

Peralta swerved out to overtake the tram, narrowly avoiding going straight into it.

'Four years of war, twelve of years of hunting Reds and the only thing that's ever scared me is your driving,' Guzmán snapped.

'Sorry, *jefe*.'

'Will you tell your wife about the shooting?' Guzmán asked.

Peralta nodded. 'We tell each other everything.'

'I hope not. Who was it said a man who talks to his wife talks to the world?'

'Some cynic by the sound of it,' Peralta said, vainly trying to lighten Guzmán's mood.

'Might have been Cervantes,' Guzmán reflected. 'Christ, it could even have been the sarge. Never mind. Just be careful what you say to her.'

Peralta stopped the car at the side of the road opposite the *capitanía general*. Rising behind them he could see trees and beyond them the ruined silhouette of the Montaña barracks.

'Here we are, sir. Sure you don't want me to wait?'

417

'I'm positive.' Guzmán opened the car door and climbed out into the thin sharp air. *Especially since I don't know if I'll be coming back.* 'Be back at the *comisaría* around seven.' He slammed the door. Across the street he saw two armed guards at the gate, saw the way one moved away from the other, spreading the target should Guzmán suddenly try anything. Further inside the main gate was a truck filled with troops. *Franco didn't get to be leader by making mistakes or underestimating the enemy. And nor will I. At least when I find out where the enemy is. If I get the chance.*

MADRID 1953, CUARTEL DEL CAPITÁN-GENERAL

The car drove away, leaving a trail of thick fumes in the thin cold air. Guzmán crossed the road to the sentry post. The soldier nearest to him stood to attention. The other waited, watching Guzmán closely.

'Good morning, *señor, papeles por favor.*'

The usual routine. The checking of the documents. Guzmán's identity papers, his special permit signed by Franco himself. He always enjoyed the impact that made. The man nodded and put down the phone in the sentry box.

'You're to proceed to the main entrance, *Comandante* Guzmán.'

Guzmán turned and crunched across the gravel towards the arched doorway. They hadn't wanted his pistol. If they had, it would have meant they no longer trusted him.

More guards at the front door. Within the elegant entrance hall beyond, a number of men in plain clothes. A young man with slicked-down hair and a painfully tight collar – again a careful perusal of Guzmán's papers.

'Are you carrying a weapon, *Comandante*?'

'Of course.'

'I must ask for it, *señor*. For the duration of your visit.'

Guzmán felt incipient rage glowing. Maybe this was where they dispensed with his services. Maybe dispensed with him. He unholstered the big Browning and handed it over. The young man weighed the heavy pistol in cupped hands.

'It will be here when you return, *Comandante.*'

'It'd better be,' Guzmán said, looking the young man in the eye until he flinched.

He followed another flunkey across the opulent carpet to a polished wooden door. The man knocked, a gentle tap that incensed Guzmán with its timidity and deference. The door opened and two large men in plain clothes came forward. One was as tall and as broad as Guzmán. His head was shaved. He stepped towards Guzmán.

'What?' Guzmán said.

'I must be sure you are unarmed, *Comandante.*'

Guzmán checked his impulse to fell the man. Shave-Head halted, sensing annoyance.

'With your permission, *Comandante?* We have a heightened level of security. With the events of last night, you understand.'

Guzmán nodded and the man patted him down professionally. Had Guzmán been armed, the man would have found the weapon. Shave-Head stepped back.

'Guzmán.' It was Carrero Blanco, the chest of his uniform glittering with medals. 'This way.' The admiral retreated into the office. Guzmán stepped forwards with a curt nod to Shave-Head who solemnly returned it. *Professional courtesy. Right now he's thinking he could have taken me if need be. He's wrong.*

The office was dark, solemn wooden panels and funereal bookshelves crowded with dark leather-bound tomes with gilded lettering. The desk caught Guzmán's eye: the papers on it aligned with a precision that made it even easier to despise the man. The admiral took a seat behind his desk and waved languidly at a chair.

'Bloody business last night, *Comandante.*' Carrero's tone was cold. 'Fourteen dead *guardia civiles*, three civilians shot dead by your *teniente*. Did we declare war?'

Guzmán outlined the previous evening's events, stressing the role of the Dominicans.

Carrero Blanco sighed. 'You'll remember the *Caudillo* was hoping there would be no problems before the signing of the trade agreement with the *Yanquis*? I think you probably do because I only fucking told you the other fucking day. And now this.'

'I'm well aware of the *Caudillo*'s orders,' Guzmán said, 'but the Dominicans attacked us, after we raided the Bar Dominicana.'

'That's what I find hard to understand, Guzmán. They attack a senior member of the security services with a heavy machine gun and kill over a dozen of the *benemérita*. Why?'

'I can't see the motive in such aggressive tactics,' Guzmán agreed, 'but it's clear these men are well trained and highly dangerous.'

'It's clear they're dangerous, Guzmán. But who's behind them?'

'I do have some information about one of the members of the trade delegation,' Guzmán said. 'A *Señor* Positano.'

Carrero blanched. 'The head of the delegation, Guzmán? What about him?'

'He has an interesting past, *mi Almirante*. Involving organised crime and murder.'

Carrero shrugged. 'That's a description that would fit most of our government, Guzmán. Including you, come to that. What do we care? He does what he wants in his country and here, in ours, we welcome him as an honoured guest with our hands open, *entiende*?'

'Most of these *Yanquis* have been against us since we won the war. They call us fascists and Nazis,' Guzmán snarled.

Carrero Blanco sighed and ran a hand over his brilliantined hair. 'Guzmán,' his voice was patient, as though talking to a particularly slow schoolboy, 'times are changing. The Nazis are gone. The British and the *Yanquis* and the Russians saw them off. Germany is rubble and America and Russia are the major powers now. The old empires have crumbled or have started to – just look at the British. But for America and Russia it's just beginning. A great game of chess. And their kings and queens will be hydrogen bombs.'

'And why will that concern us, sir?'

'Can't you see the checkmate that will emerge from such a confrontation?' Carrero asked, amused at Guzmán's failure to grasp the situation. 'They've already divided Germany. The rest of the world will follow in taking sides. It will be best if we too take sides. The *Yanquis'* side, naturally.'

'So the Americans will win?'

'No one will win. There won't be a war. Not for a long time anyway. Their weapons are too powerful. No, Guzmán, this will be a long strategic game. And best of all, we have something the Americans can use in their strategy.'

'Which is what, *Almirante*?'

'What they want from us, Guzmán, is somewhere to put their planes and their bombs. Somewhere from where they can attack the Reds.'

'There are other places, sir. Britain, France, even Italy. All nearer to Russia.'

'Spain offers them security, *Comandante*. A people who take orders, who obey the rule of law and who're ruled with an iron fist. A country officially opposed to Communism.'

'Of course.'

Carrero's voice rose as he warmed to his theme. 'It's clear, I hope, Guzmán, that this trade delegation is a forerunner to something much more important. A military agreement with the *Yanquis. Hombre*, imagine it. They get land to build bases on. There's plenty of land in Spain. We get hard currency and we also get military aid. For God's sake, Guzmán, the army is weak. Even the French could beat us if there were a war. With the Americans on our side, no one will think about trying to subvert the true and proper governance of Spain. Naturally, we want them to offer the best price possible. Our negotiators will take a strong stance.'

'Until the *Yanquis* make a good enough offer?'

'Any sort of offer. We aren't going to reject anything.'

'But these Dominicans…' Guzmán grumbled.

'Degenerate criminals.' Carrero's voice was icy. 'Which means you'll need to deal with them. But not until we order it. There's no room here for your personal vendettas. If you do anything before then,' Carrero frowned, 'we shall take severe action against you. Severe action, Guzmán.'

Guzmán glowered. Carrero was talking about death. His death. Franco's Golden Boy, the hero of Badajoz. Expendable.

'And while we're on the subject,' Carrero growled, 'the *Yanquis* say that they're missing a member of their delegation. Strangely enough a Dominican. Is that something you'd know about?'

'Not at all, *mi Almirante*. There were no Dominicans inside that bar last night.'

'Good. But remember what I said. Fuck up and you're out. In more ways than one.'

'I'll do my duty, as always.'

'Another thing, Guzmán.' Carrero stared across the desk. 'General Valverde has a suggestion as to why you're obsessed with these Dominicans. He claims you've taken money from them. That had better not be true, Guzmán.'

Guzmán didn't sweat easily. He was sweating now. 'That's preposterous. The *almirante* knows very well Valverde holds a grudge against me, mainly because I keep him under observation. On the *Caudillo's* orders.'

'I know.' Carrero said. 'But if it were true about the money, Guzmán...' He left the threat unsaid, waving a hand to signal an end to their meeting.

Guzmán retraced his steps from the office, walking across the deep carpet to collect his pistol. Guzmán replaced the gun in its holster and looked across the plush hallway. The big shave-head in the black suit was standing to one side, hands clasped in front of him, an undertaker waiting for the hearse. He saw Guzmán looking at him, and inclined his head slightly, staring at him as he walked to the door and then out to Calle Bailén. Guzmán walked down the steps, past the guards and crossed the road, still feeling the man's eyes on him. He dodged a passing tram and reached the far pavement before he turned to look back. The big man was standing at the gates. *Show the rabbit to the dog*, Guzmán thought, turning and walking towards the Plaza de España, *and the dog remembers him for ever.*

An icy wind troubled the wizened leaves of the trees as Guzmán entered the deserted plaza. He looked at his watch before slowly making his way back to the main road. He strolled past the shrubs and bushes lining Calle Asturias, towards the General Fanjul Gardens. By then it was clear he was being followed and the gardens offered good opportunities for cover and escape if needed.

MADRID 1953, JARDINES DE GENERAL FANJUL

The wind came from the mountains, raw and sharp. Guzmán stopped, took out his cigarettes and lit one, casually looking back along the tree-lined road. The man was about forty or fifty metres away. Dark hat and coat, like almost every other man in Madrid. Except that he was following Guzmán. The man gave the appearance of not being aware of Guzmán, suddenly turning down one of the narrow gravelled pathways and moving out of sight. Guzmán walked from the gardens, across the road and climbed the steps leading to Calle Cardoso. He climbed quickly, pausing at the top to catch his breath and then turned as if going to the Carmelite convent. The man following him would have to hurry in order not to lose him, and, as Guzmán knew well, when people hurry, they get careless.

The pistol left his holster smoothly, satisfying and solid in his hand. He cocked the hammer. Heard footsteps on the stone steps, climbing quickly. The man was so intent on reaching the top of the steps he looked up only as he climbed the final flight, and when he did, Guzmán towered above him, the Browning aimed at his chest.

'*Hijo de puta.*' Guzmán stared down at the man below standing frozen, his eyes fixed on the muzzle of the pistol. '*Señor* Lopez,' Guzmán said, keeping the pistol aimed at the private detective, 'I do believe you're following me.'

Teodoro Lopez nodded slowly, fear making his limbs unreliable, his movements stiff and uncoordinated. That was good, Guzmán thought. It was hard to fake that sort of fear. However, being shit-scared didn't mean knicker-sniffer Lopez was harmless.

He waved the man up the steps, lowering his pistol but keeping it pointed at the man's belly. At this distance, a round or two would destroy most of Lopez's intestines, blowing them and probably a section of his spine down the stone stairway. Lopez reached the top of the steps and Guzmán pressed the pistol against him, frisking him with his left hand.

'This is becoming a habit,' Guzmán said angrily.

'I can explain, *Comandante*.' Lopez was breathing heavily.

'You'd better.' Guzmán slipped his right hand into his coat pocket and aimed the pistol at the shivering private detective through the thick material of his overcoat. 'If you try to run, I'll shoot you. *Entiende*?'

The man nodded. '*Si*, I understand, *Comandante*, perfectly.'

'We'll take a little walk,' Guzmán said, genially. 'I want to ask you a few questions.'

'I'll be very cooperative,' Lopez said, stumbling alongside Guzmán as they began to walk slowly along Calle de Irun. The streets were still hazy with mist. On their right, a grassy bank led up to the stark ruins of the Montaña barracks.

'You followed me to the *capitanía general*,' Guzmán said.

'Not followed, *Comandante*, no,' Lopez stammered.

'Don't fuck about,' Guzmán hissed, giving Lopez a shove in the side with the pistol. 'How did you know I'd be there?'

Lopez swallowed. 'I received a telephone call.'

'From who?'

'My employer. My real employer, I should say.'

'I could lose my patience here, Lopez. You told me before you were employed by my cousin Juan. Who is this real employer?'

'It is very hard to say, *Comandante*. Every transaction has been by telephone.'

They came to a wooden bench and Guzmán ordered Lopez to

sit. The frosty grass slope rose behind them, punctuated with frozen shrubs and wizened trees. They sat, breath steaming in the bitter cold.

'Initially, I received a call,' Lopez said, 'asking me to undertake a commission requiring the utmost delicacy. A large fee was mentioned. So large I overlooked my usual ethical principles.'

'*Mierda*. You're a private detective. You don't have principles. We don't call you lot knicker-sniffers for nothing,' Guzmán snapped. 'You *huelebraguetas*, you spy on unhappy people, husbands screwing around, bored wives with too much time to themselves during the day. Am I wrong, *Señor* Lopez?'

Lopez mopped his brow with a large handkerchief. 'What you say is broadly correct, *Comandante*. And often one goes without a case at all for a considerable period of time.'

'Financial problems?'

Lopez nodded. '*Exactamente*. When this case came along, it was impossible to refuse. The money, you see. A man has to live.'

'Right now, *Señor* Lopez, whether you stay alive is not at all certain,' Guzmán said. 'But don't let me stop you. *Siga, por favor*.'

'I received a phone call asking me to undertake this work,' Lopez continued. 'It was impressed on me this was a matter of delicacy, involving a party who was extremely prominent in the maintenance of public security.'

'Me?'

'So it transpired, *Comandante*.'

'Then it wasn't my family who first contacted you – as you told me the other day?'

'No. I'm afraid that wasn't entirely correct, *Comandante*. The party I spoke to said you were to be approached at a distance and that I should use an intermediary. They gave me a name and address and instructed me to give a letter to this party to convey it to you. Following this telephone call, I was sent a sum of money.'

'How was the payment made?'

'In cash. A package, delivered to my office the same day. I was given addresses. The address of a *Señora* Alicia Martinez, and that of a hotel where I had had the pleasure of meeting your mother and your cousin Juan.'

'And what did they tell you?'

'The same as the voice on the phone. That they had recently become aware you were alive, having been presumed dead for so long. That they wanted to see you again.'

'A heart-warming story.'

'Except that *Señora* Guzmán seems to have vanished. She left her hotel and didn't return. Cousin Juan is beside himself.'

'I'll bet,' Guzmán said. 'And where is Cousin Juan?'

'At his hotel. The Barcelona. It's on Calle—'

'I know where it is,' Guzmán interrupted. 'And *Mamá* at the Alameda. Why separate hotels?'

Lopez shrugged. 'It seemed odd. But I was being paid.'

'So you suspected something strange about this?'

'I needed the money, *Comandante*. So I took the job anyway. There's no other work I can do. I used to work in an office before the war. I couldn't get a job now.'

'You were on the other side?'

Lopez nodded. 'I'm not wanted for anything. I was a prisoner for a few months and released after the necessary enquiries.'

Guzmán stood up. The street was quiet, a few cars passed them. Across the road, a mother with a pram, walking slowly, cooing to her baby, her outline soft in the wintry haze.

'There's nothing you can tell me about the voice?'

'No, a man's voice. Authoritative. Sharp.'

'That describes more than half the men in Spain, *Señor* Lopez. Including me.'

Guzmán turned and looked up the shrubbed hillside, its trees and shrubs melted by mist.

'Come on. I want to know more about this.' He jerked his head at the grassy knoll behind them.

'Up there?' Lopez asked, uncertainly.

'Yes, we'll go up to the ruins of the old barracks. We won't be overheard there. There are things you should know.'

'If you feel it's really necessary.'

'Of course I'll make it worth your while.' Guzmán reached into his jacket and produced a wad of dollar bills. 'You understand you're working for me from now on?'

'Of course, *Comandante*.' The relief was evident. 'Anything I can do to assist you. I assure you I meant no harm by any of this.'

'Yes,' Guzmán said, 'I believe you.'

They walked up the rough hillside, their feet crunching on the frozen ground. Lopez had trouble keeping up. The trees and bushes grew taller while the road below became hazy and imprecise, lost in folds of mist.

'Please, I'm out of breath.' Lopez mopped his broad forehead with his handkerchief.

'We'll stop here,' Guzmán said. He waited patiently for Lopez to get his breath back.

'You know, in my line of work, we make use of several strategies,' Guzmán started, almost pleasantly. 'One of which is never to leave a trail leading back to you. You use people as intermediaries. People who do things without knowing why they are doing it – that way they can't betray the person who employed them. People like you and *Señora* Martinez.'

'I see,' Lopez panted.

'You asked *Señora* Martinez to deliver that letter to me,' Guzmán continued.

Lopez nodded. 'I did.'

'She didn't know what was in it, did she?'

'Not unless she opened the envelope.'

'I'll take that as no. Did you tell her anything else?'

'Absolutely not. Besides, there was little I could tell her.'

'And you paid her?'

'Five hundred pesetas. She didn't want to take it. But I was instructed that she should be given the money.'

'*Señora* Martinez is a truthful woman,' Guzmán said. 'She told us about the money after an hour or two in one of our cells.'

'I never asked her to do anything illegal.'

427

'But we have no way of finding who paid you the money because you never met them.'

'That's true. I did say as much, *Comandante.*' Lopez was sweating. 'I—'

'Not true. You lied to me before. You said Juan had commissioned you,' Guzmán said.

Lopez began to bluster. He was sweating heavily. Guzmán held up his hand. Lopez stopped talking.

'You spoke with my mother and Juan. What did they say about our village?'

'They talked about when you were young, your love of music and books, the certificates you gained in first aid before the war came and you enlisted.'

'Did they talk about our house?'

'They did. The big house with the barn. Your brothers and sisters, and Uncle Pepe and Aunt Julia living in the attic.'

'In the attic. Of course.'

'Until the day the soldiers came. Juan and your mother went to market that day. Such an isolated village, it seemed a worthless target. When your mother and Juan returned, they found the house burned down, many of the villagers dead, your aunt, uncle, your brothers and sisters, all slaughtered. Your family almost wiped out. As if marked out for destruction.'

Guzmán lit a cigarette. 'And *Mamá* and Juan stayed on in the village?'

'They eventually rebuilt the house. Hoping you'd return. Later, when you didn't come back, they thought maybe you'd gone abroad or been killed.'

'The war changed me.' Guzmán threw down his cigarette. He had decided to kill Lopez when they were sitting on the bench. Lopez had been used. He knew nothing of value. Even so, he knew too much about Guzmán's business. Guzmán took his hands from his pockets. It took a moment for Lopez to see the wire held taut in his gloved hands. Guzmán recognised the look on the man's face, the sudden awareness of his impending death. But by then it was far too late to do anything because Guzmán was on him, bringing the unwelcome revelation that while killing was easy, dying was much, much harder.

MADRID 1953, CALLE DE SAN NICOLÁS

Peralta lay in a deep, timeless sleep and, for a while, the world ceased to exist. Guzmán, the ravaged *sargento*, the constant biting cold as he tramped the streets, all floated away. Even the pain in his belly subsided. And then, the sharp ring of the telephone jolted him into unwelcome consciousness. He sat up. There was still daylight outside, edging into the darkened room through closed shutters. Looking at the clock, he saw he had been asleep only a few hours.

'Paquito, are you awake?' His wife was at the door, looking at him with what seemed to Peralta to be undue concern. He didn't know she'd heard him screaming in his sleep again.

'What is it?' He swung his legs out from under the sheets. The room was icy.

'Telephone. From a call box. *Comandante* Guzmán.'

Peralta grabbed the phone, wincing at the sudden pain deep in his belly. '*Jefe, qué pasa?*'

'A job's come up.' Guzmán's voice was low. Peralta heard the sounds of a bar. 'I need you to do it, *Teniente*.'

For a moment, Peralta thought he was being asked to kill someone. His heart sank, knowing he could not refuse.

'I want you to make an arrest. It's a relative, my cousin Juan. I'll tell you why later, but get over there and pick him up now. Take him to the *comisaría*, put him in a cell and don't let him talk to anyone – even you. Understand?'

'Not entirely,' Peralta said.

'*Joder.* You don't need to. His name is Juan Balaguer and he's at the Hotel Barcelona. You know it? It's just off Preciados, opposite the Comedy Theatre.'

'I know it,' Peralta said.

'Arrest him.'

'What charge?'

Silence.

'I'll think of one,' Peralta said quickly.

'Complete isolation,' Guzmán said. 'That understood? Not you, no *guardia*, no one within thirty metres of him – not even the sarge.'

'I've got it,' Peralta said. 'Will I need any assistance?'

'No. The man isn't violent. Get the cuffs on him and take him straight into custody. I'll see you there later.' The telephone went dead.

'I've got to go out, *mi amor*,' Peralta called, and then once more a sudden white-hot spasm of pain doubled him up.

MADRID 1953, CALLE PRECIADOS

Peralta parked the car outside the Hotel Barcelona. The commissionaire stepped forward to assist but Peralta waved his identity card and brushed the old man aside. The commissionaire shrugged. The police were bad news, and if they had no interest in him, he was happy to mind his own business.

The clerk at reception looked up and Peralta produced his card once more. Whatever the man had done in a former life, Peralta thought, he had a guilty conscience, suddenly becoming nervous and clumsy, his forehead studded with beads of sweat.

'*Señor* Juan Balaguer? *Si, señor*. Would the officer like to see the register?' The clerk pointed with a shaking finger to a signature on the thick vellum page.

'Did you fill in all the necessary paperwork to submit to the police?' Peralta asked.

The man seemed to be losing control of his limbs. Papers flew onto the floor, pens rolled across the counter. If ever a man was rattled by the appearance of a policeman, it was this one. But today was his lucky day, assuming he complied with Peralta's orders.

'We have it all here, *señor*. They're submitted on a weekly basis, the officer will understand.'

'I understand this,' Peralta said, in a pale imitation of Guzmán's brusque approach. 'If this man has registered in your hotel and you have not filled in the necessary forms, you may be joining him in prison.'

The threat made the receptionist even more nervous. After a long couple of minutes, the man finally found the bundle of forms. Peralta took it from him.

'I'll need the page from the register well.' Peralta took hold of the big ledger, ripping the page from its binding. 'Room number?'

'Forty-three, *señor*. Second floor. The lift is over there by the stairs.'

'Do you have a key?'

'Of course. Here it is.'

'Come with me,' Peralta said. He had a feeling the receptionist might not be above calling this Cousin Juan and tipping him off. Probably before doing a runner himself.

The lift was slow and noisy. The receptionist looked at his shoes for most of the tortuous journey upwards. Peralta had never been in this hotel before. It was clean and well lit, a little upmarket for *Comandante* Guzmán's country cousin, he thought.

Peralta pushed the receptionist ahead of him once the man had opened the lift doors. They walked down the silent hallway in single file. The corridor was clean with only a slight air of dust and used sheets and just a faint undertone of shit as they passed the communal bathroom.

Peralta thought about making the arrest and the possible outcomes – many of them pessimistic. Cousin Juan might open the door with a gun. If there really was a Cousin Juan. Extemporising further, Peralta saw a room filled with the remaining Dominicans, armed to the teeth, high on drugs and aching to get the man who killed their comrade. And here he was, unassisted, strolling into their midst. Peralta drew his pistol, noticing the effect it had on the clerk: sweat dribbled down his sallow cheeks.

Peralta leaned close. 'What did you do? You know what I'm talking about.'

'I was a prisoner of war until two years ago, *señor*. I ran away from a work detail and came back to my wife. All I want is my job and my family, *nada más*, I want nothing to do with politics. I'll give you money. Every payday, just don't send me back.'

Peralta took the key from him. 'I don't want money. Go back to work. And make sure your paperwork is always up to date, *entiendes*? And, *hombre*, keep your head down when I come through reception.'

The man nodded and turned on his heel, walking away as quickly as he could without breaking into a run.

Peralta knocked on the door, pistol ready. He was sweating.

'*Quien es?*'

'It's the manager. Open up, please. We need to check the room.'

The door opened and Peralta pushed his pistol into the man's face. He had heard Guzmán and the sarge talking about this approach. It was a way of focusing the suspect's attention. It worked. '*Señor* Balaguer?'

'*Sí señor*, Juan Balaguer, *para servirle. Pasa algo?*'

The man stepped backwards into the room. Peralta brought up his identity card and held it alongside his pistol.

'*Policía*? Is this about my mother?'

'No. You're under arrest. Get your jacket.'

Peralta continued to aim the gun at the man as he retrieved his jacket from a chair.

'I demand to know what this is about.'

'All you need to know is that you are under arrest.'

'But this is outrageous. I demand to speak to your superior officer. I demand you give me his name. I'll explain to him.'

'*Señor* Balaguer, we don't give out our names and you can explain yourself at the *comisaría, entiende?*'

The look on Cousin Juan's face showed he understood very well.

'Does this concern the war?'

'What do you think?'

'I thought it was about my mother. She's gone missing. We're here to see a relative, a *Comandante* Guzmán. My mother went to meet him two days ago, we haven't seen her since. Please, let me explain. Maybe you can help me.'

Peralta motioned for the man to sit on the bed. 'Go on.' He pulled up a chair a metre from Cousin Juan and sat down. 'I'm listening. But make it quick.'

MADRID 1953, HOTEL WELLINGTON, CALLE DE VELAZQUEZ

The tram stopped, spilling a clutch of passengers into the brittle cold. Guzmán pushed his way out of the crowded tramcar, carefully checking for any sign of being followed. Across the street was the Wellington Hotel. Baths and telephones in every room. A hotel for the rich and the powerful – which was why *Señor* Positano and his delegation were staying there.

The opulence of the reception area was impressive: the carpet of the *capitanía general* was far inferior to the one Guzmán walked on as he made for the sleek polished reception desk with its glinting brass rails. The receptionist also clearly thought himself of a higher calibre than normal, given the way he looked at Guzmán as if he had just crawled out from under someone's shoe.

'May I help you?' The man's voice implied this wasn't likely.

'You have a *Señor* Positano staying here,' Guzmán said. 'Is he in?'

The man peered down his nose disdainfully. 'The north American gentleman? What do you want to see him about? *Señor* Positano is a very busy man.'

Guzmán nodded, resigning himself to the fact that there were so many people in the world who couldn't see trouble when it was right in front of them. Still, it was best not make a scene. Usually. He seized the receptionist by the knot of his tie and in one powerful

433

motion dragged the man across the counter, depositing him on the thick pile carpet at his feet.

'Is he in or not?' he growled, looming over the sprawling receptionist. 'Yes or no. Otherwise, I'll take you back with me to the *comisaría* and let some of my boys play football with your head if you prefer.'

The man looked at the identity card with the logo of the General Directorate of Security and realised his mistake.

'The gentleman should have said,' he panted, trying to get to his feet. '*Señor* Positano is in his suite. Please, *momentito*.'

Guzmán stepped back to allow the trembling receptionist to get up. A couple of guests across the lobby watched from a leather Chesterfield with sensible indifference. The receptionist hurried behind his desk, keeping a wary eye on Guzmán.

'Shall I call *Señor* Positano?' he asked, as if Guzmán had just walked in.

'By all means,' Guzmán said, sliding his identity card across the desk as the man dialled the number. There was a brief conversation as the receptionist announced the visitor from the *Brigada Especial*.

'*Señor* Positano will be pleased to see you, *Comandante*. Room eighty-seven.' The man handed Guzmán's ID back with a shaking hand.

'Let's hope so,' Guzmán said, walking over to the lift. The doors opened and an elderly dwarf dressed like an organ grinder's monkey beckoned him in.

'*Muy Buenas, señor*,' the man lisped through his remaining teeth. When Guzmán looked more closely, he saw there was no plural: one tooth remained, a stained solitary tombstone in the centre of the man's upper gums.

The lift whirred upwards, almost silent compared to the hotels Guzmán was more accustomed to visiting.

'The gentleman is visiting the *norteamericano*?'

'The gentleman is minding his own business.'

'They tip well, these *norteamericanos*.'

'I'll bear that in mind.'

'The Dutch. Mean bastards. No tips from them.'

'Of course not. Protestants. What do you expect?'

'Courtesy. Civility. These are things one expects.'

'And money.'

'*Hombre.* That goes without saying.'

'And the Italians?'

'They don't tip. They ask for the address of a whore, then they don't tip.'

'Perhaps the whores are disappointing? Maybe that's why they don't tip.'

'The whores are perfectly adequate. They should tip.'

'What of the English?'

'The English? Who knows? They don't speak our language. They complain a lot.'

'About what?'

'Who knows? They don't speak our language. They shout.'

'But you get by? Even with all these tight-fisted foreigners?'

'I get by. A man must live.'

'I think must is too strong,' Guzmán said, philosophically. 'There's no *must* about it.'

'As the *caballero* says: he knows more than I do about that. I press this button. This is my life. People use the lift to come in and go out. I spend my days and nights in here. I go up. I come down.'

'I understand.' Guzmán nodded. 'And having come down, you go up again.'

The dwarf nodded appreciatively at his understanding.

They reached Positano's floor. Guzmán wasn't sorry; the lift dwarf was beginning to emit bodily odours usually encountered in piles of executed prisoners. He opened the cage door and waved Guzmán out with a flourish, one hand extended hopefully. Guzmán bent and shook the man's hand.

'I wish the *señor* a good day,' the dwarf said, solemnly.

'The *señor* is very grateful,' Guzmán said. The small monkey-suited man peered at him with rheumy eyes as the lift sank downwards and slowly disappeared from view. Guzmán waited until the lift had gone. Nothing so depressing as a dispirited dwarf, he thought. They deserved no tips, the Italians were right about that.

The carpet on this floor was even more luxurious than that in the lobby. The hotel was clearly of a much higher standard than the drab austerity of most of Spanish hotels, but decor was far from Guzmán's mind as he approached the door of room eighty-seven. He had considered on his way over how to approach Positano – not least because of the possibility the Dominicans might be there. The *surviving* Dominicans, at any rate, Guzmán thought with a smile.

He wondered whether Positano might strike first. Probably not. This was a high-profile hotel. A strange place to have a shoot-out with the security services. Perhaps, Guzmán thought, he should just go in with his pistol out and see what happened. End it right here, one way or the other. But that would displease the *Caudillo* and would certainly end his career, assuming he survived.

He knocked on the door. Positano opened it at once.

'*Señor* Positano. *Comandante* Guzmán. *Brigada Especial de Policía.*'

'Ah yes, we have met. Please come in.'

The room was opulent, all dark velvet and polished wood. Positano waved Guzmán to a sofa by a large window, flanked by floor-length curtains. Guzmán crossed the room, braced for an attack.

'Nice room,' he said, sinking into the soft upholstery of the sofa.

'The US taxpayer's paying.' Positano indicated a large drinks' cabinet. 'May I offer you something? No, of course, you're on duty, I apologise.'

'This isn't America, *Señor* Positano,' Guzmán said sternly. 'I'll have a large brandy.'

Positano poured two large glasses of brandy. Guzmán took the proffered glass and inhaled the aroma. Positano sat in a leather armchair, and looked across at him, waiting for him to speak. Guzmán took his time savouring the Napoleon brandy. Perhaps a man who poured such large drinks couldn't be all bad.

'*Señor* Positano, we're very concerned about your Dominican colleagues,' Guzmán began. 'It would be helpful for my department if you could tell us their whereabouts.'

Positano took an elegant sip of his brandy and said nothing. That was good. Now Guzmán could return to disliking him.

'*Comandante*, I know you had some sort of run-in with those boys, and I know they can be a little wild, but let me explain something.'

'Those boys killed over a dozen *guardia* last night,' Guzmán said. 'Explain that.'

Positano smiled reflectively. 'I did hear about that, *Comandante*. And we deeply regret it. If it really was the Dominicans, well, that's a matter for the appropriate authorities, of course. We understand that.'

Guzmán took another mouthful of brandy, not wanting things to turn violent until he'd finished it. 'I understood these people are a part of your trade delegation.'

'A part, yes. But they are Dominican businessmen. The Dominican Republic is a great friend of the United States, *Comandante* Guzmán. They are here to promote various businesses in their own country. But they are a little unconventional, I'll grant you that.'

'So far,' Guzmán said in a patient voice, 'they've purchased properties used for criminal activities, are suspected of decapitating a police informer, selling contaminated illegal drugs resulting in a number of deaths, and murdering fourteen members of the *guardia civil*. That's more than unconventional in any country.'

'The Dominican Republic is a tough place.' Positano shrugged. 'Maybe we were unwise to take them at face value. Still, I'm sure you can cope with them – if it really was them who did these things.'

'You don't seem too concerned,' Guzmán said.

Positano waved a manicured hand. 'These things are beyond my experience.'

'Maybe these days, *señor*. But back in the day you too were, let's say, a little wild. No?'

Positano's suave expression lost its air of hospitality. 'I don't know what you're getting at, *Comandante*.'

'I'd be happy to remind you.'

'I think maybe you should.'

'Well, for starters, *Señor* Positano, I understand in your youth you had a less than romantic notion of St Valentine's Day.'

Positano glared at Guzmán. 'Well, *Comandante* Guzmán, perhaps they were wrong when they said Spanish Intelligence is a contradiction in terms?' He leaned back in his chair and laughed. 'Ancient history, water under the bridge. St Valentine? I'm sure I don't know where you got that from.'

'From your court records, *Señor* Positano.'

Positano smiled. It was a smile Guzmán recognised very well: a slight movement of the facial muscles into a caricature of normality while hiding a rapid calculation of strategies of violence and harm. It was the smile Guzmán saw every day in the mirror.

'I never think rank is an indicator of ability, *Comandante*.' Positano maintained his flat smile. 'For example, there aren't many officers of your rank who attend meetings with the Head of State or his ministers.'

Now it was Guzmán who was forcing a smile. That made him angry. *They were following me. And I never noticed. Worse, I never thought about it.*

'The *Caudillo* talks with anyone he wishes. We're all at his command.'

'Of course, that's the way dictatorship works. Franco whistles and you bark.'

Guzmán shrugged. He wasn't going to be angered by a bit of name calling. As long as it wasn't his name. 'I'm employed by the Head of State and *Generalísimo* Franco is my boss. I believe your bosses talk to their workers too, if they wish?'

Positano laughed. 'It can happen. But the Head of State chatting with a major? Let's cut the crap, *Comandante*. I know a lot about you.'

In which case you may be dead when I leave this room, Guzmán thought. 'Really?'

'Really. We can mobilise more extensive resources than you think.'

'Clearly they're less visible than your Dominicans.'

Positano shrugged. 'We borrowed those guys from the Dominican Republic to gather economic intelligence for this delegation. We thought they'd fit right in, speaking Spanish and all. We were wrong, *Comandante*. When they started getting involved in crime we tried to rein them in, but they've gone rogue. I have no idea where they are.'

'They are criminals, *Señor* Positano, and they'll be dealt with,' Guzmán growled.

'Understood,' Positano said pleasantly. 'All I want is for the trade talks to go ahead.'

'You must be desperate to have such a pressing need to trade with us.'

Positano's smile vanished. He leaned forward.

'Don't fuck about with me, *Comandante*. You know the score. Your shitty country is broke and it was Franco who broke it. How long can you keep control of a starving population with the tinpot economy you've got? Instead of development, you guys have put all your efforts into killing one another for the last sixteen years. Your agriculture's a hundred years out of date, the Church interferes in government policy and guys like you keep the war going while ex-generals get rich milking the pieces of the economy Franco gave them to keep them loyal. What you've got, *Comandante*, is a goddamned mess, and unless you get your hands on some hard cash, some of those walking skeletons out there are going to decide it's time for another war – and if there was a war, what do you think you'd fight it with? An army equipped for keeping civilians under control? They wouldn't last a week. We haven't forgotten Franco's flirting with Hitler either, I'll tell you that.'

'Thanks for the economic and military analysis,' Guzmán snarled. He glared at Positano with contempt. 'And thanks for your time, *Señor* Positano. Remember what I said: your Caribbean friends will be dealt with. This isn't Chicago.'

Positano got to his feet. He was tall, maybe a centimetre or two taller than Guzmán. Less bulky, but muscled and fit. Guzmán looked into the man's eyes with malice.

'The *Caudillo* will open the talks officially in a few days' time,' Guzmán said. 'I expect to have the Dominican problem dealt with by then.'

'I think we're done.' Positano turned his back on Guzmán and walked over to the door. *He turned his back on me.* It was the first time someone had insulted Guzmán and he hadn't responded with physical violence. He struggled for control. *If Franco hadn't been so clear about the trade talks going ahead, coño, you'd be dead now.* He walked slowly past Positano. *Try it. Make your move.*

Positano watched him leave. 'Good day, *Comandante*.'

'Until next time, *Señor* Positano.'

Outside the hotel, the wind was getting up, sending flurries of snow spiralling through the sombre light of late afternoon. Across the road a movement caught Guzmán's eye. He stopped and looked beyond the noisy tangle of traffic, seeing the crowds moving along the pavement, hunched against the cold. There was one who didn't move. Standing in the doorway of a tobacconist, framed by the dull brown paint of the woodwork and the colours of the Spanish flag over the door, the big shave-head from the *capitanía* casually acknowledged Guzmán's wave and then disappeared into the throng. *Not today then*, Guzmán thought.

The kid crawled across the gritty soil, pushing his way through sharp, desiccated shrubs. His eyes stung with sweat and he moved slowly and patiently to avoid making any noise. Then, through the sepia husks of the long dry grass, he saw them. The Moorish soldier lay on his back in a pool of blood, arms flung wide. It was as if the man had burst open. The kid had seen plenty of dead bodies and this one looked very dead. He dragged himself nearer, breathing through clenched teeth to keep from panting. He saw him clearly now, the young man they had called Guzmán. Saw Guzmán's first-aid armband, the spilled contents of the rucksack, the rolls of bandages, a canteen of water. Heard Guzmán's voice, rising and falling in a familiar cadence:

'Hail Mary, full of grace, the Lord is with thee, blessed art thou among women and blessed is the fruit of thy womb Jesus, Holy Mary Mother of God, pray for us sinners now and at the hour of death. Amen.'

The kid emerged from the long grass. Guzmán looked up and stared, open-mouthed, fear blooming on his dirt-streaked face. The kid pointed the rifle at him. 'Go ahead and shout. Everyone's dead. Where's the rest of your unit?'

Guzmán swallowed. 'There is no one else,' he said, the words catching in his dry mouth. 'We're the last of the company. The other lads got it earlier today when we advanced on the machine guns.' He looked around him. 'They're all dead.'

The kid clicked off his safety catch nervously. 'Don't move.'

'There's a column coming up from the south. They'll be here by sundown. Cavalry, artillery. Two regiments of legionaries. Surrender now and it might go easier for you.'

441

'Of course,' the kid said. 'I know how easy it goes when your lot come to town.'

'What else can you do?' Guzmán asked. 'Badajoz will have fallen by now. There's nowhere for you to go.'

'I'll go to Portugal,' the kid said. 'There's no war there.'

Guzmán shook his head. 'Portugal's on our side. Any Republicans trying to cross the border will be sent back,' he paused, 'to face justice.'

The kid tried to think of options. 'What about France? Which way is it from here?'

Guzmán looked at the position of the sun and pointed. 'Somewhere over there.'

'More than a couple of days' march?'

'Much more,' Guzmán said. 'Maybe a week. I'm not sure.'

'Where else can I go?' the kid asked, suddenly realising the position he was in.

'There's nowhere you can go,' Guzmán said firmly. 'Surrender. They'll let you see a priest and confess. Whatever happens after, at least you won't lose your immortal soul.'

It wasn't an attractive option. 'Can you help me get to France?'

'No. You're a Bolshevik. One of the Red horde. I learned all about you people when I joined up. You're on the side of the Antichrist.'

'I don't even know what that is,' the kid muttered.

'It doesn't matter. The priests told us. You want to murder nuns.'

The kid tried to think. It was difficult in the murderous heat. He was exhausted, his face was burned from the sun and his lips were cracked. He wanted to sleep. 'If I help you back to your lines, will they spare me?'

Guzmán shook his head. 'No. They say there's no point sparing Reds. They can never change. They'll shoot you. Unless the Moors get you first.'

The thought of the Moors made the kid nervous. He imagined their boots pounding on the dry red soil, marching inexorably towards him. He looked at the equipment strewn around Guzmán's feet. 'Got any water?'

Guzmán shrugged. 'I'm not supposed to give it to you. Deny all comfort to the enemy, those were the orders.'

The kid saw a canteen half hidden by the rucksack. He motioned towards it with his rifle. 'Give me that.'

Guzmán reached for the khaki canteen.

The kid licked his cracked lips. It had been hours since his last drink and his tongue felt like leather. Guzmán picked up the canteen. The kid swallowed, anticipating the cool rush of water in his dry mouth.

Guzmán hurled the canteen at the kid and leaped at him in an effort to grab the barrel of his rifle. The kid staggered back, trying keep his distance, but Guzmán pursued him, still trying to snatch the rifle. The kid stumbled and fell backwards, his finger closing on the trigger, hearing the whiplash crack of a shot. The bullet hit Guzmán in the face, blowing away the top of his head and a thin red mist hung in the scorching air as he fell. The report echoed around the yellowing hills, fading slowly until once more there was only the chirping of crickets in the simmering heat.

The kid lay on the parched soil, clutching the rifle tightly, staring at Guzmán's body sprawled a metre away. He crawled towards it, braced in anticipation of another attack. But Guzmán lay face down in the faded dust, the back of his head covered in a dark gelatinous mass that was already attracting flies. The kid rolled him onto his back and saw the bullet wound in his face. It seemed small and inconsequential. He felt tears prickle his eyes. How would he get to France now? He picked up the canteen and drank, unable to pause for breath until the last of the water was gone. He looked around as if, somewhere on this desiccated plateau strewn with corpses, there might be someone who would help him. Help him get to France.

And this Guzmán would help him after all, he realised. He went back to the body and unbuttoned the heavy khaki shirt and removed it, tossing it to one side. He unlaced Guzmán's boots and put them with the shirt. Within a few minutes, Guzmán's uniform was laid out on the dried ground. The kid took off his own uniform and dressed

Guzmán's corpse in it. A reasonable fit. When they came to bury the bodies, no one would pay attention to the Republican dead – particularly in this heat.

The kid struggled into Guzmán's uniform. It was a little tight but not enough to draw comment. He found Guzmán's kepi and put it on. Strapped on the ammunition pouches and canteen and took Guzmán's rifle. The red cross armband he threw away – Guzmán's days as a stretcher bearer were over. The kid now seemed just another regular soldier of Franco's army. Until he got to the French border, that was. He rummaged through the contents of Guzmán's pockets, finding identity papers, a faded sheet of devotional verse and several letters from relatives. He would read them as he walked. If he was challenged they might help bolster his credibility.

The kid took the curved knife from the dead Moor. The blade flashed in the white light of the sun. Guzmán's body would soon begin to rot but the kid decided to hurry the process and slit open the belly, opening a path for the flies and small creatures that would soon come. Just to be sure.

It was a long walk to the Nationalist lines. The kid passed the time reading Guzmán's letters from home. He retraced the route through the trees and shrubs he and the others had fled through hours before, walked past the bodies of his comrades, now swarming with flies. He scrambled down the narrow path that led back down from the plateau, stepping over the piles of dead Moors. Always past the dead. There were no wounded.

He was staggering now and he rested for a while, alert and cautious. If he ran into his own side they would probably kill him outright in this uniform. He also had to avoid the Nationalists, couldn't risk them identifying him as one of the enemy. If he stayed here, he would die of hunger or thirst. He would have to steal food from farmhouses, sleep rough and live off the land as he made his way towards the frontier. Wherever that was.. He kept walking.

He heard the sound of horses. The staccato drumming of hooves on the rocky soil. And singing, a martial song. 'El Camarada'. They were Franco's men. The enemy. The kid hid in a patch of dense scrub *trying to work out his options. As the sound of horses grew louder, he began to panic. He staggered through the bushes, trying to remain hidden, trying to find somewhere he could hide. The ground was uneven and he tripped and fell, his rifle clattering onto the hard ground. Horses whinnied and men shouted in alarm. The kid struggled to his feet, heard the sound of weapons being cocked. He looked up. A line of men aimed rifles at him.*

And then a shout. 'Hold your fire, he's one of ours.'

CHAPTER TWENTY-ONE

LAS PEÑAS 2009, SIERRA DE GREDOS

The road rose into a land of sun-scorched scrub, stunted trees and huge overhanging rocks. An arid landscape broken by sheer cliffs and sharp boulder-strewn ridges.

'Do you want the air con any higher, Ana?'

'*No, gracias.* I'm freezing. In any case, that's the mine up ahead, just past that sign.'

Tali slowed and turned off the road, bringing the car to a halt on the flat patch of land near the derelict buildings of the Compañía Española de Minas, *fundada 1898.* Everything seemed much as it was the last time Galindez had been there: the parched landscape, the eerie sagging outlines of the buildings in their slow decline into the dusty scrub. The heat.

'It doesn't look much,' Tali said, looking round. She raised her sunglasses to squint at the ochre surroundings. 'It's so desolate.'

'There was an important mine here sixty years ago,' Galindez said. 'Then they hid the bodies in the entrance tunnel and closed it for ever – or so they thought.'

'But why did they shoot people at a mine, of all places?'

'I think it must have seemed an efficient way of getting rid of a large number of bodies. I don't know yet whether they were dead when they brought them here or if they were killed in the vicinity of the mine. I'm not sure. Maybe there's something I missed last time. I didn't have any help that day and it took me a long time to get the skeletons out and bag them up. It would have been easy to overlook a bit of evidence.'

446

Humid, leaden heat bore down on them as they left the hermetic chill of the car.

'I want to visualise how it happened,' Galindez said. 'They must have parked their vehicles somewhere here. The plans of the place show that the track up to the quarry was rough and unsurfaced back then. It would have been too steep to drive up.'

Tali peered at the bleak landscape. 'It's not hard to imagine people being killed here. This countryside is brutal.' She leaned on the car, watching as Galindez paced the arid ground, trying to picture the scene.

'That wall was here back in 1953 and there was a fence running between the buildings and the track – you can just see the remains of it sticking out of the grass. That means that if they parked here, they'd have to go along by the wall and then up the track on foot.'

'With the bodies?'

'I suppose. Or they might have marched them up there and shot them in the quarry.'

A drainage ditch ran parallel to the stone wall, some three metres away. It must have been needed once but now it was just a rugged furrow of dirt and stones. The wall was covered in yellowing sun-blasted lichen. Many of the rough stones showed signs of weather damage. Galindez stopped. On closer examination, she saw a series of indentations on the stones. The height of the indentations varied but the spaces between them were pretty regular. Those patterns weren't caused by the weather, she thought.

Tali watched Galindez kneel to examine the marks. '*Qué te pasa*, Ana María?'

'Do something for me, Tali? Kneel down just here, by this little ditch?'

Tali shrugged, and knelt. Galindez turned her to face the stone wall. 'Bend your head, will you?' She unfastened her bag and took out a ball of string. 'Lean forward, that's it, lower your head a bit more.'

Tali laughed. '*Vaya*. Are you going to tie me up?'

Galindez handed her one end of the string. 'Keep hold of that,' she told her, stepping across the ditch to the wall. 'OK. Hold the string to your forehead.' With Tali keeping the string taut, Galindez aligned the other end with one of the marks on the wall, calling instructions to Tali to move a few centimetres to one side or the other. Once Tali was positioned satisfactorily, Galindez began to sketch diagrams and scrawl measurements in her notebook. Next came the photography: each of the marks on the wall had to be carefully recorded and its position noted – Galindez didn't want to drive out here again.

Tali drank from a plastic bottle of water as she watched Galindez work. 'Sure I can't help you, Ana?'

'Yes, you can.' Galindez smiled, pushing her sunglasses up into her hair. 'You can start digging. The spade's in the boot.'

The sun was sinking behind a dark skyline of hills by the time they had dug up the ground immediately in front of the stone wall, hacking away the dry grass and digging down several centimetres into the soil. When Galindez started to scrabble in the dry earth, probing with her fingers, Tali bridled for a few moments before reluctantly joining in. It was only when she made the first discovery she started to show enthusiasm for the task.

The dig continued as darkness fell. By bringing Tali's car nearer and shining the headlights against the wall, the excavated area was illuminated with brilliant light, enabling Galindez to examine the flat, rusty objects they retrieved from the soil.

Tali looked at her. 'Are you going to explain it to me now?'

'I'd rather wait a day or two until I've examined everything back at the lab – then I'll tell you. I want to be sure I'm on the right track.'

'As long as it's worth waiting for, I don't mind. Tell you what, I'm starving.'

'Let's go back and get cleaned up and then have a late supper. Somewhere on Calle Velázquez, maybe?'

'That's upmarket.' Tali laughed. 'Are we celebrating?'

'I won't be sure for a couple of days,' Galindez said, 'but yes, I think we are.'

MADRID 2009, CALLE DE VELÁZQUEZ

Walking up from the Retiro Metro to the restaurant, the elegance and sophistication of Calle de Velázquez was marred by the exhaust fumes of heavy late-night traffic. Tali paused to admire the luxurious Hotel Wellington. Through the front doors they could see the reception desk, where a tall man was arguing furiously with the desk clerk.

'This is how the other half live,' Galindez said.

'*Por Dios*, you trod on my foot. Look where you're going, *señorita*.' A man's voice, rising in angry protest.

Tali stumbled, clutching Galindez for support. '*Ay, perdón.* I didn't see you.'

For a moment it was hard to tell who she was talking to. Then Galindez noticed the little man walking towards the door of the hotel, brushing his coat angrily, accompanied by two young women in leather miniskirts and high heels.

'What happened?' Galindez asked, bewildered.

'I walked into a dwarf,' Tali said. 'I never even saw him coming – grumpy little sod.'

MADRID 2009, CASA DE SUBASTAS ANSORENA, CALLE ALCALÁ

'*Señor* Morales? Your ten o'clock appointment just arrived. Dr Galindez from the *guardia civil.*'

The secretary showed Galindez into *Señor* Morales' office. The room was furnished in impeccable period furniture that Galindez thought very fitting for such a leading auction house. *Señor* Morales made small talk and offered her coffee before Galindez got down to business.

'*Señor* Morales, I found this key in an old building during an investigation. I wonder if you could tell me anything about it.' She passed him the plastic evidence bag containing the key she found taped under Guzmán's desk at the *comisaría*.

449

Señor Morales put on a pair of thick spectacles and slowly examined the key. 'This is in very good condition. Did you clean it up?'

'My colleague Sargento Mendez did that. Is it damaged?'

Señor Morales laughed. 'Not at all, the only reason I ask is because it looks like a professional clean and polish. An excellent job, although I'm afraid the key isn't worth very much.'

'*No me importa*, I don't want to sell it. But can tell me something about it – maybe even date it?'

Morales walked to a walnut bookshelf and perused the shelves for a moment before pulling out an old catalogue. He showed Galindez the faded cover. *Aguado: Cajas Fuertes* 1956.

'Safes?'

'Safes *and* strongboxes,' Morales said with a defensive pedantry. 'They were a leading maker of household security boxes from the thirties until the early sixties when they were bought out by a competitor.'

'And is it possible to date this particular key, *Señor* Morales?' Galindez said. 'Or at least tell me what kind of strongbox it opened?'

Morales smiled. 'We deal with a lot of Aguado's products, Dr Galindez. I'd say what we have here is the key to the Cervantes. One of their smaller strongboxes. Here, I'll show you.' He leafed through the catalogue. Finding the page he was looking for, he passed the catalogue over to her. She saw the black and white photo of the Cervantes strongbox.

'It looks rather small. You couldn't keep much in it, could you?' Galindez tried not to sound disappointed.

'The Cervantes was for home use. They were manufactured between 1948 and 1961. Specifically designed to protect account ledgers, family Bibles and so forth. The inside was velvet lined to protect large tomes like those.'

'It was designed for books?' Galindez asked, her interest restored.

'*Exactamente.*'

After a brief discussion of the merits of the Aguado range of products and their value to collectors, Galindez excused herself and hurried out into the noise and bustle of Calle Alcalá. As she forced her way through the crowds of shoppers, her myriad thoughts began to condense around an intriguing conclusion. The key was for a specialist strongbox. And there was a book so special the key was hidden, taped under a desk. Sancho was right. Guzmán had been keeping a book.

MADRID 2009, HEADQUARTERS OF THE GUARDIA CIVIL, LABORATORIO FORENSE NO. 8[B]

The lab was quiet, the lights dimmed. The rumble of traffic that formed a constant background on other floors faded away in this room. Here, there was only silence. And the dead. All of them. Galindez pulled on her white coat as she approached the long bench in the centre of the laboratory. Mendez had done a good job in arranging the skeletons, though many of the smaller bones were just heaped to one side. It didn't really matter, Galindez thought, no one was going to reassemble them. Not even her. It was the skulls she wanted.

The cause of death was obvious. The small, precise bullet hole in the back of the skull and the gaping exit hole at the front indicated a single shot from behind. Galindez knew her initial suspicion had been correct: the prisoners were made to kneel by the ditch – just as she'd had Tali kneel there – before they were shot, the bullets impacting on the stone wall in front of them. She moved along the bench, briefly examining each skull in her gloved hands. All had similar bullet damage.

All but one. Had there not been such a long wait for a laboratory to be free, she might have been alerted to this earlier. Mendez was in charge of lab allocation and she'd refused to bump Galindez's seventy-year-old remains to the front of the queue ahead of ongoing cases. And rightly, Galindez thought. In any case, it wasn't Mendez who was at fault, Galindez knew, it was her.

Annoyingly, she hadn't noticed on that blistering day in Las Peñas. *Sloppy, Ana María. Lack of attention to detail. How could I have missed this?* She knew the answer. That day she was paying less attention to the job and much more to *Profesora* Ordoñez. Luisa's presence at the mine had distracted her from noticing this obvious detail, the one thing among these bodies indicating difference rather than similarity. *Mierda. When things are the same, identify the differences.* Where had her refreshing doggedness been when she needed it that day?

Annoying. But not the end of the world, she thought. If she didn't have an interest in the case no one else would have even looked at these skeletons. At least she'd found it now, her latex-gloved fingers running over the skull of the man whose death had been the exception amongst this group. Fourteen dead from single gunshots: a brutal improvised execution – Luisa's suggestion they had been killed by firing squad was untenable now. These men had died, waiting on their knees for their killer to work his way down the line, taking careful aim – and it was careful, she realised; there had been only one shot in each case – while the next victim had to listen to the approaching sound of the executioner, his breathing, the crunch of his shoes, the harsh crack of the shot, the metallic impact of the ejected cartridge on the ground. The victim's realisation that the executioner was now standing behind him. Galindez realised her hands were sweating inside her gloves.

And this fifteenth victim. What did he do to deserve this? Galindez looked again at the rusty wire embedded in the cervical vertebrae. Deeply embedded, by someone using tremendous force. She imagined the horror of it: the threshing of the victim as the wire bit deep, the roaring sound of imminent death as pressure increased on the carotid arteries. Unconsciousness within perhaps ten to fifteen seconds. But that wasn't enough for whoever did this: the wire would have cut deeply into the victim's throat; in fact, the man was nearly decapitated. Whoever did this was very strong. He knew what he was doing, she thought. He had done it before.

Galindez finished the examination. She tugged off the gloves and washed her hands. She stooped to catch water in her cupped hands, swilling it around her mouth to wash away the taste of dust. The taste of death. She switched off the lights, the fluorescent tubes fading in sequence until the skeletons were illuminated only by the tentative light coming through the open door to the corridor. Pausing for a moment to look back at the dead men, she let the door close. She walked along the corridor to the lift and went down to the ground floor, passing through the security screens and out into the gentle late-evening air. She thought again about the type of man who could kill like that. It was not a pleasant thought so she forced herself to think about other things. About life, not death. Trying not to think again of the elemental violence deployed in an execution like this. For seventy years, no one, apart from the killer – and maybe not even him – had given the men in that mine a thought. Now, Galindez could do little else but think about them.

The car park was a quiet pool of shadow broken by the solitary echoes of her footsteps. But not solitary, she realised. She was not alone. She felt his presence before she heard him. Sensed him sheltering in the velvet darkness. Imagined the cruel wire embedded in a man's spine for nearly a century. It was a warm night: she was shivering.

Turning, she caught the secretive movement of a black shape some twenty metres away. A match flared into life as the man lit a cigarette, his face vaguely illuminated for an instant by the flame. A man in a fedora hat. And then darkness again, with just a pinpoint of red light glowing in the shadows as she dashed to her car, scrambling inside and locking the doors, hands hurried and anxious as she started the engine. The tyres squealed as the car accelerated away from the shadows. Galindez wiped beads of sweat from her face. She knew now who was watching her. The fact that it was impossible just made it so much worse. And when she got home, secure behind her triple-locked doors, with Mendez's automatic pistol to hand, she knew there would be someone outside, watching. There always was these days.

CHAPTER TWENTY-TWO

MADRID 1953, BAR LA ALEGRIA, CALLE MESÓN DE PAREDES

The threatening sky threw the narrow street into sombre shadow. Shuffling passers-by gazed through fly-blown windows at cheap goods they couldn't afford. Guzmán picked his way through the lunchtime window shoppers. Few people made eye contact with him: anyone who looked like trouble was best avoided. Their main aim was to stay safe, Guzmán knew. Safe in their precarious lives, scoured by tides of fear and uncertainty. Fear of the sudden slamming of car doors and voices in the night, boots on cobbles. Hammering on doors. Muffled protests. Hoping it was someone else's door.

Hay calamari. The sign in the bar window caught his eye. Guzmán looked at the handwritten placard, shaking off the cloying numbness of his deep concentration. There were squid. The sign said so. And if there were squid he was having some. All of them, if he felt like it. A feeling of power surged through him: he was hungry, he was cold and he was alive. He pushed the door open and went in.

The crowded bar reeked of sweat, damp sawdust and tobacco mingled with the smell of frying fish and garlic. The air was wreathed in black tobacco smoke, voices loud and agitated in conversation about football or the bullfights. Guzmán pushed through the crowd and leaned on the counter, listening to the babble around him like someone listening to rain. He felt comfortably anonymous amongst these people. The usual groups of friends or workmates, a few couples who might or might not be married and who might or might not be married to the person they were sitting with right now. He let the conversation melt into the background. He ordered squid and a beer. The squid came, golden in fried batter, glistening with salt, pungent with garlic. He ordered another plate at once.

Guzmán munched the squid, crunching the batter and savouring the tender meat. The presence earlier of the big bruiser from the *capitanía* troubled him. If the man had been sent to kill him, he would not have been standing across the road so blatantly. He would have made an effort to avoid being detected until the time came. So what was he doing? Was it a warning from Carrero Blanco, a reminder of the price of failure? Surely not: such warnings normally followed a failure and were usually fatal. Guzmán had not failed yet.

Still, Guzmán thought, he couldn't rule out the possibility that Shave-Head had been sent to get rid of him. He knew well what such work entailed. He remembered standing in Valverde's opulent office listening to the self-important sermons the general frequently delivered to his staff. And then, in the middle of the pomp, almost without breaking the rhythm of his usual hyperbole, Valverde told Guzmán to kill the man who was his commanding officer.

Guzmán had been surprised. It seemed somehow ungentlemanly to be ordered to kill his own commander. But obedience is a soldier's virtue, and that night, as the man got out of his car, Guzmán put his pistol behind the man's ear and fired. He left the body and the car, taking only the cash in the man's wallet. It was small recompense for the long walk home.

The next day Guzmán was promoted. He used the stolen money to buy a suit for the funeral. A few months later, he was summoned to the *Caudillo*'s headquarters, where Franco gave him a new job, commanding the Special Brigade in a phony police station, his men dedicated solely to removing those who opposed the regime. Franco smiled as he outlined the work. No legal restrictions, no judicial accountability. No due process. It was something Franco had done before, following the uprising in

Asturias in 1934. It worked very well then, Franco said, and it would work well now. Guzmán would maintain the memory of the war. Nothing which had been done against Spain – meaning against Franco – would be forgotten, as Guzmán exacted vengeance upon all those who had threatened the eternal glory of *La Patria*. A Spain united, great and free, as the Falangists loved to chant, although naturally, freedom was a relative concept and was always subject to revision. Guzmán had been trained for such work and he took to it at once. The *Caudillo* trusted him and Guzmán would not betray that trust. Could not betray it.

The squid was truly excellent, its salty batter delicious, perhaps the best he'd ever had, Guzmán thought, while recalling his appointment as Franco's roving executioner. So much casual death. So much blood. So many dark times, although not for him. Who was it said the darkest hour was before dawn? Certainly whoever said it had not been in Guzmán's line of work. The hour before dawn was when you checked the rifles of the firing squad – if there was to be such a formality. It was when you watched the prisoners being brought from their confinement, their pasty faces, their innumerable cigarettes shedding tobacco as the prisoners tried to light them with trembling hands.

So many prisoners. Endless lines of gaunt faces, men and women in corpse-grey queues, waiting. Waiting to be interrogated, waiting to be judged, waiting to be lined up and then waiting to die. The mixture of emotions: some defiant, some weeping, some half mad. Sometimes the women would be raped: every execution had its own set of contingencies. The prisoners, shuffling forwards, sometimes bound, other times bound only by their own fear and the utter certainty of what was to come. No matter how many emotions Guzmán detected in their eyes as they marched past him, the one emotion he never saw was hope. There were no concessions for their feelings, no attempt to make the executions humane. These people were shot for a reason and they deserved to die.

Some deaths stood out from the rest, deaths that had some significance or which were necessary in order to make some point or other. Guzmán remembered the film star, a well-known Communist, quite a looker before the war. Her allegiance to the Republic brought her the fame she desired, although in the end she got more attention than she ever dreamed of. Her war involved making propaganda films and paying occasional visits to the front to rally the Reds in their trenches. Until the night Guzmán and his squad flagged down the car in which the actress was making another visit to the front as a boost for morale.

The driver was a fool to get lost. But then he probably knew that the moment Guzmán and his men held the car at gunpoint. The man made no attempt to defend her, surrendering with gibbering haste. It was cold that night, Guzmán remembered, cold and dark. The crowd of men around the car. Pistols pushed against the driver's forehead though the half-open window, spittle on the man's face as he struggled to control his fear. The woman was braver than him. Did they know who she was? she demanded, relying on her fame to save her. Of course they knew. Did they know how much she could be ransomed for? Naturally, they did. She was still asserting her financial worth as they pulled her and the driver from the car and shoved them to the side of the road. The driver was weeping, afraid to even look at his captors.

Guzmán speared his last calamari with a toothpick and nodded to the barman. The man turned to shovel more squid onto a plate. He brought another beer, beads of condensation running down the glass, and placed it alongside the squid.

There had been a brief discussion between Guzmán and his men as they searched the actress's car. Her fate was already decided even though she continued to try to interest them in using her as a hostage. Mainly they argued over the woman's clothes. Dressed in her finest to give the troops a show, the actress shivered in the night while the men discussed in low voices how much her clothes were worth. For Guzmán, the problem was somewhat different. Steal her clothes, leave her corpse naked, and in death she might have one last propaganda coup if the Reds gave photographs to the foreign press, enabling them to highlight yet another Nationalist atrocity. Shoot her as she stood, in her expensive outfit, and his men would resent the waste. They already resented young Guzmán's promotion and his command over them. Even for Guzmán, whose skills in leadership were underwritten by acts of sudden, elemental violence, there was still a need to keep the men motivated and obedient. A regular army commander would just have ordered them to obey. But Guzmán's men were irregulars, less accustomed to orders, more prone to contesting authority. There was a balance to be had between compliance and resentment. Later, he would have the benefit of experience as well as his lethal physical attributes, but back then he was still learning. And Guzmán was always a quick learner.

The actress began to take off her clothes, seemingly unsurprised by his order. She undressed slowly and deliberately, as if going for a swim rather than standing in front of a group of enemy soldiers. The fur coat was first, passed reverently back from hand to hand, stroked, admired, carefully placed on the bonnet of the car. The silk dress, the stockings. There was silence now, except for the sobbing of the driver. The actress struggled for a moment to unhook her camisole before sliding it from her body and handing it to be passed back to the car to be placed with her other clothing. She stood naked, pale and shivering. Someone remembered her jewellery and after a moment's hesitation the woman removed her earrings, her necklace and several large rings. The driver's sobbing became incessant and incoherent.

The men shuffled, unsettled, unsure what they were going to do with her. Some began to insult her: she was a whore, a Red bitch, she didn't know what real men could do, she would do for them what she had done for the Freemasons, the Communists, the church burners. They were becoming a mob. This needed to be over quickly, Guzmán realised. But they were near to the front lines: if they shot her, the enemy might catch them out here in the open. If they stayed to take turns raping her, they ran the risk of being discovered by enemy patrols. Leadership, Guzmán was learning, always required action. It was time to act.

There would be no shooting. Taking her with them would be too risky. A mass rape would take too long and would make them vulnerable to attack while the men shouted and jeered at the trembling woman. This was no longer about her and Guzmán decided what must happen to maintain their respect for his command. He stepped forward and the men stood aside, eager to see what the young *teniente* would do. The wire was already in his hands as Guzmán stepped behind the actress. Her head hung down as she hugged herself against the cold, unaware of Guzmán as he moved closer to her, quickly bringing the wire over her head and then pulling it tight around her throat.

For a moment she was so surprised she seemed not to comprehend what was happening. But no one who is strangled dies peacefully or with dignity and she was no exception. Her inhibition at being naked in front of the enemy soldiers was quickly lost as she flailed helplessly and hopelessly, threshing against the insistent bite of Guzmán's garrotte while the roaring in her ears drowned out the sound of her futile attempts to draw breath. There was still time to kick, to twist, to try to flee with those flailing legs, even as Guzmán's great strength lifted her clear of the ground. Still time to do all those things that seemed to offer an escape from the crimson tide of asphyxia that turned her face into a dark mask punctuated by her desperate gaping mouth as she struggled to breathe. The actress died, threshing and kicking, finally forced face downwards onto the ground beneath Guzmán's weight. He knelt astride her, his feet pinning her legs until it was over.

He had killed like this on other occasions and he had done it well here. The impression he had made on his men was considerable. They would be much less willing to dispute his authority in future. Guzmán then turned his attention to the driver. The actress had been a woman and nothing was expected of her in the manner of her death. The driver was not a brave man and he shamed himself in the way he died. The men were glad he suffered.

Guzmán chewed the hot squid, lost in thought, remembering soaking the two bodies in petrol after pushing them back into the car, the flames rising into the night sky. They heard the explosion of the petrol tank after a few minutes, but by then they were on the way back to their own lines. Guzmán took a sip of cold beer, lost in memory. The interior of the café dissolved into a comforting warm murmur. But introspection was too much of an indulgence to maintain for long. He blinked, willing himself back into the present, the smell of sweat, the thick cigarette smoke, the chatter of a dozen conversations. When he looked up from the bar, he was looking into the face of the big shave-head from the *capitanía*.

Guzmán weighed the man up. Tall, heavy and thick-set, the man's head glinted in the weak light of the bar. *Maybe five or six centimetres taller. Christ, they pick us out of a mould.* The man stepped forward and Guzmán tensed as he extended a hand.

'Gutierrez.'

'Guzmán.'

They shook hands. The bar was crowded. It was unlikely the man would make a move here. But not impossible. Pull out a gun, shoot, then leave. The only thing the bystanders would remember would be the gun. Even if they were able to describe the killer, the police wouldn't want to know. Nor the press. That was how it worked.

Guzmán warily emptied his glass. 'Have a drink?'

'Sure. You're drinking beer? I'll have one too.'

Guzmán waved the empty glass and the barman brought two glasses of flat, yellow beer. Guzmán handed one to the man and they toasted one another warily.

'You'll be wondering why I'm here?' Gutierrez asked, casually.

'I'm not stupid,' Guzmán said.

Gutierrez grinned. 'It isn't that, *Comandante*. They haven't sent me for you.'

'Just as well,' Guzmán's voice was quiet, 'for you.'

Gutierrez betrayed a moment of irritation. 'If it was that, I would hardly choose this place to do it. Although naturally, I would do it, *Comandante*. But don't let's argue – I've not got much time. There's a lot to be done, what with the *Caudillo*'s speech, the parade and then the trade meeting.'

'Sounds like you'll be busy.'

'I do my bit. Which is why I'm here. I brought you this.'

Gutierrez reached inside his jacket and then stopped, looking down at the bulge in the left-hand pocket of Guzmán's coat where the big Browning was pointing at his belly. Guzmán still held his drink in his right hand. He nodded to Gutierrez's hand, hovering halfway inside his coat.

'Very slowly, Gutierrez. Don't make me nervous.'

Gutierrez opened his jacket slowly, holding it so Guzmán could see the manila envelope protruding from an inside pocket. As he had expected, the man's holstered pistol nestled under his armpit. Gutierrez pulled out the envelope and offered it to Guzmán.

'Step back a pace.'

Gutierrez stepped back and Guzmán put down his glass and took the thick envelope with his right hand.

'That was nicely done,' Gutierrez said, 'but I really have come to help you.'

'And why was it necessary to send you?'

'I sent myself, Guzmán. As the new head of Military Intelligence I wanted to meet you. That was why Carrero had me frisk you. To get a look at you.'

Guzmán's face hardened. 'That must have been fun. So you're the new boss?'

'I am,' Gutierrez agreed, 'so fasten that tie, *Comandante*. You're on duty.' Both of them smiled with almost genuine humour, each confident that, if necessary, he could kill the other in a heartbeat.

'So what do I need help with, Gutierrez?'

'Your Caribbean friends,' Gutierrez said, reaching for his beer. 'I understand they're causing you problems. What with their property purchases and their petty crime.'

'I'm aware of all that. What I don't know is where they are.'

Gutierrez inclined his head towards the envelope. 'There's a lot there you don't know, Guzmán. Have a look at it. You should find it helpful. I had some of Carrero's best men on this.'

Guzmán scowled. 'I am one of his best men. And anyway, I've already used Exterior Intelligence Services to check them out.'

'My information comes from other sources,' Gutierrez said. 'You should find the contents of this envelope very interesting.'

'That's all very well, what am I going to do with these bastards?' Guzmán spat. 'The *Caudillo* himself said they weren't to be touched.'

'That's true, Guzmán. Officially. But from what I've seen, you need to take a wider view of things. When you see what's in the envelope you'll agree.'

'*Bueno*. I'll take a look.'

'Good. I'd hate for this to become a problem on my watch.'

Guzmán finished his beer. 'Gutierrez, when I find out where they are, they'll cease to be a problem, full stop.'

'Be subtle, Guzmán,' Gutierrez said quietly. 'The last thing you want to do is go charging in after them. If you want to keep your job, that is. And your head, come to that. I mean it.'

'*Hasta pronto*, Gutierrez. I'm sure we'll see each other again.' Guzmán stowed the envelope inside his coat and turned to the door.

Gutierrez looked up from the lengthy bill the barman had laid on the counter in front of him. 'You can count on that, *Comandante* Guzmán.'

MADRID 1953, COMISARÍA, CALLE DE ROBLES

Snowflakes fell through the late afternoon light, floating like ashes against the oncoming night. It was freezing. It seemed to Guzmán that he had never really been warm for months. The *comisaría* was as bleak as ever, shrouded in falling snow and sombre in the failing light. The lobby was dark and smelled of black tobacco and sweat. It was a familiar odour and one which put Guzmán at ease. Behind the desk the *sargento* was scrawling something in the day book.

'*Buenas tardes, mi Comandante.*'

'*Muy buenas, Sargento. Qué pasa?*'

The sarge looked down at the book. 'Still got one of the crew from the Bar Dominicana in the cells. That fat queen. Never stops complaining.'

'Speaking of which, where's the *teniente*?'

'Out.' The sarge frowned. 'Got a phone call from the *capitán-general*'s office and went over. Oh yes, earlier on he brought a bloke in. Got him in cell sixteen.'

'Name?'

'Wouldn't say, sir. The *teniente* said it was to be kept quiet – on your orders.'

'That's correct. Did you put it in the day book?'

'No, sir. Should I?'

'No. Listen, I need you to pop out on an errand for me. A little job chatting to your mates in the know.'

The sarge's evil grin widened. 'Any expenses, sir – to encourage them to talk?'

Guzmán pushed a roll of dollar bills across the counter top. 'Keep the change.'

The money disappeared into the sarge's pockets as he slid from behind the counter and pulled on his coat, pausing only to shout inside the admin room for one of the men to come and take over the desk.

'Who are we interested in, *jefe*?'

'Big bruiser attached to Carrero's staff. Shaved head, name of Gutierrez. He's the new head of Military Intelligence. That's all I can tell you.'

The sarge smiled. 'That's all I need, *mi Comandante*.'

Guzmán watched him go before returning to his office. He unlocked the door and went to his desk. Taking a set of keys from his drawer he returned to the corridor. There was no one about. No one would question him here, but it was better not to be seen. Potential witnesses were always best avoided.

The cells were quiet. Unlike prison, where the sound of

footsteps brought cat-calls, cries for food or just insults, here there was only an anticipatory silence. Guzmán's feet echoed on the stone floor of the corridor. He walked down to the great iron banded wooden door and opened it. Leaving it ajar, Guzmán went to cell sixteen. The cell was in darkness. A man was sitting on the bed. As the door opened, he looked up uncertainly, seeing Guzmán's bulk, framed against the sallow light from the corridor.

'Cousin Juan,' Guzmán said.

The man stood up, tentatively extending his hand towards Guzmán's offered handshake. It was one of many mistakes he had made recently. A powerful blow into his midriff left him gasping for breath, unable to speak. Guzmán punched him again and Cousin Juan fell to the ground, his breath rattling. Guzmán seized his feet and dragged the man out of the cell and towards the iron-banded door. Cousin Juan gasped for air, his hands clawing at the stone floor. The big door had almost closed under its own weight and Guzmán had to push it with one hand while struggling to hold an increasingly resistant Cousin Juan with the other. Finally, losing his patience, Guzmán punched him again in the belly, avoiding his head since he needed him to be conscious for what was to follow. Cousin Juan gave a visceral moan, curling up into a ball on the cold flagstones, retching and gurgling. Guzmán kicked the massive door open and Cousin Juan's wordless cries of pain went unheeded as he was hauled through the door and down into the darkness beyond. The door slammed with sonorous finality and then Guzmán and Cousin Juan were alone together, in the place below, where the angular echoes and the sound of dripping water were the only noises to break the subterranean silence. Until the screaming began, and the ancient stones echoed once more with carefully elicited cadences of human suffering.

It was seven thirty. Guzmán finished washing his hands, letting the tap run until the last swirls of blood disappeared down the drain. He dried his hands on the filthy towel. Entering the darkened mess room, he went to the armoury, unlocked the reinforced metal door and swung it open. He turned on the light and saw the bleak single bulb reflected in the reptilian glint of the weapons: the lines of rifles and machine guns, piles of batons, the boxes of ammunition. He found what he wanted and took it from the shelf. A heavy landmine. This was hardly part of the usual armament of a police station but then this was no ordinary police station. Locking the door of the armoury, Guzmán returned to his office, carrying the mine under his arm, his footsteps quiet and measured on the stone floor.

Inside the office, Guzmán placed the mine on his desk. His desk for now, he thought. By tomorrow he could be in one of his own cells with some goon from the night shift kicking his kidneys. It was a distinct possibility, the way things were going. Everything was getting out of hand. He had a feeling his luck had turned against him. Perhaps it was all those gypsies he'd punched – and worse – during his career. They'd put the evil eye on him. But he doubted their power to do that. If any of those who came into contact with Guzmán at the *comisaría* had magical powers, they would never have remained there. The first fifteen minutes would have been enough. But no one had such powers. They stayed because the real power here was his.

He had done great work here. Dealing with those people. Those who had chosen a path that led to the damp cells, where the walls echoed to the sound of shouts and blows and screaming. Familiar sounds. The annoying, slapping sound naked prisoners made when they fell repeatedly onto the flagstones. He hated them, shivering, bleeding, babbling excuses as they sprawled on the cell floor. Convoluted excuses for what Guzmán saw – and despised – as the result of their stupidity in making decisions. You made choices and you stuck with them. If you could not, you were weak. Weak, no matter how principled the arguments and excuses might be. There was no pity and very little mercy for such people. They had to die, both as an example to others and as punishment for their foolishness. Perhaps, now and again, Guzmán would be lenient, ending a wretched life quickly and unexpectedly. Such release was only for those who made a full confession and whose account did not in any way annoy him. But those occasions were rare.

He struggled to pull the heavy metal filing cabinet away from the wall. He was sweating by the time he had moved it far enough to get at the flagstone. With sufficient strength you could do anything, he knew that well. Strength was important. The strongest side won the war. Before the war, life had been against him. A blur of accusations and squabbles, pointing fingers. The priest with his stick. *Always you, boy. Causing trouble, playing too hard, hurting people.* The stick rising and falling, the priest's boot stabbing into his ribs. Later, Guzmán's attempt to play rough with the girls caused even more trouble and the beatings got worse. Especially when one girl's family got hold of him. Afterwards, when he finally crawled home, bloodied and bruised, he got another beating from his father who was just sober enough to do it before collapsing into his chair. After that, he had never gone back to school and passed the time in the woods, sharpening sticks with his big knife. Watching and waiting, without knowing what he was waiting for. Then the war came.

Guzmán removed the broken flagstone and took out the American money from the pit below. He would have to risk carrying it. If he had to flee, that cash could save him. There were other things down there: diaries, wallets, photographs, a few knives, pistols, bundles of foreign and frequently worthless currencies, a dessicated hand, some underwear, a few watches. Fragmented remains of fearful lives suddenly ended. He had other such caches, repositories of trophies and treasures. Like a magpie, perhaps. Or maybe not, considering what he had done to those birds in the woods as a youth.

And his book. Nestling in its metal box. The ledger containing the details of his murderous career, the full lists of names, dates, places. Details of the orders given and by who. Pages that would condemn him if found. He knew keeping such a record was stupid. No one in this job would do such a thing. Yet he did it. He had seen what happened to the Nazis after the war, how quickly their fortunes changed. This was his insurance, a bargaining chip he might use if ever things were to change – however unlikely that might be. In a life conducted amidst the uncertainties of perpetual war, sometimes you had to take a gamble.

The book was Guzmán's gamble. Its contents were not accessible to the casual reader. He encoded his records using a *Wehrmacht* code the Germans used to communicate with their U-boats when they made secret visits into Vigo for supplies. Guzmán had combined the German code with another, one he had found below in the vaults on one of his expeditions down there. It had belonged to the Inquisition and was like no other code he had ever encountered. That code was safe beneath the floorboards of his *piso* in Calle Mesón de Paredes and even that had been encoded, disguised as a diary, a youthful memoir of his life. He had used the real Guzmán's diary as a foundation, adding his own amendments – once he had mastered the other man's handwriting. The diary set out his strong Christian values, describing a youth who helped the local priest deliver alms to the poor, his devotion to Spain and to Franco's noble cause, his enlistment in the army the only reason he had not gone to the seminary for training. The new Guzmán had made some additions, adding in a few of his youthful experiences to reshape the journal. And to muddy the waters. It was a world of lies that recreated Guzmán in bogus, saccharine detail, though there was some truth in the later entries – the growing hatred of the villagers towards him before the war, their petty jealousies and complaints.

The diary, with all his additions and inventions that would distract the casual reader, was the key which would unlock his real chronology of horror, hidden here, beneath the flagstones. In this book there was no invention. Just lists of victims, locations where they died, sometimes the exact details if their deaths had been particularly interesting. The codes were strong and it would take great effort, whether in code-breaking or torture, to extract their secrets – assuming anyone could get hold of both parts of the code

– since the diary and the book were always kept in different locations. He took the book and placed it back in its hiding place, closing the metal box. For now it was safe. In a minute, it would be safer still.

If things went against him, he might not see this treasure again: they might take it all from him, take away the life he had fought for more savagely and determinedly than anyone else in Spain. He placed the mine into the hole below the flagstones and armed it. Using a couple of ammunition boxes, he weighted down the trigger before putting the flagstones back in place. If things went well, he would return and disarm it at his leisure. If things went the other way, then whoever came to search his office would be rewarded for their trouble. Guzmán dragged the filing cabinet back into position. It was a good hiding place, but there were always some who would persevere in their search. Those who knew that dogged persistence was the key to unlocking others' secrets. But that was their problem. Let them seek all they wanted. Let them decide if their pursuit was worth it. By the time they found this last secret, Guzmán might not even exist.

He poured a brandy and picked up the folder Gutierrez had given him, spilling out the contents onto his desk. Three photographs, secured with paper clips. He arranged them on the desk, half expecting them to be of some long-past action of his returning to incriminate him. But it was not Guzmán in the photographs, it was the Dominicans. Somewhere in the Caribbean, he guessed, noting palm trees in the background. The pictures were overexposed but he could make out their faces well enough, see the decorations and badges of rank on their uniforms, as the men stood stiffly at attention in front of the preening dictator Trujillo, at some military review. Whatever they were, they were hardly petty criminals. Nor was the man standing behind them in his dapper lightweight tropical uniform: Positano.

The next photograph was a family portrait of a young but recognisable Positano and four adults; parents and grandparents apparently. But the picture was not taken in the Neapolitan countryside where Positano supposedly lived until the thirties. There was no mistaking the familiar building behind Positano and his family. It was the White House, Washington, DC. The photograph was dated on the back: August 1922.

The telephone rang, loud and brittle in the sombre office.

'Guzmán?' It was Gutierrez. 'You sent your *sargento* to check up on me. You were rather over-confident in his abilities, I must say.'

'Is he dead?'

'No, though he deserves to be. You can have him back if you want.'

'Well, I do need someone on the desk here. Send him back. I'll kick his arse.'

'Do it later. I want to see you.'

'Just as you wish,' Guzmán said calmly.

'*Estación de* Atocha. The bar on platform two.'

'Now?'

'Right now.'

'I'll be there in thirty minutes.'

As Guzmán came through the doors into the lobby, Peralta was at the desk, signing in.

'*Buenas tardes, Comandante.*'

'I'm going out for a while, *Teniente*, don't go anywhere until I return.'

Peralta nodded. 'Did you see your cousin, sir? In the cells…'

Guzmán nodded. 'I saw him. He's gone.'

'Gone?'

'I released him,' Guzmán said. 'It was a personal matter. We never got on very well. I asked him a few questions, he couldn't help us any further so he left.'

He walked to the big wooden doors and stepped out into the biting wind. Behind him, Peralta stood grim-faced. A spasm lanced through his gut and he turned his attention from Guzmán back to his health. Picking the phone up, he dialled Dr Liebermann's number.

MADRID 1953, ESTACIÓN DE ATOCHA

Guzmán hated trains, and he hated the people who travelled on them. Passengers were either poor and stank, inviting derision, or they were well-off and self-satisfied, inviting jealousy and contempt. The station towered over him, a dark, gloomy pantheon, its huge glass roof wreathed in greasy smoke from the trains grunting into and out of the teeming platforms. He glowered at the beggars sprawled near the entrance, dwarves, amputees, the blind, the lame, men with open wounds, all keen to demonstrate the veracity of their claim for alms. Guzmán scowled at them and they scowled back, unafraid. What more could a brute like him do to them? Actually, Guzmán knew he could do quite a lot more. That thought cheered him as he picked his way through the crowds clustered along the platforms, scrambling onto the soot-stained trains that would carry them back to their hovels on the outskirts of the city. The station breathed them in and it breathed them out again, the blackened, gasping lungs of the city.

The bar on platform two was dirty and unappealing, as were its clientele, a handful of shabby businessmen waiting for their trains to grind into the station. This was the daily rhythm of their lives, Guzmán supposed, as he strained to see through the haze of smoke. Gutierrez was hard to miss: a tall burly man with a shaved head, his back to the bar, apparently intent in his newspaper. Which meant he had seen him the minute he came in. Guzmán kept his hands in his pockets as he edged through the waiting passengers towards the bar. There was a stench from the toilet.

Gutierrez looked up. '*Comandante*. Have a drink?'

'Brandy.'

Guzmán looked round, carefully scanning the customers of the bar.

'You won't see them,' Gutierrez said, casually. 'I don't go in for gunfights in bars, Guzmán, not my style.'

'And I never went to bed with an ugly woman,' Guzmán said, taking the brandy.

Gutierrez didn't have a sense of humour. 'I came alone,' he said, 'except for your *sargento*, of course.'

Guzmán shrugged. 'Where is he?'

'Taking a shit, I think.' Gutierrez nodded towards the door of the reeking toilet. 'I certainly hope he doesn't smell like that all the time.'

'You'd be surprised,' Guzmán said.

There was the sound of someone struggling with a resistant chain and then the gurgle of ancient plumbing. The toilet door creaked open and the sarge appeared, fastening his belt. People standing near the toilet door looked at him, horrified, as they moved away.

'Sorry, boss,' the sarge smirked. 'This gentleman got the drop on me when I started asking questions.'

Guzmán shook his head. 'Losing your touch, *Sargento*. Piss off back to the *comisaría* and wait there till I get back.'

'Don't you want me to hang around here, sir?'

'No. You've been no use so far. If *Señor* Gutierrez causes me any trouble I'll call the Little Sisters of the Fucking Poor because they'll be more use than you.'

'We'll have less of this *"Señor"*,' Gutierrez said, lowering his glass. '*Coronel* Gutierrez, if you don't mind, *Comandante*.'

'I didn't realise we'd become so formal in the secret police,' Guzmán scowled, 'or I'd have saluted you the moment I came in.'

'Fuck you.' Gutierrez smiled, sipping his brandy. 'And by the way, Guzmán, if you really wanted to have me checked out, why use that degenerate? I wasn't flattered.'

Guzmán lifted his glass to get the barman's attention and ordered more drinks. 'Believe it or not, he was once one of the best. Served with me in the war.'

'Ah, the war.' Gutierrez nodded. 'I could see him being of use back then. What did he do, shoot the prisoners or torture the women?'

'Very often both.' Guzmán didn't rise to the bait. 'It wasn't as if it was work for him, he loved it.' He smiled. 'Almost as much as I did.'

471

'Those days are over, Guzmán,' Gutierrez said. 'You've adapted. Psychopathic wrecks like your *sargento* may have had a use once. We're more subtle these days.'

You may be, Guzmán thought. 'We all have the same aims in our different branches of security.'

'In the *many* different branches of security,' Gutierrez corrected. 'Far too many. Still, that may change, since your unit will cease to exist very shortly and become part of Military Intelligence. And then you'll report to me. Depending on how we decide you've handled this case so far of course.'

'"We" decide?' Guzmán asked, annoyed. 'Who's "we"?'

'Carrero Blanco and myself.' Gutierrez said. 'I'll report the details to him and he'll make a decision and confirm it with the *Caudillo.*' He emptied his glass and turned to Guzmán angrily. 'You're in some fucking trouble, you know, Guzmán.'

'I've had no complaints about my work so far,' Guzmán said, irritated.

'Until now,' Gutierrez said. 'We all know the story. Your heroics in the war made you a favourite with the *Caudillo*. Inspiring stuff.'

'Certainly did me no harm.' Guzmán shrugged.

'Well, it will do you no fucking good now,' Gutierrez snapped. 'Perhaps it would help if you just listened for once?' He turned and ordered two more brandies.

'Apologies, *mi Coronel.*'

'You're aware General Valverde's not an admirer of yours?'

'It would be fair to say Valverde hates my guts.'

'Mostly due to the extraordinary independence of your command in Madrid,' Gutierrez said. 'That and your remarkable capacity for insolence.'

'My orders always came from the *Caudillo* or Carrero Blanco,' Guzmán said. 'And one of the first orders I had was that General Valverde had no authority over my command.'

'No wonder he hates you.'

Guzmán sniffed his brandy. It was cheap but smelled better with each glass. 'You know the story, I'm sure. Valverde hates me because I was his protégé until Franco took a shine to me. And because I proved useful, Franco used me more and more. And as he did, he trusted me more than he trusted Valverde. Generals are fine for fighting battles, but they don't go round knocking on doors and killing people. I do.'

'For a long time, Valverde has been worried you're spying on him.'

'Spying?' Guzmán smirked. 'Reporting, let's say. Didn't you know?'

'Of course I knew, Guzmán.'

'And is there a problem?'

'Not at all,' Gutierrez said. 'However, Valverde keeps trying to undermine you, writing letters of complaint to Franco, moaning about your lack of accountability, saying you're a loose cannon.'

'Of course he does. He fears me.'

'But he isn't stupid, Guzmán, however much you despise him.'

'I realise that.'

'And lately,' Gutierrez took a drink, 'he's had more influence with the *Caudillo*. Economic policy mainly, but he uses every opportunity to complain about you.'

Guzmán's grip tightened on his glass.

'Valverde claims you use the *comisaría* for your own ends, says you're not accountable to proper authority, abuse your position and so on. These things have a cumulative effect and that's not counting the endless letters of complaint about your insolence and insubordination.'

'Has there been anything in particular to undermine me with the *Caudillo*?'

Gutierrez nodded. 'This thing with the Dominicans has put you in a very bad light. Valverde's been banging on about how you failed to stop them shooting up half of Madrid. Not to mention of course, that these apes have intruded into business interests allocated to him by Franco himself. If it turns out you had any sort of connection with the Dominicans, it would be fatal for your career.'

'Fatal for me,' Guzmán corrected him.

'For you,' Gutierrez agreed. 'And, in light of recent events, the *Caudillo*'s getting edgy. Valverde has been making the case for social change. He produces reports and papers almost daily on what needs to be done to improve the economy.'

Guzmán snorted. 'I heard. He thinks he's better suited to lead the country than Franco. But Valverde's always been one for the long game. Never show your hand. That's his style.'

'He might be showing it now, Guzmán. This stuff about the Dominicans and you. Shit sticks. And he's making it stick. He claims to have other things on you. I don't know what yet. But I can tell you, you're heading for trouble.'

'I can handle trouble.'

'*Coño*, he's not going to challenge you to a fist fight. You don't have anything going with these Dominicans, do you?'

'Apart from a burning need to kill them? No.'

'You haven't taken cash from them? That's what Valverde's been saying.'

Guzmán felt the first stirrings of uneasiness. 'Of course not.'

Gutierrez was looking at him intently. '*Bien*. Because that would be bad. And of course, if you had money they'd given you, and we found it...'

'Money is money. How can you tell where cash comes from?'

Gutierrez shook his head slowly. 'You've had it easy for too long, Guzmán. Banknotes have serial numbers – they make it easy to trace money – and establish guilt.'

'It's not a problem,' Guzmán said, aware of the large roll of dollar bills in his pocket. 'The general's a liar. *Coronel*, I haven't taken any money.'

'Good, at least we can discount that,' Gutierrez said. 'If you had to be taken down it would seriously weaken Franco's standing internally. It would also damage the standing of the intelligence services.'

'You mean it would damage you,' Guzmán sneered.

'*Claro*. Valverde doesn't just want to be rid of you, Guzmán.

He's trying to get Franco to reorganise the security services. Simplify them.'

'With Valverde at the head of them?'

'Naturally, how did you guess? I'd be out of work as well. But that's just a part of it. Valverde is proposing massive economic change, opening up the economy to all comers, inviting foreign investment, developing the infrastructure, hospitals, roads, schools. Claims it would create a boom that would make Spain rich.'

'Spain?' Guzmán smiled.

'Quite. All those ministers and generals that Franco has given little slices of the economy would have one big payday.'

'But how would we keep control and maintain order?'

'That's the thing, *Comandante*. There would be no need to keep an iron fist hanging over the poor. There'd be so much work they'd be falling over themselves to do it. No one would care about the War, about maintaining the fear. *Joder*, the country would keep itself in line.'

'Franco would never allow that.' Guzmán said, outraged. 'All he worked for, to restore order and civilisation. The Crusade.'

Gutierrez laughed. 'The glorious Crusade. A war to restore Christian values to Spain. And what did he use at the heart of it? Fucking psychotic Moroccan mercenaries. Muslims. That tells you all you need to know about his values. If the economy suddenly explodes into life and there's money being handed out in truckloads, which values do you think the *Caudillo* will cling to then?'

'You're right,' Guzmán agreed, calling for another round. 'I'd be out.'

'That's it, look at the bigger picture,' Gutierrez sneered. '*Coño*, we'd all be out. All of us who did Franco's dirty work through the war and after. He wouldn't be loyal to us if he didn't need to be.'

'*Joder*.' Guzmán said, as Gutierrez's words sank in. 'There's a lot who'd be threatened by that kind of change, *Coronel*. Ruined, in fact.'

'*Absolutamente.* It would threaten the interests of security, the armed forces, the *guardia civil*, everyone with a stake in keeping things the way they are. You can see how that kind of change would unsettle many of them, disrupt their interests.'

'I can see it very well. Another war. Or a coup. And this time it wouldn't be us getting foreign support, it'd be the liberals. The British and *Yanquis* would probably help them bring in democracy, for Christ's sake – they all hate us. And the French.'

'Exactly. Change isn't a good thing for Spain. Nor is it necessary,' Gutierrez said. 'It needs to be introduced very slowly to adapt to our culture. And it needs to be controlled.'

'Agreed. So what do we do?'

'The talks are in two days, Guzmán. You need to have the Dominicans by then. They can't be allowed to disrupt the talks.'

'And if they do?'

'Then it's over for you. Franco said as much to Carrero Blanco.' Gutierrez finished his brandy. 'You'll be out.'

'Know what? From the start I thought the Dominicans were just a bunch of thugs,' Guzmán said bitterly, 'muscling in to get a piece of Valverde's drugs business in Madrid. I saw their criminal records.'

'And who gave you those, Guzmán?' Gutierrez raised an eyebrow.

Guzmán scowled angrily. 'Fucking Valverde.'

'There you go. But you saw the photograph I gave you. The uniforms. They're well trained for a bunch of hoodlums, I'd say. And, I might add, you can trust my sources better than Valverde's.' He looked past Guzmán, at the teeming crowds jostling through clouds of smoke and steam to get on a train. 'You've been assuming a lot based on very little, *Comandante*. And in the meantime, Valverde's been busy.' He paused. 'Of course, if it all goes belly-up, I never gave you any photographs and I never spoke to you.'

'For Christ's sake, can't we arrest him?' Guzmán asked. 'There's enough to warrant at least an interrogation surely?'

'No.' Gutierrez shook his head. '*Hostia*, Guzmán, I've got more reason to arrest you.'

'You could try.'

'Forget that kind of thinking,' Gutierrez said. 'If the shit hits the fan in two days you're finished. You'll get the blame and I have to go to plan B.'

'Which is?'

'You become a target. I'd have to act to keep my credibility. And even then, there are no guarantees. Valverde will be calling the shots after that.'

'And if I disappear right now?'

'Try it and see how far you get,' Gutierrez said. 'You're lined up to be the scapegoat. It's in no one's interests to let you retire quietly.'

'Just a thought,' Guzmán muttered sullenly.

'This is my phone number.' Gutierrez handed Guzmán a scrap of paper. 'If they come for you I'd prefer it if you weren't carrying it on you.'

'I'll make sure of it.' Guzmán nodded.

'One more thing.' Gutierrez swirled the last dregs of brandy in his glass. 'What's this thing with a *Señora* Martinez?'

Guzmán's face fell. 'What's my private life got to do with Military Intelligence?'

Gutierrez finished his drink. 'I couldn't care less who you fuck, Guzmán. But I'll tell you this, *Señora* Martinez's name cropped up in several telegrams Valverde sent recently. They were written in code, unfortunately.'

'Sent to who?' Guzmán snapped.

'Various post office boxes and then collected by someone using a fake name. What else would you expect? But you do visit this *Señora* Martinez, don't you?'

'She's a friend,' Guzmán said.

Gutierrez snorted. 'A friend? *Hostia*, Guzmán. How many men in this trade have died because of a woman who was their friend?' He shook his head. '*Coño.*'

'That's all it is,' Guzmán said, aware of how pathetic he sounded. 'And as you fall asleep in her bed? Does she take an interest in your job, Guzmán? Does she stay awake as you drift off babbling state secrets? Or perhaps she listens to your problems?'

Sweat trickled inside Guzmán's shirt. 'Absolutely not. *Mira*, we haven't even—'

'No,' Gutierrez said incredulously, 'no, please, please don't tell me you're not even fucking her. Please don't say it's love? *Puta madre.*' He scowled. 'You're a professional, Guzmán.'

Guzmán looked away, humiliated.

'Well, that's your problem,' Gutierrez said. 'I've told you what I can. I can't afford to be directly involved in any of this. Shit sticks. You need to find the Dominicans and get a grip before Valverde convinces Franco you're yesterday's news.' He put down his glass. 'I tell you what: if I was seeing some woman whose name appears regularly in correspondence from a man who wants me dead she'd have to be fucking me stupid twenty-five hours a day before I'd ignore it. Watch yourself, man.'

'I'll deal with it,' Guzmán muttered.

'I think you should.' Gutierrez turned and walked out of the door into the noise and confusion as another train pulled into the platform.

Guzmán watched him disappear into the crowds, swirls of men in shabby suits, peasants carrying wineskins, old women dressed in black. Gutierrez was slowly subsumed until only his shaven head was visible above the ragged eddies of poverty swirling around him. And then Guzmán saw him. Black hat, dark wool coat. Several metres behind, following Gutierrez across the concourse. They were watching him too.

Guzmán felt drained. Even though he had always known this moment might come, he was still surprised. He'd imagined it would be more dramatic: the arrest at dead of night, the beating in the cells, possibly a trial. He lit a cigarette and thought for a while. Gutierrez wanted the Dominicans to be prevented from disrupting the talks. Guzmán wanted the Dominicans. There were still possibilities.

Outside, a train pulled in, spouting dark acrid smoke, the tannoy announcement echoing, loud and unintelligible. People spilled from the train, jostling and elbowing. They looked like maggots, Guzmán thought with distaste, the brandy sour in his mouth. He stubbed out his cigarette and left the bar, swiftly absorbed into the crowds making their way towards the exit.

It was dark. The wretched street lighting made it hard to see very far in the freezing evening air. Guzmán passed a shop and idly glanced into the dull amber glow of the display window. The reflection in the glass overlaid the shoddy knitted goods inside but it was the reflection Guzmán was interested in. A man was following him. Discreetly, slowly, but definitely following him. *The vultures follow the sick animal before it knows it's sick.* The words of the priest who taught in the village school. He had been full of words. When he wasn't using his stick – usually on Guzmán. Until the war came. And then the villagers came for the priest. The priest's words had softened then, although by that time it was far too late.

Guzmán crossed the road and bought a newspaper at a stall. Everything was turning to shit. Valverde was much sharper than Guzmán had thought. He'd boxed him into a corner. Tricked him into taking the money and given him false information. Not to mention the poisoning of his own drugs and the shooting outside Bar Dominicana. Valverde had made a confrontation with the Dominicans inevitable, even though it was expressly forbidden. The cunning fuck. A light snow began to fall, forming soft shimmering halos around the street lights. Then there was Positano. What the hell did he have to do with all this? Guzmán was losing his grip. *Señora* Martinez complicated his life even further, so that now, everything he did required him to take her into account. So much that had seemed clear-cut not so long ago had mutated into a perplexing cluster of events, each presenting him with a new set of problems. And that was all he had right now: problems.

479

It seemed as if he was in a dream. They carried him to a wagon and gave him water. Later they brought him soup and bread. He ate hungrily, as if it were his last meal, which perhaps it would be. The men looked at him and laughed. One ruffled his hair. Another gave him a mouthful of brandy which made him splutter. They were in good spirits. As he lay in the wagon, he heard them discussing the battle. It was over: the city had fallen and now all that remained was to dispose of the losers. They were looking forward to it.

Soon they would discover who he was and then he would suffer. He was tempted to confess who he was, what he had done, to end it now and put a stop to his anticipatory suffering. But in the evening they brought him stew, thick with meat. Smiled at his hunger. Gave him more.

'No wonder he's starved, after what he went through.' He couldn't see who had spoken. From his hospital tent he could only see shadows outlined against the blazing fire. Heard them laughing, drinking wine. Heard a toast. Something about angels and swords.

The noise of a motor vehicle cut through the laughter. At once, the atmosphere changed. The kid felt it even in the tent. And he was afraid, the fear cold and cloying. They knew. They had come for him. He heard boots on the dry ground coming nearer. Heard the barked salutes of the men. 'Sí, Señor', 'A sus ordenes'. And then, worse: 'A sus ordenes, mi General.' What business did a general have with him? He knew the answer. He had come for him. Come to claim him, to remind him the wages of sin were death. Maybe the priests had been right after all.

The general entered the tent, framed by the camp fire behind

480

him. The kid lay on the bed bathed in sweat. He looked up at the general. A big man, ruddy-faced, with wild eyes burning beneath shaggy brows, a thick bristling moustache over a cruel mouth. His uniform was immaculate, medals glittered on his chest. The kid's eyes were drawn to the holster on his belt.

The general spoke. 'So you're the one?'

'Sí, señor.' The kid struggled to sit up.

'How are you, boy?'

'Bien. Muy bien.' What else could he say? He could hardly complain.

'Sad news, young man,' the general said. 'We found no one alive on the hillside. Your entire unit is dead. Every last man.' He placed a hand on the kid's shoulder. 'All except you.'

The kid nodded. That would make them even angrier. The destruction of a whole unit. There would be no mercy after that.

'The men say you pursued them to the last man. Is that true?'

The kid acknowledged that it was. More or less, he thought.

'Incredible. You never flinched in your duty. You pursued those Reds until they were destroyed. Incredible. You're a hero, son. Franco has already agreed to a medal. And you'll need to talk to the reporters – this will be a big boost for morale.'

The kid didn't understand.

'There's more,' the general said. 'We can use men like you. I've already spoken with Franco about you. We're agreed. Someone with your potential could be useful not only in this war, but afterwards. Spain has to deal with the Reds that remain – and other threats as well. We want to train you, prepare you for the role. And others like you. But I warn you, it will be hard. And we'll be watching you, lad, Franco and me, making sure you complete the tasks we set, making sure you develop the skills we need. We'll always be close by, keeping a constant eye on you. What do you say?'

'It's an honour,' the kid stammered. Maybe they'd post him near the French border.

'Do you know what the men say?' The general smiled. 'They say you pursued those Reds like an avenging angel. Followed them

through the hills until finally you put them to the sword. Like the shadow of God falling on them. That's what they're calling you: The Dark Angel of the Sword. They think you're lucky. And you must be, for us to give you this opportunity. You won't regret it. All we ask is loyalty. Loyalty and obedience. Once we've won this war, loyalty will brings rewards, believe me. What do you say lad? Are you up for the challenge?'

There was no alternative. At least until the moment came when he could flee to France. 'A sus ordenes, mi General.'

'I knew I could count on you,' the general said approvingly. 'What's your name, son?'

'Guzmán, mi General,' the kid stammered.

'Well, Guzmán, this is a great opportunity,' General Valverde said. 'Make the most of it.'

'I will, mi General,' the kid said. 'I promise.'

CHAPTER TWENTY-THREE

By the time Galindez reached the university, evening was already spilling long shadows across the parched gardens. She got out of her car and stormed across the grass towards the history building. She recalled her promise earlier in the day to Tali that she would stay cool when she met with Luisa. It wasn't going to be easy. *She mustn't suspect we know she's involved with the* Centinelas *and gave me the bugged ear stud.* That was bad enough, but there was also Luisa's attack on Galindez's work in the newspaper article. And that wasn't all: Galindez had an even bigger surprise for the *profesora.*

Galindez took the stone steps of the faculty building two at a time and hurried down the narrow corridor. Luisa's office was as chaotic as ever. Maybe she just threw her papers to the floor when she'd read them, Galindez thought. Luisa looked up, perhaps thinking this was a social visit. She was wrong.

'Ana. *Qué tal?*'

'*Bien.* You look tired, Luisa. Late night?'

'I wish. Got a deadline on this paper for the *Hispanic Journal of Socio-Historical Research.* You'd think I could get it finished easily. But can I?'

Galindez moved a pile of papers from a chair to the floor and sat down.

'I saw you on TV the other day, Ana.' Luisa frowned. 'You should have consulted me about it.'

'Why? They interviewed me because of my work for the *guardia*

483

civil. They wanted to know about our investigation of war graves and atrocities. They called my boss and he asked me to do it.'

Luisa snorted. 'What about an acknowledged expert? Someone who could put the issue into proper context and draw out the implications for society. Me, in other words.'

Her ego was astonishing. 'It was *Telediario*, Luisa. They wanted something short and succinct. You don't do either.'

'Meaning what, exactly?' Luisa's face flushed with anger.

'Meaning they wanted three minutes of interview about where a particular grave we're working on is located, and what we expect to find. Not some post-modern discussion of how we should restore the fucking palimpsest.'

Luisa stood up. 'Just remember I'm in charge of this research group, Ana María.'

'Could I ever forget it? Look, if you want to behave like a big kid, go ahead. But just remember, the government is about to announce new funding enabling the *guardia civil* to take a lead role in investigations related to Franco's dictatorship. Once that happens, we'll be in charge of those activities. We'll decide who our authorised partners will be. Partners we think will further our scientific investigations.'

'*Hija de puta,*' Luisa spat, flecking her chin with saliva. 'I welcomed you into my group and this is how you repay me – by taking it over?'

'I'm only telling you how it is, Luisa. You could find yourself on the outside when we pick our future partners. Especially since you're so antagonistic to our methods.'

'To your methods, you ungrateful little bitch,' Luisa shouted. 'I'll teach you some manners, *putita.*' She leapt to her feet, drawing back her fist as she launched herself at Galindez.

Galindez was angry now. Angry that Luisa gave her the bugged earrings and angry at what she had tried to do to her in this very office. But there was no grey mist this time, just clear-headed rage.

She sidestepped Luisa's punch, turned, and seized her wrist with one hand, the other hand moving to apply pressure on her shoulder. Shifting slightly, she forced Luisa to move off-balance or have her arm broken, and then, as Galindez released her arm, it took just a slight push to send her sprawling on the floor.

'*Puta*,' Luisa groaned, sitting amidst the disarray of papers. 'My arm.'

'Get up. I don't want to hurt you,' Galindez said.

Luisa struggled into her chair. 'Why are you being like this, Ana María?' she groaned. 'You should be grateful. I introduced you to Guzmán.'

'Only because you wanted to ridicule my work and promote your theories at my expense. Know what your problem is? You want to make Guzmán part of your academic production line, churning out paper after paper, book after book and all full of *your opinion* on Guzmán – with very little evidence to support it, *profesora*.'

'Evidence. All I ever hear from you is evidence. There's more to history than counting bullets or deciding if someone was shot from the front or the back.'

'No wonder you say that: your work, Luisa, has very little fucking evidence in it at all. *Joder*, most of it's conjecture, projection and wild interpretation.'

'Say what you like, Ana. My book on Guzmán is almost finished. Once that's published, I'll be the one defining the Guzmán narrative and doing the interviews. You and your pedantic forensic science will be excluded from all that, I'm afraid.'

'I'm happy to sit on the sidelines, Luisa. Although while I'm there I'll be throwing a couple of bits of positivist evidence into the mix,' Galindez said with a thin smile.

'Such as?'

'For a start, I'm writing an article about my investigation into Guzmán's activities. Why don't you wait until it's published? You'll be in for a surprise.'

Luisa's eyes narrowed with apprehension and fury. 'How can anything you fucking say possibly detract from a careful work of interpretive textual analysis? Tell me that, *puta*?'

'Since you're so keen, of course I'll tell you, Luisa.' Galindez shrugged. 'You think you've produced a brilliant, theoretically informed interpretation of Guzmán's rise to prominence in Franco's *Brigada Especial*. And you focus on how he had little choice in any of this – largely using the diary as evidence?'

'Absolutely. There's no evidence to implicate Guzmán directly. People like Guzmán submerged their identity in the ideals and rhetoric of Franco's cause. Personal responsibility was just a matter of sustained obedience to the State's demand for deference and conformity. Guzmán was a node in a network, a conduit for the power above him. Read the diary carefully, Ana. There are important implications in that text. What I've written is an exemplar of its kind.'

'*Bueno*, then you should know this: the diary isn't what you think.'

'What do you mean?' Luisa's expression betrayed her concern.

'You noticed there's a difference in Guzmán's writing after the war begins?'

'So? He was writing in different locations. The writing varies a little, naturally.'

'Oh, it varies, Luisa. But not naturally. In fact, my colleague, Dr María Isabel del Rio – ever heard of her?' Luisa shook her head. 'Thought not,' Galindez continued, 'Positivist scientist. A top forensic handwriting expert. World class, in fact. She came up with four pages of reasons for believing sections of the diary were written by two different people.'

'No. *Por Dios. Imposible.*' Luisa's eyes widened.

'There's more, Luisa: my colleague strongly suggests the second writer based his handwriting on the earlier style. Tried to imitate it, in fact. '

'No, no, no. *Mentira.*'

'Not lies at all, Luisa. You can see where this is going, can't you? Guzmán took over someone else's diary. In fact, he seems to have stolen someone else's life. He had the skill to try to fake this other person's handwriting. Guess which bits aren't his, *Profesora*?'

Luisa moaned. It wasn't a pretty sound.

'Let me tell you then. The Guzmán who attended church, loved music, wrote poetry, and yet was beaten and victimised, the youth who looked forward to going to war as a means of getting away from his village – that's the earlier person. The later entries in the strong angry handwriting occur once the war has begun. Around the time of the attack on Badajoz, in fact. Somewhere during the first year of the war, Leopoldo Guzmán – whoever he was – ceased to exist and a new Guzmán continued the diary after that.'

Luisa shook her head.

'I suppose you've never studied cryptography either, Luisa? Positivist science again, I'm afraid.' Galindez found her anger was almost thrilling in its intensity. 'Fortunately, I've got colleagues who've done little else all their working lives. And guess what?'

'Stop it. *Puta de mierda*, stop it or you'll be sorry.'

'Sticks and stones, Luisa. I'll tell you anyway. What's written in the diary makes sense superficially, but all those lists and details are deliberately arranged: that part of the diary is some sort of elaborate code. Our top cryptographer ran it through a series of computer tests that can decipher most modern codes in a few hours. Not this one. He's still working on it. But he's clear on one thing, *profesora*, the diary is a means for deciphering some other work. The entire thing forms the key to reading Guzmán's true secret. His book, Luisa. There was a book in which he wrote down what happened, what he did and who ordered it. His colleagues suspected he was keeping it. That skinhead – Sancho – the one who attacked me here, was looking for it. You were right that you could read Guzmán as a text, Luisa. You just didn't try to find out which text needed to be read or how.'

'It can't be.' Luisa's face was tight with anger. 'A code? That's only your opinion. You haven't cracked it.'

'Not yet, but it will be cracked, Luisa. And then we'll find his secrets with our positivist science. Find whatever his diary has hidden within it. And then we'll find the book. The *real book*, Luisa. I've already got the key to the strong box Guzmán kept it in.'

Galindez dangled the key in front of her. The metal gleamed in the light.

'No. *Por favor.* Don't colonise Guzmán with your repressive science, Ana. Don't make your work a threat.'

'Luisa, if my work seems so threatening, it's because it isn't simply eccentric or strange, but competent, rigorously argued, and carrying conviction.'

Luisa stared at Galindez wide-eyed, her mouth sagging open. '*Coño*, you're quoting Derrida to *me*?'

Galindez shrugged. 'I couldn't resist. And I haven't even got to my evidence yet, *profesora.*'

'What evidence?' Luisa's eyes narrowed.

'The evidence that shows Guzmán wasn't some innocent drawn into Franco's dictatorship by random circumstance,' Galindez retorted. 'Those bodies at Las Peñas. There's a list of men in Guzmán's diary in an entry for January the fourteenth. A list with fifteen names highlighted.'

'The *policía* were bureaucratic...' Luisa saw Galindez's expression and shut up.

'They were all arrested, according to the diary, on the morning of fourteenth of January 1953,' Galindez continued. 'By the end of the day, they were in the mine at Las Peñas, dead. In the diary, each of the fifteen names has the letter *M* by it. Presumably for *muerte*: they were all marked for death. But one was special, for some reason. There was a longer annotation against his name. Fourteen of them, Luisa, made to kneel by a drainage ditch, facing an old stone wall. Then shot in the back of the head. Not by a firing squad but by one person. One after another, all shot with a Browning semi-automatic. Guzmán's pistol.'

'It's not possible to know all that,' Luisa said angrily.

'No? I measured the victims, measured the bullet marks on the walls. I found they had to have been kneeling for the bullets to hit the wall. And they were shot by someone of above average height. Someone at least one point eight metres tall. Someone like Guzmán.'

'You can't be that precise,' Luisa protested.

'Actually, I can be. But you were right about the police being bureaucratic, *profesora*. All those invoices, receipts and requisition forms. You've got boxes of them here at the university. Shame you never looked at any. Tali went through them earlier this week and she found these within a few hours.' Galindez took a couple of faded papers from her bag.

'What are they?'

'One is a receipt dated March 1948 for a Browning semi-automatic, purchased for a *Comandante* Guzmán and delivered to the *comisaría* in Calle de Robles. The other is an order for nine-millimetre ammunition dated November 1952. And, in case you're going to say that's a coincidence, there are these.' Galindez waved the plastic evidence bag, rattling the four flattened metal stubs. 'These are nine-millimetre bullets I dug out of the ground by the old wall at Las Peñas. There is one thing I can't explain, though.'

'Which is?' Luisa asked.

'Why he shot those fourteen men but chose to garrotte the fifteenth with wire.'

'Someone else might have done it.'

'There's a name in that list, Luisa, that has more than just an *M* against it. Someone called Ernesto Garcia Mendoza. I have no idea who he was, but Guzmán must have wanted him dead very badly. He throttled him so hard the wire is still embedded in the man's cervical vertebrae seventy years later. Do you know what Guzmán wrote next to Mendoza's name?'

'*Qué?*' A string of snot dribbled from Luisa's nose.

'*Chalina.* Guzmán made a note to give him a necktie,' Galindez said. 'And he certainly did.'

Luisa was finally lost for words.

'*Lo siento*, Luisa. I think my part of this investigation is done.' Galindez started to walk to the door.

Luisa screamed after her. 'Guzmán's mine, you can't steal him from me.'

Galindez paused by the door. 'Two lesbians fighting over a man

– how ironic is that, Luisa?' She closed the door and stormed down the corridor, followed by a barrage of hysterical abuse. Still shaking with anger, she slowed as she passed the open door to the admin office. The light was on and she saw a large plan spread on a table near the door. Luisa must have been working on it earlier. Galindez looked around but saw no one. All the office staff had gone home long since. Curious, she decided to take a quick look. It was a faded architect's floorplan dated 1941 and marked *comisaría de La Policía Nacional, Calle de Robles, Madrid*. A sudden adrenalin surge. It was a plan of Guzmán's *comisaría*. The corner had been torn away but otherwise the document was in good condition. It was the work of a moment for Galindez to roll it up and take it with her. Luisa could have it back later.

MADRID 2009, TEMPLO DE DEBOD, PARQUE DE MONTAÑA

Six-thirty in the morning and the heat was already uncomfortable. Leaning against the railings, Galindez looked out over the sprawl of Madrid, its hectic contours punctuated by high rises and spires blurred by haze. Below, a path led down through trees and bushes towards the Plaza de España. Galindez watched a woman pushing a pram. Near her was a man in a dark coat, mopping his brow nervously with a large handkerchief. Other people, living other lives.

Behind her were the squat tan buildings of Franco's ancient Egyptian temple – a gift in recognition of a rare act of philanthropy by the *generalísimo*. The buildings surrounded by motionless rectangles of water, the colour of polished steel. The water threw erratic reflections over the ancient stones above. An idyllic spot to meet. Somewhere where she could spot anyone following her. This was the way she and Tali lived now: apprehensive and cautious. Meeting in out-of-the-way spots. Places with possibilities for cover and escape.

Soft footsteps on the gravel.

'*Holá.*' Tali handed Galindez a Styrofoam cup of coffee. 'It's nice here. Nicer than when the barracks was standing, I bet.' She blew on her coffee. 'As you'd expect, Luisa took the news about the diary badly. Did you tell her you knew about the ear stud?'

'No. I dropped the one with the bug down the side of my seat on the Metro. Let her chase that for a while.'

'Well, following your visit the other night, she's decided to take a sabbatical. I think she's going to work out what to do now you've pulled the rug from under her Guzmán book.'

Galindez nodded. 'Speaking of Guzmán and books, I've been thinking. Why don't we go back to the *comisaría*? I thought maybe tonight?'

'At night? Jesus, Ana, it was bad enough in the day. Why?'

'No one will expect us to go there in the middle of the night, will they? And you know what? I think you were right that there's something under the flagstone.'

'What makes you so sure?'

'Look at this.' Galindez brought out the folded floorplan she'd taken from the office. Tali watched her as she smoothed it flat before pointing out her discovery.

'*Mierda.* That's Guzmán's office, isn't it? And that little pencil mark – it's a cross. You've got me excited now, Ana María.'

'And the cross is right where the broken flagstone is. There's only one way to find out for sure. Shall we do it?'

Tali frowned. 'I'm working until seven. Exam papers to be sent off.'

'I could pick you up around then? *A eso de las siete*?'

Tali finished her coffee. She shrugged. '*Bueno.* Let's do it. Let's see if Guzmán will give up his secrets.'

CHAPTER TWENTY-FOUR

Peralta looked up from the mess room table as Guzmán stormed in, angrily throwing off his dripping hat before tossing his wet coat across a chair.

'Still snowing?' Peralta asked, before realising that a chat about the weather wasn't what his boss had in mind.

'No, it's bright and sunny, *imbécil*. Fuck the weather, *Teniente*,' Guzmán shouted, pouring a coffee from the pot on the table. He took a drink and spat the coffee out. 'Cold. Fucking cold. *Puta madre*.'

'I could make some more, sir.'

Guzmán shook his head. 'I want you on the street. Those Dominican *cabrónes* are out there somewhere. Take the sarge and go and shake up a few informers. Find an addict or two we haven't already knocked around and give them a slapping. Find out something, *Teniente*. I'll expect your report at eight thirty tomorrow. Prompt. *Me entiende?*'

'Perfectly, sir.' Peralta stood up. 'I'll go and get the *sargento*.'

Guzmán waited until the lieutenant's footsteps faded away down the corridor. He picked up his sodden coat. The corridor was silent as he walked to his office. Behind him, he heard the clank of plumbing as someone flushed the toilet. The toilet door opened and Dr Liebermann emerged, his cadaverous face accentuated by the weak light. Liebermann looked at Guzmán with concern.

'Would you come into my office please, *Herr Doktor*?' Guzmán said. Liebermann followed unhappily.

Guzmán sat at his desk. Liebermann paused reluctantly by the door.

'Come in, Liebermann.' Guzmán's voice was unsettlingly pleasant. 'And lock the door, doctor, we don't want to be disturbed.'

The pallor of the German's face increased as he turned the key in the lock. Guzmán held out his hand. 'Key.' Liebermann reluctantly handed it over.

'May I ask, *Herr Comandante*, what you wish to speak to me about in such secrecy?'

Guzmán ignored him and picked up the phone. The private at the front desk answered.

'Is *Teniente* Peralta still in the building?'

'He left a couple of minutes ago, sir,' the man said. 'Shall I go after him?'

'No. That's fine. *Gracias.*'

'*A sus ordenes, mi Comandante.*'

Guzmán put down the telephone. Liebermann was a study in concern. For himself.

'Well, *Herr Doktor.*' Guzmán smiled. 'Finally alone together.'

'Always a pleasure, *Herr Comandante.*' Liebermann bowed slightly.

'Liebermann, I'm going to give you a choice.' Guzmán stood up, and took off his jacket. Liebermann's eyes fixed on the large pistol hanging in its holster under his left arm. Guzmán began to roll his sleeves up. 'It's a choice none of the people in your camps ever had.'

'Have I offended the *comandante* in some way?' Liebermann spluttered.

Guzmán shook his head. 'No more than usual, *Herr Doktor*. But then, your very presence offends me. Which is a bad thing. For you anyway.'

Liebermann was shaking. He seemed to be having trouble speaking.

'Liebermann, what's going on between you and *Teniente* Peralta? And don't lie to me. If you do I'll have to hurt you. I'll hurt you so badly it will surprise you how much pain you can take and still remain conscious. Although you must have some idea – given the experiments you carried out on all those children. Am I making myself clear?'

Liebermann's mouth moved but the words took a while to form. Guzmán could smell the sweat on him. 'Very clear,' he stammered.

'Tell me,' Guzmán said, 'and you can leave in one piece.' He sat down and placed his feet on the desk.

Liebermann struggled to speak.

'Now or never, doctor. What is it you and the *teniente* have so much to talk about?'

Liebermann began to talk and continued for some time. When he had finished, Guzmán unlocked the door and Liebermann walked unsteadily down the corridor. Guzmán slammed his door and rummaged for Valverde's brandy in his desk. *Mierda*. He'd given it to *Señora* Martinez. The woman who blushed. Whenever he remembered that, it pleased him. But *Señora* Martinez would have to wait. Now, there was work to be done: work Guzmán did best alone.

The cells were all empty except one. Guzmán walked to the end of the corridor and unlocked the big wooden door. Then he returned to the end cell and lifted the cover on the spy hole. Mamacita was sitting on the bunk, weeping. Guzmán opened the door, saw the fat face look up, a mask of lipstick and face paint like a drunken clown. Without his wig, Mamacita was a fat man with cropped hair and wearing white foundation. And a dress, of course. '*Buenas tardes*,' Guzmán said.

'Please.' Mamacita was suddenly agitated. 'Let me go. I done nothing. Mamacita only wanted to work, never had nothing to do with those boys and their guns. Never been involved in no crime. Let me go, *Señor Oficial*?'

'All in good time,' Guzmán said. 'There are more questions yet. When you're a policeman, you have to ask a lot of questions.'

'You ain't no policeman,' Mamacita hissed, not daring to look up.

'What did you say?' Guzmán asked.

Mamacita looked up angrily. 'You ain't no policeman. This ain't no police station either. Not a proper one.'

'I think you'll find it is.' Guzmán smiled.

'I heard what you did to that man. Juan. Heard it my very self. You dragged him off down below. Mamacita heard you, heard you say his name, heard you hit him. Then you drag him down those stairs and the door close. That what Mamacita heard. And then you come back alone and lock that door. Where he at? You ain't no policeman.'

Guzmán looked at the man. 'That's what you think, is it?'

'Yes.' Mamacita looked down, his voice petulant.

'And you won't answer my questions?'

'No.'

'Well, I can't make you,' Guzmán said. 'Not here, anyway.' He reached into his jacket and produced the Browning, pushing the muzzle between Mamacita's eyes. Guzmán looked at him. 'Are you sure I can't tempt you to assist in my enquiries?' Mamacita's eyes bulged and Guzmán heard the fear in his sudden, rapid breathing. He cocked the pistol.

The noise animated Mamacita. 'I want to help,' he whispered.

Guzmán nodded. 'Of course you do. Because otherwise your brains will be all over this cell – it wouldn't be the first time.'

Mamacita moved as if in a trance, guided by the Browning now pressed against the nape of his neck. It was a powerful incentive and he walked obediently towards the big door that led down to the vaults. At the threshold of the doorway, he bridled, seeing only darkness beyond and feeling the cold dank air coming from below. Guzmán increased the pressure of the pistol and pushed Mamacita through the ancient doorway, to the long flight of worn steps. Mamacita slipped and fell, gibbering in fear. Guzmán slammed the thick door shut and then, seizing Mamacita's ankle, dragged him down the stone stairs. Pausing at the bottom, Guzmán turned on one of the feeble electric lights.

Mamacita was whimpering, half stunned and unable to breathe properly. Guzmán knelt and handcuffed the man's hands behind his back before pulling him to his feet.

'I won't tell.' Mamacita was almost incoherent. Guzmán took hold of the handcuffs and hoisted his hands up his back until he squealed. Bending, head down, he staggered forward, propelled by Guzmán's hold on the handcuffs. Mamacita raised his face upwards, seeing in terror the low arched roof, the strange obscure recesses with their ghastly carvings picked out in the sickly pale glow of the erratic electric lights. From somewhere in the darkness came the sound of fast running water.

'Where the hell is this place?' he groaned.

'Hell?' Guzmán said. 'This isn't hell. Purgatory maybe, not hell.' He pulled Mamacita's wrists higher, producing another shriek before continuing into the darkness. 'Hell comes later.'

They reached the end of the passageway and after that there were no more lights. Guzmán reached into a recess and brought out a torch. The beam was blinding and Mamacita looked away from it, seeing sudden illuminated glimpses of ancient brick and stone walls and the curved low ceiling above them. Guzmán yanked the handcuffs and with a groan Mamacita continued down the dark tunnel. The sound of running water grew louder. Guzmán stopped and let go of the handcuffs and Mamacita tried to stretch a little to ease the pain, muttering under his breath. Guzmán shone the light upwards.

'Look.'

Mamacita looked up. The arched door lintel of the passageway was covered in carvings. Grotesque, obscenely ugly carvings depicting the slaughter and savagery of some hellish massacre. Some of the figures were clearly human, both male and female, others merely infernal ciphers, improbable monsters whose role seemed to be to dismember and devour their human victims using an insane taxonomy of violence. Even Mamacita could see the antiquity of these malevolent runes, the stone so worn by time it seemed almost transparent in the beam of the flashlight. Above the carvings were words, carved in a pattern that followed the curve of the lintel.

VERITAS PER POENA

'What does it say? Mamacita whispered.

'The truth through pain,' Guzmán said, pushing him forwards again. The noise of water was much louder now, and it seemed to Mamacita that it came from below them. Filled with a sudden terrified vertigo, he leaned back against Guzmán for support. Guzmán twisted away in disgust and Mamacita fell, screaming, thinking he was falling into the torrent. Instead, he felt only unyielding stone. Guzmán switched off the flashlight and Mamacita shrieked at the sudden darkness.

'I'll talk. Mamacita tell you everything. Don't push me in. I'll do whatever you say. I won't say nothing about that Juan.'

'It's quite safe,' Guzmán said, putting the flashlight back on, 'look.'

Mamacita looked. Behind him was a high rock face, a solid, reassuring presence. In front, an ancient low stone wall. He crawled forward on his knees to the wall, leaning against it while Guzmán shone the light downwards. Twelve metres below, a fast-moving river flowed noisily from a jagged entrance in the rocks to their right, disappearing again some way to their left into a rocky chasm. The noise of the water was loud and powerful, constantly echoed by the cavern walls.

'Where does it go?' Mamacita asked, afraid of the answer.

'No idea.' Guzmán shrugged. 'At first I looked for it on maps and plans of the sewers but there was no trace of it. The files of the Inquisition don't mention it, yet they must have known it was here. I'll tell you something else. They never come back.'

Mamacita didn't like the sound of that. 'Who don't?'

'The ones who go into it,' Guzmán said. 'I used to think they'd surface somewhere, perhaps eventually turn up in the sea. But they don't. They just disappear.'

Mamacita began to wail. 'I'll tell you everything.'

'Of course,' Guzmán agreed, hauling him to his feet. Mamacita howled in useless protest, his shrill voice echoing above the incessant roar of the rushing water.

Guzmán continued to push the reluctant Mamacita along the pathway until they turned away from the river and into a small cave-like chamber carved into the rock. The chamber resembled a roughly hewn chapel, like those in country monasteries. Guzmán struck a match and a candle flickered into life, followed by others until there was one burning in every corner. He continued lighting candles until the small space was flooded with irregular, shimmering light. He sat on a packing case. From the writing on the side Mamacita could see it once held tins of tomatoes. Not everything here was ancient then. The thought was strangely comforting.

'Now,' Guzmán said, 'we need to talk.'

Mamacita was breathing heavily, and sweat made his make-up run down over his stubble. Blood trickled from his nose. 'Don't hit me, *Señor Oficial*. I swear I'll tell the truth.'

'*Vaya*. That's a good start. Because, as far as I can see, *señor*, you've been working side by side with those Dominican gentlemen. In my book that makes you an accomplice. And any accomplice gets what I'm going to give them when I find them, *entiendes*? Unless, of course, that accomplice is helpful.' Guzmán's tone was measured and even, making him even more intimidating. 'Tell me what you know about them.'

'They buy my place,' Mamacita babbled. 'I came over from the Old Country ten years ago. *Mi tio* gave me money for a ticket. I had to leave, see – some trouble in a bar where I worked. Lot of the people, they don't like my type and they very violent.'

'Sounds my sort of place,' Guzmán said.

'So I come to Spain,' Mamacita continued, 'Barcelona. Singing in bars, turning tricks. Save my money. Got my heart broke so many times but I always careful with my money.'

Guzmán snorted. 'Go easy with the details, I've led a sheltered life.'

'When I get to Madrid, at first I rent the Bar Dominicana from two guys. I hired out rooms to the whores, put on music, the place was real popular.'

'And degenerate,' Guzmán grunted.

'It was home for those who liked it,' Mamacita said defensively. 'You could get a plate of three coloured beans, just like you got back home, the colours of our flag. You could get any sort of drink. You could get a woman, or a man. Whatever.'

'And the owners gave you protection?'

'*Si, señor.* For a year or two. Then they go to jail. They didn't pay whoever they needed to pay – some soldier or civil servant: that how it works, no? One of them been in the war on the other side, got found out: he still inside now. Other guy got injured in a fight and died in prison. So Mamacita buy the place from his wife. She don't want to stay around in Madrid after that.'

'Intelligent woman.' Guzmán took out a cigarette and lit it with one of the candles.

'Mamacita really like a smoke, *Señor Oficial.*'

'You sound like my *teniente,*' Guzmán said. 'Just keep talking.'

'I buy the Bar Dominicana and then everyone pay Mamacita. Until this year.'

'What did you do with the money?'

Mamacita blinked in the flickering light. 'Tucked away, *Señor Oficial. Banco Hispano Americano.* Savings account. Someone who help Mamacita, she be very grateful to them. Mamacita always pay good money to those who help her. We could go get it now. I could change it for dollars, if you want.'

Guzmán was used to people offering him bribes. He was used to taking them as well, but money wasn't what he wanted right now. 'We'll see. Maybe we'll make an arrangement later. You said you bought the bar. What happened after that?'

Mamacita swallowed. 'This year, men come to see me. Men from the Old Country.'

'Goldtooth?'

'Yes, Don Enrique. Very nice man, strong man.'

'Less detail, *coño*, do you want me to get angry?'

'He make good offer to Mamacita. He buy Bar Dominicana. He be the boss but Mamacita run the place for him and he pay Mamacita a salary. Like a job – see?'

'Yes, I understand how it works.'

'*Perdóneme, Señor Oficial.* He buy the place and use upstairs for him and his friends. The whores, they stay and Mamacita still make money from them. All Don Enrique want is sell a little dope, play some cards.'

'Clearly the man's a saint,' Guzmán said. 'Keep going.'

'Don Enrique start asking Mamacita for information. He start using the place to meet people to buy property. Bars and cafés. Rough places, places where you do business and the law don't bother you. And they got a place in the centre where they keep their supplies, a warehouse on Calle Maestro del Victoria. I bet you never knew that, *Señor Oficial?*'

'You're right.'

'A warehouse. That where they keep all their dope. And they got a big sign that says "Pharmaceutical Products of Spain".'

'And Don Enrique bought all these places, did he?'

'He buy these places, but you know what?' Mamacita paused. 'It nòt him who pay for them. It a man. Another man, an important man. Big boss. He got plenty dinero. And he like to spend it.'

'So he bought these properties through your Dominican pals?'

'He keep his name out of the deals. Far as Mamacita see, he tell them what he want to buy, and then they send round some respectable guy to put in the offer. They use about four different guys.'

'Let me guess. These respectable types, did they use assumed names?'

'*Absolutamente, señor.* You real smart. They get these guys from Don Bartolomé's place. *Le conoce usted?*'

'No, I don't. What's his place called?'

'Café Almeja. Nice place. Lots of young guys. They have rooms.

Young guys needing money, they negotiate a price, go upstairs. Don Bartolomé get a cut. Real nice place.'

'Never heard of it,' Guzmán growled. 'What's the address?'

'It's in La Latina. Calle de la Ribera de Curtidores. Bottom of the hill. You know it?'

'Do I look like a taxi driver?' Guzmán snapped. 'Anyway, who was this important man putting up the money to buy these properties?'

'They never say his name when I'm around. Not like I can just say hey, *señores*, sorry to interrupt but please tell me who you all talking about. I can't say that now, can I?'

'You mean you don't know his name?'

Mamacita shook his head emphatically. 'Never know it. And they always go and meet with him someplace else. They keep it very quiet. I don't know who he is, I swear.'

'Never mind, you're being helpful. So what else can you tell me?'

'All these bars they buy,' Mamacita said, 'they sell their dope through them. Then one day they get a delivery, a couple of sackfuls. They take it upstairs. And one guy goes out, says he going shopping. He come back later and let me tell you, it was some weird shit he bought.'

'He showed you his shopping list?'

'I see the packaging afterwards. What you think he buy? I tell you. Bags of flour and rat poison. What you think of that?'

Guzmán lit another cigarette. 'What did he do with that stuff?'

Mamacita brightened. 'Next day, the junkies start turning up dead. They'd cut the dope. Put too much shit in it. Rat poison – *hombre*, that stuff dangerous.'

'You don't say. Why did they do it?'

'I don't know. Mamacita not going to ask questions like that. After that, we get raided by you and your boys. All that shooting. And now, poor Mamacita in jail and never done nothing.'

Guzmán stood up. 'That was quite useful.'

'I did say Mamacita help you, *Señor Oficial*.'

'You've been a great help.' Guzmán took off his jacket and

placed it carefully on a ledge. He loosened his tie and removed it before starting to unbutton his shirt.

'*Que pasa?*' Mamacita asked uncertainly.

'I'm getting undressed.' Guzmán placed his shirt carefully on his jacket.

'That fine with Mamacita, *Señor Oficial,* I give you good time. I give you all the information you want and now we have some fun, yes?'

'Yes.' Guzmán took off his shoes and unbuckled his belt.

'You a big man,' Mamacita said approvingly. 'Powerful man. Big muscles.' He watched Guzmán carefully fold his trousers and place them on the ledge. 'I give you real good time, *Señor Oficial.* Real good.'

'Yes you will,' Guzmán agreed, pulling his shoes back on.

Mamacita looked at Guzmán uncertainly. 'Don't stop now, baby.'

Guzmán took off his watch and placed it next to his clothes. 'Don't flatter yourself,' he grunted. He moved towards Mamacita, the candlelight flickering on his heavy body. 'That's a new suit,' he said.

'New suit?' Mamacita's streaked clown face looked up at him, uncertainly.

Guzmán nodded. 'It cost a lot, and I don't want to spoil it.'

Mamacita still didn't understand. She gaped as he came nearer. 'What gonna spoil your suit?'

'The blood,' Guzmán said. 'I don't want to get your blood on it.'

MADRID 1953, CALLE MESÓN DE PAREDES

Guzmán took a taxi to Puerta del Sol and walked the short distance home, stopping frequently to see if he was being followed. Even on the stairs of his building he was careful, keeping the Browning in his hand, listening for the Judas sound that would betray someone hiding on one of the landings.

He opened the array of locks on his door and entered the apartment. Pulling back the carpet in the living room, he lifted the loose floorboards. The documents of those he had killed, their money and identification, all went into the hiding place alongside his other treasures. Everything was in order. He replaced the floorboard and pulled the carpet back into position. Then he washed and put on clean clothes, before going into the kitchen in search of food.

He poured a brandy and found a chorizo which he ate in great angry mouthfuls. He checked the Browning, ensuring the action of the big semi-automatic worked smoothly, listening to its metallic cadences as he squeezed the trigger on the empty chamber. How he loved this weapon, its destructive power, the fear it provoked. He could spend hours taking it to pieces, cleaning and oiling it, ensuring it functioned perfectly. It was the possession he loved the most in this world.

Love. It was not a word Guzmán used often. It made him think of Alicia Martinez. The first woman in years who'd interested him. Normally a selection of whores kept him happy when the need took him, like any Spanish man. But Alicia Martinez was respectable and she had responded to Guzmán with politeness. A respectable woman: he tried to imagine it for a moment, them as a couple, *Comandante* and *Señora* Guzmán. Such things were not impossible. These were things people did. Other people, in other lives. It was unlikely, he knew. Given his work, how could he return home to a wife and make small talk with the blood of his victims still on him?

Guzmán still didn't understand what he felt about her. Couldn't understand. Normally, he took what he wanted. Yet with *Señora* Martinez, he hadn't even used her first name. She'd stood up to him, afraid but defiant. And he let her. He thought so much of her he'd had her tortured – within limits, of course – to ensure she'd kept nothing back about the letter from Guzmán's mother. He could trust her. And she had softened to him – or was it the other way round? He could still feel the touch of her hand on his. But could he exempt anyone from the premise which made him so good at his job and kept him alive? *Suspect everyone and no one can betray you.* The trouble was, *Señora* Martinez was different. He never thought someone like her could come into his world. And now she had, he wasn't sure how to handle it. He needed to spend more time with her. Learn her ways. Perhaps there would be time when this was over – if he survived. But, as ever, work came first. Now, he had to find this Don Bartolomé at the Bar Almeja. If Guzmán could find out who the Dominicans had used as intermediaries in their property-buying, that would at least be a start. There was just one more thing to do before he left. He telephoned the *comisaría* and asked the sarge to check the name of the owner of the pharmaceutical warehouse on Calle Maestro del Victoria.

MADRID 1953, BAR ALMEJA, CALLE DE LA RIBERA DE
CURTIDORES

The taxi slowed as it came down the steep cobbled hill. *Bar Almeja.* The sign was illuminated, but only just. From inside came a faint sound of voices and music. Guzmán got out of the taxi, taking care not to tip the driver who leaned out of his window as the car pulled away: 'I hope your boyfriend's waiting, *maricón.*'

Guzmán pushed open the door to the bar, stepping into a warm fug of cigarette smoke and cheap cologne. It was crowded and heads turned towards the door as he came in. His menacing build and hostile stare indicated he was not there to find company and he noticed how the men's eyes quickly lowered, how they turned away and attempted to resume conversations or suddenly developed an interest in their newspapers. His presence cowed the room, voices turning to whispers, hands moving away from the hands of others, a sudden desire to maintain distance where previously there had been clandestine proximity. Even the music stopped.

Guzmán made his way to the bar, the crowd of drinkers opening before him. He placed his foot on the bar rail and leaned forward.

'*Señor?*' the barman asked, uncertainly.

'*Comandante* Guzmán, police. I'd like to see Don Bartolomé.'

The barman's face scarcely moved but Guzmán saw his fear. He had good reason to be afraid.

'Don Bartolomé is working upstairs, sir. In the office.'

'Then you can show me the way,' Guzmán said evenly, 'before I start to take an interest in you rather than your boss.'

The man swallowed hard, gesturing towards a door at the far end of the bar.

'After you.' Guzmán followed the barman up the narrow stairs, his heavy steps muffled by the dusty, threadbare carpet. A landing, dark timbered and shabby, a lamp on a table providing meagre illumination. Beyond the landing, a series of numbered doors on either side of a corridor. Guzmán turned the handle of the first door and opened it. Total darkness. He pressed the light switch, spilling grey light over the sparse furniture in the room. A bed, a sink in one corner. A chair.

'You have guests here,' Guzmán said. 'I don't remember seeing a permit to run a hotel on display in the bar.'

The barman looked increasingly worried. 'These are private rooms, *señor*. They are...' he paused, 'not for accommodation.'

'I can imagine,' Guzmán sneered. 'Where's the office?'

The man pointed down the corridor. 'Near the end. Number twenty-four.'

'I'll follow you.'

Hearing a faint noise from one of the rooms, Guzmán wrenched open the door and reached for the switch. The room was suddenly illuminated in a bilious light. The two men in the bed were a twisted knot of limbs amid the tangled cheap sheets. They looked up in outraged surprise.

'Who the hell are you?' The man on top leaped from the bed, clutching a sheet to cover himself. 'I'll call the police. This is monstrous.'

Guzmán took a step towards the man and punched him in the face. He slumped to the floor groaning. The other man screamed in a voice so high even Guzmán was disturbed by it. 'Christ.' He stepped back into the corridor and closed the door. The screaming stopped and was replaced by sobbing. Guzmán pushed the barman along the corridor.

'I only serve the drinks,' the barman spluttered. Sweat ran down his face, despite the cold. 'I have nothing to do with what goes on here.'

'That's what you say.' Guzmán stopped outside the door of room twenty-four and raised a cautionary finger to his lips. 'Go on, get lost,' he whispered. The barman obeyed, moving quickly to the stairs. Guzmán opened the door and stepped inside.

It was a cramped and shabby office, a desk facing a small window at the far side of the room. The man sitting at the desk turned. Middle-aged, flabby-cheeked, balding. A thick moustache. Guzmán noted the cut of his jacket. Quality. Silk shirt and tie. Expensive shoes.

'*Quien es usted?*'

'*Comandante* Guzmán. *Policía.*'

'Bartolomé Alvarez, *para servirle.*' Alvarez looked at Guzmán impassively. 'Can I help you?'

'I'll let you know,' Guzmán said, noting the man's expensive ring and his fancy watch. 'Business is good then, Don Bartolomé?'

'I can't complain, *Comandante*,' Alvarez said languidly. He seemed very self-assured. That was reason enough for Guzmán to dislike him.

'I can.' Guzmán sat down and lit a cigarette. 'Do you realise just how many charges I could bring against you for running this place? Even renting rooms without an official permit is a serious offence. Doing so for the purposes of pederasty and prostitution as well means I could throw the book at you.'

Alvarez smiled. Guzmán was astonished. He was expecting a stumbling explanation, perhaps the offer of a bribe. Not the patronising grin of some backstreet ponce.

'I think the *comandante* is perhaps a little confused,' Alvarez said, maintaining his supercilious air. 'This is one of those businesses you have no need to worry about, *señor* – if you get my meaning.'

Guzmán felt indecisive, wondering precisely how he would begin the beating.

'What I'm saying,' Alvarez continued, compounding Guzmán's anger, 'is that these premises are protected. I don't expect to be bothered by you or your colleagues because I know one phone call will be enough to curb any interest you have in my activities. Let me make it clear: I am protected.'

'Not from me, you're not.' Guzmán had had enough. He seized Alvarez by his collar, hauling him to his feet. The man continued to protest right up to the impact of the first blow. He gasped and sank to the floor where he knelt, clutching his belly. 'Who the fuck do you think you're talking to?' Guzmán snarled. 'You're breaking the law and you try to tell me it's none of my business? *Hijo de puta.*' His next words dissolved into an angry growl as he kicked Alvarez in the ribs. Alvarez sprawled on the floor, groaning. Guzmán stood over him.

Alvarez struggled to his knees. He was having trouble breathing. 'Apologies, *Comandante*. A misunderstanding. Perhaps you're not aware of my little arrangement.'

Guzmán was having trouble controlling himself. '*Señor* Alvarez, I want to know about some of your clients. The ones who did the work for Don Enrique at the Bar Dominicana.'

'Of course,' Alvarez agreed, clutching his ribs, 'the property buying? What do you wish to know, *Comandante*?'

Guzmán hauled Alvarez to his feet and pushed him into his chair where he leaned forward, holding his stomach.

'Do you have anything to drink?' Guzmán asked.

Alvarez pointed at a small cabinet. Guzmán inspected the contents and took out a bottle of whisky and two glasses. He poured the drinks and handed a small glass to the other man who took it with a shaking hand. Guzmán filled a glass for himself and swallowed a large mouthful.

'You were aware of what these men were doing?'

Alvarez nodded. 'Assisting with the acquisition of commercial properties...'

'If you treat me like an idiot, *señor*,' Guzmán said quietly, 'I shall maim you and believe me, I'm not exaggerating: we do it quite often in the *Brigada Especial*.' He waited for Alvarez to take in the fact that he wasn't dealing with some ordinary copper. Sure enough, the man's face grew appropriately pale. Guzmán continued, 'They were engaged in buying properties using assumed names. Properties destined for use in illegal activities. You were aware of this, so we've already established your guilt. All that remains is for you to assist me by giving me the names of the men involved. If you don't, then you're under arrest and we'll continue this conversation in a cell in my *comisaría*. *Entiende*?'

'I understand.' Alvarez nodded eagerly. 'Of course I'll assist.'

'I want the names of all the men involved.'

'Of course,' Alvarez nodded, 'they weren't bad boys, *Comandante*, I assure you.'

'Names and addresses,' Guzmán growled.

'They're in my card index.' Alvarez turned to his desk and fumbled with a series of neatly written cards arranged in an ornate walnut box. After a couple of minutes, he produced four cards and handed them over.

Guzmán looked at the first card. It was written in a clear script: name, age, interests and pastimes, employment. He went through the other cards. All men aged under twenty-five, all single. Two with no known employment. One working in a library. And the final card, *Jaime Posadas*, aged twenty-five, employed as a civil servant at *Servicios de Inteligencia Exterior y Contra Inteligencia* – or at least he had been: a line had been drawn through the words.

'Jaime Posadas,' Guzmán said. 'I want his address.'

'That young man?' Alvarez said, with a flicker of a smile. 'A very popular choice, *Comandante*, in much demand. You obviously have taste in your companions. There are others beside yourself who—'

Guzmán smashed his glass into the man's face. Alvarez screamed as he fell from the chair. He lay, clutching his face with both hands, blood oozing through his fingers.

'I only want his address,' Guzmán said, brushing shards of glass from his hand.

'My address book,' Alvarez groaned, pointing at the desk. Guzmán yanked the man to his feet and pushed him towards the desk, blood spattering down Alvarez's silk shirt. Guzmán waited while Alvarez went through the leather-bound book. 'Jaime Posadas,' Alvarez said, relieved, handing the book to Guzmán.

Guzmán tore the page from the book and pocketed it. 'Why did you think you were immune from prosecution?' he asked.

Alvarez hunched in his chair, trembling with pain and shock. 'It was made clear when the premises were purchased from me.'

'You don't own this place?'

'Not any more,' Alvarez said. 'The property was purchased on the understanding that I would manage it for the new owner. And, in return, I was told that I could keep the profits with just a contribution, in return for which I was assured I was protected. I pay the money every month.'

Guzmán scowled. 'You pay protection money to the person who bought the place from you? Who is it? *Vamos, señor*, I want a name.'

Alvarez hesitated for a moment but thought better of it. 'It isn't paid directly to him, you understand. But we all know who it goes to in the end.'

'I said who?' Guzmán was getting impatient.

'The general.' Alvarez looked down. 'General Valverde.'

Guzmán wondered whether to kill Alvarez. Dead, he could do no harm, but alive, he could be even more useful.

'Thank you for your cooperation, *Señor* Alvarez,' he said. 'That will be all.' He opened the door and went back down the dingy corridor and through the now empty bar out into the street. Crossing over, Guzmán blended into the shadows of a small alley. If he was correct, Alvarez would be calling his protector about now. And, if he was lucky, someone might show up to protect him, belatedly of course. Maybe even Valverde himself, or possibly the Dominicans. It was worth waiting in the cold for a little while at least. The light from the bar's open door spilled out onto the dark cobbles. Guzmán drew his pistol and cocked it.

A few minutes passed before Guzmán heard them coming. The distant sound of a car being driven recklessly. A squeal of tyres, then the throbbing of a car engine coming down the hill. A large black sedan pulled up outside the Almeja and two men jumped out and ran into the bar. Big men in dark heavy overcoats. Not Dominicans. The driver of the car kept the engine running and waited in the road, constantly looking round him. Right now, Guzmán thought, the men upstairs would be taking Alvarez's description of his assailant. That would send a message to Valverde – at the very least it would annoy him to know Guzmán had found out what he'd been up to. What Guzmán had not expected were the two muffled gunshots inside the bar. No protection after all, then. The driver didn't turn a hair, waiting until the two men came out of the Bar Almeja before he got behind the wheel and gunned the engine. The other two were in no hurry either, Guzmán observed. Nor were they worried if they had been seen. The taller one even took off his hat before bending to enter the vehicle. The pale light from the bar was feeble, but even with such slight illumination Guzmán could still recognise Positano.

MADRID 1953, CALLE BERNARDINO OBREGON

A bustling street near the Plaza de Lavapiés. *Posadas certainly doesn't live well*, Guzmán thought. People passed him, wrapped in rags, their patched clothes a symbol of shared poverty. It was nine o'clock and some shops were closed though the street was still busy. Guzmán didn't care much. Being seen wasn't a problem when you were the Law. He found the entrance to Posadas' building. He waited and when a woman laden with shopping opened the door, he followed her into the hallway. She switched the hall light on, illuminating the stairway with a pale sourness, as much shadow as light. She moved to her door, turning to look at Guzmán who was studying the mailboxes.

'*Qué quiere?*' Her voice was harsh and challenging.

'I'm looking for *Señor* Posadas, *señora*,' Guzmán said cordially.

The woman scoffed. 'You mean *Señorita* Posadas. What do you want with him?'

'I have business with the gentleman,' Guzmán said.

'Business? *Hombre*, everyone who comes to see that gentleman is here on business.'

'*Buenas noches, señora.*' Guzmán climbed the stairs.

'Another *maricón.*' The woman fumbled for her key. 'I hope the police get you.'

Posadas' flat was on the first floor. The hallway was dingy and smelled of damp. Guzmán tapped on the door. Inside, he heard the sound of someone moving.

And then a cautious voice through the door, '*Quien es?*'

'*Señor* Posadas? My name is Alberto Loinaz. Don Bartolomé Alvarez sent me.'

The door opened and Jaime Posadas peered out, squinting in the half light.

'It's late,' he said, 'I was just going to bed.'

'Don Bartolomé said you'd be good company.' Guzmán smiled. 'For a man who has money.'

Jaime's face brightened. 'In that case, please come in. You're new to Madrid?'

'Oh yes.' Guzmán closed the door behind him and followed Posadas into the small living room. He paused by the window. The curtain was open, giving a clear view of the street. In the building across the road, he saw a cleaner at work in a dingy office. He sat by the fire and waited for Jaime to take a seat.

'There's some bad news for you,' Guzmán said. 'I'm a policeman.' He held up his identity card, watching Jaime's horrified reaction. 'I expect you to answer my questions truthfully. Otherwise we'll fall out. *Entiendes?*'

511

Posadas nodded vigorously. 'Of course, *señor*.'

'*Muy bien*. All I want to hear from you are answers to the questions I ask. *Nada más*.'

Posadas nodded again.

He was scared and keen to cooperate, Guzmán thought. This wouldn't take long. '*Bueno*. I understand you've been a visitor at the Bar Dominicana?'

'Don Bartolomé told me there was part-time work available.'

'And this involved some gentlemen from the Dominican Republic, I believe?'

'Yes. They said they wanted help with some property they were buying.'

Guzmán smiled. 'And what happened after you'd bought the property?'

Posadas looked worried. 'They were friendly at first. But they turned nasty. They knew where I worked, even where my office was. They started to bully me – said they would tell my superiors what I was. They didn't want me for their property deals at all.'

'I see,' Guzmán said, 'so they blackmailed you. And what did you do for them?'

'I had no choice,' Posadas said. 'You know how it is if they find out you're... different.'

'I don't know at all,' Guzmán said, 'but I do know the law stipulates severe penalties for deviancy and perversion. In fact, I could charge you right now, under the 1933 Vagabonds and Delinquents Act. You'd do hard labour. Twenty years, I'd guess. Of course,' he smiled, 'you'd have all the company you could wish for – maybe you'd like that?'

'No,' Jaime muttered unhappily.

'Then just answer my questions, *coño*. What did they want you to do?'

'They said a policeman was asking for information. Someone I knew, Francisco Peralta. He's a *teniente* at the police station at Calle de Robles.'

'I know,' Guzmán said. 'He's my assistant.'

'Then I know who you are,' Posadas stammered, wide-eyed. 'You're *Comandante* Guzmán. Francisco told me about you.'

'He'd better not have,' Guzmán growled.

'Nothing secret. Just that he worked with you.'

'Well, it's good to know you two had a nice little chat about me,' Guzmán sneered. 'Who knew *Teniente* Peralta was coming to see you? Which one of the Dominicans was it? Was it this one?' From his pocket, Guzmán produced the photographs Valverde had given him. Jaime looked at them and selected one. Goldtooth.

'Don Enrique,' Posadas said. 'He did most of the talking. At first, anyway.'

'Someone else took over from him?'

'Yes, but not one of the Dominicans. They said if I helped them I'd be well paid. And that I had to meet someone important. He came to the bar.'

'Who was this important person?'

'I don't know his name. But he wasn't Dominican. Or Spanish.'

'You're sure? He didn't have grey hair, big moustache, look like a soldier?'

'No, he was quite young. Very fit, muscular. Tanned as well.'

'*Joder*, I want to know who he is, not marry him,' Guzmán snapped. 'If they didn't say his name, where was he from?'

'He was a foreigner. They called him the *Americano*.'

Guzmán smiled. 'You're doing very well, Jaime. Keep this up and we'll have you back in the civil service in no time.'

'He wasn't the usual *Americano* from South America. You could tell. He was a *Yanqui*. He spoke good Spanish.'

'So this gentleman told you what to give to *Teniente* Peralta?'

'*Exactamente*. He had some cuttings and told me what I should say and how I should act. I had to get rid of the real information our people in the United States had provided and put the stuff he gave me in its place – that was easy. Then Francisco came to see me. Things went well at first. I gave him the information and he was pleased. We chatted for a while but then he turned nasty. His wife was always hostile to me and that came up. There was a scene and he denounced me in front of my colleagues. He even hit me. I had to resign.'

'I know,' Guzmán said. 'But these things can be changed – as long as you're cooperative. You just have to know the right people. Like me.'

'Really?' Jaime asked.

Guzmán nodded. 'Tell me, the material from the United States, did you destroy it?'

Posadas looked down. 'They told me to.' His face told Guzmán he was lying.

Guzmán restrained an urge to slap him. 'Jaime, if you kept any of that material, it will help you a great deal in getting your job back. Now, what did you do with it?'

'I did wonder if I was doing the right thing. So I brought it home. Just in case.'

Guzmán looked at him in surprise. 'Here? You've got it here?'

'Over there, in the drawer.'

Posadas went over to the bureau by the window and rummaged in a drawer. Guzmán followed him, and stood by the window. Snow was falling again, blurring the light of the street lamps. The cleaner was still at work in the office opposite. Guzmán turned to see what Posadas was doing.

'What the fuck's this?' Guzmán snapped, pointing to the growing pile of pornographic magazines on the table. Guzmán could see the titles; *Hombre, Chicos, Macho.*

Jaime pushed past him, shoving some of the magazines to one side. 'I'm sorry, I put the papers in these – I didn't think anyone would ever look for them in there. Look, it's in this one.' He opened one of the magazines and took out a couple of sheets of typed paper. Guzmán saw the words at the top: *Alto Secreto: Alfredo Positano.*

'And the other material?' Guzmán asked.

'Somewhere in these other magazines,' Jaime said. 'I'm not sure which. I'll find it, though.'

Guzmán looked out of the window again. The snowfall was

heavier now. The light in the office across the street went out. He turned away and took the paper over to the lamp to read it. Framed against the window, Jaime continued babbling a litany of apologies as he rummaged through his magazines.

The window exploded in a white hailstorm of shattered glass. Something wet hit Guzmán in the face and he staggered backwards, colliding with Jaime's armchair and falling heavily. He lay, winded for a moment. He looked at his hand. It was covered in blood. He looked over to Posadas. The young man was lying face down, motionless. Guzmán saw no sign of a wound until he rolled Jaime onto his back and then he understood. The sniper across the street had fired one round straight between Jaime's shoulder blades. Guzmán could have put his fist in the exit wound. He looked round the dingy apartment and saw the splashed blood on the walls. It was Jaime's blood that had blinded him momentarily.

Pushing the paper Jaime had given him into his pocket, Guzmán crawled to the door, knowing if he stood up he would make himself a target. He reached for the door handle and twisted it. The door opened and, as it did, the wood above him suddenly trembled and splintered under the impact of bullets. Guzmán heard no shots. It was a professional then, using a rifle with a silencer. He crawled forward into the hallway, scrambling to his feet once he was clear of the door. To his left, the hall led to a single window. Guzmán could see the steps of a fire escape through the glass. To his right was the landing and beyond were the stairs. He heard the sound of footsteps in the lobby. Drawing the Browning, Guzmán ran to the top of the stairs. Four men were starting to make their way up, weapons drawn. Guzmán raised his pistol and fired, hitting the nearest man in the face, sending him tumbling backwards into his comrades. Guzmán fired again, scattering the survivors as they dived for cover.

He ran back down the hall towards the window. Hearing the sound of feet on the stairs behind him, he turned and fired at the man crossing the landing. The man ducked back out of sight. Guzmán ran to the window and tried to open it. The catch was old and rusty and he abandoned it for a moment, turning to fire as the man came down the hallway after him. This time, the man fell, clutching his belly. Guzmán fired again and the man keeled over against the wall and lay still. There was no time for subtlety now, and Guzmán brought the butt of his heavy pistol down on the metal window catch, breaking it away from the rotten wood. Hearing something, he quickly turned, aiming back up the hallway, but saw no one. No one alive, anyway. He tugged the window open with one hand, still aiming the pistol down the hall. Outside the window, the flimsy-looking fire escape led down to a narrow alley running between the buildings.

Guzmán swung his legs over the sill and slid out onto the fire escape. Crouching on the small platform, he aimed down the corridor, resting his hands on the sill. Let them come, he thought, raging. They would all die. But no one came. They were either waiting for back-up or they'd gone. But whatever they were doing, they'd bought enough time for the sniper to get away from the building opposite. Guzmán briefly considered going back to Posadas' room to search for the other intelligence material but decided against it – if his attackers were expecting back-up, he would be cornered in there.

He climbed down the fire escape awkwardly, scanning above and below with the Browning as he descended the rickety steps to the alley. There was no sign of his attackers and he made his way to the far end of the alley, emerging into a small street. Seeing a bar, he went in and ordered a brandy; the barman poured it quickly before making himself scarce in the kitchen. Guzmán realised the few customers in the place were also looking at him curiously. It was when he looked into the mirror behind the bar that he understood. His face was a streaked red mask of Posadas' dried blood. Guzmán hurriedly found the toilet and cleaned up before returning to the street.

At a stall a man was frying *churros*, placing the lines of batter into the deep hot fat before covering them with sugar and salt. The smell of frying filled the cold air. Guzmán bought a paper bag full.

They tasted of salt and fat and sugar. Luxury. Guzmán strolled down the cold street, peering into shop windows, savouring the sweet-salt batter. He walked contentedly, breath steaming in the winter chill. Some people could cook *churros* just right, he thought, and when they do, there's nothing finer on a cold night like this. He wandered on, window shopping while he ate, the grease dribbling down his chin. He had one thought, and it almost spoiled his enjoyment of the *churros*. He didn't yet know how he was going to deal with Valverde and Positano. He could expect little help from Gutierrez: the *coronel* was clearly waiting to see what happened in the next two days. Even though Gutierrez didn't trust Valverde, he was biding his time, playing games with photographs, not committing himself. He had no need to take sides yet, the bastard. The man was a survivor, Guzmán thought, you had to give him that.

A shop ahead was still open. Its window was almost empty, the shelf covered with what looked like it had once been a piece of velvet. At the centre was a large glass ball with a handwritten card next to it:

Juanita, Genuine Gypsy – Fortunes told – Tarot and palm readings

Love potions – Husbands and Wives found – Luck restored

Guzmán stopped, finished the last *churro* and screwed the paper up, tossing it into the gutter. Wiping his mouth on his sleeve, he entered the shop. The room was small and draped with dark cloth embroidered with the moon and the stars in silver thread. There was a strong smell of paraffin from the single lantern that gave the room its ghastly pallor. The air felt colder than the street outside. Guzmán's eyes accustomed themselves to the gloom and, as they did, he saw the old woman sitting in the shadows. Dressed in black, ancient hands clasped on her lap, her face marked her out as the genuine gypsy her sign proclaimed. When she spoke, her voice was dry and rasping.

'*Muy buenas noches, hijo.* Can I help you?'

'*Muy buenas, señora*, I'd like my palm read,' Guzmán said, still smacking his lips from the *churros*.

'*Cómo no, hijo*? Pull up a chair. No, come nearer, *señor*, that's it, I don't bite.'

Guzmán shrugged, pulling his chair closer to the old woman. She smelled of smoke and roses: it reminded him of his time in Andalusía. There had been more smoke than roses then, he remembered. And fewer gypsies. Afterwards.

'*Qué te pasa, hijo*? Unlucky in love?' The woman took his large hand in her wizened claws. Guzmán straightened his fingers, felt her sharp nail trace the lines on his palm.

'Bad things are happening,' he said. 'I want to know how they'll turn out.'

The gypsy sighed. 'We all do, *hijo*. A *ver*.' She bent closer to his hand. 'I see a woman. Is there a woman in your life?'

'The possibility exists.'

'She wants you. She's searching for you. Dreaming of you. Yet she can't find you.'

'The woman I'm thinking of knows exactly where to find me,' Guzmán said.

'Really? So you know her already?'

'Yes. Her name is—'

The gypsy interrupted, 'I know what her name is, *hijo*. I can hear her friend talking to her, using her name: Ana, Ana María.'

Guzmán snorted. '*Joder*, she's called Alicía. What kind of gypsy are you?'

The old woman continued staring at Guzmán's palm. She frowned. 'I see great violence. Were you in the war?'

'Who wasn't?'

'And I see...' She stopped, releasing Guzmán's hand as if it had burst into flames.

'What?' Guzmán asked.

The old woman struggled to her feet, crossing herself frantically. 'Get out. *Por Dios*. Leave me alone. I can see no more.'

Guzmán stood up, annoyed. 'What did you see?'

The gypsy backed away. 'I saw the dead. All of them. *Dios mío,* how many? I saw them dying. And I saw who killed them.'

'Who?'

'You, *hijo de puta.* What are you?' She backed away and staggered, grasping at the drapes for something to keep her upright. One of them ripped from the nails holding it and she stumbled and fell to the floor, thrashing beneath the dirty black fabric. 'Get out. Get out. *Dios ayúdame.*' She began to crawl, moaning softly for the Lord to help her.

Guzmán threw a twenty-dollar bill onto the floor in front of the gypsy. 'That was rubbish. But here, get yourself something with this.'

The woman picked up the money.

'So you didn't see what's going to happen to me?' Guzmán asked, irritated.

The gypsy looked up, dark eyes reflecting the dim lamp. 'Death,' she said. 'I saw you and the others. You were bleeding and beaten. They were standing over you. Laughing.'

'*Mierda,*' Guzmán walked to the door, 'some fucking fortune-teller you are.'

After he had stormed out, the gypsy struggled to her feet, hurried to the door and locked it, fearful he would return. She shuffled back to her chair. Picking up the lamp, she held it close to inspect the banknote. It was real, enough money to feed her for a long time. Carefully holding the lamp away from the drapes, the gypsy burned the banknote and ground the ashes into the floor before spitting on them. She heard the woman's voice again, this time more faintly. The man denied knowing her but the gypsy had heard the voice clearly.

'*You're a liar Ana María.*'

She'd heard it all. Their laughter, a door opening and then the screaming. She shuddered. She was an old woman. She couldn't stand an experience like this again. When she touched his hand, she heard him wondering whether to pay her or kill her. He thought it unlucky to kill a gypsy, that was what saved her and why he left the money. Still worse, she had heard more than one voice arguing as to whether she lived or died.

She shuddered. Her sister lived in Jerez. In the morning she would pack her things and take the bus there. She could no longer stay here. Not now. Not now he knew where she lived. Not after what she had seen.

CHAPTER TWENTY-FIVE

The car sheltered in darkness beneath the strange outline of the old church. There were few people about. No one to notice two women in a darkened car.

'What time is it?' Galindez asked.

Tali looked at her watch. 'Almost midnight. How appropriate.'

'Listen, I still feel stupid for accusing you of helping the *Centinelas*. It was ridiculous. Forgive me?'

Tali shifted uneasily in her seat. '*No te preocupes*. Shit happens.'

'I'd rather you said you forgive me.'

'*Por Dios*, drop it, will you?' Tali's voice was suddenly sharp. 'I'm wound up enough already, OK? We still don't know what Judge Delgado is going to do with those papers we gave him and we've probably got Sancho and his ugly mate trailing us. And if that's not enough, now we're going back into Castle Dracula.'

'Fair enough,' Galindez sighed. 'Shall we go in and get it over with?'

'Let's. It's time we knew what's hidden down there.'

Galindez shuffled the pages of the manuscript she'd been reading by torchlight. 'I have a feeling this paper won't be going into Luisa's final report after all.'

'Publish it in a forensic journal, Ana. That will give it more credibility anyway.'

'We'll see. After tonight, I may have more to add to it.' Galindez put the manuscript on the back seat and got out of the car. Pale light from the street lamp spilled in, illuminating the title page. Bold, black letters: *Guzmán: The Vengeance of Memory.*

521

*

The street was silent. Deep layers of nuanced shadow broken by pallid street lights. They crossed the road cautiously, peering into the surrounding darkness with nervous apprehension. Tali approached the big arched doorway, taking the key from her bag. A sound across the street made Galindez turn. She saw only parked cars in dense shadow. The scrape of a shoe. She gestured to Tali to open the door. Turning back to face the darkened street, Galindez felt for the Glock, pulling it from her waistband. Holding it with both hands, she scanned the shadowed cars across the street, trying to locate the source of the noise. A shadow slowly detached itself from the rest, taking shape as it moved into the pallor of the street light. The shadow of a tall man in a raincoat and hat. The air was suddenly cold. A lighter flickered abruptly, illuminating the face of the man. Galindez felt a moment of fear. *I did see him the other night. How?*

The man spoke. '*Buenas noches*, Galindez.'

Nervous anticipation exploded into anger. 'Fuck off, Sancho.'

Even in the dark, she sensed his mocking smile. 'No can do, Galindez. You've got something I want.'

'Ana?' Tali whispered, turning the key in the lock. '*Vamos.*'

'Back away, Sancho.' Galindez's voice was tight. '*Que te vayas coño.*'

Sancho inhaled, his cigarette glowing in the dark. 'I'm going nowhere, *guapa*. We need to talk to you.'

Galindez aimed the pistol at his chest, using the glow of his cigarette as a guide. *We need to talk to you.* She thought. The bastard. What could he ever say that wasn't threats or lies? *We need to talk to you.* She tensed. *We?*

A sound to her right. Agustín Benitez was ten metres away, half crouching on the pavement by the side of a parked car. As Galindez turned her pistol to cover Benitez, Sancho started to move stealthily across the street towards her.

The silent darkness shattered as Galindez fired. The sound of the shot was bitter and loud, careering around the tall buildings in fragmented echoes. Benitez fell to the ground and rolled under the car, shouting to Sancho to be careful. Galindez turned quickly and fired across the street at Sancho who dived sideways into a pool of deep shadow, his furious curses evidence of her inaccuracy.

Galindez yelled at Tali, telling her to get inside the *comisaría*. Seeing movement in Benitez's hiding place under the car, she fired in his direction. The car's windscreen exploded in a white mist of powdered glass, the bullet shrieking away into the night. Lights began to come on in some of the buildings. Galindez started to move towards the door of the *comisaría*.

'Galindez, stop,' Sancho yelled. 'Don't go in there.' He jumped to his feet and ran after her.

She turned and aimed at him. He was only four metres away. *This time, cabrón.* Seeing Galindez raise the pistol, Sancho threw himself to the ground again. The bullet struck the ground a metre from his prone body and whined away into the darkness. Sancho's startled shout echoed around the darkened street. 'Fucking stupid dyke. Put that gun away.'

Tali pushed the big door wider. 'Ana. *Vamos, rapida.*'

Galindez rushed to the door, hearing Sancho's boots clattering on the cobbles behind her. She stumbled on the step, falling full length onto the cold tiled floor of the vestibule, the pistol clattering from her hand. Tali slammed the heavy door with a loud reverberating crash. Struggling to her feet, Galindez helped close the huge wooden latch and slide home the heavy bolts at the top and bottom of the door. The door shuddered as someone outside threw their weight against it.

'They'll never get in through that. And all the windows are barred,' Galindez said, hoping she was right.

Muffled banging on the door. Sancho's voice, angry, shouting abuse.

'Let's go further inside, we won't be able to hear him then,' Tali suggested.

Galindez looked round in vain for the pistol, realising it must have fallen to the pavement as she tumbled though the door.

Once through the double doors, in the low corridor leading to Guzmán's office, all noise from outside faded away and they were once more hemmed in by the cold and silence of Guzmán's *comisaría.*

'Are you scared, Tali?'

'No, *para nada.* You?'

'Course not.'

'You're a liar, Ana María.'

'At least there's only us in here,' Galindez said, aware she was trying to reassure herself as much as Tali. Because she knew it wasn't true. They were not – could not – be truly alone here. Even in his absence, Guzmán was always present in the dark silence. The building itself was a frozen memory of what he did. *Let's hope we don't run into him tonight.*

They came to Guzmán's office. The door was still open from their last visit.

'Ana, before we do this, shall we have one last look at the noticeboard in the mess room – in case there's something we missed?'

'Why not?' Galindez said.

The mess room was still in its dismal state of slow decay, the fittings and furniture mere cobwebbed outlines, melting slowly under layers of accumulated dust. Tali shone the flashlight at a door on the far wall. The door was slightly ajar.

'Did we look in the armoury, Ana María?'

'I think so. It was empty, wasn't it?' Galindez flicked through the papers on the noticeboard.

'I'll check,' Tali said, pulling the door open.

Galindez found nothing of further interest on the noticeboard and abandoned the old memos and notices. Something was bothering her.

'Tali,' she called, 'I just realised. We left all the lights on last time. Someone turned them off.'

There was no reply. She hesitated, listening to the silence. Something felt different. A subtle change in the atmosphere.

Something wrong. 'Tali?' Galindez turned towards the armoury. There was no light coming from the half-open door. No noise. Something rustled in the darkness.

'Natalia? *Qué pasa?*' Galindez felt the edge in her voice.

A sudden chill. The door of the armoury slowly began to open. Something scraped against the inside of the door, something moving. *Guzmán.* The strange grey mist flickered abruptly through her mind and she felt dizzy. *Por Dios, not now. Not with him here.* Struggling to keep the grey fog at bay, Galindez waited as the door opened. Waited for him to emerge.

The door opened a little more and she saw it, pointing at her from the darkness. The dull grey muzzle of a pistol. Galindez recognised the outline from weapons in the ballistics lab: a 9mm Browning semi-automatic. *Guzmán's gun.*

MADRID 2009, COMISARÍA CALLE ROBLES

The cold darkness closed in on Galindez, obscuring the bleak surroundings of the mess room. Her eyes were fixed on the muzzle of the Browning pointing at her from the shadows. The oil-sheen of the metal glinted in the sallow light, the menace of the pistol abruptly closing down choices and alternatives, holding her motionless with its reptilian hypnotic power. *He knew I'd come back.*

'Stay where you are, Ana.' Tali kept the heavy pistol pointed at Galindez as she stepped from the doorway of the armoury. 'Stay still and raise your hands.'

'Tali, that's not funny,' Galindez said, simultaneously angry and relieved. At least it wasn't *him* emerging from the darkened armoury.

But this wasn't Tali as Galindez knew her, with her golden hair softly framing her delicate features. In the short time in the armoury, Tali had undergone a transformation. Now, her hair was swept back in a tight ponytail, making her face seem gaunt and severe in the half light. A black combat jacket added to her threatening air.

'Shut up, Ana. I mean it.' Tali held the pistol in both hands, aiming it at Galindez. 'If you try anything, I'll shoot you, *te juro.*'

'I don't understand. What are you doing?' Galindez said, confused.

Tali's face darkened with impatience. 'Just do as you're told. Now, pick up that bag.' She gestured to the canvas bag containing the equipment.

Galindez obeyed, shouldering the heavy bag, her mouth suddenly dry. 'Tali?'

Tali stood back, still pointing the Browning. '*Joder*, Ana María, walk ahead of me, that's it, keep your distance. Right, go down the corridor to Guzmán's office. Slowly. *Manos arriba, mujer. Arriba, coño.*'

Galindez raised her hands awkwardly as she walked along the darkened corridor towards Guzmán's office. As they reached the door, Tali shoved her in the back with the muzzle of the pistol. Galindez fell forward with a cry of pain and the bag fell to the floor as she stumbled. Tali leapt after her, bringing the butt of her pistol down onto Galindez's head as she tried to stand. With that, Galindez went sprawling, clutching her head and groaning in shock and pain. She slowly struggled into a sitting position, tentatively examining her scalp. Her hand came away bloody. She moaned. Too dizzy to stand, she looked up at Tali through a veil of blood.

'Stay there.' Tali backed away from her. 'Don't move and don't try that fists of fury thing with me either.'

Galindez pressed the wound on her scalp, trying to stop the bleeding. 'Why are you doing this?' A thin line of blood trickled down her temple.

Tali glared at her. 'It's a stick-up, *querida.* You're being robbed.'

'I haven't got anything to steal.' There was a plaintive note in Galindez's voice. 'Besides, you can have anything of mine. You know that.'

'I want Guzmán's book.'

'But that's why we're here, isn't it? To see what's in it?'

'*Joder*, Ana María, I don't give a fuck what's in his book – unlike you with your pathetic obsession with Guzmán.' She pointed the pistol at Galindez. 'But I am taking it.'

'Why would you want it?'

'Five million euros' worth of reasons,' Tali snapped.

Galindez stared at her. 'You're going to sell it?'

'I've already got a buyer, Ana. I work to order. Steal to order, if you want to be precise – and God knows you usually do.'

'Who's the buyer?'

'*Coño*, guess. They meet in secret, wear little gold rings. Begins with *C*.'

Galindez looked at her blankly. '*Los Centinelas*? You're stealing the book for them?'

'*Venga, guapa*, don't look so surprised. Who else would want some dusty old book that's seventy years old? Besides you, of course.'

'Are you,' Galindez's mouth was dry, 'are you one of *them*?'

'Me? *Qué va*. They're not exactly an equal opportunities organisation. In fact, I don't really know who they are, apart from the guy who arranged things with me. All I know is they expect a good job. And things have to be done their way.'

'You're a thief,' Galindez blurted. She felt nauseous.

Tali scoffed. 'I'm an investigator. I investigate rare things for clients.'

'And then what?'

'Then I steal them and they pay me a lot of money,' Tali said. 'It works for me.'

'If you steal Guzmán's book,' Galindez said, 'I'll go straight to the *guardia*.'

Tali shook her head. 'No, Ana, you *would* go to the *guardia*. If you lived.'

'What?' Galindez felt blood trickle into her eyebrow. 'You're going to kill me?'

'They were very specific. You're a threat to them – as I'm sure you realise. I'm sorry, Ana. That's the way it's got to be. The deal was non-negotiable.'

'Have you done this before? Killed people?'

Tali looked away. 'These things happen. I'm sorry.'

'But not so sorry you won't shoot me?'

'No, I want the money. When I was younger, we were poor. Really fucking poor. I'm not having any of that again.'

'But your dad was a lawyer.' Galindez protested. She saw Tali's expression. 'Oh.'

'My dad wasn't anything. He left when the fourth child arrived. My two elder sisters were on the game by the time I was ten. I didn't want to end up like them. And I haven't.'

Galindez wiped her eyes. Her head was spinning. There was so much blood it was difficult to see.

'Anyway,' Tali said, 'I have to get moving. I'm booked on a flight this afternoon.'

'But we...' Galindez stuttered, her head hung down as exhaustion and pain overcame her. Blood dripped onto the cracked flagstones.

'Are you still worrying about *us*?' Tali's laugh was cutting. 'You're so slow sometimes, *chica*. We never were *us*, *entiendes*? I was faking. Christ, you've led a sheltered life.' She sighed. 'People say things that aren't true, *niña*. They're called lies. I lied to you.'

Galindez continued to look down at the stone floor, trying to think. Trying to calculate the distance between them.

Tali sensed something in Galindez's silence. She pointed to the far wall. 'I never saw that photograph of Guzmán last time we were here.'

Galindez turned to look, realising her mistake even as she did so. Tali smashed the pistol onto her head once more and Galindez pitched forward onto the flagstones, motionless. Her arms and legs twitched for a moment and then she was still. A thin halo of blood began to form around her head.

'Sorry, *querida*.' Tali stepped over Galindez's body and opened the canvas bag, searching for the big, flat-bladed screwdriver. She knelt and pushed the blade into the crack in the floor. The flagstone moved slightly and she struggled, raising the broken slab, levering it up onto its edge and then pushing it backwards. It fell with a resonant crash. It was much easier now to remove the second piece and look down into the dark space covered for so long.

A thin veil of dust rose tentatively into the anaemic light. Tali lay on the flags, peering down into the darkness. Behind her, she heard Galindez's breathing, rasping and laboured. Tali turned and looked at her for a moment. She got to her feet and stepped across Galindez's outstretched legs to get her bag and retrieve the big flashlight. The halo of blood around Galindez's head was black and oily in the white beam, making it hard to tell where hair ended and blood began. Tali lay down once more by the dark space she had uncovered, placing the flashlight alongside the opening. She could no longer hear Galindez breathing.

Tali pointed the flashlight into the cavity below, leaning further into the small space, wriggling to get her head and shoulders into the opening. She looked down, following the beam of light as it cut through the darkness. There were things down there. Things illuminated in the glare of the torch. She leaned forward, desperate to see what those things were.

'*Jesús Cristo*,' she muttered.

CHAPTER TWENTY-SIX

Peralta felt the pain twisting inside him as he crossed Calle de Robles and headed for the *comisaría*. The bottle of pills Liebermann had prescribed for him were still untouched in his pocket. He had decided he would only take them when the pain became unbearable, since the side-effects sounded appalling. Then the pain came again, a soul-burning flame of agony. Peralta felt beads of sweat break out on his forehead. He stopped, reached for the bottle of pills and took two, feeling them stick in his throat before he managed to swallow them. He fumbled with chilled fingers for a cigarette and found one tucked away in his jacket pocket. He straightened it, taking care to keep the loose tobacco from spilling out as he lit it. He inhaled the strong dense smoke and it comforted him. It was one of the few things that did these days. The church bell chimed the half hour, sending deep, ominous notes shimmering down the narrow street. There was something about the atmosphere of the area around the *comisaría*, Peralta thought, a sense of malevolence and hostility. Even the local church was run by a drink-sodden madman. The whole area was beyond redemption.

In the regular police, Peralta had a real purpose, to protect society, to enact its laws, track down murderers, arrest thieves, pimps and sodomites, and to harass gypsies or Protestants, all the activities that kept a Christian society healthy and stable. He had soon realised his work here had nothing to do with a healthy society. Though Guzmán at first seemed monstrous, Peralta had thought he was the one who needed to adapt and become tougher.

But now, he not only questioned the worth of what they did, he was repulsed by it. Perhaps many of those who Guzmán dealt with had been dangerous once. But that was in the war and the war had been won fourteen years ago. Most of the men Guzmán hunted were no longer interested in armed struggle, they were beaten and cowed, fearful of the long memory of the regime. They had seen what happened when the victors took their revenge. Peralta understood how such things happened during the fighting. But things had to return to normal, surely? Let the vanquished slink back into society, try to rebuild lives shattered in the pursuit of the misguided politics that ended with the destruction of the Republic. It was time to rebuild Spain, to replace this fragmented society in which the divisions of the Civil War were sustained by a perpetually enforced memory. And, while that memory was enforced, the present was forever a prisoner of the past.

There was no building a new society. The old men who fought the war remained in power, embedded in every ministry and department, in key industries and commerce. The country was run by men who had waged bloody war in a crusade to return Spain to a mythical golden age in which a cowed and obedient population lived lives shaped by the prescriptions of the powerful: the *Caudillo*, the military and the Church. The war had taken Spain back two hundred years. He ground his cigarette into the snow.

Peralta paused. He was thinking like a traitor. Guzmán would certainly say so, but then Guzmán would, because the corruption of this regime, its malice, its implacable intolerance of any challenge or change, all these were what gave men like Guzmán a purpose in life. Although, Peralta observed, Guzmán had several agendas. At first, he'd thought Guzmán was just a fanatic like so many others. Now, he was not so sure. Not since he had listened to Cousin Juan's story at the Hotel Barcelona. And now, Cousin Juan had disappeared, as had Guzmán's mother. Peralta didn't believe Guzmán had freed Juan. He didn't believe Cousin Juan had ever left Calle de Robles.

Things were going wrong for Guzmán. He had told Peralta

repeatedly you had to take sides. You had to choose the winning side. What if Guzmán no longer was on the winning side? What if Valverde was right and Guzmán was a loose cannon who needed to be checked? Or if Guzmán lost Franco's patronage? But worst of all, Peralta thought, was what would happen to María and the baby if he were not there. Would her uncle take care of them if Peralta went down with Guzmán? That thought stayed with him as he reached the dark wooden doors of the *comisaría*. Above him, the weather-beaten flag hung limp and lifeless. As he opened the door, Peralta began to realise what he must do. *Look after number one*, Guzmán had repeatedly told him. For once, Peralta would take Guzmán's advice.

Guzmán sat at his desk. He looked tired. His ashtray was full. Peralta had the impression he had been there for hours before he arrived. Peralta and the sarge waited for him to speak.

'So you two came up with nothing,' Guzmán said contemptuously.

The sarge took a breath to speak and changed his mind. Peralta said nothing.

'We need to look at this case again,' Guzmán said. 'In the morning, they start the trade talks. If something happens to spoil those talks, we're all fucked. Me. This unit. You two.'

Peralta frowned. He was worried enough about his future without adding to it further.

'There've been some developments we should consider,' Guzmán said. '*Teniente*, you've been writing everything down. Tell me where we are with all this.'

Peralta shuffled in his seat, feeling like a child back at *colegio*. 'It seemed pretty clear to begin with, *jefe*. Our information suggested the Dominicans were a gang of serious criminals working for *Señor* Positano – a man with connections to organised crime. Our conclusions were based on the criminal histories General Valverde supplied to you, *Comandante*, and after that, I also obtained details of Positano's early involvement in crime from Exterior Intelligence.'

'Clear cut, as you say.' Guzmán nodded.

'It was fucked up from the start,' the sarge growled. 'The *Caudillo* and *Almirante* Carrero Blanco both said not to interfere. That we shouldn't piss off the *Yanquis*. We never had a chance to get hold of the Dominicans and stop them in their tracks.'

'Exactly.' Guzmán snorted smoke. 'We couldn't do anything. Gutierrez gave me the same message as well. Mess with the Dominicans and get the chop.'

'But then—' Peralta began.

'But then,' Guzmán continued, 'it turns out Don Enrique, that gold-toothed bastard, has some high rank in the Dominican armed forces. What does that tell you, Sarge?'

'Valverde's intelligence was wrong?'

'*Absolutamente.* The *teniente* found that out days ago and what did we do, *Sargento*?'

The sarge scowled. '*Joder*, I thought he made it up to get out of that trouble downstairs.'

'You bastards were thinking of killing me,' Peralta snapped, 'and yet I'm the only one who came up with anything worthwhile on this investigation.'

'I agree, *Teniente*. We should have been more interested. And particularly in why Valverde's information was wrong,' Guzmán said.

'Intel's often wrong, *jefe*,' the sarge protested.

'It is indeed,' Guzmán agreed. 'Though not when it's from the *Capitán-General* of Madrid.'

'You're forgetting the stuff I got from Exterior Intelligence,' Peralta added.

'No, I was coming to that.' Guzmán breathed out a cloud of smoke. 'That was what did it, coming on top of the information Valverde gave us about the Dominicans. It seemed straightforward: a top trade official with links to the Mob, getting his dirty work done by a bunch of Caribbean hoodlums.'

Peralta looked puzzled. 'You don't sound too sure, *jefe.*'

'I'm not. Tell me something, *Teniente*. What's stopped this investigation from getting any further? In your opinion.'

Peralta shifted in his chair. 'You really want to know?'

Guzmán nodded.

'The problem, *mi Comandante*, has been your obsession with these Dominicans. You've been determined to get them at all costs. Even when warned off by the Head of State himself you persisted with this vendetta. You thought killing them would solve everything. And because of that, you've compromised your standing with the people at the top.'

'*Qué coño eres*,' the sarge spat. 'What do you know?'

'I know about policing.' Peralta turned towards the sarge, angrily. 'All you know is killing. Face it, your job is like Missing Persons. You find people. And when you find them, you kill them. You get leads from informers, beat the shit out of suspects and then find some poor sod who fought on the wrong side years ago and kill them. That's all you do. Which probably accounts for us being in the shit with all this now.'

'So it's all my fault?' Guzmán asked. He didn't seem too displeased, Peralta noticed.

The *sargento* sighed. 'If I'm honest, boss, you did let them get to you. And of course, you've had woman trouble.'

'The fuck I have,' Guzmán shouted. 'Leave that out of this, Sarge. *Teniente*, it pains me to admit it, but you're right. I thought it was the Dominicans we needed to take down all along. But there are other things we need to consider.'

'What? More evidence?' Peralta was affronted. 'You could have shared it with us.'

'*Hostia, jefe*, if you don't tell us stuff how are we to know?' the sarge grumbled.

Guzmán pounded his fist on his desk. 'I was about to fucking tell you, but you never shut up long enough.' He took a deep breath to calm himself. 'Someone has been giving us the runaround, *señores*.' His voice was tight with anger. 'Everything we've done so far on this case has been a waste of time. A massive decoy operation and we fell for it.'

'Decoy operation?' Peralta asked in surprise. 'Which part of it?'

'All of it,' Guzmán spat. 'One big operation to fuck us up. To fuck me up. And it worked.'

Peralta frowned. 'If that's true, this bunch of thugs must have had a great deal of intelligence on us. And on you in particular.'

Guzmán smiled. 'I agree, *Teniente*. Where do you think they got that?'

'We'd no reason to suspect the reliability of the information the general gave you. At least initially. Of course, I did get the information about Goldtooth being in the army, but you ignored it.'

Guzmán scowled. 'Yes, you've already reminded us of that, thanks.'

'And Positano? The newspaper cutting showing he had a criminal history?'

'We believed that because you got the information from the same reliable source.'

'*Servicios de Inteligencia Exterior y Contra Inteligencia*?' Peralta protested. 'You can't get more reliable sources. '

'Unless your ex-school friend gave you false information?'

'Posadas? False information? He wouldn't have the ability to do that,' Peralta spluttered. 'Not newspaper clippings. You'd need specialist equipment to forge stuff like that. Specialist staff…' His voice trailed away.

'The penny dropped?' Guzmán asked.

'I was set up,' Peralta said unhappily.

'We all were,' Guzmán said. 'We thought the Dominicans were muscling in on Valverde's business interests. I was certain they'd cut the heroin with poison to discredit him as a supplier – yet the bastard was in on it. He knew we'd take two and two and make five.'

'The shooting outside the Bar Dominicana as well. It seemed a clear attempt by them to show Valverde had lost his grip,' Peralta said.

'I agree,' Guzmán nodded, 'and what happened? I became more determined to get the Dominicans. I was sure if I got them, everything else would sort itself out. And, *Teniente*, your uncle made me think he was so threatened by them, he needed my help.

535

And all the time the fucker was funding them. And working with *el Americano.* Guzmán pulled another cigarette from his packet of Ducados. 'Positano killed Alvarez at the Almeja and then he put a bullet through Posadas while I was at his *piso.* Talented man, this *Americano.*

'Brilliant,' the sarge said. 'I'd never have suspected any of it.'

'You wouldn't suspect anything if your dick dropped off,' Guzmán muttered.

He opened his drawer and put the report Posadas had given him onto the desk. The paper was bloodstained down one edge. 'Here, look at this, it's the intelligence report on Positano that your school chum never gave you, *Teniente.* Positano was in the OSS during the war – paratroopers: secret operations, commando stuff, assassinations. A tough bunch. His record tells us he never actually left the army. The OSS became the CIA in 1947. I reckon he's either Military Intelligence or CIA. Christ knows what he's up to, though.'

'So how come he's got these Dominicans working for him?'

'They're in the army – just as you said, *Teniente.*' Guzmán placed the photograph Gutierrez had given him onto the desktop. 'The army of *La Republica Dominicana.* I expect *Presidente* Trujillo loaned them to the *Yanquis.* I'll bet he was only too glad to do a favour for them.'

'But Trujillo's our ally,' Peralta said. 'More or less.'

'I'd say less. His country's thousands of kilometres away from us, it's tiny and it's next door to the US,' Guzmán said patiently. 'Who's he more likely to do favours for?'

'And General Valverde?' Peralta asked. 'If they weren't trying to muscle in on his drugs business, what's been going on?'

Guzmán breathed out a cloud of smoke. 'The Dominicans bought up property using anonymous young men to do the buying. They made it look like a typical underworld operation. Except it wasn't. All the time we were trying to keep track of the properties they'd acquired, the drugs they were selling came from Valverde's warehouse on Calle Maestro del Victoria. All paid for by Valverde. It was a front, a big fucking front to keep us occupied. It only started to make sense when the sarge checked out the warehouse's owner – it's the general. Even the brothel where they recruited the young blokes for the property acquisitions is owned by Valverde. Whatever he's up to, it's something big – it's got to be if he's gone to so much trouble to keep us off his scent.'

'Brilliant,' the sarge said again. 'It worked a treat.'

'Enough of the professional admiration,' Guzmán growled. 'The problem now is to find them. Nothing must come in the way of those trade talks tomorrow or it'll be us who take the blame. If that happens, we're all finished. Particularly me. *Señores, me entiendes?*'

'Of course I understand,' Peralta said. 'I just don't know what to do.'

'*Entendido, mi Comandante.*' The sarge was happier now, sensing action. That cheered Guzmán. He liked to see a man who enjoyed his work.

'Valverde mustn't know we're onto this,' Guzmán said, looking at Peralta.

'I haven't said anything to him that you didn't tell me to.'

Guzmán sat forward in his chair. 'Go and see him, *Teniente*. Tell him you've some information – that I'm going to follow a lead in Barcelona because I suspect the Dominicans have outlets there. He'll think we're even further off the scent than he intended.'

'I'll call him now.' Peralta nodded. 'When shall I say you're going to Barcelona?'

'Tonight,' Guzmán said. 'Early evening. He'll think he has a free hand. We'll see what he does and then we'll act.'

The phone rang. Guzmán waited for Peralta and the sarge to leave the room before answering. It was Gutierrez.

'*Coronel.* How can I help you?'

Gutierrez kept his voice low. *It's not good if the Head of Military Intelligence is worried about being overheard.*

'Bad news, Guzmán. Positano complained about your visit to see him. Claims you harassed him. The *Caudillo's* livid.'

'I think I know what will calm him down, *Coronel*,' Guzmán said. 'I just need more time. One more night, to be exact.'

'You don't have that much time, Guzmán. You stepped way out of line. You of all people know Franco doesn't expect this kind of disobedience from people he trusts. Just to add to your problems, there's something else. I've been monitoring information requests made to the different branches of security. There's one you ought to know about. Unofficially, of course.'

'Just one?' Guzmán asked.

'Pay attention, Guzmán. I'm doing you a fucking favour, man. About twenty minutes ago, the Political Information Services of the Falange received a request for information. A person we'd flagged up for scrutiny.'

'Who's the person?'

'They requested and got, an address for a *Señora* Alicia Martinez. That's all I know.'

'Who wanted to know, *Coronel*?'

'The damnedest thing, Guzmán. No one's been able to find out. Not even me.'

Guzmán slammed down the phone and ran to the door.

MADRID 1953, PLAZA DE SEGOVIA

Peralta sat on the upper deck of the old London bus as it negotiated the Madrid traffic. Earlier, he had stopped to buy cigarettes: a novelty for him. He looked down, watching passers-by making their way along the crowded pavements. He had taken two more pills for the pain and they made him dizzy.

Posadas. How had he fallen for it? The *comandante* thought him a fool, he knew. And the sarge hated him anyway. The documents had been well done. Even Guzmán had been taken in. Now, however, Guzmán had new information. Where had that come from? Guzmán hadn't even mentioned his source, which confirmed Peralta's belief the *comandante* still didn't trust him. And yet he trusted him enough to order him to go and lie to the general. Peralta was caught between those two men, each desperate to triumph over the other. Guzmán's words came back to him again: *never end up on the losing side.* At the time, it seemed just another addition to the litany of advice Guzmán heaped on Peralta. But it was more than that. It was a code for survival. The bus stopped at Plaza de Segovia and Peralta got off into the biting cold. As he made his way to the military governor's headquarters, he realised it was time to make a choice. It was a walk of only a couple of minutes and by the time he entered the building, he had decided.

Valverde sat in a leather armchair, booted legs crossed casually. Peralta sat a few metres away. Valverde's face was as ruddy as ever, the grey moustache neatly combed, every bit the general. He was faintly cordial, making a change from his usual outright disdain. An orderly brought in coffee. Real coffee, strong and delicious.

'*Teniente,*' Valverde said, 'you said you have something for me? If not, I have to tell you there are at least a thousand things more important than talking to you.'

'Of course, *mi General.*' Peralta took a sip of coffee.

'Never mind the fucking coffee,' Valverde said. 'This isn't a social visit.'

Peralta flinched. 'First, there's something I have to ask, General. A family matter.'

Valverde snorted. 'If you want a loan, forget it. I already made arrangements to pay you for information on Guzmán and so far all I've had is shit. In fact, I wondered if he was passing on crap to you just to fuck me about. That had better not be so, *Teniente.*'

'Not to my knowledge, sir,' Peralta lied. 'But if I may just ask you this one favour…'

Valverde sighed. 'If you must.'

'*Gracias, mi General.* It's this. If something were to happen to me, my parents are dead. I have only a small police pension.'

'*Jesús Cristo, hombre,* so you do want money? You fucking beggar. *Joder.*'

'No, *mi General.* I want nothing. It's María. If something happens to me, I want you to take care of her and the baby.'

'Why? Do you think Guzmán's going to kill you? Presumably for incompetence. One could see his point.'

'I'm not joking, *mi General*. I only ask this one thing. And I have information.'

Valverde sighed. 'Of course I'd see my own niece taken care of if anything happened. I love that girl. All the more since I've got none of my own. She's a lovely child. She married badly, that's all.'

'As you say, *mi General*.'

'So that's dealt with. If you die, I'll take care of María and the baby,' Valverde said cheerfully. 'Now, you say you've got information?'

Never end up on the losing side. Peralta took a deep breath and began.

MADRID 1953, COMISARÍA, CALLE DE ROBLES

Guzmán was almost running as he got to the reception desk.

'*Sargento*. I need you to make a few arrangements while I'm out.'

'*A sus ordenes, mi Comandante.*'

'I'm going to check out the location of the Dominicans,' Guzmán said. 'To make sure they'll be in when we come calling.'

'*Muy bien, jefe.* You know where they are then?'

Guzmán slid a piece of paper across the desk. 'This is the address. It's the pharmaceutical warehouse on Calle Maestro del Victoria. I'm going to have a look. If they're there, I'll call, so have a squad on standby with the trucks ready.'

'Don't take them on alone, *jefe*.' The sarge seemed almost genuinely concerned.

'One other thing, *Sargento*.'

'Of course, *jefe*.'

'Don't give this address to Peralta and don't tell him what's going on until after I call and you're on the way. *Entendido*?'

'Understood, sir. I'll keep an eye on him.'

'*Bueno*. I'll see you later.'

Guzmán stepped out into the cold. Things were happening at last and he felt the calm that came before combat. In the street small snowflakes fell softly from a threatening sky. But the weather was of no importance. He was getting closer to them, he could feel it. They had played games with him. *Him*. No one played games with him. Very few had attempted it and they had, without exception, regretted it. So far at least.

Guzmán climbed into the Buick and started the engine. He drove as fast as possible given the icy roads. This was his fault. He hadn't thought they would go after *Señora* Martinez. He thought her a part of his life that was outside work – as if it followed that his enemies would respect such boundaries. He had been stupid and careless. Again.

MADRID 1953, CALLE DE LA TRIBULETE

Señora Martinez opened the door cautiously after his first muffled knock. She peered out into the gloomy hallway. '*Quien es?*' Her voice echoed in the darkness. She recognised the bulky shape. '*Comandante?*'

Guzmán stepped forward, melting snow dripped from his coat and hat.

'Are you all right?'

'Let me in,' Guzmán said quietly. 'You're in danger.' He stepped into the small apartment. A single lamp illuminated the table where *Señora* Martinez had been sitting. Her book was still open under the lamp.

'Danger.' Her voice caught in her throat. 'Not that *teniente* again?'

'Worse. I need to get you out of here, *señora*. They've been watching you. Get your coat on.' He looked round. 'Where's little Roberto?'

'At a friend's house.'

541

'We'll pick him up later but we have to go right now. *Ahora mismo.*'

Guzmán crossed the room to the window and looked out from behind the faded curtain. It was getting dark and the road gleamed, slick with ice and sleet. He saw his car on the other side of the road. There were few others, but he noticed one vehicle, a hundred metres down the road. There was someone in it: he saw the glow of a cigarette. Someone waiting. Guzmán scanned the shrubbery at the front of the building. From the window he saw only confused shadows pooled under the tangle of scrubby trees. One of the shadows moved. No casual observer would have seen it. A slight movement, slow and calculated.

'*Vamos, señora,*' Guzmán urged. Alicia Martinez pulled on her coat and picked up her handbag. She paused at the door, straightening her hair in the chipped mirror. Guzmán raged, but he raged in silence. He waited while she locked the door, knowing they would probably kick it down anyway. *Señora* Martinez was calm. He liked that. It was only when he took out the Browning as they descended the stairs that she began to look worried. He checked the magazine. It was loaded with soft-nosed bullets, ammunition made not just to kill but to inflict the maximum possible injury. He liked that too.

Sleet fell in slanting lines through the pale glimmer of the street lamps, the wind driving needle-sharp ice against their faces as they ran towards the car. *Señora* Martinez went first with Guzmán following, the big pistol in his hand. Guzmán pulled open the driver's door, keeping an eye on the vehicle down the road. Alicia Martinez was already in the car, looking anxiously at him as he peered into the darkness.

The shot came from the shadows across the road. There was the sound of a man running and from the shadows another shot from a handgun, the muzzle flash a white star in the darkness, the bullet whining somewhere above Guzmán's head before noisily impacting on the building behind. Guzmán brought the Browning up and fired twice, the sound of his pistol loud and percussive, the ejected cartridges rattling like coins on the ground. There was a cry of pain and Guzmán heard the man's weapon clatter onto the wet road. Guzmán climbed into the car, started the engine and accelerated forwards. There were no more shots, but Guzmán saw the sudden illumination of headlights behind them as the car down the road moved forward in pursuit. Alicia Martinez was trying to slide down in her seat to get herself below the level of the windscreen.

She placed her hands on the dashboard as Guzmán slid the car around a corner at high speed '*Dios*, what have I done?' she asked, her voice taut and anxious.

'You're safe now,' Guzmán said, putting his foot down hard. The Buick's tyres squealed in protest. He smiled to himself. *She's in big trouble and she blames herself? Any normal person would blame me for all this. For being careless.* There was only one place she would be safe: behind the reinforced door with its multiple locks at Calle Mesón de Paredes. Guzmán was taking her home. The car that had been pursuing them was nowhere to be seen in the mirror. All they needed to do now was collect the boy and then he could leave them safe in his fortified *piso*. And, once they were safe, he would pay a visit to the warehouse on Calle Maestro del Victoria. It was time to settle this.

MADRID 1953, CALLE PRECIADOS

Calle Preciados was busy, the shops bustling with customers. *There's plenty of money about*, Guzmán thought. That reminded him of Valverde's bribe and he cursed. He'd have to burn it. If they could link the money to the Dominicans, Valverde's case would be proved and Guzmán would be finished. *Joder.* He had underestimated Valverde. The general had been clever, working to increase his influence with Franco, promoting his economic plans, playing his long game as he encouraged the *Caudillo* to embrace the deregulation of foreign investment. But the poisoned drugs, killing Capuchón and the shooting of the *guardia civiles*, all those were crimes Valverde could be judged for, if a link could be proved. And proof was in short supply. It wasn't the general who was in the shit right now. It was Guzmán.

The most unexpected event had been the sudden appearance of Guzmán's mother and Cousin Juan. Whoever found them and brought them to Madrid must have known he wasn't the real Guzmán. If that came out, he was dead. He should have killed every last fucker in their village when he had the chance. But then he thought he had. Who found him out? Positano and his CIA? But why would the CIA care about someone like Guzmán? The *Yanquis* didn't give a fuck during the *Guerra Civil* when Guzmán and others like him were slaughtering anyone who even remotely was suspected of being a Red. He'd had been a quick learner back then.

At least he had ruled out *Señora* Martinez from Valverde's games, though Guzmán still didn't know why she'd been picked out to deliver the letter from his mother. Sure, it was the private detective, Lopez, who gave her the letter, but Lopez had dealt with his client at a distance and he was too poor and desperate to care that he didn't know who his client was. Someone had known Guzmán intended to return to her *piso* after the raid on her neighbours. Maybe Gutierrez? Military intelligence could easily have put a tail on Guzmán. Too many questions and not enough answers, Guzmán thought. He was unused to that situation.

In the morning they would hold the trade talks. Franco, dressed in one of his many over-decorated uniforms, would climb into the leather and walnut interior of his limousine and drive in a heavily guarded convoy from the grand country house at El Pardo. The convoy would divide as it entered the city, most of the cars heading for the Trade Ministry while Franco's car and a second, full of bodyguards, would take a carefully planned secret route, rejoining the convoy as it neared the official destination. Standard practice to avoid ambush. Gutierrez would probably be with Franco or in the car accompanying him. Guzmán would do exactly the same if he were organising it. A faultless plan. *Puta madre. Unless someone else knew.* And then it could go badly wrong. Guzmán threw the cigarette down, looking round for a phone box. He stormed across the road and into the grocery. The shop smelled of its produce: hams hanging from the ceiling, baskets of dried *pimientos* and garlic on the walls, bundles of herbs. The grocer looked up from the counter, surprised by Guzmán's haste.

'*Policía.* This is an emergency. I need to use your phone.'

The grocer looked at the identity card thrust in his face and obeyed. He led Guzmán into a small office at the back of the shop and indicated the big Bakelite telephone on the desk amidst a heap of papers, stuttering his apologies for the mess even as Guzmán pushed him from the room. Pulling out a scrap of paper, Guzmán dialled the numbers on it and heard the phone ringing.

'Gutierrez?'

'Guzmán. Where are you?'

'That doesn't matter,' Guzmán said impatiently. 'I need to ask you something.'

'Actually,' Gutierrez's voice was cold, 'I'd rather you didn't. It's not very healthy to be associated with you right now.'

Guzmán took a breath. 'What are you talking about?'

'I shouldn't even be talking to you,' Gutierrez snapped. 'Listen, Valverde has been in touch with the *almirante.* He wants you arrested – he says he's got evidence that will put you in front of the firing squad.'

'And the *almirante* believes him?'

'He has to consider the general's accusations, Guzmán. I don't know what the evidence is yet, but he says it's convincing. Listen, I shouldn't be telling you this, but what the hell. If I was you I'd be considering taking a holiday. Somewhere far away. A long holiday. Take *Señora* Martinez with you. You could try, at least.'

'Fuck that, Gutierrez. *Mira,* I just need to ask you one thing.'

'Guzmán, right now you're poison. My men may be coming for you by morning.'

'Just listen. It concerns the route tomorrow. For the *Caudillo.* Not the decoy. Franco's car. I need to know the route.'

'*Eres loco*? Or are you drunk? You think I'd discuss that with you? With anyone?'

'Gutierrez, I wouldn't ask if it wasn't important.'

'Important to who? It's important to me to stay alive. And if I start sharing operational secrets with you, what happens if you go down after Valverde meets with the *almirante*? No, *hombre*, you're asking too much.'

'For Christ's sake, Gutierrez, this is urgent.'

'Guzmán, you more than anyone know how these things work. I'm sorry, but I can't.'

'You should change the route,' Guzmán said. 'If you won't tell me, then just change it. I've got a hunch—'

'*Hostia*, Guzmán. A hunch? What am I going to tell the *Caudillo*? *Comandante* Guzmán's had a hunch? Changing the route would be massively disruptive unless there's a compelling reason. I need facts, Guzmán. Facts. Not a fucking hunch. *Puta madre.*'

'Let's try it another way, then.' Guzmán mopped the sweat from his forehead. 'I'll tell you the name of the street and you tell me if it's part of the route.'

'I'm not playing games, Guzmán.'

'If you say no, I'm wrong and we drop it. If you say yes, *bueno*, you can take appropriate action.'

A prolonged sigh. 'You're going to get me shot, Guzmán. What street?'

'Calle del Maestro Victoria.'

A long pause. '*Mierda, coño*. What the fuck is going on?'

'So the route passes down there?'

'You seem to know everything already, Guzmán.'

'I don't. But I think I know who else might.'

'And you think the *Caudillo*'s life may be in danger?'

'I do.'

'And how long have you thought this?'

'About ten minutes.'

'*Jesús Cristo y todos los santos*. Look, if I take this to the *almirante*, I'm in the shit for what I've just told you and you're already in enough trouble. Christ, I'll have to do something though.'

'Look, I'm going to Calle Maestro del Victoria now. If I'm right about this, I'll sort things out there. I've arranged for support from the *comisaría*. If there's any trouble, we'll handle it. I'll call you once it's over.'

Gutierrez sighed. 'Why not? I won't be going anywhere. I'll be here. Sorting out a new route.'

'*Gracias*, Gutierrez. I owe you one.'

'Guzmán, you owe me several,' Gutierrez snapped. 'Unless we end up standing side by side in front of a firing squad.'

'If we do,' Guzmán said, preparing to hang up, 'I'll hold your hand.'

MADRID 1953, CALLE DEL MAESTRO DEL VICTORIA

Guzmán strolled casually along Calle del Maestro del Victoria. The street was narrow, framed by sombre high buildings. Apartments, a few shops, several warehouses. It was hard to miss the pharmaceutical warehouse, the large painted letters on the side clearly spelled out its function. Guzmán loitered in the doorway of a darkened shop, watching the building. There were fewer people on the street now. He looked at his watch. Eleven forty. If Gutierrez didn't stop him, Franco would be coming down this very street around nine thirty tomorrow. Gutierrez didn't entirely trust Guzmán, that had been obvious. Changing the tightly drawn-up plan would inconvenience Franco and annoy him immensely. And, if it turned out to have been for nothing, *hostia*, someone would pay. Doubtless, Gutierrez would make sure it wasn't him.

Guzmán thought angrily about *Mamá* and Cousin Juan. They didn't just turn up by coincidence: Valverde had brought them. Cousin Juan had told Guzmán that in return for a release from his suffering in the dungeons beneath Calle de Robles. *The truth through pain.* But what Juan couldn't say was whether Valverde

547

knew Guzmán was not Guzmán. Had he known, Juan would certainly have told him.

The sky was dark. Thick clouds hid the stars. The streets were almost empty. Soon it would be time. But first, Guzmán had to make sure that there was no sloppiness in the execution of his strategy. Strolling back up the street, he found a bar and used the phone there.

The sarge answered. Guzmán ordered him to bring the squad immediately and to secure the building.

'Where will you be, *jefe*?' the sarge asked.

Guzmán's voice came down the line amidst the sounds of the bar, the sound of other people's lives being lived. Laughter.

'I'll be inside the warehouse, and if anything happens to me, Sarge,' he growled, '*dales café. Mucho café.*'

'*A sus ordenes.* We'll be there soon. Don't go in alone, sir.'

Guzmán put down the phone. He didn't need advice from the *sargento*. Nor from anyone. He was Guzmán. Whoever else he had once been was of no importance.

Guzmán stood across the street from the warehouse, finishing his cigarette. He was deep in dark reverie, unsure now if there could be an acceptable ending to this. His preferred choice would have been to triumph and return to his position of Franco's favourite executioner. But that seemed unlikely. If Valverde had given Franco the information about his past or rather, the real Guzmán's past, he was finished. The odds were heavily against him. But then the odds had been worse at Badajoz, scrambling up that hillside in the heat and dust, with the Moors clambering after them, their cruel voices sharp in the shimmering air. There had been so many of them. By the end there were none. Fuck it. Let them come. The Dominicans were the only target available to him. Flesh and blood, still living, moving around in that warehouse. Laughing at him. He could almost hear their laughter, hateful and loud, like the kids at school used to laugh. Though few of them were laughing now.

There were faint pale lights in the warehouse. The warehouse Valverde had sold to the Dominicans. He crossed the street, the cold dissipating under the raging heat of his anger, humming to himself, 'Facing the sun, in my new shirt, that you embroidered in red yesterday. That's how death will find me if it takes me, and I won't see you again.' It was 'Cara al Sol', the Falangist marching song. The Republican songs were the songs of losers, Guzmán thought, songs full of resignation, of saying last goodbyes as death fell upon them, songs of the defeated, bleating at the injustice of it all. The Nationalist songs crashed like marching boots on conquered cobbles: victor's songs.

Guzmán followed an alleyway down the side of the warehouse. He walked slowly, alert to the sounds of the night. A cat passed him, eyes glinting as it darted into the shadows. Guzmán held the big pistol by his side. His plan was simple: kill the Dominicans no matter what. He would certainly get some of them, he had no doubt. But the outcome of this battle was far from certain, because even if he won it, there was still the matter of Valverde and the *Americano*. Still, first things first.

At the end of the alleyway he came to the yard, a wire-fenced enclosure filled with a sprawl of packing cases and boxes. Piles of crates were stacked against the back wall of the building across from large wooden double doors. Sheds and outhouses lined the perimeter of the yard, offering cover. Guzmán worked his way around the outer fence slowly, getting a feel for the place. The deliveries would have to be made through the front of the building. The rear door would allow them to drive right through and unload in the yard. The wire fence was unbroken: he would have to climb it. The wall of the building backing onto the yard loomed upwards in the darkness. Assuming the sarge got the squad here quickly, there was no easy way out for the Dominicans.

Guzmán holstered his pistol and took off his coat. The wire fence was about two and a half metres high. He took off his hat and threw it over. Throwing his coat up, he managed to drape it over the top of the wire and then seize hold of the upper strand, the coat protecting his hand as he heaved himself up, his feet scrambling to gain purchase on the meshed wire. Even for him it was hard work, but finally, sweating and cursing under his breath, he managed to pull himself over the top of the fence, struggling not to fall to the ground on the other side. It was an inelegant manoeuvre and added to his simmering rage. He reached up and tugged at the overcoat. It was stuck. He swore bitterly but decided to leave it. If he was going to be shot, an overcoat wouldn't help. He put his hat back on. No point looking slovenly when paying a visit.

Guzmán went towards the big wooden door, his pistol ready in his hand. There were no sounds from inside. He placed a large hand against the rough wood and pushed. The door was locked. There were windows, but these were some six metres above him. The stacks of crates reached maybe three metres or so but Guzmán could see he would never be able to access the windows from those. He moved to the side of the building where the wall of the warehouse adjoined the alleyway. A pile of broken crates sprawled in a corner. Guzmán searched but there was nothing that met his needs. The outhouses seemed more promising and he loped over to them, blending with the shadows, breathing hard from the exertion. He was beginning to feel the cold. Here was something he could use: a ladder. It was short but if he could balance it on the crates, he could reach the window. If he didn't break his neck first.

It was easy enough to push the ladder up onto the crates before climbing onto them himself. Whatever was in the crates was heavy; they were stable and offered enough support for Guzmán's weight, as long as he kept himself pressed close to the building. Cautiously, he leaned the ladder against the wall. If it didn't move he might just do it. He placed a foot on the bottom rung and stepped onto it. The ladder held. He carefully eased himself up another rung, hands gripping the side of the ladder tightly, trying to intimidate it into staying still, avoiding sudden moves that might cause the crates below to shift. His head neared the top of the ladder. The window was still another metre or so above him.

He would have to stand on the top rung to grasp the small ledge of the window.

Leaning heavily on the wall with both hands, Guzmán inched upwards. The ladder shook. He clung to the wall face, his fingers grasping the brickwork as if that would give him any purchase if the ladder fell. Tentatively, he moved his hands up to the ledge. Somewhere a dog barked and Guzmán swayed, furious until he had regained his balance. He moved his right foot onto the top rung. The ladder was trembling now. Or was that him? He brought his left foot up, feeling sweat trickle down his forehead, stinging his eyes. He reached upwards, fingers moving over the ledge until he touched glass. A creak from below. He could feel his legs starting to cramp. He felt cautiously for a catch to open the window. There was none. Again, a creak below him. This time the ladder moved. Guzmán's fingers closed on the ledge, steadying him a little. He felt the ladder shift uncertainly as it responded to his movements. If this kept up, it would fall.

Guzmán braced, his right hand taking some of his weight as his fist crashed into the glass. There was a sharp noise as the window cracked. He tried to keep his weight supported with his right hand, trying to minimise any movement on the ladder but, as he drew his fist back for another blow, he felt it moving and he struggled to hang on as it slipped, its feet skidding off the crates below and clattering to the ground.

Guzmán hung from the ledge, feeling the strain on his hands. There was only so long a man could sustain this kind of exertion and then the muscles would go. He pulled himself up until his forearms rested on the sill. With his right arm taking his weight, he slammed his left fist into the glass again. This time, it shattered and Guzmán swore as broken shards cut into his hand. Thrusting his left arm into the hole he grasped the sill inside and began to smash out the rest of the glass with his right fist. Broken pieces tore into his arm but at least he was anchored as he knocked out enough glass to haul himself over the ledge and through the broken window. He felt clothes and skin tear as he pulled himself over the

551

jagged glass before tumbling down onto rough floorboards. He reached out, fumbling blindly, discovering his surroundings through touch and intuition. It took only a moment to realise what he was touching. A toilet. He had nearly broken his neck getting into a toilet.

Guzmán drew his pistol, fumbling with his left hand for the door handle. He edged through the door. In front of him, a wide boardwalk framed the loading bay below. Pulleys, ropes and chains hung down from the floors above. They would haul the crates up there and store them. Profit for the *capitán-general.*

He stepped into the dark silence of the boardwalk. In the muted light he could just make out the sliding doors of small offices along the outside wall. The warehouse was silent. He moved slowly and carefully from office to office, checking each small room before moving on. They were all very similar. A table, filing cabinets, a Bakelite telephone in some and occasional calendars with religious or rural images. The loading bay below was in deep shadow, and above him the obscure, tangled outlines of ropes and pulleys disappeared up into darkness. He made his way along the walkway, cautious and tense, working towards the front wall. Occasional sounds came from the street, the shouts of late revellers. They were in another world as far as Guzmán was concerned. Soon the sarge would arrive with the trucks and the *guardia civiles* and Guzmán wanted the Dominicans dead by then. He slowed his pace, peering into the dark. A pale glow spilled reluctantly from one of the small offices ahead. Faint candlelight, flickering in a draught. He edged nearer. The sliding door of the office was open and he held the pistol in front of him. Another muted step and then he swung into the office, his pistol pointing straight into the face of the Dominican sitting at the desk.

The dead Dominican. By the meagre light of the candle, Guzmán saw the bullet hole in the man's forehead. The office was too dark to make out the spray of brain tissue, the blood and the bone splinters he knew would be behind the man. He didn't need to see it because he'd seen it so many times before. He paused in the door of the office, noting the silence. Maybe they were waiting in ambush – since they must have heard him break the window earlier. He crouched, scanning the loading bay below with his pistol. Staying low, he edged his way out of the door and began to creep towards the front of the building. The boardwalk creaked loudly, making him flinch, anticipating a sudden burst of gunfire. He'd have little chance if they could see him. Six of them would outgun him easily. He'd never get all of them before they cut him down. But the darkness was on his side. As always.

He neared the end of the boardwalk, pausing outside the pool of diffuse light from the front window. There was no way to avoid passing through the light unless he went back the way he had come and he had no wish to do that. Edging to his left, Guzmán pressed against the wooden wall of one of the office cubicles. By moving very slowly he could keep most of his body out of the light, presenting less of a target. He pushed his back against the wall and crouched, putting his hand down to the floor to steady himself. He recoiled in disgust: even for Guzmán, putting a hand into what was left of someone's face came as a surprise. He had felt the teeth and part of the lips as well as the gaping wound. He reached down again and explored. The man must have been leaving the office when the killer raised their weapon and shot him in the back of the head. Guzmán wiped his hand on the man's shirt. Maybe the Dominicans fell out amongst themselves and now the winners were waiting, ready to cut him down. Let them try. Plenty had.

He began to move again, still keeping low. White light flashed from across the loading bay, the sound of a gunshot and a bullet smashed into the wood above his head. Whatever the weapon was, Guzmán thought, it was bloody powerful, its report gruff and unfamiliar. He began to move again, his pistol now aimed in the direction of the shot. Nothing. Not a sound, no click of a weapon being cocked, no sign of movement. He continued to move, a few centimetres at a time, ready to turn onto the section of the boardwalk running beneath the front windows.

The world exploded in a flickering sequence of brilliant starfire from the opposite side of the building, the sudden staccato bark of an automatic rifle, the insect-whine of bullets impacting on metal, wood and glass. He kept down, pressed against the rough board floor. And then a single shot, this time the bullet whining away to his right. Guzmán brought the big Browning up, holding the weapon two-handed, aiming in the direction of the shot. The next time the gunman fired, Guzmán would fire the murderous soft-nosed bullets at the muzzle flash. Footsteps away to his right. He swung round, pointing the Browning down the boardwalk. The footsteps came nearer. And then the world became impossibly white as dazzling electric spotlights tore apart the funereal gloom of the warehouse. Half-blinded by the intense light, Guzmán saw the outline of a man coming towards him.

Goldtooth. But this wasn't the Goldtooth who had confronted him at Valverde's reception. Now he was pale-faced, one hand holding on to the rail of the boardwalk as he staggered forwards. Guzmán saw the spreading blood on his shirt and lifted the Browning, aiming at the man's chest. At least he would have this one. And then the savage blast of the automatic rifle scythed across the warehouse again. Pieces of Goldtooth were ripped away and sprayed against the office wall, pinning the Dominican for an instant to the wooden panels, the bullets tearing through him, bloody patterns sketched around the deadly geometry of bullet holes. He leaned against the wall, swaying under the impact of the bullets. He took a step forward but his legs folded beneath him and he fell towards the single low railing of the boardwalk. The railing splintered and broke. Guzmán heard the man cry out as he fell and heard the noise as he hit the stone floor below.

There was no sign of the gunman and Guzmán stayed low, scanning the far side of the warehouse. Then he looked to his left and saw it. Erected against the wide front window on a pile of sandbags, the brilliant lights reflected in the oiled metal, the sharp nose pointing down through the dirty glass of the window to the street. Guzmán recognised it. A .50 calibre machine gun. Heavy ordnance. You could shoot down a plane with that, he thought.

And the damage it would do to a vehicle would be devastating. *Especially a limousine.* He had been right. *Cabrónes.* He stood up slowly, pistol pointed at the boardwalk on the far side of the bay. Ready to kill.

Something cold pressed against his neck.

'I'd stay very still if I were you,' Positano said. 'If I get nervous and pull this trigger your head's going to fly through that window.'

Guzmán froze, his pistol still outstretched towards the loading bay.

'Whatever you're thinking,' Positano said, 'forget it. Move and I'll kill you.'

'I get the picture,' Guzmán sneered. The rage was beginning to smoulder. He had to stay calm. Otherwise he might act too soon, might try to get his hands on Positano at any cost. And that would be foolish.

'Open your hand and let the pistol fall,' Positano said, increasing the pressure of the automatic rifle's muzzle against Guzmán's neck. Guzmán dropped the gun. The pressure on his neck eased. Positano took a step back. Guzmán waited. With his back to the American it would be stupid to try anything. Something ran down his left arm. He was bleeding from the deep cuts, but he didn't care. All he wanted was Positano. To get close enough to do some damage and then strangle him. Maybe rip him apart with his bare hands and scatter the pieces around him as he had with Mamacita. But Mamacita was just a *maricón* who became a spectator to his own death. Positano wouldn't be so easy.

'Listen carefully,' Positano said.

'I can't wait,' Guzmán snarled.

The rifle butt smashed against the back of Guzmán's head and searing lights exploded across his vision. He staggered forward, his foot connecting with the Browning, sending it sliding over the edge of the boardwalk and down into the loading bay six metres below. The guard rail shook as Guzmán staggered against it. He clutched his head, trying to pull back from the drop in front of him. Positano again used the rifle as a club, holding it by the barrel and smashing the stock into Guzmán's back. Guzmán gave a howl of pain and pitched forward against the barrier. The wood disintegrated in a series of dry percussive cracks as he plunged through it into the loading bay. There was a sudden impact and the air was knocked from him. He lay, fighting to breathe, hands gripping the coarse burlap of the pile of empty sacks he was lying on, his head flooded with pain worse than any he had known. He struggled to his knees, his vision awash with flashing lights. He ran a hand through his hair, feeling blood and the swelling on the back of his head where the rifle butt had struck him.

There was a heavy impact on the pile of sacks as Positano jumped down from the boardwalk above. The man rolled smoothly, uncoiling in a single fluid motion, still holding the automatic rifle, keeping it aimed at Guzmán as he stepped towards him.

'Paratrooper?' Guzmán struggled to conceal the pain in his voice. 'I recognise the—'

Positano brought his boot savagely up into Guzmán's crotch. Guzmán's involuntary cry of agony choked on itself as he suddenly vomited, folding over, clutching himself. The pain was an excruciating revelation, holding him a prisoner of his own body, unable to move without discovering new intolerable constituencies of nauseating agony. He snorted back another cry and made a fierce effort to sit up but the pain was too much. He retched and fell back onto the sacks.

'Now we can talk,' Positano said, the automatic rifle dark and menacing, aimed straight at Guzmán's chest. 'I didn't think you'd be much trouble.' He laughed. 'Big fuck like you, used to roughing up old men and women. First hint of trouble and you roll around moaning and puking. Typical of this country. Just like your *Caudillo*, Guzmán, him and his pathetic army, his pathetic government and all the other shits who hang onto his coat tails. All talk, all bluff and no balls.'

'Fine,' Guzmán panted, 'throw the rifle over there and let's see if you're right.'

Positano laughed. 'If I did, I'd still win. I trained as a soldier, Guzmán. And I keep in training. Not like you. You beat the Republic because the fucking army turned traitor and the Nazis and Italians pitched in on your side. And to fight what? Peasants, commies and vegetarian anarchists. You must have known all along you were on the winning team.'

'Not quite.' Guzmán smiled grimly. 'No one could be sure back then. Sometimes you had to pick sides according to circumstance.'

'Well, you sure picked the right one,' Positano said.

'I did.' Guzmán wiped a lock of hair from his eyes. 'We won. End of story.'

'I don't think so.' Positano stood up. 'Sure, Franco's had thirteen years of fun: shooting the losers, dressing up like the king, looting the economy. But know what, Guzmán? It's no way to run a country.'

'I like it,' Guzmán said, measuring the distance between them. 'It suits me very well.'

Positano moved quickly and without warning. The rifle butt cracked into the side of Guzmán's temple and as he rolled back clutching his injured face, Positano again brought his boot slamming down into his groin. This time, Guzmán's cry was a primal, uninhibited articulation of pure pain. He curled in a ball, fingers digging into the sacks, unable to move until he had to lift his head in order to puke.

'It must have been great fun for you, Guzmán, doing this to all those half-starved bastards you tracked down.'

'I did my job,' Guzmán groaned.

Positano shook his head. 'You were just a *campesino*, Guzmán. A poor peasant, doing his master's bidding. You were – and you still are – a nobody.'

'What happens now?' Guzmán's voice was thick with pain.

'If it was up to me, *Comandante*, you'd be dead already.' Positano lifted the rifle to his cheek and pointed it. 'I'd shoot you in a heartbeat. But it isn't up to me. I'm just,' he hesitated, struggling to recall the Spanish word, 'I'm just a facilitator. I help people achieve things.'

'Really?' Guzmán asked. 'Who have you helped achieve anything lately?'

Positano laughed. 'Oh Guzmán. Your worst nightmare, *amigo*.'

Guzmán scowled. 'Valverde?'

'Spot on.' Positano grinned, his teeth gleaming in the half light. 'A man with a vision of the future, Guzmán, instead of the past. He sees the need for change, new ideas.'

'He's a traitor,' Guzmán spat. 'He just wants a share of whatever's going. *Nada más.*'

'Well, they say "to the victor the spoils", don't they?' Positano's laugh was cold. 'Except in Franco's case, he took it literally and spoiled the country. With outside funding and help Spain could become a real country, not this shit-heap with bad plumbing and more spies and security men than doctors.'

'Why would Valverde help you *Yanquis*?' Guzmán asked. He coughed and bile ran down the side of his chin.

'Work it out, Guzmán. He helps us. We help him. We get airbases. We put our planes here. If the war with Russia comes, we bomb the Soviets from here. Much faster and much more effective.'

'And they drop their bombs on us?' Guzmán asked.

Positano shrugged. 'Who cares? Listen, once the US starts trading with you, the rest of the world will join in as well. Hell, there'll be all sorts of rewards. Maybe we'll get the Brits to give you Gibraltar back.'

'Just like that? The country has to change to suit you *Yanquis*?' Guzmán stared malevolently at Positano. The pain made him lower his head and he saw the piles of sacks, the pool of his vomit on the dark mildewed burlap, and amongst the undulating folds, the dull sheen of the Browning.

'Just like that, Guzmán. What do you think will happen when this country wakes up to find there's enough food for everyone? Even the strictest party member is going to think we did him a favour by machine-gunning the *Caudillo*'s car.'

'I grasped that part of the plan,' Guzmán said. 'Although I thought that it was going to be the Dominicans doing the shooting.'

'There you go, Guzmán. Wrong again. The plan was for them to keep you busy. Get you so mad you wouldn't see what was going on right under your nose.'

'They did that all right,' Guzmán said, grudgingly.

'The Dominicans did a good job,' Positano continued. 'In their country they were part of the special forces. We just borrowed them from old General Trujillo. Another dictator. Completely fucking mad. But a great ally. Until we say different.'

'So why don't you get rid of him?' Guzmán struggled not to look at his pistol. There was no way he could reach it. Not yet. Not from where he was. Not in this pain.

'Well, that's the thing.' Positano smiled. 'He may be a son of a bitch, but he's our son of a bitch. Franco isn't. Makes all the difference.'

'If your Dominicans did such a good job, what happened here?'

'Well, comes a time, Guzmán, when people become surplus to requirements. I had to terminate their employment.'

'You killed all of them?' Guzmán asked, with sudden professional interest.

'All but one,' Positano said. 'One disappeared a few days ago. You wouldn't know about that, would you? Just so we know where to send the medal.'

'You know where you can put it,' Guzmán said. 'Shame he was the only one.'

Outside, someone pounded on the front gate.

'Expecting anyone?' Positano asked casually.

'No one in particular. Just my *teniente*, *sargento* and a squad of the *guardia civil*.'

Positano grinned. 'I think you may be disappointed. Look behind you.'

Guzmán turned. Even as he did, he realised his mistake. The rifle butt cracked across the back of his head and another mist of shimmering pain tore through him, blinding him. He sprawled face down, unable to move. He cursed and struggled, but by the time he could see again, Positano had opened the front door and returned to cover Guzmán once more with the automatic rifle.

Guzmán lifted himself, taking his weight on his forearms, and saw the newcomer.

'*Buenas noches*, Guzmán. I see you've met the welcome committee.'

Guzmán raised his head. Sweat dripped from his face.

'*A sus ordenes, mi General.*'

'Please, Guzmán,' Valverde said, a triumphant smirk beneath the white moustache, 'no need for formality now, *hijo de puta*. Not now you're about to die.'

Positano was still aiming the automatic rifle at Guzmán.

'Have our friends from the Caribbean been looked after?' Valverde asked.

'Just as you asked, General.' Positano nodded.

'No trouble? No one escaped?'

'Not one. I told you. I do a thorough job, General. They won't be talking to anybody about this operation.'

'At least you saved me this one.' Valverde stepped towards Guzmán, unfastening his holster. 'So rare as a general one gets to shoot anyone these days,' he crowed, the revolver in his hand.

'You haven't got the guts,' Guzmán said. 'You let others do the business while you watch. I'm sure you have a similar arrangement with your wife.'

Valverde's cheeks flamed as he struggled to keep control.

'Guzmán, Guzmán. Always thinking you have the upper hand. Franco's favourite assassin. His Dark Angel of the Sword. But not now, *cabrón*. We've played you like a bull and now it's you who is waiting for the sword. But first, *cabróncito*, let me show you just how fucked you are. Then we'll get rid of you once and for all. Come in, *señores.*'

Guzmán looked at the big doorway and any last vestige of hope drained away. A gust of wind blew in a small cloud of snow, the icy chill sharp on his sweat-soaked body as Peralta entered, pale and cadaverous as ever, the collar of his cheap overcoat turned up against the biting wind. At least he looked suitably shamefaced, Guzmán noted.

'*Buenas noches, Teniente,*' Guzmán sneered. Peralta stood a pace or two behind the general and said nothing. 'I always had you down for a traitor,' Guzmán spat, taking some comfort from Peralta's pained expression.

'But not *you,*' he said as a second figure emerged from the darkness of the doorway, closing the big wooden door behind him.

'Sorry, sir. Nothing personal. Just the money, see,' the sarge said. 'Too good to turn down.'

'Well, I hope you got your thirty pieces of silver out of this fuck in advance,' Guzmán said, struggling unsteadily to his feet.

'Really, Guzmán, I think comparing yourself to Christ is perhaps a little too much.' Valverde raised the revolver and shot Guzmán in the thigh. He cried out and fell back onto the sacks, pressing the wound with his hands to staunch the flow of blood.

'He's to be taken alive,' Peralta shouted angrily. 'You promised he'd have a fair trial.'

Guzmán gritted his teeth and continued to squeeze the wound. He was dizzy. If he lost too much blood he was finished. His strength would ebb away and with it his chance of – what? Escape? That was impossible now. The best he could hope for was getting his hands on Valverde and the general was still keeping his distance, flanked by Positano and his automatic rifle.

'What did you get, *Teniente*?' Guzmán asked. 'A few dollars for drink like the sarge?'

'Some things are more important than money, *mi Comandante,*' Peralta said.

'*Teniente* Peralta needed some assistance with his personal finances.' Valverde looked mockingly at Peralta.

'I bet he did,' Guzmán said. 'His wife won't manage on his pension when he dies before the year's out. Terrible thing, cancer, *Teniente*. Very painful way to go. Agony, they tell me. Still, you'll find out soon enough, I hope.'

Peralta's mouth fell open. 'How could you know that?'

'Didn't your *mamá* ever tell you?' Guzmán grunted. 'Never go to a Nazi doctor.'

'Splendid.' Valverde beamed. 'Your *teniente* betrays you for an insurance policy and your *sargento* sells you out for the price of a four-course meal.'

'It was a bit more than that, sir,' the sarge said. Guzmán nodded appreciatively.

'And you, Guzmán, you betrayed your country, fought for the ungodly and you've lied to everyone from the *Caudillo* downwards. *Joder*, if Christ had returned you'd have lied to him.'

'I've always been consistent,' Guzmán muttered.

'Can we get on with this?' Positano said. 'I need to make sure the machine gun upstairs is ready. And you need to be out of here, General, ready for when the news of Franco's assassination breaks.'

'Indeed,' Valverde said. 'If I could have that rifle for a second, I'll just send *Comandante* Guzmán to hell, where he belongs.'

'I'll be waiting when you arrive,' Guzmán growled, 'fucking your mother. Again.'

Positano kept the rifle aimed at Guzmán until the general had taken it from him.

'Heavy beast.' Valverde weighed the rifle in his hands. 'Is it on single shot?'

'Yes. But can we get a move on?' Positano said again. 'I need to be ready for when your Head of State drives past. It has to go smoothly.'

'Of course,' Valverde agreed. 'Although, there's been a slight change of plan.'

He turned and fired the automatic rifle from less than a metre into Positano's chest. The blast threw Positano backwards, the immense spray of blood on the wall behind him black in the half light. Cordite smoke rose from the body and, for a moment, his shirt flickered with flame around the wound.

'*Yanqui* bastard,' Valverde said. 'Telling me to hurry.'

'What the fuck?' The sarge stared at Positano and then back at the injured Guzmán.

Clearly Peralta wasn't going to tell him: the *teniente* stood motionless, shocked.

Valverde laid the automatic rifle by Positano's body and took out his pistol.

'*Teniente*. Draw your weapon and keep Guzmán covered, would you?'

Peralta reached into his coat and produced his service revolver.

'What are you going to do with that, *Teniente*?' Guzmán sneered.

'Move and I'll fire, *Comandante*. Remain still and I guarantee you'll receive medical help and a fair trial.' Peralta's face showed too much doubt to take him seriously.

'Are you going to shoot the *Caudillo* yourself, *mi General*? Or will you order the *teniente* to do it?' Guzmán called to Valverde.

Valverde walked across the loading yard, pistol in hand. 'No one is going to shoot the *Caudillo*,' he said. 'Not now. I know you've probably tipped off Gutierrez in Military Intelligence. So we have to change things. *You* were going to shoot Franco, Guzmán. You were in league with this *Yanqui* and his Dominican accomplices. There was a fallout over the money and you killed them. The *teniente* and I arrived and managed to stop you carrying out your planned attack. No one will question your guilt. There's more than enough evidence, I've made sure of that. And of course there's also the matter of who the hell you are. Because I understand your so-called mother and cousin had grave doubts you were any relation of theirs.'

'Call them as witnesses.' Guzmán smiled. 'And the private detective.'

Valverde raised his eyebrows. 'Well, well. A few new stars in heaven tonight, then, Guzmán? You've been busy. But do you know what? The witnesses you didn't kill, Positano did. Alvarez and Posadas. That means you're the last one.'

'So this was all your idea?' Guzmán grunted, sweat coursing down his face. He was trying not to vomit. 'A diversion to keep me off the scent?'

'All of it.' Valverde nodded. 'You wouldn't understand. At heart you're just a thug. No subtlety. But you do – *lo siento* – did, have

Franco's ear. Not any more. Positano helped plan it: the CIA are good at these things. We knew the Dominicans would enrage you so much you'd decide whatever else happened, you had to kill them. They would probably have seen you off anyway, given they were some of the finest of the Dominican Republic's armed forces.'

Guzmán spat bloody phlegm onto the sacking in front of him. 'I'm always up for a fight, *mi General*. Some things don't change.'

'Of course, Guzmán, and you're one of them. By taking my bribe, you cut yourself off from Franco, and even then, you never saw what was happening. We had you watched constantly, waiting to add to your troubles. We watched you at the *comisaría*, and when you visited *Señora* Martinez. All the time we had our eye on you.'

'*Señora* Martinez?' Guzmán asked, feeling his stomach sink.

Valverde laughed. 'Ah yes, the lovely *Señora* Martinez. We thought she would appeal, Guzmán. It was Positano's idea. *Hombre*, for a man who's been under surveillance for years, you behave as if you didn't care who knew your business. We'd long known that whenever you met a woman who took your fancy in the course of a raid, you'd return and fuck them. Not that they had any choice. The French call it *droit de seigneur*.'

'I call it admirable,' the sarge muttered. Valverde glared at him.

'When you arrested *el Profesor*, you also spent some time intimidating *Señora* Martinez,' he gloated. 'Once your *sargento* tipped off my man, we popped in and had a word with her.'

'*Gracias, Sargento*,' Guzmán said coldly. The sarge looked down in discomfort.

'You aren't much of a policeman, Guzmán,' Valverde chortled. 'Even before we put pressure on her, she'd been playing you for a fool. You thought she was a widow?'

'She is,' Guzmán muttered.

'Her husband's doing fifteen years in a prison camp near Pamplona,' Valverde laughed. 'Any idiot could have found that out without much effort. But not you, Guzmán. One sniff of her and you thought with your dick. Let me tell you, by the time you returned that night, we'd spoken to her, discussed terms and she was ready to play you like a gypsy's fiddle.' Valverde paused, his face florid now, triumphant. 'But if you don't believe me, you'd better hear it from the horse's mouth. *Adelante, señora.*'

Guzmán peered through the stinging sweat. The darkness around the warehouse entrance moved, and a figure emerged into the pale light encircling Guzmán and his tormentors. Guzmán stared, bewildered. *No. Please, not this.* No matter how bad things got, he could not have imagined this.

'Say hello to the *comandante,* my dear,' Valverde instructed *Señora* Martinez.

Guzmán stared, helpless as she came forward, face pale, hands clasped in front of her. She looked hesitantly at Peralta. The *teniente* looked away, keeping his pistol aimed at Guzmán.

'See, Guzmán?' Valverde cackled. 'I gave that woman five hundred US dollars to fuck your brains out. You perhaps thought it was love, *Comandante?*'

'Not you,' Guzmán whispered. He couldn't think clearly. Not now the world had changed so fundamentally. It was all wrong: they had won and he had lost. He heard Valverde laughing, laughter congested with pride and hate, the laugh of someone accustomed to winning.

'Was he good, *señora?*' Valverde snickered. 'Five hundred dollars gets a man a lot, I imagine. Did he take full advantage of what you had to offer? Perhaps not, since you seem to be walking normally.'

Guzmán hung his head. Sweat dripped from him. His leg was bleeding badly. Better if it all ended now. He remembered briefly the times in the village when they would heckle him: 'Where you going, *culón?* Hey, fatty. Oddball. *Gordo de mierda. Culón, culón.*' The difference was that he'd had the chance to revenge himself on most of them later.

Señora Martinez spoke. There was fear in her voice. But there was something else, a determination that made Guzmán look up, blinking the tears and sweat from his eyes. 'The *comandante* behaved like a gentleman, General. He never touched me once in the way you suggest. Not once. And amongst all of you here, he was the only one who ever treated me with common decency.' She looked viciously at Peralta and then back at Guzmán. 'You wanted to keep me safe,' her voice broke for an instant, 'and I betrayed you.' She hung her head. 'To save my husband. That was the only reason. I'm sorry.'

'How did they get into my apartment?' Guzmán's voice was a hoarse whisper. 'You were safe there. No one could get in, surely?'

'Exactly,' Valverde said. 'No one could get in. But she could get out. To warn us.'

Guzmán coughed and tasted blood. He was finished. He just wanted it to be over.

'*Comandante*, I had to help my husband, I couldn't let him rot.' *Señora* Martinez's voice was strained and its anguish touched him, just as once her hand had gently touched his in one brief shared moment.

'Well, you messed that up, you bitch,' Valverde snapped. 'We wanted Guzmán to keep himself busy between your thighs so we could do our business undisturbed. Christ, this new man at Military Intelligence, Gutierrez, has been all over the place. If he'd got wind of any of this it would have been all over for us. You were paid to be a whore but you kept your pants on because Guzmán behaved like a gentleman? *Puta madre.* Your husband will stay locked up in the wilds of Navarra until sometime in 1986.'

Alicia Martinez moaned. 'You promised.' Her voice was sharp with recrimination. 'You disgusting man. All of you, you disgust me.' She looked at Peralta. He avoided meeting her eye.

'*Señora. Ven aca,*' he said, his pistol still clasped in both hands and aimed at Guzmán. 'Come over here. Stand behind me. I'll make sure you're safe until we can sort this out.' *Señora* Martinez looked at Guzmán. He saw her pale eyes, the high cheekbones. He nodded and she moved slowly past Peralta to stand a few paces behind him, her eyes fixed all the while on Guzmán.

The *teniente* looked at Valverde. 'This is intolerable, General. A Spanish officer always keeps his word, surely?'

Valverde flushed puce. '*Joder*, Peralta, mind your own business. I've sorted your arrangements out. Keep your nose out of the rest. You're a dead man anyway.'

'No one but a fool would trust you, General.' Guzmán's voice was thick with pain. He looked at Alicia Martinez. 'Unless they were desperate.'

'Quite. But it's an ill wind, Guzmán,' Valverde said. 'In a few minutes Peralta will make a call to the *guardia civil* for help. They'll find the *teniente* and me here, surrounded by carnage. And the story of how we stopped the plot to assassinate the *Caudillo* will increase my influence enormously with Franco and with the people. And in time, that influence will shape Spain's future direction. Particularly as our American trade partners will soon make it clear they would rather deal with me than the *Caudillo*. Although obviously, *Teniente*, you'll only be able to enjoy any of this success for a very short time.'

'Thank you,' Peralta said, glumly.

'As for you, *sargento*,' Valverde smiled, 'you don't figure in any of my plans now. I'd be grateful if you would go over and stand with *Comandante* Guzmán. I think you'd be more comfortable with him. And in any case, it will be easier to kill you.' The general raised his pistol. 'Now.'

'Bad choice, Sarge,' Guzmán said, as the sarge shuffled towards the sacks.

'Always bad at making choices, sir.' The sarge smiled at Guzmán, his disastrous teeth foul in the half-light. 'Sorry I let you down, *jefe*. You've been good to me. Well, sometimes.'

'Yes,' Guzmán agreed, 'I got you out of the fucking asylum, for one thing.'

'You did,' the sarge said. 'And I owe you.' He grinned and Guzmán saw his coat fall open, saw the pistol in his belt.

'Even with me gone, Military Intelligence still suspect you, *mi General*,' Guzmán said.

'You think so? There's no one who'd believe your version of events – even if you lived. And you won't. Nor this halfwit *sargento* of yours.'

'I resent that, *mi General*,' the sarge said. '*Con su permiso*.'

'Protest noted,' Valverde scoffed.

'I made another call after I called you tonight, *mí General*,' the sarge said quietly, still with his back to Valverde, his hand moving slowly inside his coat.

'Good for you,' Valverde mocked. 'Was it to your dentist?'

'I called *Coronel* Gutierrez,' the sarge said, winking at Guzmán as he spun round, pulling the pistol from his waistband. As he turned, Valverde shot him. The sarge staggered drunkenly, struggling to keep the pistol raised. He fired and Valverde fell sideways, steadying himself against a crate. Valverde fired again and the *sargento* clutched the wound in his chest in surprise as he fell to his knees and pitched forward, face down into the sacking. Valverde dropped his gun, grasping with both hands at the bloody hole in his side. He slid down the crate, cursing.

'*Mierda*. Shoot Guzmán,' he gasped, a thin stream of blood coming from his mouth.

Guzmán hurled himself forward, stretching for the pistol nestled in the burlap sacking. He fell heavily and searing pain jarred his battered body. He reached out a hand but the pistol was still centimetres from his grasp.

'Stop or I'll fire,' Peralta shouted. Behind him Valverde was clinging to the packing case, trying to stand. Guzmán was losing yet more blood; he felt it pumping from the wound in his leg.

'Shoot him, *Teniente*. Kill the bastard. That's an order,' Valverde shouted.

'Leave the gun, *Comandante*. There'll be a trial. I guarantee it.' Peralta aimed his revolver at Guzmán, holding the weapon two-handed as if on the firing range.

Guzmán tensed. There were always choices to be made. Always had been. He reached for his pistol, fingers scrabbling on the burlap, gripping the big Browning, the pistol he loved. Around him, the noise of combat: Peralta shouting a warning, aiming his revolver, Valverde raging in pain and anger, *Señora* Martinez's sudden cry as she threw herself towards Peralta, clutching at his arm. All his life had been combat, Guzmán thought. His finger fumbled for the trigger, his hand shaking and unsure.

Peralta fired first.

*On arriving at the prison, the commandant asked him to make his
will and assured him in due course it would be taken to a person of
his choosing. Naturally, he named her: the woman he had always
planned to leave it all to. They gave him a pencil and paper. When
he had written the will and the commandant had witnessed it, it was
sealed in an envelope. The commandant again promised him it
would be delivered shortly. Afterwards, of course.*

*In the cell he passed the time smoking and listening to the sounds
of prison, sounds charged with the rhythms of life and death. The
noise of the officials and soldiers who passed up and down the
corridors chatting, shouting, giving and obeying orders, who
laughed, as men laughed outside, about women and drink, about
the radio shows they listened to. Their boots clattered on the hard
stone, echoing sharply, blending with the slower, more reluctant
tread of those who were being accompanied to the cells or to
interrogation or just death. From time to time he heard muffled
shots but they were too faint to convey further information. There
was a slight commotion when they took away a body and once more
the shouted orders, the clatter of obedient boots and the walk of
captor and prisoner. The metal bolt of a door sliding open and then
closing again. Gunfire.*

*He lit a cigarette. His hand was shaking, though he was not
afraid. Even so badly wounded, he would not show emotion. This
was a game and there were always winners and losers. True, he had
entertained for a while the notion that he might find some way out
of this, that someone, somehow, might intervene or might discover
erroneous evidence which would render his guilt questionable. But
it would not happen now. Life did not contain such episodes, and*

besides, there was little time left. The judgement had been made almost at the same time as his arrest.

His wound pained him greatly and he wondered with only slight interest whether he might bleed to death in the cell. But they brought a doctor. They offered that quack Liebermann. As if he would be treated by that Nazi charlatan. He demanded a Spanish doctor, one who would speak with him in a Christian tongue and finally, they found one. The man put iodine on his wounds and dressed them. There was little else he could do, the usual doctor's admonitions to take care, to come back for a change of dressing: those things were oriented towards the future and the future was no longer relevant to him.

It was afternoon now. He asked the commandant if he might have clean clothing in which to die. His request was refused. There was little time left and the commandant did not want the trouble or the expense of trying to find clothing that would then be ruined.

They came for him shortly after dark. Not because this was an act that must be done at night but because the shift changed then. They helped him from the cell carefully, not out of respect but out of a fear he might produce some hidden weapon – unlikely though it was, since they had searched him thoroughly. He growled that he would walk unassisted and they stood back, allowing him to stagger, occasionally resting a hand on the wall while he caught his breath. At the door to the courtyard, a civil guard saluted as he stepped through the ancient doorway. He almost spat. Military regulations and formalities now were a thing of his past, no longer of importance to him. He was to die and that was an end to it. Fuck them.

The courtyard was dark and the high walls were topped with spirals of barbed wire. At the far end, against the chapel, they had built a wall of sandbags. He saw the patterns of bullet holes in the hessian sacks, sand spilling from the holes onto the cobbles of the courtyard. They had thrown more sand down to soak up the blood.

In the War he had watched as the African troops shot hundreds of prisoners in the bullring at Badajoz. He had watched dispassionately, as if they were exterminating vermin. There were no such witnesses now, only one man with a camera, no doubt to assure the veracity of the execution. Even as the guards turned him to face the courtyard, his back to the sandbags, the firing squad was forming a hurried line. There was no time to lose, it seemed. And yet, time was such a little thing to lose, he thought, as the officer shouted commands to his men. The priest approached and blessed him. He muttered back, the words suddenly thick in his throat. The priest hastened away, seemingly worried the firing squad might open fire before he withdrew.

Twelve men in tricorne hats. How foolish those hats looked, how bulky their capes. How white those faces peering down the rifle barrels. These were the sort of men he had commanded. He was a better soldier than any of them. How dare they pass such summary judgement on him? He should never have trusted Franco, should never have faithfully supported him as he had. After all his years of faithful service, to be dragged out to be shot like a dog. At least he had seen combat, had known it and embraced its violent arts. He had killed and was glad of it. That thought consoled him and, as he pondered on what would be a fitting final curse to bark at those quavering faces behind their rifles, the officer gave the order to fire.

From that distance, it was hard for a man with a rifle to miss and the twelve shots hit him simultaneously, tearing apart his chest and blowing a vast hole in his back. He toppled against the sandbags, his feet slipping forward as he slid into a sitting position, his back pressed against the crimson hessian sacks. The officer stepped forward, aimed his pistol and fired one shot into his temple. It was over.

CHAPTER TWENTY-SEVEN

The summer night air was thick and warm. Though the history building was almost entirely shrouded in shadow, someone was working late. Vague lights showed in the windows of the *profesora*'s room. Luisa's office was cooled by a large electric fan, window blinds closely drawn as she arranged the plan on the table. A faded plan, drawn with the formal linear precision architects bring to their work. Over sixty years old, created just after the war, when they had begun to rebuild the damage done to Madrid. The plan must have been commissioned when the police took over the building, converting it to a *comisaría*.

She looked again at the plan, the same plan Ana María Galindez was carrying around the *comisaría* on Calle de Robles right at that moment. Though Ana María's copy didn't have the handwritten information in its bottom left-hand corner. Crucial information, written in the broad angry handwriting both she and Galindez knew so well. What was it Galindez said? That Luisa was obsessed with the world as a text. She'd spurned Luisa's love of words, just as she spurned Luisa. Galindez had rejected words. Yet words could have saved her. These words. Words written boldly and simply beneath the stamp of the architect's office:

Cracked flagstone in the far corner of the office beneath filing cabinet.
The book and other items are below
Lift the left half of the flagstone to disarm the mine.

573

How delightful of Guzmán to leave his treasured text so lethally protected. It confirmed what Luisa had long suspected: that Guzmán had a certain artistic flair, thwarted by historical circumstance. Guzmán, a man trapped within the machinery of the dictatorship. Of course, this description involved a certain amount of creative speculation but still, Luisa had a strong feeling about the *comandante*. A far stronger intuition than Ana María's rigid assumptions and her sterile, joyless methods of inquiry. Such an approach could never do justice to the rich narrative of history.

All along, Luisa realised, Ana María had intended to exploit her work – to exploit *her*. Luisa recognised Ana María's sneaky approach with hindsight: worming her way into Luisa's bed after their meeting at Las Peñas, ingratiating herself and getting a secondment from her uncle. All aimed at securing things for herself – even at her first meeting with the project team, she flirted shamelessly with Tali. A pair of sluts together. They would have had a hard time of it in Guzmán's cells. He would have known how to punish them for their impudence in trying to secure his book.

Luisa had been surprised by Ana's discovery that the diary was the key to his secret code. Although what Guzmán had encoded, Luisa didn't know. Or care. Certainly his secrets would all be in there. Finding Guzmán's book would be the final jewel in Ana María's crown. Once it was deciphered, that information would give an intolerable boost to her status. She'd be a media sensation, no doubt. There'd be photographs of the young forensic scientist of the *guardia civil* all over the news. And worst of all, her star would rise just as surely as Luisa's would fall, as Galindez demolished her work with her baleful evidence. Luisa's position as head of the university's new research centre would be short-lived if her life's work was suddenly refuted by an upstart like Ana María Galindez.

That couldn't be allowed to happen, Luisa had decided. Guzmán's book must remain a forbidden mystery – one to enthral her from afar. Just as Ana María enthralled her once, with the angry fire of those deep brown eyes. Until she cast Luisa aside and tried to steal her subject matter – the real love of her life. Ana María should be punished. She probably thought she'd suffered already in her short, sad life. She hadn't suffered nearly enough.

Ana María and Tali, such a perfect couple, tripping off together to Guzmán's *comisaría* – where they found nothing on their first visit. But that wasn't true. They must have found Guzmán's memo, the one Luisa pinned on the noticeboard as a test. And surely Ana María's pushy positivism located the graffiti in the cells? No one with any real interest in him would miss any of that. But they said nothing. They thought Luisa was stupid. That was their choice. They were tested and they failed. They would be punished accordingly. And conveniently, it wouldn't be Luisa who had to do it. Still, it was a tragedy. Or rather, it would be later tonight.

There was a certain comfort in knowing that at least Ana María and Tali would have found what they were looking for. Of course, their destruction would also see the end of Guzmán's book. Without that, his diary would remain a text in need of an interpreter – Luisa, naturally. Ana María and Tali's sacrifice would enable Guzmán to speak again – through Luisa's authorial voice. Their loss was of no real importance. They wouldn't be the first people to have been sacrificed below the *comisaría* in Calle de Robles.

CHAPTER TWENTY-EIGHT

The sun was brighter this morning and despite the cold it seemed as if spring might be getting closer. The hearse and the funeral cars formed a line along the roadside and the breath of the pallbearers wreathed the coffin in white clouds as they bore it to the grave. The priest walked ahead of them, reciting solemnly, his voice firm and clear above the crunch of the pallbearers' boots. A small attendance for a funeral. Besides the soldiers, a few portly men in dark coats and hats standing in distinct groups. A woman weeping, all in black, her hand moving under her veil from time to time to dab her eyes with a handkerchief. Like a broken crow, she leaned against an elderly woman whose arm circled the younger woman's waist to keep her standing.

The firing party aimed up into a pale blue sky flecked by irregular strands of cirrus cloud. Shouted commands. The explosion of the shots. And then the bleak angular sadness of the bugle. Around the grave, the men in uniform stood at attention until the last haunting echo died away. The soldiers moved off, marching down the avenue beneath the skeletal chestnut trees. The men in dark coats began to drift away, intermingling with other groups of mourners. A few handshakes, an embrace here and there. One man broke away from the others and went to the weeping young woman who made a vague gesture with her gloved hand before collapsing against the older woman in a renewed storm of tears. The man leaned nearer to her, speaking softly, the woman nodding vigorously without interrupting her sobbing. He patted her on the arm and stepped back, leaving her to say her last goodbyes before the older woman half carried her to the waiting car. The driver jumped from his seat, tugging open the rear door and helping bundle the young woman into the back of the vehicle. The car moved away slowly. At the graveside, two men looked down into the open hole. Fifty metres away, the grave-diggers waited patiently, leaning on their spades, smoking.

'How is *Señora* Peralta?' Gutierrez asked.

'As you'd expect the widow of a fallen hero to be.' Guzmán took out a packet of cigarettes and offered one to the other man. They lit up and exhaled clouds of blue smoke into the thin air. 'Devastated, naturally. But at least there's the knowledge her husband gave his all in the line of duty.'

'Shot down in the service of Spain by an unknown criminal while protecting an innocent woman.' Gutierrez nodded. 'A tragedy.'

'At least he got off a round,' Guzmán said. 'But the other guy was a better shot.'

'He had a better weapon, I believe? Probably a nine millimetre?'

'An altogether more powerful weapon. And loaded with soft-nosed bullets. I put a hole straight through him. Several, actually.'

'The unknown killer did,' Gutierrez corrected. 'Keep to the official version, Guzmán.'

'As you say.'

'It's deeply regrettable *Señora* Martinez died,' Gutierrez said. 'I know you had feelings for her.'

Guzmán inhaled deeply. 'She was too involved, *Coronel*. Stand next to the fire and you get burned.'

'She did that all right. Anyway, you couldn't have missed her at that range. And with the ammunition you were using – well.'

'True. I had to fire or let Peralta shoot me. It was just unfortunate she was behind him.'

'Tragic,' Gutierrez agreed. 'But you had no choice. In any case, it's much tidier with you as the only witness. For all of us.' And then, changing the subject, 'Returning to the issue of the Widow Peralta. There'll be a full pension. That should be a comfort.'

'And the medal. Not to mention her inheritance from the late general. The *teniente* wanted her to be well provided for and now she is. I should say the *capitán*, of course. Another nice posthumous touch, *Coronel*.'

'What was that I heard you say to her about adoption?' Gutierrez asked.

'They wanted another child,' Guzmán said. 'With Peralta gone, it will console her. I found her one. Alicia Martinez had custody of her late sister's son. If he isn't adopted, he'll be sent to a children's home.'

'Better a good home than to be locked up with a bunch of queer priests.'

'I think so,' Guzmán agreed. 'It's what his aunt would have wanted.'

They walked up the gravel path, surrounded by cracked gravestones and withered rose bushes. Gutierrez slowed his pace to accommodate the limping Guzmán.

'How's the leg?'

'I can walk.' Guzmán grimaced as he put weight on his injured leg. 'Slowly, anyway.'

'The admiral wants to see you.'

Guzmán nodded. 'I expected that. Has he decided what happened to Valverde?'

'Oh yes. A sudden heart attack on holiday near Barcelona. Naturally, the family were so upset they requested the *Caudillo* not to hold an official funeral and to let them inter him privately. He's buried and the headstone's already up. Hero of Badajoz. Warrior of Spain. Veteran of the Crusade. All of that.'

'I wish I could have attended the heart attack,' Guzmán said. 'I would have loved to give the order to fire. Just to see the look on his face.'

'I know. But the doctors were still digging his bullet out of your leg when we put him against the wall. Franco wanted it done fast.'

'You were there then?'

'Professional interest. If it helps at all, he died frightened and tongue-tied.'

'I'm only sorry it was so quick.'

Gutierrez smiled. 'We took photographs. I thought you'd like a souvenir.' He reached into his coat and pulled out a manila envelope.

Guzmán took the envelope and put it into his coat pocket. 'Thanks, *mi Coronel*. I owe you a drink.'

Gutierrez stopped as they reached the end of the pathway. Across the road was a dark Hispano-Suiza with white-wall tyres and tinted windows.

'You owe me a couple, Guzmán. The files he kept on you have been burned. I didn't read them. He was a traitor, so they'd be lies anyway, no doubt. *Hasta la proxima.*' They shook hands.

Gutierrez walked away down the road towards Ventas. Guzmán crossed to the parked car. The rear window rolled down and Carrero Blanco leaned forward.

'Guzmán. How are the wounds coming on?'

'Very well, *mi Almirante*. I'll be back at work in no time.'

'You did a good job, Guzmán. I thought for a while you didn't have a grip on things but I was wrong. Well done.'

Guzmán smiled. 'Everything I do is in the service of the *Patria*, *Almirante*.'

'It's always been so, Guzmán. That's why the *Caudillo* has a new role for you.'

'A new role?' Guzmán's mind raced. *So they're getting rid of me after all.*

'Times are changing, Guzmán,' Carrero said. 'Madrid is secure now. Your work has ensured that. But this is a big country. There are places which aren't so secure, where the rule of law isn't as strong as it should be. The *Caudillo* thought you would relish a chance to travel. Instead of a dingy office in Calle de Robles, you can be out in God's own country, taking the fight to the Reds and the godless ones. Action, Guzmán. You'll love it. And with a pay rise, naturally.'

Guzmán hesitated. Leave Madrid? He had spent so much time creating the web that emanated from Calle de Robles. These streets were his battleground. But then, so what? The *almirante* was correct: there were traitors out there, new enemies to conquer. And opportunities too, in the anonymity of travelling. New faces. New prey.

'That's more than generous, *mi Almirante*,' Guzmán said. 'I look forward to the challenge. I can pack my things at the *comisaría* within the week.'

'No, forget that, Guzmán,' Carrero said. 'We want you out there. Immediately. Go home and get packed. Forget the *comisaría* and just get on your way. Now we've reached an agreement with the *Yanquis*, the hard hand has to be a little more hidden. We're going to return the *comisaría* to the police. The *Brigada Especial* will have to be a bit more secret in future. The tourists won't like it, you see.'

'Tourists?'

'They're the future, Guzmán. Foreigners flooding in, filling the hotels, spending their cash. Even that fat bastard Hemingway is going to return this year. The country will be awash with money.'

Guzmán nodded, thinking of his stash of dollars. They were safe, but the treasure trove underneath the flagstone at the *comisaría* would have to stay where it was. Maybe in a month or two he could return under some pretext, disarm the mine and collect his treasures.

Carrero handed Guzmán a large envelope. 'Here are all the details, Guzmán, and a list of contacts. The same autonomy as before – your contact will be the new head of Military Intelligence, *Coronel* Gutierrez. Unless the *Caudillo* or I need to talk with you directly, of course.'

Guzmán took the envelope.

'One more thing,' Carrero continued, 'we've sorted out Valverde's mess as far as we can. Is there anything you need to do before you leave Madrid – to tidy up, I mean? Loose threads?'

Loose threads. As if, Guzmán thought. Carrero should know

how he dealt with those. Everyone implicated in Valverde's scheme had been dealt with. None of those who entered the warehouse that night were alive, except for Guzmán. Most of them deserved it. At least the sarge had recognised the need for sacrifice, redeeming his betrayal in blood. Guzmán tried not to think about *Señora* Martinez. *Señora* Martinez, with her chapped hands and threadbare clothes, living in her cheap flat, posing as a widow to avoid problems about her husband's choice of sides in the war. She had seen something in Guzmán, something, if not good, then at least acceptable to her. Valverde had paid her to be a whore and she had taken his money but, when the time came, she'd refused to play the role. That was her gift to Guzmán and he appreciated it. Apart from her deception, she had behaved properly – as, remarkably, had he. She had changed him. Showed him he could be something else. As well as someone else.

At least there was no pain for her at the end. That was his gift. An end to her sad existence, killed by the deadly fire that cut down Peralta. She could never have lived in his world, Guzmán realised. And he would never have changed enough to live in hers. It was impossible. The boy would be well looked after by *Señora* Peralta, once he got over the shock of the Jesuits and their Christian discipline. By the time he was delivered to *Señora* Peralta he would be house-trained. The *teniente* said he wanted a son and now he had one, albeit posthumously.

'Everything has been dealt with,' Guzmán said. 'Thoroughly.'

'Excellent,' Carrero said. 'Your work has always been most reliable.' The car window closed smoothly. Guzmán saw Carrero speak to the driver and the limousine glided forward, the engine purring as it picked up speed. It turned a corner and was gone, leaving Guzmán alone in the cemetery. He lit a cigarette and limped back to his car near the main gate, leaving the dead behind him. As he always did.

CHAPTER TWENTY-NINE

Tali pulled back from the opening to the pit and crawled over to Galindez's body. She had been wrong: Galindez was still breathing. It was time to honour the clause in her contract with the *Centinelas*. She rolled Galindez onto her back. Her face was dark with congealed blood. Tali placed a finger against her neck, feeling for the carotid artery. The pulse was steady, in fact it seemed to be getting faster. That was a shame. It would have been easier if Ana had just slipped away quietly rather than being a problem. But then she always was. Always had been, Tali thought. Complicating the lives of everyone around her without ever seeing that it was her who was the problem.

'You won't be a problem much longer, Ana,' she whispered.

Tali undid the buckle of Galindez's belt and pulled it free from her jeans. She slid the belt under Galindez's neck and tightened it, hearing her breathing alter as the thick leather began to compress her throat. Tali braced herself and began to pull harder.

'It's all right, *niña*. Just let go. Go away now, Ana. It's not so bad.'

Galindez opened her eyes. The darkness of her pupils glinted with radiant anger, the surrounding whites a sharp contrast to the mask of dried blood smeared across her face.

'*Puta madre, Ana Mar—*' Tali's voice stopped abruptly as Galindez closed her hand around Tali's throat with terrifying strength. Tali scrabbled with both hands, trying to loosen the fierce grip, struggling to breathe. Galindez sat up, still keeping her grip. She brought her face close to Tali's. She smelled of blood.

'Surprise.' Galindez stared into Tali's amber eyes, seeing fear

582

and pain where once she had seen other emotions. After a moment, she released her grip and Tali rolled away from her, her shoulders rising and falling as she gasped noisily for air.

'Fucking hell, Ana,' Tali gasped.

Galindez ran her hand over her scalp and winced. She pointed towards the dark open space of the pit. 'What's down there?'

Tali smiled weakly. 'There's loads of stuff, Ana María. *His* stuff.'

Galindez glowered, taking the belt from her neck. 'So you thought you'd strangle me to celebrate?'

Tali shrugged. 'I thought you were already dead. Anyway, that stuff is all yours now. I'll settle for something else, though.'

'Like what?'

'Fuck it. You keep it all and I disappear into the sunset.'

'Why would I let you go? I could easily put you behind bars.'

Tali shrugged again. 'Because of how you feel about me.'

'I wouldn't count on that.' Galindez said. 'Where's the pistol? I don't want you changing your mind again.'

'Here.' Tali pulled the Browning from her belt and handed it over.

Galindez removed the magazine and threw it across the room into the shadows. After checking the chamber was empty, she tossed the pistol aside.

'There's one thing,' she said, picking up the big flashlight, 'if you try any more tricks, I'll kill you.' Tali nodded. Galindez pointed to the opening in the flagstones. '*Bueno*, after you, *Señorita Castillo*. I'm not turning my back on you.' She paused. 'When we've seen what's down there I'll give you two hours before I call the police. You're on your own after that.'

'I knew you liked me.' Tali smiled.

She lay on the flagstones and Galindez eased herself alongside her, holding the flashlight at an angle, shining the beam into the bottom of the pit below. Boxes, papers, wires, bundles wrapped in waxed paper, all testimonies of Guzmán's presence. Fragments of evidence, the truths of his life assembled in the cold darkness, long guarded by the sullen stones of this ancient building. The things Galindez always hoped to find, now just an arm's length away.

Reaching down, Tali tried to lift one of the files. A brittle metallic sound. A thin wire reached up towards the light, like some cave-dwelling worm, its end broken from where it had been attached to the flagstone. Galindez saw the wire, saw how it emerged from the metallic khaki object placed at the centre of the bundles and packages. She called out, though her voice was strangely muffled and distant. And now Tali was shouting, struggling to get back up, but with the two of them jammed together it was hard to move quickly. Time seemed so strangely slow, Tali's voice distorted and unfamiliar, although suddenly it was too late for that to matter, too late for anything to matter as the sudden revelatory power of Guzmán's secret was released.

This was Guzmán's gift, Galindez realised. The gift he left here long ago, a gift she had never really been sure existed. She had wanted to know Guzmán and now she would experience the very essence of the man in this dusty mixture of empirical evidence and lethal technology as it sent out Guzmán's final message to the world: *you can never know me.*

Galindez and Tali stared, frozen in surprise and horror, shouting warnings neither of them would ever hear as Guzmán's terrible gift was revealed, released in all its malignant intensity from its long confinement beneath the *comisaría*, in a furious rage that even Guzmán's office had never seen, nor would again. In a moment of frozen fire and flame, time itself burned, as Guzmán's secrets were carbonised and destroyed, fragmented truths hurtling in the irresistible violence of their ascent. It was a game, this search for Guzmán. But it was always Guzmán's game, his final card should things go wrong and he never return to collect his treasures. And the game was over: this was his reality and that reality now raged around them, before it disappeared for ever. *The truth revealed through pain.*

The immense volcanic fury of the blast channelled upwards from the confined space, blowing out windows, smashing doors from their hinges and bringing down plaster and fittings from the ceilings. For a moment, the ancient building trembled before the rage released by Guzmán's handiwork. The reverberations of the explosion hammered through the narrow corridors, shaking the bars of the cells, pounding against the ancient door leading down into the forgotten depths of the *comisaría* where Mamacita and so many others were sacrificed to the perpetual greed of the darkness. And then, as the smoke billowed around the rubble, small flakes of plaster from the ceiling began to fall, floating in the draught from the shattered windows like snowflakes as the *comisaría* slowly reverted to its usual state of brooding and sullen silence.